COME NINEVEH, COME TYRE

BY ALLEN DRURY

Fiction

ADVISE AND CONSENT

A SHADE OF DIFFERENCE

THAT SUMMER

CAPABLE OF HONOR

PRESERVE AND PROTECT

THE THRONE OF SATURN

COME NINEVEH, COME TYRE

Non-fiction

A SENATE JOURNAL

THREE KIDS IN A CART

"A VERY STRANGE SOCIETY"

COURAGE AND HESITATION, *With Fred Maroon*

COME NINEVEH,
COME TYRE

The Presidency of Edward M. Jason

ALLEN DRURY

Doubleday & Company, Inc., Garden City, New York

1973

Grateful thanks are expressed to Carla Koss
Roberts for kind permission to use her poem
"Remembrance," on the Dedication page.

Allen Drury

ISBN: 0-385-04392-9
Library of Congress Catalog Card Number 73–9347
Copyright © 1973 by Allen Drury
All Rights Reserved
Printed in the United States of America
First Edition

To

FLORA ALLEN DRURY

1894   1973

Here lies a heart,
Dead not half a year;
I shan't defile her grave
With half a tear.
I would, instead, recall
The many times she paced
This ground to meet
Her love's embrace . . .
Remember her smiles,
Easily won . . .
Remember how her hair
Shone in the sun . . .
Remember how great beauty
Brought her tears . . .
Remember that she loved me
Many years.

MAJOR CHARACTERS IN THE NOVEL

In Washington

Edward Montoya Jason of California, President of the United States
William Abbott, ex-President of the United States
Mrs. Beth Knox, widow of the Secretary of State
Representative Harold Knox, their son
Robert A. Leffingwell, Secretary of State
Ewan MacDonald MacDonald, Secretary of Defense
George Henry Wattersill, Attorney General
Fred Van Ackerman, Senator from Wyoming, Chairman of the Committee on Making Further Efforts for a Russian Truce (COMFORT)
LeGage Shelby, Chairman of the Defenders of Equality for You (DEFY)
Rufus Kleinfert, Chairman of the Konference on Efforts to Encourage Patriotism (KEEP)
Mr. Justice Thomas Buckmaster Davis of the Supreme Court
Patsy Jason Labaiya, sister of the President
Robert Durham Munson, Senator from Michigan
Dolly, his wife
Tom August, Senator from Minnesota
Arly Richardson, Senator from Arkansas, Majority Leader of the United States Senate
Representative J. B. "Jawbone" Swarthman of South Carolina, Speaker of the House
Representative Bronson Bernard of New York
Roger P. Croy of Oregon, Vice President of the United States
Lafe Smith, Senator from Iowa

Mabel Anderson, widow of Senator Brigham Anderson
Cullee Hamilton, Senator from California
Lady Maudulayne
Celestine Barre
Walter Dobius, a columnist
Frankly Unctuous, a commentator
Other members of the media
Members of NAWAC (the National Anti-War Activities Congress.)

At the United Nations

Lord Claude Maudulayne, the British Ambassador
Raoul Barre, the French Ambassador
Krishna Khaleel, the Ambassador of India
Nicolai Zworkyan, Ambassador of the U.S.S.R.

In Moscow and Washington

Vasily Tashikov, Chairman of the Council of Ministers, U.S.S.R.

NOTE TO THE READER

THIS NOVEL, like others in the *Advise and Consent* series, is not a prediction of what *will* happen. It is a prediction of what *could* happen if certain attitudes and trends in America and the world proceed unchecked to their logical conclusion.

As such, it will of course receive the usual shrill denunciations from that sector of the media whose members have done so much to help create the attitudes and encourage the trends. . . .

COME NINEVEH, COME TYRE: THE PRESIDENCY OF EDWARD M. JASON, is the first of two sequels to *Preserve and Protect* which will conclude the *Advise and Consent* series.

Its companion volume, THE PROMISE OF JOY: THE PRESIDENCY OF ORRIN KNOX, is scheduled to appear in 1975.

Most of the characters in this novel, and the background of most of its events, have appeared in its predecessors, *Advise and Consent*, *A Shade of Difference*, *Capable of Honor* and *Preserve and Protect*.

In *Advise and Consent* (written in 1958, published in 1959) will be found the nomination of Robert A. Leffingwell to be Secretary of State; the accession of Vice President Harley M. Hudson to the Presidency; the successful Soviet manned landing on the moon; the death of Senator Brigham Anderson of Utah; the appointment of Senator Orrin Knox of Illinois to be Secretary of State following Bob Leffingwell's defeat by the Senate. There also will be found the marriage of Orrin's son, Hal, to Crystal Danta, the marriage of Senate

Majority Leader Robert Munson of Michigan to Washington hostess Dolly Harrison, and many other episodes leading into later books.

In *A Shade of Difference* (written in 1961, published in 1962) will be found the visit to South Carolina and New York of His Royal Highness Terence Wolowo Ajkaje, ruler of Gorotoland, with all its explosive effects upon the racial problem in the United States and the United Nations; the beginnings of the war in Gorotoland; the early stages of Ambassador Felix Labaiya's activities in Panama looking toward seizure of the Canal; the opening moves of California's Governor Edward Montoya Jason in his campaign for the Presidential nomination; the death of Senator Harold Fry of West Virginia and his decision to entrust his son, Jimmy, to Senator Lafe Smith of Iowa; and many other episodes leading into later books.

In *Capable of Honor* (written in 1965, published in 1966) will be found the bitter convention battle between President Hudson and Governor Jason for the Presidential nomination; the selection of Orrin Knox for the Vice-Presidential nomination; the escalation of the war in Gorotoland, the outbreak of war in Panama, and their effect upon the Hudson-Jason battle. There also will be found the ominous formation of the National Anti-War Activities Congress (NAWAC) which turns the convention into a near battleground and puts Edward M. Jason increasingly in pawn to the lawless, the sinister and the violent.

In *Preserve and Protect* (written in 1967, published in 1968), there will be found the violent aftermath of the sudden and mysterious death of just-renominated President Hudson; the furious contest in the National Committee between Orrin Knox and Governor Jason in their struggle for the nomination; the open civil rebellion of NAWAC in its drive to nominate—and dominate—Ted Jason; and the climactic episode at the Washington Monument Grounds where Orrin Knox, nominee for President, and Edward M. Jason, nominee for Vice President, meet the destiny that furnishes the basis for COME NINEVEH, COME TYRE and THE PROMISE OF JOY.

Running through the first four novels, through this and its successor —as it runs through our times—is the continuing argument between those who would use responsible firmness to maintain orderly social progress and oppose Communist imperialism in its drive for world dominion; and those who believe that in a reluctance to be firm, in permissiveness and in the steady erosion of the law lie the surest path to world peace and a stable society.

Far-called, our navies melt away,
On dune and headland sinks the fire.
Lo, all our pomp of yesterday
Is one with Nineveh and Tyre!

—"Recessional," Rudyard Kipling

COME NINEVEH, COME TYRE

BOOK ONE

1. NOW THE AUGUST DAY has come when he and Secretary of State Orrin Knox are to go to the Washington Monument Grounds and there before their countrymen pledge their lives, their fortunes and their sacred honor—and as much cooperation with each other as they can manage.

It is also the day when Edward Montoya Jason, Governor of California, may find out whether he can control the violent elements that have gathered behind his campaign and run rampant in his name.

As he finishes shaving and prepares to rejoin his wife, Ceil, in the charming guest suite of his sister Patsy's house in Dumbarton Oaks, he is confident of his ability to control the violent. But he does not know just how much cooperation with Orrin there will be.

However, he has given Orrin his word and he intends to keep it: There will be as much as he can conscientiously contribute.

He will make a genuine effort.

Ambition and the country have a right to expect no less . . .

Ambition and the country!

How much he has done for both, in these recent hectic weeks that have seen the wildly violent national convention; the mysterious and still unexplained death of President Harley M. Hudson; the accession to the Presidency of Speaker of the House William Abbott; and the hasty reconvening of the National Committee, whose deliberations, surrounded by a violence even greater than that which shattered the convention, have finally resulted in Orrin's nomination for President and Ted Jason's for Vice President.

Some have said that Ted Jason, Governor of California, descendant of grandees and shrewd Yankee traders, darling of all that aggregation of uneasy citizens whose hopes and fears are symbolized and given voice by radically activist NAWAC—the National Anti-War Activities Congress—has played too much with violence.

Some—and they include his running mate and the President—have said Ted Jason has put himself in pawn to violence. Some—and they include the lovely Ceil, who only last night abandoned her self-imposed exile at the great Jason ranch "Vistazo" north of Santa Barbara and flew back to be at his side for today's ceremonies—have said that he has betrayed something essential in himself in so doing. And some—and they include all of these and many more besides, in Washington and throughout the country—have made plain to him their fear that he may never be able to break free from violence and the begetters of violence, no matter how he tries.

Well: those who think that do not know Ted Jason, so favored by heritage, character, brains and physical presence. Even Ceil, astute and perceptive as she is behind the screen of her striking blond beauty and sweetly entrancing personality, does not know Ted Jason. Only Ted Jason, he tells himself with a certain grim defiance that shows for a second in the deep-set dark eyes hooded in the beautifully tanned face, crowned by the distinguished silver-gray hair, knows Ted Jason. And what he knows does not dispose him to be frightened of the hobgoblins of minds less self-assured and certain than his.

Not, of course, that his mind has been that way consistently in the past few weeks and days. During the convention when Orrin's daughter-in-law, Crystal Danta Knox, was beaten by rowdies supporting the Jason cause, thereby losing her unborn son; during the final hours of that same convention when President Harley M. Hudson attacked Ted mercilessly in his final speech from the platform accepting renomination and then named Orrin as his Vice-Presidential running mate; and again when NAWAC's sullen ranks burst into Kennedy Center and attempted to actually assault the National Committee because it named Orrin its Presidential nominee after Harley's death—on those occasions Ted Jason had come very close to terror and despair as he contemplated what seemed to be the abyss opening beneath his own and his country's feet.

But it had not taken him long to recover.

The violence that culminated in Crystal Knox's tragedy had been, he soon convinced himself, as much Orrin's responsibility as his. The savage berating by Harley Hudson had been wiped out in an instant in the crash of Air Force One that took Harley to his death: instantly Ted had been back in the running for President. The mood that had prompted the NAWAC-led "Great Riot" at Kennedy Center had melted like magic when Ted appeared after Orrin's nomination to receive the fervent adulation and obedience of the mob. And now Orrin, making the only compromise possible in view of the circumstances facing him in the nation and abroad, has invited Ted to be his running mate.

So Governor Jason has come safely through; and may yet, if something should happen to Orrin—or even without that, just in the normal course of time and politics—sit in the White House himself.

He realizes as he gives Ceil a quick smile and begins methodically putting on trousers, shirt, cuff links and tie, that all of this could be interpreted as sheer ambition and the ruthless sacrifice of everything to it—and nothing more. It is clear enough what many think, at least others in his immediate vicinity—the vicinity of power. Out in the country and across the world, most of the reaction is more charitable, and more in line with his concept of himself.

KNOX BOWS TO PEACE DEMAND, TAKES JASON FOR V.P., the New York *Times* has it; GOVERNOR EXPECTED TO USE INFLUENCE TO SEEK SWIFT END TO WARS IN GOROTOLAND AND PANAMA. . . . ANTI-WAR FORCES WIN, the *Daily Telegraph* agrees; JASON RETURNS KNOX TICKET TO POSTURE OF PEACE . . . IMPERIALIST WARMONGERS FAIL, *Pravda* avers; JASON HAILED AS WORLD PEACE HOPE ON KNOX WAR TICKET . . . RUNNING DOGS OF WAR CRUSHED, the Peking *People's Daily* maintains; JASON THWARTS KNOX DRIVE FOR WORLD DOMINION.

An overwhelming majority of the headline writers, editorial writers, news writers, columnists and commentators of his native land, and the world, agree. He finds this very comforting, for it is exactly the way he sees it himself.

There come into his mind once again the bitter conversations he had with President Abbott and with Orrin during the course of the National Committee's deliberations—conversations in which he kept insisting, patiently and for the most part in good temper, that he spoke for, and was responsible to, only the sincere and worthy elements of the country as they protested with an earnest and genuine dismay the twin catastrophes of Gorotoland and Panama.

For who could not sincerely and genuinely oppose those two ghastly follies, begun by President Hudson and carried forward with a ruthless determination by President Abbott?

When rebel forces in far-off Gorotoland in central Africa had risen in rebellion against "Terrible Terry"—His Royal Highness Prince

Terence Wolowo Ajkaje, 137th M'Bulu of Mbuele—they had also killed some forty American missionaries of both sexes and burned a Standard Oil installation in the north of the country. Their leader, "Prince Obi"— Obifumatta, Terry's cousin and challenger for the throne—had defied the United States, called on the United Nations, the Soviets and the Chinese for help, seemed for a few days to be succeeding in his drive to topple Terry. Then Harley Hudson had sharply escalated the number of American forces in the country—after Harley's death Bill Abbott had escalated them even further—and now Obi was in exile and Terry appeared to be reestablishing firm control. But American forces were still there, the situation was still fluid, Obi was still trying to gather support wherever he could for a try at reinvasion. At any moment the whole thing could explode again. Who could not condemn it, for all the two Presidents' pious pretenses that they must "stop Communist aggression?"

Few believed that old chestnut in this day and age.

And Panama. There the situation was even worse, for hostilities were not diminishing in Panama. Clever Felix Labaiya-Sofra, Ted's almost-ex brother-in-law (his sister Patsy Jason Labaiya's divorce action being now in its final stages), had formed his Panamanian People's Liberation Movement, attacked the Canal and launched, also with help from both Communist giants, an all-out drive to rid his country once and for all of the hated Yanquis who had created it. In Felix's mountainous and difficult terrain American efforts had so far not been successful. Nor had President Abbott's bluff—for surely it must be one, he wouldn't dare follow through—to blockade the country against the supplies being shipped in not only by the Communists but by Britain, France and other good friends of the United States.

Bill Abbott's threat had produced no decrease in hostilities. It had only brought a further uproar in the United Nations which, in the hectic debates over Gorotoland, had already come very close to expelling the United States because of its racial troubles at home. Most of the UN was still vocally and violently opposed to U.S. actions, even though Gorotoland appeared to be subsiding. Panama most certainly was not.

Naturally out of all this there had come great domestic uneasiness and disturbance throughout America. Ted was willing to concede that the protest had been inflamed by such organizations as DEFY—Defenders of Equality for You—headed by the brilliant, bitter black LeGage Shelby; COMFORT—the Committee on Making Further Offers for a Russian Truce—whose spokesman was one of Ted's most active supporters, Wyoming's strange and near-psychotic Senator Fred Van Ackerman; and KEEP—the Konference on Efforts to Encourage

Patriotism—headed by its Knight Kommander, oil-rich Rufus Klein-fert. It was true that his own idea of consolidating the three, plus all others who wished to make their feelings known, under the single broad umbrella of the National Anti-War Activities Congress had perhaps increased the tension to some degree. The leaders of NAWAC, some obvious and open, some more clandestine and mysterious, did seem to have a tendency to encourage violent rather than peaceable methods of protest.

But still, Ted was convinced that the vast majority of citizens for whom NAWAC now appeared to speak were decent, loyal, concerned and deeply troubled. And, as he had maintained throughout to President Abbott and to Orrin, he felt he had both a right and a duty to defend and represent them.

He had conceded to the President in their first conference on the subject, shortly before the National Committee began its meetings, that some forces of protest involved in the demonstrations and violence "are not sincere or genuine or perhaps even loyal to the country.

"But there are many, many millions more," he had maintained, "who honestly, earnestly and sincerely deplore and abhor the policies your Administration is following in world affairs. Now, these people are not kooks. They are not crackpots. They are not wild-eyed radicals or subversive Communists. They are decent Americans, deeply and genuinely disturbed.

"Am I to repudiate them, when they look to me for voice? Am I to say to them, 'Sorry, run along. I agree with Big Daddy, everything's 100 per cent O.K. and you're just a bunch of disloyal rats?' I cannot do that, Mr. President. I don't believe it to be true."

"What do you believe?" Bill Abbott had asked, as others had asked and others would continue to ask. "That's what I don't understand. Perhaps if I could, I'd understand better where you think you're going and what you think you're trying to do."

"I think, if you will forgive me," Governor Jason had said quietly, pointing to the massive Presidential desk, "that I am going right to that desk over there."

But that had only made the President angry and he had repeated some of the tired old clichés people on his side of the issue liked to repeat:

"These things backfire. Violence feeds upon itself; presently all order and all certainty are swept away. You cannot control these forces. . . ."

And at last in desperation he had turned to the personal attack upon Ted so reminiscent of Harley Hudson when he, too, was trying to divert the Governor from his campaign for the White House:

"I wish I could believe you were sincere, Ted. I wish I could believe you know what you're doing, when you run with that pack. I wish I could honestly think your method would bring us through. I might get out of your way if that were the case. But I cannot for the life of me believe you to be anything but overly ambitious, taking desperate chances with the very fabric of the nation, flirting and perhaps even conniving with forces whose capacities for destruction you just don't understand. I think you're the product of your upbringing. I think you think that just because your name's Jason you can ride any whirlwind, control any holocaust, put any genie back in the bottle. And, my friend, I just don't think you can."

"I thank you for worrying about me," Ted had said dryly. Bill's reply had alienated him even further.

"Oh, not you. I don't give a damn about you. But quite a lot of my fellow Americans are involved in what you do—possibly the fate of the country itself is involved. And that makes it a worrisome matter, for me. You have the power to lead or mislead. Right now, you're misleading, in my estimation, because you're misled—by ambition and greed for office and people who are taking advantage of those two weaknesses to trap you into being a stalking horse for their own purposes."

Shortly thereafter, deeply angered and offended, Governor Jason had terminated the interview and withdrawn, depressed by his inability to penetrate so closed and prejudiced a mind.

And then just two days ago, in their final interview before Orrin had chosen him for Vice President, he and Orrin had gone at it again. Orrin too had parroted the clichés, and again he had held his ground—though yielding a bit as a concession to Orrin's obvious sincerity and his own decision that he must compromise in some degree if he were to receive the nomination and so be able to assist Orrin in bringing the country back to some sane middle ground in foreign policy. For Orrin had been adamant:

"Much as I want to win this election—much as I feel that I can bring my country back to some sort of reasonable sanity if I do win it—I am not going to win it at the price of taking on the ticket a man who either honestly or willfully refuses to recognize the desperate dangers in the violent elements that support him. . . . There *is* an element of conspiracy in the country; it isn't all just innocent, democratic, happy-as-a-lark, spontaneous protest; there *are* enemies of America who are trying to use it to bring America down. Good God, man, they'd be fools if they didn't! And one thing they definitely aren't, is fools. . . .

"Therefore, if you come on this ticket, Ted, I want from you tomorrow, before the National Committee and before the world, a flat-out repudiation, with no equivocations whatsoever, of NAWAC, DEFY, COMFORT, KEEP and any and all other elements of organized violence in the country. Ever since Harley's death you have had repeated opportunities to do this and you haven't done it. Each time there have been qualifications and a lot of tricky words. . . .

"I won't have it, Ted," he had concluded quietly. "I'm simply not going to have it. . . . Either you cut those connections altogether or you don't come along with me.

"You decide."

And Ted had decided.

He had relented and met Orrin's objections part way, conceding that there might be deliberately subversive elements among his supporters, emphasizing that if so, he did not know of them, and that if they existed, "Of course I shall repudiate them.

"If there is proof of their subversion, I shall denounce them as vigorously and relentlessly as you. If it is impossible to accept their support without jeopardizing the country, of course I shall cut them off."

"At what point will you admit the danger?" Orrin had persisted. "What sort of proof do you have to have?"

It was then that Ted interrupted the conversation to ask for a couple of hours to consider his answer. He had gone back to Patsy's and thought it out . . . and he had hesitated at the moment of lifting the telephone to call Orrin and capitulate, because when all was said and done, he had too much faith in the country. He was confident he could control the violent and bring them back to safer channels of democracy. He felt that Americans had a right to protest policies with which they did not agree. He honestly believed that the great majority who did so were sincere, earnest and loyal.

He actually had his hand on the receiver, about to lift it and tell Orrin to forget the Vice Presidency, when Ceil had called from "Vistazo." In his happiness over her return—although no quid pro quo had been requested or thought of—he had realized that the only way it could last was if he conformed to what she believed best, and joined Orrin.

Next day before the National Committee and the world he had given his pledge:

"If, in the organization known as NAWAC or in any of its member organizations such as COMFORT, DEFY, KEEP or any of the others— there be any whose purposes are not within the law—who do not wish to keep their dissent within the law and within common decency—

then I repudiate them here and now and declare that I wish their support of me to cease forthwith. . . .

"There is a place for decent and honorable protest and dissent. I shall defend it always. But to those others," he had concluded sternly—"if others there be—I give notice and fair warning."

And although this seemed to leave a good many people, including Orrin and Ceil, still wondering exactly where he stood, it seemed to be enough both for the noisy ranks of NAWAC waiting outside the Center and for the Committee. Within five minutes he had been nominated by acclamation to be Orrin's running mate. . . .

"My goodness," Ceil says lightly now, ruffling the hair on the back of his neck, startling him out of the intense concentration into which he has fallen as he stands before the mirror absent-mindedly knotting his tie, "that's a brown study. What are you doing, going over your speech at the Monument?"

"No," he says, coming out of it with a smile, turning to take her in his arms and give her a quick kiss. "Other speeches."

"All right," she says cheerfully, moving away to pose by the window, "*don't* tell me. . . . How do I look? Like a proper Vice-Presidential wife?"

"Much more beautiful than that," he says firmly. "In fact, there's never been another in the same league."

She chuckles.

"You candidates will say anything for a vote. What *are* you going to say, by the way? Or is it a secret from me as well as from your great panting public?"

"I hope they aren't panting quite as hard as they have been," he says with an odd moroseness in his tone, sitting down on the bed and surveying her thoughtfully from head to foot. "They've got me now—or Orrin's got me. I don't quite know which."

"Orrin has, I suspect," she says more seriously. "Which is the way it should be, isn't it?"

"Is it?" he asks, again with the odd little melancholy in his voice. "I don't know. I couldn't say, at this point. I just wish he were a little less rigid about things, that's all."

"And he wishes you were a little less—" she begins, and then softens it with a smile. "You'll be good for each other. You'll find the middle ground. I'm sure of it."

"Are you?" he asks dryly. "That's nice."

"You've got to," she says, suddenly serious, coming to sit down beside him, taking his hand. "You simply must. So—what are you going to say? Or must I wait and hear it, just like everybody else?"

He gives her a quizzical look and squeezes her hand.

"What is this? Did Orrin put you up to something?"

She shakes her head, returns the squeeze, gets up and moves to an overstuffed armchair by the window; shoves it around briskly so that it faces him; sits down and studies him with a characteristically intent and thoughtful expression.

"Now," she says, "what's it going to be? Around corners, or straight down the street?"

For just a second he looks annoyed. Then he laughs.

"We have to leave for the ceremonies in ten minutes. I couldn't possibly tell you in that time."

"You could give me an idea," she says, but he only smiles and shakes his head.

She looks momentarily flustered but manages to respond lightly.

"Now, don't make me beg. That wouldn't be nice to your poor old wife who's come all the way from California to be with you in your hour of triumph."

"Not a poor old wife at all," he says, rising and coming over to lean down and kiss her again. "Only the most beautiful wife in American public life today. *And* the wittiest. *And* the most intelligent. *And* the most perceptive. That's what scares me, really—you see through me so."

"That will be the day," she says with a rueful little smile, accepting his proffered hand, rising to stand beside him and look straight into his eyes. "I hope, my dear friend," she says very quietly, "that you are going to be today what everyone hopes and believes Edward M. Jason is."

For just a moment he returns her look with a gravity as deep and naked as her own. Then the protective curtain of banter she has come to know too well in these recent months of his campaigning for the Presidency comes down once again. She had hoped when she returned last night that it might be gone, and for a while it had seemed that it was. But she realizes now, with a sinking heart, that here it is again.

"If you will continue to be the Ceil Jason I believe you are," he says lightly, "then I shall be able to be the Ted Jason everyone wants me to be. Is it a deal?"

She returns again the rueful little smile.

"If it's the best one I'm going to be offered . . . I guess it is."

But at this, surprisingly, the banter vanishes and he speaks with an absolute and almost desperate honesty.

"If you were not beside me," he says softly, "I honestly do not know what I would do, Ceil. I honestly do not."

Now it is her turn to speak lightly, though he can see she is deeply moved.

"I guess that's a good enough deal for any girl. I'll try to be worthy of it."

"Oh, you are," he says gently, taking her face between his hands. "There's never been any doubt of that."

"HEY, up there!" Patsy calls in her raucous way. "Can't you hear the limousines and motorcycles revving up in the driveway? Your parade's about to begin, hero. *And* heroine. Let's GO!"

And so not even his wife knows what he will say when he stands before the enormous crowd at the Monument Grounds to commit himself beyond retrieving to the cause of Orrin Knox and the difficult and dangerous road Orrin thinks will lead to national stability and world peace.

So the hour of acceptance comes, bright and hot and clear, and from all the corners of Washington's two cities—the one shining with legend and hope, the other dark with blasted promise and harsh reality—from all the corners of the nation, all the corners of the earth, the great throng gathers on the Monument Grounds around the stark white obelisk honoring the fatherly first President.

Krishna Khaleel, Ambassador of India; Vasily Tashikov, Ambassador of Soviet Russia, and his "agricultural attaché," who is really the head of the KGB intelligence apparatus for eastern United States; the British Ambassador and his wife, Lord and Lady Maudulayne; the French Ambassador and his, Raoul and Celestine Barre; and almost all their colleagues of the diplomatic corps, are there.

Somewhere in the enormous multitude that laughs and yells and chatters, shoves and pushes and jostles in amiable contest for position, are LeGage Shelby, Rufus Kleinfert and most of their fellow members of NAWAC. (Only Senator Van Ackerman is missing. Whispering now, he is in his fourteenth hour of filibuster against the Administration-backed *Bill to Further Curb Acts Against the Public Order and Welfare.*) The Chief Justice is there, his wife already upset because she can tell from the way Mr. Associate Justice Thomas Buckmaster Davis is bustling about near the platform that he must have some preferred assignment she doesn't know about. Senate Majority Leader Robert Durham Munson of Michigan and his wife, Dolly, are there, along with Stanley Danta of Connecticut, the Majority Whip and Crystal Knox's father, and more than half the Senate. From the

House, Representative J. B. "Jawbone" Swarthman, chairman of the House Foreign Affairs Committee and a possible strong contender for the Speakership next year, and his wife, "Miss Bitty-Bug," are rubbing elbows not too comfortably with California's giant young Negro Congressman Cullee Hamilton and his soon-to-be wife, Sarah Johnson. More than two hundred of their fellow House members are also on hand. All members of the National Committee have already taken their seats on the platform.

Television crews are everywhere, and through the crowd there are many television sets in place to bring the ceremonies to the farthest reaches. Police with walkie-talkies are also everywhere, moving constantly, efficiently, yet amicably, their presence giving rise to a few catcalls but otherwise no indication of hostility. At regularly spaced intervals groups of four soldiers stand back-to-back facing their countrymen, guns, bayonets and gas canisters ready. Around the flag-decked platform and the dignitaries' circle at the foot of the Monument, a tight cordon of Marines stands guard. Overhead the ubiquitous helicopters whir and hover.

Yet somehow, despite these precautions, there seems to be something in the air that indicates they will not be needed. Press and police estimate more than four hundred thousand present on this day that belongs to Orrin Knox and Edward Jason, yet with no visible exceptions they seem almost to be on picnic, so happy and relaxed do they look and sound. Even NAWAC's banners are good-natured, and this seems to put the final touches on it:

ORRIN AND TED: THE UNBEATABLES . . . HEY, HEY, GREAT DAY! BAD TIMES, GO AWAY! . . . TED AND ORRIN HAVE GOT US ROARIN' . . . WE'LL HAVE PEACE TOMORROW AND NO MORE SORROW . . .

Presently from far off there comes the sound of sirens, hailed with a great roar of greeting and approval. The sleek black limousine from Orrin's house in Spring Valley comes along Constitution Avenue in the center of its police motorcycle escort, turns into the Monument Grounds and proceeds slowly to the foot of the obelisk. Two minutes later, more sirens, another great roar. The sleek black limousine from Patsy's house in Dumbarton Oaks, in the center of its police motorcycle escort, comes along Constitution Avenue, turns into the Monument Grounds, proceeds slowly to the foot of the obelisk.

Out of their cars step the nominee for President and the nominee for Vice President, and their wives, and for a moment in the midst of a wave of sound that seems to blot out the world, they stare at one another with a questioning, uncertain, hesitant yet friendly look. Then

Orrin steps forward and holds out his hand, and as the picture flashes on all the television sets, a silence falls.

"Ted," he says, and his words thunder over the Monument Grounds, the nation, the world, "Beth and I are glad to see you."

"Orrin," the Governor replies, "our pleasure."

Impulsively and with a completely natural friendliness, Ceil steps forward and kisses Beth and then Orrin. Beth gives her a warm hug and then turns to embrace Ted. The television cameras zoom in, the still photographers push and shout and scramble. A shout of happiness and approval goes up from all the vast concourse.

Orrin links his arm informally through Ted's and leads the way to the platform, through the dignitaries' circle where friends and colleagues, opponents and supporters, greet them with an eagerly smiling, unanimous cordiality.

"It seems to be a happy day," Orrin says quietly, words no longer overheard as the police hold back the press. "I'm glad."

"So am I," Ted says. "I think we have a great responsibility."

"We do," Orrin agrees. "I'm going to make a conciliatory speech."

"I too," Ted says. "I had thought of sending it over for your approval this morning, but—"

"Oh, no," Orrin says quickly. He smiles. "I trust you." The smile fades, he looks for a moment profoundly, almost sadly, serious. "We've got to trust each other, from now on."

"Yes," Ted says gravely. "We must. I think we can."

Orrin gives him a shrewd sidelong glance as they reach the steps of the platform.

"I have no doubts," he says quietly.

"They're going to need our help," Beth says to Ceil as they, too, reach the steps and start up after their husbands.

Ceil smiles, a sunny, happy smile.

"I think," she says with a little laugh, "that you and I can manage."

The wild, ecstatic roar breaks out again as they appear together on the platform, standing side by side, arms raised in greeting, framed by the flags and the backdrop of the gleaming white needle soaring against the hot, bright sky.

"Mr. Secretary and Mrs. Knox! Governor and Mrs. Jason! Look this way, please! Can you look over here, please? Mr. Secretary—Governor—Mrs. Jason—Mrs. Knox—this way, please! Can you smile and wave again, please?"

Finally Orrin calls,

"Haven't you got enough?"

And from somewhere in the jostling tumult below them, of heads, hands, flailing arms, contorted bodies and cameras held high, there comes a plea of such anguished supplication that they all laugh.

"*Please,* just once more, Mr. President! All together again, *please!*"

"The things we do for our country," Orrin says with a mock despair as they all link arms and step forward once more.

"Yes," Ceil says happily. "It sometimes seems as though—"

But what it sometimes seems to Ceil at this moment will never be known, for they are interrupted.

No one in the crowd hears anything, no one sees anything. For several moments the full import of the sudden confusion on the platform does not penetrate.

It is so bright and hot and sunny.

It is such a happy day.

They cannot quite comprehend, in this bright, hot, sunny, awful instant, the dreadful thing that has occurred so swiftly and so silently before their eyes.

It is not clear now, nor perhaps will it ever be, exactly what those who have planned this intended. But whatever they intended, by some perhaps inadvertent and unintentional miscalculation they have accomplished even more.

A husband and wife—but they are not the same husband and wife— stare at one another for a terrible moment suspended in time and history. Then she begins to scream and he begins to utter a strange animal howl of agony and regret.

Their puny ululations are soon lost in the great rush of sound that engulfs the platform slippery with blood, the Monument Grounds sweltering under the steaming sky, the two cities, the nation, the horrified, watching, avid world.

ORRIN KNOX, CEIL JASON SLAIN . . . PRESIDENTIAL NOMINEE, RUNNING MATE'S WIFE ASSASSINATED IN WASHINGTON . . . GOVERNOR JASON, MRS. KNOX WOUNDED, NARROWLY ESCAPE DEATH IN MELEE AT MONUMENT GROUNDS . . . POLICE HOLD FAKE PHOTOGRAPHER SUSPECT . . . NATION'S LEADERS JOIN IN MOURNING SECRETARY OF STATE AND MRS. JASON . . . PARTY THROWN INTO CONFUSION BY LOSS OF NOMINEE . . . CONGRESS IN RECESS . . . WORLD APPALLED BY NEW VIOLENCE IN U.S. . . .

And the second day:

KNOX, MRS. JASON LIE IN STATE AT CAPITOL . . . STATE FUNERAL FOR BOTH TO BE HELD TOMORROW . . . GOVERNOR, MRS. KNOX "IMPROVING," REMAIN IN SECLUSION . . .

PRESIDENTIAL ELECTION SCENE CLOUDED . . . PARTY HEADS CONFER ON NEW STANDARD-BEARER . . . PRESIDENT ABBOTT RECONVENES NATIONAL COMMITTEE FOR DAY AFTER TOMORROW. . . .

And the third day:

ORRIN KNOX, MRS. JASON INTERRED AT ARLINGTON IN SOMBER STATE FUNERAL . . . GOVERNOR, MRS. KNOX UNABLE TO ATTEND . . . PRESIDENT SAYS GOVERNOR "ABSOLUTELY CERTAIN" TO BE NOMINEE . . . WORLD STILL STUNNED BY HORROR OF DOUBLE ASSASSINATION. . . .

And the fourth:

JASON UNANIMOUS CHOICE OF NATIONAL COMMITTEE . . . FIFTEEN-MINUTE MEETING CONFIRMS "INEVITABLE DECISION" . . . PRESIDENT ABBOTT PREDICTS "OVERWHELMING" JASON VICTORY . . . PARTY HEADS TO MEET TONIGHT WITH GOVERNOR, STILL IN SECLUSION AT SISTER'S HOME . . . RUNNING MATE IN DOUBT . . .

And life and history, as they must, move on.

"Bob," the President said with a heavy sigh as the long black limousine swung out of the West Gate of the White House promptly at 6:30 P.M. and began its swift motorcycle-escorted glide through the black-draped streets, "sometimes I feel mighty old."

"Yes," Senator Munson agreed with an equal heaviness, "and this is the worst time of all. What's going to happen to this country, anyway, Bill?"

The President sighed again and shook his head.

"I don't know. I swear I don't. Except that I do know one thing: you and I and all of us who have the responsibility are going to have to be a damned sight better than we have ever been, if we're going to bring her through."

"Will *he* be better than he's ever been?" Bob Munson inquired gloomily and answered his question with others. "How can he be, after this? It's enough to shatter any man. Are you sure the Committee did the right thing yesterday? What kind of a nominee have we got now? And what can *he* do to pull us through?"

"He'll get over it," the President said bluntly, not as unkind as he sounded for a moment: just practical and pragmatic, as he had always been when he was Speaker of the House, and still was in the White House. "Events knock a man down and events stand him up again, in life and politics. He'll get over it. Things are moving so fast for him that he'll have to get over it or he'll go under. And crushed as he is, I can't see Ted Jason going under. As for the Committee, what else could we do? For the sake of public stability we had to act immediately—there was only one logical claim we had to satisfy—we couldn't possibly have passed him by at such a time, the country just wouldn't have stood for it—and who else was there? We didn't have room to maneuver. It was inevitable."

"You could have taken the nomination," Senator Munson said. But the President only snorted.

"Oh, yes. Sure I could. Me and who else? They would have given it to me last week if I'd wanted it, but after this horror and all the sympathy it's created for Ted, they would have run me out of town on a rail if I'd dared to ask. And anyway, Bob, you know I mean what I say: I don't want it. I'm going to get re-elected to the House from Colorado and then I'm going to be Speaker again and then I'll see what I can do from up there on the Hill to help this fellow." He sighed again. "He's going to need it."

"Yes," Bob Munson said grimly. "That he is."

"How will things go on your side?" the President asked. Bob Munson, who had been Majority Leader of the United States Senate for twelve years, looked thoughtful as he contemplated his ninety-nine fellow egotists with all their faults and foibles, their good points and their bad.

"Probably quite easily, to begin with. The tragedy will help him a great deal at first—we'll go along with pretty much anything he wants. Then the checks and balances will reassert themselves and he'll be in trouble again. But I imagine he'll do all right until we get over the hump."

"Same way with the House," the President said. "With one big if: *if* he doesn't go too fast and too far in the direction he seemed to be going before this happened."

"That's our personal reaction, Bill," Senator Munson said. "*We* didn't like what we thought he was doing, playing along with the violent at home and apparently favoring a new appeasement abroad. But we're a little old-fashioned, you know. We're not really in the trend of things. We still believe in America acting like we think America ought to act. A lot of our fellow citizens don't agree any more. Ted speaks for them, you know, not for us. How sure are you that Congress won't follow him, even down that road? I can think of quite a few on my side who will."

"My side too," the President conceded. "But I'm not going to let them get away with it."

Senator Munson gave a wry little laugh as the car and its outriders left Pennsylvania Avenue and started up Wisconsin.

"We think we aren't, my friend, but the days when you and I could pass miracles on the Hill are pretty well over, I think. It's going to be a hard fight from now on, particularly if we have a President who's pulling the other way."

"Then we'll just have to keep him from it," the President said firmly. But again his companion uttered a wry little laugh.

"Mmhmm," he agreed. "We'll try, Bill, there's no doubt of that. But I have a feeling we won't get much help from him or his staff."

"That's why we've got to fight like hell to see he doesn't get himself surrounded with the wrong crowd," the President said. "This Vice-Presidential nomination is the first step."

"Yes," Bob Munson said, "and who's going to be at this little huddle about it? Who has he called in to advise him?"

"Who has Patsy called in, you mean," the President suggested dryly. "I got the call from her, not from him."

"But presumably—"

"Presumably," the President agreed. "But maybe he really is too shattered to take a hand."

"Well," Senator Munson said tartly, "if Patsy Jason Labaiya is going to be the new powder-room President of the United States, then I'll lead the revolution myself. Anyway, he knew we had to come and see him as soon as possible. It couldn't be delayed."

It was the President's turn to say, "Mmmhmm."

"I can understand his calling in Roger P. Croy," he said, grimacing slightly as he thought of Oregon's silver-haired, demagogic former Governor who had led the Jason forces in convention and in the National Committee. "And Tom August. And even Jawbone Swarthman. But George Wattersill? And Walter Dobius? And LeGage Shelby? And Rufus Kleinfert? And *Fred Van Ackerman?* My God, man!"

"That's all right," Bob Munson said. "We have Bob Leffingwell and Stanley Danta and Cullee Hamilton and Lafe Smith. And maybe one or two more. And that's not too bad a company."

"Outnumbered," the President noted. "But prepared to put up a gallant battle, no doubt. Who do *we* want for Vice President, Robert? Do you have any ideas?"

"Let me startle you," the Majority Leader offered, not entirely in jest. "Since you don't want it, how about me, just as a practical matter of party harmony?"

"You don't shock me at all," the President said, "I'm 'way ahead of you. But we have to convince Ted, you know. And there'll be plenty of other voices there tonight saying No."

"And who will they propose?" Senator Munson inquired sarcastically. "Fred Van Ackerman?"

"I won't be a bit surprised if the name is mentioned," the President said. His companion looked genuinely shocked.

"That would be insanity. Utter, rabid insanity."

"We live in an utterly rabid age in which insane things happen," the President pointed out. "I have the feeling we aren't more than a hairline away from something like it. These next few days and weeks are going to be critical."

"These next few hours are going to be critical," Bob Munson said. A sudden profound sorrow touched his face.

"Ah, hell. I wish Orrin were here."

"I don't let myself think about that too much," the President said. "Or anyway, I try not to. Don't succeed very well, I'm afraid. It's too awful."

"I have no words for it," Senator Munson said simply. "It's almost beyond comprehension, still. Do you think that guy they're holding did it?"

"It looks like it," the President said. "The FBI tells me there's a pretty strong presumptive link between this and Harley. His plane crashes, I move in, Orrin's nominated, Orrin's killed, Ted moves in. You could make a strong case that somebody is out to arrange the American succession to suit himself. Or themselves."

"Who is it? The Communists?"

"Now right there," the President said with a return of a little of his customary wryness, "you're sounding like the same old reactionary bastard you always sound like. How can you be so conservative and crude?" His expression changed and became somber as their little cavalcade turned off Wisconsin and started west on Massachusetts Avenue, rolling swiftly past the few startled citizens who were on the streets to see its hurried passage. "Could be that bunch in NAWAC. Could be 'Gage Shelby's friends, or Van Ackerman's friends, or Kleinfert's friends. Could be somebody working behind or through them. Could be somebody they've never even heard of. Could be Tashikov and the Russians. Could be the Chinese. We intend to find out."

"And when you find out," Bob Munson said with a sudden bitterness, "what good will it do you? If it involves the Communists, you can't convince anybody, the media won't let you. Walter Dobius will write columns and the rest of his crowd will go wild. You can state it until you're blue in the face and all they'll do is pour on the ridicule until they bury you under it. Even now, I suspect, Walter and his friends will still maintain that no outside power could possibly have any interest in the American Presidency or could possibly intervene in any way that would affect it. Particularly so kind and friendly a power as the Communists. *Even now*. It surpasses belief. But there it is."

"The special investigating commission and the Justice Department have their orders," the President said. "If we find out, we'll state it. Walter and his friends can rant and ridicule all they like. We'll state it and we'll keep on stating it. Eventually some of it will get through."

"But not to enough people," Senator Munson said. "Never, in these recent years, to enough. They've got us on the run, Bill. I'm not so sure as I used to be that we're going to break through."

"We've got to," the President said grimly, "and we will."

"Stout words," Bob Munson said, "but only as valid as the next President makes them. . . . I only wish Warren Strickland had a chance."

At this reference to the humorous, astute and dignified Senate Minority Leader, senior Senator from the state of Idaho and almost certain Presidential nominee of the other party, the President smiled for a second before the unhappy weight of the unhappy day closed down again.

"Warren's smart. He doesn't want it and he won't run very hard for it. . . . And anyway, there isn't a force on this earth that can beat Ted Jason now, with the sympathy vote he's going to get."

"Not a force except himself," Senator Munson suggested. But the President shook his head.

"Not even that. As long as he's alive and able to stand on his two legs, wave a little, smile a little, open his mouth and state the time of day, he's going to get it. Ceil gave him that when she went."

"Gave him that," Bob Munson agreed somberly. "And took with her —what? She was a marvelous girl, Bill. She may have been the last balance wheel Ted had. Without her, who knows what he will do?"

"I'll tell you what he'll do," the President said with a sudden uncharacteristic contempt that revealed how little he really liked the man he believed would be his successor. "He'll get himself elected any way he can and then he'll run this country the best way he knows—for Ted Jason. And devil take principle and patriotism and everything else. That's what *I* think he'll do." Then he sighed and shook his head. "No," he said, more quietly, "I mustn't be that hard on him. Mustn't be so harsh. There's got to be more to him than that. We've got to believe there is."

"With Ceil around," Senator Munson said slowly, "yes. At least there would have been somebody at his side working all the time to keep alive the good instincts, which I think he has, and the good character, which I think he started out with and maybe still has underneath. But now . . . I don't know." He stared with a sad expression at the trees relaxing limply from the fierce summer day. "I'm really scared, Bill. For the first time in all my years in this town, I really don't know whether a President of the United States is going to take care of his country. And that's not a very nice feeling."

"I don't go quite that far, yet," the President said softly, "but I tell you, I don't rest very easy, either . . . which is why," he added abruptly, pragmatism returning, "we have all got to support him and help him just as much as we can. The country's been traumatized by these deaths—Harley, Orrin, Ceil, all in ten short days—it's too much, we're reeling. And the only real element of stability right now is the sympathy for, and the popular support for, Ted Jason. Whatever our doubts, we've got to suppress them for the sake of the country. We've got to present a united front for the election and then we've got to help him be a good President. And the start of all that process," he concluded as the sleek black limousine and its whirring escort came to Spring Valley, left Massachusetts Avenue and began to climb the gentle ridges toward the comfortable house where the aftermath of tragedy awaited them, "comes right here."

"I know," Bob Munson said bleakly. "I hope she'll understand."

"Beth Knox?" the President said. "She'll understand. She always does."

Dimly she was aware of noise outside, of movement downstairs; somebody seemed to be coming, but she did not know who it was nor did she want to know. She wanted only to be left alone, to sleep, to forget, to die if she could: she did not want to stay in a world of such horror as had come to her three days ago at the Washington Monument. Thirty years of public life had come to this, and if she had her way, she would be quickly out of it and on her way to rejoin the good-hearted, volatile, impatient and idealistic soul at whose side she had lived for so long.

Except that she could sense dimly, through the enormous black mass that seemed to overhang everything, crushing down upon her heart and mind and physical being, that they apparently did not want her to leave. They were apparently trying to keep her alive. They apparently were determined that she should stay with them and share the horror, instead of going away. It seemed terribly, awfully, dreadfully unfair. But it was obvious that this was their intention.

Somewhere back down the day—or was it yesterday, or the day

before?—she remembered vaguely that someone had come to the door, looked in, entered, taken her hand gently, said something. Had it been a nurse? Had it been—who had it been? And what had she said?

With a great effort and for the first time since—since *it* had happened—she made a deliberate effort to force her mind into some coherent pattern; and for what seemed a very long time, while she again became conscious of some stirring and movement downstairs, distant, muffled, infinitely far away, it did not appear that she was going to succeed. All she could think of over and over, like some sickeningly insistent broken record, was a voice desperately demanding attention—some sort of amused reaction to this—a quick half-heard retort by someone she sensed rather than knew to be her husband—the start of a laughing rejoinder in a woman's voice—a sound, a flash, a blur, a searing pain in her right side—and then horror, back again full strength as it had returned to overwhelm her ten thousand times while she drifted heavily in and out of sedated sleep. She wanted to struggle, cry out, move, protest. But bleak and awful came the knowledge that it would do no good, and that the terrible dead weight that suddenly sagged against her, spurting blood, would never again respond to human voice or know a sentient thought.

But now the noises below seemed louder, more insistent; and slowly, desperately, protesting every step of the way yet beginning at last to bow to the automatic disciplines of a trained and well-ordered mind, she began at last the long return to the condition of knowing she was Beth Knox, who had a certain being, a certain personality, a certain way of thinking and looking at things—and a certain responsibility. She had never wanted responsibility again, but the habits of three decades of public life were too ingrained to permit her to drift away forever. Finally they were beginning to reassert themselves.

For the first time in seventy-two hours she had a conscious, deliberate thought that moved in a consistent uninterrupted progression. She remembered who it was who had come in and what she had said. It was Lucille Hudson, herself only ten days widowed, and what she said was what had to be said, the only thing that could be said to a public wife in their condition. The words did not come back too clearly to Beth even now, but the import was the import neither could escape. The import was Duty; and to Duty, after so long a time in public life, there could be only one answer, and the answer was Yes.

So she must rouse herself and try. Louise had managed and so had others; and so could Beth Knox. She had been unable to attend the funeral for on that day she was still, although her wound was beginning to mend, in such shock that the doctors would not permit it; and she might not have attended anyway, for hers had been a genuinely close and loving marriage, and instead of going through the public charade the more honest thing might well have been to stay away. It was a choice she had not had to make, so she would never know.

But now she did have a choice to make, and knowing it, knew her decision already. She could not leave the hurrying world, for all the horror and pain and anguish it had brought her in a second's frightful passage. She had to come back, for much still depended upon Elizabeth Henry Knox.

Now the noise and stirrings below were still louder, she knew people were entering the house, knew instinctively that they must be coming to see her; knew that somehow she would find the strength to see them, whoever they might be. With an effort that at first seemed enormous but decreased in difficulty as she proceeded, she raised herself slowly to a sitting position—swung slowly around until her feet rested on the floor—suddenly saw her face in a mirror, red-eyed and swollen with weeping—stopped abruptly and felt for a moment that she could not possibly go on—but did, because she knew she must.

A few minutes later when her daughter-in-law, Crystal, and Lucille Hudson knocked gently and entered, she was standing and already partially dressed. A few minutes after that, trembling with the physical effort and emotional strain but with head held high and mind steadily clearing, she was able to come slowly down the stairs on her son Hal's arm and greet her guests as Beth Knox should.

"Dear Bill," she said managing from somewhere a reasonable ghost of her old, comfortable smile as she saw their sadly troubled faces, "dear Bob—what can I do to help?"

He too had heard voices, much the same: somewhere an outcry, exaggerated in its intensity, begging their attention—a quick rejoinder by someone he knew must be Orrin Knox—the start of a laughing reply by someone he knew (though even now he fought himself desperately not to admit it) must be his wife—a sound, a flash, a blur, a jarring impact, momentarily too fast for pain, in his right shoulder— and at his side a strange little cry, a flowering mist of blood, a crumpled movement so fast he could not understand what it was —until it was finished, when it became all he could understand, over and over and over again, without surcease or mercy.

So passed three days in which the world moved on without Edward Montoya Jason, though high and mighty were the proceedings in his name. Dimly he had been aware—for Patsy had tried to rouse him to go and would have succeeded had the doctors not intervened with emphatic alarm—that a funeral was held. Dimly he knew—for Patsy crashed triumphantly through his drugged cocoon to tell him—that he was now his party's nominee. Dimly he sensed—though his exhausted mind could not really grasp the fact—that he had become someone very important, even more important than Jasons always thought themselves to be. Dimly he understood, with a great and infinite weariness, that this meant that the world that had killed his wife would now be demanding many things of him. And flatly, furiously, with an almost animal fear, he rejected them all and turned his back upon the world.

But now three days were gone and this was the fourth; and somewhere below, in and around the big old house in Dumbarton Oaks, he began to realize that there was a stirring, a restlessness, a change, and knew instinctively that it was for him. People were coming and he knew they were coming to see him. He did not know who they were, or what they could want (although Patsy had tried to tell him this morning somewhere in the haze of steadily decreasing sedation), but he knew, as surely as Beth had known, that he must respond.

Abruptly he had a sudden sharp revelation of where he was and who he was. In that moment, for the first time since the horror at the Monument Grounds, Ceil Jason really began to die and Ted Jason began to live again.

For what purpose, however, he did not really know as he got slowly and painfully out of bed, his shoulder still on fire, his mind still shuttered, his heart still stunned. He realized now that he was the Presidential nominee, and off in some other world this probably should make him very pleased, for God knew he had desired it more fiercely than he had ever desired anything. He realized also that this meant he must make decisions, choices, resume the active direction of his own destiny and that of his country. But one thing more he realized now, implacable and without appeal, and that was that he must do all this without Ceil. And without Ceil, as he had told her just before they left the house for the last time together, he did not know what he would do.

Yet it was obvious that he must do something. The noises and stirrings and excited sounds were growing louder. It was apparent that quite a few people must be arriving. He had nearly completed his slow and awkward dressing before he finally remembered Patsy's words and understood the reason. And then only because he happened to think of the words "running mate," and remembered finally that he had none.

Struck by the fact, which suddenly hit him with all its implications, he paused and listened to the babble below and then went slowly over to the window and looked down at the porte-cochere and the winding drive. The parking area was crowded with the paraphernalia of an obsessively communicative age. Sound trucks were drawn up, television cameras were in place, reporters he recognized stood about. The house was under siege and now he knew what he was supposed to do and why they all were here. They had come to report his first decision.

For a moment he felt a sharp annoyance with his sister, who presumably had arranged it all; but then he knew, with an increasingly swift return of political awareness, that of course it had not been Patsy, it had been the imperatives of the situation. A Vice-Presidential nominee had to be chosen and chosen at once, the moment the doctors declared him able. He wondered briefly why they had not given him more time, but decided that perhaps it was some kind of therapy. Maybe they felt it was best that he be brought out of grief with the abrupt challenge of having to do something. If that was it, he told himself with a certain wryness, it seemed to be working. For the first time in seventy-two hours he was looking forward instead of back. A little excitement and anticipation began to stir in his heart. Who was waiting and what did they seek of him? And what did *he,* the nominee for President, intend to do about it?

Carried by the excitement of this he moved back, more quickly now, to the closet, completed his dressing with tie and coat, turned toward the door just as Patsy knocked vigorously and called out, "Ted, can you come down soon? Some VERY interesting people are here to see you!"

"I'll be down in a minute," he called back, sounding, she was thrilled to hear, much like himself again. "Make them comfortable."

"I've had a conference table set up in the ballroom. I'll tell them you're on your way."

"I'll be right along," he promised and turned back to study himself in the mirror for a moment. His eyes were dark-ringed and sad, his face drawn and thin beneath its tan, but the over-all impression of silver-haired, commanding force and dignity was unimpaired. If anything, sorrow seemed to have made it more impressive. For just a wry, split second he thought: *Tragedy becomes me.* And instantly was overcome with shame that he could think such a thing, even in jest, at such a time. Sorrow rushed back upon him, adamant, implacable, overwhelming. He sat slowly down on the bed again, his head in his hands.

"TED!" Patsy bellowed from below.

Somehow he stood up.
Somehow he moved to the door.
Somehow he managed the stairs.
Somehow.

"There are times," Frankly Unctuous said in his rich plum-pudding tones, looking out with a simple candor from the little screen as he concluded the nightly news roundup with the usual portentous moments that were officially designated "Opinion," "when the world narrows down.

"Tonight is such a time.

"Even as we bid one another farewell on yet another fateful day in the onrushing history of this confused but well-meaning land, party leaders and top advisers of Governor Edward M. Jason are gathering at his sister's home here in Washington to confer with him on the selection of a Vice-Presidential candidate.

"Few meetings in recent years have been more important for the nation than this consortium of brains and influence. What they say to the candidate for President—what he says to them—the decision he reaches after considering their views and matching them against what he believes best for the country—all will have vital bearing on our nation and the course she is to pursue from now on in world and domestic affairs.

"Dreadful as were the events of four days ago which struck the late Secretary of State Orrin Knox from his party's leadership, it is yet possible for many to anticipate a turning of enormous significance for American life. Feeling, as they do, a deep horror and sadness at his loss; sympathizing, as they do, deeply and sincerely with his bereaved family—still they can perceive, awful though the occasion may be, some glimmering of hope for the future that could give the terrible sacrifice a meaning worthy of its shattering dimensions.

"It could, in fact, well mean an end to all those dangerous policies of foreign intervention, manipulation and war with which the Secretary and the last two administrations in which he served were so closely identified in popular thinking both here and abroad. It could mean the turn toward final peace with which Governor Jason is so closely identified, and for which he had been expected to work as Vice President in a possible Knox Administration.

"Now his subordinate position has been changed by some hand or hands as yet unknown; and shocking and unexpected as the transformation has been, still it has brought what almost amounts to a revolution of hope to the nation and the world.

"Now the war in Gorotoland, begun on what many have regarded as the phony pretext that American citizens and American big business investment in that far-off African land had been attacked, can be speedily concluded on a just and honorable basis. Any such conclusion would, of course, as a majority of the United Nations clearly desires, result in the removal of Prince Terence Ajkaje from the throne to which he has now been precariously restored by American arms, and the substitution of his enormously popular cousin, Prince Obifumatta, now temporarily in exile, as head of a truly liberal and democratic government.

"Now the war in Panama, launched by the last two administrations to prevent the Panama Canal from being returned to the hands of its rightful owners, the Panamanian people, can also be speedily wound down on a similarly just and honorable basis. This would, of course, mean recognition by the United States of the legitimate claims of the Panamanian People's Liberation Movement led by Felix Labaiya-Sofra. It would mean the establishment of the PLM as the ruling force in the nation, with Señor Labaiya as President. It would mean a speedy end to the present Administration's imposition of a unilateral blockade on such friends of America as Great Britain, France and the Soviet Union, who are shipping supplies to the PLM. It would mean that democracy, for the first time in many decades, would once more control the Isthmus.

"It is true, of course, that Governor Jason has not yet been elected President, and that if he is, there will still ensue a transition period of more than two months before he can be inaugurated. But every indication now is that he will win triumphantly, and that his very presence at the head of the ticket will have an immediate and enormous influence on President Abbott and the remaining five months of the present Administration.

"And if Governor Jason has a Vice-Presidential running mate who agrees with him 100 per cent, of course, his influence will be even greater. The party will speak with one leadership and one voice and after the election the nation will do the same. There will be no divided counsels, no hesitations, no holding back from the great goal of peace.

"That is why Washington waits tonight, tense and anxious, for the outcome of the fateful discussions with the Governor. Will he yield to those who may propose a running mate from the party's war camp, on the spurious argument that this would somehow bring about 'party harmony' and 'national unity?' Or will he decide, with the courage and integrity that have always characterized his public career, that he must have beside him as second-in-command and political heir a man as firmly and selflessly dedicated to genuine world peace as he?

"Washington waits—the nation waits—the world waits.

"None of the three really expects to be disappointed in Edward Montoya Jason."

For a few moments as he reached the bottom of the stairs, she was all he could see. All the rest were a blur, no other face came into focus. Their eyes met, hers filled with tears, his responded. Spontaneously she held out her arms and he came forward. For a brief and fleeting moment they were united in grief, before politics, ambition, philosophical divergence and the crowding world rushed in again.

"Ted," she said, almost in a whisper. "I hope—I hope—"

"Yes," he replied, equally low. "I'm managing. And you?"

"Yes," she said. "I think so. I think so."

"Good," he said, and before he could say more,

"WELL!" Patsy exclaimed brightly. "Here's everybody, so I guess we can get to work!"

For a second longer they remained staring into each other's eyes. Then he shook his head, a quick, regretful movement as if to say, *You see? I have no choice.*

And from somewhere in the accumulated depths of character Beth was able to nod quite matter-of-factly and say calmly, "Why, of course, Patsy. So we should."

At this, seeming to gain strength from her example, he was able to move forward, hand outstretched, and begin the ritual of greeting. Blurs became faces, faces became collections of ideas, beliefs, principles, prejudices, personal and political ambitions and associations: the living, powerful people with whom he must organize the future.

"Mr. President," he said gravely, and Bill Abbott shook his hand with all the dignity of Mr. Speaker and Mr. President combined. Senators Bob Munson, Stanley Danta and Lafe Smith came next, standing together in a concerned yet friendly grouping; Tom August, chairman of the Senate Foreign Relations Committee, with his usual awkward, shy and nervous manner, almost shuffling forward; Bob Leffingwell, focus of so many bitter emotions from one side during the time when the Senate defeated his nomination for Secretary of State—focus of bitter emotions still from the other side, now that he had swung over to support of the Administration and its war policies; Walter Dobius, stocky and stern and, as always, pompous and faintly, yet inescapably, smug; George Harrison Wattersill, that glamorous and well-publicized young attorney, defender of the sick, the misfit, the lost and the headline favored; Cullee Hamilton, California's powerful young Negro Congressman, his handsome face and thoughtful dark eyes troubled and unhappy; J. B. "Jawbone" Swarthman, chairman of the House Foreign Affairs Committee, his usual ebullience momentarily suppressed but likely to break out again at any moment; Roger P. Croy, ex-governor of Oregon, smooth and bland and confident in his power with words and crowds; LeGage Shelby, chairman of Defenders of Equality for You (DEFY), dark and scowling, particularly when his eyes met those of his onetime friend and college roommate, Cullee Hamilton; Rufus Kleinfert, pasty-faced and dumpy, head of the Konference on Efforts to Encourage Patriotism (KEEP); and Senator Fred Van Ackerman of the Committee on Making Further Offers for a Russian Truce (COMFORT), carefully standing apart from his fellow legislators, insolent and unyielding.

This was the oddly assorted aggregation that would help him select a Vice President. There shot across his mind the thought: *God help me, I don't believe it.* But the old habit of command was beginning, though still somewhat raggedly, to return. It was with a passable authority that he said politely, "Mr. President, Mrs. Knox, gentlemen, if you will come into the ballroom and be seated, please, we can begin."

There would come a time when he would look back and decide that to accept this strange hodgepodge of people and not demand the removal of some of its more extreme members such as LeGage Shelby and Fred Van Ackerman might very well have been his first decision of all, and perhaps his most serious and fateful one, considering all that was to flow from it. But he was in no mood or condition to understand this now, and it did not occur to him until much later, when it was too late.

When they were seated around the long conference table that Patsy had directed the servants to put together from two dining tables and a green baize cloth, himself at one end, the President at the other, a silence fell and he realized that they were all staring at him intently. The President broke the silence to ask the question they all wanted to ask.

"How are you feeling, Governor?"

He managed a small smile, for their interest was genuine enough and, for the moment, quite removed from politics.

"Not too bad," he said and added slowly, "under all the circumstances." Then he seemed to draw himself together, took a deep breath and leaned forward to speak as he knew they wanted him to speak.

"I want to thank you all," he said gravely, "for your concern for me at this time, which I believe far transcends any political situation in which we find ourselves. I know how you must be feeling about my —my bereavement—and I want you to know that I am deeply grateful for your sentiments. I thank you and I know that—" for just a second his voice broke, but he recovered and went on firmly—"she is grateful to you too. . . .

"I know also," he added, and for a moment his eyes met Beth's and she was able to murmur her thanks, "that I speak for Mrs. Knox as well in expressing our gratitude to you. It is a great help to us both. . . .

"Well, then—" his tone deliberately stronger and more impersonal— "so you are here, I take it, to give me advice on the Vice-Presidential nomination. I don't know who invited you—" Patsy shifted slightly in her chair, halfway down the table, and he smiled slightly—"but it was a good move, Pat. I have to make a decision and I know it can't be delayed, and so I think it is just as well you are all here to help me. I had always thought," he added, a certain dryness entering his tone, "that this sort of thing was done in a series of small conferences instead of one large one, but maybe these are unusual times and we should use an unusual method. Anyway, you are here and I am happy to have your ideas."

He stopped and again there was a silence as they all watched him intently. Again it was the President who broke it with his customary directness.

"You have no one to suggest yourself, then."

He shook his head and began to make some frivolous rejoinder—"If you only knew—" perhaps, or, "I can't even think straight yet"—or something of that nature. But he knew this revelation of the chaos that lay behind his outward calm would only shock and dismay them. And they wouldn't believe it anyway. He suppressed the impulse and continued to perform as he knew they wanted him to.

"Not at the moment, no. I had rather get your thinking first. Possibly, if I might suggest, Mr. President: there seems to be a pretty clearly defined division here, just as there was in the convention and the Committee and, indeed, in the country. So why don't you act as spokesman for the one group, if you like, and someone else—Governor Croy, possibly, or Senator August, or whoever is agreeable—might speak for the others. With everyone, of course, having the right to state divergent views if he so desires. Is that agreeable?"

He looked around the table, took silence for consent.

"Very well then, Mr. President. You have the floor."

For a moment the President did not reply, staring thoughtfully at Ted Jason as he leaned back, appearing tired but effective: handsome, dignified and in command. *He looks the part, anyway,* the President thought dryly. *Maybe I can wake him up. Maybe I can wake them all up.*

"I think," he said slowly, and to him, too, they gave their intently watchful attention, "that the most logical candidate for Vice President, the one who would be the most popular choice and would do most to unify the party and the country, would be the one who best exemplifies the philosophy and the character of the late candidate for President. I think you'd be making a mighty smart move if you took Mrs. Knox."

There was a complete, stunned silence as he sat back and stared impassively around the table at expressions which ranged from Lafe Smith's sudden grin to LeGage Shelby's scowling dismay to Patsy's scornful disbelief. He had invited an explosion and knew it was coming. Its source did not surprise him.

"What kind of crap," asked Fred Van Ackerman with a deliberate insolence, "is that?"

"Spoken like the boor you are," the President said coldly, and whatever fragile peace had existed in the room was abruptly ended.

"Now, Mr. Chairman," Senator Van Ackerman said, and his voice suddenly sailed up in the sharp psychotic whine his colleagues in the Senate knew all too well, "now, Governor, I don't think you should permit that kind of language. I don't think you should permit this used-up old man who temporarily fills, and yes, unworthily fills, the office of President, to talk like that. He is unworthy, Mr. Chairman, and he is politically passé. He is on his way out and the sooner the better. I suggest, yes, I suggest, that he be asked to leave this conference, Governor, Mr. Chairman, unless he can offer something that makes some sense and has some bearing on what we're trying to do here. I so move, Mr. Chairman!"

"Now, Mr. Chairman—" Senator Munson began angrily through the babble that began all around the table. But the President's calm voice got through before Ted could act; if he had been going to act.

"Let him talk, Governor. Let him rave on. This is what we are confronted with in this party and we had all better have it spelled out clearly for us once again before you make your decision. I offer you a true lady, one of the great ladies in American public life, and back comes this rude, crude, intolerant, boorish behavior. That summarizes the issue for you, right there. We might as well realize it right now."

"Governor," Senator August said from down the table in his hesitant way. "Mr. Chairman, if I might say something—?"

"Yes, Senator," Ted Jason said, and added in what seemed, curiously, almost an afterthought, "the meeting will be in order, please. Proceed, Senator."

"Well, Mr. Chairman," Tom August said, "I don't want to inflame the discussion any further, but I do think, if the President will forgive me, that there is much more to the issue than the unfortunate remarks of the Senator from Wyoming. I do regard them as unfortunate, Mr. Chairman," he added stoutly as Fred gave him a black look, "and I agree with the President that they probably deserved the epithet 'boorish.' But, Mr. Chairman—I don't think we should permit our discussion here to be influenced too much by unfortunate turns of phrase or ways of speaking, for no doubt we will all be guilty of some exaggerations as we go along. I think we must stick close to what the real issue is, and on that I offer you what may be a simplification, but which I nonetheless believe to be a sound one. The issue is peace or war, Mr. Chairman. It is as simple as that.

"What has confronted us all along?" he asked, as all down the table his listeners either nodded agreement or looked stubborn and uneasy, according to their philosophies. "In the whole long-running argument over this party's leadership? That argument really began, you will remember, with the nomination—and rejection—of Mr. Leffingwell, here, to be Secretary of State. It appeared to go in one direction when President Hudson succeeded to office and began the actions in Gorotoland and Panama. It appeared to go even further that way when you, Mr. President, moved into the White House and increased and made more emphatic both those involvements. And it appeared to go entirely in your direction when the recent convention nominated President Hudson for re-election and then, after his tragic death, nominated Secretary Knox for President.

"But you will remember, Mr. Chairman," he said quietly, "that each of these steps along the way was violently and bitterly opposed by almost a majority of the party and of the population; and you will remember that their opinion was so strong and so inescapable that the late Secretary was virtually forced to accept as his running mate Governor Jason, the man who now, through yet more tragic fate, carries our party's standard as Presidential nominee.

"There was nothing open and shut about it at any point along the way. The 'war party'—if I may use that invidious term for convenience only—was opposed every foot of the road. Its control was marginal at best—tenuous, fragile and uncertain. At each turning point it could have reversed itself and changed the pattern of events; and great numbers of the citizenry wanted it to turn back. Now we have come to one more turning point, tragic and unexpected but nonetheless here before us—a fact. And we have what may be the last, the only, the ultimate chance to turn back. I think," he said softly, peering about the table in his gentle, almost wistful fashion, "that is the real issue, Mr. Chairman and Mr. President. It is war or peace, and the choice of Vice-Presidential candidate will indicate to the country and the world more surely than anything else which it is going to be."

He paused and looked about vaguely for water. Patsy rang a bell, there was a brief pause while two maids hurried in, distributed pitchers and glasses along the table, withdrew. Tom August drank slowly; wiped his lips carefully on a handkerchief; went on, his audience silent and intent.

"It seems to me, Mr. President, that if a so-called 'war party' candidate agreeable to you and some others in this room were to be chosen, a great feeling of dismay and disaster would sweep over the country. Not all the country," he said hastily as the President gave him a sudden frown in which skepticism and annoyance were equally mixed, "but a very substantial portion of it. Indeed, I think it may safely be said, a majority of it. Whereas a so-called 'peace party' candidate—"

"Ah," said Lafe Smith with a knowing intonation, and for a second Senator August looked quite offended.

"You can say, 'Ah,'" he retorted with a rare asperity, "but the fact remains that a Vice-Presidential candidate leaning generally in that direction is obviously what the country desires. At least," he added with a defensive irony, "in my humble estimation."

"Mine, too," Fred Van Ackerman said with a harsh contempt. "It's so obvious I don't see why we have to waste time on a lot of pious crap about it."

"I beg your pardon—" Tom August began, his face flushing. But Bob Munson forestalled him.

"You people fascinate me," he said. "You cannibalize each other, don't you? You can't even be decent with each other long enough to achieve what you all want. It's amazing. And very revealing."

"We'll achieve what we want," LeGage Shelby said with an ominous scowl. "Don't you worry about that."

"Yess," Rufus Kleinfert agreed in his peculiar accent. "Don't you worry about that."

"I'm worried as hell about that, if you want to know," Senator Munson said bluntly. "I can't imagine anything worse for the country than to have this ticket beholden from top to bottom to people like you and what you represent."

"And what's that, Senator?" Fred Van Ackerman inquired coldly. "It's only common sense, isn't it? It's only what's best for the country, isn't it? It's only peace, which is what this country wants, from top to bottom and from one end to the other. That's all it is, Senator. *Peace,* if you aren't too stupid to know it."

"This is one of your principal sources of strength, Governor," Bob Munson said, and his reference called their attention suddenly to how silent Ted Jason was being through all this. "I hope it pleases you."

For a moment Ted did not answer, seeming far away and abstracted. Then he shook his head as if to clear it and spoke with a calmness that reassured them all, even those who were greatly fearful of what he might decide this day. The man who would be President *had* to be calm: how else could they?

"I think I can assess my support for what it is, Senator. Insofar as it sincerely represents the desire of all patriotic Americans for peace, I am not worried about it. I am, in fact, proud to have it. Senator August, are you through?"

"Well," Tom August said doubtfully. "Well—yes, I guess I am. I guess I have stated the issues, basically. As I see them, anyway."

"Good," Ted Jason said. "Mr. President, did you wish to add anything further in support of your position and your nomination of Mrs. Knox?"

The President gave him a look as thoughtful as his own and spoke with an equal calmness.

"No," he said slowly, "I don't think I have much to add—except possibly this. We are still confronted here, as Tom says, with exactly the same issues we were confronted with at the convention and in the National Committee. Violence masquerading as peace on the one side, a genuine concern that the country remain strong in spirit and in fact on the other. And, as before, no real compromise possible between the two unless there is genuine desire for compromise on the part of those most directly involved." His face became grave, his voice touched with sorrow. "Until four days ago, that meant two people. Now it means just you. Maybe you should tell us how much *you* want to compromise between these two points of view. Our opinions and desires, after all, are probably academic alongside yours."

But Governor Jason, as the President surmised, was not to be drawn into a revelation of his position just yet.

"I am open to suggestion at this point," he said quietly.

"Very well, then," the President said, somewhat tartly. "I have suggested Mrs. Knox as the best candidate to unify the party and the country. How about it?"

There was an uneasy, and in some cases angry, stirring along the table and before anyone could respond Roger P. Croy had his hand up and his mouth open.

"Governor—" he said. "Governor—if I may. It seems to me there are further things to be said before we can proceed—*you* can proceed —to a decision. Possibly also there are other candidates to be proposed. With all respects to one of the most gracious, most attractive and most intelligent ladies in American politics"—Beth gave him a wry smile, but he was, as usual, impervious—"the President's suggestion may be too pat. It may be too neat for the grave problems that confront the country. It may be one of those solutions which, seeming on their faces perfect and profound, exacerbate differences rather than settle them. How would the selection of Mrs. Knox, one wonders, settle anything, any more than the selection of her husband did?"

"He had the choice," Cullee Hamilton said with a sudden anger, "and he chose Ted Jason. You thought that solved plenty at the time. Now that *your* boy is on top, you don't see it that way. You're a great man, Governor Croy. You've got real character, that's for sure."

"Well, Mr. Chairman," Roger P. Croy said blandly, "I really see no need to indulge in personalities. I am sure the Congressman will not deny that the situation has sharply and tragically changed from what it was when the late Secretary of State had the choice he refers to. For one thing, even conceding Mrs. Knox's many virtues—which all of us concede, all admire and none deny—there is no single figure of her husband's stature remaining on the national scene to represent his point of view. Unless, of course," he said with a sudden soft blandness, "the President himself might wish to step down and run for Vice President, as a contribution to national unity?"

But at this, to Roger Croy's obvious delight, both Ted and the President answered together.

"I have said repeatedly—" the President began.

"The President has said repeatedly—" Ted began.

Then they stopped and laughed a little, while varying degrees of amusement flickered down the table.

"Obviously we agree," the President said, "so that ends that ploy— that Croy ploy, perhaps I should say. We could, on our part, give you alternatives, despite your kind statement, Governor, that we are so devoid of brains and ability that we have none. There is, for instance, Congressman Hamilton. How about a black on the ticket? Surely that would please a great many. How about Mr. Leffingwell, here? He has quite a constituency among those who are honest enough to appreciate an honest man who has had an honest change of heart.

We have the Senate Majority Leader, certainly a man who has proved through many a long season and many a legislative battle that he is deeply and devoutly devoted to the preservation of America. . . . We have candidates, you see, Governor Croy. It is not as though we are completely devoid of anyone at all. Who, might I ask, do you propose? Yourself?"

At this Roger P. Croy, who had indeed indulged such ambitions at the national convention a couple of weeks ago when it appeared Ted might beat Orrin for the nomination, uttered a deprecating laugh.

"Mr. President," he said, "your humor does you credit. But it is not to my poor person that Governor Jason should turn for running mate. Surely he has better alternatives than that. We might, for instance, propose the distinguished chairman of the Senate Foreign Relations Committee. How about that?"

This time the President shared his reaction with Tom August.

"What?" he demanded with an indignant disbelief, and,

"*What?*" cried Tom August with a ludicrous dismay.

"Certainly," Roger Croy said calmly. "Who more fitting? He has just given us a most cogent and effective statement of the issue before the country. He has just shown himself a most reasoned and powerful spokesman for the point of view held by many of us, including, I believe, our candidate for President. So, why not?"

"Well, if you really want to know—" the President said; and then he smiled. "But that would take too long. Anyway, you don't really want it, do you, Tom? I seem to have that impression."

"Gracious," Senator August said. "My gracious! I never thought—"

"Neither did anyone else," Fred Van Ackerman agreed with a brutal flatness, "so that takes care of that."

"Well—" Tom August began indignantly, stung out of his usual meekness. "Well, I—" But no one came to his aid, and after a moment his voice trailed away.

Into the silence there intruded the flat, heavy voice of Walter Dobius in his most pompous, Moses-leading-the-Israelites-out-of-difficulties manner.

"Governor Croy is too modest," he said calmly. "Surely he is far and away the most qualified candidate of the group which, I believe, represents the present mood and intention of the country. And we do not yet know how Mrs. Knox feels about it. Perhaps—" he turned to peer at Beth down the length of the table—"she is not as eager as her supporters."

Called thus directly to their judgment, she returned his look with a gaze which she hoped was as bland and steady as his own, though she felt a sudden desperate trembling inside. *If you were only here,* she thought; but the other half of the great Illinois team of "Orrin and Beth" would never be with her again. She drew a deep breath and spoke in a voice that shook only slightly.

"Yes, Walter: perhaps that would be advisable, to find out what I think. Looking at it from a strictly pragmatic political point of view—" and even the harshest critics of her husband around the table listened with close attention, for Beth Knox had the reputation of being as shrewd and practical a politician as any in Washington—"having me on the ticket would of course greatly strengthen Governor Jason's chances, because it would bring to him all the many Americans—and they are not, perhaps, so much in the minority as Tom assumes—who supported my husband and believe in the policies he stood for. On the other hand—" and she gave a small, rather wistful smile—"does Governor Jason need any strengthening? Isn't he already so strong that his election is a certainty? And where else can my husband's supporters go, if not to him? And so why does he need me?

"I will leave aside any question of whether or not I would like to be on the ticket, because I regard that as quite academic under the circumstances. It is not a necessity for victory, and so what I might feel about it myself is really not important at all. If *you* should wish me to serve—" and she looked straight at Ted to emphasize the choice of pronoun—"I should of course be willing to do so. If you decide otherwise, I should of course support your choice and the ticket.

"I would, though," she said, as they all listened intently, studying her pleasantly attractive, comfortable face, "like to make just one point about it. You do have the power, Governor, of course. You can choose anyone you like. You don't have to choose anyone from the 'war party,' if we have to use Tom's rather unpleasant way of putting it. But you perhaps ought to keep in mind that there *are* a great many people who believe in these policies, and that they are not bloodthirsty, not ravenous for war, not irresponsible. They just have a different way of looking at the same set of facts involving Communist power, particularly Soviet power; and they see a different solution and a different way of meeting the challenge. Basically, maybe, the difference is that they *admit* the challenge, while many on your side of it—or so it seems to us—will not.

"So: I think you would be taking quite a gamble, and perhaps be making quite a mistake, to dismiss them summarily and ignore them completely in making your choice for Vice President. You can do it, your power of selection is absolute; but it might be really a very ungracious thing, and also one that would weaken your hand in the

White House. Because the country really should be unified, Ted; we need it desperately, after these recent months and years; and it can't be done by deliberately ignoring a great segment of the population. . . .

"That, at any rate," she concluded quietly, "is how I see it. Those are my thoughts on it. I offer them to you for what they are worth."

And she sat back with a little sigh, brushing a stray gray hair with a hand that trembled slightly, as Governor Croy leaned forward again to speak in a calm and well-reasoned voice.

"Which, if you will forgive me, Mrs. Knox, is not, perhaps, as much as they should be worth at such a time and given such a serious situation in the country.

"We all appreciate, I am sure," he went on smoothly as the President and Bob Munson showed signs of protesting his comment, "the great patriotism with which you speak, and the profound and sincere concern that prompts your remarks. You have made a most generous and becoming offer—to serve or not to serve as it suits Governor Jason's pleasure; and there is no one of us, I am sure, who has any doubts whatsoever that you have the ability, the intelligence and the character to fill the high office of Vice President of the United States if Governor Jason should so desire. I for one would rest very comfortably with it, I will state to the group—*under present circumstances*. But, Mrs. Knox and ladies and gentlemen—" and his voice sank to a hushed and thoughtful low—" as we all are so tragically aware in these times —circumstances change.

"Twice in recent days hands unknown have struck down the leaders of America. And even you, Governor, may not be immune. . . .

"I don't want to raise hobgoblins," he said firmly, as an uneasy stirring greeted his remark, "but it is necessary for us to face these things. If by any tragic mishap, yet a third leader should be removed from us—and if he were then in the White House—and if Mrs. Knox were his Vice President—then she would be President."

"And would that be so bad?" Bob Munson demanded with a sudden sharp impatience.

"Ah, Senator," Governor Croy said gently, "it would not be bad in the sense you mean it, or in the sense that the country would not have a wise and steady leader. But don't we come back, right here, to Mrs. Knox's own point? Aren't we faced with the possibility that the vast numbers who place their faith in Governor Jason and his policies would thereby be, in a very real sense, summarily disenfranchised?

"Would his policies, even with the best will in the world on the part of his successor, not be inevitably and perhaps harshly reversed in some major degree? Should he not in short, have someone beside him who would continue to carry out his policies of peace, the policies which I happen to believe are favored by the great majority of our countrymen?

"It is, I suggest, something to think about. It is something to consider most carefully. It is, to me, the kernel of what we are discussing here. It is not so much continuity of office. It is continuity of ideas."

"Well, I'll be damned," Bob Munson said. "And isn't that what's involved right now? Continuity of Orrin Knox's ideas—continuity of the ideas that won endorsement of the national convention and the National Committee—continuity of the ideas that won the victory and took control of the party not a week ago?"

"But are not," Roger P. Croy pointed out softly, "in control of it now. That is what you must remember, Senator: which are not in control of it now."

Again there was a silence as all along the table they studied one another carefully and then turned at last to the silent figure at their head. But from the handsome face, the distinguished profile, the tired, deep-set eyes, they did not, for several moments, receive response. Then abruptly Ted spoke, passing across his eyes a hand which, like Beth's, trembled slightly from emotion and fatigue.

"You have all been very kind to come here today," he said, "and I appreciate your giving me your advice. But, as you truly say, Beth, it *is* my decision, and I think I have to make it—alone.

"I am aware," he went on, as again there was the fitful, restless, demanding movement along the table, "that time is of the essence. I am aware you need—the country needs—I need—a decision at the earliest possible moment. The things you have said, particularly the President, Mrs. Knox, Senator August, Governor Croy, have needed to be said, they are important and I have had to have them in order to make up my mind. But now I—" and he repeated the pronoun and gave it a slight but unchallengeable emphasis—"*I* must make up my mind. And no one can do it for me.

"Also," he added with a sudden little smile that foreshadowed the return of his considerable charm, "I am feeling a little tired and a little rocky still, and I think maybe it's time for me to take a little snooze and gather myself together. But I promise you," he concluded, abruptly grave again, "that I shall have a decision for you by tomorrow and no later. And now—" he stood up, slowly and somewhat awkwardly, but managing reasonably well; and they perforce stood with him.

After they had come forward to shake his hand and pay their respects, and just before they began to move slowly and somewhat uncertainly toward the door, he held up a hand and smiled again.

"Keep the wolves outside at bay," he commanded. "No statements, please, no interviews, and no comments on me, my appearance, the Vice Presidency or anything."

"What do you think?" Bob Munson murmured to the President as they left the room and started along the hallway to the front door.

The President shrugged.

"Who knows?" Then he frowned. "He'll call in Croy and Dobius and the NAWAC crew again later, I suppose, and they'll decide it without us."

But in this the President was mistaken, for no one was called back to Patsy's house that night, no one was telephoned, and all who tried to telephone were politely brushed off. And at Press Club bar and Georgetown cocktail party, in humble home and stately mansion, on tube and airwave and printed page, the speculation raged and grew through the night and into the morning and on into the afternoon of the following day, while the nominee for President rested and repaired his health further and, not entirely without calculation and not entirely without enjoyment, let the world dance to the tune he set.

2. THE ANNOUNCEMENT, when it finally came at 6 P.M. on the day after the meeting at Patsy's, was surprising to some, anti-climactic to others, worrisome to many, and for all those around the world whose plans and strategies were geared to the troubles of what they regarded as the West's bemused, uncertain and declining giant, a pleasing and encouraging sign.

Dutifully, at home, the build-up began.

"The selection of ex-Gov. Roger P. Croy of Oregon as Vice-Presidential running mate for Gov. Edward M. Jason of California," Walter Dobius wrote busily in his 436-newspaper column at beautiful "Salubria" in the steaming Virginia countryside near Leesburg, "gives great and justified hope to a war-weary nation and a war-weary world that the United States is finally going to turn away from the international aggression and adventurism which has characterized these past few frustrated years.

"The endorsement of the National Committee, given in a brief pro forma session immediately following Governor Jason's formal announcement of his choice for running mate, makes the fact clear for all the world to note: A peace ticket is in the field in America, and in America a peace ticket is going to be elected.

"This fact is as certain as anything in American history has ever been.

"With it come still wider certainties, more profound and more gratifying to all who believe in the concepts of lasting peace among nations and the ability of mankind to live in harmony with itself.

"Now the unjust decisions of the war in Gorotoland will inevitably, in due course, be reversed by a Jason-Croy Administration. Liberal, democracy-loving Prince Obifumatta will be assisted to replace his corrupt, reactionary, fascist-minded cousin, Prince Terry.

"Now, more importantly, the shameful conflict in Panama, which is threatening to turn into another Viet Nam on America's very doorstep, will be ended. Canal and country will be placed in the hands of their rightful owners, the democratic and forward-looking Panamanian People's Liberation Movement led by Felix Labaiya-Sofra.

"And most importantly of all, new, genuine and really good-faith negotiations will begin with the Soviet Russians, whose military might increasingly surrounds us and whose earnest desire for genuine world peace is apparent everywhere their ships, subs, missiles, planes and bases encircle and embrace the earth.

"All of these, and more, will come from the triumph of Governor Edward Jason and Roger P. Croy, the very able man he has chosen to run with him and assist him as Vice President. . . ."

"We would be remiss indeed," said the *Times* in the magisterial tones with which it liked to confer its blessings—or its disapproval—upon the wayward nation for whose destinies it felt such personal responsibility, "if we did not make the point that some have overlooked in their comments on the selection of Gov. Roger P. Croy as Vice-Presidential candidate:

"This is a good man.

"These simple words sum up why the nation, we submit, should be delighted with his nomination as running mate for Gov. Edward M. Jason of California. It is not only the fact that his choice makes of the Jason ticket—and the Jason Administration-to-be—so single-minded, so united and so bright a promise of world peace.

"Dwell for a moment on the qualifications of this man who has come out of the West: Phi Beta Kappa student, Rhodes scholar, brilliant lawyer, husband, family man, civic leader. Major political figure of the great Northwest, twice governor of Oregon. Prime mover in many national causes, committees and campaigns in the ceaseless quest for peace. More recently, principal lieutenant of Governor Jason in his quest for the Presidency. Liberal, progressive, forward-looking, staunch, undaunted, never-tiring fighter for human justice.

"Citizen of America.

"Citizen of the world.

"Roger P. Croy.

"We do not think Governor Jason could have made a sounder choice. We wish him and his running mate—and America—well, in their certain election and their certain Administration, to which all decent men everywhere can look forward with bright and confident hope. . . ."

"It is rarely," Frankly Unctuous informed his viewers on the evening news roundup, "that the selection of a Vice-Presidential candidate is an occasion for genuine rejoicing in the land. Far too frequently these men—who, in one of history's most shopworn but most accurate clichés, stand only one heartbeat away from the Presidency—are simply the leftover choices of party politics. All too often they are selected to appease one party faction—to 'balance,' as they say, the ticket.

"Well, tonight, in former Governor Roger P. Croy of Oregon, appeasement of party faction has been tossed out the window and a true balance of integrity, honor and hope has been achieved.

"Not for Edward M. Jason the shabby compromises of conventional politics. Not for him the appeasement of defeated political enemies. Not for him an artificial 'balance' which could only hamper, hinder and handicap his Administration as it goes forward.

"He has grasped the overriding necessity of his candidacy in these desperate times—a running mate who sees things as he does, 100 per cent. He has him, in Roger P. Croy. *We* have him, in Roger P. Croy.

"If, as seems likely, Governor Jason is a shoo-in for election, the nation can rest easy. Whatever happens in the future, the cause of peace is guaranteed in the nomination of a Vice President made today."

In similar vein crowed *The Greatest Publication That Absolutely Ever Was,* the *Post* and Percy Mercy in his new magazine, successor to *View* (named, of course, *Overview*). In similar vein caroled networks, newsprint and all thinkers of Right Thoughts in politics, the arts and sciences, drama and academe. So thought they, overseas. So sang NAWAC.

It was not surprising at all that most of these trumpeters of the Vice-Presidential nominee really had only the haziest idea of what he was all about. It was not surprising that this sudden and overwhelming flood of praise should have come quite automatically, simply because he was running mate of the man they wanted for President. It was not surprising that they should thus give this lavish and enormous build-up to a man who was, for many of them, a pig in a poke. He was *their* pig in *their* poke, and it was not the first time in American history that the self-same process had occurred. And this time, of course, he was on the Right Side of *everything*. That really made it perfect.

There were some, of course—illiberal—stupid—enemies of peace—in love with war—imperialistic—short-sighted—antediluvian—dangerous—reactionary—"conservative"—who had some doubts.

Naturally they included the President and Senator Munson, who, however loyal a face they put upon it in public, could not conceal from one another their profound misgivings about the basic character of Roger P. Croy; Robert A. Leffingwell, who said, No, he was not, when Patsy called triumphantly to ask if he wasn't simply THRILLED TO DEATH by Roger Croy's selection; Beth Knox, who had seen in the gesture of her own nomination really only a symbol of genuine balance, which she now feared was gone altogther; some few journals, commentators and columnists, terribly reactionary, who felt uneasily, in an old-fashioned and out-of-date sort of way, that balance at such a time was indeed vital, and that the nomination of Roger P. Croy might well open the gates to excesses they could not help but worry about; and some older members of Congress, who took the experienced long view that the violent elements backing Ted Jason needed the checkrein that a more middle-of-the-road and vigorously skeptical Vice President might provide.

Not the least of those who worried, though no one who had been at Patsy's that night, or indeed anyone of those who now so loudly welcomed the Croy nomination could have believed it, was the nominee for President. Even as the chorus swelled throughout the land and overseas (JASON PEACE TICKET CONFIRMED BY VICE-PRESIDENTIAL NOMINATION, said Paris *Soir;* PEACE CAMPAIGN BEGINS WITH CROY NAMING, said *Corriere della Serra;* WAR FORCES IN U.S. FACE FINAL DEFEAT, said *Aftonbladet;* RUNNING-DOGS OF IMPERIALISM LOSE U.S. HOLD, said the *Indochina People's World* published simultaneously in Hanoi, Saigon, Phnom Penh, Vientiane and Bangkok), he was engaged in a conversation with his newly chosen running mate which was to come back to him many times later, so significant did it become in retrospect.

It took place two days after the nomination in the book-lined den at Patsy's house, where a temporary office had been set up. In those familiar surroundings he had thought he was at home with most things in his world, but discovered he was not.

The first indication he received of this was word that Roger P. Croy was not arriving alone. The reaction when he objected brought the start of an uneasiness which grew, softly but insistently, throughout their talk.

"Governor," he said when Roger Croy was shown in, "I hope you will forgive my insistence that we talk alone. But it seemed to me that this early in the campaign—and also, this early, really, in our personal knowledge of each other—it might be best."

"As you like, Governor," Roger Croy said calmly. "Although," and the clever, intelligent eyes clouded a moment with an obvious hesitation, "I had thought perhaps Senator Van Ackerman, Mr. Shelby and Mr. Kleinfert might be able to contribute something of value to our discussion. They do represent, after all, probably the major elements in our support. However, if you think best— . . ."

"I think so," Ted Jason said.

"I see," Roger Croy said thoughtfully. "I would assume, however, that when we begin detailed planning for the campaign and the Administration, you will wish to consult them—and, of course," he added smoothly as a little glint came into Governor Jason's eyes—"many others as well, as to plans—programs—strategies—personnel—"

"I would expect to receive their ideas and suggestions, yes," Ted agreed.

"But not right now," Governor Croy said slowly.

"Not right now," Ted agreed pleasantly.

"Well," Roger Croy said briskly, a candid smile replacing the faintly regretful, almost wistful expression, "then I suppose they will just have to wait until a more propitious time."

"Perhaps they will," Ted said, still pleasantly. "Tell me, Governor," he inquired with a sudden calculated curiosity, "why did you bring them with you in the first place? Doesn't it seem to you a little odd that the first meeting between the Presidential nominee and the man to whom he has given the Vice Presidency should be—cluttered up, as it were—by outsiders? Don't we have the right to get acquainted a bit, and to plan basic strategy alone, at least in the opening stages? I'm a little puzzled."

"Governor," Roger Croy said with a smile, "you have a right to be puzzled and a right to seek clarification. I suppose they wanted to be here—and, quite frankly, I thought their presence would be helpful to us—because, in a sense, you would not have 'given' me the Vice Presidency as you so accurately state it, if it had not been for the pressures of public opinion in the country which these gentlemen so vigorously represent. I suspect if it had not seemed best to you to—shall we say, cooperate—with these elements, you would not have made me this 'gift.' You would have 'given' it to Mrs. Knox, or to someone equally worthy to speak for that particular faction of the party and the country. In the eyes of Senator Van Ackerman, Mr. Shelby and Mr. Kleinfert, you chose, in a sense, 'their man.' As, of course," he added smoothly, "you yourself are 'their man.' Isn't that correct?"

For just a second a genuinely angry expression came into Ted's eyes; all the arrogance, determination and fierce pride of his indomitable grandmother, Doña Valuela, and all his other Montoya and Yankee-trader Jason ancestors flared out for a second. Roger P. Croy thought he might have gone too far.

But almost as soon as the spark flared, it died; and Governor Croy breathed easier. This was, after all, a man still desperately shattered by the horror of his wife's death. For quite some time, in all probability, he would not really be very difficult about things.

"Anyway," Ted said rather lamely, "they have no right to be with us now."

"Certainly not," Roger Croy agreed. "But perhaps a little later—after we have had a chance to talk—their advice could be quite helpful, I think. Perhaps we can consult with them then. After all, there would be no point in deliberately antagonizing them. They do represent many millions of votes which must be considered. But more importantly, and more worthily, they represent a genuine desire for peace which I am proud to say *you* and *I* represent. That, I think, is the perspective from which we must view them."

Ted nodded, passing a hand that still noticeably trembled over his eyes.

"Yes, of course. Their views will have a proper place in the campaign."

"And, I would assume, in the Administration," Roger Croy suggested. But this time the nominee for President sounded more Presidential and less compliant.

"We shall see. . . . Tell me about yourself, Governor. We've never really had much chance to talk, in these last few hectic weeks. I have appreciated your support, as you know, at the convention and in the National Committee, but there certainly hasn't been time to get acquainted. You're fifty-seven, right?"

Roger P. Croy gave a little mock bow and a graceful little laugh.

"I have you outdistanced by a handful of years. But I think there's life in the old boy, yet."

Ted smiled.

"Oh, I'm sure of it. I wouldn't have chosen you for running mate if I weren't—support from our friends," he added with a trace of acid, but amicably, "or no support. And you have, of course, a family, and you are in favor of love, motherhood and the flag."

Governor Croy chuckled.

"I was in favor of love at twenty-two when I married, and promptly expanded this to include motherhood when my darling Katherine began presenting me with a steady sequence of offspring which finally numbered, as you no doubt know, seven. Five of them happily married, the sixth engaged and the seventh and last soon to graduate from Stanford and no doubt embark upon the same quest. I only regret, Governor, that you yourself did not have children to comfort you in this most tragic— . . ." His voice trailed away with a certain sympathy whose unctuousness Ted was unable to perceive as his face twisted suddenly with pain.

"No," he replied, staring out the window into the still, hot day, eyes suddenly clouded with emotion. "We were not that lucky."

"So sad," Governor Croy said gently. "So terribly sad. It would have been such a comfort to you now."

"I know," Ted said in a choked voice. "I *know*. Now please go on . . . tell me more about yourself."

"Not much to know beyond the public record," Roger Croy said matter-of-factly. "Lawyer, public servant like yourself, twice Governor of Oregon, leaving office three years ago. 'Activist,' to use the jargon term, in politics—at least activist in the sense that I had, I think, a very good reform record in the state house and have always been very vigorously engaged in campaigns for world peace. The *Times*," he added comfortably, "summed it up pretty well in their editorial."

"Yes, I saw it," Ted said, sounding more himself again. "They like you."

"I flatter myself they do," Roger P. Croy said with a certain complacency. "It is comforting to know I have such support. As, of course," he added suavely, "do you."

"Which of us, do you think, has more?" Ted asked with a certain quizzical note in his voice. Roger P. Croy gave the only answer possible.

"You, of course," he said flatly. "What would I be without you?"

"If I thought you really meant that, Governor," Ted said with a certain moody pleasantry, "I might have no worries at all about anything."

"Do you have worries?" Governor Croy asked in a disbelieving tone. "And if so, what are they, for heaven's sake? Certainly they don't revolve around me, I hope!"

"No, of course not. Except as I wonder—"

"What?" Roger Croy demanded with the start of an indignation, whether real or faked, Ted could not tell. "What is it you wonder, Governor?"

"I keep coming back to your traveling companions this morning," Ted said. "They puzzle me. You puzzle me. I wonder," he said with an ironic echo, which he did not at first realize, of the President and Orrin Knox talking to him before the nomination, "how closely you can identify with those elements without becoming beholden to them in some way that could affect the campaign—and perhaps even the conduct of the Administration afterwards."

Governor Croy was ready for him.

"Governor," he exclaimed with a growing amusement. "Governor! This is not Africa, you know. No sinister plots revolve around Vice Presidents. I can't conspire against you. You won't be deposed by me, God knows! And anyway," he went on, less humorously, more reasonably, "it isn't just myself they support, is it? They support you too, far more than they do me. If anybody has problems, it's you. But, of course, I utterly reject and denounce the idea that you do."

"Do you?" Ted Jason inquired, almost as though he didn't believe it. "Do you really?"

"Certainly," Governor Croy said, surprised. "Don't you?"

"I don't know," Ted said slowly, and his running mate was intrigued to note the slow and almost hesitant way in which he spoke. "I know the President and Orrin were always very— . . ." and his voice trailed away.

"Very what?" Roger P. Croy demanded. "Governor—Mr. President—surely you aren't going to let their attitudes influence you now? You are the nominee. The Secretary of State is gone and the President is going. What could they possibly have said to you that could be allowed to hinder you now?"

"They have always been very worried," Ted said more strongly, "that in the forces that comprise NAWAC I might be aligning myself with things really dangerous to the United States. I know," he said, raising a cautionary hand as Governor Croy started to interrupt, "all the reasons you and others produce to argue that this isn't so. God knows I used them myself in my talks with Orrin and the President. I *know* there are many, many millions of sincere and loyal people who disagree with the war policies of the Administration. I *know* there are many, many millions of genuinely patriotic and genuinely uneasy Americans who oppose the methods and the manner of American intervention in world affairs. I *know* all the arguments for democratic dissent and protest, and I *know* many of those who dissent and protest are perfectly democratic and perfectly loyal. I *know* all these things, Governor . . . and yet—"

"And yet what?" Roger P. Croy inquired, and his tone now was sympathetic and understanding.

"And yet there has been enough violence of a sinister nature," Ted Jason said quietly, "enough protest of a deliberately organized and deliberately anti-democratic sort, enough protest and dissent of a deliberately anti-American kind, that I think—I think we had best be very careful, you and I. Because while I am not about to antagonize or lose the support of the genuinely loyal and genuinely concerned—as I told Orrin and the President—I am also not about to place myself in bondage to those who really want to destroy America, if I can help it. They do exist, you know."

"'Destroy America,' Governor?" Roger Croy echoed in disbelief. "Who could 'destroy America?'"

"Oh, 'America' wouldn't be destroyed. Something with that name would still be around, of course. Nobody would be stupid enough to change that. But it would be a far different country from what you and I have grown up in."

"Isn't that assurance enough?" Roger Croy inquired thoughtfully. "That we *have* grown up in it, that it *is* part of us, that we would never knowingly betray it in any way or surrender it to its enemies? That as two Americans charged, or about to be charged, with control of the destinies of America, we simply could not conceive of letting it go down?"

"Yes, Governor," Ted Jason said, still quietly, "but look at what we inherit if we win. We have mounted an effective, and mercifully short, engagement in Gorotoland. We are fighting to hold Panama and the Canal. But how much margin does that leave us, these days? How strong are we, really? How much have our predecessors, even Bill Abbott and Harley, who certainly have wanted to act in the tradition that America had power, left us to operate with? Defense has been cut back steadily in recent decades—the Soviets have consistently spent twice as much of their national budget as we have, all the while certain very vocal and powerful elements of our people have been demanding we cut back. And some past Congresses and administrations have bowed to this, and have cut back. Soviet power surrounds us in all the oceans and lies deployed and ready, if still hidden, not only in and under many areas of the earth's surface but in the skies above. In a good many vital ways we are *second-rate*, Governor. The facade remains but what lies behind it? And how do we protect America when the knock comes on the door and history says, 'This is the moment. It

is now or never'? What do we do then? Particularly if we have let ourselves be persuaded or controlled by elements inside the country who
clamor, 'Don't fight—be safe—do it the easy way—*open the door!*'"

For several moments after he concluded, his expression somber and
moody, his eyes far away down the lush byways of the formal garden
beyond the windows, Governor Croy said nothing, simply staring at
him with an open disbelief and dismay, as though he could not possibly have heard what he had just heard. When he responded it was
with a very careful slowness and a very careful choice of words.

"Is this Ted Jason whom I hear?" he inquired softly. "I cannot believe it. It seems such a complete and abrupt reversal of everything
you have been saying in all these recent months. It just doesn't make
sense. Suddenly you sound as militaristic, as dependent upon armed
force, as wedded to outmoded concepts of 'national power' and 'national prestige' as—as Orrin himself. It astounds me, Governor. I can't
believe it. Surely I must be mistaken in what I hear? Surely this does
not represent your final and considered judgment on these things?"

Ted sighed and shook his head.

"Maybe I'm beginning to believe my own publicity," he said with a
wry little smile. "Maybe I'm beginning to think like a President already. But they are things we must think of, you and I. . . . No," he
said, more positively, with an abrupt shake of the head. "I don't agree
with all of that, of course. I'm not turning my back on everything I've
advocated and spoken for in these recent months. I'm not betraying my
true believers, Governor. But I *am* saying that these are things to consider, and that they make it even more imperative that we be very
careful about certain people and certain forces and how intimately
we let them participate in what we do."

"But even that is quite a change," Roger P. Croy said with some
dismay. "Does it mean you are not going to redress the dreadful
wrong done in Gorotoland—you are not going to restore Prince Obi
and a truly democratic government? Does it mean you are not going
to end the conflict in Panama and recognize the government of Felix
Labaiya? How can you turn your back so completely on the people
who believe in you, Governor! I am shocked and dismayed, I will tell
you frankly. Shocked and dismayed."

"You can always resign," Ted remarked with a sudden tartness that
momentarily halted Roger P. Croy in his oratorical tracks. But as usual
it took him only a moment to recover.

"And abandon the man I believe in, the only one in America who
can lead us back to a position of dignity and justice and peace in this
world?" he inquired blandly. "It is hardly likely. Having accepted the

high honor of being at your side, Governor, I could not so rudely abandon it now. But I can, I trust, express from time to time my thoughts—and my misgivings, if it should come to that. I trust I am not to be foreclosed from candid and helpful comment. It seems to me that would be a betrayal of one of your truest 'true believers,' indeed!"

"Governor," Ted said with a smile, "I can see I have met my match."

"Oh, I hope not!" said Roger P. Croy with an amiable good will. "I hope not!"

"I'm not so sure," Ted said with a quizzical look. "I'm not so sure. . . . Governor," he said, suddenly serious again, "of course I mean to do what I can to correct what seems to me an unfortunate outcome of the conflict in Gorotoland—"

"Which will mean withdrawing American forces from support of Prince Terry's government?" Governor Croy suggested.

"Which will, in the long run, have to mean that," Governor Jason said, "providing it can be done without turning over the government to a successor who would invite the Soviets into that most strategically located African state. We can't just cut and run, I'm afraid. It will have to be done gradually."

"Again, the militaristic concept," Governor Croy said sadly. "Why is Gorotoland 'strategically located,' Governor? Why must we bother ourselves with a local quarrel in a little country in the bush, far away? Why can't we simply let democratic elements prevail, and take our chances? . . . But—no argument now. No doubt the policy will have to develop as we go along. . . . And Panama?"

"Panama," Ted said thoughtfully, "is a different matter."

"And why is it different?" Roger Croy demanded. "Is it not the same militaristic concept of imposing American wishes by force? Are we not confronted with the same phony, hysterical arguments of 'military necessity,' 'national defense needs,' 'strategic requirements'? When what we are really confronted with, as we are in Gorotoland and indeed wherever else we have unfortunately seen fit to blunder in, in recent years, is simply the sincere desire of smaller nations and peoples to be free and independent and work out their own destinies. . . . Governor," he said, suddenly deeply earnest and intent, "I beg of you—do *not*, now that you have finally achieved the power to lead the world, abandon the millions of Americans and the millions everywhere in the world who desperately want peace. Do *not* go back to the old, outmoded, bloody way of doing things. There must be a better way, Governor! *There must be.* A troubled humanity looks to you to find it. Do *not* weaken, do *not* yield, do *not* turn back. To do so would be a dreadful betrayal of us all. Simply—unbelievably—

dreadful. . . . That is why," he went on presently, in a less fervent tone but grave and earnest still as Ted watched him attentively but without expression, "I do hope you will be able to consider, even if you are unwilling to consider them now—for reasons which I grant you," he acknowledged smoothly, "are valid—the views of the gentlemen who were to have accompanied me today. The views and, I might add, the assistance of these gentlemen in the difficult times ahead."

Ted frowned.

"'Assistance?' How so?"

"I would expect," Governor Croy said somberly, "that we may be in for serious troubles when it becomes clear that you really are going to reverse past mistakes and restore American policy to a basis of sanity in the world. Those who favor the harsh approach—the radicals of the right—may not take it lying down. There may be genuine trouble."

"In which case," Governor Jason said with a thoughtful slowness that told his running mate nothing, "your friends may be able to help in some way. What way?"

"*Our* friends, Governor," Roger Croy corrected pleasantly. "And I don't know what way, exactly. But I do know that I would rather have them on our side than against us. They do represent a very strong and very vocal element. And if there is trouble—"

"If there's trouble, they know how to create it, right?" Ted inquired with a sudden dryness that momentarily shattered the earnest composure of the distinguished visage before him. "Governor," he said firmly, "we must think about these people very seriously."

"You were not so hesitant to accept their support when you were seeking power," Governor Croy said quickly. Governor Jason nodded.

"And now I have it," he said quietly, "or at least you all tell me I soon will. And that illumines many things." Abruptly, startling his running mate, he stood up and held out his hand. "Well. Thank you for coming, Governor. We shall talk again. Many times."

"But—" Governor Croy began, for once nonplussed. "But—"

"I believe Patsy is expecting us for dinner," Governor Jason said. "And then I'm off to 'Vistazo'—and a little rest—and a lot of thinking."

And he did fly out later that night, in the larger of the family planes, to "Vistazo," the great Jason ranch that sprawled along the soft brown coastal hills north of Santa Barbara, its comfortable old ranch house still controlling the remaining six thousand acres of the once enormous land grant held by his Montoya ancestors in the days of Spanish California. But before he left he had one thing to do; and after he had said goodbye to them all (refusing Patsy's offer to keep him company, saying he wanted to be alone for a little while at the ranch), he made a telephone call from the car and then spoke to the chauffeur. Obediently the car turned and headed west across town.

"Why does he want to see you now, the tricky bastard?" Hal Knox inquired bitterly. "I wouldn't let him in the front door, if I were you, after all he's done to hurt this family."

"Well, I don't think—" Beth said slowly "—I don't think *he* has done it, so much as the people behind him. I think he's very genuinely shattered by it."

"By losing Ceil, maybe," Hal said, unrelenting, "but not by losing Orrin Knox. It's going to make him President. Why should he feel shattered about that?"

His mother shook her head.

"You're too harsh. Too harsh. I can't hold him personally responsible."

"Not personally responsible?" Hal demanded with an angry disbelief. "My God, how charitable can you be? If he hadn't encouraged the violence at the convention and kept it going during the National Committee meeting, Dad would—would—" his voice broke a little and then strengthened again with indignation. "And you don't hold him 'personally responsible!' Well, *I* do, I can tell you that."

Beth sighed.

"Yes, I know. Maybe you'd better take him away somewhere when Ted gets here, Crystal. We can't trust him to behave, I guess."

Crystal Danta Knox smiled a little at her husband, vigorous and indignant and so much like his father in that righteous moment that Orrin might almost have come back to them.

"He'll behave. It's just the Knox in him running rampant."

"I will not behave," Hal said firmly. "I think he is an evil man, and even more fundamental than that, I think he is a fool."

"And of the two," Crystal said gently, "Knoxes may abominate evil but they absolutely *despise* a fool. Right?"

"Well," Hal said, smiling a little in spite of himself, "you can make fun of me, but by God, he *is* evil and he *is* a fool. And he's going to run this country right into the hands of God knows what, now that he's got the chance."

"But not deliberately, I don't think," Beth suggested.

"I said he was a fool," Hal reminded her tartly. "Of course it won't be deliberate. He won't know what he's doing. They'll take him and us to the cleaners before he even knows what's hit him."

"I think you underestimate him a little," Crystal remarked. Beth nodded.

"So do I. Ted Jason isn't a fool, he's a very smart man and in some ways a very shrewd one. And I happen to believe that down underneath it all he is very deeply and genuinely concerned for this country and very determined to be a success as its President."

"'Underneath it all,'" Hal echoed scornfully. "Underneath what? Buddy-buddying up to all the NAWAC crew? Playing along with violence until it cost Crystal and me our baby and my father his life? If that's an example of Jason judgment, I don't want any more of it, thank you very much!"

"She didn't say he had judgment," Crystal pointed out quietly.

"No," Beth said, "I didn't. And that's where the problem comes. And that's where the Knoxes have to help, if they can. And they can't help, my dear child, if you're going to remain hostile and antagonize him the minute you set eyes on him. That isn't going to help anybody accomplish anything. It's going to ruin whatever chance we have to encourage him to be the President he's going to have to be to save the country. And I mean 'save' quite literally. So calm down, Harold, and approach the strategic problem like a true Knox would, after all the puffing and blowing is over."

"You two," Hal said, again smiling a little, "you're a pair. You can soft-soap a man into anything . . . except Ted Jason," he said, abruptly somber again. "You can't soft-soap him, because he's gone already—long gone. And he isn't coming back, the road he's gone down to get where he is. It's too late to save the country, Mother. He's given it away already, by accepting the support he has. Roger Croy, for God's sake! And Fred Van Ackerman. And LeGage Shelby. And Rufus Kleinfert and George Wattersill and all the terrible elements they represent, of violence at home and weakness abroad." His face contorted with a sudden pain. "It's too late. When they killed Dad, they pulled the plug on everything that held us together. And," he concluded simply, "I hate them for it. I hate them with all my heart and all my being. And if I have a chance to kill some of them before they kill us, I will."

But at this his mother shook her head with an expression as close to real anger as Beth Knox ever allowed herself.

"Stop that. Stop that crazy talk. Nobody is going to kill anybody—"

"Oh, no?" Hal remarked bitterly. "Somebody did."

"Well," she said flatly, "nobody is any more, we hope. We hope that's all over, in America."

"You said yourself we have to save the country," her son reminded her, his expression stubborn, unyielding, 100 per cent Knox. "What did you mean by that?"

"I meant we have to work together with Ted and anyone else we can find to restore sanity and calm and reasonable cooperation to the country. We have to work out a middle ground. That's always been the salvation of America, it still is. We can't do it by talking about killing more people, or their killing us, or any other crazy talk. We've got to bring the country together. We've got to help Ted, because he's the man who's going to be elected to do it. And we've got to start right now, by receiving him in this house as we would any other friend— because that's how we've got to think of him from now on, as a friend. We can't help him if we think of him as anything else."

"He wants our help, doesn't he?" Hal inquired dryly. "Roger P. Croy for Vice President, hey, hey. Why didn't he take you, if he's so dedicated to love and harmony? That would have helped some. A lot, in fact, don't you think?"

"Yes, I do think," Beth said quietly. "But I also can see his point of view. Knoxes aren't perfect, you know. Many millions of people take that mirror you're using and turn it right around. To them, we seem to be the awful ones and the ones whose continuance in power would mean the destruction of the country. There are actually a good many, I suspect—" and for the first time her voice quivered a little—"who actually think it is a good thing that your father—that he isn't with us any more. So, don't be too smart about it. From his point of view, Ted made the choice he felt he had to make in order to calm things down. I'm sure he considered our viewpoint very carefully, but he didn't really have to take it into account. It was his choice."

"But now we must help him," Hal remarked softly and found himself outnumbered two to one.

"Yes," said his wife and mother simultaneously.

He shrugged, somewhat helplessly, his expression still stubborn. "I hear a car in the drive," he said. "I think I'll go upstairs for a while."

"You will do no such thing," Beth said, and again Crystal came to her aid.

"I think we'd all better meet him," she said quietly, putting aside the half-knitted sweater she had been working on, standing up and sliding her arm firmly through her husband's. "Come along, Mr. Knox. You're going to be elected to the House in November and you might as well learn to work with your President, right now."

"Honestly—" he said, shaking his head with an angry frustration. "You two—" But the doorbell rang and cut him off.

Instinctively they drew together in the center of the living room to form a small, almost defensive group, as they heard one of the Secret Servicemen still on duty in their house open the door and say calmly,

"Why, good evening, Governor. Won't you come in? The family is expecting you."

"He is," he said wryly as the car swung away from the house toward Canal Road, the lazy winding river, and Memorial Bridge, "a very positive young man." Beside him the positive young man's mother uttered an agreeing sound.

"He's like his father," she said quietly. "He reacts strongly to things . . . and to people."

"I'm sorry they wouldn't come with us," he said gravely. "I'm sorry he holds me so responsible for—what happened."

"I'm afraid he does," she said, "but I expect in time he'll get over it."

"Will you?" he asked and for several moments there was silence as the big car and its following car of Secret Servicemen rolled smoothly down the brightly lighted, near-deserted streets.

"Ted—" she began, and paused. Then she spoke more firmly. "I think so. Because I don't hold you responsible in quite the personal way he does. And also," she added softly, "I think you have paid amply for whatever your responsibility might be."

It was his turn to remain silent for a time, because the emotions that suddenly seized his being were so confused, chaotic and intense that he probably could not have spoken coherently had he tried.

"Yes," he said at last, very low. "I think I have. . . . Beth—do you really blame me for everything that happened at the convention, everything that happened during the Committee meetings, everything that—everything? I've—been trying to think it through. I've been trying to face up to that, and to—a lot of things. How much blame do you think I really ought to shoulder?" He turned to look at her, his sad face illumined for a moment as they passed beneath a street light. "God knows," he said quietly, "nobody has a better right to tell me."

She shook her head with a frustrated sadness equal to his and turned away to stare out the window as the car swung down into Canal Road and turned left on its way to the Potomac.

"How can I tell you?" she asked. "I could repeat all the things you've heard a hundred times about the risks implicit in certain people who support you—but you *have* heard all those things, Ted. You've heard them for months, from a lot of people, and it hasn't changed you one bit. Why should you want to hear them again from me now? And what difference will it make to you if you do? So why should I bother?"

"I met with Roger Croy a couple of hours ago," he said. "I told him we must be very careful about certain people. I don't think he was impressed. But I meant it."

She sighed.

"I'm sure you did. But I can see his point. Why should he believe you? The concern comes a little late. And are you really sure you mean it? And how can anyone be sure you're sure?"

"Am I that empty?" he asked in a curious, musing tone. "Am I really that shallow, that lacking in principle?"

She hesitated before she spoke. When she did it was in a voice that did not hold out much comfort.

"I don't know, Ted," she said quietly. "I think you're the only one who can answer that."

And because there was no real answer he could make, and because there was nothing further she felt she could say, a silence fell and they did not return to the subject, or indeed to any subject, as the car moved swiftly down into Georgetown, along the freeway past Kennedy Center to the Lincoln Memorial, and so across the gentle river to their objective.

It was not an unamiable silence or a hostile silence, for indeed there was every consideration of shared tragedy and mutual sympathy to draw them together. Though each was lost in thoughts increasingly agonized and increasingly inward as they approached Arlington, each was profoundly glad of the other's company on this visit, which would be the first for both of them, to the two new graves on the haunted hill.

"I think," he said in a voice that trembled yet tried desperately to be humorous as the car drew slowly to a stop at the foot of the little incline, "that we have managed to avoid the press, in spite of Hal's assumption that I wanted this to be a—a Roman holiday, as he put it."

"He didn't mean it," she said. "Don't think about it. There are other things to think about."

"Yes," he agreed, his voice suddenly choked, almost inaudible. "Yes."

Side by side, Beth leaning on his arm, they walked slowly up the gentle rise, stood for several moments, bowed and silent, before the simple tablet that said CEIL HALL JASON; walked presently along the little pathway that led to a neighboring knoll; stood silent again before the tablet that said ORRIN KNOX; turned at last and walked slowly back down to the waiting limousine and its silent escort.

Only once did either of them speak.

"Did I do this?" Ted asked in an agonized whisper as they turned from Orrin's grave. *"Did I do this?"*

But Beth, lost in tears and sorrow, was unable to give him answer, except to shake her head in a sad and hopeless gesture that was no answer.

Later neither of them could remember any details of the ride back to Spring Valley. But their final words as he said good night and left for the airport neither of them would forget.

"*I will try,*" he said with a desperate, naked earnestness, as though throwing himself completely on her mercy, not knowing exactly what he meant but making some sort of desperate promise of something—to her, to Ceil, to Orrin, to himself.

"I hope so," she said, compassionate yet with a kind of distant judgment in her tone that placed the responsibility squarely where he knew it lay. "You are the one who must."

He nodded, unable to speak further. For a long moment they stared at one another across great chasms of politics and belief, great bonds of sympathy and pain. Then he turned away and was taken swiftly to the airport where he boarded his plane with an almost hunted haste. It swung out over the beautiful city, gave him a last glimpse of glowing Capitol, Washington Monument, Lincoln Memorial, Kennedy Center, Arlington and all, and then turned toward the continent and "Vistazo" lying on its western edge.

He did not read, or talk, or sleep, or even think very much, during the long journey across the night reaches of America. "Vistazo" was home. He was going there like an animal, wounded, and hoping to recover.

3. FORTUNATELY in his own view, not so fortunately in that of some others, the campaign rushed him forward, bringing its own hectic therapy even as it forced him into choices and decisions he perhaps was not quite repaired enough to make. He did not have time to worry about this, though some did. He had three days to himself at "Vistazo," haunted by Ceil's presence everywhere as he rode faithful Trumpet over the softly crumpled hills and down to the rocky shore where the cold Pacific hammered in. Then he had to fly east again to make his wildly successful kickoff speech in Philadelphia. Its theme was his preconvention slogan: *Conscience must decide the issue.*

Two months remained until election. For him and for many others in his own country and around the world, they were busy times.

"Out here," Lafe Smith wrote hurriedly to Mabel Anderson one mid-September night in Des Moines, "it looks as though everybody is right: Ted's in by a landslide. If so, I wonder why he is still talking—and acting—as though he were afraid to offend the violent. He's too gentle with them still, in my estimation. He's got it in his hands, he doesn't have to appease them. *I'm* not making that error, as you may have noticed. I think I'm in by a landslide too, but I'm not playing with that crowd. Every time they try to kick up a fuss I pick up another fifty thousand votes. Let 'em go right ahead raising hell with me because it's all to my advantage to raise hell with them.

"That's why I can't understand Ted—or, really, understand the voters, many of whom deplore some of his people but still are all-out for him. It's that 'my-hero-isn't-to-blame-it's-the-guys-around-him' syndrome that every skillful President in our history has managed to use to his advantage. And I don't say Ted isn't using it, and very deftly. But the fact remains that the odd-ball crowd is sticking very close. In my mind it's also a somewhat sinister crowd. I was very dubious when he picked Roger Croy for V.P., but I managed to swallow that. Then came George Wattersill as campaign manager, along with 'Gage Shelby as head of the minorities division and assistant to Frightful Freddie Van Ackerman, who emerges as head of 'campaign security,' whatever that means. As near as I can gather, it seems to mean turning out the gangs of NAWAC whenever you need a big demonstration; and while they're a lot better behaved—at the moment—than they were at the convention and after, it still makes me very uneasy. And it makes a lot of other people uneasy, because they tell me so when I go around the state. But they always wind up smiling rather uncertainly and saying, 'But I imagine the Governor knows what he's doing.' That blind faith people have in public figures! It will be the death of us yet.

"Myself, I'm still not sure he *does* know what he's doing.

"Anyway, one thing is certain: that crowd isn't mixing into my campaign, even if they have been around already trying to butt in. Fred called me the other day offering help 'if you have any trouble with anti-Jason demonstrators.' I've barely spoken to that bastard, if you'll pardon my French, since Brig's death. I cut him off in a hurry, said I didn't want any help of any kind from him or any of his gangs. He snarled something about, 'Don't sound so high and mighty, smart boy, you may need us yet.' Well: I won't. I'd rather go down to defeat than accept anything from that crowd.

"But it's typical of the way the campaign seems to be going. There are elements that shouldn't be in there. They can't push me around. But can they push Ted? One likes to think they can't, that it's all campaign expediency, that once a guy is President he can control anybody or anything. That's the way we used to hope it was. Maybe we're into an era now when it isn't so certain. I worry about it. So do lots of people. But Ted welcomes them into his campaign organization and seems unaware of the danger. What does that portend?

"Which is a gloomy way to sound to my two sweet gals in Utah. I hear you're going great guns on the campaign trail yourself—I know they appreciate having Brig's widow speak to them, and it's good to have you active again. I know all the candidates are very grateful for your support. And as for Pidge—she's really an electoral threat. That little monkey is probably the most powerful six-year-old campaigner in the country. Tell her Uncle Lafe said, Give 'em hell! All I can say is, I'm glad she's not working for my opponent here in Iowa. I'd be trailing instead of him, if she were.

"I'll try to call you Saturday night from Marshalltown. Once the election is over—assuming I win, which, perhaps arrogantly, I am assuming—I have plans. I intend to bring Jimmy Fry down from that sanitarium on the Hudson. And then I intend to marry Mrs. Brigham Anderson and install her and her charming daughter in a nice house, maybe on Foxhall Road, if you'd like that. And then I intend to live happily ever after. So how about *that?*

"Take care of yourself and your young lady. You're both very important to

Old Lafe."

JASON MAKES TRIUMPHANT TOUR OF WYOMING, GIVES FULL SUPPORT TO SENATOR VAN ACKERMAN FOR RE-ELECTION. NEAR RIOT AS ARMED CAMPAIGN GUARDS ROUGH UP DISSENTERS. TWO INJURED, ONE SERIOUSLY.

After furious arguments in the privacy of their editorial offices between those who were openly worried and those who were afraid to admit, just yet, that they were, *The Greatest Publication*, the *Times*, the *Post* and several other major newspapers across the country expressed the first glimmerings of a mild concern about this. But all refrained from condemning it outright. It was, in the words of the *Times*, "perhaps one of those unfortunate little episodes that occur occasionally in the heat of a campaign—nothing more. We are sure it has no relation to the true intentions of the Jason campaign or the great hopes of the country which that campaign embodies."

"Warren," the President said cordially from the Oval Office a week later, "how are you getting along? Making a lot of headway out there?"

From the Picturephone the shrewd and kindly face of the Senate Minority Leader, Warren Strickland of Idaho, gave him a candid look and a sudden wink.

"You know perfectly well how I'm doing, Bill. I'm conducting a holding action. That's why I accepted my party's nomination for President. We had to lose with dignity and I thought I knew how."

"And so far," the President agreed with an amiable grin, "you're managing it beautifully. . . . Tell me," he said, suddenly serious, "are the bullyboys bothering you?"

Warren Strickland frowned.

"They're beginning to show up. Not very many, and not in too many places, and not, so far, with any open activity. But they're increasing."

"How about Bert?" the President inquired, and at the thought of the earnest, good-hearted, rather bumbling Governor of New Jersey who was going through the motions of running as Warren's Vice President, they both smiled.

"He's getting the same."

"Odd," said the President dryly. "The fact doesn't seem to be turning up on the television screens or in the news stories. How does that happen, I wonder?"

"It happens, "Warren Strickland said crisply, "because a), the media don't want to admit that this sort of thing is appearing again in the Jason campaign, and b), the more intelligent and sensible of them are beginning to get scared about it. They're hoping it will go away before they have to mention it."

"Do you think it will?"

"It had better," Senator Strickland said, "because if it doesn't, sooner or later it will get to them. And the more farsighted can see that. Actually, no, I don't think it will go away unless or until Ted drives it out and really means it."

"Time's running out on his option," the President observed. Warren Strickland nodded.

"It is indeed."

"Well, watch yourself. Do you need more Secret Service protection?"

"No, I don't think so. I feel it's adequate. How is your campaign getting along in Colorado?"

The President smiled.

"No opposition. I'm making one visit to Leadville, and that's it. Since you folks were afraid to run anybody against me—"

"I want you back on the Hill," Warren Strickland said with a chuckle. "When you return to the House, maybe we can get some sense into Ted's head and help him get the country back on the right track."

"Maybe," the President said with a sudden gloom. "But it won't be easy."

"No," Senator Strickland agreed gravely. "But it must be done."

The President nodded.

"It must be done."

"Meanwhile, back at the ranch," Senator Strickland said, "how are things really going in Panama and Gorotoland?"

"Not too well," the President admitted. "About what the papers say. Terry's still very shaky in Gorotoland and Felix Labaiya is still riding high in Panama."

"And our dear friends and kindly enemies are still threatening to run the blockade."

"May try it, too. Which will pose some sticky problems."

"You know we've got to get out of that, Bill," Senator Strickland said gravely.

"Got to get out of them both," the President said grimly, "but not at the toe end of somebody's boot, and not until we're sure the situation's stabilized in both places. Particularly Panama. Gorotoland sits at the crossroads of Africa and that's a long-range worry. The Canal is right here and that's a now worry. I'm not abandoning it and neither would you. Ted may, and if so, more fool Ted and God help the United States. That's what we've got to stop, when and if the matter comes to Congress."

"Maybe we can't," Senator Strickland said thoughtfully. "Ever think of that? We may not be miracle workers any longer, once the new dispensation takes over."

"That's what Bob Munson tells me," the President acknowledged. "I hate to admit you both may be right, because I think it would be literally deadly to the future of this country, in the long run."

"So do I," Warren Strickland said. "I'll be in there fighting. But we have to face the possibility we may lose."

"I have four months left in this White House," the President said, "and I'm going to do what I can to fix it so the question's academic by the time it comes to him. Congress is dispersed, and until January I'm the guy in charge. And I have a few ideas."

"Good luck with them," Senator Strickland said with a combination of irony and encouragement.

"I'll need it. What I really called to tell you was that I've just received intelligence of a big shake-up in Moscow that will probably be announced tomorrow. Thought you might like to be forewarned because you'll be expected to say something about it. Our old friend Tashikov has pulled some sort of coup and has taken over as Chairman of the Council of Ministers."

"And what does that mean?" Warren Strickland asked, thinking of the shrewd, ferret-faced little fanatic who had been Ambassador to the United States and the United Nations these past several hectic years.

"Trouble," the President said grimly. "Plain, ordinary, hell-fire trouble. He knows this country like a book and plays the media like an organ. There'll be a merry tune in our ears and some tough gambling with the world along with it. . . ."

"The news from Moscow concerning the selection of Ambassador Vasily Tashikov to head the government of the Soviet Union," Warren Strickland said next day in a carefully worded statement, issued in Minneapolis, *"must be greeted with a cautious and thoughtful reserve by the American people. Chairman Tashikov has known this country intimately and well as ambassador. We must hope his familiarity has given him an understanding and appreciation of America's genuine desire to preserve and strengthen world peace. It would be tragic indeed if his memories of our weaknesses outweigh his memories of our strengths, for that could lead to errors dangerous for all of us."*

"All Americans genuinely anxious for peace," Governor Jason said in a statement issued from the Jason estate "Harmony" in Charleston, South Carolina, *"must welcome with a heartfelt enthusiasm and hope the selection of Vasily Tashikov to be head of the Soviet Government. He knows us, he understands us, he has given evidence during his years as ambassador here of an earnest desire to work out our mutual differences in peaceful and constructive ways. Insofar as I may speak for those Americans who believe in peace, I welcome him to the supreme position in his government. If I am elected in November, I shall look forward with genuine enthusiasm and high hope to the challenge of working with him to achieve the friendly cooperation of our two great countries, and world peace."*

POLLS SHOW JASON AHEAD 27 PER CENT AS CAMPAIGN HITS HIGH GEAR. "LANDSLIDE OF ALL TIME" PREDICTED BY PARTY LEADERS . . . GOVERNOR REQUESTS WHITE HOUSE CONFERENCE AS PRESIDENT ORDERS BIG ECONOMIC AID TO CONSERVATIVE GOROTOLAND GOVERNMENT, SAYS TROOPS WILL REMAIN UNTIL COUNTRY FINALLY STABILIZED. PRESIDENT STANDS FIRM ON BLOCKADE OF PANAMA DESPITE UN PROTEST, THREAT BY ALLIES AND SOVIETS TO RUN IT. COAST GUARD IN NEW BRUSH WITH SOVIET FISHING FLEET OFF ALASKA. VIOLENCE MARS

STRICKLAND RALLY IN L.A. AS NAWAC GUARDS SEEK TO BAR GATE TO SENATOR'S SUPPORTERS. SIX HURT IN BLOODY SKIRMISH.

"Whoever controls the forces of NAWAC," the *Post* said cautiously next morning, "if there is such a thing as 'control' over that amorphous peace-seeking aggregation of interests, it does seem to us that he, she or it should clamp down a bit on the excessive zeal which seems to infuse the lower ranks. We cannot believe that any responsible authority condoned the shameful bullyboy tactics that erupted suddenly in Los Angeles last night at the Strickland rally, but we do believe that it should not be allowed to happen again. It does not help Governor Jason, if that is the purpose; and it does not hurt Senator Strickland.

"It hurts, if anything, the cause of peace for which NAWAC presumably labors, and for which Governor Jason in fact does labor. NAWAC's somewhat sinister willingness to resort to force in the suppression of those with whom it disagrees should not be encouraged. It should be condemned, for by implication it carries in its train many things of serious import to the future of a free democracy.

"We hope those who value that democracy will utter such condemnation, and we hope those who guide the somewhat peculiar destinies of NAWAC will see to it that such things do not happen again. . . ."

Two hours later that morning the general director of the *Post,* trying to be casual but betraying his uneasiness to the searching eye of the Picturephone, called the gentle old man who was executive chairman of *The Greatest Publication That Absolutely Ever Was.*

"Frederic," he said without preliminary, "have you received any threats from NAWAC?"

"Not yet," the executive chairman said with a smile. "Why?"

"Well, we have," the general director of the *Post* said, not smiling, "and it wasn't a make-believe one. I thought our editorial this morning was perfectly reasonable—"

"Perfectly," the executive chairman agreed. "I've just been reading it."

"—but apparently even that was too much for NAWAC. Somebody tossed a dud grenade into the foyer this morning, and I've just received a blank-screen call that next time we criticize them it will be the real thing."

"So will you stop criticizing them?"

"We will not," the executive director said stoutly. "But I just wanted to alert you that we've got something ugly on our hands."

"Oh, I know that," the executive chairman of the *G.P.* said gently.

"I tried to convince my boys here of that during the convention and the Committee, but they never quite believed me, I think. They don't like violence but in general they like the objectives of the violent. It makes it rather difficult for us to take a stand. As you noticed, we were quite tender with NAWAC this morning—far more so than you, and God knows you weren't exactly savage. Maybe this has saved us. No hand grenades here, so far. But—" his tone became more firm, his face stopped smiling—"the time is rapidly coming, I fear, when we must take a stand, and a very positive one, too."

"Yes," the general director of the *Post* agreed unhappily. "I wish Ted Jason—"

"Talk to him," the executive chairman suggested. "I wish so, too. He was, and he remains, an enigma to me. But I think we must first be honest with ourselves: we must not evade the fact that it is we who created the enigma and wanted desperately to place it where it is. Once we accept our share of the responsibility, then perhaps we can begin to effectuate the cure."

"If we can," the general director of the *Post* said moodily. "We also have to recognize the danger to a free press, it seems to me. Maybe we were too kind to violence in the beginning. Maybe we should have seen the danger then."

The executive chairman of *The Greatest Publication* nodded.

"Yes," he agreed gently. "That could be."

Far down the lush valley of his childhood, youth and maturity, he could see the mountains rise against the sky, soft and mysterious in the aftermath of rain. At the rambling stone hacienda of "La Suerte" —named by fierce old Don Jorge, his grandfather, for "La suerte esta enchada," or *The die is cast*—Felix Labaiya-Sofra, oligarch of Panama of the new style, knew that it was indeed cast, and, he believed, in his favor. Not only was his Panama People's Liberation Movement successfully holding the troops sent by that old man in the White House, but the old man had trapped himself, with his silly attempt at blockade, into a position in which he was daring Felix's powerful friends to break through and come to Felix's aid. The challenge made it almost imperative that the friends try to do so. Then would come the unthinkable confrontation, and since it was indeed unthinkable, after it would come the irreversible retreat of the United States that had been inevitable for so many years.

And then would come the final humiliation of the hated colossus of the North, no longer so colossal in these days of its waning power in the world, and with it the final triumph of Felix Labaiya, who had known since childhood at Don Jorge's knee that it was his destiny to drive the insufferable Yanquis into the sea forever.

One month to Election Day in the United States, three to the inauguration of his former brother-in-law as President: Felix knew he had only to hang on and wait. There had been a long period, while he was married to Patsy, when he had been in considerable awe of Ted Jason, the overwhelmingly wealthy, the golden, the invincible, who had risen with such destined inevitability to become, first, Governor of California, and then nominee for President of the United States. Ted was overawing, in those days, and Felix, though he never admitted it to Patsy and only very secretly to himself, had been overawed. Then came Ted's race for the nomination and he was overawed no longer. Now he regarded Ted with the same contempt with which he regarded them all, the managers of the great Republic as it floundered from one desperate position to another in what its enemies believed to be its steady drift downhill. They all sought power, or came into power, thinking they could reverse the drift; they all succumbed to self-interest, the desire for election or re-election, the constant nagging of their critics in Congress and the media; and the drift went on. Ted would be no different. He had tipped his hand in the compromises he had made, and was still making, with those within America who desired America's death. It was clear to Felix that this was their intention and he could not understand why Ted could not see it.

In Felix's judgment, they were backing Ted because they believed he would be unable to stop their plans and would, indeed, either knowingly or unknowingly, assist them. In Felix's judgment, Ted was a weakling who would do exactly that. And his first step would be to give in and retreat from all those positions around the world where America still held forth the promise that she would defend her own independence and that of others against the ravenous Soviet imperialism that threatened to bring down upon mankind the endless night of the death of the mind.

Not that Felix, of course, really feared this latest and most ruthless of history's imperialisms, deep-rooted far in Russia's past. He was convinced that he and his country could survive. He was one of the many around the world who thought they could take communism's help without incurring communism's domination. His slogan was *It could never happen to me;* and because he was brilliant and clever and, both personally and intellectually, supremely self-confident, he thought he could play both ends against the middle and emerge unscathed amid the ruination of the great contending powers. It was a heady belief and one which encouraged certain errors by the unwary, who thought they were shrewd but were actually only arrogant.

So now at "Suerte," Felix, grandson of Don Jorge, was content with what he saw in mind's eye as he looked far down his beautiful valley to the distant range. He could see the difficult jungle terrain where the Americans were bogged down; he could envisage, as vividly as though he were present, those long, agonized, frustrated debates in Washington, which he remembered so well from his days as ambassador, about the wisdom or unwisdom of using national power to the fullest; he could imagine, coming on a distant sea, the subs and planes and warships that would run the American blockade. And he could see the victory of all his lifelong plans and hopes, guaranteed, certified and made irrevocable by the coming electoral triumph of Edward M. Jason. Felix Labaiya was quite content.

Not so another figure, who also stood on a terrace and stared far into the distance—not, in his case, at green jungles and misty mountains, but at the flat, dusty plain that surrounded his ramshackle capital of Molobangwe in the heart of Gorotoland. His Royal Highness Terence Wolowo Ajkaje, 137th M'Bulu of Mbuele, was a worried and uncertain man; and this was not an easy thing for "Terrible Terry" to be.

Life, in fact, had played rather roughly with the M'Bulu in the past year and a half. First had come his smashing victory at the UN, when that body had demanded by an overwhelming vote that the reluctant British speed up their withdrawal and grant immediate independence to Gorotoland. Along with it had come the near censure of the United States, which Terry had virtually stage-managed, from his intervention in the school situation in Charleston, South Carolina, to his dramatic appearances prior to the knife-edge vote in the General Assembly. Those were the days when Terry had been the darling of the American and world media, hero of every headline, central figure, with his giant stature and shimmering colorful robes, of every television show and commentary.

Then, abruptly—disaster. The friends from China and Russia, who had stood so kindly by his side when he was trying to break away from Britain, had suddenly proved themselves fair-weather indeed. Without warning they had turned to his cousin Prince Obifumatta, that scurrilous and rotten offshoot of the royal tree. A brief clash had occurred, a "coalition" government of the classical Communist pattern had been installed; and in the usual scenario for such things, Obi and his friends had promptly tried to seize power. Desperately Terry had called upon the British whom he had so recently ousted. They had responded with assistance, as had the United States. The situation had abruptly escalated when Obi's forces slew American missionaries and destroyed a Standard Oil installation in the highlands; and with suddenly aroused American aid, Obi had been driven out and Terry had been re-established in his hodgepodge capital, sitting, as he had been portrayed in one of the *Daily Telegraph's* most recent cartoons, not too comfortably upon American bayonets.

Not too comfortably, and not too certainly, and not with any guarantee as to how long even this uneasy support would last. It was true that President Abbott appeared to be as firm in his commitment as President Hudson had been; but it was also true that all of that group and all of that thinking in America was about to be swept away by the imminent apotheosis of Ted Jason. Terry had no more doubt than Ted himself that Ted would be elected a month from now, and when he was, American aid for Gorotoland would almost certainly cease. Terry was convinced of this—perhaps more convinced than Ted himself—since all he had to go by was what he read in the papers and heard on the air. It placed before him a bleak and chilling prospect.

It was true that Ted's campaign speeches so far—to the obvious dismay of such as Walter Dobius and some of Ted's more famous supporters of newsprint and tube—had been somewhat equivocal on the point. "In Gorotoland," he had said in Cleveland just two nights ago, "as in Panama, we will immediately hold the most stringent review of past policies, present commitments and future necessities. And I promise you that we will not just talk. We will do something!" Ted had not said what, exactly, but the implication eagerly and widely spread by his supporters was that the United States would get the hell out, and no dilly-dallying. While this made Felix happy it filled Terence Ajkaje with a profound gloom; more than he should have felt, perhaps, but as so often on so many things with Ted—one simply did not know.

And even more frustrated than Terry, if possible, was the powerful and worried old man who faced Ted now across the massive desk in the Oval Office. He too had been thinking deeply and staring thoughtfully—in his case at Abraham Lincoln, who, from his place of honor on the wall, stared thoughtfully back. This was the continuity of America, the President thought dryly: except that there were times these days when he was not at all sure the continuity would continue. Certainly it might not if his visitor performed in office as he seemed to be performing on the way to it: still uncertain, still wavering, still equivocal, still slipping like quicksilver through the body politic and the awful imperatives of the world. He had thought that might be finished as the day of victory neared. If anything, in his estimation, it had grown worse.

"Ted," he said abruptly when the Governor was seated, "what did you want to see me for? Just to make more points with the votes you've got sewed up already? I don't get it."

For a moment Governor Jason returned him appraising look for appraising look. Then he smiled and leaned forward.

"Mr. President," he said calmly, "I wish you could concede, for just one moment, that my motivations might be as noble and as devoted to the best interests of America as yours are. I really do."

"Hmph," the President said. "I'll concede that on the day I see it. If you disagree with my policies, it occurs to me the way to do it is to take them up privately with me, not to arrive here trailed by a hundred reporters and fifty cameramen like Hannibal crossing the Alps at the head of his herd of elephants."

"I've taken your policies up with you privately before," Ted pointed out in a reasonable voice, "and a fat lot of good it's done me, if I may say so with a candor to match your own. You imply that I don't care about the country. You think this is all an ego trip. I think it's an attempt to focus public pressure in such a way as to prevent you from tying my hands completely when—if—I enter this office."

"No 'if' about it," the President said. "You know that as well as I do."

"Then why—?" Governor Jason asked with a certain restrained exasperation.

" 'Why' what?" the President demanded with an equal annoyance.

"Why do you persist in placing us deeper into the Gorotoland mess? Why do you persist in trying to blockade Panama, daring the rest of the world to try to break it, which could only mean a most serious confrontation? You're playing an extremely dangerous game, Mr. President. I don't like it, and I don't think the country likes it."

"Living in this world nowadays *is* a dangerous game," the President said. "Have to be as tough as the other side or go under. Not much of a game for cowards."

"Which I am," Ted said dryly.

"No, of course not," the President said impatiently. "But you don't play with your gut, which is what you have to do to survive. You play with your mind. And right now your mind is all involved with how you can satisfy that crowd over there in the Press Room, and how you can hold onto the NAWAC crowd, and how you can—well, basically, Ted, how you can please people you don't have to please. That's

what gets me. It *isn't necessary* for you to put on this kind of grandstand stunt. Why do you do it?"

Again there was a silence while they studied one another. Finally
the Governor spoke, very quietly.

"Does it ever occur to you, Mr. President, that I might sincerely believe in what I'm doing? That I might feel genuine concern because
of your activities? That I might really believe that they are ill-advised,
and that I might really, genuinely feel that my ideas are better for the
country and the world?" He paused and shook his head with a sigh.
"But, no. Obviously not. That isn't Ted Jason, is it? At least, not your
Ted Jason." He sat back in his chair and spoke with a growing firmness. "Now, understand me, Mr. President. I don't like what you are
doing. You are trapping me fearfully in what you think ought to be
done, when in actual fact, in three months' time you will be out of this
office and back on the Hill and the whole responsibility will be mine.
You can't make me a prisoner of your policies. It isn't fair, and I won't
let you."

"Oh? How will you stop me?"

"By walking out that door and repudiating you," Ted said calmly.
"By removing myself completely and entirely from any support whatsoever for what you are doing. By turning on 'the leader of my
party,' because now *I* am the leader of my party. I don't have to wait
three months, if you force me. I can begin right now."

For several moments they gave one another look for look. Finally
the President spoke softly.

"That's right. But I don't think you even have the guts for that—or
at least the decisiveness. Five weeks into the campaign, and you still
don't know who you are. You still don't know whether you want to
set this foot here or that foot there. You're still trying to play to people
you don't have to play to, because you've got 'em already, and you're
still flirting with the safety of this country and the independent nations
because you think that will make you popular with the media and
the violent. Isn't it time you settled down and decided what you're
going to be, Ted Jason? Look here!" he said with a sudden vehemence,
taking up a heavy blue-jacketed folder and tossing it across the desk.
"Those are the reports I get on the infiltration and the invasion plans
that are still going on in Gorotoland and in those great peace-loving
black neighbors of hers who ring her like a flock of vultures. There
are the plans for another Russian attempt at take-over, which may
come at any minute. There are all the reasons why Gorotoland, lying
at the heart of the continent, has to be saved for the independent
world, all the strategic reasons why she is, in many practical ways,

the key to Africa. And this!"—and he tossed another, in a red jacket, after the first—"here are the Russian plans for taking Panama after that egotistical fool Felix Labaiya has done their work for them. Here are the names of the people around him who are going to get rid of him as soon as he succeeds in kicking us out, *if* he succeeds in kicking us out, and here are the details of how they're going to do it. Study those for a while, and decide who you are!"

For several minutes, turning the pages thoughtfully and carefully, first of the blue book, then of the red, Ted Jason did so. Then he closed them and pushed them back across the desk.

"If these are true," he suggested quietly, "why don't you publicize them? Why don't you make a speech and tell the world about them? Why keep them quiet, if they are such perfect justification of what you are doing . . . and if they are true?"

"'If they are true,'" the President mimicked bitterly, an angry and exact echo of Ted's quizzical tone. "You've just told me why I can't make a speech. *Because you and your friends in this country have got us so conditioned to disbelief in everything that proves Communist duplicity that I couldn't make a sufficient number believe me if I did.* You try it, my friend, when you get behind this desk. You try it! You'll know then that it's true, but you'll find you can't do much about it, because not only will your friends disbelieve you, but you've made yourself one of theirs and you won't dare take a public stand that flies in the face of their beliefs and their purposes. *You won't dare.*" He paused abruptly and demanded with a harsh impatience, "Why are you smiling?"

But Ted shook his head and sighed.

"I'm not smiling, Mr. President; not really. I was just thinking that five weeks ago, when my nominee for Vice President came to me in Patsy's house for our first private talk together, I said to him much the same things you have said, and are saying now, to me. I was smiling about life's ironies—because, understand me, Mr. President: I *know* Gorotoland is important. I *know* Panama is important. I *know* elements dangerous to this country and to independent nations everywhere are seeking to drive us out of them both, as they have tried— and have succeeded—in driving us out of many other vital areas around the world. I *know* a great part of this—a great unnecessary part—has been caused by many of our own people, many sincere, some not so sincere, in many areas of American life, from the media to the universities, and back again. I know all this and I told Roger Croy that we must be careful, of our support and of our policies."

"Then why in the hell," the President demanded in a tone compounded equally of bafflement and exasperation, "aren't you honest enough to say so? You've got the election won."

"Not yet," Ted Jason said softly. "You know how they'd turn on me, if I said these things now. They could conceivably cost me the election. They could conceivably—" and suddenly his eyes darkened with pain, and the President realized for a brief and fleeting moment of human sympathy that he was dealing with a still deeply wounded man—"cost me my life. . . . Wait until I'm in, Mr. President. I'll say these things then. And they'll take them from me, then."

"Want to bet?" the President asked quietly. "Do you really want to bet?"

"And of course," Ted Jason said, ignoring the question, "there is another thing for you to remember, Mr. President: I agree in principle with much of what you say, but I do honestly believe that there are areas in which a different approach—"

"Oh, yes," the President interrupted sarcastically. "Oh, yes. Here it comes."

"In some areas," Ted repeated calmly, "there are fair arguments to be made about the ways in which we should do things. And there we begin to run into all the sincere and loyal and patriotic people—quite aside from anyone you may single out as disloyal and dangerous— who really disagree. Some disagree on methods and some disagree on the basic premises. And I have the job as candidate, and will soon have it as President, of trying to lead them all—"

"And still save the country."

"And still save the country," Ted agreed quietly.

"In other words," the President said, "they've gotten to you, haven't they? In your heart of hearts you don't really believe what you say about Gorotoland and Panama. They've managed to make you just a little bit unsure, just a little bit uncertain, just a little bit unable to act as the next President may have to act in this office. Well, good for them. You're the one man they had to convince, and they've done it. That's all they need. If they can get the President of the United States really intimidated and unsure of himself, they've got us."

"I'm not intimidated," Ted replied quietly, "but I may be a little uncertain of my absolutes. I told Roger Croy we should be cautious and careful, and I am trying to be. Isn't that enough for you? Really, Mr. President!" And he shook his head as if to clear it. "This is really an extraordinary conversation. You are saying the most extraordinary things to me, the most extraordinary attacks upon my beliefs and my integrity, and I am taking them with the most extraordinary patience, really, considering I don't have to, when all's said and done. I wonder why I should, any longer?"

"Who's been pressuring you, Ted?" the President inquired with an unimpressed bluntness. "The usual? NAWAC and Van Ackerman and Georgie Wattersill and Walter Dobius and all that crowd? You haven't asked for this conference to try to make me change my mind or moderate my policies. You've asked for it to set yourself up for some big dramatic headlines about breaking with me over the war. Isn't that right?"

Once more Governor Jason did not answer for a while. When he finally did it was in a thoughtful, almost remote tone.

"Mr. President," he said quietly, "you want motives to be so simple. You want everything to be so cut and dried, because, I suppose, that's how your generation has always looked at things. Yes, I'm prepared to break with you and get big headlines, if you force me to. But I also, as I said, am seriously interested in not having you tie my hands before I even get into office—in not having you create such a tangle in world affairs that I have no options to move—in not having you create such a strait jacket that I can't reverse my field and turn us around, if I feel I must. I thought when I came here that maybe we could work out some compromise: announce a gradual reduction, with a definite time limit—six months, say—on aid to Gorotoland. Say that second thoughts have indicated that a blockade of Panama may not be the best way to achieve our objectives. Call for an international conference of the interested maritime powers, maybe, and try to get some voluntary reduction of aid to Felix and his group. Try to bring Felix to the negotiating table. . . . In other words, try to find a middle ground that would protect the United States and still make some reasonable concessions to her critics both domestic and foreign, who can't go along with the way you're trying to handle it. . . . That seems reasonable to me. I know it doesn't to you, but—there it is."

"And there are your headlines," the President suggested.

"Yes," Ted agreed. "If you make me do it."

"What are you going to do about NAWAC?" the President asked abruptly. "What about their trying to break up Warren's rally last night? What about these reports I get—"

"What are they in?" Ted couldn't resist. "A *black* folder?"

"They should be," the President said grimly. "These reports I get that these so-called 'campaign security guards' of yours are beginning to turn up at other people's rallies? Lafe Smith tells me he's being increasingly bothered because he isn't 100 per cent for you. And Cullee Hamilton called me the other day to say he's beginning to run into the same flak in California. Bob Munson's been shouted down a couple of times and some in his audiences have been roughed up. Why," and his smile became sarcastic and a trifle savage—"even my old buddy the general director of the *Post* called up yesterday, scared peeless because he's received a couple of blank-screen calls on the Picturephone threatening dire events if the paper doesn't stop even its mildest type of pittypat criticism of NAWAC. . . . Now, in the first place, Ted: what in the hell are 'campaign security guards' of *yours* doing at somebody else's rallies? And in the second place, have you learned a damned thing from the convention—or the Committee meeting—or—" and he said it with a deliberate sledgehammer bluntness that he knew would make his listener flinch, and it did—"the Monument Grounds? For God's sake, man, cut loose from it! *Stop it!* I beg of you."

"Mr. President—" Ted began, then paused and started over again slowly and carefully. "I know there have been—excesses—here and there. I am aware of them. I have given orders they are to be stopped. I have been assured by Senator Van Ackerman, who is head of the campaign security division, and by LeGage Shelby, who is his assistant, that they will not occur again. I have that assurance."

"But you won't fight them on it," the President said. "Not really. You won't have an open break and big headlines with *them*, will you?"

"Because," Ted said, a stubbornness in his tone, "they do represent the point of view held by millions of peaceable Americans. They do believe as I do on these great issues of foreign policy. They may be misguided and overenthusiastic—" the President snorted, but he ignored it—"but they represent the opinion that supports me and the people I have to work with."

"The point is," the President said quietly, and it was obvious it was a quietness obtained only by the use of a great deal of will power, "the point is, you *don't have to do it. It isn't necessary.* It's a concession to dangerous elements far beyond what any necessity of political campaigning or political victory requires you to do. You don't *have* to temporize with evil: it is *your personal decision* to do so. And frankly, my friend," he concluded, even more quietly, "it scares the holy hell out of me."

Again there was a silence, the last of the many that had punctuated their conversation, as his visitor stared out at the Rose Garden, his face troubled but unyielding, his thoughts obviously far away in some region where the President, and perhaps no one, could accompany. Finally he replied, in a grave and thoughtful voice that conceded little.

"Mr. President, thank you for seeing me. I appreciate your thoughts on these matters and I will take them under advisement. In the meantime I am going to be expected to make some statement when I leave this place. This is probably the last time we shall talk privately before the election. It would look better if we could show some sign of agreement. What would you suggest we say?"

"Say," the President suggested coldly, "that in January I shall be back on the Hill as Speaker, and that you realize that if you adopt a policy of retreat abroad and appeasement of the violent at home, you will have me and the Congress of the United States to deal with."

For a moment he and Ted Jason stared at one another almost blankly across the huge desk that symbolized their similarity and their differences. Then Ted spoke his last word.

"Maybe," he said quietly. "Maybe . . ."

Five minutes later in the Press Room he met their clamorous friendly questions, their friendly flattering cameras. Within half an hour he had his headlines.

JASON BREAKS WITH PRESIDENT, REPUDIATES "PRO-WAR" POLICIES OF ADMINISTRATION. SAYS HE SEEKS "MIDDLE GROUND" FOR SOLUTION OF WORLD'S ILLS, CONDEMNS FURTHER AID TO GOROTOLAND, BLOCKADE OF PANAMA. PROMISES TO WIN "WITH OR WITHOUT SUPPORT OF PRESIDENT'S MEN." GOVERNOR'S DRAMATIC MOVE IS FIRST OPEN REPUDIATION OF SITTING PRESIDENT BY CANDIDATE OF OWN PARTY. WHITE HOUSE SILENT.

"Rarely—indeed, almost never," Walter Dobius wrote busily that evening in "Salubria's" softly lighted, book-lined study, "has there been a political event of such dramatic magnitude as has just occurred here in a capital that has seen its share of them in recent years. In an act of unparalleled statesmanship and courage Governor Jason has acted, not on a basis of oversentimentalized 'party loyalty,' but on the basis of fact:

"*He* is the leader of his party, and it is time the whole world knew it.

"At one stroke he has freed himself of the obsessive and oppressive burden of the fearfully misguided, mismanaged war policies of the late Secretary of State Orrin Knox, the late President Harley M. Hudson and President Abbott himself. If he has not yet pledged himself to do what the overwhelming majority of his countrymen expect and want him to do—get out, immediately and entirely, once and for all, of the world's wars and the world's insoluble and never-ending troubles —at least he has taken a giant step in that direction. He has shaken off the crippling and imprisoning past—he has made way for the peaceful future. His fellow citizens and the world can await with a serene confidence the inevitable next step in his policy of complete and enlightened disengagement from hopeless quagmires into which no American Administration should ever have dragged us in the first place.

"There remain now only the triumphant concluding weeks of Governor Jason's great campaign—the ratification by the electorate of his inevitable victory—an uneasy but mercifully short interregnum during which President Abbott and his discredited advisers will have no choice but to cooperate in their own dismissal from control of the government—and the dawn of the new day. 'Conscience must decide the issue,' Governor Jason states it, in the most felicitous and appealing slogan of his campaign. Conscience has indeed decided this major act of political courage, and, if there were degrees of inevitability, has made an already inevitable triumph even more so. . . ."

Walter paused, reached over and poured himself a glass of iced water from the pitcher Arbella had left on the desk, after a dinner he had consumed alone at the big candlelit table downstairs, complete with his usual one Manhattan and one glass of wine. He sat back thoughtfully for a moment. There was something else in the Jason campaign he did not like quite so well—in fact he was beginning to find it quite disturbing—and he debated for several minutes whether he should say something about it, or let the great adoring multitudes Out There rest satisfied with a few more innocuous comments about Ted Jason's courage, integrity, foresight, statesmanship, peace-loving nature, etc., etc., etc.

He had a window open on the gently cooling, Indian-summer October night. Now that his typewriter had stopped there was nothing to break the quiet of the house or the silence of the beautiful Virginia countryside that stretched away on all sides of the little rise where "Salubria" had stood for the better part of two hundred years. He shivered suddenly, for no reason he could tell, and turned back to flick the machine on again and tackle it with his pudgy, determined fingers.

"Given so notable and so noble an affirmation of decisiveness and integrity on Governor Jason's part," he wrote, and the words flowed right along, as they always did for Walter, "it is to be hoped, by all who value democracy and the place in it of decent and honorable dissent, that he will now turn his attention to the one flaw in an otherwise perfect campaign.

"This is the unfortunate incidence of violent and near-violent 'roughing-up' of those who disagree in the slightest with the Governor's philosophies and oppose, however reasonably, his bid for office. It seems, even to those observers here most favorable to the Governor's cause, that such episodes are increasing. It is, if truth be known, a disturbing if not, indeed, a sinister, thing.

"Certainly no fair-minded man can charge that Governor Jason himself knows of in advance, or sanctions or in any way excuses or condones, such episodes. Yet the roll of their occurrence is growing: disturbances when he spoke in Wyoming on behalf of the re-election of Senator Van Ackerman; disturbances in Iowa, where Senator Lafe Smith has apparently annoyed the Governor's most partisan backers with his occasional criticisms; disturbances in California, where black Representative Cullee Hamilton, apparently well in the lead in his race for the Senate, is running into increasingly bitter heckling and some violence because he dares voice reservations about the Governor's policies; disturbances in Illinois, where Hal Knox, the late Secretary's son, is running for the House of Representatives under the party label but with a strongly independent approach—and now, most recently and most disgracefully, in Los Angeles, where Senator Warren Strickland, carrying his party's standard honorably in a losing race, found his supporters balked and threatened and in several cases physically molested by forces purporting to be 'campaign security guards' for Governor Jason.

"Sincere supporters of the Governor can legitimately wonder—and the wonder is certainly no personal reflection at all upon him—why 'campaign security guards,' other than the Secret Service contingent furnished all candidates by the federal government, and the forces customarily furnished by the states and municipalities where he speaks, are necessary. One wonders why 'campaign security guards,' supposedly directed by Senator Van Ackerman of COMFORT and LeGage Shelby of DEFY for the safety and protection of Governor Jason, should be turning up at other candidates' rallies across the country to indulge in violent or near violent tactics. One must wonder if there is some significance, some message, intended in these carefully timed and carefully staged episodes, and whether they presage something unclean and unhealthy, possibly even dangerous, which could flower under the shield of the coming Jason Administration.

"If there is even the remotest possibility of this—and again, one can only absolve the Governor himself from all responsibility, for he is an honorable and decent man—then it may perhaps be time for him to caution his more intemperate supporters against their intemperance. Zeal for a given candidate can be a fine and productive thing; even excessive zeal, if not carried to violent or harmful lengths, can be fine and productive. But zeal carried beyond the bounds of democratic principle and a decent respect for those who disagree with you can be something else.

"Governor Jason has shown great courage in breaking with the burden of past political mistakes by his own party. The many millions who see in him the world's greatest hope for peace can only wish that he will show a similar courage in breaking with the present danger and future possibility of serious damage to the oft-battered but still worthy democracy which he soon will lead."

And for the next few hours, Walter Dobius—who on occasion did have the integrity to rise to the sobriquet of "Walter Wonderful" conferred upon him long ago by Lyndon Johnson—felt very well satisfied with this. He was not all that bedazzled by Ted Jason, whom he had come to regard, after several close contacts in the pre- and post-convention period, as a devious and slippery individual, even if headed in what Walter believed to be the right direction. He was not a blind believer in the Jason myth, even though he industriously helped promulgate it every day because he considered it necessary to the country's stability and the world's peace. He admired many of Ted's policies and actions, particularly the break with that stubborn old fool in the White House, but he was not at all bemused by the basic character that had to be dealt with, underneath. Though the President would have been much surprised to know it, Walter Dobius regarded Ted Jason pretty much as he did: as an individual with a good many fine qualities, but essentially opportunistic, arrogant, overconfident of "the Jason luck," and weak—the weakness increased by the fact that he was still, behind the charismatic figure that managed to smile and wave, make a powerful speech and go through the motions, deeply shattered by the tragic death of his wife. Such a man required guidance, in Walter's estimation, and it was not just the usual guidance that Walter normally gave to Presidents and other world leaders who needed it. It was guidance that would prevent the essential weakness from being played upon and taken advantage of by forces that did not see the future of the Republic as the free and still idealistic thing Walter felt both he and Ted believed in.

So for approximately fourteen hours, while he read the papers over a leisurely breakfast, pleased to see his column featured in *Times*, *Post* and *Greatest Publication*, the three he read most faithfully every day, he felt he had discharged his responsibility as journalist and citizen well. He continued to feel that way later on while Roosevelt drove him at a leisurely pace through the lush and smiling land to Washington. He continued to feel that way until he stepped inside the door of Sans Souci half a block up Connecticut Avenue from the White House, where he was meeting the general director of the *Post* for lunch. Then he stopped feeling that way.

"Monsieur Dobius, how nice to see you," Paul said, as he always said. "You have a telephone call, Monsieur Dobius, and then we will seat you."

Arbella's familiar face, plain and honest and now deeply disturbed, appeared on the Picturephone. A sudden premonition gripped his heart.

"Mistah Waltuh," she said, words tumbling over themselves. "Oh, Mistah Waltuh—"

"Hush," he said sharply, moving to shield the screen from the hat-check girl. "Calm down and tell me what it is."

"They called, Mistah Waltuh," she said, and he could see she was almost crying with worry and fright, "they called—"

"Who called?" he demanded in an intense whisper, while the French Ambassador and the Secretary of Defense passed by with cordial smiles on the way to their table. "Arbella, I order you to calm down and speak slowly and tell me what it is. Now, who called?"

"Don't know," she said hopelessly, "except I know they bad—real bad, Mistah Waltuh. They threaten to burn this house down, Mistah Waltuh, that's what they did. They threaten to burn this house down."

A terrible pain for lovely and beloved "Salubria" knifed his body, even as he remembered the frightful threatening interview there with Fred Van Ackerman, LeGage Shelby and Rufus Kleinfert during the Committee sessions two months ago.

"But *why?*" he asked, and she looked more desolate still.

"They say you wrote somethin' this mohnin', Mistah Waltuh. They say you write anythin' like that agin, they goin' burn this house down. They mean it too, Mistah Waltuh. I went out right after they call and that little shed out by the barn—you know that little tool shed, Mistah Waltuh—"

"For God's sake," he said in an explosive whisper, "*I know the tool shed.* What about it?"

"They told me to go look and there was a little smoke goin', Mistah Waltuh, a little pile of rags and some kerosene on it. I put it out and I looked all around, but I didn't see nobody. But they was there, Mistah Waltuh, off in the pond woods. I know they was there. Maybe they still there, just waitin' to come agin." The honest face did finally crumple into tears. "Mistah Waltuh, what I goin' do? Shall I call the police, or what?"

"*Salubria*" he thought; and then: *America!* and finally with an agonized wonder: *What are we getting into?* But he spoke with a reasonable calmness.

"Now, Arbella," he said, keeping his voice carefully lowered and even managing to smile a little at the Undersecretary of State and Supreme Court Justice Thomas Buckmaster Davis on their way to a table, "you're a very brave woman and I think you've done wonderfully well. Roosevelt and I won't be back until about four o'clock, so I think you had better lock up the house and go next door to the Randolphs' and just stay there till we get home. Don't worry about 'Salubria.' I think," he managed to say reassuringly, though his mind said, *Oh, God, I hope so—*"it will be all right. I think it was just a threat. It isn't going to scare me and I don't want it to scare you, either. So you lock up and go on over, and don't worry. We'll be back soon, and I'll get some guards if I have to. We won't let anything happen to us or to 'Salubria.' You go along now."

After she hung up, terribly troubled and uncertain, he stood for several moments breathing deeply and firmly until his nerves quieted and his face, while somber, regained most of its public composure. Then he turned to cross the upper dining platform and descend, through the customary barrage of shrewd and knowing eyes, to the restaurant floor.

Somehow he managed not to show it, but he was really very upset indeed; and after he had talked for a few moments with the general director of the *Post* and told him the cause of it, they were very upset together; although they managed to put a reasonable face on it even then, so that the fact passed almost unnoticed in that small, crowded, self-important, self-preoccupied room.

CAMPAIGN ROARS INTO FINAL WEEK WITH JASON IN COMMANDING LEAD. POLLS SHOW DROP OF SIX PER CENT IN GOVERNOR'S SUPPORT AS STRICKLAND HAMMERS DOMESTIC VIOLENCE, DANGER OF "WEAKNESS" IN DEALING WITH COMMUNISTS. NAWAC DEMONSTRATORS FORCE SENATOR TO LEAVE PLATFORM IN DETROIT, MAR RALLIES OF JASON CRITICS IN SEVEN CITIES. PRESIDENT MAKES SOMBER SPEECH TO COLORADO CONSTITUENTS, WARNS OF "EVIL MEN ACTING IN GOVERNOR'S NAME WHO MUST BE STOPPED," ASSAILS "POSSIBILITY OF NEW TURN-TAIL ERA IN FOREIGN POLICY," BRITAIN, SOVIETS STILL HESITATE ON PANAMA REBEL RECOGNITION AS PRESIDENT STRENGTHENS BLOCKADE. GOROTOLAND AID GOES FORWARD. U.S., SOVIETS REACH "INFORMAL UNDERSTANDING"

ON LATEST BERING STRAIT FISHING SPAT. GOVERNOR CROY
HOLDS TO LANDSLIDE PREDICTION DESPITE "SOME LOSS
OF MOMENTUM." GOVERNOR JASON REAFFIRMS STAND.
CONTINUES TO DRAW HUGE CROWDS EVERYWHERE.

But as Roger Croy accurately said, Ted was indeed "losing some
momentum," and knew it; and now on the Saturday night before election, as he prepared to make his final campaign speech, in his native
city of San Francisco, he was for the first time in two months a slightly
worried man. Not greatly worried, for Ted Jason did not succumb
easily to worry about his own course, nor did he worry, really, about
the outcome on Election Day. He might have lost six points as a few
polls showed (others, more friendly, acknowledged only two or three,
although all conceded decline), but he was still so far ahead that not
even the most drastic reversal could stop him now. No cause for such
reversal was anywhere in sight. He was coming home safe; but still
he was a little worried. Just a little.

He knew why, as he stood thoughtfully at the window of his suite in
the Fairmont and looked across the Bay to the diamond lights of Oak-
land and Berkeley strewn across the hills, while behind him his remaining family bickered and argued as they always had, as long as he
could remember. Below on the rapidly darkening waters the ferry
boats to Sausalito and Tiburon crisscrossed on their cheerfully lighted
way; through the Golden Gate a long bolster of fog crept slowly in;
the lights of Fisherman's Wharf and North Beach glittered their gaudy
promise. To the north he could see the string of lights that marked the
Richmond-San Rafael Bridge. Beyond, the Bay faded out of sight in
the deepening twilight as it stretched on up toward his capital of Sac-
ramento, where he had not been much lately. The lieutenant governor
was having to mind the shop a good deal these days: which was all
right with him, because he was running for governor and soon would
have full charge of it anyway.

"Sweetie," Patsy said, coming to stand beside him, martini in hand,
"Fred Van Ackerman just called from the Cow Palace. He says it's
already full, and we still have two hours to go before you speak. I'd
say THAT's something."

"Very gratifying," he agreed. Behind them their aunt, Selena Jason
Castleberry, she of the constant fund-raising parties, demonstrations
and causes, gave a derisive snort and demanded in her whiskey voice,

"Is that all you can say, Ted? 'Very gratifying,' he says. I'd say it's
damned exciting and thrilling, myself."

"He's bored with it already," remarked their other aunt, the painter

Valuela Jason Randall, she of the villa at Positano and the steady string of never-quite-permanent young men. "He'll probably go to sleep at his own inauguration."

He uttered the quick, and quickly gone, explosion of semi-mirth that had passed for a laugh with him ever since the dreadful day at the Monument, and turned to face them as his uncle Herbert Jason came out of the bathroom, eyes apop and hair afrizzle in his customary fashion: perfect picture, Ted thought dryly, of a Nobel Prize-winning scientific nut, which was exactly what he was. Here they were, the five of them, odd terminal branches of the once vigorous Montoya-Jason tree: what a family! But his.

"Are you and Selena prepared to demonstrate, Herb?" he asked. "I don't want this to be just a nice, peaceful, unanimous evening, you know. I want the Jasons to put some snap in it."

"Dear boy," his uncle said blandly, "Sel and I have our banners ready and our noisemakers poised. Say the word!"

"It's hard for them this time," Valuela observed, "because for once they agree with something, you see? They aren't in opposition. They really think it's good for the world to have Edward Jason elected President."

"And don't YOU, Val?" Patsy inquired indignantly. "I didn't know YOU objected."

"*I* DON'T," Valuela said with a deadly parody of her niece's exaggerated way of speaking. "*I* think it's GREAT. But it might be humbling for us all, particularly the President-to-be, to remember that there are some who aren't so ecstatic."

"I know that," Ted said with a sudden moodiness, sitting down on the window seat and turning to stare at the lights of the fabulous city glowing below. "I've had indications."

"There won't be any tonight," Patsy promised flatly. "Fred and NAWAC are going to see to that."

"What's with this NAWAC, Ted?" Valuela asked. "I just flew in from Europe yesterday, you know. Over there we get a rather mixed impression of NAWAC. It seems to be somewhere between Hitler's storm troopers and the Russian KGB. Are you sure it's good for you?"

"It stops a lot of frivolous interference," Herbert Jason pointed out, pouring himself a scotch and soda at the bar. "Refill, Sel?"

"Not just yet, thanks," she said. "I'm doing fine. And it does keep a lot of reactionary elements from interfering with Ted's campaign."

"It shows them," Patsy said with considerable satisfaction, "who's boss."

"Is that what we're out for?" Valuela inquired, with something of the persistence which must once have distinguished her grandmother, fabled Doña Valuela, founder of the family. "To show people who's boss? Who bosses the boss?"

"Very funny," Patsy said, totally unamused. "I could stand one more small martini, Herbert. About half."

"Whoever," Herbert inquired, "had 'about half' of a martini? But I shall do my best. The thing is, Val, that this all began really, you know, during the convention when—well, you do know, you were here. Ted thought it would be a good idea to coordinate all these anti-war groups into one organization, the National Anti-War Activities Congress. More manageable."

"And more managing, no doubt," Valuela remarked. "Do you find it so, candidate?"

Ted, who appeared not to have been listening—and indeed he had not been, being away in the charming streets below, hand-in-hand with Ceil in the enchanted days of their courtship—started and looked around.

"I said NAWAC might have been more manageable once but could be more managing now," Valuela told him. "Is that your experience?"

"Oh," he said, and paused thoughtfully, studying the question. "No," he said slowly, "I don't think so."

"You find that Senator Van Ackerman and Mr. Shelby and Mr. Kleinfert, and the others in charge, go along with what you say," his aunt suggested. "You have no problems keeping them under control."

He hesitated and half-smiled.

"Who's been talking to you, Val? What *do* you hear in Europe?"

"Nothing specific," she said, handing her glass to her brother with a terse, "Another"—"but there have been some reports that you have tried to stop these interferences with Senator Strickland and some of the others, and that NAWAC has virtually ignored you. I didn't worry when *Der Spiegel* had an article entitled 'AMERICA'S BROWN-SHIRTS RISING?'—with a question mark. But when the *Guardian* went so far last week as to suggest gently that 'Governor Jason should perhaps attempt a little more diligently to moderate the apparently over-enthusiastic efforts of a small minority of his supporters,' I really began to get worried. So: are they giving you trouble?"

"Valuela," Patsy said firmly, "that is stupid. Just simply STUPID."

"No, it isn't," Ted said mildly. "It's a valid question. It concerns me. It's right to have it asked."

"How do you answer?" Valuela inquired, and Herbert and Selena betrayed by their uncharacteristically silent attention that his answer interested them too.

"Publicly, I say nothing. Here in the family, I say it worries me some. The day I broke with the President we had quite a conversation, which included that; and I told him what was the truth, that I had protested to Fred and 'Gage and the rest and that they had assured me there would be no more attempts to break up other people's meetings, no more bullyboy tactics, no more threats of violence. However," he said, somewhat bleakly, "there have been. Some have been public knowledge and some have been reported to me privately. They have not kept their word."

"So why don't you repudiate them?" Valuela demanded bluntly, sounding so much like the President for a moment that her nephew started and could not entirely suppress a small smile. "And what's so funny? I think it's very serious for you—and for everybody, really. Actually," she said, leaning forward with an intent thoughtfulness which showed that despite the villa and the young men the practical shrewdness of her forebears ran in her yet, "I think you could really sew it up completely if you would repudiate them. Straight out, with no equivocations. I think it would be enormously popular, and it would certainly strengthen a lot of people's respect for you. It has seemed to me, watching you at the convention, and then from Europe since I went back, that the story of the last two or three months has been a long succession of attempts on your part to make up your mind about them. Sometimes it's seemed as though you might be drawing away from them, other times you seemed to be swinging back. The end result has been that they act as though they control you rather than vice versa, and you seem to be unable to destroy the impression. I think there's only one way to do it, and that's just what I said: repudiate them, flat out. This is your last speech tonight: let them have it. You don't owe them a thing—it's dangerous to let them think you do—*get rid of them!* That's my advice, anyway."

"Valuela Jason Randall," Selena said dryly, "political adviser par excellence. Don't you realize how the price of your paintings will go up when you have a nephew in the White House?"

"Oh, Sel," her sister snapped, "stop being a damned fool. This is serious business. Damned serious."

"I think," Patsy said tartly, "that Ted has to make his own decisions without us worrying him with half-baked uninformed opinions. He knows what he's doing!"

"Indeed," Valuela said coldly. "Would it were more obvious."

"Well, now," Herbert Jason said in his bland and comfortable voice as Ted again turned to stare moodily down into the lighted streets, like the thoroughfares of a toy town laid out before him there below. "I don't see there's any need to get heated about it. I believe Ted feels that for all its—er—imperfections, you might say—NAWAC still represents, in the most cohesive form, the great sentiment for peace and harmony in the world which is going to sweep him into office next Tuesday. I believe he feels he can't repudiate that sentiment, Val: how could he? It would destroy the entire basis for his campaign. It would destroy everything he stands for. It would *shatter* the people who believe in him so, who have given him their faith and their trust. It would be a dreadful blow to peace."

"Yes," Valuela said dryly. "'We're for peace, and by God you'd better do it our way or we're going to beat your head in.' Very peaceful. Very noble. Very worthy of trust and faith. Herbert, you sound like an ass."

"You've had too many, old girl," Herbert said imperturbably. "Just a few too many. I do hope you can manage to stagger to your seat on the platform all right."

"Ted," Valuela said earnestly, and again she sounded so much like the President that this time it did not amuse him, only sent an eerie little shiver along his spine, "*I beg of you.* No one else in this family seems to have the elemental sense of an alley cat about this. It's tonight or never. You must break them or in due time they will try to break you. How can you not see that?"

He turned back to face them, framed against the dramatic bay and beautiful city: gray-haired, tanned, handsome, distinguished, powerful. His voice was thoughtful as he spoke directly to Valuela.

"Val," he said soberly, "I appreciate your comments very much—I really do. Believe me, it has given me a lot of wakeful nights, starting with the convention and running right on through. I am still not really in charge, you see, at this moment: I am not yet the President, and even after next Tuesday, I won't be—not until January. So that inhibits me. Then there's the other thing: Herbert is right, in a basic way. These people do speak for many, many millions here and abroad whose pressures on this government have been strong enough to give me what appears to be the making of a great victory."

"But you wouldn't have had it if Orrin Knox were alive," she pointed out quickly. For a moment he stopped dead; then nodded.

"That's true. That is very true. But he isn't, Val, and so—I can't worry about what might have been. I've got to be concerned with what is. And that's the fact that all these millions do believe in me, do want peace, do think I can get it for them—and I mustn't tamper with that faith, in any way, because it's what's going to sustain me when I do what I think has to be done, starting next January. If I were to repudiate a group which—while sometimes showing a tendency to be 'over-enthusiastic,' as some say—" he conceded to her grimace—"yes, even violent—nonetheless represents the largest organized body of leaders of the peace movement, then I would be upsetting the delicate balance that underlies my campaign and my Administration. They'd probably still vote for me all right—I don't think I'd lose any great swatch of votes, it really is too late to stop me now—but it would cause great questioning and great uncertainty among a lot of perfectly sincere people who form the broad base of NAWAC. My problem is to separate them from their leaders, and the time to do it isn't until I actually get in the White House, as I see it. Until then, I'll be needing those leaders to keep things moving in the direction I want to go."

"Not as much as they need you," Valuela said, her tone already conceding she had lost the argument. "Not as much, Ted."

He shook his head soberly.

"I don't know. I don't think anybody can say. Anyway, that's how I see it and that's how I've been playing it. I'll ride with them now, get rid of them later. I may be mistaken, but I think I can do it."

"God help us if you don't," she said. "You play for high stakes."

"Don't Jasons always?" he asked with a sudden charming grin, the first genuinely relaxed one any of them had seen from him since the death of his wife. "Come on," he said, moving forward to give her his hand and pull her to her feet. "They'll be coming to take us to the Cow Palace in a minute. Powder noses, zip zippers, and let's go, family!"

"I just KNOW everything's going to be all right," Patsy said earnestly.

"Of course it is," Selena said impatiently. "Honestly, Val!"

"Why, *certainly*," Herbert agreed in his comfortable voice.

The doorbell rang, the guards and Secret Service appeared, they descended to the enormous glitter-gilt-and-red-velvet lobby of the Fairmont.

A great shout went up as they appeared from the hundreds who jammed the lobby and spilled over into Mason Street. Happy excited voices called out words of good luck and good cheer, happy, excited faces beamed upon them. The violent world of NAWAC's leaders seemed far away.

He still, as he smiled and waved and went through the motions, wished he could have some sign that his course was the right one and that he would be strengthened in what he wanted to do; not aware that within an hour he would have one, and from a most unexpected source.

Swiftly they were escorted down the Bayshore Highway, off at the Cow Palace exit and back through the hills, lights flashing, sirens screaming, their progress hailed by the excited waves and shouts and horn poundings of the many motorists they passed and met along the way. As they neared the huge auditorium, glowing in the center of a dozen giant searchlights stabbing the sky, they began to pass many thousands moving on foot through the quiet residential streets. Swiftly they were recognized and a great murmur of sound, welcoming, adoring, proprietary—*hungry* in a way that was frightening to those who listened perceptively, as he did—began to accompany his approach. He thought, as Beth had thought: *I wish you were here.* But Ceil was not, and he must return to the scene of the bitter convention, his great defeat and humiliation, and now his great triumph, essentially alone, though Patsy chattered briskly by his side and in the car following his uncle and aunts waved and smiled and greeted the multitudes right royally.

When the Secret Service escorted him backstage through the solemn rows of NAWAC and the uneasy rows of state troopers, there was an instant's hush, then pandemonium as the words *"He's here!"* raced across the great hall. Sound rose, doubled, redoubled, redoubled again. The world cracked in two. He stepped upon the platform, was introduced, walked slowly to the lectern. The universe collapsed amid screams and yells and the loud, ironic thunder of the gods. He opened his notebook carefully, lifted the handsome, commanding head in a short, decisive gesture. Sound stopped, save for the distant echo of Harley Hudson's voice in bitter denunciation, Orrin Knox's in vigorous challenge, the President's in angry frustration, Ceil and Valuela's in worried puzzlement. He drew a deep breath and began. Sound was reborn and the galaxies exploded with his opening words:

"I am here to bid you welcome to Tomorrow."

Five minutes later, some semblance of order restored, he went on: "Conscience must decide the issue, and on Tuesday next—*it will.*"

Five minutes later, some semblance of order again restored, he was allowed to proceed for another twenty-five words before approval overwhelmed him. Then another fifty words—a hundred—seventy-five—"Six ovations in twelve minutes!" the Los Angeles *Times* cried ecstatically to the Kansas City *Star,* who could only shake his head in awe—and so on, bit by bit, line by line, little by little, for almost thirty fantastic minutes. George Wattersill had written a good speech for him, his own editings and polishings had made it into a genuinely powerful one. But still it would have been, as he knew with a certain inward melancholy, just another typical campaign speech by a Presidential candidate assured of victory had there not come, just before he was about to launch into his peroration, the dramatic interruption that was to make of it a speech never to be exceeded, on a night never to be forgotten.

At first, when Fred Van Ackerman appeared abruptly from the curtains at his right, there was a gasp of alarm and fear from all the many thousands who filled the Cow Palace and stood in further thousands on the grounds outside, watching him on giant television screens. It was repeated in a great continent-leaping susurrus wherever men watched around the globe. *"Oh, my God, not again!"* the *Times* whispered in agonized protest to the *Post.* But they need not have worried. Immediately it was perceived that it *was* Senator Van Ackerman, that he *was* grinning broadly, that high above his head he waved triumphantly what appeared to be an envelope, and that there was nothing here but joy and happiness for Edward M. Jason.

Nonetheless, he did not, at first, take kindly to being interrupted.

"What *is* it?" he demanded in what began as an angry, low-voiced question but was instantly boomed around the world by all the means of communication available to man. Equally loudly came Fred Van Ackerman's excited reply.

"Governor, I have here a communication which I have just received from the Soviet delegation at the UN—"

"What an odd channel for them to use," the London *Times* murmured gently to the *Daily Mail.* "Extraordinary," the *Mail* murmured back.

"—to be delivered to you personally—and, the instructions said, prior to the finish of your speech. They tell me it is good news, Governor. Good news!"

With a puzzled frown, while his worldwide audience quieted down in a tensely watchful silence, Tod Jason slowly opened the envelope, carefully unfolded the single sheet within, read it slowly. Then he too looked up with a pleased smile. Instantly a great rush of sound, applause and shouts, happy, excited, relieved, welled up to embrace him in warm and loving approval. When it had finally died away, he spoke with an undercurrent of excitement that communicated itself instantly. Great expectations rose.

"Ladies and gentlemen," he said slowly, "I have here, as Senator Van Ackerman has announced, a message from the Soviet delegation at the UN—or rather, I should say, a message transmitted by the

Soviet delegation at the UN. It is addressed to me and comes from the newly elected Chairman of the Council of Ministers. My old friend Vasily Tashikov writes to me as follows:

"Dear Mr. President: My sincerest congratulations on your inevitable triumph!"

There was a great shout of applause. He glanced up with a smile and waited patiently for it to subside.

"Your victory opens a new era for our two countries and for mankind. On behalf of the great Soviet peoples, I say we welcome this with eager minds and overflowing hearts. Peace now comes nearer—much nearer, Mr. President.

"It is within our grasp at last."

Again there was the approving roar. Again he waited and went on.

"Mr. President: Let me make clear to you at once on this historic occasion what I, as Chairman of the Council of Ministers, foresee. Under your Administration, I foresee:

"An end to the unfortunate intervention by United States imperialist-militarist circles in the two unhappy nations of Gorotoland and Panama.

"An end to all other unfortunate imperialist-militarist interventions by the United States in the affairs of the world.

"An end to the arms race which has forced both our countries to divert funds much needed for domestic development into a futile and hopeless attempt to overtake one another.

"An end to the mutual suspicion and mistrust which have too long divided and embittered our two great peoples.

"I see an end to all these things, Mr. President. *I see the start of peace!*"

Once more, hopeful, happy, excited and approving, the roar went up. Ted smiled, nodded, let it run its course.

"Mr. President, I want to tell you what I would like to have happen when you take office. I speak to you as your friend, who has known and admired you over the years. I feel we can talk frankly to one another. This is what I hope:

"I hope we will sit down somewhere and discuss our differences with trust and confidence as old friends should.

"I hope we will agree to abandon hatred and suspicion as a basis for our policies.

"I hope we will, with ruthless speed, dismantle and destroy all arms except those needed strictly for self-defense.

"I hope we will withdraw from all useless militaristic-imperialist interventionist adventures.

"I hope we will bring to our two nations and the world a new era of calm and lasting peace in which our two great peoples can work together in harmony and brotherhood for the betterment of all mankind.

"This is what I hope, Mr. President. And this is what I know can be achieved.

"It can be achieved because you are a man of great and farseeing wisdom.

"It can be achieved because you are a statesman of absolute courage and integrity.

"It can be achieved because you are a man of peace.

"It can be achieved because you are my friend!

"We look with hope to your Presidency, my friend. You will find us ready for a new start. Let us achieve it together!"

Ten minutes later by press corps count, silence again returned, humming, vibrant, wildly excited, alive with hope and the desperate yearning for peace. Ted stood for a long moment looking out upon his countrymen, his gaze candid and earnest as he stared into the cameras that took his commanding figure across the globe. Then he lifted the two remaining pages of his prepared speech, held them up so all could see, and tore them in two.

"I say to the Chairman of the Council of Ministers," he said, and his voice rang out solemn, strong and proud, *"Let us begin!"*

And when the last wild shout had finally subsided, he smiled and concluded with a grave yet happy confidence, while in Moscow Vasily Tashikov studied his handsome face on the little screen and smiled to himself a small, self-satisfied smile:

"My friends, we have a date on Tuesday.

"Good night!"

After that, of course, it was indeed all over but the shouting. There were, here and there in some few old-fashioned journals and from some few old-fashioned political figures and members of Congress, some uneasy grumblings about this blatant intervention in American affairs. But from the great majority who wrote, broadcast, editorialized, commented, there came only an ecstatic chorus of approval, congratulation and relief. It was true that there had once been a much-treasured tradition that foreigners should not intervene in American politics, ratified almost into principle in a dozen Presidential contests of the past. But in this case, almost everyone agreed, it was a wondrous and marvelous event, absolutely God-sent. This time the intervention had come on the Right Side of Things, and when anything happened on the Right Side of Things, tradition could be happily abandoned and principle speedily forgotten.

Two nights later he and Warren Strickland appeared on television in succeeding fifteen-minute segments to deliver the customary election eve statements. Both were dignified, commanding, statesmanlike. Warren looked a little older, a little tireder, a little less handsome; but an impression of great solidity, understanding and integrity came across. Many millions who intended to vote for Governor Jason told one another that, "It's just too bad Senator Strickland had to run against him, because Senator Strickland's a damned fine man." But the sentiment was obviously not going to be enough to help Warren Strickland, as he had known from the moment he had reluctantly agreed to undertake the thankless job of running for his party.

Ted spoke calmly, quietly, hopefully and with complete confidence. He referred very briefly, somberly, touchingly to his wife; very briefly, hopefully, stirringly to Chairman Tashikov; very quietly, firmly, movingly to his hopes for peace and his plans for the country. The luck of the draw had placed him first, but all through Warren's speech the memory of Ted's grave and commanding figure against a slowly rippling flag haunted the screen and dominated the viewers' minds.

Next day in their millions the free Americans went freely to vote: and as the sun and the tally swept on west to the Pacific shore an "inevitable outcome" became history's certainty.

JASON-CROY LANDSLIDE! IT'S T.J. ALL THE WAY! GOVERNOR WINS 479 ELECTORAL VOTES, TAKES 45 STATES IN MASSIVE SWEEP. POPULAR VOTE 119,563,000 TO 72,333,061. CARRIES BOTH HOUSES OF CONGRESS BY BIG MARGIN. MANY LEADING CONSERVATIVES DEFEATED. LIBERALS IN SADDLE AT LAST. STRICKLAND, PRESIDENT ABBOTT PLEDGE FULL COOPERATION. JASON THANKS U.S. FOR SYMPATHY AND SUPPORT. PRESIDENT-ELECT GIVES PLEDGE TO WORLD:
"TO END ALL WARS AND THREATS OF WARS IS MY FIRST PRIORITY."

4. "IT IS ONE of the more frustrating constitutional necessities of our land," Frankly Unctuous remarked on his final election roundup at two o'clock in the morning, "that a newly elected President, even one elected with such an overwhelming mandate as the nation has just

given Edward M. Jason, must wait two months before he can exercise the power his countrymen wish him to exercise.

"How fortunate we would all be if President-elect Jason could move immediately into a position to influence policy. How much unnecessary delay and confusion could be avoided if only there were some way to make his talents immediately available to the nation. How unfortunate there is no one of sufficient vision and foresight to get around this barrier and bring President-elect Jason, even if only on an informal basis, immediately and directly into the government he will shortly head."

In the Lincoln Bedroom, which, like his two immediate predecessors, he allowed himself the quiet historical satisfaction of using, the President snorted and snapped off the machine.

"I get your message, little man," he said aloud to the empty room as he began getting ready for bed, "and your Old Daddy Bill is just the man of vision and foresight you're looking for. . . . Although," he added more somberly, his voice trailing away, "God knows what it will portend for all of us. Including you, smart boy. Including you . . ."

At midnight, when returns from California and the Pacific Coast began to come in full strength and it was apparent that Ted Jason's victory was to be as triumphant there as it was almost everywhere else, the President had issued his congratulatory statement. It was brief, businesslike and to the point. It did not dwell on their policy differences nor did it in any way concede that the results were a repudiation of himself and the last two administrations. It congratulated Ted, pledged him full support, invited him to a conference at 10 A.M. Thursday, promised they would meet the press together at its conclusion. Then he had put in a private call to "Vistazo," where Ted and his family were waiting out the returns. Within five minutes the Governor's face appeared on the Picturephone, pleased, excited, yet somehow curiously serene, as though something inward had been decided for him by his countrymen. He spoke first.

"Thank you for your call and your statement. I've just watched it come over. I appreciate your support."

"You have it," the President said.

"All the way?" Ted asked pleasantly.

The President smiled.

"Within reason."

Ted smiled in return.

"Who determines the reason?"

"For two months," the President said, "I do. However," he added, as his successor's pleased expression dimmed a bit, "I don't intend to

be too arbitrary about it. In fact, what I should like to announce after
our meeting on Thursday is that you are going to move into the White
House immediately and begin to share my office with me as virtual co-
President. How does that strike you?"

For just a second it was apparent that this struck the President-elect
very well. Then caution took hold, a veil came down. He spoke with a
careful slowness.

"Mr. President," he said, "I appreciate the offer. But . . ."

"But what? Seems to me I'm being mighty generous, all things considered."

"Oh, you are," Ted agreed hastily. "Indeed you are. I'm very grateful for it, I don't minimize it for a minute. Nor do I minimize the wonderful opportunity it would be for me to learn the inside of it before
I actually have to move in there. It's just that—well, it goes back in a
sense to the same basic issue that came up in our last talk together."

"You don't need the headlines now," the President pointed out with
a wry smile. "You're in."

"It isn't so much headlines. It's the matter of fundamental policies.
Having cut myself loose from them—"

"They've been repudiated," the President acknowledged much more
bluntly and candidly than he ever would in public. "So what have you
got to worry about? You've won the argument. I've got to help you
devise new policies now. And you have to help me dismantle old
ones."

"Yes?" Ted inquired warily. "Which old ones?"

"Take your pick."

Ted smiled.

"With how many exceptions?"

"Two," the President said cheerfully. "We will not cut and run in
Gorotoland, and we will not abandon the Panama Canal to the Communists."

Ted's smile faded.

"I thought so."

The President raised a conciliatory hand.

"Let me amend: we will not get out of Gorotoland unless we can do
it safely, leaving a secure situation behind us; and we will not get out
of Panama until the Canal has been secured for unrestricted peaceful
passage of all vessels. Can you go that far with me?"

Ted hesitated and the President could see that he was calculating all
options, possibilities, advantages and disadvantages in half a minute's
time. When he spoke it was slowly and deliberately.

"If you will let me have a free hand to write the statement confirming this and let me give it to the press for both of us on Thursday."

It was the President's turn to hesitate and calculate. He, too, responded slowly and deliberately.

"You're going to be my President. I'm going to have to be helping you on the Hill when I become Speaker again. I guess I've got to start trusting you. . . . Very well. I shall rely on your good faith and your good judgment. And now, one favor to me, please."

"Yes?" Ted said, and the President could tell from a certain defensiveness in his eyes that he knew what was coming.

"Will you now, as President-elect of the United States, repudiate NAWAC and the violent elements that supported your campaign?"

Again a silence fell while Ted gave him a thoughtful stare whose import the President could not define. Finally he spoke with an almost angry impatience.

"Mr. President—no. I'm not going to go over all the reasons again. Just—no. Partly because I may still need their help in some ways, and partly because I simply no longer regard them as a danger to anyone, now that I've won. They're just not that important any more." His tone became almost contemptuous. "They've got their hero elected now. He's going to be in the White House where they wanted him to be. Their purpose has been achieved, and now they'll gradually disband and disappear into the general population. I'm willing to bet that within two weeks after inauguration NAWAC will have folded."

"Are you really willing to bet?" the President asked quietly. "What if they stay together—and wait to see how you act?"

"They'll be satisfied with the way I act," Ted said flatly. "And anyway, some of their—" he stopped abruptly and concluded somewhat lamely, "anyway."

"Anyway, what?" the President demanded. "You're not going to keep some of them around you, are you? You're not going to appoint any of that crew to anything, are you? Come on, now, Ted—"

"Mr. President," Governor Jason said firmly, "I thank you for calling, I thank you for proposing an agreement you and I can live with for the next two months—and on into the new term, for that matter. I thank you for suggesting that I take an office in the White House, which I greatly appreciate and which I accept. I look forward to seeing you on Thursday and making clear to the world that there will be no difficulties or frictions in *this* transition. And now there are many people here waiting to see me—"

"Give my love to NAWAC," the President told him with an angry bitterness. "You take a fearful gamble, Mr. President."

"Much less than you think, Mr. President."

"I hope you're right," the President said grimly. "God help us if you're not."

"He's helped me pretty well so far," the President-elect replied. "I don't see any reason why He shouldn't continue."

But, of course, no one at that moment, including the President-elect himself, could really be sure. And so, as a direct result of their talk, two more conferences were held that night before famous and weary poll watchers could at last go to bed.

The first, filled with concern for the country and firm pledges of mutual support, took place via a three-Picturephone link-up of the President in the White House, Senator Munson at beautiful "Vagaries" in Rock Creek Park, and Senator Strickland at his rambling old home in Boise, Idaho. The principal decision reached was that there should be further meetings and discussions as soon as their friends in Congress who had survived the Jason sweep got back into town. There was a most disturbing moment for them all when the President disclosed that he was actually much less sanguine about his chances of being re-elected Speaker than he had maintained to the President-elect. Bob and Warren agreed with this. It was on a note of uneasy foreboding that their talk concluded.

The second conference began at midnight, California time, in the rambling, redwood-paneled library at "Vistazo." There in the room he had known from infancy, filled with the worn leather armchairs and sofas that had supported Montoyas and Jasons down the years, the President-elect stood at an open window during the slowly creeping minutes before his guests arrived, listening to the faint recurring roar of the Pacific, miles below. It was the background of his life, that distant, restless, implacable sound—on rare occasions soft, soothing and gentle, far more often angry, somber and harsh. It was somber tonight, and so was his mood as he listened. Three hours after final confirmation that he had won one of the great political victories of American history, he was as uneasy and uncertain as though he were a hunted soul instead of the next President of the United States. And so he was hunted, he realized, by ghosts, by the past, by history, by the future.

How typical of the President, to fight to the last for his point of view on NAWAC; and how effective he had been, in these past few weeks and months, in implanting his own fears and worries in his successor. Ted would never admit it to him, but his words had struck home far more often than he knew. There had been a number of occasions when Ted had been on the very point of openly repudiating his unruly and unpredictable supporters, but always he had backed away, for reasons he had patiently tried to explain to the President, to Valuela, to all the many others who had written him or questioned him during the campaign, troubled and concerned lest he let himself become too much beholden to elements they feared. He had never fully acknowledged to anyone, even himself, the ultimate reason for his hesitation, the reason that had lived with him ever since that dreadful moment at the Monument:

He feared them too.

And that was a most unusual and unnerving emotion for Edward M. Jason to experience.

He was not exactly afraid of them in a personal, physical sense, although that was a large share of it, as he had come very close to admitting to the President in their talk before the election. But somehow, although that fear did exist, as it would for any sensible man, it went far deeper, to a general fear for the country, and for what the violent might do to it if he did not handle their dismissal from his cause and from public life with the greatest astuteness, firmness and skill. There had been times before in America, not too long ago, when the violent had run amuck, had begun to organize deliberately to destroy democracy, had begun to coalesce behind candidates for President who had been either too complacent, too naive or too self-confident to worry about the ultimate implications of their support. In one way or another fate had intervened, using strange instruments, and none of those candidates had reached the White House. No one would ever know how they would have handled the problem (if they even realized it was a problem) that he faced now. He knew that many of his countrymen believed that he also had been too complacent, too naive, too self-confident about it. But he had not been, really. He had been trying, as best he could, to mask a constant concern, conduct a winning campaign, and simultaneously decide on the best time and place to get rid of NAWAC.

Tonight the President had finally won his point, though he did not know it as he fell at last into a troubled sleep in the Lincoln bed. His successor had decided that this was the time and this was the place.

Now he waited for the leaders of the National Anti-War Activities Congress to come to him at "Vistazo." The Vice President-elect was flying down from the Croy home in Portland. Senator Van Ackerman was flying in from Cheyenne after his squeak-in, 106-vote majority re-election in Wyoming. George Harrison Wattersill, LeGage Shelby and Rufus Kleinfert were driving up from Jason campaign headquarters in Los Angeles. Very soon, now, they would be here. What would he say to them, and how would they receive it?

He did not know, on either score; but he did know his mind was made up beyond reversal, and he knew that he would never have a better opportunity. If he was not in position now, on the very night of his overwhelming victory, to bring the violent to heel, when would he ever be?

Far below he heard the sullen sea crash in. So they found him, back to them, head erect and shoulders squared, staring out the window into the empty night, listening to the sound that would always mean home to him.

"Mr. President," Roger P. Croy exclaimed, hurrying forward, "heartiest, *heartiest* congratulations on your wonderful triumph!"

He turned to face them with an air of grave dignity that said, as clearly as though the words came to them aloud: This is a President. For a moment the sheer magnitude of his achievement overwhelmed them. Then he smiled, and the magic dissolved a little—just enough for them to remember that he was Edward M. Jason, a man whose weaknesses they thought they knew. And a certain moment passed.

"Mr. Vice President," he said, returning Roger Croy's fervent handshake, "don't minimize what you did to bring us victory. It wouldn't have been possible without your help."

"Anything would have been possible to you this day," George Wattersill assured him, coming forward in turn to take both of Ted's hands in his with an equally fulsome fervor. "*Anything!* What a rout!"

"Right on," LeGage agreed, shaking hands with less ecstasy but with what appeared to be a reasonable respect.

"Marvelouss," Rufus Kleinfert mumbled, following suit; and finally, coming forward with his expansive, self-conscious swagger, Fred Van Ackerman gave him a satisfied and somewhat savage grin and said, "We showed the bastards, didn't we?"

Abruptly Ted's smile vanished.

"Did we?" he asked in a voice so cold and so Presidential that for a moment, again, even Fred was momentarily awed. But his recovery time was very fast.

"Yes, *we* did," he said, the usual insolence in his voice. "I hope your supporters can take some credit, Governor."

For a moment longer Ted continued to look at him with a cold and skeptical glance; and again there was a chance to take command, the sort of chance that a President Abbott or an Orrin Knox would have seized. But soon his expression changed, became less stern, more friendly. Having appeared firm, he seemed subtly to waver. And the magic dissolved a little more.

"I think my supporters can take a great deal of credit," he said quietly, "but I don't think there should be any vindictive spirit about it. That, in fact, is why I wanted to talk to you tonight, even though it means imposing on exhausted men the burden of further discussion, when all any of us wants to do right now is sleep. But this seemed to me so important that I took the liberty of asking you to come here."

"Whatever you say, of course, Mr. President," Roger Croy assured him cordially. "It is our pleasure to oblige."

"Sure thing," Fred Van Ackerman agreed with a heartiness exaggerated just enough to mock Roger Croy's elaborate manner, which Roger Croy perceived and did not like. "Can we sit down?"

"Please do," Ted said a trifle dryly. "Forgive me for not suggesting it. Would anyone like a drink? . . . No? Is the room too cold for anyone? I'm used to these Southern California evenings, but you may not be. . . . Everybody fine? Good." He paused and looked around the semi-circle of attentive, shrewd, professionally impassive faces that confronted him. "I think it is time," he said calmly, "to dissolve NAWAC and get back to a more peaceful and democratic emphasis for the new Administration."

"That seems like a perfectly reasonable re—" Roger Croy began, but Fred Van Ackerman interrupted.

"Don't move too fast, Governor," he said, deliberately emphasizing the old title with a lazy arrogance. "You may need us."

"Now, why," Ted inquired with a thoughtful slowness, "would I need you?"

"Can't tell what's going to happen when you switch things around," LeGage observed. "Some of these nice folks may not take it so well."

"When you end our endless entanglements in foreign warss," Rufus Kleinfert remarked with the heavy Pennsylvania Dutch accent that thirty years in Texas oil had never changed," there may be violent responses. Speaking as Knight Kommander of the Konference on Efforts to Encourage Patriotism, I think KEEP would be prepared to assist in putting those responses down."

"Likewise DEFY," 'Gage said.

"And COMFORT," Senator Van Ackerman agreed.

"What do you mean, 'put' them 'down?'" Governor Jason asked quietly. "You mean they don't have a right to protest if they want to? You've always claimed that right, haven't you?"

"Sure," Fred Van Ackerman said with a lazy smile. "But now we're on top."

"What I think they mean—" Roger P. Croy began, somewhat nervously, but Fred interrupted in the same lazy, insolent way.

"He knows what we mean: just what we say. There's no mystery about it."

"Well, now," George Harrison Wattersill said with the fluid suavity that had made him such a courtroom sensation in helping the misfit and the violent escape the just punishments of a troubled society, "there's no point in creating any issue about it. I think the Governor—the President-elect—is well aware of the uneasiness that may occur in some quarters when it becomes apparent that he really means to have a peace Administration. But certainly no one here has any intention of denying those who oppose such a course their right to express their opposition. I have always fought against restraints on those on our side of it, God knows, and I hope to God I am prepared to be consistent."

"You were a good man when we needed you, Georgie," Senator Van Ackerman told him with a patronizing cruelty, "but who needs you now? You forget: we've won."

"Edward M. Jason has won," Roger Croy snapped, "and that perhaps should be remembered here this morning."

"We're not forgetting," LeGage Shelby said with a sudden scowl, "and we don't want him to forget who helped him do it, either. We're only trying to save him trouble. What's everybody complaining about?"

"Maybe he doesn't want your help," George Wattersill suggested bluntly. "Maybe he can do very well without it."

"Yes, and maybe he can let the dissenters and the protesters run wild and raise too much hell, too," 'Gage said in a dour tone. "Can't let 'em tear things apart, if you want to govern this country. You've got to be firm."

"And you don't think I can be firm, I gather?" Governor Jason inquired.

"We mean," Rufus Kleinfert said, "*really* firm."

"Yes," Fred Van Ackerman said with a comfortable insolence. "Like you weren't with us."

Again Ted started to look angry, but this time he abandoned it with an expression of ironic disbelief.

"You gentlemen," he remarked, "are quite amazing in your consistency. You are really calling, I take it, for a serious attempt to suppress dissent in America, after taking advantage of America's tolerance toward dissent in all these recent months. To say nothing of *my* tolerance, I might add. How do you square that with what you're proposing now?"

"Governor," Senator Van Ackerman said, and a cold bluntness entered his tone, "you were tolerant of us *because we helped you get elected.* And that's the only reason. And don't try to get high and mighty *now* and try to convince us it was anything else. Because we don't believe you, and neither does anybody else."

And looking around the circle of faces, in what he suddenly realized was a cataclysmic moment, the President-elect could see that Fred spoke the truth. It was a revelation so profound in its implications for his future, and for his whole concept of himself, that for several moments he was unable to reply. When he did it was to echo Fred's final remark as though he did not want to accept it but knew he must.

"You don't believe me, and neither does anyone else," he repeated slowly. He shook his head with a strange little smile. "When all along, I was defending your right to dissent to the President—to Orrin—to my aunt—to—" his voice broke for a second "—to my wife . . . when all along, I was arguing, even when NAWAC's methods became dangerous, that the basis for its support and the principal purpose of its leadership was to give voice to valid, genuine, loyal, democratic protest . . . and it was all a fraud. You never really—it was all a fraud. Just as they said. And I was terribly, terribly mistaken. . . ." He repeated the words, so low they could hardly hear, as if to himself alone: "Terribly, terribly mistaken . . ."

He rose suddenly, a movement so abrupt it startled and almost disturbed them—almost; but they felt sure of their man, and so it did not disturb them very much. He turned away and went to the open window. Far below, distant and insistent, the somber sound of home gave its melancholy intimations of man, mortality, the inexorable flow of history and the vast, impersonal sea.

So he stood for what must have been at least five minutes, while behind him Fred and 'Gage and Rufus Kleinfert exchanged an occasional glance that ranged from the satisfied to the smug, and George Harrison Wattersill and Roger P. Croy looked at one another with a genuine alarm, shaken by the sight of a President apparently foundered before he had even entered office. But they had all underestimated their host. He was not a Jason for nothing, nor could his lifelong self-confidence be so easily broken.

Presently he turned back.

"George," he said in a tone of such normal conversational quality that they could never be sure, later, whether this was something he had contemplated right along or something he had only thought of in the last five desperate minutes, "I intend to appoint you Attorney General of the United States. When I do," he went on, hardly allowing George Harrison Wattersill time to utter his gulp of surprise, "I want you to prosecute these people with all the legal weapons at the government's command. Have I your assurance that you will do so?"

Instantly the parade of Washington ambition, the endless game of boxes-within-boxes, began as he had known it would.

"Why," George Wattersill said, stumbling over his words in his surprise, cupidity, concern and confusion, "Governor—Mr. President—I —I could not be more—words cannot express—I am honored—overwhelmed—I should be proud and happy—I accept, Mr. President! I accept!"

"With my condition?" Governor Jason asked softly, and on the other side of the circle the junior Senator from Wyoming stirred.

"And with my opposition to your confirmation in the Senate, if you do?" he asked with an equal softness.

Boxes-within-boxes began to tumble around in George Harrison Watersill, as they all could see. Ted decided to help.

"I doubt very much that your opposition weighs very heavily with the Senate nowadays, Senator. Ever since your censure following Brigham Anderson's death, I don't think your colleagues have paid too much attention."

"Ah, but I can make trouble," Fred said, the vicious note that his colleagues knew and feared coming suddenly into his voice. "I can make trouble, Governor. And not only for Georgie, here—for many things. *Many* things."

"I repeat, George," Governor Jason said calmly. "Do you accept with my condition?"

"Well," George Wattersill said hastily. "Well—I—this catches me quite unprepared, you understand, Mr. President—quite unprepared—"

"I know," Ted agreed. "I thought a state of unpreparedness might elicit a candid answer. I can always withdraw the offer. Nothing's firm until I send it to the Senate, after all."

"Don't—don't act hastily," George Wattersill said. "It takes a moment of thought, I submit. This is a profound question you raise here, Mr. President."

Ted nodded.

"On a profound issue," he agreed. "The most profound, perhaps, that I may have to resolve. At least domestically. Maybe in the foreign area, too. So don't accept."

"Oh, now, Mr. President," George Wattersill cried, and for once the daring young battler for the downtrodden, the anti-establishment, the finger-in-the-face-of-society crowd, he who was the Right Thinkers' hero and the media's darling, sounded genuinely dismayed. "Now, Mr. President—"

"Mr. President," Roger P. Croy said in a respectful but urgent tone, "if I may be permitted a thought, just for a moment—not that I have much to contribute, but perhaps as a relatively objective observer, so to speak—aren't you, perhaps, forcing too much of an issue here? Aren't you possibly being just a trifle—in the heat of the moment, only, but still—just a trifle unfair to both George and our friends of NAWAC? Is it quite fair to force them to confront one another so bitterly, when they have so recently been comrades in arms in the great cause of peace? Is it possible for him to prosecute them, Mr. President? Wherein lies their crime? Is it opposition to war, Mr. President? Then if so— what was your platform, in the great victory just won?"

There was a silence while Ted studied him thoughtfully.

"My platform," he said at last, "was not the violent suppression of those who disagreed with me. It was not brutalizing my opposition and attempting to drive them under with threats and fear."

"But also, Mr. President," Roger Croy said softly, while his colleagues watched intently and far away the sea roared on, "it was not opposition to peaceable assembly, was it? It was not denial of any American's right to dissent, was it? If we were to allow for a moment, for the sake of argument only, that there may be grounds for concern in some of the more robust activities of NAWAC—" Ted smiled wryly, but his running mate continued, quite imperturbable "—then, on what ground would you have the Attorney General proceed against them? In recent decades the courts, as you know, have handed down such broad interpretations that nowadays 'peaceable assembly' means almost anything except outright murder, does it not? Where in the laws as the courts now interpret them do you find the warrant for any such vendetta as you would require of our good friend George against our good friends of NAWAC?"

Again Ted studied him with great care, as though seeing him for the first time, as perhaps he was.

"You are very fluent, Governor," he said at last. "And as far as the courts are concerned, you are right: the protections of the average citizen against the violence of the mob, providing the mob can put a thin claim of reason on its initial motivation, are virtually gone. Possibly I'm approaching it the wrong way. Possibly I should work to reestablish those protections."

"We have a proposed law," Senator Van Ackerman said dreamily, "which I filibustered to death in the last session of Congress, which would establish a Federal Riot Control Board to approve the use of 'any facilities within one mile of any Federal building or installation' for gatherings of three or more people, and would define as illegal any such gathering of three or more 'if there is obvious intent to create civil disturbance and/or riot.' Maybe we're all approaching this the wrong way. Maybe that's the way to handle your opposition from now on, not with the help of crude old NAWAC, but with the help of the law. Maybe I should change my position on that bill. Maybe all liberals should. Maybe we should get behind it and push it through in the next session. . . . What do you think of that, Mr. President?"

Ted shook his head, hard, as if to clear it of fogs and frights and fearful things.

"You open abysses beyond abysses," he said quietly. "You enter areas where not I, nor any American President, should ever be prepared to go."

"Bill Abbott was willing to enter those areas a couple of months ago," Fred said with a vicious anger, "when it was *us* he wanted to get. What's so wrong," he asked softly, "with turning it back on him and all the rest who will be working against you when you make your moves for peace?"

"Abysses beyond abysses," Ted repeated harshly. "I forbid you to think of it."

"You can't forbid anything," Senator Van Ackerman told him with an unimpressed contempt. "You can only do what the law allows, and as Roger says, it doesn't allow very much . . . unless we get a new one. . . . I'm not afraid of abysses," he said, still softly. "How about you, 'Gage, and Rufus?"

LeGage shrugged.

"Law or no law," he said, "isn't anybody should be permitted to get in the way of peace."

"To end these monstrous interventions in foreign wars," Rufus Kleinfert said in his flat, unemotional voice, "nothing, in the judgment of KEEP, can be too severe."

"That is not true," the President-elect said in a brooding almost-whisper. *"That is not true."*

"Well, Mr. President," Roger Croy said smoothly, "it is obvious that there is something of an impasse here, and it seems to me that by far the better way to handle it is not by forcing Mr. Wattersill to initiate actions he could not win, in the courts as now constituted, against his comrades of your campaign; nor by passing extreme legislation whose dangers you yourself, Senator Van Ackerman, so brilliantly and exhaustively explained during your recent filibuster; nor by threatening, on any side, to do anything. Rather, it seems to me, it is by working out an informal agreement here, in the privacy of these old walls that mean so much to you, Mr. President, as our homes mean to us, which will bring us all back together to work in harmony for the great cause for which you and I have just been elected.

"I am sure George would, of his own volition, do his best to control unnecessary and unworthy acts of violence on the part of NAWAC or, indeed, of any American of whatever political persuasion. By the same token, I am sure our friends of NAWAC will soon perceive that there is no need for them to indulge in any such actions against anyone as they perhaps, in their less thoughtful moments, may have been contemplating. I don't think there will be any need for a commitment to prosecution, because I don't think there is any need for a commitment to violence.

"I would remind our friends, Mr. President—and indeed, I would remind you—that you, after all, have just been elected overwhelmingly on a simple, forthright and unequivocal platform. Not five hours ago you stated it yourself with crystalline clarity: 'To end all wars and the threat of wars is my first priority.' Very well. We are agreed. And so is the country. That is what they expect you to do. That is what they want you to do. You are now the only man who can lead a complete and speedy reversal of past policies. It is your clear mandate to do so. Very few, if any, will dare protest too vigorously against it. So there will be no need for anyone to organize to stop that protest. The protest won't exist—the need to stop it won't exist. So where is the argument?"

And looking satisfied with himself, for he had stated a middle ground and in his estimation stated it very well, Roger P. Croy sat back with a firm nod of his distinguished white head and looked about him blandly.

"I do think, Mr. President," George Wattersill ventured presently, "that Governor Croy—the Vice President-elect—is right. There really is no need to force the issue. I shall be vigilant—I am sure our friends of NAWAC will be moderate—for the very reason the Vice President-elect so succinctly states: there will simply be no cause for trouble. Isn't that so, gentlemen?"

"Why, of course," Fred Van Ackerman agreed with a blandness close to mockery. "Everybody's going to be good boys." He shifted in his chair and leaned forward. "Just remember, though: if there is trouble, we're ready for it."

"There will be no trouble," Roger Croy said comfortably, "and all we need be ready for is a new era of good will and friendliness in the nation and the world as this great mandate is exercised by our President. Isn't that so, Mr. President?"

Thoughtfully, again, Governor Jason studied them, face by face, with a curiously distant manner that made even Fred begin to feel uncomfortable. Then he appeared to come out of whatever private world he was in and spoke with what appeared an adequate firmness.

"I have your word, then," he said. "COMFORT's word, DEFY's word, KEEP's word, NAWAC's word—that there will be no more violence, no more disruption, no more interfering with the legitimate right of others to protest, even if they should protest against the policies I intend to put into effect. I have your personal word, and your word as head of your respective organization. Is that right, Senator?"

"You have my word," Fred Van Ackerman said solemnly.

"Mr. Shelby?"

LeGage shrugged.

"Why not?"

"Mr. Kleinfert?"

"Certainly," Rufus Kleinfert said.

"I hope I do," Ted told them quietly, "because if I don't and if you betray my trust in your cooperation, I shall spare no expense and no effort on the part of the government to bring you to book and destroy your organizations. Is that clear to you?"

"Couldn't be clearer," Fred Van Ackerman agreed. "Can we go now?"

"When I tell you!" Ted snapped, and for a moment Fred looked at him with an expression so genuinely startled that it was ludicrous. In a second, however, it became deliberately ludicrous, and when he responded it was with the usual mocking edge.

"Well, well," he said softly. "Yes, *sir. May* we go now?"

"I don't think the President has made a decision yet on Mr. Wattersill, has he?" Roger Croy suggested smoothly. "Perhaps he would like to let us know what he—?"

"I will let Mr. Wattersill know in due course," Ted said. Abruptly he stood up. "It is very late and we are all very tired. There's no reason for any of you to drive back. The servants will show you to your rooms and you can leave in the morning."

"Do you wish to see any of us then?" Roger Croy inquired. "If so, I am sure we can all arrange—"

"No, thank you. I expect to get as much sleep as I can, myself, and then leave directly for Washington and my conference with the President on Thursday. I expect I'll be in Washington pretty much straight on through to inauguration. If any of you wishes to see me there, I believe the White House switchboard is going to take calls for me. So good night, gentlemen. Thank you for coming."

"Don't let that old man talk you 'round," 'Gage said with a sudden harshness. "He's a mighty smooth one and hard to overcome."

"Not," Ted said with a bitterness so dry and unexpected that it stunned them momentarily, "a weakling like me, is that it? All right, 'Gage, I'll be careful. And now I really must suggest we go along to bed. It is past one, and I for one am exhausted."

"Yes, of course, Mr. President," Roger Croy said, gesturing them vigorously out as Maria and Tomas appeared at the door to take them to their rooms. "A good trip to Washington, good luck with the President, and we will see you soon."

After they had gone he turned to the silent room and studied it for a long moment: these old familiar walls, books, chairs, lamps, tables, sofas, Persian rugs, ancestral portraits, a hundred years of Montoya-Jason living. Doña Valuela hung in her usual honored place beside the fireplace, Ceil in hers on the other side. Two months from now they would be in the great hall of the White House, the first two portraits the visitor would see as he entered from the North Portico. The honor would have pleased Doña Valuela's independent and indomitable spirit, though Ceil might have been more modest and content with a lesser place.

He sighed, a lonely and vulnerable little sound. Grandmother and wife: would it be comfort or judgment they would give him now, could they only be here? . . . For he knew he had not succeeded in doing what he had intended to do, and the knowledge brought a deep foreboding.

He walked again to the open window, stood listening again for a moment to the somber sea before he closed the panes against the now sharply chilly night. Unchanging and unchangeable, the Pacific advanced . . . withdrew . . . advanced . . . withdrew . . . advanced again, in the eternal, inexorable attack that always takes from the shore and adds to the sea—but does not always, or of necessity, take from the sea and add to the shore.

PRESIDENT NAMES JASON "INFORMAL CO-PRESIDENT" DURING TRANSITION PERIOD. GOVERNOR TO OCCUPY ADJOINING WHITE HOUSE OFFICE IN EXTRAORDINARY GESTURE OF AMITY BY OUTGOING PRESIDENT. TWO EXECUTIVES PLEDGE COOPERATION IN "GRADUAL RESTRUCTURING" OF U.S. POLICIES DURING TRANSITION AND NEW ADMINISTRATION. JASON ANNOUNCES FIRST CABINET APPOINTMENT: WATTERSILL TO BE ATTORNEY GENERAL. CONGRESSIONAL DISCONTENT INDICATES PRESIDENT AB-

BOTT MAY FACE STRONG OPPOSITION TO HOPE OF REGAIN-
ING SPEAKERSHIP. NAWAC PLEDGES "VIGILANT AND CON-
TINUING SUPPORT" OF JASON PEACE PLANS. SENATOR VAN
ACKERMAN WARNS OF "POSSIBLE VIOLENT RIGHT-WING
REACTIONS WHEN PRESIDENT JASON REALLY TRIES TO
MAKE PEACE." SUGGESTS LIBERALS "RESTUDY" RIOT CON-
TROL BILL "IN LIGHT OF DEVELOPMENTS THAT MAY UN-
FOLD."

"We are pleased," *The Greatest Publication* announced next morning to all those, and they were many, whom years of faithful reading
had conditioned to be pleased when the *G.P.* was pleased, "with
President-elect Jason's nomination of the distinguished attorney George
Harrison Wattersill to be Attorney General of the United States. If
this first appointment is indicative of the stature of those to follow, the
Jason Cabinet will be scintillating indeed.

"The career of George Harrison Wattersill, only thirty-seven years
old as he moves to the top judicial administrative post in the nation,
is one that will stand in the annals of these times as a perfect example
of enlightened public service in the legal profession. From his first appearance on the national scene—his brilliantly successful defense of
the so-called 'Statue of Liberty Bombers' eleven years ago—his life has
been dedicated to the protection of democratic freedoms and all those
who challenge the sometimes frightening ways in which the American democracy has twisted and perverted them.

"When he succeeded in destroying the government's case against the
'Statue Bombers' (their 'crime' not really a crime at all in the sense
most understand the term, but only the destruction of the torch in the
statue's hand as a means of protesting what they believed to be in-
equities in the American system), he was projected immediately into
the national spotlight as the youngest, most dynamic and most effective legal defender of the loyal dissident in the country and perhaps
in the world.

"He has never looked back. Having set foot on that courageous and
sometimes lonely path, he has trod it with a fervor and dedication
which have made his name a byword wherever true friends of freedom
congregate. Many an alleged draft-card burner, bomber, rioter, radical and 'pornographer' walks the streets a free man today because of
the brilliant defense provided him by George Harrison Wattersill.
Many a threatened miscarriage of American 'justice' has been
thwarted by his shrewd mind, dedicated perseverance and sure-footed
mastery of his profession. He is in the great tradition of those sons of

democracy who believe that the cure to its ills is more liberty to do more things, not less liberty to do fewer things. He has helped to open American doors and free the American spirit. We think he will continue to do so. We think he will be like a breath of fresh air as he presides over the administration of those laws that remain on the books. We are sure he will continue to seek their steady relaxation to permit more and more citizens to have more and more liberty to do more and more things.

"Having said that we are pleased with Mr. Wattersill, we must, in all honesty, now inject a couple of less jovial notes into these thoughts on the opening days of what will soon be the Jason Administration. Two things concern us, and quite deeply.

"The first is the surprising, disturbing and indeed, in our estimation, quite ominous statement by Wyoming's Senator Fred Van Ackerman that he thinks liberals should 'restudy' the anti-riot bill which he himself filibustered to death in the last Congress scarcely two months ago.

"And the second is the continuing failure of President-elect Jason, now that the election is safely won, to repudiate and seek a permanent disbanding of the hodgepodge National Anti-War Activities Congress whose violence and intolerance brought so many untoward incidents across the country during the recent campaign.

"Senator Van Ackerman's announced intention to 'restudy' the ill-omened *'Bill to curb further acts against the public order and welfare'* and his call upon all liberals to do likewise have to be taken in context with his further remarks that he expects there may be 'possibly violent right-wing reactions when President Jason really tries to make peace.'

"Is the Senator implying that this bill, which he rightfully opposed and literally talked to death when he conceived it to be directed at NAWAC and all those who genuinely protested past administrations' war policies, should now be revised for use against those who might conceivably oppose the peace policies he favors?

"That way, we submit, lies a dangerous toying with forces so hostile to democracy that we are amazed any United States Senator would espouse them. It is true that they were espoused, briefly, by President Abbott and some of his friends in Congress; but this, we think, was basically just a gesture, ill-advised but in context understandable, to try to calm the violent activities of NAWAC which so disfigured the national convention in San Francisco and the subsequent meeting of the National Committee in Washington. The bill was never designed to be a serious legislative proposal, as witness the way in which all Abbott Administration support for it swiftly ceased and the Senator was permitted to filibuster it to death without opposition or hindrance.

"Senator Van Ackerman suggests that 'liberals' restudy this so-called 'Riot Control Act.' We consider ourselves 'liberal,' and we do not think any amount of 'restudying' of this dangerously undemocratic legislation could convince us of its worth. We most strongly urge all liberals, as we urge the President-elect himself, to repudiate the bill and along with it the shadowed and somewhat unsavory Senator who now appears to be emerging in the surprising and ominous guise of its converted defender.

"By the same token, we call on President-elect Jason to repudiate once and for all NAWAC and all its works. We note that it has announced that it will give him 'vigilant and continuing support' as he moves to turn the country away from war and toward that general peace which is the hope of all mankind. We do not like the word 'vigilant' with its overtone of 'vigilante'; and we suspect, on NAWAC's record, that this is exactly why that word was chosen. This nation does not need NAWAC's vigilante vigilance to protect it, nor does Edward M. Jason need it. It is time now, we submit, to put an end to the kind of games NAWAC has played with the public order and safety.

"NAWAC had a worthy birth in legitimate protest against sincerely hated war policies of past administrations. Those policies are about to be ended. They are already, in President Abbott's and Governor Jason's delicate phrasing, beginning to undergo a 'gradual restructuring.' Without question the restructuring will be speeded as soon as Mr. Jason enters upon the full powers of the Presidential office. He does not need, nor does any of us need, the heavy hand of NAWAC to help in the task.

"He should, we submit, get rid of this uncomfortable and potentially dangerous organization, with its sinister overtones of theatrical crudity and storm-trooper violence that have marred the precampaign and campaign periods. We will support him heartily, as will all true Americans, liberals and conservatives alike."

GREATEST PUBLICATION COMPOSING ROOM SHATTERED BY BOMB. THREE DEAD, TWO PRINTING PRESSES DEMOLISHED. POLICE FIND NO CLUES. TOP EXECUTIVES ATTRIBUTE BLAST TO "DISGRUNTLED EMPLOYEES" DISCHARGED IN RECENT ECONOMY MOVE, DECLARE "TACTICS OF THIS KIND WILL NOT CRIPPLE OR STOP THE PAPER." PLEDGE FULL PRESS RUN TOMORROW, REFUSE FURTHER COMMENT "NOW OR ANY TIME."

"Gentlemen," the executive chairman of *The Greatest Publication* said gently to the three troubled faces that stared back at him from the Picturephone link-up between Washington and New York, "I think we all have a problem. I am wondering if we of this paper have your support in trying to meet it."

"You certainly have mine," the general director of the *Post* said stoutly, and from the worried editorial director of the *Times* and a Walter Dobius looking grim and upset there came agreeing nods.

"Then you think it was who we think it was," the editorial director of the *Times* said. His friend of *The Greatest Publication* nodded.

"Who else?" the *Post* inquired dryly. "You don't mean to tell me you didn't get your quota of threats during the campaign?"

"We did," the *Times* admitted somewhat stiffly.

"So did I," Walter Dobius said. "I guess a lot of us did."

"And did you yield to it?" the executive chairman of *The Greatest Publication* inquired in his wispy old man's voice that could ask such disconcerting questions, as his staff had long ago found out.

"You know none of us did," the *Post* began indignantly. Then he stopped with a shamefaced little smile. "We went a little easy," he admitted. "Let's be honest and say we all did."

"We expressed concern on several occasions," the *Times* said stoutly.

"But gently," the *Post* noted. "Gently. Isn't that right?"

"There were so many other things to write about in the campaign," Walter said, "that I really didn't find the subject coming to mind very often."

"And when it did, you carefully told it to stop bothering you," the executive director of *The Greatest Publication* suggested with a little smile. "And that, I guess, is about what we all did."

"My first reaction was to tell them to go to hell and do it in a front-page editorial," the *Post* remarked.

"We all felt that way," the *Times* agreed.

"Then," the *Post* admitted, "I started to think. And once I began to think, I guess I had lost the battle. I'm not proud of it. I don't think any of us should be."

"No one said we were," Walter Dobius observed somewhat testily. "It isn't fun to know you're being a coward—even if you tell yourself it's because you're helping the candidate you like and don't want to hurt or embarrass him by raising difficult questions."

"That's how we rationalized it too," the *Post* said. "We felt we shouldn't trouble him when it was so important that the public believe in him and give him full support in what he wanted to do."

"And doesn't that rationale still apply?" the executive director of *The Greatest Publication* inquired. "Should we not perhaps have evaded the point by not raising it, even in our editorial today?"

"Three would be living and two presses would be running if you had," the *Times* observed. "But the question is still valid: what do we do about it now?"

"Exactly," the executive director of *The Greatest Publication* agreed. "At this moment, of course, we have no physical proof whatsoever that NAWAC perpetrated this atrocity this morning. Probably we will never have any. All we have is the call I received after it occurred, in which a mailed fist—these people have a positively Hitlerian sense of staging—simply held the NAWAC emblem up before the Picturephone, and then hung up. And how can I ever prove *that* occurred, and who would believe me? Things like this simply don't happen to the American press." He smiled with a certain irony. "Nor, in fact, do its leading members ever confess, even to each other, that they might have let themselves be intimidated—and that they are actually considering whether or not to let themselves be intimidated further. No one at all would believe it, we have convinced the public so well of our fearless integrity."

"That great element of skepticism concerning the evils that do really exist in the world!" the *Times* said moodily.

"Which we have done so much to create," the executive director of the *G.P.* pointed out quietly. "Let us be really honest, at least with each other, about that. . . . Well: I am wondering if you think it would do any good for us to form a deputation and ask for a conference with the President-elect. What is your feeling about that?"

"I think," Walter Dobius said slowly, "that we could put together an impressive group. Frankly Unctuous and some other friends in the networks have been getting it, too, you know. Frankly told me he was actually quite badly roughed up on leaving the studio after his broadcast on the Strickland rally in Los Angeles. He had made one or two critical remarks about NAWAC, not very severe by any standard. Of course he never reported the incident."

"Nor did he ever really attack NAWAC again, did he?" the *Times* inquired.

"No," Walter said, "because, as he told me, he decided that to do so would be to embarrass Ted Jason and perhaps cost him votes. And none of us," he pointed out with a dry bitterness, "did any better. None of us wanted to cost him votes."

"Now he has the votes," the executive director of *The Greatest Pub-*

lication observed. "Do we still want to avoid causing him the embarrassment?"

"I think we *must* defend the rights of a free press," the *Post* said.

"I couldn't agree with you more," the *Times* told him.

"Nor I, of course," Walter Dobius said. "But do you think it will do any good to call on Ted Jason? Do you think he really has any control over the situation?"

"If he doesn't," the executive director of the *G.P.* remarked, "then God help America, because she will need it. Yet I suspect you have a point. I suspect he really does not. I suspect he may already have tried and been unsuccessful."

"You think more highly of Ted than I do," Walter Dobius said grimly. "I think he's an opportunistic lightweight and a weakling. I think if it came to a showdown with NAWAC, he'd give in."

"That's what you think of the man you told your readers they should elect President," the *Times* said wryly. "My, my."

"We all did that," Walter said sharply, "and you know why we did it: we didn't want the other guy. It's that simple, and that's the way it always is, isn't it? So why be smart about it? This is serious business."

"Gentlemen," the executive director of the *G.P.* said with a pleasant firmness, "at the risk of curtailing fascinating postmortems on how we got where we are, I must remind you that we *are* where we are, and the question now is how we go about extricating ourselves and the country from it. I am prepared, as I say, to go to Washington immediately and talk to him about it."

"If we're going to do that," the *Post* said, "I think the best thing to do would be to get up a deputation that *is* a deputation—get the American Society of Newspaper Editors in on it, get a delegation from Sigma Delta Chi, maybe some of the Pulitzer Prize judges, invite the top men of the networks—make it really impressive. Because if we're correct in the way we assess this thing, it's a most serious threat to all of us. And the time to stop it is now, before it gets any bigger."

"It may be too late already," the *Times* said in a morose tone, and Walter nodded.

"It may be. And again we face the question: could we possibly have such a meeting without embarrassing him? Could we possibly keep it a secret from the press?"

"Could the press keep a secret from the press?" the executive chairman of *The Greatest Publication* inquired with a wry humor. "I imagine we could if we confined it to a few top people. But that would defeat the purpose, too, wouldn't it? We don't want to embarrass him or put him on the spot, yet at the same time the only way we could really be sure of getting action is to do just that: make the appeal public and give it so much publicity that he would have to do something."

"Have you considered the possibility," the *Post* asked, "that he can't?"

"That he may be under physical threat?" Walter responded. "He may be. I know"—and his eyes turned moody at the thought of beloved "Salubria"—"that I am. So are we all, I suppose, directly or indirectly. But if we are to actually contemplate a situation in which the President of the United States hesitates to do what is right for this democracy because someone threatens him—then, gentlemen, we are a long way further down the road than I for one like to think we are."

"We may be," the executive chairman of the *G.P.* remarked with a moodiness of his own. "Which is why I have called you to raise the question: shall we try to stop it now, or shall we be silent and not rock the boat of a man whose policies we all believe in and want to have succeed—whose policies require unshaken public support?" He shook his head, his fine eyes troubled. "We here on this paper are prepared to act—"

"Are you prepared," Walter interrupted bluntly, "to drop this polite cover-up about 'disgruntled employees' and state in a front-page editorial your convictions about who bombed you, and what their threat is to this country? And repeat the appeal you have already made to him, in your editorial this morning—the appeal that brought the bombs? Are you prepared to spell it all out so nobody can mistake the import of it?"

"If one of us does it, we all should," the *Times* said. "We ought to get on the phone and call our newspaper friends all over the country, contact the networks, get them to agree to it too, let go with a coordinated nationwide barrage. . . . Or," he concluded quietly, "we had better face the honest fact of it, which is that a private appeal probably won't work, while a public appeal will greatly embarrass and hamper him in the work we all believe in, the search for peace."

"The only way it could really embarrass him," the *Post* said slowly, "is if the appeal were made to him—and he did nothing about it. And that raises the fundamental question: do we really believe in Ted Jason, and do we really have faith in his ability and willingness to be as tough as he may have to be? Because he, too, has two choices: he can either back down or he can go all out, get the country behind him and give NAWAC real hell. Which do we think he would do?"

"Do we really have faith in Ted Jason?" Walter echoed somberly, and a silence fell and lengthened as they stared thoughtfully at one another and wondered about it. . . .

Finally Walter spoke again.

"Then if we don't," he said crisply, "we had damned well better forget any ideas about appealing to him either publicly or privately, and concentrate instead on protecting his image so he can proceed with full public support to carry out the peace policies we believe in."

"And take our chances," the *Times* said, "that he will presently, when he feels himself strong enough, deal with NAWAC as we hope he will."

"Yes," the *Post* said unhappily. "That appears to be about it."

"And what do we do in the area of our own responsibility, gentlemen?" the executive chairman of *The Greatest Publication* inquired. "Do we stand together and fight, or do we become cautious, careful, water down our criticisms of NAWAC, invite no more retaliations—and hope?"

"Since we seem to be agreed that it would embarrass him if we condemned NAWAC too strongly," Walter pointed out with a bleak candor, "there is evidently only one answer to that."

"I only hope," the executive chairman said, "that NAWAC will understand our reasons and will not be encouraged to further excesses by what may appear to be its success in intimidating the American media. That is what *I* hope."

"I think we all know how good a hope that is," the *Post* said glumly. He sighed. "Perhaps we should have thought a little more carefully before we gave NAWAC so much publicity in its early stages. Perhaps we should have condemned it when it first began, instead of going along half-fascinated and half-admiring. It might not be such a potential Frankenstein's monster for us now."

Walter Dobius made a dry, ironic sound.

"Yes. But we can always use the great apologia of our age: *it seemed like a good idea at the time.*"

"And of course," the *Times* pointed out with a sudden nervous heartiness, "we do have to protect Jason. He's the only President we've got. As you said yourself, Walter, if we aren't going to appeal to him, we'd better forget all this and concentrate on assuring public support for his peace policies. Those, after all, are a hell of a lot more important than us or our problems."

"I thought that might be the final consensus," the executive chairman of *The Greatest Publication* said gently. "But I thought I should find out for sure."

After they had bade one another farewell and faded from the screen, he turned back to his desk and stared long and moodily, with a deeply troubled face, at its shining surface. And in their own handsome offices, the editorial director of the *Times* and the general director of the *Post* did likewise. And at beautiful "Salubria," Walter Dobius stepped outside on the back lawn and stared, long and far away, down the chill November reach of Virginia countryside, before he turned back with a sudden, involuntary shiver and went in to the typewriter that had done so much in its time to help bring his country to its present parlous and uneasy state.

It was at times like this, the busy little figure bustling briskly up the curved drive to the East Portico of the White House told himself with a considerable satisfaction, that he really enjoyed being exactly who he was. He wouldn't, in fact, be anybody else, so interesting did he find his life and so full of surprising and exciting events.

No one would have dreamed three months ago, for instance, that the President-elect of the United States would be calling in Mr. Justice Thomas Buckmaster Davis of the Supreme Court for a private consultation on anything. Three months ago Mr. Justice Davis had ruled against the President-elect when his lawyers, George Harrison Wattersill and Roger P. Croy, had petitioned the Court for an order reconvening the national convention. Mr. Justice Davis had ruled against that petition, and as a result the matter had gone back to the National Committee and Orrin Knox had been nominated. After that, Mr. Justice Davis had heard no more from anyone in the Jason camp.

He realized now, however, that Ted Jason must have finally understood why that ruling had been inevitable on a point of law. He must have finally acknowledged to himself that Mr. Justice Davis had spoken the truth when he had said from the bench that he would have liked to uphold the Jason petition, but could not in honesty do so. He must have realized that Tommy Davis was what Tommy Davis believed himself to be: a man of consistency, a man of honor and a man with a good head on his shoulders, too. Otherwise, why would the President have sent for him on this gray day to consult on a matter of highest import whose nature Mr. Justice Davis could only guess and speculate about as he trotted briskly along?

It was not until he got inside the door and was going through the formalities of giving his name to the police officer on duty that he suddenly perceived, like a bolt from the dull December sky, what the occasion must be. At the other end of the hall, sitting on one of the sofas in the waiting area, he saw a familiar figure who spotted him at the same moment and waved, with a wry and somewhat rueful smile. Beaming with pleasure, Tommy Davis hurried forward, hand outstretched.

"My dear boy!" he exclaimed. "My *dear* boy! Do I dare think what I am thinking? Does your presence here indicate—"

"My presence here indicates that I *am* here, Tommy," Robert A. Leffingwell said, "and as far as I know, that's absolutely all it does indicate."

"But surely," the little Justice said, "surely it indicates more than that. Surely it must mean that he has decided—"

"Sit down and keep your voice down, Tommy," Bob Leffingwell ordered, looking about uneasily; but nobody was around except the cops on the doors and a secretary or two hurrying by on the endless treadmill of White House paper work. "I don't know what he has decided. I haven't spoken to him since the convention. I haven't wanted to and he obviously hasn't wanted me to. So I'm just as much in the dark as you are about this."

"But you will take it if he offers it to you, won't you?" Tommy Davis asked anxiously, dropping his voice to a conspiratorial level. "It would be *such* an encouraging thing to the whole country, *such* a worthy action on the part of both of you. It would be a truly noble act."

"Would it?" Bob Leffingwell asked moodily, his expression turning somber as he stared out at the winter-bare Rose Garden under the leaden sky. "I can't imagine anybody who would be pleased. The Secretaryship of State and I are an old, old story by now, Tommy. Orrin and the Senate didn't want me—and so I lost. Then Orrin as candidate decided he wanted me—but he died. I started out on the 'liberal' side of foreign policy, if you want to call it that—I ended up on the 'conservative.' I've been to the well twice and wandered all over the lot and finally wound up in a bitter personal argument with Ted Jason. And you think he's going to offer me the job on the third go-round? Not very likely, Tommy. Not very, I think."

"I don't know why not!" Justice Davis said stoutly. "There still isn't anyone better equipped than you are, or one who has been more educated—and chastened, I think one can fairly say—by events. You have the support of Orrin's friends, you are still highly thought of by the genuine liberals in the country, and—" he finished with a triumphant little smile—"you are a good man and I like you, and so how could he go wrong if he took you into his Cabinet?"

"Maybe he couldn't go wrong taking me into his Cabinet, Tommy," Bob Leffingwell said wryly, "although that's a matter of considerable argument, it seems to me. But the question arises, and very seriously, in my mind: couldn't I go sadly wrong if I accepted? Even if it were conceivable that he and I could yet come to an agreement on foreign policy, what about the general atmosphere and climate that is apparently going to surround his Administration? I made very clear to him in our last talk what I thought of that. Where do I fit into it now? That's what I'm wondering about."

"When you accept a President," Tommy said thoughtfully, "you accept everything about him. You select the things you particularly believe in and you support him on those; and you close your eyes, gulp hard and swallow the rest in return for what you think he can do in the areas you're interested in. I doubt if anybody is ever completely satisfied with everything about a President. How can you be? They're human."

"You're assuming," Bob Leffingwell said, "that I accept this President. I fought this President to the bitter end, and I don't like what he's doing now. On what grounds, therefore, do I join his happy group?"

"On the grounds of serving your country," Justice Davis said shrewdly, "which is something you still believe in, I think."

"Yes," Bob Leffingwell agreed moodily. "But is this the way to do it? . . . Anyway," he added with a sudden impatience, "this is all nonsense. Strictly speculation. And pointless speculation, at that."

"I can't think of any other reason for both of us to be here at the same time," Tommy Davis said. "He wants you to take it and he wants me to help persuade you. I'll bet you."

And when, five minutes later, a brisk young man from the appointments office came to get them, taking them along the long corridor past the Rose Garden, through the hushed and busy hallways and so to the door of the Oval Office, it began to seem that Tommy must be correct. When the door was opened for them and they were shown in, he could not suppress a triumphantly murmured "You see?" as they walked forward to greet the two men who awaited them. "I told you so!"

"What are you muttering about, Tommy?" the President inquired with a smile as he shook hands. "Always something. Always some gossip or other! Don't you ever stop?"

"He couldn't," Governor Jason said, coming forward to shake hands in his turn. "He'd die." He turned to Bob Leffingwell and for a moment they stared at one another virtually without expression. Then he held out his hand. "Bob—thank you for coming."

"Thank you for inviting me, Governor," Bob Leffingwell said in a level voice, shaking hands briefly and then turning to the President. "Mr. President," he said with a genuine cordiality, "good to see you."

"We are glad you could come," the President said, emphasizing the pronoun in a way that indicated he had decided to give this project his backing. He gestured to chairs across the room. "Now," he said, when they were all seated, "the President-elect has something to say."

"Bob," Ted said without preliminary, "I would like you to be Secretary of State in my Administration."

"Oh, I think that is marvelous!" Justice Davis exclaimed. "Simply *marvelous!* What a stroke of genius, Governor! I'm sure Bob will accept. He will accept at once!"

In spite of the solemnity produced by the fact that Bob Leffingwell looked as though he thought the idea anything but marvelous, the President could not suppress a chuckle.

"Are you sure now, Tommy?" he asked. "Doesn't look to me like much of a foregone conclusion at this moment. Have you consulted Bob about this?"

"I most certainly did," Tommy said stoutly, "while we were waiting. Isn't that what I was brought here for? I told him it would be the chance for a great public service."

"Well?" Ted asked, his eyes unwavering upon Bob's. Presently Bob looked away, his eyes wandering over the portraits of Washington, Jefferson and Lincoln on the cream-colored walls. Then he sighed heavily and looked back.

"Why should I?" he asked quietly. "To bail you out of something? Take the heat off Wattersill? Stop the flak about NAWAC? Lend respectability? Provide a suspect character to serve as lightning rod when you turn the country around 180 degrees in foreign policy? Why, Governor? I don't get it. I thought you and I parted company forever several months ago. Why go into the political graveyard and resurrect this old skeleton? Surely you can do better than that?"

Ted smiled, a small, unamused grimace.

"I'm not asking you to like me," he said with an equal quietness, "so I think we can abandon all the small dramatics about it. I'm asking you to serve with me as Secretary of State because I believe we have a tough job ahead and I believe you're the man to help me do it. Now, if there is some service more vital to the country that you can perform, or something in private business you'd rather do, then of course I shan't try to persuade you further. But if you agree with me that the search for peace is more important than anything else, then you'll come along."

"But why me?" Bob Leffingwell asked.

"Because you have the brains, the ability and the breadth of vision —and also, to be completely honest with you about it—because you're the nearest thing to a political heir that Orrin Knox has, and I want the people behind me that you can bring."

Bob Leffingwell gave him a quizzical glance.

"What more do you need than you got on Election Day?"

"I want them to stay with me," Ted said. "Besides which," he added dryly, "leaving all else aside, I think you're a man of character and a man of integrity who would be good for the country."

"Well," Bob Leffingwell said with his first show of humor, "that's a mixed bag of motives if I ever saw one."

Ted smiled.

"Aren't Presidential motives always mixed?"

The President grunted. "You can say that again. . . . I think you'd better do it, Bob. The Governor here wants to make various changes, and since they're going to be considerably different from what's been going on, he's going to need a man at State that a lot of puzzled and upset people can put their trust in. A lot of them who were Orrin's friends may not trust Ted Jason—but they've got to have somebody. You'll serve a real purpose."

"How worthy a one?" Bob Leffingwell inquired, his eyes again distant and unyielding. "To assist in the abandonment of every principle of foreign policy I have come to believe in—that *you* have come to believe in? This President is coming into office pledged to dismantle our entire foreign policy and turn it all around. That's what he told the country he would do, and knowing that, the country elected him overwhelmingly. I assume they want him to do it and I assume he's going to. How can *you* cooperate with that—let alone me?"

It was the President's turn to look moody, but his answer came without flinching.

"Because of exactly the reason you say—he was elected overwhelmingly; he made no bones about what he intended to do, it was a fair decision in a free election—and that's that. I'm too old a war horse to start balking at the popular will now, Bob. When the voters speak, I listen. That's been my lifelong training and habit, and I'm sticking with it. He's the man in charge, and what he wants goes—within reason, of course." He smiled at Ted with a certain quizzical tenacity, and Ted smiled back in the same spirit. "It's no secret to him that I still have a very lively interest in seeing that whatever changes are made, whatever withdrawals or rearrangements are worked out, should be done with the best interests of the United States in mind. I think he agrees. We've had some talks about it in the last few days, and I'm satisfied he is basically just as concerned as I am with the safety and preservation of this nation. Campaign oratory and campaign supporters sometimes get a little more dramatic and arbitrary than things can afford to be in actual practice. Isn't that right, Governor?"

Ted nodded.

"That's right. I don't suppose I will be believed or get much credit for it, in this room, but in my first talk with Roger Croy after he became the Vice-Presidential nominee, I said that we must get out of Gorotoland, but we must do it in a way that would not jeopardize the strategic interests of the United States or the strategic balance in Africa. And I said that we must try to work out an arrangement in Panama that would respect the wishes of the Panamanian people and at the same time protect our own security and interest in the Canal. So I'm not as rabid about it as some of my supporters—" he smiled—"or maybe even some of my campaign oratory would lead you to believe. I doubt if it will be 180 degrees, Bob. More like 90, I suspect. Or even 75."

"But, Governor!" Justice Davis said in a tone of such open dismay that they all looked at him, startled. "Mr. President-elect! How can you say such a thing? How can you go to the voters, as you did, on a complete anti-war platform, accept their votes, accept your victory which has come to you in a spirit of complete good faith on their part—and then turn right around and indicate that you're going to make a mockery of their good faith and betray their trust? I beg of you, Governor —you must not do it! How can you? *You must not!*"

A silence followed his words and into it Bob Leffingwell uttered one crisp word:

"Exactly."

"Well," Ted Jason said after a moment, and he spoke with a careful slowness, "you must understand, Mr. Justice, that there are ways of doing things which are more—subtle—than the words that describe them, perhaps. There are also many different ways of doing things. Now, it is entirely possible that things could be worked out in such a way that even a change of government in Gorotoland would not, in the long run, be hostile to us—that we could help to bring it about in such a way that whoever took control would do so with a friendly feeling toward us and that we could thus have good friends who were not reactionary or illiberal or dictatorial, and who at the same time would be friendly toward our attempts to maintain the strategic balance in Africa. By the same token, it could well be that we could accept a change of control in Panama, but do it with such friendliness and encouragement of the liberal forces led by my brother-in-law that they likewise would emerge feeling friendly and cooperative toward us in our desire to maintain free passage of the Canal.

"You see, I believe these things can be done. I don't believe everything has to be a head-to-head confrontation. I think we can concede a great deal, and in the very fact of doing so emerge with strengthened friendship and strengthened ties with those who are now our enemies around the globe. That is how I see it."

And once again, though heavily and moodily this time, Bob Leffingwell said:

"Exactly . . . Governor," he said, shifting in his chair. "Ted—do you really believe that? Do you really, honestly think that we can assist Obifumatta's Communist-backed movement to take control in Gorotoland and have him give us *anything* in return? Do you really, honestly think that if we assist Felix in Panama, he will have *anything* but contempt for us as a result? In fact, do you really, honestly think that the Communists would allow either Obi or Felix to stay in power for a year, or even a month perhaps, after their forces take control?" He shook his head in a baffled, uncomprehending way. "Obviously you really do believe that. I wonder on what grounds?"

"I, too, wonder that," the President said somberly, "especially when I have shown you the evidence. I really do wonder."

"*I* don't wonder," Tommy Davis said triumphantly. "*I* think it is a most farseeing, worthy and noble spirit in which to approach world problems. I think it is truly Christian and wonderful. I think it will succeed because it is the good-hearted desire of a good-hearted man. And after all: doesn't he already have the personal pledge of the new leader of the Soviet Union to cooperate in a genuine attempt to achieve world peace? *You* don't have that pledge, Mr. President. *You* don't have it, Bob. *I* don't have it. But the next President of the United States does. Suppose you were he, having received such a pledge. Wouldn't you be optimistic and finally, at last, freed from the fears that have dogged this country and plagued the world for a generation?"

"If you're asking me," the President said tartly, "I'd be damned suspicious and scared to death."

"Well," Ted Jason said quietly, "I am not. In the last analysis, that is what I place my faith in. I was reasonably optimistic before, but when I received his letter in San Francisco that night I decided that it came in good faith and I must accept it in good faith. And suddenly the way grew clear and I stopped worrying so much. Because, after all—how could he put himself on record that way, before the whole world, unless he intended to keep faith with me? The reaction of the world would be too violent if he betrayed me. The damage to him and his country would be too great. He wouldn't dare."

"Ted," the President said in a voice that combined the explosive and the hopeless in a barely controlled mixture, "Governor—Mr. President-elect—*Mr. President*—for *God's* sake look at the world as it exists, will you? Just look at it! Let me take you around the globe in two minutes and show you what your friend is up to, behind his pretty words.

"Take Gorotoland. I showed you the intelligence reports on the build-up that threatens to overwhelm the country again the minute the Communists think they can get away with it. That has not ceased since Vasily Tashikov took over. It has increased.

"Take Panama. I showed you the intelligence reports that prove the conspiracy that is waiting to assassinate Felix Labaiya the minute he has finished his job for them. Those plans have not been scrapped since Tashikov took over. They have been perfected further.

"Take the Middle East. I can show you other intelligence reports that prove the conspiracies that wait to take over Egypt and the Arab world the instant the time seems propitious. Tashikov has ordered them stepped up.

"Take the Far East. I can show you the intelligence reports that document the build-up for a pre-emptive strike against China the minute Moscow thinks it can get away with it. It continues, with Tashikov's cooperation and approval.

"Take India. I can show you the reports on the conspiracy that waits to take over there. Tashikov approves.

"Take South America. There are a dozen reports on a dozen countries there. Tashikov approves.

"Take our own situation vis-à-vis the Soviets. You have already seen the reports on relative military strength and the desperate situation we are in—and will continue to be in, unless you build up our defenses just as fast as you can. And look at the reports I get about domestic subversion, about elements in your own campaign—" he held up his hand at Ted's movement of protest—"yes, elements in your own campaign that you won't believe and won't do anything about. Take the report that is coming soon on the death of President Hudson, the death of Orrin Knox, the death—" Ted flinched but the President drove inexorably on—"if you will forgive me, but this is no time to be gentle, of your own wife. Take the reports on all the deliberate disruptions around the globe all the time, from these little pinpricks in Alaska on the fishing question to the latest riot against an American embassy someplace this morning—I don't know where, yet, but I'm sure there's been one—this constant, incessant drive to stir up every trouble that can possibly be stirred up, inflame every hatred that can possibly be inflamed, destroy every hope of peace that can possibly be destroyed, because war is the climate they thrive in and peace is the last thing they want. They couldn't live with real peace in the world. It would destroy them. . . .

"No, Ted. Your friend is a monster, and for the sake of this country I plead with you—*don't you ever forget it.*"

For several moments after he concluded the characteristic muffled silence of the Oval Office seemed more profound than ever. Outside the afternoon was turning rapidly to twilight under the heavy, leaden sky that means snow. Very faintly there came the sound of voices in the corridors, a sense of the continuing busy life of the White House; but it seemed very far away in this tense and earnest moment. It was Mr. Justice Davis who finally broke the mood.

"Well!" he said indignantly. "*Well*, Mr. President! I may say as one citizen that I think it is just as well you are leaving this office and going back to the Hill, if that is the sort of blind, reactionary, hopeless attitude you take toward things! I have known you many years and you know I say that as a friend, but I am glad, Mr. President. Glad! I can't think of anything worse for our country and the world than a continuation of these old, worn-out, hopeless clichés at a moment in history when we have a chance to open a whole new chapter—when we have a chance at last to work with the Soviet Union toward a genuine and lasting peace. Governor," he said earnestly, turning to Ted with a desperate sincerity, "*I* plead with you, too: ignore these harmful, hindering, hampering thoughts that freeze us in old hostilities and old terrors. Have faith in the future! Have faith in friendship! Have faith in good will! *Have faith in yourself!*"

Again there was a silence while they waited for the President-elect. When he spoke it was quietly, calmly and with a self-confidence that was quite obviously serene and unshakable.

"Thank you, Tommy," he said gravely. "I appreciate your support and your faith in me. I don't intend to betray it, nor do I intend to betray that of any man—including the Chairman of the Council of Ministers. Mr. President, I appreciate your sincerity and your concern, and I acknowledge your patriotism and your devotion to the country's best interests as you see them. Obviously the country does not agree, or it would not have elected me by the margin it did. Therefore I have a mandate to seek new solutions to old problems—to thaw the ice—to break the logjam—to use whatever clichés one wants to use to indicate a new and good-faith approach to the achievement of world peace. Chairman Tashikov, new to his office as I am to mine, has given me that opportunity. I intend to take it. I believe I can succeed. I hope you will presently come to believe that I can, when you return to the Hill. By the same token, I hope all Americans of good will will help me—beginning," he concluded quietly, "with the man I have asked to be my Secretary of State."

"Bob," the President said into the hush that followed, "I think you'd better."

Bob Leffingwell nodded, his expression troubled and unfathomable. "Yes," he said quietly. "I think I had."

Ten minutes later, Ted having left to return to Patsy's for the night, the President having bade them farewell to retire to the family quarters on the second floor and get ready for the state dinner he was giving for the President of Nicaragua, the Secretary of State-designate and the little Justice were walking together down the curving drive to the East Gate and the taxis that would take them home. At his side Tommy was bubbling, as Bob had known he would be.

"My dear boy!" he said happily. "My dear boy, what a magnificent step forward! How much he needs you and how splendidly you have responded! And what a great man he is! I truly believe," he said, suddenly solemn, "that his Administration is going to do more for world peace than any in a hundred years. I really do, Bob. I honestly, really do."

"I hope you're right, Tommy," Bob Leffingwell said. "We'll all have to pray that you are."

"I shall pray," Mr. Justice Davis promised as the guards wished them a pleasant "Good night!" and they passed through the gate.

"I, too," Bob Leffingwell told him. "Constantly."

It was beginning to snow, in the persistent way that indicates that Washington is in for it. Instinctively, as they reached Pennsylvania Avenue, they turned west and walked along the fence until they could see the White House sitting amid its floodlights, full and clear. It looked white and ghostly in the steadily increasing swirls of snow, secret and mysterious with power: an omen and a talisman, though of what, at that moment, neither they, nor in all probability anyone could have said with any surety.

JASON FILLS AGRICULTURE AND TRANSPORTATION POSTS TO COMPLETE CABINET ON EVE OF INAUGURATION. LEFFINGWELL, WATTERSILL HEAD WHAT NEW EXECUTIVE CALLS "GATHERING OF EXCELLENCE." BATTLEFIELD LULL FALLS ON GOROTOLAND, PANAMA AS WORLD AWAITS LEADER PLEDGED TO END ALL WAR. NATIONAL MOOD

SOBER, HOPEFUL AS AMERICANS FORESEE DRASTIC CHANGES IN FOREIGN POLICY. JASON AIDES HINT "DRAMATIC, REVOLUTIONARY" PEACE MOVE IN INAUGURAL.

"I have called you together," the President said with a little twinkle, "for this final, private dinner in the White House before we must all pick up our worldly goods and flee from the advancing forces of change and dissolution. As leader of the government-in-exile I thought it might be fun, before we all go underground, to meet for the last time in these hallowed halls and plot our future course. Before we do, though—" and the light mood died, he looked suddenly somber and completely serious—"I think we should drink one toast, in which I know you all will join me." He raised his glass and down the table they raised theirs, abruptly as serious and concerned as he. "To the next President of the United States. May God give him the strength he will need to lead us safely in the paths he proposes."

"Hear, hear!" said Beth Knox, widow of Orrin, and Lucille Hudson, widow of President Harley. "Hear, hear!" said Senator Lafe Smith and Mabel Anderson, widow of Senator Brigham. "Hear, hear!" said Cullee Hamilton, Senator-elect from California, and his bride-to-be, Sarah Johnson. "Hear, hear!" said the President's sister and brother-in-law who had lived with him in the White House during the six hectic months of his tenure. "Hear, hear!" said Senator Elizabeth Ames Adams of Kansas. "Hear, hear!" said Senate Majority Leader Bob Munson and Dolly, who had come with Senator Stanley Danta of Connecticut, the Majority Whip. "Hear, hear!" said Stanley and Stanley's daughter, Crystal Danta Knox. And "Hear, hear!" albeit with a note of annoyance that amused them all and lightened the mood again, said Representative-elect Harold H. Knox of Illinois.

"I suspect I should tell you also, quite confidentially," the President said, "that the incoming Secretary of State sends his warm regards and affection to all. I invited him to come and he wanted to, but we agreed that it might not be too diplomatic, under the circumstances. He said he was going to need all the diplomacy he could muster, and had best start now."

"I still don't see why he took it," Hal said moodily. "I still don't see why—"

"Because," the President said crisply, "as of approximately twelve noon tomorrow, Edward Montoya Jason of California is the only President we have, and Bob Leffingwell feels, I believe, that he has got to help him in every way he can if Ted is not to be crushed by the pressures of the events he is going to set in motion—starting, probably, at approximately 12:05 P.M. tomorrow. I might add," he said with a certain affectionate severity, "that I think we had all better do the same. And that includes rambunctious new Congressmen from the state of Illinois."

"I've tried to tell him," Beth said, ruefully amused, "but he finds it difficult to listen."

"His father would have, I think," said Lucille Hudson softly, looking, as always, plump, lacy-pink and grandmotherly.

"Would he?" Hal asked, still moodily. "I wonder."

"Oh, I think so," Senator Munson said. "He fought many a fine fight, did Orrin, but when it came right down to the basic needs of the country, he stopped fighting and pitched in."

"And you think Ted Jason is going to serve the basic needs of the country?" Hal inquired with a sudden asperity so reminiscent of his father that several of his elders exchanged amused glances. "I don't."

"Of course he is," Elizabeth Ames Adams said with an answering asperity that made Hal blink for a second. "Not according to your lights or mine, maybe, but according to his. Which he's been handed the right to do, remember. Maybe you'd better repeat that fact to yourself several times a day. It might help you get along more comfortably on the Hill."

"Now, Aunt Bessie," Hal said with a sudden charming grin that he had learned years ago could mollify the Senator from Kansas and most others of his father's close Senatorial friends, "don't lecture me. I'll do my best to support him . . . I guess. But it won't be easy."

"I didn't say it would be for me, either," Bessie Adams said, responding with a smile. "So don't think you're alone, young scamp. But I'm going to try. I'm going to go just as far as I can, give him the benefit of every doubt right up to the limit, probably swallow my oath to uphold the Constitution until it chokes me—and hope we can keep him from taking us too far down roads I don't believe in and worry about."

"Good for you, Bess," Bob Munson said. "One vote I can count on to support the Administration, anyway."

"And how about you, Uncle Bob?" Hal inquired. "Are you going to be right in there every minute, rounding up those votes and cracking that whip, being the very model of a model Majority Leader, no matter what the guy does? I suppose he's that lucky."

"No," Bob Munson said slowly, "I wouldn't put it exactly like that. . . . I'll help him to the limit, just like Bessie: surely. That's my job, not only as Majority Leader but as United States Senator. After we reach the limit—" he looked suddenly grim—"other considerations will apply."

"And who sets the limit?" Lafe Smith inquired from down the table, almost as moody as Hal. "You—me—the next guy? Where do we draw the line, Bob? I'd like to know."

"Conscience," Cullee Hamilton suggested dryly, "must decide the issue. . . . But whose conscience?" He too looked moody. "His or mine?"

"A collective conscience, maybe," the President said. "We'll know, on the Hill. Instinct will tell us when to stop."

"Do you and Bob really think you can hold this new Congress in line?" Cullee asked. "More than half of this Congress rode in on Ted's coattails. It's going to be his Congress. It may not be yours at all, this time."

"We know that's a possibility," the President conceded with a troubled frown in which Bob Munson joined. "We know we may have to fight for it."

"You may not be re-elected Speaker and Bob may not be re-elected Senate Majority Leader," Cullee persisted, "even if the boys have been temporarily decent enough to delay organizing the two houses until you can get back to the Hill. . . . Then what?"

"I'm not ready to concede that, yet," the President said shortly. "I'll know more about that day after tomorrow. I'm damned if I can see myself getting beaten by Jawbone Swarthman."

"Or me by Arly Richardson," Bob Munson said.

"We can't see it either," Lafe Smith agreed, "but sometimes these things happen. If Ted throws his support to Arly and Jawbone—"

"If Ted is smart," Senator Munson said bluntly, "he'll damned well keep his hands off both houses of Congress when we organize."

"Do you think he has, in the past few days?" Beth asked. "There seem to be rumors—"

"If he's smart," Bob Munson repeated, "he'll keep his hands off. If he isn't—well—" he looked grim—"then Bill's right, there *will* be a hell of a fight. I don't *think* he wants to add that to all the other problems he's going to have to handle right off the bat—but maybe he does. We'll just have to see. If so, I'm ready for him on my side, and I think Bill is on his."

"If either of you has the say," Stanley Danta reminded quietly. "What's going to be in the inaugural address? Does anybody know yet?"

"An end to all wars," Lucille Hudson said with a gentle irony. "For which I am sure we must all be very grateful."

"I would be if I thought it were anything more than a grandstand stunt," Cullee remarked.

"I too," Lafe agreed. "But I don't see how—"

"He's been very secretive with me," the President said, "but I get the impression that it won't be too great a wrench from past policies. We're both still pledged to 'gradual restructuring,' remember. I haven't seen any indications of a change in that."

"But you don't really know, do you?" Hal pressed.

"No," the President admitted. "I don't really know. But I repeat, I haven't seen any indications."

"He never did repudiate NAWAC, did he?" Lafe Smith asked. "And he forced you to halt aid to Gorotoland. And relax the blockade on Panama."

"He did no such thing," the President said sharply. "I've made that quite clear to everybody. I did agree with him a couple of weeks ago, in the statement you all read, that as my contribution to 'restructuring,' I would not *increase* aid to Gorotoland during the interim period. And I agreed privately with him that I would not make any more statements of any kind about the blockade. But I certainly haven't *diminished* aid to Gorotoland, and I certainly haven't relaxed the blockade."

"But you have permitted him to establish the impression," Stanley Danta pointed out, not unkindly, "that there has been a slackening, a falling-off, a change. You have allowed him to appear to have slowed down the momentum to a point where he now has all sorts of options and can move in almost any direction. Isn't that the fact of it?"

"Look," the President said, with a certain frustrated annoyance, "let's all remember one thing, shall we? The man *is* about to become President. I haven't been able to ignore that fact, much as I would have liked to. He has had *some* right to say what should be done. I have had to take *some* account of his views, after all."

"You could have told him to go to hell and kept right on with what you were doing until the moment you left this house," Hal Knox said bluntly. "Others have."

"Yes, so they have," the President said with a show of real anger, "and a hell of a mess it's made for their successors and for the country. I sometimes think you young hotheads on our side of it are just as ruthless, intolerant and impractical as the hotheads on the other side of it. . . . I have tried to cooperate as much as I could, consistent with my own convictions," he went on more calmly. "That has been my concept of it and that has been my training and tradition, and that is how I have done it. I know some people haven't liked it. I know I haven't liked it myself, sometimes. But I am still enough of a Christian and a gentleman, I hope, so that I will do unto others as I would like them to do unto me, were the situation reversed. I'm not ashamed of it."

"But you don't have any real promise from him, do you," Cullee Hamilton said, also in a not unkindly fashion, "that he won't kick the whole thing over the moon tomorrow, if he wants to."

The President shook his head.

"No," he said quietly, "I don't have any promise. All I have is the faith that he will take his oath of office seriously and won't make too many violent changes."

"Just faith in Ted Jason," Lafe Smith said in a musing tone and the President gave him a steady look.

"That's right," he said crisply.

"Good luck," Hal Knox remarked grimly, and his mother leaned forward.

"Listen!" she protested. "Try to be objective about it, will you? The President has done the best he can to work with Ted. He has had to work with him. I think he has done a fine job of it, in a very difficult situation. What Ted does with it now is his problem, and whatever comes of it is on his hands and on his conscience. I applaud what the President has done. And," she concluded quietly, "I think your father would have approved, as well."

"Well—" Hal began, but his wife forestalled him.

"I couldn't agree with you more," Crystal said quietly. "I think you have done a fine job, Mr. President. And I'm not afraid of Ted Jason. I don't think he's all that bad."

"After all his people did to you and our baby," Hal began in bitter disbelief. But again she spoke with a quiet firmness.

"He didn't do it and I will never think he wanted it. I'm not so sure he's entirely wrong. I would like a world of peace for our children to grow up in, too, you know. I'm willing to give him the chance to try for it. The overwhelming majority of our fellow citizens think he can. Who am I to stand in his way and cast suspicions on his plans before we even know them?"

"I agree," Mabel Anderson said abruptly, and Sarah Johnson said firmly, "So do I." Mabel pushed back a lock of hair with a hand that trembled with nervousness. But her voice was equally firm.

"The thing I hate about politics is that it always sets people so *against* each other. I saw what it did to—" her voice trembled for a second, then strengthened—"to my husband, and after Brig died I said I would never have anything to do with it again. Lately I've changed my mind, because I've decided it's the way we do things in this country, and if I wanted to have any influence at all I'd better get back in and play my part. But I still hate the suspicion and the backbiting and the tearing-down of men before they even have a chance to show what they can do. I agree with Crystal. I don't like Ted Jason in lots of ways but we've got to have peace and he thinks he knows how to get it. So let's give him a chance. It seems to me that's only fair."

"I say so too," Sarah Johnson said as Mabel sat back looking flushed but doggedly determined while Lafe smiled at her encouragingly and took her hand. "I say give him a chance. I don't know him like you-all do, not having worked with him in politics so long as you have, but to me he seems to be well-meaning and sincere. Certainly lots of other folks think so, his vote shows that. I say maybe he *can* get peace. I believe he really intends to try. Let's let him. Isn't that the fair way to go about it?"

"Of course it is," Dolly Munson said firmly. "Of course it is."

There was a silence, increasingly amused on the part of their gentlemen companions.

"It appears to me," Cullee Hamilton said presently, "that Ted has the ladies' vote and we'd better shut up."

"He didn't have mine," Dolly said, "but that isn't the point. The point is, just as the President said a while ago, that Ted is about to become the only President we have. So let's wait and see and wish him all the luck in the world. After all, we drank to that. Let's do it."

"It does appear," the President said with a chuckle, "that us old cynics are outnumbered, so perhaps we had best surrender, gentlemen. And maybe we should repeat that toast, before we end this farewell banquet of the Lost Cause." His face became grave, his voice filled with a sudden deep emotion, his aspect turned solemn. He raised his glass and they raised theirs. "To the next President of the United States. May God give him the strength he will need to lead us safely in the paths he proposes. . . ."

A few minutes later they stood together chatting and laughing under the North Portico waiting for their cars to drive up and take them back to their respective homes. A heavy snowfall had started while they were dining, blown in on a new storm from the west.

"Will you be on the platform tomorrow?" the President asked Beth Knox. She nodded.

"He wants the Knoxes and Lucille to be there."

"I shall be," Lucille Hudson said quietly. "I don't like him, but it seems the thing I should do. If he feels it will strengthen him in his task, then I feel I must help him."

"The Knoxes feel the same way," Beth said, turning to her son and daughter-in-law. "Isn't that right?" she demanded firmly.

"Well—" Hal began, but Crystal took his arm and gave it a shake.

"We'll be there," she promised. "Including Storm Cloud, Jr. Right, Storm Cloud, Jr.?"

"You women!" Hal exclaimed, but smiling a little. "Yes, damn it, we'll be there. And he'd better be good, damn his guts."

"He will be," the President said. "I think we can count on Ted for a real spectacular—whatever it may be."

Cars came, friends departed. Bob and Dolly Munson were the last to leave.

"You'd better get back in or you'll catch your death of cold," Dolly urged the President as their car drew up. "We'll see you at noon tomorrow."

"We will indeed," Senator Munson said. He turned back after Dolly got in the car.

"You really don't have a guarantee of any kind from him, do you?" he asked quietly. The President replied with an equal quietness.

"Not a damned thing." He sighed. "Frankly, Bob, I'm scared to death."

The Senate Majority Leader nodded.

"Yes," he said grimly. "So am I."

And so, in a sense, though they would never believe it and he would never admit it, was he. Not in a panic sense or a paralyzed sense or even in a hesitant sense, but rather in some deep underlying way that came, he supposed, from the fact that his limitations, measured against the job he was about to undertake, seemed suddenly substantial. It was the first time in his life that Ted Jason had ever felt any doubt about his ability to do anything; and since he was about to embark upon the biggest challenge of them all, it was perhaps a healthy thing, for him and for his country.

Lying awake in the guest suite at Patsy's, as the clock crept slowly past midnight and on toward 1 A.M., he reflected that at this time tomorrow night he would be sleeping in the Lincoln bed. This would symbolize a great change, he thought wryly, but to the White House staff it would probably just mean a new set of clean sheets. Maybe that was all it would mean to history, too—here he comes, there he goes, change the sheets and away with him—but he did not really think so. He thought, and it was a solemn and profoundly sobering thought, that this time it would mean a little more than that. This time it would mean one of the sharpest breaks ever between one Administration and the next.

No one, not even George Wattersill, Roger P. Croy and the others who had submitted their suggestions and drafts for the inaugural address, knew what he would do twelve hours from now when, oath taking completed, America and the world quieted down to hear the words of the new President. He had written the heart of his speech himself and had shown it to no one. He had, in fact, kept it on his person, in the breast pocket of his suit, ever since the moment two nights ago when he had completed it in the privacy of this same room.

In spite of his conviction that what he intended to do was right, and his continuing awareness that the overwhelming majority of his countrymen presumably wanted him to do it, he could not escape a feeling of mixed elation and uncertainty. *Was* it the right thing? Did his countrymen, operating on that faith in Presidents which is all they have to go on when they vote, really want him to act in the specific fashion he intended? Would the events flowing from it confirm his own convictions and permit him to enter history as a strong and worthy leader—or would they shatter all his hopes, make of his intentions a shambles and write large across his record the single word *DISASTER?*

He was not, he knew, the first man in the White House to undergo such doubts and agonies on the eve of great decisions, and presumably he would not be the last. The knowledge was reasonably comforting but not enough to answer the fundamental question. Each in his time, apparently, had to meet his responsibility in his own way and on his own terms. There was no easy answer for Presidents. Yet reviewing his course in the last two months, he was not unhappy with it. He felt that most things he had done led logically to what he was about to do.

Toward the President he felt that he had conducted himself with considerable skill, not provoking him to an open break, yet at the same time firmly keeping his own options open. There had been a brief period, after he himself had taken the initiative in arranging a break during the campaign, when he had thought he might have alienated the President permanently. But he might have known that he could count on the old man's devotion to party and concern for country: lifelong political instinct told him he must come back to Ted's support in the end. After the one sharp speech in Colorado, he had done so. No one could have been more decent or more cooperative than he had been as soon as the election was over. The "informal co-President" arrangement had worked very well. Their relationship had eased many transition situations and their differences on foreign policy, even though sharp, had not resulted in any further public friction. Again the President's instinct had come to Ted's assistance. The rapidly gathering mystique of Ted's swiftly approaching accession to power had guaranteed an outward show of harmony. And he in turn had agreed to accept the President's term "gradual restructuring," aware that the words and their application provided a necessary face-saving, not only for the President, but for all the millions who still, despite his massive electoral triumph, were wary of Ted Jason.

The important thing was that Ted had kept open his options and his freedom to act when the time came. Quite deftly, he thought, he had kept the President and the conservatives reasonably mollified during the transition period. With equal deftness, he thought, he had satisfied his own followers, not giving them as much as they wanted as fast as they wanted it, but daily reiterating and strengthening the vigorous promise of action to come, along the lines they believed were best.

The problem of NAWAC to some degree remained, but it was his firm belief, as he had told the President, that it was a diminishing problem that would vanish permanently with his inauguration. He was not aware of much recent activity from the organization, and after Fred Van Ackerman's statement on the Riot Control Act, nothing much had been heard from the Senator. He had come in several times to see the President-elect about jobs for constituents in Wyoming, but each time he had been businesslike and as pleasant as Fred Van Ackerman could manage. He had not referred to the legislation again, nor had he discussed anything in the area of foreign policy. Ted could only conclude that the statement had been just a form of bluster—the sort of thing that Fred might like doing just to make some people uneasy, but no real threat to anyone or anything.

Nor had LeGage Shelby or Rufus Kleinfert, or DEFY or KEEP, lifted their heads above water in these recent weeks. As far as Ted knew or had been told, all was quiet.

In the media, too, a pleasantly flattering calm prevailed.

The *Times,* the *Post, The Greatest Publication,* Walter Dobius, Percy Mercy, Frankly Unctuous, NBC, CBS, ABC—a happy expectancy filled their pages and dominated their commentaries. Finally they had their ideal President, the man who would pull their country away from the world and turn it once more inward in the great new isolation they had all, for one reason and another, desired with such hysterical persistence for so many years. Their news stories, their editorials, their "news specials" and "roundups" and solemn "analyses" glowed with an eager anticipation. They, too, seemed to have abandoned an earlier uneasiness about NAWAC.

The same mood echoed through the world, where journal after

journal, statesman after statesman faced toward Washington with high hopes and confident expectations. The things they expected varied as widely as their own self-interests, but of one thing they were certain: Edward M. Jason meant peace, or at least the absence of war. For most, this was the extent of, and the answer to, their concern.

From his countrymen, too, he had daily received letters running into the many thousands—over 3,673,000 pieces of mail since Election Day, so the overburdened White House mail room told him. The tenor of nearly all was the same:

"Dear Mr. President-elect: We place in you our hopes for a world re-born and free from the monster of war. . . . To our dear President Jason: As the parents of two teen-age sons, we look to you to end the awful threat which hangs over them and their generation. . . . Dere Mr. Jasson: God bless you and kepe you to lede us forever in the ways of Christan peece. . . . Dear Mr. President: It is hard to escape the conviction that you have been Divinely chosen to lead the world's un-happy peoples into a genuine, war-free Promised Land. . . ."

And from some few, of course, perhaps 300,000, so he was told, out of the 3,673,000, a more worried note:

"Dear Mr. President: As concerned citizens who have always be-lieved that America should play her rightful and responsible part in the world, we wish to suggest most earnestly . . . Dear Mr. President-Elect: You say you want peace and an end to war. We believe you. We do not believe, however, that peace should be achieved at the expense of . . . Dear Governor Jason: We most earnestly request that you weigh with the greatest care all the implications of the policies you propose. We think that peace at any price is too great a . . . Dear President-Elect: We pray with all our hearts that you will always keep firmly before you the knowledge that the very life of the United States itself may be at stake in . . ."

To all he had arranged to have the staff send the same reply:

"Dear——I am deeply grateful for the patriotic concern which has prompted you to let me know your thinking on the task that lies ahead for all of us. You may be sure that your views will be of great assistance to me as I enter upon my new duties. With your support, and the help of Almighty God, I shall strive to do all things for the honor and well-being of our beloved country."

Hope, doubt, faith, fear, worry, concern—but the strongest of these which came to him from his countrymen was hope. Second only to it was faith—a deep, blind, absolute faith in him as a leader and as a human being, which could not help but move him profoundly many times every day as he went about the fascinating, if sometimes tedious, business of putting together a new Administration. To some extent he took this as his due, but often enough to start the growth of a decent humility he realized that it was a rare and voluntary tribute by his fellow men and women. He was determined not to betray it. And he was confident, as he had told the President, Justice Davis and Robert A. Leffingwell, that with the help of his counterpart in Moscow, he would not.

He had reviewed Tashikov's letter many times in his mind, had gone through his periods of doubt about it, emerged on the other side serene in the conviction that it was a genuine and irreversible signal to him that the Communists, too, desired a real and lasting peace. At first, inwardly as wary and skeptical as the President, though he would not admit it to him and could not admit it to his supporters, he had tried privately to get a reaffirmation from the new Soviet Ambassador in Washington. That gentleman (whose military rank of general had caused a little mild, quickly dropped speculation in the press) had received him in the gloomy electric-fenced embassy with a bland and impassive countenance and a firm refusal to transmit his request to Moscow. "Mr. President-elect," he had said calmly through an interpreter, "the Chairman has made his views completely clear in his letter. What could be clearer? To seek further clarification or repetition could only be considered, I am afraid, an expression of disbelief in the Chairman's word. Is that the desire of the new American President? If so, it would seem to my government, I am afraid, a most drastic betrayal of the sincere peace-loving hopes of Chairman Tashikov and the entire Soviet people."

"No, indeed," he had replied hastily, while the general and the interpreter stared at him with bland, opaquely interested eyes, "that is not my intention at all. Such a thing is farthest from my thoughts. Please convey to the Chairman my apologies if any such interpretation can be placed on my request. Tell him I withdraw it and that I shall proceed firmly and with great hopes in the spirit of San Francisco."

"To the spirit of San Francisco," the general said with grave approval, and, "To the spirit of San Francisco," he was given time to reply before the interpreter rose and politely showed him out.

So he could not betray Tashikov either, nor had he, of course, any such intention. Reviewing the conversation later, he found that he was almost ashamed of himself for ever having entertained for a moment any doubts of the Chairman's good faith. After all, Tashikov had done exactly what his new envoy said: he had made his views completely clear before all the world, and it was, in truth, an unfriendly and unfair thing to doubt them for a second. It might be the fact, as the President had asserted, that certain aggressive Soviet designs appeared to be going forward; but that, after all, was perfectly understandable. Tashikov was new at the job. He faced an entrenched bureaucracy and a military that had been moving together in an aggressive direction for several decades. He could not justly be expected to reverse things overnight. No doubt he was as determined as Edward M. Jason to change the course of events as soon as he was sufficiently strong in his new position to do so.

Again Ted felt ashamed of himself for questioning for even a moment so honorable and peace-loving a man. He determined then and there that in dealing with the Soviet Union, he would, if necessary, bend over backward to assist and encourage the leader whose task was as difficult, and whose motivations were as idealistic, as his own.

Now as he lay in Patsy's guest suite and felt himself at last beginning to grow drowsy despite the great excitements of the coming day, the uneasy underlying fears vanished altogether. He was satisfied with the things he had done in preparation for his Administration. He was satisfied that peace was no longer a mirage, but something that he and Tashikov together could achieve. As his part of the bargain he felt to exist implicitly between them, he was determined to take the steps he would reveal to the world in his inaugural address, now only eleven hours away.

There would be in it, he knew, some surprises for many of his countrymen: but they were surprises just and right and long overdue. He was confident they would be accepted by his fellow citizens and the world as the great and constructive forward steps to peace that he sincerely believed them to be.

As he drifted quietly off to sleep, he was inadvertently, if honestly, overlooking something he could not have known before but now was about to learn: that Presidents are sometimes full of surprises; and that sometimes there are surprises for Presidents.

And so Inauguration Day arrived, sharp and bright and sparkling. The storm, ending just before dawn, had left the great white city covered with more than a foot of snow. Hasty crews had worked desperately all night to keep Pennsylvania Avenue open for the triumphal passage of the new President to the Hill, his return to the White House and the parade that would follow. For the sake of the parade their endeavors were necessary, but for the general public they need not have bothered. Not since Franklin Roosevelt's first inaugural in March of 1933 had there been such a fervent outpouring as now was making its way to the Hill. No amount of snow, clogged roads, skidding cars, minor accidents, traffic jams was going to stop it. If streets were blocked, cars were locked and left and their occupants proceeded on foot. By 10 A.M. all the main arteries from Maryland were closed, all the bridges from Virginia were solid with abandoned cars. Vehicular traffic had come to a halt save for the police, Army, Secret Service and other official cars that skimmed nervously up and down Pennsylvania Avenue between White House and Capitol prior to the ceremony. Sometimes silent but more often singing, the believers in Edward Jason trudged toward the Capitol, happy and hopeful and greatly excited, in the cold clear sun.

From those whose business it was to engage in the tricky and inaccurate game of public guessing, there came the customary dutiful estimations. One million were in the city as noon approached, said Associated Press. One million five hundred thousand, said UPI, not to be outdone. Probably close to a million and a half, agreed CBS and ABC. At least a million anyway, said NBC, sounding slightly miffed. Probably five hundred thousand along the mile from White House to Hill, said UPI and AP, agreeing. Pushing five hundred thousand, conceded NBC and CBS. Well over, said ABC. In front of the Capitol, filling the temporary wooden stands, spilling out across the park, solid to the very steps of the Supreme Court a block away, at least another five hundred thousand, said everybody. And still they came, plowing through the trampled drifts, pushing in behind those already in place along the Avenue, breaking through police lines again and again—but happy. Always happy. Here and there a few wore the mailed-fist-superimposed-on-dove emblem of NAWAC, but even these were smiling and excited, if wary, on this wonderful day. Even they for once seemed happy. Nothing but good was expected by this crowd, and nothing but good, it seemed to those trained observers who watched it with microphone or pencil along the line of march and before the East Front of the Capitol, could be expected from it.

At the Mansion the great glass doors were swung open promptly at eleven-thirty, and out onto the North Portico stepped the outgoing and incoming Presidents of the United States, the one big, solid, plain, outwardly serene, smiling pleasantly into the cameras, the other slightly shorter, trimmer, handsome, distinguished, giving a sudden wave and eager grin that brought a responsive roar from the crowd that stood across the Avenue in Lafayette Park and from all those, and there were many, who carried small portable television sets in the crowds along the route. A vast shout of pleasure and anticipation echoed from White House to Hill; and for the next ten minutes, while the cavalcade rolled slowly out the gate, turned right on Pennsylvania, made the jog down past Treasury and then turned left and proceeded to the Hill, the roar never stopped, but only grew in its wild, ecstatic, animal intensity.

Because there was really, at this moment, nothing left to say, neither of them said anything until just as their cavalcade reached the foot of the Hill and started the gentle climb up. Then the President who had fifteen minutes of office left turned to the President who had—how long? An hour? A year? Four years? Eight?—still ahead, and said with a little smile, "They seem to like you. Don't let them down."

"I don't intend to," Ted Jason said with a sober yet happy expression. "You have my word on that."

"May God give you strength to keep it," the President said.

"I think He will," the President-elect replied, suddenly completely serious. "I really do think He will."

Then they were swept up again in the constant roaring, and both turned again to smile and wave as the procession proceeded on up the Hill to the East Front, where they entered the doorway under the arch on the Senate side and proceeded between double rows of police to the great Rotunda. There they spent the remaining few minutes until noon exchanging greetings with leaders of Senate and House, smiling and waving to Cabinet members, members of the Supreme Court and distinguished guests as they made their way through the doors and down to their seats on the steps.

It was noted, by all the eyes whose job it is to note such things and relay them via voice and tube and newsprint to the dazzled world, that the sister and brother-in-law of the outgoing President, those two simple folk who knew with a perfectly genuine relief that in one more day they would be shut of official life forever and back in retirement at their home on Lake Tahoe, were already neatly in place at the right of the platform. It was also noted that members of the family of the President-elect were in place at the left, Patsy and Valuela glittering with Jason family jewels, Selena touslod and determinedly unadorned in a simple thirty-thousand-dollar mink coat, Herbert if anything more rumpled than usual in his elfish disarray.

Comments were also dutifully made upon members of the Congress as they straggled in and took their places on the stands right and left; upon the members of the outgoing Cabinet and the members of the incoming Cabinet; upon the Supreme Court and particularly Mr. Justice Thomas Buckmaster Davis, burbling and bouncing and waving excitedly to friends all over the place; upon the Vice President-elect, entering on a wave of friendly applause with Mrs. Croy; upon the President-elect's recent opponent, Senator Warren Strickland of Idaho, dignified and friendly; upon the members of the Joint Chiefs of Staff, gleaming like four scarabs in all their braid and finery; upon the distinguished relics of past administrations, particularly the eternal Presidential daughter, great hat swooping, famed tongue still acrid, now within hailing distance of her first, but surely not last, centenary; and on all the other less recognizable souls, some there by virtue of long-standing friendship, some there by virtue of campaign contribution, and some just mysteriously *there*, who always fill in the nooks and crannies of the East Front at all inaugurations.

At approximately 11:50 A.M., the four empty seats next to the seat reserved for the President-elect were filled, and after a moment's hesitation when the news was relayed to them, another great shout of applause and approval went up from the crowds all along the way. Beth Knox, wearing a pale blue dress, a small blue hat and a white coat with a single purple orchid, came slowly down the steps on the arm of her son, who wore a dark suit and dark blue tie. Behind them came her daughter-in-law, also dressed simply in a peach-colored dress, peach-colored coat and peach-colored hat; and Lucille Hudson, in pale pink dress, pink hat and plain pink coat with a single white orchid.

As they took their seats the shout gradually diminished and for several moments an avidly attentive silence fell. To the cameras, which zoomed in upon them with merciless but understandable attention, it was clear that all were under considerable strain. Beth and Crystal managed small smiles and quick little waves to those immediately around them and to the reporters standing on their benches in the press area just below the platform. Lucille Hudson bowed gravely to both sides and to the front, but did not smile. Hal's face was somber and remained so, a fact which prompted comment, not charitable, from both NBC and CBS. But when they were all seated, the significance of their presence, its generous and implicit acknowledgment of Edward Jason, suddenly struck the multitudes again, and again there came a deep, relieved, approving roar.

It was then 11:55, and abruptly the clamor fell away and a hushed, expectant silence gripped the city, filled with many things, not least of them the memory of what had happened the last time these people had been gathered together in one place, in August, at the Monument Grounds.

The memory was in Ted Jason's face, too, and in that of his predecessor, as they came through the great bronze doors and started down the steps to the podium; and for just a second, as the cameras faithfully found these most important figures of the day, the silence held. Then it broke in a steady, rolling thunder of welcoming shouts, screams, applause, ecstasy that overwhelmed and consumed the world.

It continued as they moved slowly down the steps, their first somber expressions quickly dissolving in the necessity to nod, smile, beam, wave to, or shake hands with, those they passed along the way. By the time they reached the level of the podium and separated, the President to take his seat alongside his sister, the President-elect to take his next to Beth Knox, the roar was still rolling but beginning to die away. Presently it was gone and again the quivering hush settled over all.

It lifted for brief applause when Roger P. Croy was sworn in as Vice President. Swiftly and respectfully he resumed his seat and turned to look, as did they all, with a profound and almost hungry expectancy at his running mate.

For one further moment the world hung suspended in a watchful, waiting silence. Then the Chief Justice rose and moved solemnly to the podium from one side, Edward Montoya Jason rose and moved solemnly to the podium from the other. The Chief Justice opened the ancient Spanish Bible that had come to California more than a hundred years ago with Don Carlos Alvarado Montoya. The President-elect placed his left hand upon it, raised his right; and so became, in the brief, traditional, moving catechism, the President.

As he concluded with the pledge to preserve, protect and defend the Constitution of the United States, repeating it gravely after the Chief Justice, the great roar rose again—swelled—thundered—died presently away. Again the quivering silence fell. Into it the President began quietly to speak.

"My countrymen," he said, his voice booming out across the plaza, the city, the nation, the world, "we are met on a day of import for America and her friends. On this day, America leaves the ancient battlegrounds of futile war and turns, we hope for all time, to the hopeful and productive uplands of fertile peace."

("Nice work if you can get it," murmured the Chicago *Tribune* to *Women's Wear Daily*, and, "I sense the flowery rhetoric of the Vice President," *W.W.D.* murmured back. But from the eager multitudes there came a deep, believing shout.)

"I do not say to you," the President continued solemnly, "that this will be an easy or a quickly accomplished task. But I do say to you that *it must be done.*"

Again the approving shout.

"I pledge to you all the resources of my being, and all the resources of the government of the United States, to get it done. Not two years from now—not one year from now—not one month or one day or one hour from now—but *now.*"

("Yes?" Senator Munson murmured dryly behind his hand to Senator Danta, and Stanley Danta, possibly too hasty in his amusement, replied, "Watch my miracle, kids!")

"My countrymen," the President said as the third great shout subsided, "one thing I would make clear to you, and to all our friends and all our enemies—for alas, we do have some. And that is that *this* Administration brings hope, not a sword. *This* Administration brings optimism, not despair. *This* Administration brings vision, not blindness. *This* Administration brings an eager and affirmative welcome to the future, not a desperate and self-defeating clinging to the past.

"It does so because it is my conviction—as the votes of so many millions of you have shown that it is yours—that we cannot longer continue to live in a world dominated by fears of aggression and expansion. We cannot endure further in the shadow of imperialism and hate. Neither we nor any other land can survive much longer in a world society racing faster and faster toward final self-destruction.

"The world must stop its folly and return to sanity.

"The madness must end.

"All nations, and particularly those three or four that are greatest, must realize that those peoples that have the most to lose from war have also the most to gain from peace. It is to them that the world looks for leadership. Upon them falls the obligation. Upon *them*—and perhaps most heavily of all—upon us.

"It is in that knowledge, and in that spirit, that I address you today."

He paused to take a sip of water. Quickly the cameras panned across the ex-President, the Knoxes, Lucille Hudson, the Jasons. All were solemn and intent. Hastily the cameras raced back to the President.

"I address you in that spirit because I have received, as you all know, a most encouraging indication of cooperation and support from the distinguished Chairman of the Council of Ministers of the Union of Soviet Socialist Republics. Let me refresh your memories. ("And Tashikov's," Lafe Smith whispered to Cullee Hamilton, who nodded with a somber look.)

"These are the concluding words of the message he addressed to me on the eve of the election. I quote from Chairman Tashikov:

"'This is what I hope:

"'I hope we will sit down somewhere and discuss our differences with trust and confidence as old friends should.

" 'I hope we will agree to abandon hatred and suspicion as a basis for our policies.

" 'I hope we will, with ruthless speed, dismantle and destroy all arms except those needed strictly for self-defense.

" 'I hope we will withdraw from all useless militaristic-imperialist interventionist adventures.

" 'I hope we will bring to our two nations and the world a new era of calm and lasting peace in which our two great peoples can work together in harmony and brotherhood for the betterment of all mankind.

" 'This is what I hope, Mr. President. And this is what I know can be achieved. . . .'

"And the Chairman concluded:

" 'We look with hope to your Presidency, my friend. You will find us ready for a new start. Let us achieve it together!'

"Those of you who were listening on that night will remember my brief, yet I think all-important, answer—and again I quote:

" 'I say to the Chairman of the Council of Ministers—*Let us begin!*' "

At this familiar collection of statements, which had drummed upon his countrymen from thousands of billboards, newspaper advertisements and radio and television spots during and after the campaign, the eager, approving roar again went up. While it was gradually dying away, the cameras had time to notice, and the commentators had time to voice their excited speculations, that the President had taken from his breast pocket several sheets of paper, unfolded them carefully and placed them over the body of his prepared text on the lectern. When he resumed speaking it was with a deeper note of solemnity, mixed with an underlying excitement that communicated itself instantly to his listeners.

A silence even deeper, more profound, more expectant than that before, enclosed the world.

The ex-President and many of his friends, off camera, noticeably braced themselves.

"My countrymen," the President said gravely, "what I now undertake to do is not, I grant you, the usual procedure. The usual procedure might be for me to wait until I am established in the Oval Office—to wait until later today, or tomorrow, or next day or next week to do what I am about to do.

"That would be the usual procedure.

"But these are not usual times.

"These are times that demand action, and action now.

"Accordingly, by virtue of the authority vested in me as Commander in Chief—"

(The ex-President's face was a study, and so were Senator Munson's, Robert Leffingwell's, Hal Knox's and many another's. But the cameras had no time for anyone in all the world but the man who was speaking into the deathly silence that hung upon his words.)

"—I am directing the appropriate officers of the government to carry out immediately the following orders."

He paused for an almost imperceptible moment, took a deep breath and went on, voice filled with emotion but firm.

"To end immediately all aid, economic and otherwise, to the reactionary and undemocratic government of Gorotoland headed by Terence Ajkaje."

A wild, delighted shout responded, and in far-off Gorotoland, watching the little screen, a gaunt and glittering figure dropped head in hands in a gesture of sudden abysmal despair.

"To withdraw immediately all American military personnel presently stationed within the areas of Gorotoland claimed by the aforesaid government of Terence Ajkaje."

The shout doubled—tripled—redoubled—retripled; and behind him the ex-President uttered, though no one heard him in the uproar, a heavy sigh.

"To cancel immediately the present ineffective and, in my judgment, inexcusable blockade of the People's Republic of Panama."

There were no voices left, no breath, to express the ecstasy. But somehow sound emerged, triumphantly drowning out the world. And in the drawing room of "La Suerte," far to the southwest, the trim and dapper figure of his brother-in-law leaped to his feet with a sudden triumphant shout.

"To withdraw immediately all American military personnel now stationed on the territory of Panama, in the skies above it and on the seas adjacent."

And again the sound—"The Sound" as Walter Dobius and his friends would think of it later, something they would always associate with Ted Jason and this marvelous, fantastic day when all their hopes at last, after so many long, reactionary years, appeared to be coming true.

The President paused, took another sip of water, waited for The Sound to subside. He looked excited, triumphant, happy. The response was proving him right. Man and Moment were truly met.

"Nor, my friends," he said, in a quieter, more conversational tone, "is this all. These are but the peripheral actions to turn this nation toward peace. More fundamental things remain, going to the heart of America's posture in, and toward, the world.

"Therefore in the pursuit of peace and in the sincere belief that the following actions, taken together with those just announced, will provide the basis for an immediate international conference, or series of conferences, which will be able to deal at last with the substance and reality of a genuine world settlement, I am further ordering:

"An immediate suspension, to continue for a period of sixty days, of all U-2 and satellite surveillance of the Soviet Union and its associated states."

(This time the ex-President turned with an expression of genuine alarm to seek the eyes of Senator Munson in the tier above; and this time, to the audible chuckles of many in the media, the cameras caught the gesture and carried it to the world.)

"An immediate withdrawal, for a period of sixty days, of all American air and naval forces, including submarine forces, from Mediterranean and Atlantic waters to their respective home bases."

The Sound was astounded beyond itself into realms of noise normally unknown to man. The confident voice continued.

"An immediate withdrawal, for a period of sixty days, of all American air and naval forces, including submarine forces, from the Indian and Pacific oceans to their respective home bases."

The Sound, helplessly ecstatic, but still trying, surged again.

"And, finally, an immediate study, starting tomorrow morning, by the Secretary of Defense and his appropriate aides, looking toward reduction of the Army of the United States by not less than one million men, and a comparable reduction in the personnel and planes of the Air Force and the personnel and ships of the Navy; the purpose being to restore the military forces of the United States to what they were originally intended to be—*defense forces,* in a world where men may live at peace with one another, freed from the fear of war."

Now The Sound, exhausted at last by so much surprise, delight, exuberance, approval and expended energy, began to trail away; and into the murmurous quiet that succeeded it he continued on a graver note that soon hushed the world again.

"Now, my countrymen," he said—and the handsome head came up in the challenging, fighting gesture they had come to know so well during the campaign—"I should be a poor President indeed if I did not accompany these actions, which I think no honest man anywhere in the world can call less than generous, friendly and cooperative, with two provisos.

"I would not only be a poor President, in fact: I would be a fool.

"The first thing is that when I make these far-reaching and voluntary decisions, I assume—and I expect—that they will be honored in the spirit in which they are made; and that when American forces strike their colors and begin their immediate withdrawals, they will be allowed to depart without harassment, attack or any kind of action at all that will in any way endanger them.

"The second thing is that I should be a poor President, and derelict in my duty, if I did not accompany these decisions with a most earnest and serious appeal to others to act in the same spirit for the sake of the peace of the world.

"Specifically, in Gorotoland, I call upon the faction of Prince Terry and the faction of Prince Obifumatta, together with other interested powers such as the United States and the Soviet Union, to begin immediate good-faith negotiations looking toward the establishment of a unified and democratic government.

"Specifically, in Panama, I call upon the faction of Señor Labaiya and the faction of his opponents, together with all maritime powers interested in unobstructed passage of the Canal, to begin immediate good-faith negotiations looking toward the establishment of a unified and democratic government and a responsible international consortium for control of the waterway.

"In addition, and most importantly of all, I call upon the Chairman of the Council of Ministers of the Union of Soviet Socialist Republics to take immediate steps involving Soviet armed forces which will be comparable to mine.

"And I call upon him, together with such of his colleagues as he may select, to meet with me and my colleagues at the earliest possible moment, at a mutually agreed-upon place, to begin the serious negotiations for peace to which my actions, and comparable actions by them, will have contributed so much in the way of trust, good faith, hope and practical reality.

"I submit to reasonable men everywhere that my proposals and appeals are honest, decent and fair.

"I assume—and I expect—that they will be accepted in the same spirit and with the same willingness to cooperate with which I have made them. I assume—and I expect—that they will be received with a comparable honor, decency and fairness by these to whom they are addressed.

"I say to the Chairman, and indeed to all world leaders everywhere:

"Together let us create the climate of peace.

"Together let us create the *inevitability* of peace.

"I have every reason to believe," he said with a solemn confidence, "that this appeal will be answered affirmatively. My colleagues and I will await with you, my countrymen, the indication from Moscow that it will be. We hope, and we expect, that it will not be long delayed.

"Then at last, I think, the world will know that America has truly turned to peace as a way of life; and men, women and children here and everywhere will be able to look ahead with confidence and certainty to a world in which wars and the threats of wars have at last been removed from the backs of mankind.

"This has been my pledge to you in my campaign and this is my redemption of that pledge. God giving us strength, you and I will see it through together. And the new day will dawn and remain with us, unto the last generation.

"Thank you very much."

And with a grave and solemn expression as The Sound once more outdid itself, he picked up the pages of his speech and put them in his pocket; shook hands with the Chief Justice, with William Abbott, with Beth Knox and Lucille Hudson; and nodding to his family, took Patsy's arm and led them slowly up the steps, past the congratulatory outstretched hands and the fawning, excited smiles, through the bronze doors, and once more into the depths of the Capitol; from which he emerged an hour later, after the customary luncheon with leaders of the Congress, to enter his limousine and start the slow, triumphal progress back down Pennsylvania Avenue to the White House, the reviewing stand and the long hours of the parade—now joyous far beyond the dreams of all the hard-working souls who had labored for so many weeks to make it ready for Edward Montoya Jason's Inaugural Day.

Forty-five minutes after the address ended, having proceeded downtown on foot because there was no other way to get through the excited crowds and the sparkling snow, Walter Dobius was typing rapidly in the office kindly lent him by his friends of the Washington *Post*. His friends of the *Post* were also typing rapidly, and so were his friends of the *Times*, *The Greatest Publication* and most other editorial staffs across the country. Equally busy were Frankly Unctuous and his colleagues of NBC, ABC and CBS, their delighted and approving words pouring forth incessantly upon the populace from every channel and wavelength. Walter, as happened so frequently, could have served as spokesman for them all, so well did he synthesize their thoughts, hopes and emotions on this gloriously satisfying occasion.

"Rarely," he began, the machine seeming to leap under his hand with the speed and happiness of his thoughts, "has a President kept faith with his countrymen as has Edward Montoya Jason today. Rarely has a President redeemed his campaign pledges so quickly, so specifically, so dramatically and with such breathtaking sincerity and completeness.

"Edward Jason pledged an end to all wars and threats of wars. In a reversal of American position so total that it will take the mind—and the world—a long while to grasp all its dizzying implications, he has done in fifteen overwhelming minutes everything an American Chief Executive could possibly do to achieve that end.

"Decades of stupidity, a generation of error, have been wiped from the books in a quarter of an hour. It would be unbelievable—had not the nation and the world been witness. Edward Montoya Jason, not yet a day old in office, has placed himself already among the immortals.

"And now he, and we, await the word from Moscow. It may be another day or two, perhaps even a week, before we hear, for our friends in the Soviet Union are slow and cautious to move. But there can be no doubt of the response. Such simple honesty and directness as the new President has shown can only be answered in kind.

"Now the Communists have a President who speaks the language they understand: the language of honest negotiation—the language of fearless and sincere concession—the language of peace.

"This is the opportunity they have been waiting for.

"We need have no fears or doubts that within a very short time they will let us know in unmistakable terms that they have seized it. . . ."

And in this, of course, Walter was, as usual, right; although it would be another few hours before his countrymen would be able to realize once again how truly prophetic he was. Meanwhile Washington danced—or at least tried to dance, for the four inaugural balls were, as always, more push-and-shove than wiggle-and-hop.

Ball No. 1—"the one *he's* going to come to first, at 9:30 P.M., and where he'll come back to conclude the evening"—was held at the Kennedy Center. Approximately six thousand would squirm their way to the bars and canapés there.

Ball No. 2—"where *he's* due at 10:30 if his schedule doesn't get fouled up"—was held at the Museum of History and Technology at 14th Street and Constitution Avenue. Perhaps four thousand were expected there.

Ball No. 3—"where *he'll* be around 11:30 unless he gets delayed at the Museum"—was held at the Washington Hilton, on up Connecticut Avenue. Another three thousand to four thousand had tickets there.

Ball No. 4—"where *he'll* be right around midnight unless he gets delayed at the Hilton"—was held at the Sheraton-Park, still further up Connecticut at Woodley Road. Close to five thousand were expected to squeeze in there.

There were statistics for these affairs, too, and dutifully the compilers of figures sent the story out on the wires and over the channels: so many bottles of liquor, so many tons of food. But the important thing, and the thing that pushed statistics far into the background, was the mood. The mood, as everyone who observed, reported upon, described or attended those historic galas would vividly and wistfully remember, was one of such excited happiness and uplift as Washington had rarely seen; and, after approximately 12:53 in the morning, would not, in all probability, see again.

When the evening began, however, nothing could have been more ecstatic or more heart-warming than this first social contact between the new President and those of his countrymen who had been fortunate enough to beg, borrow, steal, or pay through the nose for, a ticket to one of the balls. From the moment his arrival was announced at Kennedy Center just before 9:30 P.M. until shortly after his return to the same cavernously beautiful surroundings at 12:45 A.M., it was one long euphoric ride for Edward M. Jason. Euphoric too were Patsy, who had changed to a shimmering scarlet dress which beautifully set off the great emerald "Star of Boonarapi," most famous of the Jason jewels; Valuela, who wore several lesser emeralds, a clutch of rubies and her late mother's diamonds; Selena, who had abandoned her humble thirty-thousand-dollar mink simplicity and now appeared almost literally drenched in a shower of diamond brooches, necklaces, rings and bracelets; and Herbert, who, though still determinedly homespun of manner and hair arrangement, did wear an obviously expensive tuxedo, a ruffled blue lace shirt and a set of diamond-and-ruby studs and cuff links that must have set him back a good thousand smackers at Tiffany's.

Euphoric also were Vice President and Mrs. Roger P. Croy, his distinguished gray head bobbing constantly as he acknowledged the cheers and applause, hers turning rapidly from side to side as she smiled with a careful graciousness upon all these new and overwhelming friends. Euphoric also were the George Harrison Wattersills, Secretary of Defense Ewan MacDonald MacDonald and his lady, and all the other Cabinet members who, in a burst of confidence in Ted Jason, had been speedily confirmed by the Senate in its brief one-hour session during the afternoon. All euphoric, that is, save one, and he too was able to muster sufficient will power to make his way for the most part smiling through the evening. Only when the Secretary of State happened to catch the eye of the ex-President and the Munsons as the Presidential party passed through the Hilton was there a change in his carefully set expression; and then his momentary look of recognition and worry was noticed only by a drunken few who swiftly forgot it as his determinedly pleasant expression returned and he moved on gracefully through the crowd.

Neither the Knoxes nor Lucille Hudson appeared in the city on this glorious evening, feeling that they had contributed sufficiently by their appearance at the Capitol. Other members of "the government in exile" felt they must, for various reasons, attend. Lafe Smith and Mabel Anderson joined Cullee Hamilton and Sarah Johnson for dinner at the Jockey Club and then went to Kennedy Center. William Abbott, the Munsons, Stanley Danta and Bessie Adams dined together at "Vagaries," the Munsons' beautiful home in Rock Creek Park, and then went to the Hilton, planning to go later to the Center for the President's final appearance.

Some members of Congress who had either been defeated in the Jason sweep, or disagreed too violently with his dramatic peace moves, stayed deliberately away; and a few other diehards—four or five former Secretaries of State and Defense, a handful of retired columnists and commentators who had always believed that walking softly and carrying a big stick was not such a bad policy for America to follow—found themselves, somewhat to their surprise, too embittered to attend. But for the most part, everyone who was anyone or had ever been anyone in Washington political life was there. Doddering relics from as far back as the Theodore Roosevelt and William Howard Taft administrations mingled with their successors clear down the years to the outgoing Abbott cabinet. Ancient bejeweled harridans who had vied savagely for the title of "Washington's No. 1 hostess" generations before Dolly Munson and "Vagaries" came on the scene, mingled happily with grinning stalwarts of NAWAC and well-fed campaign contributors whose donations to this campaign, as to all others of whatever political persuasion, always guaranteed them a welcome at the seat of government. As the night wore on and the hilarity became increasingly unrestrained and amiable, a great ooze of fellowship, love and good will swept over the official city.

And constantly, of course, in the way of Washington, there were comments on what was referred to simply as "The Speech," varying in intensity and approval according to the ear of the beholder. "Great speech, hey, boy?" cried Ewan MacDonald MacDonald, ex-national committeeman from Wyoming, new Secretary of Defense, passing

Blair Hannah, national committeeman from Illinois, in the lobby of the Shoreham-Park. Blair Hannah scowled and snapped, "Giving us away on a silver platter and then some, isn't he?" But Esmé Harbellow Stryke, national committeewoman from California, spying George Harrison Wattersill in the crush at the Museum, screamed, "George! *George!* Congratulations! Marvelous! Simply *marvelous!*" And George, who had been as surprised and amazed as anyone at what had come out of the President's mouth in place of his own carefully polished rhetorical suggestions, bowed and preened and cried back, "I guess we showed 'em, eh, Ez?"

In general—indeed overwhelmingly, as it seemed to the many newsmen who worked their way through the crowds buttonholing as many famous names as they could find—official Washington was as thrilled and captivated by "the New Day" ("He has given us at once," Frankly Unctuous had told his listeners two minutes after The Speech ended, "the name for his Administration: this is the New Day.") as the rest of the country seemed to be. Hourly, indeed minute by minute, the conviction grew that Ewan MacDonald MacDonald, Esmé Harbellow Stryke and George Harrison Wattersill had the right of it: it *was* the most exciting thing that had ever happened, it *was* the greatest blow for peace ever struck, it did, as the *Times* announced in its lead editorial, "gloriously and without equivocation give Americans once more the right to stand unashamed and proud in the eyes of the world." By the time the President and his family came back downtown from the Sheraton-Park to Kennedy Center at half after midnight, the overwhelming majority of his countrymen were ready to give him one great big universal kiss and put him lovingly to bed.

So, too, it seemed, was the rest of the world, where in almost every capital The Speech had been hailed with popular approval and official congratulations worthy, as Hal Knox remarked when some of them appeared on the home screens, of the Second Coming. And now, even as Washington danced, the world watched via Telstar, waiting, like his countrymen, for the final comments ("The ecumenical blessing," Bob Munson labeled it dryly to Bill Abbott as they arrived at the Center just ahead of the Presidential party) he might wish to make before bidding them all good night.

When he and his family entered the Center, Selena and Valuela somewhat the worse for wear but himself, his sister and his uncle amiably under control, The Sound was heard for the last time—a great, rolling, roaring shout that swept over them, growing and rising and rising and growing, until it seemed the universe must come asunder. When it finally began to die away he allowed yet another full, patient minute to accommodate the last drunken yells and the last happy screams. Presently even they were gone. A silence of complete absorption and intensity ensued. Into it he spoke in a pleasant, almost conversational way.

"My friends," he said, "my friends here in this lovely capital—all over America—all over the world—"

There was a renewed burst of cheering.

"—this has been a great day—and I think we have all enjoyed it—and I for one am exhausted—and I think we all ought to go home and go to bed!"

Laughter, warm, approving, embracing, filled the cavernous halls and found its echo in smiles and chuckles wherever men and women heard his voice and watched his dignified, handsome face.

"Before we do, however"—and at his words they abruptly stilled—"I think I will let you in on a little secret. When I made my proposals today, nobody knew I was going to say them—nobody. They were my own idea. I consulted no one. I wrote them myself and I offered them because I thought that *some*one, *some*where must break through the deadly stultifying morass the world seemed to be in. It seemed to me I was the logical one to do it, and that this was the logical time. So I acted, hoping you, my countrymen, might approve."

A great cheer, wholehearted and loving, told him that Yes, yes, he had done the right thing and they adored him for it.

"They tell me at the White House that they have already received so many wires and telephone calls that the circuits have broken down and they can take no more tonight. They tell me that almost without exception these are favorable. And from the State Department they tell me something else—they tell me that they are receiving a constant stream of cables from heads of state, and that these, too, are almost universally favorable. The world is so *relieved,*" he said into the applause and cheers that were beginning again, "to have an American President who not only talks peace but *acts* peace, that it is as happy as—" he chuckled with a contagious delight—"well, as you and I are!"

It was at this moment, with laughter and applause rising joyfully around him, that Bob Munson happened to notice the Secretary of State, standing far to the side in one of the archways, and pointed him out to Bill Abbott; and so it was that they, first of anyone but the Secretary himself, became aware through some combination of experience, instinct and hunch that something was about to go wrong.

"Bill—" Senator Munson said, closing a hand tightly on the arm of the ex-President; the ex-President uttered a peculiar sound.

Not moving, looking carefully vague as they continued to glance at Bob Leffingwell, they saw the new Undersecretary of State, managing to look reasonably casual but revealing to the trained eye a considerable agitation, approach and hand him a folded sheet of paper. They saw him open it, scan it rapidly, turn pale. Quickly he glanced around to see who might have noticed, caught their eyes and with a sudden, savage forward movement of his head that said as clearly as words, "*Follow me!*" began to push his way as rapidly as possible through the amiably resisting crowd to the platform. Automatically and without question they began to do the same.

"My friends," the President went on, not at first noticing the little eddies of increasingly vigorous protest that began to accompany their desperate progress toward his side, "three capitals we have yet to hear from, and of these the most important, of course, is Moscow. But there is no reason for alarm in that: I've given them quite a mouthful to digest and it may take them a little while!" Again there was a burst of amusement and approval. "But," he said, more solemnly, "I have no doubt what their answer will be. If honor and decency and cooperation have any place at all in human affairs, then their response can only be as disinterested and farsighted as I like to think your President has been. I am very confident that before many more hours have passed—" he paused, his attention distracted finally by the commotion on the floor. "Wait a minute," he said in a pleased tone. "Don't I recognize those distinguished gentlemen coming my way? Of course I do! It's the distinguished ex-President of the United States—and the Senate Majority Leader—and the new Secretary of State. Let them through, ladies and gentlemen, please! I want them beside me on this historic night."

And obedient to his words, there was a murmur of recognition, a wave of good-natured cheering and applause, a stepping aside and making way. But as they came nearer the platform the applause suddenly died, for it became apparent to all who could see them that these were desperately worried men.

"What is it?" the President asked uncertainly. "Let them through there, hurry it up! What is it, Bob? Senator? Mr. President?"

Senator Munson and William Abbott could only shake their heads and gesture to the Secretary of State as they clambered to the platform, assisted by a hundred helping hands. And he could only hold up the folded piece of paper.

"Bring it here!" the President said sharply. "Gentlemen—" he reached out and pulled Bill Abbott and Bob Munson to his left side, Bob Leffingwell to his right. "Now, Bob," he said as a sudden agitated hush descended, into which his order, puzzled and concerned, rang clear, "put it on the lectern here and let's see what it is."

For several minutes after the Secretary of State complied, the silence, increasingly worried, beginning to be frightened, held the room. It could be seen that all four men read, reread and read again, that all were obviously dismayed by what they read, that for just a moment, glancing quickly at one another, they looked completely horrified and even, momentarily, afraid. But the realization of where they were and who they were swiftly reasserted itself, so that when the President finally spoke, it was in a voice that managed to be reasonably steady, though obviously carrying a great emotion.

"Ladies and gentlemen," he said quietly, "I'm afraid I must return at once to the White House. Mr. President—Senator—Bob—come with me. Please go on dancing and enjoying yourselves, ladies and gentlemen. There will be an announcement in due course."

"Of what?" some woman screamed as the Secret Service swiftly formed a flying wedge and rushed them to the waiting limousines. "My God, *of what?*"

But nobody knew; and within a minute's time, at the Center, at the Museum, at the Washington Hilton and the Sheraton-Park, the babbling crowds were pushing hysterically toward the cloakrooms, claiming their coats, whistling up their cars, scurrying out and away as quickly as possible. The instant rumor, of course, was war; and though no home would be safe in such an event, home was where they wanted to be.

Within fifteen minutes all four ballrooms stood empty and desolate. Desolate was the watching nation, too, and desolate the world; and desolate the heart of the man who now sat in the White House Situation Room, head in hands, looking suddenly much older as he read the dispatches and intelligence reports that were pouring in.

WHITE HOUSE ANNOUNCES MASSIVE SOVIET ASSAULT ON U.S. WORLDWIDE POSITIONS.

U.S. TROOP WITHDRAWAL IN GOROTOLAND TURNS INTO ROUT AS COMMUNIST TANKS, MIGS LEAD OFFENSIVE. MORE THAN 100 AMERICANS BELIEVED KILLED BY REBEL FORCES, AT LEAST 500 CAPTIVE AS PRINCE OBI SEIZES COUNTRY, PRINCE TERRY FLEES TO EXILE IN ENGLAND. . . .

LABAIYA FORCES IN PANAMA SEIZE CANAL AND COUNTRY AFTER SOVIETS LAND PLANES, TROOPS, SUPPLIES. RETREATING AMERICAN FORCES CORNERED ON SEACOAST. U.S. FLEET RESCUE TRY BARRED BY RUSS BLOCKADE. . . .

NOME, POINT BARROW IN ALASKA OCCUPIED FOR TWO HOURS BY SOVIET PARATROOPS AS MOSCOW DENOUNCES "INSUFFERABLE AMERICAN INTERFERENCE WITH FREE-DOM OF SEAS." INVADERS WITHDRAW AFTER "UNARMED" RED TRAWLERS UNVEIL MISSILES, SINK BULK OF U.S. FISHING FLEET. MANY CREWMEN FEARED CAPTURED OR DEAD. . . .

SOVIET NAVAL FORCES STREAMING THROUGH BOS-PHORUS, MALAY STRAITS, NORTH ATLANTIC AS U.S. FLEETS SAIL OUT. . . .

TASHIKOV ASKS UN SECURITY COUNCIL MEETING, INVITES PRESIDENT TO MOSCOW CONFERENCE "IMMEDI-ATELY, TO SETTLE OUTSTANDING DIFFERENCES, ELIMI-NATE IMPERIALIST U.S. AGGRESSION AND ESTABLISH GENUINE PEACE. . . ."

WAR FEAR GROWS AS STUNNED NATION AWAITS WORD FROM PRESIDENT JASON.

BOOK TWO

BOOK TWO

1. STUNNED NATION, stunned world; and stunned President, too, awaiting as desperately as anyone the word . . . any word.

But there is no word.

Only the awful confusions and terrors of the catastrophic end of a policy destroyed forever by the harsh realities of a world many wishful Americans had always pretended did not exist.

But here it is.

And here he is.

And where is the Word?

Somewhere around 2 A.M. he became conscious of a hand on his shoulder, a pressure not unkind but firm enough to get his attention. He looked up with exhausted eyes into the equally exhausted eyes of his predecessor.

"Mr. President," William Abbott said, "come away for a little. We've got the picture. It isn't going to change. Let's go to the office and do some thinking. They'll let us know if anything new develops." The slightest reminiscent smile came into his eyes before they became somber again. "They're very good about that, here in the Situation Room. They let a man know."

"Yes," he said in a voice too tired to respond to even that small humor. "You're right, Bill. Thank you. Are the others—" and for the first time in an hour he turned away from the huge clutter of paper that covered the desk at which he had been sitting.

"They're here," Bill Abbott said, gesturing. And there they were, standing together around the teletype machines, exhausted also but still staring as if hypnotized at the words that came incessantly, inexorably, implacably clattering over: Roger P. Croy, George Henry Wattersill, Robert A. Leffingwell and Ewan MacDonald MacDonald, the new Secretary of Defense; Senator Strickland, Senator Munson, Senator Danta, Senator Hamilton, Senator Smith; Senator Tom August, chairman of the Senate Foreign Affairs Committee, Representative J. B. "Jawbone" Swarthman, chairman of the House Foreign Affairs Committee; and an added starter, who had come in sometime at somebody's suggestion, he did not know whose, Representative Harold Knox of Illinois, pale, strained and looking a lot older.

In a week or two, no doubt, he would have all the paraphernalia of crisis to assist him, National Security adviser, National Security Council, National Security Agency, CIA, armed forces intelligence, Special Action Group—but not now. His enemies, sophisticated and shrewd in the ways of the world's most open society, had struck too fast to allow him all those comfortable and sometimes helpful cushions. Now all he had were thirteen hastily assembled men to help him decide, quite possibly, the fate of America. He hoped with a bone-weary, self-lacerating bitterness that their ideas were better than his, which had not, in recent hours, proved to be noticeably successful.

His eyes returned for a moment to Bill Abbott's and he said in a low voice,

"Sometime, if there ever is time again, maybe you can forgive me for—"

"Nonsense," the ex-President interrupted impatiently. "Nonsense. Nothing to apologize for. You acted as you thought best. We all have to, in this house. No time, now or ever, to apologize to me. Come, Mr. President, let's go in the office and get busy on the best way to get out of this mess. That's what we've got to do now."

"Yes," he agreed. "Yes, we must." He stood up, feeling the movement in every inch of bone and ounce of flesh; straightened his shoulders, lifted his head, surveyed them all. Automatically they turned to him, intent, expectant, obedient, waiting to be told—waiting to be led.

"Gentlemen," he said, his voice getting stronger through the tiredness because it had to, there was no other voice to do it, "please come in the Oval Office with me and let's talk this out a bit. Captain," he said to one of the military aides, hurrying by with still more papers, still more reports, "ask the kitchen to send some coffee and something to eat up to the office for us, will you please?"

"Yes, *sir!*" the officer said, tossing his papers on the desk and jumping to a phone.

"You know," he said with a small attempt at wryness as they entered the big, silent room where Washington, Jefferson, Lincoln and Jackson looked gravely down from their safe harbors in history, "you may not believe this, but this will be the first time I've tried out that desk. I was going to save it until 9 A.M. today when I thought—" the wryness cracked and for just a second, alarming them all, his voice wavered, "when I thought regular business would begin."

He walked slowly over and stood for a moment, one hand on the chair, looking down at the gleaming expanse, utterly empty of documents, pictures, souvenirs, ash trays and ideas.

"Please be seated," he said finally, sitting himself. When they had complied, drawing up chairs and sofas into a semi-circle in front of the desk, he looked slowly from face to face, uttered a tired sigh and asked quietly, "Well, what shall I do? Go to war?"

"Oh, Mr. President—" Tom August began in his alarmed, uncertain and diffident way. But Bill Abbott forestalled him.

"That is an alternative," he said crisply.

"But unthinkable!" Roger P. Croy exclaimed with an almost frantic distaste. "Absolutely unthinkable!"

"Is it, Ewan?" Bill Abbott asked. "You've been getting all those briefings at the Pentagon these last few weeks. How unthinkable is it?"

"Well," Ewan MacDonald MacDonald said slowly in the gentle burr that still lingered, an elusive ghost of Deeside childhood, after fifty-one years of citizenship and commercial success in the United States, "I wouldn't want to think about it too much."

"Nor I," Bill Abbott agreed. "But it could be done, I think, if it were done fast, surgically and with limited and specific targets—if, in short, we operated exactly as they have. I know we have strength enough for that."

"Although," Bob Munson remarked, and he could not entirely keep the bitterness out of his voice, "thanks to the combined efforts of some people in this country who should have known better over the past few years, we haven't been left the wherewithal to do much more."

"I expect," William Abbott said soberly, "that there are going to be recriminations enough without us starting them here. The basic fact is that a lot of determined people for one reason or another managed to carry the day in the media, the Congress and sometimes in the White House, and so they were able to force a steady reduction of our military strength. I have an idea," he added with a certain grim satisfaction, "that they're scared silly tonight just like the rest of us."

"Now that it's too damned late," Hal Knox said bitterly. "Now that they've left us to pick up the pieces."

"Me," the President said quietly, startling them a bit for he had listened so silently that they had almost forgotten he was there. "Left *me* to pick up the pieces."

"Well, pick them up, then!" Hal snapped, so frightened and angry and upset that he momentarily forgot all protocol and respect. "It's what you wanted, and you've got it, so do something!"

"Well, now," Bob Munson said in a conversational tone into the shocked little silence that followed, "Bill and I called you to come over here because we thought there should be a little bit of Orrin around to help us out tonight. You're the man of the house now, so we asked you. We didn't invite you over here to insult the President of the United States, or to act like a schoolboy. So if you can't contribute something constructive, don't say anything. All right?"

Hal's face was a study, first paling, then flushing. But finally, in a choked voice, the little bit of Orrin came through.

"Yes, sir," he said, very low. "I'm sorry, Mr. President."

The President sighed and managed a small smile.

"That's all right. We're all under great strain. I'll probably be lucky if you're the only one who jumps on me before we're through. . . . I still haven't received an answer to my question, gentlemen: shall we go to war?"

Again a silence fell as they contemplated the word and all its implications.

"I'm inclined to agree with the Vice President," Bob Leffingwell said finally. "It is unthinkable."

"Why," Cullee Hamilton wondered, in a musing not a combative tone, "is it always so unthinkable for us and so thinkable for them? Why do they always take the gambles and why are we always afraid to?"

"Because we've permitted them to find out that we won't gamble," Stanley Danta suggested quietly. "Isn't that really it?"

"And it isn't so much a matter of armed force, either," Lafe Smith remarked gloomily. "It's a matter of will. They know they've paralyzed the will of America."

"Americans have paralyzed the will of America," Bob Munson said in a bleak voice. "Our friends in the media and our friends in the colleges and our friends in the clergy and our friends in the drama and our friends—"

"And our friends in the Congress and our friends in the White House, just as you said a minute ago," Roger P. Croy interrupted sharply. "And they acted the way they did because of our friends in the country. You have a President and Vice President here who have just been elected by our friends in the country, and we were elected overwhelmingly, too. And it was on a policy of peace, isn't that right? It isn't our fault that we've been betrayed by those we trusted to help us make peace, is it?"

"The betrayal isn't your fault, Mr. Vice President," William Abbott said slowly. "But maybe the trust is."

"I had to trust them," the President said with his first show of anger. "What else could I do? I believed they wanted peace as much as I did."

"Their peace," Cullee said, "giving them control of the world, on their terms. Lafe and I saw it every day at the UN. Hell, any foo—anyone could have seen it. If he had been brave enough to see it."

"And face the consequences of seeing it," Warren Strickland said. "That was the next step."

"It does seem to me," George Wattersill said abruptly, "that it is a great thing for men who have led the United States Congress for years to be so high and mighty about it, particularly when one of them actually sat at this desk and had the power—"

"For six months," Bill Abbott interrupted coldly. "And with what I had, which wasn't very damned much after being overruled in Congress all these years when I tried to argue for a bigger defense, I used the power. Don't talk to *me*, Georgie boy."

"Well," George Wattersill replied with a frustrated anger, "I still think—"

"I still think," the President interrupted in a tired voice, "that you were right a few minutes ago, Mr. President, when you called for an end to recriminations. So let's proceed, shall we? What do we do?"

"I've told you what I would do," Bill Abbott said, not yielding very much. "I would take out their so-called fishing fleet up there *at once*. No discussions, no talk, no messages to Tashikov or anything. Our bombers and subs should be on the way right this minute, without any warning or by-your-leave to anybody. Then I would immediately cancel all withdrawal orders in Gorotoland, Panama, the Med, the Pacific, the Indian Ocean and everywhere else on God's green earth. I would instantly reinstate all U-2 and satellite surveillance. Basically, I would dig in *and stay where I am*. . . . Except," he observed softly, "that you aren't there any more, are you? You're already in retreat, so how can you turn around? I think you can if you move *right this minute*. But the longer we sit here and talk, the more the moment passes in which you can do anything at all—the more you approach a condition in which you will have only two alternatives, both absolute. One is, not the essentially limited response that I have just described, but all-out war to the death on both sides. And the other," he concluded even more softly, "is the imminent, if not the immediate, sur-render of the United States of America." He stared at the man who had succeeded him. "Tough choices, Mr. President. But you did, as the youngster of the crowd pointed out, ask for them."

For a moment there threatened to be a long and uncomfortable silence as Ted Jason returned his stare from haunted and unhappy eyes. But Jawbone Swarthman broke in with that voluble verve that had long ago, in his maiden speech to Congress, won him his nick-name. The press noted then that Franklin Roosevelt, having been belabored by everything else, had now been belabored by the jawbone of an ass.

"Well, now, Mr. President," he cried. "Mr. Presi*dents*, sir. Sirs. What's become of that little ole pledge about recriminations, now, Mr. Presidents, sirs? Seems to me everybody's recriminatin' right and left, and not least you, Bill, Mr. President, Mr. Speaker, *sir*. Stop it now, I say! Best everybody stop it right now, I say! We've got to find ourselves a way out of this little ole tangle, and we're just not goin' do it with ev'body slammin' away at ev'body, here! We've got to *think*, Mr. Presidents, sirs, and that's for certain sure, we've surely got to *think*.

"Now, then, let's just take a look at that little ole proposition you just made, Bill, Mr. President, sir. Why, how they goin' to look at that, over there in Moscow? They goin' to look at it as an act of *war*, Bill, they surely are. Of *war*, I say! They goin' to say—and the rest of the world goin' say it with them, you *know* the rest of the world, now—they goin' say, Look at that old United States, aggressin' again! Look at that old United States, jes' tearin' up ev'body's hopes for peace, they goin' say! Lookit, you-all! There she goes *agin*, they goin' say, re-sortin' to arms, sendin' bombers, sendin' subs, *aggressin'*, they goin' say. *Aggressin'*, that's what they—"

"Good *God* Almighty," Bill Abbott said in a grating voice, "you are beyond belief, Jawbone. *Who* has sent in troops and bombers, *who* has sent in subs, *who* has launched new offensives, captured prisoners, sunk American vessels, invaded American territory? Tell me that, you blithering idiot."

"Call me anythin' you like, Bill," Jawbone Swarthman said with a sort of merry, relishing doggedness, "but you know it don't make one damned bit of difference to the Communists or the world what the *facts* are. They goin' attack the U.S. of A. *regardless*, Bill, you know that. They goin' fly right in the face of the facts and lie themselves silly 'bout us, Bill, you *know* that. They all bein' doin' that for years, Bill, all those Communists and all our dear friends and ev'body else, and they goin' keep right on at it. And *we all know it.* Now, isn't that right, you-all? I submit it to you. Isn't that right?"

He paused, demanding argument; but of course there could be none, for he was entirely correct; and so after a moment, tossing his shaggy gray hair triumphantly, he proceeded apace and atumble in the carefully cultivated cornpone rhetoric which covered up the Phi Beta Kappa, *magna cum laude* graduate of Duke University Law School.

"So, then: we got us a condition to face here, not a theory; we got us a *reality.* We got, first, the world's deliberate refusal to admit we have a case, and its sure-certain readiness to jump on us if we so much as budge in our own defense. So that's a hurt and a hindrance. Then secondly, we got our own military condition, which condition I grant you isn't so hot, although I don't think it's quite so apple-pie simple to explain as you make out, Bob, I really don't. But anyway," he hurried on as Bob Munson showed signs of a sharp reply, "anyway, be—that—as—it—may, we got us a condition and a reality there, too, and they's simply no point in debatin' it now, Bob, simply *no* point. And that's another hurt and hindrance. And thirdly, we got another big 'If' nobody's mentioned here yet in all these free-swingin', dashin' outlines of how tough we ought to be. Jes' supposin' now, Bill, that they *really mean it* this time. Jes' supposin' they finally made up their minds *this is it.* Jes' supposin' they decided they got us on the run and *they goin' keep us there.* Then what?

"Supposin' we come back with bombs and subs and war-makin', Bill —*and supposin' they don't back down?* Supposin' they say, O.K., you asked for it, *we goin' let you have it?* Then what's goin' happen to us, Bill, and you other tough guys here? What's goin' become of dear ole America *then?* Think about that now. Think about it!"

And he sat back dramatically and stared brightly around the circle of their tense, unhappy faces. Finally Warren Strickland shifted in his chair and began to speak in the quietly reasonable way that had been his contribution to Senate debate for twenty years.

"Then what you propose, Jawbone, *is* surrender, isn't it? Because if we were really to accept your third point, and put it in context with your second and first points, then there would really be no use in trying any kind of defiance at all, would there? We'd be licked before we started.

"Well—" he sighed and rubbed a hand across his tired eyes for a moment, then resumed in a stronger voice, "maybe we are. But I don't like to proceed on that assumption just yet. I am not, as it turns out—" and a touch of his usual relaxed humor crossed his face for a second—"

the President of the United States, but if I were, this is what I think I might do:

"I should, first of all, proceed on the assumption that there is, in the long run in this world of ours, some balance between evil and good which does come down finally, when all is said and done, on the side of good. I should proceed on the assumption that evil wins most of its victories, at least its early victories, by bluff; and that even though we are very late in the game now with our Communist friends, and even though they have advanced very far by bluff, that bluff can still be called *if we will do it*. I said a little while ago that the problem is facing up to it. I think you all know me well enough—or at least my colleagues of the Congress know me well enough—to know that I would. I can only hope—" and for a moment he paused and studied Ted Jason as though seeing him for the first time—"that the man who sits in that chair now will do the same. . . .

"Now it seems to me," he went on as the President moved slightly but did not otherwise respond, "that there is one thing we cannot afford to ignore, and it is to some extent over and above, possibly even greater than, considerations of the Panama Canal in hostile hands, or a friendly government toppled in Gorotoland, or American troops captured or about to be captured, or a fishing fleet decimated, or two American cities successfully 'occupied,' if only for two hours' time. And that is the basic *nerve* of all these things—the basic *dare*—the basic taunt, almost childlike in its terrible simplicity, which says, 'We're doing these things to you *because we don't think you have the nerve to respond*. We think *you* think that we're strong enough now *so that you won't dare to answer back*. We're contemptuous of you and we're insulting you because we don't think you have the guts to do anything about it.'

"Particularly do I think that this applies to the situation in Alaska, grave though the others are. Alaska is part of us, and they intend for the world to see that we're too weak now to defend our own.

"If that is true," he said quietly, "then we are lost, and there's no way of glossing it over. America is *lost*, and that's that. . . . But I like to think that perhaps America is not, just yet. And so for my own contribution, I would like to offer this:

"In many ways there are arguments to be made against our involvements in Gorotoland and Panama and there are arguments to be made for allowing those situations to work themselves out, providing it can be done with all interested parties negotiating in good faith toward the goal of a stable Africa and an internationalized Canal. But we cannot allow Alaska to pass without the most immediate and drastic response, in my humble judgment.

"So I would agree with President Abbott on that. I think President Jason should order *at once* exactly the kind of retaliation Bill proposes: an all-out death strike against any and all Soviet ships and planes in—or adjoining—Alaskan waters. I do not think this will bring war with Russia, because I think she half expects this strike and she knows she deserves it, and so I think, though there will be a lot of saber rattling and a great deal of teeth gnashing, that she will lick her just and well-deserved wounds, and withdraw.

"I would couple this with a flat and unequivocal demand for at least $150,000,000 in reparations for damages to our fishing fleet.

"At the same time, I would announce *at once* that all surveillance activities have been resumed, and that all American air and naval forces are returning to their stations around the world.

"I would also announce *at once* that American prisoners in the hands of Obifumatta's forces in Gorotoland will be freed immediately—or we will resume full-scale aerial strikes on the country.

"And I would announce that threatened American forces in Panama will be evacuated by the American Navy—period. I would not hesitate, I would not equivocate, I would not apologize for it, I would simply say calmly that they will be saved as we have a right to save them, and it will be done.

"I would then call for immediate negotiations in both countries by all interested powers including us and the Russians.

"And I would then join in the Russian call for a Security Council meeting, lodge the strongest possible protest against their actions and introduce a resolution condemning them for aggression. . . .

"That way has risks," he concluded quietly. "But in my judgment, inaction has more."

"I think you have given us a prescription for world war," Tom August said in a taut, aggrieved voice into the silence that followed. "I really do, Warren. And I regret it, because I don't think we could possibly do what you propose."

"Why not?" Hal Knox asked abruptly. "Just why not?"

"Because it is impossible," said Roger P. Croy.

"It would never work," said George Harrison Wattersill.

"We haven't got the strength," said Ewan MacDonald MacDonald.

"And what," asked Warren Strickland gently, while the President remained silent, studying their faces, "says the Secretary of State?"

For a long moment Bob Leffingwell returned him stare for stare. Then he too sighed, but spoke in a firm voice.

"I say we must do something," he said. "I say we *must* respond. How strongly it should be leaves the area of certainties and gets into the area of gamble. But all things considered—" he paused and they studied him and his employer as he resumed—"I should not be afraid to gamble, and quite strongly, I think, for I too think that this is, essentially, a testing—perhaps the final testing—and a contest of wills. . . . But," he concluded quietly, "it is of course not my will or yours which holds the answer here. . . ."

And so finally it came back to the man behind the desk, as it had to. "The buck stops here," Harry Truman had put it, at the start of an earlier difficult era whose erratic braveries and inconsistent equivocations through succeeding administrations had led straight to this more terrible, more difficult age. And so the buck did.

"Gentlemen," he said, his voice dragging a little with the weariness that now, at almost half-past three in the morning, was beginning to affect them all, "I thank you for your very thoughtful discussion, which has been most helpful to me in clarifying my own ideas. I think everyone has spoken out of genuine conviction and real love of country and concern for the world, and I hope I may act in that spirit as we move through the days until this thing is settled.

"I am, as you can understand, most—" his voice faltered a little, then strengthened—"most terribly disappointed by what has occurred. I acted in good faith for a goal in which I honestly believed, the goal of world peace. I think even those of you who disagree with me most severely accord me that. At least—" and he gave a slight, almost hesitant smile to which they all responded with vigorous nods, so important is it in times of crisis to preserve the confidence of the man who sits behind that particular desk in that particular house—"I hope you do. . . .

"I agree with the Secretary of State, with you, Warren, and with Bill, that a response must be made. I think," he said, as they began to watch him with a hopeful anticipation, "that I have the channel through which to do it. I have the excuse, you might say, to hang it on." And for some of them, the anticipation died.

"Excuse?" William Abbott echoed blankly. "What 'excuse' do you need, Mr. President?"

"I think," the President said slowly, "that I need something that will permit me to respond without directly challenging the Soviet Union."

"Exactly," Senator August said happily. "That is exactly it, Mr. President!"

"But—" the ex-President began in a dismayed voice. Then the dismay overcame it, and it trailed away.

"Shortly before we came in here," the President said, "I received an appeal from the Governor of Alaska. It was, as you might expect, somewhat hysterical in tone. But the gist of it was, of course, an appeal for immediate assistance. This I propose to give.

"I propose," he said firmly, while the faces of his predecessor, of Senators Munson, Danta, Hamilton, Smith and Representative Knox, gradually froze into expressions of dismayed disbelief, "to declare Alaska immediately a disaster area. I propose to dispatch immediately the sum of fifty million dollars for the relief of civilian distress caused by this unfortunate incident—"

"Is that how you are going to refer to it, Mr. President?" Bob Munson asked in a strangled tone. " 'This unfortunate incident?' "

The President nodded.

"I think so. I don't think there's any need to say anything inflammatory. The whole world knows what's happened."

"But—" Bob Munson began; and then he, too, gave it up.

"I also propose," the President continued calmly, "to dispatch another fifty million dollars to compensate the owners for any damages that may have been suffered by the American fishing fleet. And another fifty million dollars to assist the families of any men who may have been lost. That, I think, will take care of that. And it will also," he said, his tiredness seeming to disappear and his tone growing increasingly stronger as his thinking on it became moment by moment more clarified and more firm, "permit me to work logically into the next phases of it, which I think will be these:

"After I have outlined the aid I shall send to Alaska, I shall then go on to say that I agree with the Chairman of the Council of Ministers that a conference should be held to settle the outstanding problems which are aggravating the world.

"I will propose that this conference, instead of being held immediately in Moscow as he proposes, be held in some neutral point, probably Geneva, at a date, say two weeks from now, that will allow adequate time for all parties to prepare.

"I will propose that it consist of two working groups, one to deal with the situation in Gorotoland and the other with the situation in Panama.

"I will propose that the meeting on Gorotoland include representatives of both factions in that country, and that the meeting on Panama have the same composition.

"I will propose that both work toward an end to the fighting and toward the establishment of temporary coalition governments which will, in due course, hold free plebiscites to determine the final composition of the governments that will control those two countries.

"I will propose further that after those objectives have been achieved, each group should then proceed to work out agreements in their respective areas for the neutralization of Gorotoland and for the establishment of a fair and democratically selected international body to administer the Panama Canal.

"And finally, I will announce that all surveillance activities by U-2 and satellites have been resumed. Which," he concluded with an air of satisfaction, "they already have been, isn't that right, Ewan?"

"That's right," the Secretary of Defense agreed. "An hour ago, just as you told me."

"Good," the President said with a triumphant little smile. "This, then, is what I propose. I think it will give us a way out that will bring ultimate agreement on these problems and an ultimate easing of these tensions that will contribute greatly, perhaps decisively, to world peace. I hope you will all agree and support me."

"What about reversing our withdrawals of naval and air power?" Warren Strickland asked quietly. "You didn't say anything about them."

"I think an abrupt reversal now would be too inflammatory and too warlike," the President said. "I've thought of that, but I think my way is better. I think the re-establishment of surveillance will indicate to them that we mean business. We can always send the fleets back later if things get worse."

"Can you?" William Abbott asked with equal quietness. "Can you really, Mr. President?"

"Why not?" the President inquired. "I'm the Commander in Chief. All I have to do is say so."

"Is that all?" Bill Abbott asked, still quietly. "Is that all it takes, once they've begun to leave?"

"I think so," the President said firmly. "I believe my way is best. I think this is a combination of whip and carrot that will bring our friends in Moscow around and get things on the right track again."

"You really think you're using a whip," Stanley Danta said in a musing voice that did not ask for answer. Nor did the President give a direct one.

"I think I am proposing a way out which will bring agreement and help to establish a lasting peace. I really think I have found a middle ground."

"Assuming both sides want a middle ground," Bob Munson said, as quietly as his colleagues. "What, in the past six hours, leads you to believe they do?"

"What makes you think they don't?" Roger P. Croy demanded with a sudden belligerence. "What do you mean, attempting to destroy the President's confidence in his course of action, which he must believe in if he is to carry it off successfully? What do you want, Senator, a Third World War?"

"That's right, Bob," Senator August said before the Majority Leader could articulate his angry reply. "You people do sound awfully belligerent to me."

And Jawbone Swarthman agreed, "Surely do. Surely do, you-all."

"I think," George Harrison Wattersill said before anyone could respond, "that the President has proposed a most reasonable, most diplomatic and most farsighted solution for the situation that confronts us. He is acting firmly and I think shrewdly and wisely. I for one am proud of him and proud of my country that it has chosen such a wonderful leader in times like these!"

There was silence for a while, as the President's men nodded agreement to one another and the ex-President's men regarded one another with dismay.

Finally Bob Munson spoke in a reflective, distant, almost disinterested fashion.

"You want to go to Geneva," he said, his eyes and his thoughts far away. "I went to Geneva once with another President, Harley Hudson, a couple of years ago. And when we got there, we were confronted with all the wildest dreams of the Communists wrapped up in one package—demands that we get out of this and get out of that, withdraw here and withdraw there, cut back our armed forces to the bone, give in to Communist imperialism entirely. We were threatened that if we did not there would be instant retaliation against our cities, presumably atomic, from orbital bombs, from the submarines that are stationed permanently off our coasts, and in other ways. And the world knows what Harley said. He said they were crazy and he was going home. And he got up and led us out of that hall, and we did come home. And nothing happened. . . . I wonder," he said, still in a distant, musing way, but with his eyes now coming back to focus steadily on those of the President, "if you would have the guts to do that. And I wonder further why you think it is that you aren't going to be confronted with something very similar to what Harley got, in view of what has already happened out of Moscow in these last few hours?"

For a long moment the President returned his gaze, unwavering. Then he glanced up, as if seeking some reassurance, at his predecessors on the wall. Then he glanced back at the Majority Leader and framed his reply in careful yet confident words.

"In the first place, I cannot tell you what I would do in such a situation, for I have no certainty—nor do you—that it will be presented to me. I would hope that whatever I did would be done with the same courage and the same dignity as that shown by President Hudson, God rest his soul. We owe him a very great debt for what he did on that day, and whether you think so or not, Senator, I am not forgetting it. . . .

"Now: you ask me why I think there is a middle ground to be found. I will tell you why. Because I believe that Chairman Tashikov—"

"Christ!" Hal Knox said in a muffled whisper, but the President, though an icy look came into his eyes for a second, ignored it and went calmly on.

"—is not the man who originated these actions of the past few hours. I do not believe that the man who sent me the message on the eve of my election is the man who ordered these frightful things. I do not believe the spirit of San Francisco can be that lightly dismissed. I believe he still adheres to it, and I think it is up to me to help him come back to it.

"I think," he said, and his voice too became contemplative and far away, "that he is a prisoner of his military. I do not believe that any sane man would condone, connive or cooperate in doing what has been done. I think he had no choice. I think in a very real sense he is trapped. I think it is up to me to get him out so that we can all breathe safely again. I think I can do it if I pretend to go along part way—if I show a spirit of peace and cooperation—if I provide the standard forms of diplomacy and play the game with a straight face as it has always been played.

"Then, I think, there will be hope. Then, I think, we can work it out. If I can just get him to Geneva, out of Moscow, into the public spotlight, away from what I believe to be his captors—then I think I can do it.

"You talk to me," he said, quietly but with a certain indignant bitterness just the same, "about taking gambles. I submit to you *I am* about to take a gamble; in my way, just about as brave a one as Harley Hudson took. I submit to you that the alternative *is* world war and the end of everything. I would appreciate it, if I may say so once again, Mr. President and those who agree with him, if *just once*"—and the bitterness became more sharp and open—"if *just once* you would grant me *my* integrity, *my* patriotism, *my* good faith and *my* intelligence. I really *would* appreciate that."

"Hear, hear!" the Vice President said harshly.

"I say amen!" Jawbone Swarthman echoed. "I certainly say amen!"

"I, too," Tom August agreed.

"And I," George Wattersill and Ewan MacDonald MacDonald offered fervently together.

"And I," said Bob Leffingwell quietly, at last. "Personalities don't help. If this is the decision, this is the decision."

"Well, then, Mr. President," William Abbott said with an equal quietness, "I think you should know that when Bob and I run for reelection to the leaderships on the Hill this afternoon, we will make this the issue and it will be a clear-cut vote by the Congress of the United States on whether they approve of your handling of this or not."

For several moments the President stared at him with an expression that yielded nothing. Then he put out his arms straight against the edge of the desk and pushed himself back to his full seated height.

"Very well," he said in a quiet but unyielding tone that showed he was completely committed at last. "If you do, you will lose."

And in the afternoon—after he had appeared on television at 11:30 A.M. to announce and explain his message to Moscow, concluding just two minutes before the sessions began at noon in Senate and House—he proved to be right, though it was a bitter battle and one with ominous overtones to come.

In the Senate, sarcastic Arly Richardson of Arkansas, triumphing by a vote of 63–34 over the man who had beaten him for the job a dozen years ago, toppled Bob Munson at last from the Majority Leadership in which he had become a Washington fixture.

And in the House, exploding all precedent, an ex-President just returned to his Congressional seat was handed a sensational slap in the face when his colleagues voted 323–102 to deny him the Speakership and gave it to a bouncing, beaming, ecstatically voluble J. B. Swarthman of South Carolina.

In all the terms in which what remained of "the old Washington" thought and operated, both defeats were almost unbelievable. But this was the New Day, and it had arrived with a vengeance that left even the most delighted and approving of commentators floundering. Walter Dobius and his colleagues sought, bemused, for words. Frankly Unctuous and his colleagues gulped and stammered in the astounding glare of events. They wanted the New Day but found it almost impossible to grasp. In his first test with the Congress, their man in the White House had won two sensational victories, hands down. They almost could not believe it.

Nor, as he walked slowly back to the Old Senate Office Building with Dolly and Stanley Danta, could Robert Durham Munson, senior United States Senator from the state of Michigan; now, as he had to keep reminding himself through the gloom of a shattering and unprecedented rebuff, just another Senator. It had been a long, long time since Bob Munson had been "just another Senator"; and considering all the implications to be found in his defeat, and in the manner of it, he considered that the event held a significance far beyond one bruised ego. It did indeed indicate the New Day, and he found the fact profoundly disturbing. He had seen the future, to paraphrase a famous ubiquitous saying, and he didn't like it. In fact, as he had just put it to his wife and Stanley, it scared the hell out of him.

The debate had begun mildly enough, as such things customarily do at the start of each new Congressional session. First had come the swearing-in of new Senators. Then John DeWilton, senior Senator from Vermont, had risen in his likably pompous way, like some silver-topped cockatoo, to move the name of the Minority Leader for the Majority Leader's job. Warren Strickland, back in his front-row seat as Minority Leader after his foredoomed fling at the Presidency, had smiled and bowed with a suitable irony to acknowledge the equally ironic applause of the sixteen Senators left on his side of the aisle after November's Jason sweep.

At that point Stanley had arisen at his desk beside Bob Munson, who sat comfortably relaxed across the aisle from Warren, to make the customary amendment to the motion, substituting Bob's name for Warren's. At that point things began to go wrong with a sensational suddenness.

"Mr. President!" Fred Van Ackerman cried from his seat in the second row behind Bob. "Mr. President, I wish to further amend the amendment of the Senator from Connecticut to substitute for the name of the senior Senator from Michigan the name of the senior Senator from Arkansas, the Honorable Arly Richardson. I so move, Mr. President!"

"Mr. President—" Stanley Danta began in surprised protest. But before he could proceed further the new junior Senator from Oregon, a thirty-year-old so youthful in appearance that the guard on the door literally had challenged his entry a few minutes before, was on his feet to cry, "I second the motion of the Senator from Wyoming, Mr. President!"

And from at least a dozen of his equally freshman colleagues, springing up all over the majority side, as Johnny DeWilton expressed it disgustedly later, "like a pack of damned chorus boys," came cries of "Second! Second! Question! Question! Vote! Vote!"

"Mr. President!" Stanley Danta shouted, aided now by Lafe Smith, Cullee Hamilton and half a dozen others, also on their feet and shouting. "Mr. President!"

After a pause, during which he studied Stanley with a bland look so close to insolence that Stanley could hardly believe it, Roger P. Croy, presiding for the first time as Vice President, rapped twice with a deliberately languid gavel.

"For what purpose," he inquired, elaborately polite, "does the senior Senator from Connecticut arise?"

"The Majority Whip," Stanley said with a rare show of anger (while from somewhere behind him someone said mockingly, "But not for long") "arises to protest the railroading tactics which are apparently being resorted to by some in this body."

"Mr. President," Fred Van Ackerman demanded with a sarcastic laugh, "isn't the Majority Leader's election *always* railroaded? Hasn't the Senator from Connecticut been conniving for a decade in railroading the Majority Leader's election? What's the sudden noble fuss about, Mr. President? What's so new here?"

"Mr. President," Stanley said, and the anger was suddenly raw in his voice for a man he utterly despised, "I did not yield to the junior Senator from Wyoming, a man known all too well to this Senate—" there was a murmur of boos across the floor, echoed and increased by the packed galleries—"to make his usual flippant, obstructive and ungentlemanly comments. The Senator is proposing a fundamental change in the organization of the Senate and I think it should be debated."

"Have your debate, Senator," Fred Van Ackerman advised disdainfully. "We have the votes."

"And who," demanded Stanley Danta harshly, "are 'we?' Are they Senators who have sat in this body long enough to know the junior Senator from Wyoming for what he is, a man censured by his colleagues two years ago for his part in destroying one of the most decent men who ever served here, the late Senator Brigham Anderson of Utah? Are they newcomers here who have no knowledge as yet of the customs and the traditions of this Senate—" there was a sudden explosion of laughter, harsh, sarcastic, so unexpected that for a moment he hesitated and almost lost his thread of thought—"no knowledge of our traditions and customs, Mr. President, and therefore easy game and easy prey for a fast talking freebooter—"

"Now, Mr. President!" Arly Richardson exclaimed, rising to his feet abruptly while around him the boos and laughter for Stanley Danta grew louder. "The Senator from Connecticut is impugning the personal honor and integrity of a fellow Senator. I demand he be required to apologize, Mr. President!"

"The Senator from Connecticut," Stanley Danta said, angrier than his colleagues had ever seen him, "does not see, he will say to the Senator from Arkansas, how he can impugn something which does not exist. The Senator from Connecticut—"

But now the booing, filled with an anger as great as his own, hummed and buzzed not only from the floor but from the galleries where it could now be seen that a number of the black-leather-jacketed thugs of NAWAC were scattered through the audience. Apparently they had not disappeared quite as readily as Ted Jason had prophesied. After they had expressed themselves sufficiently the Vice President put a stop to it with a sudden sharp rap of the gavel.

"The Senator from Connecticut," he said calmly, "will proceed in order. If he wishes to proceed."

"Yes," Stanley snapped, "I do! The Senator from Wyoming, as I say, is attempting to overturn here a man who has served with great distinction and integrity as Majority Leader for a dozen years. He is attempting—"

"Oh, no, Mr. President," Fred Van Ackerman interrupted, not even bothering to seek recognition. "That is not the man I am seeking to overturn, I will say to the Senator. The man I am seeking to overturn is the man who will, if he is re-elected to this powerful position, do everything he can to thwart and defeat the plans of the greatest leader for peace this nation has ever elected to the Presidency. *That* is why I wish to defeat Robert D. Munson!"

There was a burst of applause and cheers from many Senators and from the galleries. He looked about with a grim satisfaction as Bob Munson, half turned in his seat, studied him with an impassive face— too impassive for Fred, who suddenly jabbed an accusatory finger in his direction and sent his voice into its familiar, psychotic whine.

"There he sits, Mr. President! Yes, there he sits, this man who would destroy the plans of our great new world figure, our great new architect of world peace who wishes to relieve humanity of its burden of war! There is the enemy of Edward M. Jason, nurtured in the bosom of this Senate like an asp and an adder to sting and destroy! I say to you, Mr. President, we cannot *afford* to re-elect him Majority Leader! The Senate cannot afford him—the country cannot afford him—the world cannot afford him! He cannot honestly serve with this President because he does not believe in this President! The effrontery of him, Senators, the effrontery! The ego, the awful ego! He wants to *be* Majority Leader just because he has *been* Majority Leader! And that isn't all, I say to you. He wants to hang onto his office like a dog in the manger so he can hurt and obstruct this great new President. He doesn't want to serve and help this great new President, he wants to hurt and obstruct him. That is his reason, Senators! Strip him of his influence and *get him out of the way of Edward M. Jason!* . . .

"I defy him," he said, making one of his sudden baffling shifts to a quite ordinary conversational tone, as his colleagues and the galleries stared at him, fascinated, "to look this Senate straight in the eye and tell us that he approves of the policies of Edward M. Jason 100 per cent and will work for them 100 per cent.

"I defy him, Mr. President. I do not think he can do it."

And abruptly he sat down with a grimly satisfied little nod of his head and a smile so tight and tense it looked like death.

There was a renewed burst of applause from the galleries, led ostentatiously by NAWAC and joined by what the Congressional Record referred to next day as *many Senators.* The Vice President made no attempt to control it. Presently it was succeeded by a humming, buzzing, waiting silence as Bob Munson, still outwardly impassive, looked thoughtfully straight ahead, and in the Family Gallery above, Dolly, accompanied by Beth and Crystal, twisted her handkerchief, unknowingly, into tatters.

Finally, just as Roger P. Croy was about to say something, the Majority Leader rose slowly to his feet, straightened his shoulders and gave him a stare as bland and unyielding as his own.

"Mr. President," he said slowly, and the crowded old chamber became instantly hushed and attentive, "I see that we have here, indeed, the New Day, in which no attempt is made by the Chair to control these demonstrations from the galleries, which are against the rules of the Senate."

There was an angry booing, mostly from the representatives of NAWAC. He spoke into it with a flat, blunt anger, his eyes holding Roger P. Croy's.

"Why don't you perform your duties, Mr. Vice President? I am sure you would if they were applauding me."

For a long moment the Vice President, flushing to the roots of his silvery mane, gave him angry look for angry look. Then his eyes dropped, he rapped the gavel as half-heartedly as he dared, and said, in a muffled voice, "The galleries will be in order."

"What?" Bob Munson demanded sharply.

"I said the galleries will be in order!" Roger P. Croy repeated loudly.

"And what else?" Senator Munson asked with an ominous quiet, as the parliamentarian hastily scribbled a sentence and shoved it under Roger Croy's angry nose.

"The-galleries-are-guests-of-the-Senate-and-they-will-be-requested-to-leave-if-there-are-any-further-demonstrations!" the Vice President snapped, so rapidly the words tumbled upon themselves.

"Very well," Bob Munson said. He reached down, lifted a glass of water from his desk, took a sip, replaced it. "Now, Mr. President," he said, "since we have here an issue raised by the junior Senator from Wyoming which I did not wish to touch upon, but which he wishes to, I will answer him. In a way, perhaps, he is right to raise it, for it goes to the fundamentals of what this Senate is, and what it wishes to be, during the Presidency of Edward M. Jason.

"I will say at the outset that I do not find too much in the events of recent hours to lead me to believe that the new President of the United States has yet found his way in foreign affairs."

There was the start of a boo, but this time Roger P. Croy did use his gavel slightly more than lackadaisically. The boo subsided, reluctantly.

"He has made a beginning only, and in the opinion of a good many, I believe, including myself, it is at best an extremely controversial and uncertain one. His opening decisions, promulgated from the steps of this Capitol yesterday at noon—and promulgated, I will grant, in complete good faith and good will on his part—have been greeted with a reaction of the most violent and hostile kind from the Soviet Union. He has just attempted to respond, in the message to Moscow which he described to us over television less than an hour ago. No one at this moment can say what the future holds. The fate of peace—the fate of this nation and the Russian nation—perhaps the very fate of the world itself—quite literally hangs in the balance at this moment.

"It is against this difficult backdrop that we must perform our duties here this afternoon.

"Now the Senator from Wyoming, in his customary kind and generous fashion, has accused me of wanting to hold onto my office because I am a dog in the manger, I am on an ego trip, I want to hurt and obstruct the President as he attempts to find the way to world peace.

"How can I be a dog in the manger in an office which is entirely at the disposal of the Senate, and from which the Senate can remove me at any time by simple majority vote? And how can I be motivated by ego when I have had from this Senate, and from the people of the great state of Michigan, honors and responsibilities that would humble any man in the knowledge of his own unworthiness?

"But, Mr. President," he said, and his colleagues and the galleries became more intent at the change in his voice, "there is an argument to be made—and it is an argument far beyond the simple shallow sophistries of the junior Senator from Wyoming—on his third allegation. I will address myself to it very briefly, and then as far as I am concerned, let us vote.

"It is not my purpose, I will say to this Senate, to 'hurt and obstruct' the President of the United States. I have dealt with a good many more Presidents of the United States than have most who now occupy this floor, and I will say that my purpose has always been to help and assist them in their almost impossible task. That is the basic purpose, I submit, of any good United States Senator; and in recent decades there have been a good many good United States Senators. May those who are freshmen here today—and we now have more, as the result of a single election, than we have ever had in my experience or lifetime—measure up as well to their responsibilities.

"Hurting and obstructing is not my job, Mr. President. But helping to maintain a balance is. And there we come to the fundamental question of how Senators regard this body, in which they are more honored and more fortunate than some of them know, perhaps, to have been given membership by their people.

"There are two ways of looking at the Senate and its Majority Leadership, and those two ways have always conditioned the selection of the man who sits in this seat. One view is that the Senate is simply an arm of the Executive and its Majority Leader simply the man who speaks *for* him *to* it. And the other view, of course, is that we are an equal and coordinate branch of the government, working in cooperation with him to run the country, and that our Majority Leader basically speaks *for* us *to* him.

"This latter view, of course, with a few exceptions here and there over the years—" and for a moment a fleeting amusement, unanswered by Roger P. Croy or his solemn, mint-fresh, suspicious young colleagues, came into his eyes—"has been my own. It still is."

He paused again, again took a sip of water. Around him the Senate shifted restlessly but heard him out.

"I repeat, and I am not trying to deceive you, that I have many misgivings about President Jason's new policies. *But—*" and his emphasis stilled the uneasy murmuring that began again through floor and galleries—"they *are* his policies—he has put them into effect as he had the power to do—he now faces a very great crisis as a result—*and I have got to help him.*

"As have we all. . . .

"I ask you, Senators," he said softly, turning his back on Roger P. Croy so that he faced his silent, attentive colleagues (how strange it was, he thought with a knifing realization that made him feel suddenly very old, that for the first time in memory, he did not know at least forty of them at all), "I ask you: does the President not need the most skilled and experienced leadership to stand by him in this fearful crisis which now confronts us—the crisis *right out there*, Senators, the crisis which exists *right this minute?* Does he not need a man who can lead this Senate as it should be led, to work with him and alongside him, as an equally concerned and responsible partner, to save this Republic? That is what it comes down to now, Senators—*to save this Republic.* I have done a good deal to assist in that endeavor in past years. I trust you will let me continue now."

And abruptly, surprising them all, he sat down, while in the Press Gallery AP murmured, "I never thought I'd live to hear Bob Munson beg for votes." "The mighty have fallen," the *Times* replied with satisfaction. "And that ain't all," the Kansas City *Star* observed, not kidding.

Here and there across the Senate, from Stanley at his side, from Cullee and Lafe, from Warren and Johnny DeWilton and Bessie Adams, from Lacey Pollard of Texas, B. Gossett Cook of Virginia, Magnus Hollingsworth of Wisconsin and some other loyal, familiar friends, there came handclaps and applause. But many of the old faces were gone, after this election—many, many were gone. He sat down with a cold hand on his heart, though he managed an encouraging smile at Dolly, who managed an encouraging smile back. Neither believed it.

"Mr. President," Arly Richardson said, the disapproval and dislike he had felt for Robert Durham Munson for a decade and more vivid in every angle of his grizzled head and tall, storklike old body, "that was no doubt a noble and moving speech. And it had no bearing on what confronts us today.

"The Majority Leader—the Senator from Michigan—has maundered on about the two ways of looking at the Senate, and about how much he has helped past Presidents. He has tried to cover over with pious platitudes exactly what he thinks of this President. But we know, Senators—we know. Those of us who know where he has stood in the past know, and those of us who understand what lies behind his famed seductive phrases at this moment know. We also know what this President thinks of him. But perhaps out in the country they do not know.

And so I wish to read to the Senate a brief letter which was delivered to me just before we convened at noon today."

There was a sharp intake of breath, a heightened tension in the room. Years of training kept Senator Munson's face blank, but only just.

"It is dated this morning," Senator Richardson said, "and it comes from the White House. It reads as follows:

"'Dear Senator Richardson,

"'I am informed that the Senate will meet this afternoon for the purpose of selecting a Majority Leader. It is imperative for the success of my Administration that I have in that position a man upon whose loyalty, willingness and complete cooperation I can depend in these most difficult times.

"'I do not know whether your other duties would permit you to seek the office, but if so, and if you should be chosen for it, I would look forward to working with you.'

"It is signed," Arly Richardson said, "'Edward M. Jason,' as Senators may clearly see." And with a gesture both impatient and contemptuous he stepped forward from his place just behind and to the left of Bob Munson, and tossed it on his desk. Then he stepped back, looked about like some tall, old, peering bird, and said with considerable satisfaction, "Mr. President, if it is the Senate's desire that I fill this position, I shall be happy to serve."

Above in the Press Gallery the wire-service reporters dashed out to send their bulletins, in the Family Gallery Dolly, Beth and Crystal looked stricken, elsewhere in the galleries and on the floor an excited babble began. Cullee Hamilton was on his feet in the back row shouting for recognition. After a moment of bland delay the Vice President gave it to him.

"Mr. President," Cullee said, "I am a freshman in this body, but even to a freshman it seems an extraordinary thing for the President to try to intervene in our business here. What does he want, a rubber-stamp leader and a rubber-stamp Senate? It seems to me that's what he's after, and as one Senator, Mr. President, I don't like it, I resent it, and I don't want it!"

There was a sudden burst of boos from NAWAC and many others, this time with a certain ugly, personal note. He swung about angrily on its nearest perpetrator, the new junior Senator from Ohio, a middle-aged swinger swept in from the governorship on Ted Jason's coattails.

"Yes, I will say to the Senator, I resent it and I don't want it! And if he has an ounce of regard for the authority of this Senate and for his own authority, he will oppose it too. Because I tell you, Mr. President, the road lies clear ahead if this is done. A rubber-stamp leader. A rubber-stamp Senate. And a President with no restraints who can do anything he wants any time it pleases him. A constitutional dictator, Mr. President, that's what's down the road if we go this way. And don't make any smart mistake about it!"

Now the boos rose louder and angrier, including Bob Munson's friends, responding at last with an equal, bitter vigor. Fred Van Ackerman and at least a dozen others were on their feet shouting for recognition when the Senator from Michigan rose slowly to his. The tumult hesitated, faltered, died. One by one the Senators, even Fred Van Ackerman, sat slowly down. Bob Munson turned and deposited the President's letter, neatly folded, on Arly Richardson's desk. Then he turned back and began to speak.

"Mr. President," he said quietly, "if the Senate pleases, I would like to say a word. . . . It is obvious, Mr. President, that very deep and angry emotions are involved here, and it is equally obvious that if allowed to continue, they are going to tear this Senate apart. The Senate is making a spectacle of itself, Mr. President, and as one who loves the Senate, I deplore this. I think it is a very ominous thing, and what it portends for the future, I do not know. Whether it is what the junior Senator from California foresees or whether it is something less drastic, I cannot tell. But I do know it means bad business, for the Senate, for the country, and perhaps for our democracy itself. . . ."

There was an uneasy stirring from the ranks of NAWAC. But he went steadily on.

"It is particularly ominous, it seems to me, because obviously what is involved here goes much deeper than my political fate or that of the Senator from Arkansas. It obviously goes directly to the policies of the President and whether we agree with them or not. He has polarized this Senate and very shortly now, I am afraid, he is going to polarize this country. We not only have the crisis outside our doors, but very rapidly, I am afraid, we are going to develop a very serious crisis within them. And all of this, unhappily and ironically, because he has acted in perfectly good faith, as those of us who oppose him—and yes, I will say to the Senator from Arkansas," he said sharply as the booing began to rise again, "I will say I *do* oppose him—are also acting in perfectly good faith. . . .

"Mr. President," he said gravely as the noise subsided into grumbling murmurs, "I have been considering in these past few moments what I should do. It is quite obvious, I think, to anyone who knows the Senate that it is not the Senate it was last session. It is not the Senate it was before the election of last November. To a considerable degree, at least at this moment—and this moment, right now, with the crisis outside our doors, is what counts, for it will help to decide everything that follows in future months and years—it is President Jason's Senate. And it is obvious that what he wants here will be done.

"I have considered, in these few moments, withdrawing from the contest for Majority Leader which it is now quite apparent I am not going to win. But, Mr. President, I have decided not to do so—" sharp booing rose again but he continued calmly—"because that would not only be abandoning a fight I believe it important to make, but it would be failing to make a record I believe it important to make. Those of us who disagree should make our position known, for history's sake if nothing else. And because there are, I believe, a good many millions of our fellow Americans who feel the same way, I am going to let things stand and make the record I believe should be made, in order to indicate to them that they are not without hope and not alone, that some of us in Congress will continue to fight against policies we believe to be desperately dangerous to this country"—again the hostile noise arose, and into it he concluded with emphasis—"and against the mood in the country which these ugly sounds—not heard very often in this room, in our history—represent. I pray to God this sound does not indicate the mood of what is going to happen to us all, over the policies of this President. But I am not so sure—I am not at all sure. And it frightens me, I will say candidly to Senators: it frightens me.

"Mr. President," he concluded quietly, "I ask for a quorum call, and then for the vote."

"Without objection," said Roger P. Croy, matter-of-factly trying to keep the triumph out of his voice but not managing too well, "it is so ordered. The Clerk will call the roll."

And on the other side of the Capitol the same pattern of events prevailed. There, too, the galleries had their quota from the raucous ranks of NAWAC. There, too, many new members were eager and impatient to carry out the will of Edward M. Jason. Most of them did so in the sincere conviction that what they were doing was for the good of the country; and therefore the division over policy was just as sharp, and the determination of the President's men just as ruthlessly adamant, as it was in the Senate. This was a day, as the ex-President could sense the moment he set foot in the big brown chamber abuzz with excitement, in which William Abbott would have to make the fight of his life if he wished to regain control of the House of Representatives.

This he did. But he realized very soon after the Acting Speaker, Richard S. Morgan of Missouri, gaveled the House to order, that it was not going to be good enough. Even as Stanley Danta was placing Bob Munson in nomination for Majority Leader of the Senate, Asa Mc-Murtry of Colorado was placing Bill Abbott in nomination for Speaker of the House. And just as Fred Van Ackerman leaped to his feet to nominate Arly Richardson, a newcomer, twenty-six-year-old Bronson Bernard of New York, was on his feet to nominate Jawbone Swarthman. After that, things proceeded just about as they were proceeding across the Capitol.

Out of the welter of bitter charge and countercharge that ensued, while the galleries and many members booed or clapped or hissed or sneered despite Dick Morgan's ineffectual attempts to quiet them down, the two major statements of the day came, of course, from the ex-President and his opponent. Unlike Bob Munson, whose opposition to Ted Jason's policies was intense but at one remove, William Abbott was faced with the immediate prospect of a second repudiation of his entire policy while President. Ted Jason had repudiated it once yesterday in his inaugural and now it was clear—because Jawbone, too, had a letter from the White House which he read to his colleagues—that he wanted the House to repudiate it a second time. The memory of the haggard man in the Situation Room who had begged his forgiveness with a seeming humility scarcely ten hours ago, together with the memory of his own generous and forgiving response, was in the forefront of his mind as he began to speak. It rankled, and bitterly. And so it was that he, unlike Senator Munson, made no pretense of being able to work with the President. He embarked instead on the much riskier—and, the instinct of thirty years told him, foredoomed—course of attempting to swing the House behind him in a direct challenge to the Chief Executive. He knew that he would fail. But like Bob, for the record—and for himself—he had to make the try.

"Mr. Speaker," he said, when all the secondary leads and supporting players had strutted their oratorical way across the well of the House, "it is quite apparent that the House is most sharply and bitterly divided on this issue. It is quite apparent that it has come down now to a contest between the new President and the ex-President and what they believe. So be it. I didn't want it to happen this way, but his direct intervention here has made it that way. And so be it.

"Let me say first of all—" and the House at last was very quiet, for he had been many years on the Hill, served his country well, about him still were the great twin dignities of having been both Mr. Speaker and Mr. President—"that I give to the President every iota of respect and acknowledgment of the sincerity of his motives and his intentions. I think he really was selfless in what he thought he was setting out to do. I think he genuinely believed he could achieve peace by the means he announced scarcely twenty-four hours ago in front of this Capitol. I think he still thinks so, in spite of the response he has received from the Soviet Union. In fact, I know he does, because I was in the White House with him until four o'clock this morning, and I know how he is thinking. But it is my judgment, and I think it is the judgment of many here and in the country, that he has completely and abysmally failed."

The boos which had risen and fallen so many times during the debate rose again, the tenuous fabric of respect for his years and position was ripped apart, largely, he knew by his own decision. He welcomed it. He was in no more mood than they to temporize or be gentle.

"Yes," he said, and the iron in his voice was as harsh as any they could muster, "completely and abysmally failed. We know he failed yesterday and I am convinced he is going to fail today in this new proposal he has made to Moscow. He is going to fail because while he may still have hopes of making a deal, they won't deal. He wants to dicker and they don't. They haven't the slightest intention of easing up on the pressure one little bit, for one little minute. Wait and see!" he said sharply into the angry, protesting clamor. "Just you wait and see. . . .

"Now, Mr. Speaker," he went on bluntly when order finally returned, "what is the responsibility of this House, in this situation? Let me tell you what it is, seeing it as one who has been both Speaker of the House and President of the United States, something no other man in our history, as I recall, has ever been. As I see it, it is this: we have the obligation to support the President and help him in every way we can when he is engaged in protecting this country against her enemies. But we have no obligation to support and help him when he is saying to those enemies, 'Come ahead, walk over us, we believe you aren't a bully when you are a bully, we believe you're honorable when you're dishonorable, we believe we can appease you when you telegraph us as clearly as actions can possibly telegraph that you can't be appeased.' That Mr. Speaker, is not our obligation."

The booing and the hissing broke out harshly again, ugly, sustained, personal. Dick Morgan in the chair rapped futilely for order but William Abbott turned to him with a dismissing wave of the hand and a scornful expression that brought silence more quickly than the gavel could.

"Don't bother to try to control this mob of two-bit would-be storm troopers, Mr. Speaker," he said scornfully. "This is the New Day and this apparently is how it's going to be from now on in our national life.

We might as well get used to it. I fear for America because of it, but apparently they don't. So let them howl down opinions they don't like, if they really think that's worthy of what used to be a great Republic—if they really think that's the way to make *themselves* safe, when the day comes that somebody doesn't like *their* opinions. . . . Now," he went on more calmly into a sulky but subdued silence, "there *is* an obligation resting on this House, in my estimation, and that is for us to do whatever we can to help this President extricate himself and us from the situation we find ourselves in—the situation, to state it truthfully because God knows I didn't do it—that *he* got us into. And how can we do that?

"We can do it, it seems to me, by first of all passing a resolution stating most strongly the position of the House that we do not agree in toto with the President's policies but that we support him 100 per cent in his efforts to repel this unprovoked vicious Soviet aggression—" There came again the rumble of disagreement through the chamber and with a sudden blaze of anger he snapped, "For God's sake, what do *you* call it? What is your fancy term? What is your rationale, if it isn't aggression? By God, I think there is insanity in this House and in this nation today, to try to excuse and cover over such inexcusable acts of naked aggression! *How can you do it and still hope to have this nation survive?*" And now they were shouting, many members were on their feet trying to get the floor. In the galleries the black-jacketed knights of NAWAC were standing, booing, gesticulating angrily at the stubborn old man who glared up at them, unimpressed and unafraid, from the well of the House.

"Yes!" he cried into the uproar, and some last vestige of respect quieted them long enough to hear his final words. "Look at them and listen to them, my fellow countrymen! Here they are on this floor, and there they are in the galleries, these Americans who would give up their own country because they don't have the guts to defend her! Listen to them rationalize, listen to them pussyfoot, listen to them tiptoe and hide and evade and duck out from under the burden history has put upon them! Listen to them howl down dissent! It is all they can do in a crisis, Mr. Speaker. It is all they have left. . . .

"Mr. Speaker," he said when the uproar had ended as suddenly as it began, as though someone somewhere had turned a switch, "I will not proceed further with this, because it is obvious the House has made up its mind. But I will say this: I was Speaker of this House for more than a decade. I have but lately been the President of the United States. I say to you most solemnly that unless the policies of the new President are reversed, unless he moves drastically and at once to restore America's position in the world, then this Republic is lost and all our liberties will very rapidly be lost with it. And once this process has begun," he said into the skeptical and mocking laughter that greeted this most time-worn and hysterical cliché of America's doom-saying conservatives, "it will proceed far more swiftly, my scornful, all-knowing and self-confident ones, than you can possibly imagine. . . .

"President Jason at this hour is a confused, uncertain and desperately frightened man. He has been handed the worst challenge any new President has ever been handed. He needs a powerful Congress behind him. Not a Congress bemused and knocked off base like he is, but a tough-minded Congress that will help to push him in the way he has got to go to save the country.

"If anybody has any doubt that I would provide tough leadership for a tough House," he said, with a little smile and a brief return of something of his accustomed wry humor, "he hasn't followed my career. . . .

"This is a fundamental decision you are going to make here this afternoon, I say to the House. This time, I think, God has stopped being patient with America. This time we aren't going to have the luxury of being able to take our own sweet time to reverse mistaken decisions. This time it's now or never."

And raking galleries and floor with a last grim, challenging, unyielding look, he sat down amid the frantic applause of what an experienced ear told him was well under half the members of the House.

And of course, Jawbone Swarthman thought as he jumped to his feet and strode down the aisle to the lectern on a wave of warm, appreciative, enthusiastic applause that drowned out Bill's meager claque, uniting floor and galleries in a bond of welcoming brotherhood, how could it be otherwise? What made Bill think he could swing the House, particularly this new Ted Jason House, with that kind of antiquated, outworn, demagogic oratory? Bill, Jawbone realized with a sudden thrill, was all through—finished—*kaput*—out to pasture at last. And who should be waiting right here to take over but happy, excited, progressive, forward-lookin', peace-lovin' ole Jawbone hisse'f?

Never, in all the months since he had reached the difficult decision that he would stay in the House instead of seeking the empty Senate seat of the late Seabright B. Cooley, had Jawbone been so absolutely certain that his decision had been right. Seab and a lot of other folks had always considered Jawbone something of a fool even if he did have a mind certified by Duke and Phi Beta Kappa to be bright as a pin. But he bet ole Seab wasn't laughin' at him from the grave right now, any more than ole Bill was laughin' at him from the front row, there. Be-

cause Jawbone Swarthman had what it takes: he had the backing of
the President. And that meant that Jawbone Swarthman, sure as God
made little green apples and brand-new coattail-ridin' freshmen
Congressmen, was about to become Speaker of the United States
House of Representatives. There wasn't any way to stop him now. Not
no way, nohow.

Secure and elated in this knowledge, he stood for a moment beaming
and smiling as he leaned an arm comfortably on the lectern, surveying
the House. He could see ole Bill lookin' grim in front, and 'way toward
the back he could see that young smart-aleck Hal Knox lookin' dismayed, and there were quite a few others he remembered from past
battles who had looked down on Jawbone Swarthman but weren't
lookin' so superior now. This was his day and everybody knew it. But
if they expected him to act the buffoon for them this time, they were
downright mistaken. He knew that Bill, sensing his own defeat, was
playing for a constituency far beyond the confines of this chamber. It
was up to Jawbone, as the President's man in the House, to play to
the counterconstituency—the one which even now, although uncertain
and frightened by the shattering events of the past twenty-four hours,
was still desperately anxious to believe in, trust and follow Edward M.
Jason. Jawbone's task was one of reassurance. He intended to discharge
it so that the President would know he had made no mistake when
he sent the letter that made certain Jawbone's imminent victory.

"Mr. Acting Speaker, sir," he began gravely, deliberately making his
approach somewhat less cornpone than usual, "I'm sure everybody in
this House loves and respects our former President and former
Speaker—" there was a skeptical titter from somewhere in the back but
he frowned and repeated firmly, "yes, sir, loves and respects our former
President and former Speaker. And that's why, Mr. Speaker, all of us
here who have admired and followed him all these years can only feel
sad, yes, sir, downright sad, when we hear him say the sort of things
he has just said here today."

From the general area of the titter there came a spurt of approving
applause, quickly joined by the galleries. Jawbone let his tone become
more stern.

"Yes, sir, Mr. Speaker," he said reprovingly, "downright sad and upset and per—turbed, that's what we are. We just don't see how any man
who has held the highest office in the gift of this House, plus the highest office in the gift of this people—even though, Mr. Speaker, he of
course didn't get it as the gift of the people, like some have done, most
recently our great new President, Edward M. Jason, he just got it
in the line of succession—" this time the applause came as he wanted

it to, quick, loud and spontaneous—"anyway, Mr. Speaker, we just don't see how any man who has held these offices can be so pinchin' and minchin' and yes, Mr. Speaker, downright sub—versive to the President of the United States. We just don't see, Mr. Speaker.

"Now, Mr. Speaker!" he cried with a sudden indignation, banging his hand sharply on the lectern while the ex-President studied him with a cold and ironic regard that didn't faze him the least little bit, he told himself, not the least little bit, "what is he tryin' to do to our great President? He's tryin', and I say deliberately tryin', to weaken public faith and confidence in the President, that's what he's doin'. And I say it's vicious, Mr. Speaker, right down vicious!

"What's he sayin' to us here? Why, he says, he stayed with the President until four o'clock this morning, and how does he describe him to us? Why, he says he's 'a confused, uncertain and desperately frightened man.' Yes, sir," he cried as the dutiful boos began, "that's what he says about our great President and I wrote it right down so I'd have it straight—'a confused, uncertain and desperately frightened man.' What a thing to say, Mr. Speaker! For shame, now, what a thing to say!

"Supposin' it were true, Mr. Speaker and I deny 100 per cent that it is, but just supposin' it were—is *that* how to comfort and encourage the country, Mr. Speaker? Is *that* how to keep us calm when we got such big things worryin' us as we got right this very minute, right out there 'beyond our doors,' as he puts it? Is *that* how to make us feel better and help us along, by tearin' down our great President and tryin' to picture him to the American people as some sort of weaklin', Mr. Speaker, some sort of scaredy cat? *That's* helpin' America? For shame, I say again, *for—shame!*

"He wasn't the only one who was with the President until four o'clock, I'll say to this House. Some of the rest of us were, too. *I* was there, Mr. Speaker! And I see another who was, too. The new Representative from the Third District of Illinois, that fine young man who is the son of his late great daddy, Mr. Harold H. Knox. No, *wait* a minute, now!" he exclaimed hastily as booing began. "*Wait* a minute, now, I want him to corroborate me in something here!" Obediently the booing stopped and a little tentative applause began. "I say to Congressman Knox, isn't it true, now, that our great President was perfectly calm and perfectly steady this morning? Wasn't he in complete command of everything, now? Your daddy wouldn't lie about something like that and I don't think you will, either! Isn't that true about our President? I yield to the gentleman to tell me if I'm not tellin' the truth to the House!"

Hal looked white, tense and upset as he got to his feet and came forward a couple of paces to the nearest microphone. But he spoke in a steady and straightforward voice.

"He impressed me at first as an extremely agitated man," he said, and at once the hypersensitive booing began. His head came up sharply and a cold anger came into his tone. "Damn you," he said flatly, "let me finish! . . . So were we all, Mr. Speaker—all agitated. Later, when he began to outline his plans for the message he has just sent to Moscow, it seemed to me that he became much calmer, almost serene. I do not know why," he said dryly, "but that was my impression. Extremely agitated first—calmer later. Whether this was bravado or will power or real conviction, I have no way of knowing. Nor do I have any way of knowing how he really felt underneath. President Abbott has known him longer and more intimately than I have. He may be the better judge."

Again the booing came, puzzled, uncertain, annoyed at his lukewarm comment, as he smiled a quick, humorless smile and returned to his seat.

"Very well, then, Mr. Speaker," Jawbone cried indignantly, "if that is the best the gentleman can do for our great President, I thank him and wish him well for being so ungracious. I guess I have to ask you to just believe me, then, when I tell you President Jason was calm, confident, every inch the leader America elected him to be, Mr. Speaker. Yes, sir, just as calm and confident and every inch a leader as anyone could possibly wish! Do you believe me when I say that," he demanded with an abrupt harshness, "or am I lyin' to you?"

"NO!" roared House and galleries.

"You do believe me then, that he's our calm and confident leader?"

"YES!"

"All right, then!" he said with an indignant satisfaction. "All right, then! . . . Now, Mr. Speaker, let me dispose of a couple of other things our beloved ex-Speaker and ex-President is tryin' to do here, and then I'm through and we can vote on him or me, Mr. Speaker—him or me.

"He says the President has failed already, Mr. Speaker, failed in the things he set out to do in his inaugural yesterday, and goin' to fail in his message to the Soviet Union today. Well, has he failed? And is he goin' to fail? Let's see about that for a minute, members of the House, let's just see about that.

"Just because they's a little group in Moscow doesn't want peace and friendship with the U-nited States, does that mean Edward M. Jason is any less a fine and worthy man who wants to save the world from war and bring it peace, Mr. Speaker? Does that mean he's any less to be admired for tryin' to save mankind from all these horrors we've been sufferin' through in recent years? Do you condemn *him* for what *they* did? How can you be so unfair, Mr. Speaker? *How can you treat this great man like that?*

"Now, then, I grant you he's received a little setback, Mr. Speaker. They's a good-sized monkey wrench been thrown in by our friends in Moscow, Mr. Speaker, can't nobody deny that. But, Mr. Speaker, that's only *some* of our friends in Moscow, it isn't *all*. And it doesn't mean that if we proceed patiently and firmly and keep our goal of world peace every minute in mind, we can't come out of this in good shape with everything right side up again.

"That's all he wants to do, Mr. Speaker, just take it easy—just keep calm—just be patient and give 'em a chance to come around and work it all out. Not with *war*, Mr. Speaker, because that isn't what Edward M. Jason was elected to do—and elected by one of the biggest land-slides in history, I'll remind this House and the ex-President. He was elected to make *peace*, Mr. Speaker, and he's tryin'. *In the name of God, let's give him a chance!*"

Excited applause, shouts, whistles endorsed him. He nodded his head vigorously, shot a quick look of satisfaction at William Abbott watching somberly in the front row, and plunged on.

"The ex-President says this House should pass a resolution condemning the Soviet Union, Mr. Speaker. Talk about what was said at 4 A.M. this morning! You should have heard *him*, breathin' fire and brimstone, sendin' out ships and bombers and American *boys*, Mr. Speaker, yes, sir, *American boys!* God save this House from that sort of thing, Mr. Speaker! God give this House sense enough to keep hands off when our President is tryin' to make peace! We elected him, now let him do the job! Keep this House off his back, Mr. Speaker! That's our job! Keep this House off his back!"

Again he was endorsed and again he tossed a triumphant look at Bill Abbott, whose expression did not change.

"And finally, Mr. Speaker, what does the ex-President say when he gets a little feedback from these fine and honorable Americans sitting on this floor and in the galleries? When he finds his warlike ideas don't have the support of this body or his countrymen? Why, he gets nasty, Mr. Speaker. He doesn't believe in America's right of dissent. He calls us a mob. He says we're insane. He loses his temper and rants and raves, Mr. Speaker. I never thought I'd live to see the day," he said with a sudden sorrow, "when Bill Abbott, my old, dear friend Bill Abbott, would talk like that to his fellow Americans, Mr. Speaker. I never thought he would say such terrible things to this House which has given him so much.

"Mr. Speaker," he concluded gravely, "I expect a lot of this here today is quite confusin' to new members who have come here, elected in the first flush and idealism of their youth, elected in the traditional processes of this great democracy, elected to support a great President, only to find him attacked and degraded and have their own motivations and even their sanity questioned. I say to them: don't you be dismayed, hear? This House has a function all right, and it is a noble function and you have a noble part to play in it.

"That function is to support what may well be the greatest President we've ever had as he attempts to lead this nation and this world to peace. Don't be ashamed of that, I say to the House, and don't be afraid to do it. He's countin' on you and America's countin' on you. *Don't you let 'em down,* no matter what anybody says!"

And with one last triumphant look at William Abbott, he left the lectern and returned to his seat halfway up the aisle as House and galleries again burst into prolonged and vociferous applause. In the midst of it the ex-President got to his feet. Instantly the applause changed to a heavy, hammering chant of VOTE! VOTE! VOTE! After a moment during which he turned and stared around the chamber as though he were seeing it for the first time and was appalled by what he saw, he sat down again.

Now, in fact as well as assumption, it was Ted Jason's Congress, and it was obvious that it would support him by overwhelming majority in whatever he found necessary to do.

The thought was profoundly heartening at this moment, late in the evening of his first full day in office. He was busy with many things, for the machinery of the United States Government ground on in a thousand areas large and small, whatever outside crises might impend. But basically he was doing just one thing as he sat alone in the Oval Office going over studies, reports, proposals, problems: he was waiting for Moscow to reply to his message.

And the clock had dragged slowly on from 9 P.M. . . . to 10 P.M. . . . to 11—and there was no reply.

Nor, as the intelligence reports coming steadily up to him from the Situation Room indicated, was there any diminution in the harassment of withdrawing American troops in Gorotoland and Panama, or the steady outflow of Soviet naval and air power through all the arteries of the queasy globe.

But he would not—could not—permit himself to yield to the dismay these facts might otherwise induce. Nor, indeed, did he really feel any particular dismay. He was convinced that his interpretation was correct, that Tashikov, aided by his message, was in process of gaining the upper hand over hawks and war lovers in Moscow just as he had gained the upper hand over them in Washington, and that he would receive in due course a message as conciliatory and constructive as his own.

This was what he believed. It was, in fact, what he had to believe. To believe anything else would be to open abysses he could simply not afford, as man or President, to acknowledge or look into.

In this position he was mightily and comfortingly confirmed by the actions taken during the afternoon in Senate and House. Had not the Congress repudiated with crushing finality the two men who symbolized and represented, not only in Congress but in the nation, his principal opposition? Did not Bob Munson and particularly William Abbott speak for the war party? And had not the representatives of the American people in Congress assembled, acting under the national mandate delivered two months ago at the polls, flatly and completely rejected everything they stood for?

The votes had come on Senator Munson and Congressman Abbott but the man at issue, of course, was Ted Jason. The free Congress of a free people had told him with overwhelming enthusiasm that he was right. Right to do what he had done yesterday in his inaugural, right to do what he had done this morning in his message to Moscow.

Events of the past twenty-four hours had not shaken his hold on the country: he was secure.

Now the question arose, secure to do what? And the only answer possible came back: exactly what he was doing. He had offered the Communists not a sword but conciliation; he was confident they would respond in kind; and now he had only to wait, in the certainty that he had the full support of all the elements in his country that a President had to have to move forward in the direction he wanted to go.

He was pleased to realize, as one more earnest young military aide knocked discreetly, hurried in to leave his burden of reports from the Situation Room, and as discreetly departed, that there was no doubt he had the support of the media. Walter Dobius and friends, Frankly Unctuous and pals, had recovered with gleeful rapidity from their first bedazzled astonishment. Walter, the New York *Times* and the Washington *Post*, had rushed advance copies of tomorrow's comments and editorials to his desk; and during dinner, which he had eaten with the family on trays in the solarium, he had made it a point to watch

Frankly and his colleagues of the little screen. Nothing could be more flattering or encouraging than the praise he was receiving from every side.

"We do not remember," the *Times* would say tomorrow morning, "a President who has responded with greater courage or more farsighted statesmanship to the difficult challenges which confront him than has Edward M. Jason in these first difficult hours of his Presidency. He has given the world an example of leadership so powerful in its application and so moving in its implications that we think he has already moved into the ranks of America's greatest Chief Executives.

"Faced with an erratic and inexplicable—except as a possible Byzantine captivity of Chairman Tashikov explains it—démarche by the radical military elements of the Soviet Union, he has resisted the advice of the most bloodthirsty—Senator Munson and ex-President, now Representative, William Abbott. He has not wasted time on recriminations, rantings or revenge. He has moved swiftly and sure-footedly to remove the threat to peace, ease tensions and open the door to a genuine conciliation with the peace-loving elements in the Communist leadership.

"We applaud him for his statesmanship, his courage, his integrity and his calm and fearless dedication to world peace. . . ."

The *Post* was equally triumphant—not quite so high-flown but getting at what, in its editorial board's opinion, was the guts of it:

"Edward M. Jason with a sure-footed mastery has moved to consolidate his control of the American Republic so that he may lead it in the ways of peace. There is no question about it now: he is the boss and whatever he decides will be done. We could not applaud more heartily than we do the events of the past twenty-four hours which have established him as both the world's greatest peacemaker and the nation's most responsible leader.

"Momentarily—but only momentarily we believe—he has received what appears to be a slight setback at the hands of what is apparently a military clique in Moscow as rabid and stupid as our own. To it he has responded with calmness, with courage, with farseeing statesmanship and Christian good will. We await as confidently as he does the response which will, we know, tell us he is on the right road to the great goal of world peace.

"And we congratulate him a thousandfold on his defeat of its enemies.

"Be it known to all the fainthearted, the reactionary and the subverters of peace: Edward M. Jason is in charge. It would be wise of them to acknowledge the fact. . . ."

Walter Dobius' summation was as flattering and encouraging as Frankly Unctuous' final words:

"Edward M. Jason," Walter said, "having made a great gesture and received an unworthy rebuff, has responded in the tradition of history's greatest peacemakers. The nation waits—the world waits—for an answer from Moscow that will be worthy of his own integrity and courage. The world must have such an answer, for any other kind would be absolutely unthinkable.

"President Jason has shown the way to peace. A noble Congress and a united people stand behind him, inspired by his shining example. Not in all her history, perhaps, has America been blessed with a leader of such integrity, such courage, such statesmanship. He must not fail— he cannot fail—he will not fail, else there is no God in heaven, and no hope for the just."

And Frankly, gravely concluding that portion of the evening news roundup that viewers were officially told was "Opinion," proved equally encouraging.

"Thus," he said, "Washington waits, tonight. But it waits in the calm certainty that it has in the White House a statesman and leader of far-seeing vision and far-ranging hopes. Briefly, perhaps, those hopes may have received a temporary setback. But in the march of mankind toward universal peace, he knows, as most Americans know, that the setback is infinitesimal, the goal of peace almighty. Confidently he waits for the accommodating answer which must come. Confidently this capital and his nation wait with him. Rarely have man, moment, the fate of America and the fate of the world been so surely met. Rarely has there been reason for greater optimism that all will in due course come right. . . ."

And just now one more ubiquitous young man had approached the President's desk, this time carrying advance copies of *Time* and *Newsweek.* Ted's head, handsome, distinguished, confident, steady, appeared on the cover of both. Across the corner of *Time* a slanting double banner: PRESIDENT EDWARD M. JASON . . . THE SPEECH THAT INSPIRED THE WORLD; across the corner of *Newsweek:* EDWARD MONTOYA JASON . . . THE GREAT LEAP TOWARD PEACE—neither magazine, of course, having had time to receive the Russian response, but both devoting many pages to the inaugural and the thrilling decisions that would, in the unqualified opinion of their editorial boards, open the gates to the Promised Land and let all God's chillun in.

Add to that the letters, telephone calls and telegrams that had already brought the mail room and the switchboard to a stop with their eager messages, running approximately 10 to 1 in his favor, and he had every reason to feel loved, endorsed, supported.

Everything, in this late hour in the Oval Office, combined to confirm in the mind of the President of the United States the conviction that all would, as Frankly had said, come right. How could it, indeed, be otherwise? His decisions had been inspired by sincerity, idealism and good will. Therefore they simply *had* to bring good, because God *was* good and He *recognized* goodness, and therefore He would not abandon America, which was so good, or her President, who was so good.

It was almost midnight, just as he was on the point of calling it a day and turning in to get some badly needed sleep, when there finally came the knock on the door that he had been waiting for, and with it the realization that the President of the United States and his perennially hopeful country had once again overlooked the one thing they never quite understand and never quite dare acknowledge to themselves: the endless and unrelenting malevolence of those who, unlike Deity, wish them ill.

Once again the hand of the Secretary of State thrust a paper beneath his eyes. Once again euphoria crumbled, certainty died, confidence fled.

MOSCOW REJECTS U.S. NOTE, DEMANDS "IMMEDIATE CONFERENCE OR DEVASTATING CONSEQUENCES." RECOGNIZES NEW GOVERNMENTS IN GOROTOLAND AND PANAMA. ANNOUNCES SOVIET UNION TO ACT AS "CUSTODIAN" OF AMERICANS TAKEN IN BOTH COUNTRIES, SAYS "HUNDREDS" OF PRISONERS ALREADY BEING AIRLIFTED TO CAMPS IN UKRAINE.

REDS MINE BERING STRAITS AND AREAS OFF ALASKA "TO PREVENT IMPERIALIST WARLIKE ACTS IN CONTIGUOUS WATERS OF THE SOVIET UNION." WILL "CONTINUE TO SINK ALL VESSELS WHICH INTERFERE WITH INTERNATIONAL SHIPPING."

UNITED NATIONS SECURITY COUNCIL SETS EMERGENCY MEET FOR 10 A.M.

ANTI-JASON PROTESTS ERUPT IN LOS ANGELES, CHICAGO, MIAMI. NAWAC BATTLES DEMONSTRATORS IN BLOODY CLASHES.

WHITE HOUSE SILENT.

White House silent and President silent, as he wandered, with an air his frightened but admiring aides took to be casual and untroubled, across the Rose Garden to the Mansion shortly before 1 A.M. His face had appeared impassive, his manner calm, when he had bade them good night. Nothing in his brief conference with Bob Leffingwell, Ewan MacDonald MacDonald and the hastily summoned Chiefs of Staff had disclosed any undue agitation or any noticeable diminution of purpose.

To the agitated counsel of the Chiefs of Staff, supported by a nervous Secretary of Defense MacDonald, that he ask Congress to declare war immediately, he had simply said the one word *"No!"* in such a terrible tone that none of them had dared repeat the suggestion. To Bob Leffingwell's alternative plea that he at least authorize an all-out fight for world opinion in the United Nations and launch it with an address to the nation, he had been more amenable.

"I think," he said, looking tired and a little pale but otherwise resolute, "that we'll take it one step at a time, first the UN and then, if necessary, the talk. Who do we have at the UN now?"

"President Abbott," Bob Leffingwell said hesitantly, "had Lafe Smith and Cullee Hamilton. If I might suggest, it might be best to keep them on, because they have the experience—"

"I doubt if they're loyalists," the President interrupted, using a rather odd term that he hadn't intended, really, but which just came out. He smiled grimly. "In fact, you and I know they disagree with me 100 per cent. I need loyalty, in this situation. Wake up the Vice President and George Wattersill and tell them they're to be in this office at 7 A.M. and in the Security Council at 10. And call the secretary of the delegation, whoever he is, and tell him to have all the necessary position papers ready for them when they get there. All right?"

"Yes, sir," Bob Leffingwell said. "Do you want me here at seven, or—?"

"Certainly," the President said. The briefest of smiles crossed his face. "I don't intend you to be a bypassed Secretary of State. Unless you'd rather."

"No," Bob Leffingwell said. "I'd rather be here, thank you."

"Good," the President said. "Then I guess that does it for now. Unless you have something more, Ewan? Gentlemen?"

And when the Secretary of Defense and the greatly worried but still deferential Chiefs responded with dutiful if uneasy disclaimers, he said, "Well, then, let's all go home and get some sleep. We're going to need it."

With their rueful agreement the hasty little conference ended, leaving him approximately seven hours until 7 A.M. to decide what he would do, prepare his instructions for the Security Council, begin thinking about the talk he would inevitably have to make to the nation sometime in the next forty-eight hours, and get some sleep.

Get some sleep: that was probably the most important for the moment, but as he entered the silent Mansion, speaking quietly to the guards on duty at this lonely hour, he did not know how soon this would come, even with the pills the White House physician had given him earlier in the evening.

He had intended to go straight up to bed, but as he paused for a moment after receiving the guards' greeting—hushed, respectful, somehow curiously tender and protective—a pull he had felt all day but had been unable in the midst of turmoil to answer, drew him along the great central hall to the portraits of his wife and grandmother, side by side facing the doors to the North Portico.

He stood looking up at them and for the first time a desolation of soul so great that he felt he must actually stagger beneath its weight surged out of the events of the past thirty-six hours and savaged his heart.

Ceil! he thought, crying to her desperately inside like a little child. *Oh, Ceil, what shall I do?*

And turning, half-blinded by emotion, to Doña Valuela, impassive and indomitable alongside, *Grandmother! Help me! Counsel me, counsel me!*

Neither responded, not Ceil in her perfect, shining beauty nor Doña Valuela in her fierce and hooded courage, and for a moment it seemed he must actually cry aloud in the silence of the vast corridor where so many of history's mighty had passed in different times, and where now only the silent guards, deeply troubled, watched him from their posts.

As he stood thus, paralyzed by emotion, he became aware that someone was approaching from his right. He turned to see the present-day Valuela. He could tell from long experience that she had consumed her usual quota for the evening, but he knew instinctively that if there was any help to be had from his living family, it would come from her, who was, in her rather offbeat and raffish way, as tough an old bird as her mother.

"Ah, Teddy," she said softly, placing a hand on his arm as she, too, looked up at the portraits on the wall. "I grieve for you, dear heart. It all began so wonderfully, didn't it, and already it's come to this. *But,*" she said, and a firmness came into her voice and into her grip, "here it is and it's your job to meet it, and us Jason gals all expect you to do it." She shot him a sudden keen look from under her tall red wig. "O.K.,

Mr. President? You aren't going to let Ceil and the old lady and me down, are you?"

For a moment he stared at her almost as though he did not see her. Then his face softened, he smiled and placed a hand over hers.

"Dear old Val," he said quietly. "No, I'm not. . . . I don't quite know how it's going to happen, yet, but—somehow—it's going to work out."

"Good," she said. "I'm sure of it. Want a nightcap before you turn in?"

"A very little one," he said, sounding more cheerful than he had since the inaugural ball, taking her arm and walking her toward the elevator to the solarium. "I've got to have a clear head in the morning. But don't let that stop *you.*"

"When did it ever?" she demanded and chuckled, and so did he, their amusement echoing lightly and encouragingly through the cavernous hall.

The guards silently watched them go, nodding gravely to one another, feeling better.

2. UP AND DOWN the East River patient tugs and barges passed. Gulls swooped low over the grimy swift-flowing water. January's bleak sun tried halfheartedly to find a way through the sullen overcast, as delegates and staff members, coated and muffered against the freezing wind, hurried into the gleaming glass shaft of the Secretariat and the crouching hulk of the General Assembly. It was a cold, gray, impersonal day in New York. Inside the plush and overheated headquarters of the United Nations fear and relish suffused the agitated air.

Fear on the part of those who still looked to American strength as a necessary balance in the world.

Relish on the part of those whose purpose for many years had been the permanent destruction of that necessary balance.

The fearful and the relishing were agreed: if the time had come for the balance to be knocked permanently askew, this would be the day.

Standing thoughtfully for a moment in the door of the Main Delegates Lounge shortly before 10 A.M., the British Ambassador, Lord Claude Maudulayne, surveyed the long, buzzing room with a speculative concern that was not lost upon many of his colleagues. Two in particular, the Indian Ambassador, Krishna Khaleel, and the French Ambassador, Raoul Barre, noting his rather gloomy aspect, detached themselves from their coffee companions and came toward him through the colorful crowd. Krishna Khaleel, Lord Maudulayne noted sourly, had been deep in a confidential chat with the Ambassador of the People's Republic of China. Raoul Barre had been chummily hob-nobbing with the new Soviet Ambassador, Nikolai Zworkyan. He could not resist a dig when they had found a table together in a relatively secluded spot beside one of the great windows.

"Well, gentlemen, I see your alliances are in good shape. Are you all going to vote together today?"

"I," Krishna Khaleel announced with dignity, "shall vote according to the best decisions of my government, Claude. You know that."

"I, too," Raoul Barre said, staring quizzically at a group of East Africans going by in gorgeous robes and voluble clacking conversation. "The outlook is not favorable for our friends in Washington. I assume you will support them as usual, however."

"Not 'as usual,'" Lord Maudulayne said mildly. "As common sense and survival require, I should say."

"I do not see that," Krishna Khaleel said, somewhat stiffly.

"I do," Raoul Barre remarked. "That does not mean it will control the vote of France, however."

"How can it not?" Lord Maudulayne demanded with a gloomy though unsurprised disbelief. "Something must be done to save this President."

"It will not be," the French Ambassador said flatly. "Anyway, what good are votes here? Never very important—now, even less so. The deed is done, only the coup de grace remains. It is immaterial what happens here or anywhere except where American power meets Russian. And this President does not want them to meet. Oh, he will talk, he will meet that way. But to meet strength with strength—no, he prefers to run away, this President. Ergo—" He shrugged. "There will be no real meeting and therefore no turning back and therefore no stopping the Russians. It is already history, it is inevitable. The script was written many years ago when the Americans grew tired and lost their nerve. The only difference today is that now, at last, they are being forced to admit it. All that is left them to determine is the style with which they will do so. That, I think, is their only option."

"And where does that leave the rest of us?" Lord Maudulayne inquired with some asperity, "assuming your gloomy scenario is correct? If the linchpin is really gone, what of us?"

"Adapt or die," Raoul Barre said with a sort of bleak indifference. "I do not think this is pleasant or nice, you understand. But it may be advisable."

"Not for India," Krishna Khaleel said stoutly. "India has her own road to follow, I will say, gentlemen, her own responsibility to world peace. India will not adapt to anything that does not further world peace."

"Except as it affects Pakistan and Kashmir, K.K.," Lord Maudulayne could not resist. "Always excepting those."

"I am speaking in terms of centuries," the Indian Ambassador said with dignity, "not of passing episodes in which India is right."

"Yes," Lord Maudulayne said. "But the issue at the moment is not whether or not India is right, but whether, if the American counterweight is gone, anything can stop a Russian conquest of us all. What, really, will stand between? I think there is no doubt of the answer: nothing. Nothing at all."

"India," Krishna Khaleel said blandly, "is not afraid. India has been India for a very long time, I think, and she will continue to be, for a very long time on. We do not think the Russians can conquer us. We have absorbed and ejected conquerors before, after all, Claude."

"Yes," Lord Maudulayne agreed with equal blandness, "when they were willing to go. You may not find this the case with our friends in Moscow."

"We are not afraid," the Indian Ambassador repeated firmly.

"We are," the French Ambassador said, "but we do not see, at the moment, what can be done about it as long as our American friends will not stand firm. That is our problem, and it frightens us more than the Russians do. They are besotted with the word 'peace,' the Americans. They do not realize that in all of human history peace has never really existed: there has only been an occasional uneasy absence of war. The fact does not fit comfortably with the clichés of the President and his people. To acknowledge it is too difficult and too demanding. Clichés are more comfortable. Americans want comfort above all things. Ergo," he said again with a shrug, "ergo, history proceeds."

"Toward what?" Lord Maudulayne inquired somberly, more to himself than to them.

"The New Day," Raoul Barre responded with a sardonic distaste. "For us all . . ." He paused and looked with interest down the long room to the entry. "There is a spokesman of the Old Day." He raised an arm and waved. Lafe Smith nodded, waved back and started toward them through the hands suddenly outthrust to grasp his.

"One would almost think they were glad to see me," he said as he reached them, "if one didn't know better. Claude—K.K.—Raoul—how are you? Nothing changes at the UN, I see. Except the American delegation."

"You aren't still on it, are you, old boy?" Lord Maudulayne inquired delicately. "I mean—I don't know what President Jason may have in mind, but—"

"He doesn't have *me* in mind, that's for sure," Lafe said, pulling up a chair. "No, the staff stays about the same, and most of the delegation. The principal changes are those announced at the White House this morning. Cullee and I are out, permanently, and the Vice President and Georgie Wattersill are in, for this special session. He was decent enough to call and explain to both of us before the news was released. Nothing personal, he said, and I believe him: just the need for spokesmen who were completely in accord with what he is trying to do."

"Which is what?" Raoul Barre inquired dryly. "Relegate the United States overnight to a second-class power?"

Lafe made a grimace of disgust and frustration.

"I wouldn't know quite how to describe it."

"Well," Krishna Khaleel said stoutly, "*I* would. I think it is the most noble, the most generous, the most statesmanlike and humanly *decent* policy any President of the United States has tried to follow, at least in my time in Washington and at the UN. To us he seems a spirit of true nobility and grandeur. We think, if you will forgive me, dear Lafe, that he is infinitely better, from the world's standpoint, than the last two Presidents. That is *our* opinion. I know yours differs."

"Fundamentally," Lafe said with a moody scowl. "But, then," he said, more lightly, "don't you and I always disagree on things, K.K.? It's endemic."

"What really happened in Congress yesterday?" Raoul asked. "Was it genuine support for President Jason, a personal rebellion against President Abbott, a protest of youthful members, a general malaise—?"

Lafe shrugged.

"Very simple and exactly what it seemed. His landslide overawed them, a great many of them owe their election to it, and, let's face it, a great many of them sincerely and genuinely believe in what he is trying to do. You and Claude and I may think he's relegating the United States to a second-rate power so fast it makes the head swim but a lot of people still don't see it that way. Even with things as they are. My God!" he exclaimed with a sudden savage despair that turned the heads of two Israelis, four Papuans and the Ambassador of the Maldives, sitting nearby. "At *this moment* those bastards are raking in American prisoners, choking off Alaska, taking up war stations everywhere around the globe and demanding that Ted Jason crawl to Moscow. And there he sits issuing pious statements and indulging futile hopes. And a majority of the Congress and the country still supports him 100 per cent. It's unbelievable . . . or it would be," he concluded somberly, "if three decades of constantly being torn down and weakened by our own people hadn't laid the groundwork for it. That's where they've caught us. A lot of awfully shrewd minds have been doing their work for them for an awfully long time. Now it's paying off."

"Oh, come, Lafe!" Krishna Khaleel said with a sudden uncharacteristic asperity. "Surely you are not going to give us that old chestnut about Communist conspiracy, again!"

"Oh, no," Lafe said. "There's been some all right, but basically it's a lot simpler than that, K.K. Basically it's been a conspiracy of intellectual bias, arrogance and stupidity conducted by a bunch of closed minds who think they're so superior that they can tell everybody else what's good for them. It has not been good for them, in my estimation. It has brought us to where we are now, which is one hell of a place to be."

"Possibly something can be worked out here," the Indian Ambassador suggested. "I do not think it is entirely gloomy, not by any means. I believe the Russians will be willing to compromise now that they know the United States is not going to indulge in any warlike gestures."

"Now they know the *United States* is not going to indulge in warlike gestures!" Lafe began with a frustrated loudness, but then abandoned it abruptly with a wondering shake of the head. "K.K., *you're* unbelievable."

"But I have much company," the Indian Ambassador pointed out with some smugness. "Much, *much* company."

"Yes," Lafe agreed, "and you'll all have to live with what's left after we're gone."

"After you're gone!" K.K. echoed with a tinkling laugh. "Dear Lafe, how dramatic. The United States is not going anywhere but right where it is. How absurd to think otherwise!"

"Some do," Lord Maudulayne observed with a certain bleakness.

"They have so little faith in mankind's goodness," Krishna Khaleel said comfortably. "So little faith!"

"Yes," Lord Maudulayne agreed dryly. He turned to Lafe with an ironic wink. "What brings you here today, anyway? Sentiment, old times' sake, spying on the new delegation—?"

"I think my country should have *some* mourners who understand her terminal condition," Lafe said dourly. Then he shifted in his chair and smiled in a more relaxed way. "No, seriously, I'm on my way up the Hudson to Oak Lawn to get Jimmy Fry and bring him down to Washington. It seemed only natural to stop in for a bit."

"How is he?" Raoul Barre asked with the sympathy they all felt for the plight of the son of the late U.S. delegate, Senator Harold Fry of West Virginia. The boy was locked in some mental world of his own that no one yet had been able to unlock.

"The same," Lafe said, his eyes unhappy as he thought of the legacy Hal had entrusted to him just before his death—the handsome youth, pleasant and smiling and so far unreachable. "The doctors think that getting him down to Washington and having him closer to me will be a help."

"The doctors think or you think?" Claude Maudulayne inquired, and Lafe responded with a little smile.

"*I* think and *then* the doctors think. Also, Mabel thinks so too. She agrees, and since she's willing—well, there's no reason why we shouldn't go ahead, since they don't think it could possibly do any harm and might conceivably do some good."

"How is Mabel?" Krishna Khaleel inquired. "Is she coming back to Washington, then?"

"I told her during the campaign," Lafe said, "that after I had won re-election, which I did, that I was going to buy a nice house, which I have, and that then I was going to bring her and Pidge to Washington and marry her. Which," he said, smiling again, "I am."

"Alas, what a loss to womankind!" Raoul Barre exclaimed. "They will miss you, Lafe, everywhere."

"Yes," Lafe said. "Well. They can miss, as far as I'm concerned. I've had it. I've got more important things to do, now—namely, Mabel, Pidge and Jimmy."

"He says it as though he means it," the Indian Ambassador observed with a smile. "I believe our Lafe is about to become thoroughly domesticated."

"And not a minute too soon, I gather," Lord Maudulayne said.

"Not," Lafe said with a sudden gravity that indicated that the UN's *chasseur formidable* had finally exhausted all the possibilities of his restless hunt and concluded with complete finality that there was nothing to it, "a minute too soon. . . . Say!" His expression changed abruptly, he gestured down the room, they all swung to gaze at the entrance where there was a sudden stir, a sudden hurrying forward, a noise and a babble. "Don't I see the outriders of the New Day, come to claim the triumph of justice and sweet reason?"

"How exciting!" exclaimed Krishna Khaleel. "We must go and greet them!" And leading the way, he pushed forward vigorously through the rapidly growing throng of delegates until he stood face to face with the new Vice President and Attorney General of the United States.

At first, overwhelmed by a flurry of handshakes, back thumps, arm grabs and general frenzied welcome from their fellow delegates, Roger P. Croy and George Henry Wattersill did not observe Senator Smith, standing quietly behind K.K. with the British and French ambassadors. When they did, their expressions for a moment were classics of surprise, chagrin and disapproval. Lafe studied them with a quizzical, deliberately annoying smile; and then he too stepped forward with an enthusiastic expression that exactly parodied all the white, black, brown, yellow, in-between faces around them, and held out his hand to Roger Croy.

"Mr. Vice President!" he said, while the babble stopped abruptly and everyone craned to hear. "Congratulations, and welcome to the United Nations! How much you can accomplish for our country—assuming, that is," he added dryly, "that we still share it."

For a moment he was rewarded with that rare sight, Roger P. Croy nonplussed. But, as always, it did not take the Vice President long to recover.

"I hope so," he said coolly, "but of course, if not, I daresay the Jason Administration can survive it."

There was an approving titter from the delegates nearest, and the whispered report went shushing back through the room on a little wave of laughter. The Vice President looked satisfied, Lafe impassive.

"I think we should try to continue to keep our unity," he said, "because there are many here who would be delighted to see the country split apart."

"Speak to *your* friends, Senator," Roger Croy suggested blandly. "Ours are quite united behind us."

"And intend to stay that way, too," George Wattersill remarked stoutly.

Lafe nodded gravely.

"Well, good. I'm glad. I wish you success with your endeavors here, where you will find you are not surrounded by friends of the United States."

"Lafe!" Krishna Khaleel said indignantly. "I must object to that. I must indeed object most vociferously to that! That is your impression of the United Nations because you were here for two administrations that *defied* world opinion. The distinguished Vice President and his colleague are here for an Administration that *heeds* world opinion, that *respects* world opinion, that *supports* world opinion and in return is supported by it. *That* is the difference, Lafe! That is why the United States has nothing to fear here today! That is why the United States is among friends today! That is why all will go well for the United States here today! Is it not so, my friends and fellow delegates?" he demanded, turning to search the full circle of surrounding faces, his eyes appealing, his hands outstretched. "Is it not so?"

With spontaneous cries and friendly applause they endorsed his remarks. Triumphantly he turned back to Lafe.

"You see?" he asked happily. "What has America to fear?"

"It is in that spirit," said Roger P. Croy with a gracious warmth that dismissed skeptical Senator Smith, "that we come here today."

"You see?" K.K. cried happily, while all around the delegates applauded vigorously with an eager, kindly approval. "You see?"

Wafted gently in on the wave of such generous and sincere support, the Vice President and the Attorney General took their seats at the green baize circle of the Security Council at approximately ten-fifteen. For a few minutes, while other members strolled in casually, while delegation staffs bustled about busily with their papers, and while the crowded galleries (here, as in Washington, filled with a solid and well-prepared representation from NAWAC's sturdy ranks) ogled and exclaimed at famous names and familiar faces, the new American delegates received the full attention of the media, whose insistent members wanted to know specifically what the United States intended to do in this most serious and fateful moment.

To all inquiries Roger Croy and George Wattersill returned bland smiles and unrevealing answers, except to say repeatedly that they had confidence in the fairness of the United Nations, trust in the good faith of the Soviet Union and a profound conviction that "the collective intelligence of mankind," as the Vice President put it, would see their country safely through. It was not until Australia, this month's Council president, gaveled the meeting to order at ten forty-five that their pleasant expressions and air of insistent optimism began to disappear, to be succeeded by a growing, and to many delegates somewhat comic, dismay, as they underwent a crash course in what the world nowadays was really all about.

When Australia's gavel fell, the Vice President smiled cheerfully at the Attorney General and prepared, in a comfortable and rather stately fashion, to raise a hand for recognition. Unfortunately there was no time for such a courtly gesture. The gavel's crack and the Soviet Ambassador's raucous shout for recognition were simultaneous; and after hesitating for a moment while the Americans looked at one another in obvious confusion as to what they should do, Australia reluctantly bowed to another angry shout from across the circle and said, "The delegate of the Soviet Union," in a disapproving but helpless voice.

"Mr. President of the Council," Nikolai Zworkyan said, as dark and dour as all his predecessors on the Council including Vasily Tashikov, speaking with a tumbling rush that was obviously intended to batter down all opposition, "Mr. President, the government of the U.S.S.R. rejects utterly and out of hand any attempt by the imperialist capitalist warmongers of the vicious United States regime to justify their actions against world peace in Gorotoland, Panama and the contiguous waters of the Soviet Union. The government of the U.S.S.R., being confronted with aggressive and inexcusable acts on the part of the imperialist capitalist warmongers of the United States in these areas, has taken appropriate action on behalf of the United Nations and in the best interests of all peace-loving peoples of the world to halt these inexcusable acts.

"The government of the U.S.S.R. demands that the Security Council approve this resolution, which I send to the President of the Council with a request that it be read to the Council by the Secretary-General."

"Well," Australia said uncertainly as one of the Soviet delegation staff stepped briskly around the circle to hand him the resolution, "well, I—this is rather irregular procedure, to have the resolution read without prior submission to the Council. But if no other delegation—"

His voice waited tentatively and, "*Why don't the Americans do something?*" Claude Maudulayne demanded in a fierce whisper of no one in particular. But it appeared that Roger P. Croy and George Henry Wattersill were too new at the game and too filled with innocent dreams of fair play and good will to know what to do.

"I demand that it be read, Mr. President!" Nikolai Zworkyan snapped with a contemptuous look in their direction.

"Very well," Australia said obediently. "The Secretary-General will read."

And obediently the Secretary-General, that stately, tired old man from Nigeria, did so in his beautiful, grave voice, his solemn manner and deeply impressive tones serving for a moment or two to camouflage and lend respectability to the sheer terrifying insolence of it— terrifying and insolent to the minds of the remaining friends of the United States, that is, if only right and fitting to the minds of her many enemies.

"Whereas," the S.-G. read, "the government of the United States of America has been guilty of consistent violations of world peace in the countries of Gorotoland and Panama, and in the contiguous waters of the Soviet Union; and,

"Whereas, these unprovoked aggressions and warlike acts by the government of the United States have continued for many months in direct defiance of the United Nations and its coordinate bodies, the Security Council and the General Assembly; and,

"Whereas, the United Nations and its coordinate bodies have several times attempted to restrain and terminate these aggressive and warlike acts by the government of the United States, only to be thwarted by vetoes of the government of the United States in the Security Council and open defiance of obvious overwhelming sentiment in the General Assembly; and,

"Whereas, the government of the Union of Soviet Socialist Republics, determining as a charter member of the United Nations that it must come to the aid of this body in the face of these aggressive and warlike acts by an international outlaw, has proceeded to take such necessary steps as it deems advisable to repel aggression and restore world peace in all areas threatened by the government of the United States;

"Now, therefore, the United Nations, acting through the Security Council, does approve, endorse and support the necessary steps taken by the Soviet Union to halt United States aggression against world peace, and pledges its support in all ways required to assist the Union of Soviet Socialist Republics in maintaining world peace and order in Gorotoland, Panama, the contiguous waters of the Soviet Union and all other areas of the world where peace is threatened by aggressive designs of the government of the United States; and, further,

"The United Nations approves, endorses and supports the request of the government of the U.S.S.R. that the President of the United States of America meet with it in Moscow at once to settle outstanding problems threatening the peace and stability of the world. The United Nations joins the government of the U.S.S.R. in requesting that the President of the United States of America respond affirmatively and immediately to this invitation."

When it became obvious, after a tense and silent moment, that this was the end of it, there came a sudden noisy burst of clapping and approval from the galleries and from the delegates of Ghana, Zambia, Cuba, Egypt and Chile around the table. The American representatives still seemed stunned to the point where, for the moment, neither the Vice President nor the Attorney General appeared able to answer. In the awkward little silence that followed, the Soviet Ambassador looked around triumphantly and then seized the opportunity offered.

"Vote, Mr. President!" he cried. "Vote! Vote! Vote!"

Promptly the chant filled the room, drowning out the few opposing shouts, drowning out thought:

"VOTE! VOTE! VOTE!"

For several minutes this continued, as Australia banged futilely with the gavel and some delegates, notably Lord Maudulayne, Raoul Barre, Krishna Khaleel and the delegates of Norway and Lesotho, turned to stare up with angry disapproval at the noisemakers. Presently the sound subsided and into it Australia spoke with an angry firmness.

"The Chair will advise the galleries," he said, as indignantly as though he were in Congress and with about as much effect, "that they are here as guests of the Security Council and are not to interfere with the Council's work by unseemly demonstrations. The Council must demand order and decorum in the chamber, otherwise the galleries will have to be cleared."

"Mr. President!" Nikolai Zworkyan said indignantly. "On behalf of the peace-loving peoples of the world, I object to the attempt to silence free and honest dissent. Let them express what they think of the imperialist warmongers, Mr. President! Let them express it freely!"

Into the new burst of excited and approving sound that automatically greeted this, Claude Maudulayne turned directly to the Vice President sitting beside him and in a low voice grated out, "For God's sake, man, are you going to let him have *everything* his own way?"

And finally, acting a little as though he were fighting up through water to find air, as in a way perhaps he was, Roger P. Croy at last leaned forward, raised a somewhat tentative hand and called out in a voice that eventually made itself heard through the racket, "Mr. President, the United States requests recognition. Mr. President, the United States requests recognition."

"The delegate of the United States, the distinguished Vice President," Australia said with a sigh of relief that came clearly over the loudspeakers and touched off another little wave of sardonic amusement. When it too had settled, Roger Croy grasped the microphone in front of him and began to speak with a growing firmness that brought expressions of relief from his colleagues of Britain and France, Australia, Norway and Lesotho. For the moment the other members of the Council—China, the U.S.S.R., Ghana, Cuba, Zambia, Egypt, Rumania, India and Chile—also looked impressed.

"Mr. President," Roger Croy said slowly, "the United States is not prepared to accept this kind of tactic in this Council." There was a disparaging little titter in the galleries. He shook his head with a sudden impatience, and went on. "The United States has come here today in the same spirit in which its new President and new Administration have acted since Edward M. Jason was inaugurated in Washington two days ago—the spirit of peace." This time the titter swelled into scornful laughter. "Yes!" he said angrily, and for the first time there was a note in his voice which indicated that he was at last beginning to understand what faced his country here: though he still attempted to be conciliatory, for that was his conviction as well as his commission from the President. "Yes, the spirit of peace. That is what prompted the President's most generous actions in withdrawing so much of America's military strength two days ago. That is what prompted his conciliatory and hopeful message to the Chairman of the Council of Ministers of the Soviet Union yesterday. That is what prompts our appearance here today, and the course of action we wish to propose to this body. The spirit of peace, which we assumed, perhaps in our innocence, distinguished both this body and the Chairman of the Council of Ministers of the Soviet Union.

"We still believe this, Mr. President. That is why we come here today, in peace instead of bearing arms, in response to the actions of the Soviet Union; why we hope that compromise and conciliation in the interest of all mankind will be possible here today. . . . It will not be possible," he said with a sudden crispness that for a moment gave heart to all those—and there were still a good many—who placed their hopes in America, "unless we are met with that same spirit on the part of the Soviet Union, and on the part of a majority of the members of the United Nations. We cannot do it alone, although I think all but the most deliberately prejudiced will concede that we have gone a long way toward it. . . .

"I, too, Mr. President," he said, looking squarely into the television cameras which were carrying their words and faces to the great globe's limits, "have a resolution to propose. I offer it as an amendment to the resolution of the distinguished delegate of the Soviet Union, and I ask that it too be read by the Secretary-General."

And pushing back his chair, he carried the paper himself around the circle to Australia, who received it with a nod and a rather nervous smile and handed it to the Secretary-General. When the Vice President came back around the table Nikolai Zworkyan glowered with an elaborate disdain, not bothering to pull in his chair or to acknowledge Roger P. Croy in any way as he resumed his seat.

"Whereas," the Secretary-General read gravely in his clipped West African-British accent, "the government of the Soviet Union has called the attention of the United Nations to what it believes to be aggressive actions by the United States of America—"

("Wow!" murmured the Chicago *Tribune* in the Press Gallery. "Some way of 'calling attention to'!" "Strong enough so even your stupid government can't overlook it!" the *Guardian* snapped from the row behind.)

"and,

"Whereas, the government of the United States, while rejecting as unfounded the criticism of the United States implicit in such actions by the Soviet Union, does not wish to inflame further a difficult international situation by replying with acts of a similar military nature, but instead wishes to dedicate itself to the pursuit of a genuine and lasting world peace; and,

"Whereas, the government of the United States, believing the United Nations to be the proper forum and agency for the settlement of disputes, urges the United Nations to call an international conference of all interested parties to be held under the auspices of the United Nations at a mutually agreeable time and place for the discussion and settlement of problems arising from the differing positions of the two powers; now, therefore:

"The United Nations agrees with and accepts the call of the government of the United States for a conference and directs the Secretary-General and other appropriate arms and agencies of the United Nations to begin immediate planning for such a conference to be held at a mutually agreeable place outside the respective territories of the Soviet Union and the United States at a date not later than three weeks from the date of approval of this resolution."

Again there was a silence as the Secretary-General concluded and into it Australia said hastily,

"The amendment of the United States to the resolution of the Soviet Union has been offered and read. As an amendment it automatically becomes the first order of business to be voted upon. Is there further debate, or do members wish to vote now on the resolution of the United—"

But of course this deliberately naive ploy did not work. Cuba, Egypt, Zambia, the U.K. and the U.S.S.R. all raised hands and demanded recognition. After a moment's hesitation Australia said, "The delegate of the United Kingdom."

Scornful booing came from the galleries. Lord Maudulayne turned to stare with an impassive and deliberately infuriating contempt. Then he turned back to his microphone and spoke in level and unhurried tones.

"Her Majesty's Government," he said, "wishes to state that in our opinion the position of the United States is so reasonable as to be almost suicidal. It is reasonable beyond belief. It is reasonable beyond any call of conscience or any duty to the United Nations or any duty to the goal of world peace. It is," he said flatly, as the booing began again, "so decent in impulse, so idealistic in concept and so generous in purpose that it puts to shame all those, here or elsewhere, who condemn the government of the United States with the shabby clichés of the shabby past."

Again the booing. This time he rounded on it angrily.

"What is this 'government of the United States' that my friend from the Soviet Union attacks so savagely and some here seem to be treating with such contempt? Why, it is none other than the new President of the United States, the man so many of you wanted to see in the White House, the man so many of you hailed as the world's great new leader for peace. It is Edward M. Jason, it is not Harley Hudson or William Abbott. It is the man who in his inaugural just forty-eight hours ago voluntarily laid down many of the arms of the United States as his contribution to world peace. It is the leader who did more than any single leader of any nation has ever done to prove by deeds rather than words that he believes in a decent and hopeful future for mankind.

"And what has been the result? Did the Soviet Union welcome this most generous and noble action in the spirit in which it was offered? Did it offer a similar decency, a similar idealism and a similar restraint? It did not. It moved immediately to take military advantage of it, in the most ruthless, most deceitful and, yes, most evil way imaginable. Yes!" he exclaimed into the chorus of boos that arose once more. "Most evil. Most monstrously evil. And as excuse its representative sits at this table and condemns American administrations and an 'American Government' which no longer exists, because now a new and genuinely peace-loving one sits there.

"Mr. President," he said somberly, "how far from the truth can this world get and still survive? How far can it afford to let the Soviet Union and her friends persuade it that black is white, up is down, yea is nay, evil is good? There has to be a point at which the world calls a halt and gets back to sanity. Otherwise we are indeed doomed, not only to the tender physical mercies of the Soviet Union but to the death of the free and inquiring mind—that death of the mind which a complete and unchallenged Communist hegemony has long since imposed on the great Russian nation and will impose on all of us, if it can. From that long night, Mr. President, the world would be a long time waking . . . if ever. . . .

"Mr. President, Her Majesty's Government supports the amendment of the United States of America to the resolution of the Soviet Union. Her Majesty's Government believes the President of the United States has been extraordinarily patient, decent and good. Her Majesty's Government rejects the unfounded and deliberately untrue Soviet condemnation of the United States and it will support an international conference only on the basis proposed by the United States. Her Majesty's Government will, if necessary, veto the Soviet resolution."

And he sat back, chin on hand, shrewd face unyielding, while again the galleries spewed forth their hatred, mingled with a few defiant sounds of approval. Around the table a majority of the delegates looked openly annoyed and antagonistic.

"And we," the Soviet Ambassador spat out, not bothering to seek recognition, "will veto the resolution of the United States! And so where will we be then, I ask the distinguished representative of the Government! And the U.S.S.R. standing alone to protect the world open aggression of the imperialist capitalist warmongering American government! And the U.S.S.R. standing alone to protect the world against it! So be it, Mr. President, if that is what the distinguished representative of the U.K. wants, so be it! We shall see who imposes hegemony on whom, if the American warmongers are permitted to run free!"

"I waive the right of reply, Mr. President," Lord Maudulayne said in a bored tone. "My words, I'm afraid, would be too intelligent to counter such gibberish."

"Mr. President!" Cuba said, swiveling his roly-poly little body around and twisting furiously at his drooping mustache, "Mr. President, Cuba would like to comment before the vote. Cuba, Mr. President, is a neighbor of the war-mad American oligarchs and we know from long experience how to evaluate the words and the deeds of those strange people.

"It is true we heard the words of the new President Jason two days ago. It is true we heard those fine words. We are aware of promises to withdraw troops and ships and planes, and we know that there was an apparent beginning. But, Mr. President, it was only apparent! The Soviet Union has shown Cuba, Mr. President, the intelligence reports which disclose that American withdrawals were only a pretense, that after a little gesture, a little smoke screen, they intended to stay where they were. They intended to make only a token showing, Mr. President. They intended to retreat an inch and then when the world was lulled into inaction, come back a mile. It was all a fraud, Mr. President, to catch us all off balance!"

"But that isn't true!" George Wattersill protested half-aloud in a dismayed voice. "That just isn't true!"

"Tell him, then," Claude Maudulayne demanded in an urgent whisper. "You have *got* to answer him. You *cannot* let the lie stand."

"Mr. President—" George Wattersill said obediently and not quite firmly enough. Cuba rushed on in his high, staccato tones.

"Mr. President, what do these documents prove? They prove that the words of the new President were a fraud, just as the words of the other Presidents have been. They prove that the imperialist American warmongers were simply trying to hide behind this new man who claims to be for peace. They prove that he himself is part of them, that he is a fraud, too. It was all a conspiracy, Mr. President, all a joke. Only now," he said, and a grim relish came into his snapping little eyes, "the joke is on someone else. Because of the great courage and decision of the Soviet Union, because *one* power, at least, believes in the charter of the United Nations and will come to its assistance, the fraud has been exposed and the warmongers have been driven away. They are in retreat, Mr. President! They are in retreat everywhere! Because of the fearless actions of the great peace-loving Soviet Union, the world can finally hope, Mr. President, that they are in retreat *everywhere and forever*. That is the great hope which comes to us with the fearless actions of the great Soviet Union, Mr. President.

"Now let us examine the proposal of the government of the United States, which one must confess, Mr. President, looks to be the last, desperate gasp of an outmoded imperialism trying frantically to hide its evil deeds behind a smoke screen of piety and peaceful pretense. What does the distinguished Vice President of the warmongering imperialist American regime offer?

"Why, he says the government of the United States is innocent, Mr. President! It is honest, Mr. President! It is decent and forbearing, it does not want to inflame international tensions. It wants the United Nations to pull its chestnuts out of the fire, now, it wants *us* to come to its rescue, now that the fearless Soviet Union has revealed its betrayals and stopped its sinister purposes. That is the fraud it seeks to put upon us here.

"After nearly a year, Mr. President, of defying the United Nations, of spitting on world opinion, of engaging in deliberate aggression and warlike attacks against the free peoples of Gorotoland and Panama, after compounding these crimes by adding the further crime of interfering with the free passage of shipping in the contiguous waters of the Soviet Union off Alaska, the American Government comes here and tries to tell us its hands are clean just because it has a new man in the White House.

"Do his pious words wipe out a year of betrayal and aggression, Mr. President? Yes, do they wipe out even more—all the long sad story of American aggression in Viet Nam, in Korea, and everywhere else Washington has seen fit to meddle around the world? How pious can you get, Mr. President? Not pious enough to wipe out a filthy record,

I submit. Not pious enough to make the world believe American policy has changed overnight in one great, glorious change of heart. Oh, no, Mr. President! Edward M. Jason may be a pious and well-meaning man, but he is the prisoner of his imperialist military clique, Mr. President. He mouths fine words, but the hands of America are not clean. He cannot convince us of that!

"Here, Mr. President!" he cried, suddenly holding up a sheaf of papers. "Here, *here* is the proof of what a fraud is this Pious Curtain the American Government has put up! Here is the proof of American perfidy just as Soviet intelligence has discovered it. Here—take them, pass them along, read for yourselves!" And he handed a fistful of papers to China on his right, to Egypt on his left. Each took one and passed the rest on around the table.

"Here is the proof, Mr. President," Cuba concluded, "and because of it, and because of the perfidious deeds of pious, pretending America, I submit that this Council should speedily defeat the amendment of the government of the United States and give overwhelming approval to the resolution of the U.S.S.R."

And with a satisfied shake of his head and one more furious twist on his mustache, he slumped back in his seat while the galleries and many of his fellow delegates applauded long and vigorously.

"Does anyone else wish to—" Australia asked. Again the chant of "VOTE! VOTE! VOTE!" began. It changed rapidly to booing when it was observed that the Vice President, after a hurried whispered conference with the Attorney General and the British Ambassador, was holding up his hand for recognition.

"The galleries will be silent!" Australia said indignantly, banging furiously with his gavel. Finally he was able to recognize Roger P. Croy, who looked around at the still murmurous crowd with a strangely mingled expression of supplication and anger, and began slowly to speak.

"Mr. President," he said, "my government is aghast and appalled at the attitude here today."

"You should be!" someone shouted and there was a burst of raucous amusement. The Vice President flushed angrily for a second but decided to ignore it.

"We feel to some degree that we are in the midst of an insane situation in which, as the distinguished Ambassador of the United Kingdom says, there is an attempt being made to convince the world that black is white, up is down, yea is nay and evil is good. We are, I repeat, aghast and appalled at this; and yet we still do not believe that we should reply in kind, because to do so would be to join in what seems to us a *real* betrayal of world peace. We think we should respond simply by correcting the facts for the record. We do not think we should imflame the atmosphere here further by replying with hostility to the hostile charges and hostile actions against us. We still believe that the government of the United States can best serve mankind by turning, if you please, the other cheek."

"That is too bad," Raoul Barre murmured to Egypt at his side, "because if you do, you will get slapped."

"Yes," Egypt agreed with a happy relish. "Yes, indeed."

"Mr. President," Roger Croy said, and his voice showed more strain and tiredness than he knew, "we are somewhat at a loss where to begin, so many are the falsehoods that have been hurled our way in the past hour. Yet perhaps the best place to begin is with a frank admission of past errors, which this Administration repudiates as vigorously and completely as many of you do. This Administration was not responsible for those errors in Gorotoland and Panama, nor was it responsible for errors, if errors there have been—" he paused and emphasized the next words, which caused the Soviet Ambassador to stir restlessly—"in waters contiguous to the Soviet Union. They are not, I might add, 'contiguous waters *of* the Soviet Union,' which is a wordage attempting to establish a claim to sovereignty which we do not recognize, since these are international waters."

"Good," Claude Maudulayne murmured to George Wattersill. "I wondered if you were ever going to get around to that."

"But, Mr. President," Roger Croy went on, "after acknowledging that past administrations in Washington have perhaps been guilty of certain actions which have been opposed by many members of the United Nations, and which we of the new Administration have opposed, I must insist upon the plain and simple truth that this *is* now a *new* Administration, which comes to office with a fresh page to write upon. And it does come, I will say to the distinguished delegate of Cuba, with clean hands. And it does come with generosity, candor and decency to offer a new procedure to the world in mankind's endless search for a viable peace.

"The President of the United States *is* sincere. The Vice President of the United States *is* sincere. Our Administration *is* sincere. We *do* want peace, and in the President's inaugural and in the actions he took on that occasion, as well as in his message to Chairman Tashikov yesterday and in our resolution here today, I think we have proved it to any fair-minded man.

"The United States, I submit to you, has been subjected to aggression of the worst kind by the Soviet Union—the most blatant—the most ruthless—the most unprincipled—"

But now the booing which had begun to rise through the galleries reached a crescendo that drowned him out, and for several moments he remained grim-faced and silent while a NAWAC-led chant of "FRAUD! FRAUD! FRUAD!" filled the chamber and pounded from the world's television screens. Presently it diminished and he went on.

"Yes, Mr. President," he said managing to sound relatively calm, "the most unprincipled and most inexcusable aggression. We offered peace and we were met with instantaneous armed hostility. Governments not perfect but at least reasonably stable were immediately overthrown in Gorotoland and Panama. Rebel forces backed openly by Soviet arms were immediately installed. Using the pretext of fishing disputes, which are always recurrent in the Bering Straits and always resolvable by peaceful negotiation, the Soviet Union destroyed American fishing vessels, actually landed briefly on American soil, and now has attempted to mine the waters around Alaska. Instant and complete atomic annihilation, under other circumstances and under other administrations, would perhaps have been visited upon the Soviet Union for such actions.

"With great forbearance and with a genuine devotion to peace which must be apparent to all but the most willfully self-blinded, the government of the United States did not retaliate in this fashion, though we could have. Instead, we have adopted a conciliatory posture and have placed our faith in the basic good will and honor which we believe still exist in the Soviet Union, and in the great majority of the nations and peoples throughout the world.

"Because we do feel good will and honor to exist in others as we believe they exist in us, we feel it is not necessary to waste very much time on an attempt to answer the charges made by the Cuban delegate concerning any alleged bad faith on the President's part in withdrawing American forces around the world. We note that the Cuban delegate claims he has been shown some purported intelligence document by the delegate of the Soviet Union. If there is such a document, it is a forgery. We do not believe it represents the true intention or attitude of those forces of good will and decency which we believe exist in the Soviet Government."

The Vice President paused to take a sip of water and Raoul Barre raised his hand.

"Does the distinguished delegate of the United States," he asked, "believe that the delegate of the Soviet Union is here under false pretenses? Does he think he was not appointed by his government? Does he think the delegate would present a document, even a forged document, without the specific knowledge and approval of his government? Is that the distinguished delegate's concept of how the government of the Soviet Union functions?"

For just a moment Roger P. Croy gave him a disturbed and startled look. Then a stubborn expression closed it out.

"It is the belief of my government, of the President and of myself," he said firmly, "that the action of the Soviet delegate, and the intent of those who sent him here, differs substantially from the elements desiring genuine peace with America that we believe are presently engaged in a struggle for ascendancy in the Soviet Union."

"Is that correct, I will ask the delegate of the Soviet Union?" Raoul Barre insisted blandly.

"Rubbish!" Nikolai Zworkyan snapped. "Childish rubbish!"

"That was my impression," the French Ambassador agreed. "Perhaps the delegate of the United States should concentrate on the forgery rather than on the presumed good will, or lack of it, of those who directed that it be placed before this body."

"We have said that this document is a forgery," the Vice President said stiffly. "We reiterate that statement. We must leave it to the world to judge."

"I think I might warn my friend from the United States," Raoul Barre said with a certain philosophic sadness, "that the world is judging, and quite severely, at this very moment."

"I do not know what the delegate is talking about," Roger Croy said with a sudden show of anger, "but I do know that the government of the United States comes here with clean hands, in good faith, with good will, in honor, decency and integrity, to seek a peaceful solution for the difficult situation created by the Soviet Union. I know we do not want war, we want peace. I know we have submitted a resolution to this Council which, without indulging in invidious name-calling or false and unfounded charges, seeks to establish the machinery for solving the situation and furthering the cause of peace. We cannot believe that members of the United Nations are so blind to the facts, so prejudiced in their feelings toward us, so completely willing to ignore all the evidence, so frivolous with the peace of the world which lies in their keeping, that they will support these unwarranted attacks on us and block our efforts to save the peace. *We cannot believe that*, I will say to the delegate of France."

"The distinguished delegate," Raoul Barre said with something of the same philosophic melancholy, "I am afraid does not know this body as well as some of us who have served a little longer in its unique

and ineffable atmosphere. Mr. President, if the delegate has concluded—?" and he paused and looked politely at Roger P. Croy, who
started to say something angry and then thought better of it and subsided "—and if no one else has anything to say, I would suggest
we vote."

"VOTE! VOTE! VOTE!" cried the galleries obediently, and around
the circle there were nods and gestures of agreement.

"If that is agreeable—?" Australia inquired. "Good. The question
comes on the amendment of the government of the United States to
the resolution of the government of the Soviet Union. The Secretary-
General will call the roll."

"Australia," the S.-G. said gravely.

"Yes," said Australia.

"Booooo!" said the galleries.

"Chile."

"No," said Chile.

"Hooooray!" said the galleries.

"China."

"China," said China with a bland and affable little smile, "abstains."

"Cuba."

"Cuba votes *No!*"

"Egypt."

"Egypt votes No!" said Egypt loudly.

"France."

"France votes Yes," Raoul Barre said, as blandly as China.

"Ghana."

"*No!*"

"India."

"India," said Krishna Khaleel, looking about brightly, "abstains."

"Lesotho."

"Lesotho," said its representative, an enormous chieftain of the
Sotho tribe, "votes Yes."

There was a moment of booing, quickly stilled and then renewed
as Norway was called and also voted Yes.

"Rumania."

"Rumania votes No."

"The United Kingdom."

"Yes," said Lord Maudulayne, to more expressions of distaste from
the galleries.

"The Union of Soviet Socialist Republics."

"*Nyet!*" Nikolai Zworkyan spat out, and a burst of applause, cheers
and yells approved him.

"The United States."

"Yes," said Roger P. Croy and received the expected boos.

"Zambia."

"Zambia votes NO!" shouted Zambia as a final happy cheer went up.

"The vote," said Australia, "is six Yes, seven No, two abstentions. The resolution of the United States loses because a permanent member, the Soviet Union, has voted No. It also loses by simple majority. The question now comes on the original resolution of the government of the U.S.S.R. The Secretary-General will call the roll."

"Australia."

"Australia votes No!"

Boos.

"Chile."

"Chile votes Yes!"

Cheers.

"China."

"China," said China, bland little smile unchanged, "abstains."

"Cuba."

"*SI!*"

Cheers.

"Egypt."

"Yes."

More cheers.

"France!"

"France votes No," Raoul Barre said calmly, and again the boos broke out, angry, contemptuous, disgusted.

"Ghana."

"*Yes!*"

"India!"

"India votes *Yes*," said Krishna Khaleel crisply and there was a happy roar.

"Lesotho."

"Lesotho votes NO!"

Boos.

"Norway."

"No!"

"Rumania."

"Yes!"

"The United Kingdom."

"No," Lord Maudulayne said quietly, and the disgusted sound was renewed.

"The Union of Soviet Socialist Republics."

"*DA!*" shouted Nikolai Zworkyan defiantly. The roar of approval was repeated.

"The United States."

"The United States," said George Henry Wattersill with an earnest, almost prim air of forbearance that produced astonished looks from his colleagues of Britain and France—amazed and then pleased grins from many others around the table—a delighted yelp from the galleries —"abstains."

"Zambia."

"Zambia votes YES and death to all imperialist warmongers!" Zambia cried with an exaggerated flair that brought a laughing, hand-clapping, floor-stamping roar of approval.

"The vote," said Australia quietly, "is eight Yes, five No, and two abstentions. Since two permanent members of the Security Council, France and the United Kingdom, have exercised their right of veto, the resolution of the Soviet Union is defeated. Twice defeated, in fact," he added with a small attempt at humor that fell thinly to the ground in the suddenly tense and quiet chamber. "Does the delegate of the United States seek recognition?"

"Yes," said George Wattersill earnestly, "I do, to explain the action of my government in the vote just taken. On direct orders from President Jason, in which the Vice President and I wholeheartedly concur, it has been determined that the United States under this Administration will never exercise its right of veto in the United Nations. We feel that the exercise of the veto by the United States during the past two administrations represented a fundamental weakening of the United Nations, which we regret, and we have determined that this Administration will not be party to any such further weakening."

("Christ!" said the New York *Daily News* in the Press Gallery. "How noble can you get?" "A question," agreed the New York *Times*, gesturing at a number of baffled but ironic faces around the green baize table, "which has obviously occurred to quite a few others.")

"I thank the delegate for his explanation," Australia said politely. "If there is no further business—ah! The delegate of the Soviet Union."

"Yes, Mr. President," Nikolai Zworkyan said dourly, "the delegate of the Soviet Union. The delegate of the Soviet Union wishes to announce that he is departing this chamber at once to go to the General Assembly, which I am informed is presently meeting, to introduce an identical resolution. We shall see what happens then, away from this peace-defying temple of the veto!"

"Which the delegate's country has only exercised some two hundred times," Lord Maudulayne observed acidly. The Soviet Ambassador shot him a black glance but made no reply; shrugged, picked up his papers and, trailed by his delegation and staff members, marched stolidly out of the room on a wave of frantically approving applause.

"Please," said Australia patiently for the last time, "the galleries are advised they must be in order. If there is no further business—the delegate of the United States."

"The United States," said Roger P. Croy, unable to appear anything but anticlimactic, "wishes to announce that it, too, will introduce its resolution of amendment immediately in the General Assembly."

And to a chorus of scornful hoots, he and George Wattersill and their worried delegation and staff members also arose and walked quickly, and somehow almost apologetically, from the room.

"I take it there is no further business at this time," Australia said in a relieved tone, "so the Security Council stands adjourned subject to call of the Chair."

"And what do you make of that?" Claude Maudulayne murmured as he and the French Ambassador walked slowly along in the midst of a hurrying, jostling, excitedly talking crowd of delegates and newsmen to the General Assembly.

Raoul Barre gave a tired shrug.

"I told them the world was judging, and I am afraid it has. And I am afraid it will now begin, for the sake of sheer survival, if survival there be, to make other arrangements."

"Yes," Lord Maudulayne agreed glumly, "I am afraid you may be right. Or perhaps I should say: I am afraid, period."

"Now," he said—comfortably, he hoped, not too heartily, not too anxiously—"How about that?"

But beside him, as always, the handsome boy smiled his kindly, impersonal, all-embracing smile and made no response. Not even so much as the flick of an eyelid, Lafe thought bitterly, to indicate that he was alive, was being moved, had left familiar surroundings, was going somewhere else. The sensation of being in an automobile should itself be a major new thing for him, but there was nothing . . . nothing. Poor Hal! Lafe thought. To have been given such a son, outwardly so perfect, inwardly so absent—somewhere, where no one yet had ever been able to follow.

Or hadn't they? He could still remember with an aching vividness the flickering moment when he and Cullee had come up to Oak Lawn six months ago to escape the savage contentions of the UN. The youth Hal Fry had entrusted to his care had been sitting under one of the giant old trees on the beautiful lawn that sloped down to the Hudson.

They had talked to him for a while, as usual without eliciting response, and presently had started to go. They had said goodbye cheerfully and for just a second—a thrilling second—Jimmy had seemed to respond. There had been the start—almost the start—the intimation, the hint, the barest possibility—that he had tried to say goodbye in return. They had been elated, standing there on the lawn while he returned again to his placid smiling silence. Almost, they thought—almost—he had tried to come out of it. And if he could do so once, could he not again?

So far, in the several visits Lafe had been able to make to him since, during the rising crescendo of the campaign and the busy weeks of transition, he had never again done so. The indications were that he would not do so now—or, quite possibly, ever again.

And yet it was very important to the Senator from Iowa, just as it had been important to Cullee that day, and as it was important to Mabel, and to Claude and Raoul and K.K. and to many other people. They would all be as pleased as he, he knew, if the day came when he could say to them triumphantly, "Jimmy talked today. He responded. We've broken through. We've won!"

It would be a small—a very small but in its way a very big—affirmation of life. And affirming life, Lafe thought with a somber grimness, was something that suddenly seemed overwhelmingly important, right now.

How many millions there were—how many billions—for whom life's affirmation rode uncertainly on the increasingly somber news that even now was coming over the car radio from the garish blue chamber where the races of man sat assembled in their bitterness, suspicion, anger and hate. The Soviet Union, true to its word, had taken its resolution to the General Assembly. The United States had done the same. This time Roger P. Croy had bestirred himself, been a shade more fleet-footed than Nikolai Zworkyan, introduced the American resolution first. Zworkyan had introduced his as the amendment this time. The results, it was clearly apparent as the debate raged on, were going to be no different.

Right now Tanzania had the floor, and over his clipped and savage denunciation of corrupt, imperialist America the suave tones of Frankly Unctuous, broadcast simultaneously on radio and television, put it in a perspective that to Lafe, and he surmised to many millions, was chilling. Perhaps the most chilling thing about it, he realized as he piloted the car skillfully down the Garden State Parkway, was Frankly's calm and indeed almost approving tone of voice. Many Americans, Lafe realized with a desperate heart, were relishing this day along with their enemies. Frankly for the moment, at least, appeared to be one of them.

"It is evident," he said in his smooth, rich, rolling tones, "that the vote will come very shortly on the Soviet amendment condemning the United States. It is also evident that it will be overwhelmingly approved.

"The reasons for this have been made amply clear in the day-long debate that has included nations from all parts of the globe. With very few exceptions the United States has been vigorously, even harshly condemned. The exceptions have included nations such as Greece and Spain, tied to the United States by treaty or by hope of economic or military favors. America's critics have included such notable spokesmen of the non-aligned world as India, such progressive republics as Libya, such outstanding leaders of world opinion as Chile and Indonesia. The cry, whether or not one may agree with it, has been clear and well-nigh universal: end American imperialism and restore world peace!

"In this situation," Frankly went on suavely, as in the background Tanzania concluded and the translator could be heard rendering Bulgaria's harsh gobble into English, "the efforts of the United States so far have continued to be controlled and conciliatory. Obviously there is every determination on the part of the Jason Administration to avoid direct attacks upon the Soviet Union which might foreclose talks and agreement later. In a way which might seem surprising—were not America's past record of impulsive aggression so well-known and bitterly remembered here—the United States appears to be receiving very little credit for the President's forbearance. The Jason Administration is evidently carrying the unhappy burdens of the Hudson and Abbott Administrations. This is regrettable but, apparently, inevitable. It may well be—as this American and many others sincerely believe—that in his turn-the-other-cheek approach President Jason has found exactly the method to draw the teeth of the crisis and bring about that mutually respectful and mutually constructive conference with Russia's leaders which he is seeking. But it is quite apparent that this approach will not receive the sanction or the ratification of a vote in the General Assembly, any more than it did earlier today in the Security Council. The reasons for this, resting upon the American record in the past twelvemonth, may be painful but, as Americans perhaps need to recognize and face up to, they may also be fully justified in the eyes of the world. . . ."

And obviously in yours too, you undercutting son of a bitch, Lafe thought with a savage contempt. . . . But maybe all was not so well with arrogant, intolerant old Frankly, after all. Rumors were beginning to get around Washington that Frankly and some of his very powerful colleagues of tube and newsprint had received threats during the campaign, that pressures had been attempted and had been at least partially successful—not coming, thank God, from the opponents of Ted Jason but from his "friends," so called: from NAWAC and the fascist-minded left. These hints had taken a while to surface in Washington, but ultimately most things do surface in that ingrown, gossipy climate. Now they were the subject of common—and to those who really cared for the democracy—genuinely concerned discussion.

How much of the support of Frankly and his friends for the Jason position was genuine and how much was dictated by the instinct of self-preservation, he did not know. Theoretically the media were staunch, fearless, upright, steadfast, courageous, undaunted, noble and true. Actually, confronted by a really genuine threat to themselves and their businesses—and that was the kind of threat that some astute minds had long felt to be implicit in NAWAC and the violent elements supporting Ted Jason—they were as capable of trimming to the wind as anyone. There comes a time with most men when self-preservation cancels all else; and he thought, with a certain relish he tried to keep from being too vindictive, that even for the smug know-it-alls who had for so long lectured and directed the world with their superior wisdom and slanted news, the day could come.

He hoped with a shiver that it was not here yet, because if it were, it would be one of the surest and most obvious signs that the American Republic, as it had been founded and as it had endured, was to be irrevocably changed. Ted Jason, he knew, had no such intention; the great majority of his supporters in the media had no such intention; but there were people in the world who did have such an intention, and some of them were working as busily inside America as others were working out, to bring it about.

The terrible situation that now confronted the country could very well provide the quickest and most efficient chute to hell for all the democratic traditions and still worthy—if, as always, confused—ideals of the great Republic.

He sighed and glanced quickly at Jimmy. Eyes straight ahead, apparently not even noticing the countryside racing away on either side, he smiled his gentle and embracing smile. Lucky bastard, Lafe thought with a sudden deep bitterness, lucky bastard, to be out of it. And then, of course, was deeply ashamed of himself and said aloud, "I'm sorry. I didn't mean it." And received from Jimmy nothing save the placid, mindless, heartbreaking smile.

For a moment, riding along with his silent burden at his side, the Senator from Iowa had a sudden apocalyptic vision of people all over the earth with their worries, hopes, fears, concerns, going about their business while a little band of insane men pirouetted on the top of the heap in their dance of mutual death. Right now all over the globe people were getting up or going to bed, eating or making love, being born or dying, getting ready to go to the store, talking to their neighbors, waiting in hospitals worrying about their loved ones, vacationing at the beach, climbing mountains, working in the office, building dams, cutting down timber, stopping for a hamburger and milk shake, driving down the street, gossiping with friends, sitting in restaurants, looking at beautiful views, cleaning the house, going to the movies, watching television, going to the supermarket, walking the dog, planting the crops—doing simple things, getting along from day to day, living, making plans. Some were working on small areas of hope, such as getting Jimmy to talk; some were working on larger areas, such as trying to save the Republic and the peace of the world. But most were just going along with their lives, doing the best they could, nothing very dramatic or special, just the things that made sense to them, trying to find some purpose in life, trying to survive and keep on going.

And 'way up above, 'way up top, the dance of death, where the dancers must be extremely sure-footed or bring themselves and all, even the great globe itself, crashing down forever into the final silence.

He became aware of a new note in Frankly's voice, hushed and expectant.

His attention stopped wandering and came back, concentrated and intent, to the contentious hall of nations he knew so well.

"At the insistence of the Soviet delegation," Frankly said, "the vote will be recorded by poll instead of on the voting board where the votes of all delegates are recorded instantaneously when they push the proper button at their seats. The President of the Assembly, Ceylon, has drawn lots to determine who will cast the first vote. The Secretary-General will now call the first name and proceed alphabetically thereafter."

"The Maldives!" came the steady voice of the S.-G., and the Maldives voted Yes on the Soviet amendment to the American resolution.

Interrupted repeatedly by excited, approving demonstrations from the galleries, again dominated by NAWAC, and by occasional dismayed outcries from a few unfashionably out-of-date friends of America, the tally mounted steadily to its inevitable climax.

Somewhere along the way, Lafe became aware that an odd thing was beginning to happen to Frankly Unctuous. His running commentary appeared to be just as smooth and effortless, his conclusions just as dogmatic, positive and knowing, but now and again there began to be evident a curious, unexpected little hesitancy; a surprising, almost candid, moment of open disbelief; an inadvertent, surprisingly honest glimpse of genuine dismay, that this should actually be happening to his country and to the man whose Presidency he had so vigorously supported, in whose principles and policies he so determinedly believed.

It was covered up very smoothly with years of practice, but to an astute ear like Lafe's, it was apparent that for the very first time, ever, Frankly Unctuous was actually beginning to be a little frightened by what the world was doing to his country. He believed desperately in the UN. He believed desperately in Edward M. Jason. He believed, though very grudgingly most of the time, in the United States of America.

And now suddenly all these beliefs were at sixes and sevens with one another, and underlying his comments Lafe could sense the beginnings of the agony of a man who must at last make a real, Doomsday choice—a man who was beginning to suspect, terrifying though it might be to the lifelong assumptions of a rigidly closed mind, that he might have to decide in favor of the awful, blundering, despised America he had criticized with such implacable diligence for so many long and profitable years.

If Frankly was beginning to feel this, Senator Smith was sure, so were all his friends and fellow mind benders of the media. Walter Dobius, too, must be having very disturbing second thoughts at "Salubria." In the editorial conference rooms of the *Times,* the *Post,* the networks, and all their imitators across the land, men must even now be looking at one another with an uneasy surmise as NAWAC shouted in the galleries and on the floor of the General Assembly hatred spewed forth upon their country while the world proceeded solemnly to vote on the exact opposite of the known facts. In all those arrogant minds and all those intolerant hearts there must even now be growing the terrifying question: could we possibly have been wrong all these years? And if we have been, and if as a result the country is now beginning to slide out from under us at last in response to pressures both foreign and domestic, then *God,* what shall we do now to save ourselves and the society which has given us, and suffered us, so much?

Well, he thought bitterly: let the bastards sweat—except, of course, that this was not a very sensible attitude either, because, as Ben Franklin had remarked with a wisdom not remembered of late by his mutually cannibalizing heirs, if we do not hang together we shall all hang separately. And when we have hanged separately, either at the direct hands of NAWAC or something like it—or at the indirect hands of an Administration too shattered by foreign and domestic pressures to control the violent who would destroy the freedoms of all citizens on the pretext that Edward M. Jason must be supported—what then will be left of the marvelous experiment of Ben and his remarkable band of brothers?

He supposed, Lafe thought as he drove along with an automatic carefulness while the tally mounted in the Assembly and Frankly sounded increasingly strained, that Hal Fry had probably summed it up best six months ago, not only for the world to which he was speaking at the time, but for his own countrymen as well. The United States had cast its vetoes in the Security Council, the last bitter battle over Gorotoland and Panama was moving to its climax in the General Assembly. The Senator from West Virginia, chief United States delegate, was dying of leukemia. He had made his way by sheer will power to the podium of the Assembly and made a speech many preferred to forget, though its peroration still lay uneasily on the conscience of the world—as it should lie, Lafe Smith reflected grimly, on the consciences of his countrymen as well. The message applied to America too, now, as it had never applied before.

"Oh, Mr. President!," Hal had cried, mustering from somewhere a last desperate energy that carried him through. *"How does mankind stand, in this awful hour? Where does it find, in all its pomp and pride and power, the answer to its own fateful divisions? Where on this globe, where in this universe, is there any help for us? Who will come to our aid, who have failed so badly in our trusteeship of the bounteous and lovely earth? Who will save us, if we will not save ourselves?*

"I say to you, my friends, no one will. No one will. We are wedded to one another, it may be to our death, it may be to our living. We cannot escape one another, however hard we try. Though we fly to the moon and far beyond, we shall take with us what is in our hearts, and if it be not pure, we shall slaughter one another where'er we meet, as surely on some outward star as here on earth.

"This is the human condition—that we cannot flee from one another. For good, for ill, we await ourselves behind every door, down every street, at the end of every passageway. We try to remain apart: we fail. We try to hide: we are exposed. Behind every issue here, behind the myriad quarrels that make up the angry world, we await, always and forever, our own discovery. And nothing makes us better than we are.

"Mr. President, I beg of you, here in this body of which men have

hoped so much and for which they have already done so much, let us love one another!

"Let us love one another!

"It is all we have left."

"On this vote," said Ceylon with a smug satisfaction, "the yeas are 99, the nays are 28, and the amendment of the Soviet Union to the resolution of the United States is agreed to."

A savage whoop of triumph rose from Assembly and galleries, and in the aisles various Africans began to dance.

"They like us," the Secretary of State observed dryly. It was the first voice that had broken the silence of the Oval Office in fifteen minutes and the Secretary of Defense, the Majority Leader of the Senate and the Speaker of the House all looked a little startled. Arly Richardson and Jawbone Swarthman, in fact, even appeared annoyed by his flippancy. But if a man could not be flippant in such an hour, what could he do?

Apparently, if he was President of the United States, he did not do anything, at least outwardly. Bob Leffingwell had studied that impassive face for some minutes now as the tally in the General Assembly rolled steadily higher against America, and its owner was still as much enigma to him as he had always been. How does a man look, how does he feel, when he has led his country into something like this? Ted Jason's expression, attentive, alert but otherwise completely unrevealing, gave no clue. The President remained a mystery, the Secretary of State conceded with an inward sigh. Whether the mystery would ever have an explanation no one but the President, in all probability, could say.

Except that it must have an explanation. *It must.* Even as they sat there the world, or whatever passed for "the world" in these chaotic and hopelessly fragmented times, was attempting to drive the final nails in the American coffin. And here sat the man who bore the responsibility of response, his idealism betrayed, his hopes shattered, his options narrowing down with terrifying rapidity to—what? What were his remaining options, and what could he possibly do, now that he had let so much precious time slip away, had sacrificed forever the only thing that really mattered, under all the missiles and bombs and monstrous armaments of war—the Moment. The moment to act— the moment to be decisive—the moment to be brave—the Moment, which was all that ever really counted in the chance-filled, unpredictable affairs of men.

The Moment, of course, and the character: that was what it came down to, when all else was tossed in the balance and found wanting. In the slow, patient, inexorable judgment of history, these alone mattered. The moment came, and if you did not have the character to grasp it, history bade you a dispassionate farewell and moved on to someone else.

By this cold standard, in the opinion of Robert A. Leffingwell, the new President of the United States was already far, far down the road to final failure, for himself and for his country. The moment had come and the character had not been there to match it. In the last analysis all an international confrontation really involved was character—one man's guts against another man's guts: or the collective guts of one group of men against the collective guts of another. Tashikov and his colleagues were tough; Edward M. Jason and his—or at least a good many of them—apparently were not. Therein lay the tale of a lost republic, unless things changed very, very drastically and the Lord vouchsafed some last-minute miracle to those who perhaps had not really earned it, except that they knew in their hearts that they were so noble, so well-meaning, so innocent, so *good.*

Bob Leffingwell was very skeptical, in this bleak moment, that the Lord would still be that generous to America. He felt that he himself was tough, and he had tried insofar as he could in a subordinate position to urge the President to be likewise; but there was only so much a Cabinet officer could do, or indeed that anyone could do. So he had for the time being submerged his very great fears and worries about the course Ted Jason was pursuing and done his loyal best to help him carry out his policies.

Now they had all apparently failed, in the span of three terribly short, terribly long days. Surely there would be something now, some desperate last-minute turning, some response finally unleashed. Then it would be the Secretary's job to try to hold back, to counsel moderation, to urge a middle ground. When Edward M. Jason reacted in anger at last, it might well be a fearsome thing.

The President turned away from the telecast of grinning black figures cavorting in the aisles and instantly all such ideas died.

"They really *don't* like us," he agreed with a wry little smile. "But I suppose, from their point of view, they're justified."

"And what do you propose to do about it, Mr. President?" Bob Leffingwell ventured, sounding more impatient than he meant to. "What do you intend?"

"What do you want him to intend?" Senator Richardson snapped before the President had a chance to answer. "What is he supposed to do, blow up the world? I get the distinct impression you'd be a lot happier if he did."

"Anyway," Jawbone remarked dourly, "a lot happier with some other Administration, I'd bet you that."

"Well, I'm with this one," the Secretary replied sharply. "Unless, and until," he added with an equal sharpness, turning directly to face his employer, "the President prefers otherwise."

The response was a mild and somewhat surprised little laugh.

"No, I don't prefer otherwise. Why should I? You've been a good Secretary of State in our vast three days of experience together. Why should I make a change at this late juncture? I have no complaints. You've supported me loyally in what I've tried to do."

"Which brings me back," Bob Leffingwell said in a more amicable but still insistent tone, "to my original question." He gestured to the little screen where the grinning puppets still rollicked and cavorted in the aisles. "What are we going to do now?"

For a moment the President stared up at the impassive portraits of his predecessors. Then he spoke one word softly:

"Wait."

"For what?" Bob Leffingwell asked blankly, and even Arly and Jawbone looked genuinely puzzled for a moment before loyalty covered it up again.

"For the only thing that really matters," the President said. "Word from Tashikov himself."

"And suppose it doesn't come?" the Secretary persisted.

"It will," the President said with serene confidence. "After the military clique in Moscow realizes they can't push him or me around."

"The military clique in Moscow," Bob Leffingwell pointed out, "now has the official sanction of the world for whatever it has done, is doing and may wish to do. Are you going to say anything at all about this? Shouldn't we make some official response? At least reiterate our position—restate our principles—set the facts straight again in a formal statement? Do *something?*"

"There are times," the President said, "when simply waiting can be the best kind of something. I feel this is one of those times." And he glanced for the first time at Senator Richardson and Congressman Swarthman as if seeking reassurance. It was given with loyal promptitude.

"Couldn't be more right!" the Speaker exclaimed. "No, sir, couldn't be more right! Best we jest sit tight and see what that great statesman in Moscow is goin' do, I say. Best we not rush into anything, now, Bob.

Best we play it cooool and cautious. The President's right. You know he's right, Bob!"

"I don't know he's right," Secretary Leffingwell said, but mildly. "That's why I'm asking."

"The curse of this Administration, like that of so many others I've seen," Senator Richardson remarked, "is apparently going to be divided counsel. And there's no need for it to be divided. The Congress is behind him, the country is behind him—"

"*Some* of the country is behind him," Bob Leffingwell interrupted. "Some are beginning to turn, and that's going to mean trouble, too."

"The country is behind him," Arly Richardson repeated firmly, as though saying would make it so.

"And the world is against him," Bob Leffingwell responded tartly, "in spite of the fact, as Claude Maudulayne and the Vice President have just pointed out in New York to no avail whatsoever, that he is the President the whole world wanted. Doesn't this discrepancy suggest to you that maybe we're 'way out there all alone with only ourselves to depend upon—and that maybe it is now time for the United States of America to act instead of react? I just don't want us to be so damned *passive*. That's what's beginning to bug me."

"If we are really under all this pressure," the President said, and his voice was still confident, though weary, "and I agree with you, we are—then, as I tried to point out, waiting—'being passive,' if you like—is a very strong act of affirmation in itself. They aren't stampeding us. We aren't scared. We aren't panicking—"

"We're just being driven back everywhere," the Secretary of State said bleakly, "and we aren't responding in the only way these people understand, which is with decisiveness and strength."

"There!" the Senate Majority Leader cried triumphantly. "You see? He really belongs to the war party after all, Mr. President! He isn't your man at all!"

"Arly," Bob Leffingwell said, "I am grateful to you for your past support of me in the Senate on various occasions. But there are times when I think you are a fool."

"Well, now!" Jawbone protested loudly. "Well, *now*—"

"You, too," Bob Leffingwell said, turned on his heel, left Jawbone gasping, and walked to the doors leading to the Rose Garden where he stood gazing somberly out into the snow-hung trees.

Behind him there was silence for several minutes, broken at last by the President.

"Come back and sit down, Bob," he said quietly, "and let me put all this in perspective, if I may. Will you let me do that, in fairness to myself? . . . Now," he said, after the Secretary of State had complied, though without moderating in the slightest the annoyed expression with which he glanced at, and dismissed, the Speaker and the Majority Leader as he returned to his chair, "let us suppose that any President you like had been sitting here when these things happened. Any hero you want, Kennedy, Eisenhower, Truman, Nixon, Wilson, Lincoln, Jefferson, G.W., you name him. And suppose the Soviet Union had done the things it has done. What do you think any one of them would have done, really? What *could* any one of them have done? The event happens, and instantly you think—even I," he remarked dryly, "think: it's an act of war, how dare those lying bastards, damn their souls in hell, I'm going to let them have it! But then instantly you think: over what? Reports that a few fishing boats have been sunk? Reports that a couple of friendly governments have been overthrown? A little harassment of withdrawing American troops—now, wait!" he said, holding up a restraining hand as the Secretary of State started to offer angry protest. "Wait! This is at the beginning, remember—the first moment it happens. All you have to go on are these first, fragmentary reports, probably true, but not quite—not *quite*—substantial and conclusive enough so that you can in good conscience order retaliation. Particularly knowing that the only kind of retaliation that would be really effective would be atomic—and that would mean the end of everything.

"So. You don't proceed quite as fast and quite as dramatically, in those opening hours, as many of your countrymen would like you to do—as you yourself, perhaps, would like to do. You act cautiously— and the next reports are worse—and the enemy has advanced even further and is moving very rapidly—and again, there is a way to stop him. But again you think: is it worth it? Is it really justified? Should you really do this awful thing? And you wait a little longer—and you don't do it. And he keeps coming. And things get worse.

"*Except!*" he said with a sudden vigor and a light of inner conviction that brought to the Secretary of State the sudden chilling thought that the desperate need for hope had overreached itself in a mind always accustomed, except in these last few chaotic months, to having things its own way. "*Except,* that in your heart of hearts you know—you *know*—that there must be rational men still operating on the other side—that there *must* be men of good will—even more importantly, of *sanity*—who no more want the world to blow up than you do. You know, *because you have to know,* that there *must* be men to whom it is as unthinkable as it is to you that they would quite literally end the world if they are not careful.

"And to them," he concluded quietly, "you pin your hope, and with them in mind you conduct your policies, and reaching out to them across the gulfs of suspicion and hatred that isolate the races of man upon their bristling, fortified, embattled mountaintops, you say, 'Friends, we cannot commit this final awful insanity, we simply *cannot*.'"

He stopped, and the Secretary of State realized suddenly that Ted Jason, the wealthy, the ambitious, the pragmatic politician and avid Presidency seeker, had somewhere along the way undergone a most startling and apparently genuine conversion to an almost Messianic concept of his mission in the world. The Senate Majority Leader and the Speaker broke into hearty, prolonged, genuinely emotional applause.

In it the Secretary of State did not join, sitting quietly, elbows on arms of chair, chin on fingertips, staring moodily at the floor. A silence fell and into it Arly Richardson said in a spiteful voice,

"He won't even applaud you, Mr. President. A loyal Secretary indeed."

As though coming back from some far distance, Bob Leffingwell raised his eyes slowly from the floor until they met the Senate Majority Leader's full-on.

"Arly," he said in a tired voice, "again you are a fool. I don't think the President really doubts my loyalty, do you, Mr. President?"

The President studied him thoughtfully for a moment and then shook his head.

"No. And I hope you don't doubt my sincerity, either, Bob."

"Not at all," the Secretary said. "Not at all. I just find one thing missing in your historical equation, and that is that, of all those you named, of all who have sat in this house, *all* of them—you are the very first who came into office and deliberately and immediately began to dismantle America's power and position in the world. And from *that*, it seems to me, flow our present perils and the great trouble we are in. It was not a sudden decision by the Russians to move—until you made it clear to them that they could do so with impunity. And *then* they moved—and kept moving—and are still moving—and will, I am very much afraid, keep right on moving, because from your very first moments in office you made clear to them that you will not stop them. And the world, which I am afraid is really not a very idealistic place, assesses this accordingly. And so we have these votes just now, and dancing in the aisles.

"That," he said in a tired and unhappy voice, "is where I fault you, Mr. President. Not for idealism. Not for honesty. Not for courage. Not for a sincere vision of what you sincerely believe—what any sane man sincerely believes—to be the only safe dream for mankind—but because you did it too fast—by yourself—without adequate preparation—and without getting from them, first, a quid pro quo, *some* sort of guarantee, *some* sort of bargain, *something* that would give us a little influence left on our side, which would at least keep them a little bit uncertain as to what we would do, a little bit uneasy, a little bit cautious, a little bit restrained. But you didn't do that. You voluntarily gave up all our advantage which, shaky and shopworn though it may be by now, still had some inhibiting effect. And now—how, and where, do we stop them?"

The President gave him a long look and then he smiled,

"I say what I said at the beginning, Bob," he said pleasantly. "We wait."

"And rightly so, in my estimation," Arly Richardson said bluntly.

"That's what I say, too, Mr. President," Jawbone Swarthman said stoutly. "Rightly so, now. Rightly so!"

"And you will not even authorize," the Secretary of State said in a disbelieving voice, "a statement in response to these votes which would set the historical record straight. I do not understand it, Mr. President. I simply do not understand it."

"Wait," the President repeated gently. "Wait, Bob. The answer will come."

And within fifteen minutes, during which they engaged in desultory small talk while Frankly and Walter Dobius and various others analyzed the UN votes in a way which disturbed the Secretary even more, because for the first time in all his years of knowing them he could tell they were disturbed too—though the fact did not seem to reach his companions, or bother them—the answer did come.

Once more of what Bob Leffingwell was beginning to think of as those endless young men in uniforms and crew cuts who seem to live in the White House woodwork knocked on the door and was admitted. Being strictly schooled in protocol he held strictly to it, ignoring the President save for a dutiful quick salute, handing the paper he was carrying to the Secretary of State.

Bob Leffingwell read it through hastily and then said, *"Christ!"* in a tone of such terrible anger, disgust and sheer frustrated exasperation that even his colleagues, whom he regarded now as distinctly euphoric if not unbalanced, looked startled and upset.

He reached across and placed it in front of the President, and keeping his voice carefully drained of expression of any kind, inquired,

"And now?"

TASHIKOV DEMANDS IMMEDIATE MOSCOW CONFERENCE WITH U.S. [the headlines would scream in half an hour as the news reached the world.] IGNORES WHITE HOUSE, ISSUES STATEMENT TO PRESIDENT THROUGH SOVIET UN DELEGATION. POINTS OUT "OVERWHELMING INSISTENCE OF WORLD OPINION" THAT MEETING BE HELD. TELLS JASON "YOUR DELAY IS INEXCUSABLE AND CAN ONLY LEAD TO IMMINENT CONSEQUENCES OF GRAVEST AND MOST FINAL NATURE." RUSSIAN LEADER ASSERTS "MY GOVERNMENT AND I HAVE BEEN MOST PATIENT WITH YOUR INTRANSIGENCE BUT OUR PATIENCE HAS RUN OUT. WE MUST INSIST UPON AN IMMEDIATE AND AFFIRMATIVE REPLY."

In the Oval Office, where at the moment only two men knew all this, there was again a silence—this time a very lengthy one as the President read, reread and read again the piece of paper while his companions regarded him with an intent and worried concentration.

Finally he glanced up and, ignoring Senator Richardson and Representative Swarthman, asked Bob Leffingwell,

"What do you think?"

"I think he thinks he has you on the run," the Secretary said bluntly. "This is no message, this is a public humiliation. I think he thinks he has you licked."

"Ah, but he doesn't, though," the President said softly.

"What will you do?" Bob Leffingwell inquired, his voice beginning to fill with a hope that now, at last, something—he did not know exactly what at this desperately late date, but something—would be done to stop the headlong downward rush of events.

"I shall go to Moscow," the President said serenely.

"But, Mr. *President*—" the Secretary said, his face and voice nearly ludicrous with dismay.

"I shall go to Moscow," the President repeated with a sudden sharpness that disclosed a strain so deep that it chilled the Secretary, though it seemed to escape their colleagues from the Congress. It was gone as swiftly as it had come. "And then," he concluded calmly, "we shall talk this over face to face and settle it once and for all."

"But, Mr. President—" Bob Leffingwell tried again, his voice this time attempting to be patient and reasonable but only sounding completely tired and completely hopeless.

"I shall go," the President repeated firmly, and again for just a second the Secretary was convinced he was seeing a glimpse of hell in the fine eyes that stared out at him with an almost frantic anguish before again becoming opaque and unreadable, "to Moscow. You will go with me. You two will also go with me, so that the Congress may be represented. I may even take Bill Abbott, though I don't know yet. But I do know I shall go before Congress tomorrow as I depart and tell them and the country why I am going and what I intend to accomplish. So you two may get back up to the Hill and get things started on that, if you will. And you, Bob, may stay here and help me start drafting the speech, if you will."

"Anything I can do, Mr. President," the Secretary of State said, very low, "God knows I will do."

"That applies to me too," the President said with a little smile and some return, from somewhere, of a small, amazing gleam of humor. Then his expression changed to one of calm, if somber, confidence.

"I think He will help us," he said quietly, "for we go in good heart."

"By ding-dang-doozy," Jawbone Swarthman said with a sudden explosive emphasis which disclosed for the first time that even his loyal and ebullient soul was beginning to be shaken at last, "He'd *better*."

Far in the distance came the put-put-put and larger and larger in the chill winter sky grew the little whirling speck as all the thousands crowding around the Capitol stared with a strained and anguished intensity down the Mall toward the White House hidden in its trees. Once before a President had arrived by helicopter to address the Congress, but then it had been at night, in spring, warm and steaming, and he had not been going to Moscow but returning—tired, but as he told the Congress and his countrymen, hopeful and encouraged. Those —ah, those had been the heady days!—of peace and love and cynical dreams, and many, many solemn agreements writ in many, many solemn words on many, many solemn pieces of paper that now lay folded and forgotten in silent and untroubled archives far from the dreadful deceits of clever, clever men who all thought, alas for the world, that they could outsmart one another. They had not been able to, for all their devious trying, and so now another President was coming by helicopter to the Congress, to tell its members and his countrymen about another mission to Moscow.

What would he say?

What *could* he say?

Such being the imperatives of Presidents, it could hardly be an intimation of defeat.

Hope must go with this President, as with all Presidents, to Moscow or wherever they might travel; and hope, desperate hope, was what awaited him at the Capitol, to be inspired and strengthened and gathered together to add to his own so that it all might fortify him for his fearsome, inscrutable journey. Something waited, there beyond, for Edward M. Jason and his people. What were they to make of it, on the day of his departure?

Some had already decided, and perhaps they were the lucky ones, for they, at least outwardly, had no doubts.

"I would accept the invitation of the President to go with him to Moscow," said ex-President, ex-Speaker William Abbott, "if I thought that anything I might have to offer would change in the slightest the way he is proceeding in this matter. But repeatedly in recent days I have tried to offer advice and it has been consistently and arrogantly refused. Nothing leads me to believe the situation is any different now. I can be better employed here doing what I can to arouse public opinion, either to support him if he comes back with a reasonable compromise of views with the Russians, or to oppose him if he shall have proved to have given them all they want, which is our heads.

"History has known for more than half a century that the United States only had to lose its nerve once—just once—and the jackals would be at our throats.

"We have and they are.

"I wish the President God's help but I wish our unhappy country even more. My presence in Moscow would be empty window dressing. Here at home, I can perhaps be of some help to him—or to the country. Whichever needs it most."

Senator Fred Van Ackerman, speaking as chairman of the Committee on Making Further Offers for a Russian Truce, and for its fellow branches of the National Anti-War Activities Congress, was equally firm.

"It is with a feeling of genuine relief and a deeply loyal appreciation of his great and farsighted statesmanship that the affiliated groups of NAWAC wish the President of the United States Godspeed on his mission to Moscow. We are delighted to note that he will be accompanied by the Hon. Arly Richardson of Arkansas, Majority Leader of the United States Senate, and the Hon. J. B. Swarthman of South Carolina, Speaker of the House. We are also pleased to note that his delegation will be free of the critics, the carpers and the faint of heart.

"The three principal organizations which have merged their identities in the single entity of NAWAC—COMFORT, for which I speak, the Defenders of Equality for You (DEFY) and the Konference on Efforts to Encourage Patriotism (KEEP)—wish to give their wholehearted, 100 per cent endorsement to President Edward M. Jason and his policies. We believe his inaugural address and the actions he announced at that time, to change the course of the United States and redirect it into the paths of world cooperation and peace, will go down in history as one of the great American state papers and one of the great American policy decisions of all time.

"We believe his responses to the apparently hasty and ill-advised actions of certain segments of the government of the Soviet Union has been moderate, statesmanlike and farsighted. We regret those actions and we do not believe they represent the true intent of the Soviet peoples or the genuine peace-loving elements within the Soviet Government. One of the great potentials we see in the trip of the President to Moscow is that he will be able to assist the genuine peace-loving elements in the Soviet peoples and Government to regain control of the destiny of their country.

"We expect President Jason's example of statesmanship to have a profound effect upon the Soviet leaders. We expect them to respond with forthrightness, practicality and candor to the opportunity afforded by his presence in the Soviet capital.

"We wish him Godspeed, a safe journey and an achievement worthy of his own statesmanship and the hopes of his loyal countrymen.

"One further thing we of NAWAC pledge. We pledge to support the President loyally and completely in whatever he may do in his search for peace. We pledge him our full and unqualified assistance in the carrying-out of his policies and their swift, efficient and orderly application both abroad and at home."

Which rang uneasy bells in the minds of many, not the least of them, though they too gave outwardly encouraging and fulsome praise, being the clever minds in the world of Walter Dobius. The words that flowed suavely in editorial columns and friendly news stories, that purred smoothly from news specials and roundups and commentaries, were dutifully approving and hopeful. But in the hearts of many in the media, a worm encouraged by the various uncomfortable things that had happened during the campaign was beginning to gnaw. They did not know, as many of them stood observing the crowds outside the Capitol, or awaiting the President's arrival in the standing-room-only galleries of the House, how fast its insidious mandibles would work upon their arrogance and certainties before this day was over.

"Mistuh Speakah," shouted Fishbait Miller, grown gray in the service of his country and this one, familiar bellow, "the Prezdent of the Yewnined States!"

And down the aisle he came, closely followed by the Secretary of State, the Secretary of Defense and the rest of the new Cabinet. His face was solemn as he entered the House chamber but it swiftly relaxed as hands were outthrust from both sides and eagerly smiling faces looked fervently into his. Here and there men stood silent and unapplauding, the ones whose disapproval was expected: William Abbott and Senator Munson, Lafe Smith and Cullee Hamilton, Warren Strickland, Hal Knox and perhaps a hundred more. Yet even their expressions were not hostile, only gravely worried and prepared to be helpful, if he would only tell them how. It was still Ted Jason's Congress, and as he stood at the rostrum to hear the other famous phrase about what a high privilege and distinguished honor it was for the Speaker to introduce the President of the United States—which Jawbone lingered over as lovingly as had all his predecessors—the desperate emotion that welled up to him from the absolutely full and now absolutely silent room was a palpable thing. It came from beyond the chamber, too, from outside the doors, as though the television cameras that searched floor and galleries for prominent and familiar faces were somehow bringing in as well as sending out. And what they brought was hope: willing to be encouraged, anxious to be strengthened, respectful of his sincerity but demanding reassurance with a desperation he knew he could not evade.

He had known this, in fact, ever since Tashikov's first harsh message two days ago; and in spite of the way in which he had managed to come through the various challenges he had received from within his own official family as well as outside of it, he had known from almost the beginning that it was indeed, as Valuela had perceived, up to him. His had been a risky and supremely lonely course in the desperate days since inaugural; and so, too, had it been a risky and supremely lonely life. Val had come closest in that period, but even their amicable nightcap in the solarium after midnight had ended in a moody silence as both had stared out across the Ellipse at the Washington Monument and the muted gleam of the Potomac. Only the headlights of a few late-passing autos broke through the misty, faintly luminous glow of the snow-covered world. All else was unmoving, ghostly and still.

"Well, my dear," Val had said finally, rising a little unsteadily to give him a brief but heartfelt kiss on the forehead, "good night now, I must get my beauty sleep. Try not to worry too much. Tomorrow will be better."

"Good night, Val," he had said, giving her hand a sudden, almost desperate squeeze, and returning the kiss on her weathered and heavily made-up cheek. "You're not only an aunt, old girl, you're a friend. . . . I think it will."

But of course tomorrow had not been better, nor had any of the succeeding hours, or minutes or even seconds, when all was said and done. There had been periods when inner tension had seemed to relax, when there had come a sudden surge of calmness and certainty, when, abruptly, there had appeared to be no problems and he had *known* that all would come right. Quickly they had passed. He had recognized them for what they were, the mind's necessary relaxation before having to face the next bout of tension. Even though they had helped, they had not helped for long. Always the terrifying realities he faced came rushing back.

Yet he felt, as he stood now smiling a little and bowing gravely first to one side of the aisle and then to the other while the Congress, the Cabinet, the Court, the media and the galleries stood applauding with a wild and insistent enthusiasm, that he had managed pretty well to conceal this from those around him. From somewhere in the crucible of these awful three days Edward M. Jason had gained substantial strength—at least the strength to put a good face on it, which was one of the major requirements of the Presidency in all crises, and this one most of all, the crisis to end crises unless he handled it exactly right.

Somehow, he thought, he had managed to, so far.

Somewhere in this terrible tangle of days and nights almost without definition, in the onrushing flow of events precipitated by the military masters of the Kremlin, he had undergone what Bob Leffingwell had dimly and somewhat skeptically surmised—an inner change, a reformation almost spiritual, a conversion from politician trying to satisfy a ravening ideological constituency to a man profoundly convinced of his own mission.

Even though tension had been succeeded by calm, and calm again by tension, and even though there had not been much real slackening of the mental and emotional tightrope he was walking, somewhere far below in the inner citadels of his many-citadeled personality there had grown the genuine conviction that he did have a mission: to show to the world by precept and example that an American President could do what both the honestly idealistic and their cynical and politically motivated leaders demanded of him—offer the world a complete and genuine act of peace, without reservation and without guile.

The conviction did not remove the tensions or the constantly waning and returning terrors, or the nervous strain, or the need for a couple of sleeping pills every night and an occasional tranquilizer during the day from the worriedly hovering White House medical staff. But it did give him, somewhere underneath, a foundation that he had never had in all his political life. The last two generations of Jasons had always had money as a foundation for their personal lives, but he knew there had not been much real foundation for his political life except a growing, finally all-consuming, desire to be President. This was sometimes enough to get you there but it was never enough to support you once you had achieved the ambition. Now he had found something—at what cost to his country, history would have to decide. But he had it.

Buoyed up by this, while the desperate applause, yearning for miracles, continued to inundate him in supplicating waves, he was able to continue to stand there, a dignified, statesmanly, commanding figure from whom it appeared miracles might well be expected. Presently there was evident a growing impatience for this. The applause at last began to falter, some voices began to cry, "Enough!" and "Let him speak!" And finally, at last, he did.

"Mr. Speaker," he said, half-turning to Jawbone and to Roger P. Croy, seated behind and above him, "Mr. Vice President—my friends and colleagues of the Congress—" he turned back and faced them full-on—"we must indeed be friends in the cause of America, and colleagues in the cause of peace."

They applauded again wildly as he had known they would. The Secretary of State, to whom this line, like many others he was about to hear, was a stranger to the text on which he had collaborated until almost 4 A.M., remained impassive to the searching cameras; though at quite a cost, for he knew in that one sentence that while Edward M. Jason had seemingly agreed with him on a plan of action, he was about to elude him once again.

"We meet," the President said gravely, "at a time of crisis. Yet I think it is not a crisis of despair. It is a crisis of hope."

Again they applauded, save for those few, like William Abbott and Harold Knox, whose lack of response the cameras noted with a lingering and obviously disapproving attention.

"Hope, because at last, I think, we are going to come to grips with the forces within the Kremlin which have precipitated this situation— the forces which have precipitated many such situations, lesser in degree but equally dangerous to world peace, on many occasions in the recent past. And we are going to find out who really rules Russia, and whether men of good faith and good will can find their counterparts in that land, and work with them toward the great goal of world understanding and world peace."

("Two," murmured UPI in the front row of the Press Gallery above, making a mark on his notepaper. "Two what?" whispered AP beside him. "Two 'world peaces,'" UPI explained—"or world pieces, as the case may be." "Funny," whispered AP. "Oh, funny.")

"I believe this can be done," the President said calmly. "That is why I am accepting the invitation of Chairman Tashikov and am going directly from this chamber to Andrews Air Force Base and from there, with only a brief rest stop in London, to Moscow.

"*Not* as a yielding to the threats that have been made to me and to the United States in the name of Chairman Tashikov—but as an acceptance of the invitation to rational discussion and good-faith negotiation, which I know to be the true purpose and intent of Chairman Tashikov himself."

Applause came again, a little uncertain this time, a little more dutiful, but still with him wholeheartedly.

"Together, I believe," he said firmly, "Chairman Tashikov and I can cut through this tangle of unfortunate events of the past seventy-two hours. Together we can find a solution that will satisfy the best interests of both our great countries. Together we can find peace."

("Three," murmured UPI, making a mark. "Doesn't count," AP objected; "he left out the world." "Don't great peacemakers always do that?" UPI inquired innocently. "I'm giving him three." "Ho, ho, ho," said AP.)

"My countrymen," the President said, and a new note of gravity entered his voice and held them spellbound, "I would be less than candid with you today if I tried to pretend that I embark upon this journey without considerable handicap. You are all familiar with the ill-advised and impulsive actions taken by military elements in the Russian Government since my inauguration. You are familiar with the harsh statements which have followed upon those actions. You know that a majority of the nations of the world, acting in the United Nations, have chosen to place your country in the category of international criminal, and to give support to those military elements of the Soviet regime. You know that a deliberate attempt has apparently been made by those military elements to place me in the position of threatened supplicant going to Moscow, instead of the position of seeker after world peace ("Four," said UPI.) which I like to think I occupy.

"I not only like to think that," he said with a challenging lift of the head, "but I like to think that my countrymen and decent men and women of the world *everywhere* regard me that way too!"

The roar of applause that he wanted rose up to him in full measure. He held the fighting pose, the buoyant angle of head, the fearless and determined look of eye, until at last it died away.

"In that spirit," he resumed quietly, "I go to Moscow. Not as a supplicant, but not defiantly, either. Not as a man who believes that he has all the right on his side"—the eyes of William Abbott, glancing sideways along the aisle, met those of the Secretary of State and glanced quickly away again—"for I do not think any American President can go anywhere and claim that—" there was a sudden little burst of applause, startled and pleased, from some of the younger members on the floor and from those members of NAWAC who had managed to gain admittance to the galleries. Again the Secretary and the ex-President exchanged glances, more openly troubled now—"but as a believer in world peace ("Five," said UPI.) who has faith that honest negotiation can settle honest differences.

"I know there are some," he said, and a trace of scorn came into his voice which brought an appreciative murmur across the chamber, "who favor a different course. They favor oratory. They favor bombast. They favor defiance and threats of retaliation and waving the big stick. I am leaving them," he said, and a roar of happy laughter greeted the sally, "at home. . . .

"No, Mr. Speaker, Mr. Vice President, my friends and countrymen—I do not go as a warrior but as a man of peace. ("Six," said UPI. "How about 'Prince of Peace?'" suggested AP. "It's been done," said UPI.) I go in the belief that while the United States is not perfect—indeed, far from it—neither is any other government or nation on the face of this earth. I go in the belief that whatever has happened in the past three days at the direction of the military elements in the Russian Government has not had the true endorsement and support of those other, equally important elements in that government which are peace-loving. I believe those elements do exist and I believe that I can talk to them. And I believe that when I reach Moscow I shall find that what I and many of us have suspected right along is correct: that Chairman Tashikov, though his name has been used to endorse what is seemingly a militaristic course, is in reality as dedicated as I, or any other sane and responsible leader, to the cause of world peace." ("Seven," said UPI.)

Applause rose again, wholehearted, encouraging, approving: they, too, or at least most of them, had faith in Vasily Tashikov.

"So I go," the President said, "secure in your affection and secure in your support—both here in the Congress and, I like to think, throughout the country."

"Yes!" someone shouted, and applause welled again,

"I do not go thinking it will be easy, or comfortable, or even, at times—" and he smiled, a wry but confident smile—"even pleasant. But I go convinced that it must be done. *Not* because I and my country have been threatened. *Not* because I am giving in to what might appear to be bullying tactics. *Not* because I believe that we will suffer any dire consequences if I do not go. But just because it seems to me the simple—and the honest—and the trustworthy—and the decent— thing to do. Just because I believe in world peace ("Eight," said UPI.) and just because I believe there are decent men in Russia who believe in it too; and because I believe that together we can work out our differences and resolve our disputes and, honoring one another's genuine interests and the need of all men everywhere for a steady and a stable world, arrive with honor at an accommodation that will permit us all to live in harmony, in friendship and in peace."

"Nine, and the ball game," UPI told AP as they leaned together over the gallery railing to watch the President, directly below, close his loose-leaf notebook and raise his arms, fingers of both hands forming the V for victory, in answer to the tremendous roar that met the conclusion of his speech. Again the cameras noted that some few sour and skeptical souls did not applaud. But they were quickly brushed aside as the cameras panned over the shouting, stamping, wildly applauding occupants of floor and galleries. Inside the Capitol it was Edward M. Jason a thousand to one. Outside was another matter.

"Hello, New York, hello, New York," the young network reporter said insistently to his intercom from his vantage point near the steps of the East Front. "God damn it, New York, I'm telling you there's trouble here. . . . I don't give a God damn if they gave him an ovation inside, I tell you there are people out here who don't like him and they mean business. The damned right-wing reactionaries are organized out here and so are the NAWAC people. There's going to be one hell of a fight the minute he comes out. I don't give a good God damn if the whole farting Congress *is* shaking hands and saying goodbye, I need at least three cameramen out here right *now*. Oh, God damn it, don't argue! I'm *here*, and I know what I'm talking about! *Hurry!*"

But neither in New York nor anywhere else where the shrewd purveyors of the instant's happenings directed their far-flung and, as in this instance, sometimes anguished cadres, was there any anticipation of what would happen when the President appeared on the balcony of the East Front to begin the long walk down the gently inclining steps to the cleared parking area and his waiting helicopter. Certainly Edward M. Jason himself was probably the least prepared of all, for the cameramen who were running along beside his official party did manage to capture one thing—quickly banished from the screens, destroyed, and never shown again anywhere—the expression of utter disbelief, disorientation and dismay that momentarily crossed his face as there came from somewhere a loud, harsh, angry, obviously well-organized roar of hostility and contempt.

It was followed at once by a concerted rush from somewhere to the right among the trees. Slipping and sliding over the icy ground came perhaps three hundred men and women, some carrying banners which, hastily glimpsed, seemed to indicate that not all his countrymen loved Edward Jason or approved of his actions since taking office.

STOP BETRAYING AMERICA! demanded one. DON'T BE A COWARD—FIGHT MOSCOW! insisted another. MILLIONS FOR DEFENSE, a third appealed to history, BUT NOT ONE CENT FOR TRIBUTE! NO RUSSIAN BLACKMAIL! urged a fourth, and HELL, NO, DON'T GO! demanded a fifth.

Frantic, red-faced, not so well organized as the young TV reporter had thought but obviously in desperate earnest, the little crowd continued to stumble forward over the treacherous icy pavement. The Secret Servicemen around the President instantly closed ranks. One group of Capitol and District police formed a cordon to rush him and his traveling companions to the already revving helicopter. Another group formed a line to face the oncoming protesters who, their gesture made, now began to hesitate and waver. But from around the other side of the steps came a response far more effective. Black-suited, black-helmeted, perhaps no more than fifty in number but carrying guns, clubs and grenades, completely organized and ready, came what could only, now, be called a detachment of the troops of NAWAC.

"Get us out of here!" the President snapped to the head of the Secret Service detail, and in less than two minutes they were airborne and looking back down upon a steadily receding mass of struggling little figures, dark against the snowy esplanade in front of the Capitol.

Over the beautiful building the beautiful flag flew briskly in the cutting wind as they swung away north and east toward Andrews Air Force Base. Behind them they left a new hemorrhaging from the disease upon whose likely disappearance Edward M. Jason had congratulated himself, perhaps a bit too soon, more than two months ago.

TWO DEAD, DOZENS BEATEN AS NAWAC "TROOPS" BATTLE PROTESTERS AFTER PRESIDENT'S SPEECH. BLOODY RIOT ERUPTS AT CAPITOL AS RIGHT-WING GROUPS OPPOSE MOSCOW TRIP. PRESIDENT'S FAREWELL MARRED BY OUTBREAK AS CONGRESS, NATIONAL LEADERS UNITE IN HAILING "JOURNEY FOR PEACE." FURTHER PLANNED DEMONSTRATIONS AT ANDREWS FORESTALLED BY

THOUSAND-STRONG NAWAC "HONOR GUARD" RINGING
PRESIDENTIAL DEPARTURE.

VAN ACKERMAN TO INTRODUCE NEW ANTI-RIOT BILL
TOMORROW. SENATOR SAYS "THIS SAVAGE OUTBREAK OF
RIGHT-WING REACTIONARIES" HAS CONVINCED HIM TO
ABANDON OPPOSITION, EMBRACE MEASURE TO GIVE GOV-
ERNMENT VAST NEW PEACE-KEEPING POWERS. CHARGES
NATION IN "STATE OF SEMI-WAR" AGAINST POLITICAL DIS-
SENTERS OPPOSING PRESIDENT. HINTS HE WILL PROPOSE
"AMENDMENTS AND PERFECTIONS" TO GIVE ADMINISTRA-
TION IRONCLAD CONTROL OF ALL PUBLIC MEETINGS. OP-
POSITION EXPECTED FROM CONGRESS CONSERVATIVES.

"It is possible to heartily applaud the President's courage and the
course he is following," Walter Dobius wrote rapidly in the study at
"Salubria" later that afternoon, "while at the same time deploring the
excessive zeal with which his supporters, particularly in the ranks of
NAWAC, seem to be treating all who raise any question about it.

"This does not, it seems to this correspondent, aid the cause of democracy at home, nor does it really strengthen the President for the
overwhelmingly difficult tasks he faces, now and in the days ahead.

"This is a time for deep and fervent prayer for the Chief Executive
in all the troubles he must resolve. It is also a time to remind him most
respectfully that he has the sincere and heartfelt support of vast numbers—indeed the overwhelming majority, still—of his countrymen. If
there are those who disagree, that is their privilege. Patient education
and the accretion of loyalty based upon understanding are the means
to win them over. These are the only means, it seems likely, consistent
with the democratic heritage of these United States."

He paused for a moment to stare out, hardly seeing, upon the gentle white-clad hills and valleys of lovely Virginia. "These United States"
indeed! When had he last used that corny old phraseology? It must
have been twenty years ago, at least. Why was he reverting now to
such unsophisticated, such hayseed rhetoric? He had noticed this
tendency in his columns more than once in the past few weeks; a sort
of harking back, as it were, a sentimental return, to an old-
fashioned way of thinking about the country that he had not seriously
entertained in decades. He had noted it also in the works of his closest
colleagues, and he knew they were thinking, as he was, of their conversation prior to the election, and of the troublesome hidden events
of the campaign. He knew they were all uneasy and disturbed. And
he knew the events of the past three days had done nothing to allay

the uneasiness or remove the disturbance, even though all of them were still loyally, in printed word or spoken message or carefully selected photograph, giving their support to Edward M. Jason in this most difficult and frightening hour.

But not all the frightening things right now were overseas, Walter knew; and he knew that many of his old friends and comrades of the genuinely liberal cause were aware of it too. Only a couple of hours ago, after the busy cameras had brought the tragic details of the catastrophe at the Capitol (which had begun, he was sure, innocently and earnestly on the part of the protesters, only to be turned deliberately by black-jacketed bullies into something dreadful and savage, in a moment's time), he had received a call from one worried old friend.

"Walter!" Mr. Justice Thomas Buckmaster Davis had said abruptly, his anxious little face staring urgently from the Picturephone. "Which of us will they try to murder next?"

"Who, Tommy?" he had asked, although he knew.

"NAWAC!" Tommy Davis said. "Those thugs, those despicable, worthless people! Walter, mark my words: they will be after the press next, and they will be after the Court, too. None of us is going to be safe if they are permitted to run on unchecked."

"You saw Freddie Van Ackerman's statement," Walter said dryly. "He's going to put in a bill to take care of all that. It will stop public disturbances."

"Absolutely unconstitutional," Tommy Davis said sharply. "Absolutely!"

"I haven't heard the Attorney General or the President denouncing it yet," Walter observed, still dryly. "Although, of course, there hasn't been time. Tomorrow, perhaps."

"They had better," Mr. Justice Davis said, an unusual and uncharacteristic harshness in his voice. "They had better, because if it ever comes up to the Court—and it will very swiftly if it passes, I'll predict— I shall certainly vote against it. And I think the rest of us will too."

"We may be borrowing trouble unnecessarily, Tommy. It may not even get through Congress. Perhaps we shouldn't worry."

"This Congress?" Justice Davis asked with a snort. "Anything will get through this Congress. They scare me to death. Aren't you scared, Walter?"

"Yes," Walter Dobius said, and he looked at his old friend without equivocation or evasion. "Yes, Tommy, I am. I don't like this re-emergence of NAWAC. I thought it was a campaign phenomenon that had been buried and forgotten. I don't like the President's way of handling that subject, and I don't really like his way of handling the Russians, although of course I can't say that in my column. I approve of his patience and his refusal to be thrown off base by it—if that's really what his attitude indicates—but I do not approve of his apparent refusal to fight vigorously to place our side of it before the world. He's doing something no smart world leader ever does—he's letting the enemy make the record. And that's no good, Tommy. That's really no good."

"Do you suppose he's *afraid* of NAWAC?" the little Justice asked hesitantly, as though the thought was so awful it should not even be mentioned. Walter frowned.

"I don't really know," he said thoughtfully. "But I have a hunch the two are related—or soon will be—or, in fact, are already, given this thing at the Capitol today and that farewell scene at Andrews. 'The NAWAC honor guard!' An American President going off between a row of storm troopers! I never saw anything like it in my life."

"Well, I don't suppose he could really control it, could he?" Tommy suggested in the same hesitant way. "I mean, in fairness—maybe, suddenly, there they were, and what could he do? He couldn't stop and make a scene, he was on his way to the plane, and so—"

"And so they just took him over, by default," Walter Dobius said somberly. "It's happened in other countries. I think he *should* have made a scene, Tommy. I think he should have delayed the plane right there and ordered the Army to clear the area and not departed until it *was* cleared. He wasn't in all that much of a hurry. And if that makes me sound like a damned reactionary," he added as the little Justice gave him a sudden startled look, "then I'm afraid that's what I may be turning into. I am, as you say, getting scared."

"Of course, though," Justice Davis said with a typical quick, reviving optimism, "we have to remember that NAWAC *does* represent what you and I believe, basically. It *is* against war, and it *is* for a peaceful accommodation with the Russians, and it *does* support the President, who *is* trying to keep the world at peace. We have to remember all those things, Walter. It does represent the liberal point of view, basically."

"I'm beginning to think it doesn't represent my kind of liberalism," Walter said slowly. "Nor yours, either, really. We don't believe, for instance, in killing our opponents. I may write harsh columns and you may hand down tough decisions, but we do it in the context of this democracy, not in the way this NAWAC crowd is doing things. We give the conservatives hell and they give us hell, but there's a basic tolerance and a basic compromise, a basic *compassion*, if you like, for each other's views. At least we're fair-minded."

"Have we always been, Walter?" Tommy Davis asked quietly. "Really, now? Haven't we been just as rigid and just as arbitrary and, in our way, just as ruthless as NAWAC? Haven't we opened the door to this, over the years, by being too willing to forgive excesses as long as they agreed with our point of view?"

"Isn't that what you were just doing?" Walter Dobius demanded with some indignation. "You were just defending NAWAC, Tommy, not I! Be consistent, now!"

"Yes," Justice Davis said with a sigh, "you're right, Walter, as always: I am just rationalizing. But I think I have a point. They *are* bad—very bad. And we did help to open the way for them, and so I think it's up to genuine liberals like us, more perhaps than to others, to be in the forefront of the fight to stop them and bring them under control again."

"You interrupted a column in which I was about to say just that," Walter remarked.

"Oh, my goodness, I'm sorry!" the Justice said, and his face was quite comical in its dismay. Walter smiled, somewhat grimly.

"No, I'm glad you called, because you've helped to clarify my thinking. . . . I think," he said, and his eyes were suddenly distant and in-turned as if foreseeing many things, "that we have some difficult battles ahead, in this old Republic. I think we're rapidly getting to the time—with an insane rapidity, really, so much has changed in three long days—when men must show their colors."

"I shall do so on the Court," Tommy Davis said stoutly.

"And I, and I think most of our friends," Walter agreed, "on the printed page and on the air. I just have one nagging question at the back of my mind."

"So do I," Justice Davis confessed, and after a moment, with a candor almost defiant, stated it. "What colors will he show?"

"Exactly."

"But of course," Tommy added quickly, "he has so *much* on his mind, Walter. We must be patient. We must be tolerant. We must be understanding. We must help him. He has *so* many things."

"I wish he'd say something about NAWAC," Walter replied glumly. "I really do, Tommy. I'd feel a lot, lot better."

"Maybe he will," Justice Davis said comfortingly. "Give him time."

"He should have already!" Walter snapped, an odd desperation in his voice. "Timing is what escapes this man—the sheer importance of timing. He's letting everything slide out from under him because he doesn't understand *timing*."

"He's hopeful," Tommy Davis said, somewhat forlornly. "He hopes. It always used to be important, to be hopeful."

"It is now," Walter agreed grimly, preparing to end the conversation. "But hope needs help."

And so he urged, as he turned back now from the empty countryside to his column, things that he might not otherwise have urged. They were things which represented chance—taking of whose dangers he was fully aware as he sat in beloved "Salubria." But they were things he felt must be said, chances he felt must be taken. Already in the *Post*, the *Times, The Greatest Publication*, the networks, the newsweeklies, the note of warning to the President they had all worked so hard to elect was becoming more and more open, more and more insistent. His own concluding paragraphs were strong, and in the new circumstances rapidly arising in the country, dangerous, but he felt with a curious, suddenly reckless defiance that he would not be true to twenty-five years of being Walter Dobius, Molder of Thought, if he did not state them.

"And so," he wrote, "it seems to this correspondent, as it seems to many of us who have for many years professed and, we believe, stoutly defended and maintained, the true liberal faith, that another profoundly grave matter waits upon the President for decision.

"Heartily as we applaud his patience with the Russians, desperately as we believe that he *must* succeed in persuading them to abandon their present military follies, we yet cannot refrain from expressing another worry, equally deep, here at home.

"We do not agree with NAWAC's presumptuous attempt to 'capture the President,' in a sense. We do not agree that its members have any right to appoint themselves guardians of his policies or guardians of his person. We think he is encouraging a most dangerous and un-American [*There I go again*, he thought] trend when he does not speak out at once and repudiate their attempts.

"For years this correspondent, like so many of his friends, has been persistent and unrelenting in warning against the fascism of the right. We have been equally scornful of what has seemed to us a smoke-screen term, a right-winger's bugaboo, a deliberately thought-confusing expression—'the fascism of the left.' We have not thought such a thing was possible, and particularly not in America.

"Now, we are not so sure.

"It may be happening here. There were episodes during the campaign that the public knew about—and private incidents that never reached print. Now come these latest events surrounding the President's departure for Moscow. Hard on their heels comes the announcement by Senator Van Ackerman, one of NAWAC's most powerful leaders, that he no longer opposes the dangerous and ill-advised 'anti-riot bill' that died in the last session of Congress. Now he favors it and will introduce a new version with 'amendments and perfections' to give the government 'ironclad control' of public meetings.

"Whose public meetings?

"And why?

"President Jason has more on his mind at this moment than any mortal man should have to bear. But when he returns home, we respectfully urge, he should have one overriding priority: to break completely with NAWAC once and forever, and to repudiate the vicious, inexcusable and desperately dangerous Van Ackerman bill."

And now, he thought, tearing the paper out of the typewriter with a sudden savage motion, you do your damndest, you bastardly sons of bitches.

But the defiance did not last long, as he rose and went again to the window to stare far down "Salubria's" softly rolling acres. It was succeeded by something that had happened very, very rarely to Walter Dobius. The last time had been three months ago when he had visited the grave of his estranged former wife Helen-Anne Carrew, society columnist for the Washington *Star-News*, assassinated because she was getting too close to what lay at the heart of NAWAC and its influence on the Jason campaign.

Not since then had tears come into his eyes.

"I don't care if you burn the whole place down," he cried out suddenly, weeping because he knew he didn't mean it, it would kill him to have "Salubria" destroyed. But the tears of anger and anguish were coming now because he realized finally that he had to write these things, he *had* to. Tommy was right, they had all been responsible for what was happening, and he more than a great many, for he had held much greater influence and power.

Like many already in this unhappy hour for the United States, and like many more yet to come, Walter Dobius was one of the proud, self-confident and arrogant whom the Presidency of Edward M. Jason was forcing to face themselves, at last.

Rising at 8 A.M. London time, partially rested but still not really refreshed, he found Walter's anguished urgings among the many journals and commentaries transmitted to the embassy for his perusal from all over the world. He skimmed it rapidly, tossed it aside; the smallest of grimly ironic little smiles touched his lips. Across his desk the screaming headlines sprawled, describing his speech, the disturbance, his departure. Here and there he saw concern like Walter's, but mostly he saw, particularly in the world press, an almost unanimous tendency to minimize the dissent and concentrate instead on his journey.

Miraculously, even in Russia and her satellites, even in China, Africa and Asia, he saw very little contempt for his journey as such. On the contrary, he sensed a great relief, as though they had not been quite sure but what he would do something drastic and dreadful. He was behaving as they wanted him to, and in return they were sensible enough to give him praise. There was almost no reminder that he was going under threat, almost no hint that this could be considered humiliation, hardly a word to convey anything other than that the world wholeheartedly admired, respected and applauded his patience, his statesmanship, his good will and his determination to work for peace.

At his elbow the Secretary of State picked up Walter's column as the President tossed it aside, and read it through. Then he remarked quietly,

"I'm afraid that for once I find myself agreeing with Walter, Mr. President. Your decision still stands? You still don't feel you should issue a statement deploring the riot and criticizing NAWAC?"

The President looked up with a sudden sharp impatience, and Bob Leffingwell felt a little shiver of genuine fear, because for the first time since he had known him, there was an expression almost vindictive in Edward M. Jason's eyes.

"Those dissenters did their best to ruin my departure and cast a shadow on the whole trip," he said with a harshness that brooked no argument and accepted no answer. "I don't find it possible to feel very sorry for them."

Forty-five minutes later the helicopter had taken them to Heathrow and they were airborne for Moscow in Air Force One.

It was not a particularly talkative journey. Frequently during its silences Robert A. Leffingwell found himself staring down moodily at the farmlands of eastern Europe speeding away beneath.

O my President, he thought; and after a while, with a deep, profound and growing sadness, *O my country.*

In Moscow the reception was very formal, very cold. The President of the Soviet Union, a tired old party hack looking ostentatiously grim and unyielding, met the American party. The Foreign Minister and five minor, unidentified officials accompanied him. Tashikov was nowhere to be seen. One American flag and twenty Russian flew in the subarctic breeze that the small accompanying corps of twenty American newsmen blamed, in their reports, for cutting the ceremonies short. But they knew what Edward Jason knew: nothing in the weather cut the ceremonies short. They were short. President Jason shook the old man's hand, the old man shook his. President Jason started to read a prepared statement, the old man cut him off with an impatient wave of the hand. One small ten-piece military band played the two national anthems, the Russian first. Then the American delegation was led to waiting limousines and rushed away to the Kremlin through snow-piled, carefully empty streets.

That night there was a "working dinner" between the American President and the Chairman of the Council of Ministers and their aides, lasting until 10 P.M. After that the aides were dismissed and the two men continued alone. Newsmen were not given access either before or after to any of the principals and spent their evening at the National Hotel getting progressively more drunk and progressively more worried. At 4 A.M. they were notified that the meeting was over and were told to go to bed. At 7 A.M. they were roused from uneasy sleep and told to get ready as fast as they could, the American party would be departing Moscow at 9 A.M. Baffled and deeply troubled, they filed hasty bulletins and complied.

At the airport they were hustled aboard the plane by blank-faced Soviet soldiers prior to the arrival of the President. Shortly thereafter another limousine whirled up with the Secretary of State, the Speaker and the Senate Majority Leader. Peering out, the reporters could see that all three looked grim and openly worried. Seconds later the last limousine rolled up through the now lightly falling snow. The door opened and the President stepped out, followed by Vasily Tashikov, his wiry little figure and clever little face peering owlishly up at the President who towered above him.

It was very obvious that the Chairman was smug, triumphant, almost openly jubilant. It was equally obvious that the President was ashen, shaken, so profoundly depressed that he made only the most perfunctory of attempts to conceal it. Tashikov shook his hand fulsomely, laughed merrily, said some last thing no one heard. The President blinked and shook his head as though trying to clear it of some heavy weight, managed a small nod in return. He turned and started up the steps of the plane. He did not turn back to wave. His eyes met those of the watching reporters in the after cabin. They felt, as the New York *Times* expressed it in a hushed whisper shortly after they were airborne, as though they had seen a man coming out of Hell.

The official communiqué was issued simultaneously two hours later in both capitals and at the United Nations. It told the world nothing of what it wanted to know.

"Following a conference held in Moscow between the President of the United States and the Chairman of the Council of Ministers, the President and the Chairman are pleased to announce that many outstanding differences between their two countries have been settled. Further explorations of those problems still outstanding will be held at a mutually agreed date in the near future.

"The Chairman of the Council of Ministers wishes to state on behalf of the Soviet Union that he is satisfied his country's objectives in the search for world peace have, in major degree, been achieved.

"The President of the United States reserves the right to comment on these matters at a future date."

But no future date was given, and this time there were no plans for a speech to Congress or a press conference. At Andrews the President and his party were hurried directly from Air Force One to a helicopter. The media were kept back. No reporter was allowed to come close or interrogate. Telescopic lenses zeroed in on the somber faces of somber men, none of whom bothered to try to smile or pretend cheerfulness. On the White House lawn when the helicopter landed, newsmen pushed with sheer weight of numbers through the protective police lines. "Mr. President—" many of them cried as the guards hurriedly pushed them back. A haggard man gave them a haggard glance from haggard eyes.

"Get away and leave me alone!" he snapped in a voice so savage they recoiled as if physically struck. They did not dare venture further word nor did he and his party offer any as they walked hurriedly into the Diplomatic Entrance and disappeared.

Around the world speculation bloomed, blossomed, raced, roared.

In the United States of America, palpable fear was suddenly everywhere.

BOOK THREE

1. PROMPTLY on the convening of the Senate at noon the next day, Senate 1776, "A Bill to Strengthen the United States Against All Enemies, Foreign and Domestic," was introduced by Fred Van Ackerman. Its identical companion, House of Representatives 1776, was introduced a few minutes later by youthful Representative Bronson Bernard of New York. They referred to it in their brief joint statement as "the Help America Act." The media instantly picked up the phrase, which was handy, colloquial, had immediate recognition value, and looked and fitted well in headlines. By nightfall opponents led by ex-President William Abbott, ex-Senate Majority Leader Robert D. Munson and Minority Leader Warren Strickland had begun to call it "the dictatorship bill." But the positive emphasis of the words "Help America," with their appeal to patriotism in a deeply troubled time, had already given it a substantial advantage in the public mind. This advantage, however, did not extend to a great many thoughtful citizens. Thus the stage was set for a tense and extraordinarily bitter debate.

By the same nightfall the impression was beginning to seep into the national consciousness and across the world that there were to be no immediate dramatic consequences of the Moscow meeting (unless, as some were beginning to suspect, S. 1776 was a consequence). Sporadic Soviet-supported fighting continued through the day in Gorotoland and Panama under the new anti-American governments. The airlift of American prisoners apparently was continuing to flow into Kiev. Word came in from Alaska that three American fishing vessels, though not sunk, had been driven back into Anchorage when they tried to venture out, by a Russian trawler now openly armed with weaponry sophisticated beyond the knowledge of American intelligence.

In Lafayette Square a new and much larger anti-Jason crowd assembled during the afternoon. This time many of its members were fully armed. They constantly shouted warning threats across Pennsylvania Avenue to the rows of NAWAC guards who stood along the White House fence, openly and successfully defying the police who tried, in a gingerly and cajoling fashion, to persuade them to move on. At 6 P.M. a line of army tanks rolled down Pennsylvania Avenue, closed it to vehicular traffic, and took up position between the two contending factions.

In seven cities across the country from New York to San Francisco, impromptu parades of protesters, carrying signs denouncing the President, clashed bloodily with NAWAC and others supporting him.

An anxious clamor that he address the nation, led by those who had been his most ardent and active supporters, began to rise in the media. But no word, save a terse announcement by the press secretary at 7 P.M. that telegrams and telephone calls were running 4 to 3 in his favor, issued from the hooded Mansion. Shots of its brooding, floodlit front, looking somehow suddenly awesome and forbidding, appeared frequently on television. No word came from the man inside, though he was receiving many words and many more were being said of him as uneasy day crept slowly into frightened night.

"Bob," William Abbott said, and the Secretary of State could tell from his expression on the Picturephone that he was in no mood to accept any nonsense, "I want you to level with me. What in the hell happened in Moscow?"

"Mr. President," Bob Leffingwell said, "—Bill: I'm damned if I know. And that's the God's truth. You heard it exactly as it went. Arly, Jawbone, Ewan and I accompanied the President to Tashikov's office. Tashikov was flanked by the Foreign Minister and the Minister of Defense. They looked grim and so did we. There were no courtesies exchanged. Tashikov launched into a tirade that lasted almost an hour about all our crimes and sins of commission and omission. I would say it was about one-half show and one-half genuine indignation. The President replied at almost equal length—"

"How was he?" Bill Abbott interrupted. "Show any guts?"

"Oh, yes," the Secretary said. "In fairness to him, he was calm, unhurried, polite and firm. And also, at that point, unafraid. He seems to have been supported by some inner vision these last few days—"

The ex-President interrupted again.

"Is he supported by it now?"

"I don't know," Bob Leffingwell said gravely. "He is a very badly shaken man, that's for sure. Anyway, after this exchange of pleasantries, Tashikov abruptly dismissed his men and indicated with a gesture I can only describe as arrogant, impatient and unpleasant, that the President do the same. The President started to protest but Tashikov looked around with an elaborately sarcastic air at the empty seats on his side of the table and then gave the President a deliberately insolent stare. So after a moment the President gave in. I suppose you could say Tashikov shamed him into it, but there really wasn't much he could have done, under the circumstances. So we left them alone and were shown back to our quarters. Four hours later we were awakened and told to be ready for departure at 9 A.M. He remained in his cabin for the entire trip and did not speak to any of us. We barely spoke to one another. It was a somber journey."

"Has he seen any of you since?"

"Arly, Roger and Jawbone briefly—"

"Probably to prepare this hell's brew we have up here now," Bill Abbott snorted. "By God, I tell you, Bob . . . and who else did he see? Surely he's given you and Ewan at least a nod during the day?"

"He had us in at 4 P.M. for about fifteen minutes. His instructions were vague and he didn't seem to focus very well on what he was saying. He gave us no idea what happened after we left. He gave us, really, no idea of where we go from here. Right now I'm afraid we're drifting, Bill—an obviously shaken President—a brand-new Cabinet whose members hardly know each other yet—and nobody in charge."

"The senior member of the Cabinet ought to carry a little weight," the ex-President said. "Don't let Roger grab the wheel."

"I have some ideas," the Secretary of State said firmly. "I don't intend to, if I can help it. . . . What's going to happen in your bailiwick?"

The plain, massive old face before him twisted in a savage, almost despairing, grimace.

"Have you read this monstrosity yet?"

"I saw the text in the *Star-News*. It *is* monstrous."

"You're damned right it is. 'Help America,' my hat! Destroy America is more like it. First we have all the features of the old anti-riot bill—"

"Which you yourself proposed," the Secretary could not resist. William Abbott shook his head with an angry impatience.

"Only to scare NAWAC, you know that. I never intended to push it at all, otherwise that little monster Van Ackerman wouldn't have been able to filibuster against it for ten minutes, let alone twenty hours. I'd have crushed him in an hour with the Congress we had then."

"Which isn't," Bob Leffingwell pointed out, "the Congress we have now."

"The Congress we have now will do anything," Bill Abbott said darkly. "It's composed of kids, kooks and incipient Ku-Kluxers out to lynch everyone who doesn't agree with them 100 per cent. Such is the noble dispensation that rode in on the Jason coattails, conditioned by many years of careful education and propaganda to consider the Russians just kindly old bears and their own country history's most nauseating villain. Quite a job they've done on us in these past few decades, Robert; quite a job. Anyway, such is the Congress, as you know, and such is the bill we now have before us. Except that Freddy has tightened it up a bit. You now have the restrictions on public meetings, plus a couple of nice new phrases that lay us wide open to an absolute dictatorship and no kidding.

"'In order to preserve domestic peace and tranquillity, the Attorney General is empowered to establish and administer a new Special Branch'—why do police states love that term 'Special Branch,' I wonder? So many of them seem to use it—and this 'Special Branch' is to work 'in close conjunction and cooperation with the Federal Bureau of Investigation, the Internal Revenue Service, the Central Intelligence Agency, the intelligence branches of the respective military services, and any and all other governmental or private agencies engaged in the collection of data concerning American citizens.' The purpose of this 'collaboration' is so that the Special Branch may 'more speedily and effectively meet the threat posed to democracy by citizens found, suspected or deemed to be, subversive to the best interests of the government of the United States.'

"'Found' to be by whom?" he demanded with a sudden surge of anger. "'Suspected' to be, by whom? 'Deemed to be' by whom? 'Best interests of the government of the United States' as determined by whom? I tell you, Bob, this thing is dreadful. *Dreadful*. And in addition to that we have censorship proposed too, as our friends in the media are desperately, and I'm afraid too late, beginning to realize.

"'In order to create a more favorable public climate for the solution of foreign and domestic problems confronting the government of the United States,' there will be established a 'Domestic Tranquillity Board' which will 'advise, suggest and encourage' a 'positive, constructive and affirmative approach on the part of all sectors of the nation toward the policies deemed necessary for the solution of such problems by the government of the United States.' Again, 'positive, constructive and affirmative' by whose standards? Administered *how* in order to 'advise, suggest and encourage?' Violation of the regulations

—not spelled out—of this 'Domestic Tranquillity Board' to carry a penalty of $10,000 fine for each offense, 'and/or not less than one nor more than five years' imprisonment in a suitable place of detention.' What 'suitable place of detention'—an insane asylum, like our Communist friends, those vicious, awful people? I tell you, Bob, this one is a doozy. And I'm not at all sure we can lick it."

"You're going to have some powerful help when the media finally get the message," Bob Leffingwell said.

"Why don't we have some powerful support from *him?*" Bill Abbott demanded. "What kind of a President is he, to give such a measure his endorsement and backing?"

"I'm sure he hasn't," Bob Leffingwell said mildly. "They slipped it over on him and he just hasn't had time to rally and denounce it, what with everything else that's been going on."

"He damned well better had," Bill Abbott snapped. "He should have this afternoon, the minute it was put in. Anyway," he added dourly, "it's too late. Too late."

"You aren't going to give up, I hope?" the Secretary asked in some alarm. The ex-President gave him a sharp, implacable look.

"I certainly as hell am not. We're mounting quite a battle plan up here. Roger recessed the Senate, you know, at Freddy's request, almost immediately after the bill was put in, and Jawbone did the same on our side. So we couldn't start the debate today, which they no doubt thought was smart. Actually it gives us until noon tomorrow to get organized—and for the full import of the bill to sink in to the country. We're working on it. I've got Hal Knox and a few other old and new hands helping me here, and Bob Munson and Warren are hard at work over there. I think sentiment is roughly 60–40 against us at the moment in both houses, but there are a lot of parliamentary tricks we can use, and Bob and Warren are certainly going to use them in the Senate even if they don't succeed over here.

"Meanwhile, we'll work on time. *Time* is what we want to achieve. Time is our ally, time is our friend. Time, time, *time:* the more we can manage, the more opposition we can build up in the country and the nearer we'll come to success. . . .

"But," he said, and his voice sobered and grew lower, "time isn't your friend down there, is it? Basically, I can't see that a thing has been accomplished overseas. The longer time runs overseas without something from us, the worse off we're going to be, aren't we? What is the U.S. going to do, Bob? Got any ideas?"

"Why don't you try to see him?" the Secretary suggested. William Abbott dismissed it with a shrug.

"Already have tried. He's turned me down, speaking through George Wattersill, who obviously enjoyed every minute of it. Anyway, what could it add to what I've already said to him a hundred times? He knows where I stand."

"Somebody's got to get him out of this lethargy," Bob Leffingwell said with a sudden, almost angry insistence. "Somebody *must*."

"I suspect that the only one who might is dead. So he's on his own, I guess. . . . Let's see how it's running in a day or two. Then if he hasn't snapped out of it maybe enough of us can get together to demand that he see us, and he won't be able to refuse. Will you join us?"

"Oh, yes," Bob Leffingwell said quickly. "But in the meantime—"

"Keep trying, you and Ewan," Bill Abbott advised. "Sooner or later he's *got* to snap out of it. Let's hope to God it's sooner."

But he did not know whether he could, as he slowly walked the second floor of the fabled old house, brooding and alone, nodding absent-mindedly to the guards, pausing from time to time to stare at the portraits of his predecessors hung in conspicuous places along the walls. Valuela and Selena had gone to New York to do some shopping together; Herbert was keeping a speaking engagement at the University of Chicago ("I am sure my nephew is doing what he believes to be right for the country," he had declared stoutly on the early evening news, in a film clip taken during his arrival at O'Hare); Patsy had returned to Dumbarton Oaks to put things in order before leasing the house and moving into the Mansion as his official hostess. Only soldiers, secretaries and servants were around for company now, and although all were friendly, worried and sympathetic, none was really the kind of human contact he needed. None was a friend.

He realized suddenly, as he turned on an impulse into the Queen's Room and walked slowly to the windows overlooking Pennsylvania Avenue, that outside of his family he really had no friends—that he had never really had any, save one, since he had left Stanford. The standard Presidential crony who pops up—simple, rough-cut, unsophisticated—even, occasionally, a little crude—perfect counterpart to the suave, accomplished Presidential figure as they boat together, fish together, escape the madding crowd and enjoy the remote, well-photographed joys of nature together—did not pop up in his life, because there was none. The inner aloofness of the Jasons had been most pronounced in him, and only a few friends, transitory and not particularly intimate, had ever managed to break through. None had been quite the type who lasts to become, ultimately, the officially recognized Presidential Pal; nor, indeed, had he ever felt the need for one. He had always been confident, self-possessed, powerful, decisive, assured. He had always been in command of his world. Until now, when literally everything depended upon his retaining command, and when a friend he could really unburden himself to would be a benison beyond price.

He had possessed one—just one; and the ache of her absence was sharper than he thought he could bear, as he raised the curtain and stared down at the somber line of tanks dividing the Avenue. The mobs had dispersed in considerable degree, without violence, but both in Lafayette Park and along the White House fence many of the antagonists were still arrayed. In the cold antiseptic glare of the street lights he could see the soldiers moving uneasily around their vehicles, the guards of NAWAC holding their ostentatiously rigid poses, the anti-Jason forces facing them across the way. An enormous placard meant for him caught his eye.

ARE YOU ASLEEP? FOR GOD'S SAKE, DO SOMETHING.

He let the curtain drop and turned back to resume his restless pacing of the silent halls. Do what, my friends? he wondered. If you knew what I know—

But that way lay the dragon, and he must not let his mind go there again. It could only confuse him further. He could not afford to be confused. Or, at least, he could not afford to let those out there, and all the millions and billions over the globe whose clashing opinions they represented, know that he was confused.

In due course, he supposed, he must speak to the nation. In due course he must decide what to do. In due course he must act. In due course he must be the President again, instead of what he was now, a lone and shattered man.

In due course.

But not now.

Outside, America drifted.

Inside, he drifted.

He knew he must stop it, he knew he must take the one decisive action that might somehow turn today into yesterday—into some day prior to the time when, idealistic, well-meaning and thinking to play to the gallery of his ravenous supporters, he had deliberately yielded up all of his advantages.

Somehow he must find his way back.

But not now.

"I think," Beth Knox said quietly as they sat in a comfortable semicircle of chairs and sofas before a crackling fire in the enormous living room at "Vagaries," the Munsons' beautiful home in Rock Creek Park, "that it's time *we* formed a committee. I think our side has got to do something and do it fast. It seems to me the best way is to organize, raise funds, form a speakers' bureau, start advertising, focus public opinion. I think there'd be plenty of support for it around the country. Because we've got to stop it, you know. We've got to stop the bill, and we've got to show him that there's a great segment of the nation that wants him to take a more forceful stand abroad."

"It's so late," Bob Munson said gloomily. "Things have moved so fast. But you're right, of course. There's got to be *some* counterweight."

"You wouldn't get into the sort of thing NAWAC's doing, would you?" Warren Strickland wondered. "We wouldn't find our people arming because NAWAC's armed, would we?"

"Some of our people are already armed," Lafe Smith pointed out unhappily. "I hate to see it, but if somebody comes at you with a gun, you don't have too much choice, do you?"

"But that isn't America," Crystal Knox protested.

"What is America?" William Abbott asked moodily. "America is a fragile web that people have been trying to tear apart for a couple of decades, now. 'The consent of the governed.' That's really all it is, you know—the consent of the governed. Once somebody realized that all you have to do is persuade enough of the governed to withhold their consent and you've got it made, then America began to change into something a lot different from what she had been. I hate to think of Americans taking up arms against each other, too, but they've started it, we haven't. . . . My God!" he added with a sudden explosive bitterness. "What has that man got us talking about? Civil war?"

"Suppression of dissent, I think," Hal Knox said. "You come to power on a wave of dissent, proclaiming the right of dissent as loudly as you know how, and then once you get into power, you turn around and suppress dissent—when it's against you. That's the routine of it, and that's what Jason's little pals are up to right now. And he's condoning it, if he isn't openly pushing it."

"Maybe he is, with this damned bill," Cullee Hamilton said. "'Help America, but woe to you if you don't go along with *us*.' Why doesn't he say something about it? He should have issued a statement against it the minute it was introduced. In fact, he should have prevented it from being introduced."

"In fairness to him," Senator Strickland said, "he may not have known it would be."

"Van Ackerman certainly made no secret of it," Lafe said sharply. "He announced his intention."

"But the President was involved with the Russians," Warren Strickland pointed out mildly, "and, like all of us, he may have had no idea of what Fred really had in mind."

"But surely just the innate nature—just the simple conscience—of the American people will prevent such a thing from becoming law," Dolly Munson said. "It's unthinkable Congress could pass it."

"It would be unthinkable if two things happened," William Abbott said. "*If* he opposed it—and *if* he reacted strongly and positively to the Russians. The two go together. As long as he doesn't do anything about the Russians, protest and dissent are going to grow very rapidly. As long as protest and dissent grow very rapidly, Van Ackerman and NAWAC and the rest are going to be able to argue—and get real support for it—that protest and dissent are dangerous to the conduct of government in these parlous times, and therefore a law must be put on the books to control them. The two things dovetail very neatly."

"And both come back to him," Beth Knox remarked quietly. "What *is* the matter? He seems paralyzed."

"I talked to Bob Leffingwell a while ago," William Abbott said. "Bob thinks he may be. Nobody knows what went on in that conference with Tashikov. Maybe Tashikov threatened him with the end of the world."

"Even if he did," Cullee said with some contempt, "Ted should have threatened back. You have to be tough with them, it's all they honor, in the long run."

"Maybe this time we don't have a tough President," Senator Munson said softly, "and maybe they know that. But I agree: somehow we've got to force him to do something. What do you want to call your committee, Beth?"

"I've been thinking," Beth said, and her eyes narrowed with the shrewdness that had always made the Knox team so politically formidable in Illinois, "that it might be called 'In Defense of Liberty.' Or if you prefer, 'the IDL.' How does that sound?"

"No good," William Abbott said promptly. "The next step would be to refer to it as 'Idle.' We certainly don't intend to be that, I hope."

"All right," Beth conceded with a smile. "I defer to superior judgment. What do you suggest?"

"I don't exactly know, now that you pin me down," Bill Abbott said. "Lafe, you're clever. Come up with something."

Lafe smiled.

"Not very. And rarely on command. I think Beth's got the germ of it."

"In Defense of Freedom," Hal suggested. "The IDF. Not very swinging, but typical of us on this side—earnest, well-meaning, a little awkward, a little funny. But determined."

"Fine," Bill Abbott said quickly. "And to chair it, who more fitting than the widow of—"

"Oh, no," Beth said hastily. "I'm not suggesting it for my own aggrandizement but because I think it's something we've got to do. Who more fitting than the ex-President of the United States?"

"Let's make it a joint effort, then," William Abbott said. "We need your name and most of all, your abilities. How about two co-chairmen—"

"Might as well hit all the bases," Cullee Hamilton said with a rather dry smile, "and I don't say this for *my* own aggrandizement, or just because I'm black. On the other hand, you have that damned LeGage Shelby and COMFORT on the other side. Don't you need a house nigger?"

"Well," Bill Abbott demurred as they all looked startled and somewhat embarrassed. "I wouldn't exactly say that."

"I wouldn't either," Cullee agreed cheerfully, "but some will. Anyway, it makes sense, doesn't it? And I'm not afraid to lay my convictions on the line. I want to, in fact. How about a triumvirate? You can handle the political and financial side of it, Beth can handle the women, I can talk to the minorities—"

"Perfect," Warren Strickland said and they all concurred with hearty approval.

"Now all we need is two expensive floors on Connecticut Avenue," Hal remarked, "and we've got it made."

"We'll need an office, all right," Bill Abbott said, "but let's keep it small. An administrative director and a couple of secretaries ought to do it."

"If we're not being overly optimistic," Bob Munson said with a smile, "it's going to grow a lot faster than that."

"The faster the better," Beth said.

"I've thought of the ideal location," Lafe said. "How about the northeast corner of Connecticut and L?"

"That's where NAWAC is," Crystal objected.

"We can spy on them," Hal said wryly. "I've no doubt they're spying on us."

And so they were, though not in quite the basically good-natured and humorous way in which Hal and the others were still able to contemplate the situation. At NAWAC's newly established headquarters on Connecticut Avenue they meant business. And none meant it more than the individual who stared down at the snow-clogged, slow-moving, home-going traffic with a moody expression on his customarily tense and restless face. Fred Van Ackerman, recently re-elected junior Senator from the great state of Wyoming, was, as usual, at war with the world. Only this time Fred had the feeling he was going to win.

The methods by which he intended to do so might not, in another time, have appealed to a United States Senator. There had been a very few to whom the idea of actually destroying the traditional democratic processes of the country in order to establish something drastically and even dreadfully different had appealed, for a time. But none had possessed quite the inner drive and inner conviction that Senator Van Ackerman had, and none had operated in quite the strange climate that he was operating in now. And almost none had quite the incredible brashness and contempt that permitted him to challenge and dismiss, quite sincerely, all the assumptions of a free society upon which America had lived for more than two centuries.

Had the nation's politically minded psychiatrists turned their attention to analyzing Fred Van Ackerman with half the zeal with which they publicly analyzed statesmen whom they considered more conservative, they would perhaps have found many harsh explanations for his behavior. Since he had always been on the Right Side of Things they had never given him such kindly treatment. Yet, in many ways, the junior Senator from Wyoming was a classic example of all that they alleged, and condemned, in others. And now it appeared that he might be about to get away with it all, at last.

He had come, of course, from a broken home. He had been, of course, a loner as child and youth. He had not, of course, participated in games, achieved with any particular distinction in school, succeeded in acquiring or keeping friends. His attempts at romance had been, of course, sporadic, feeble, unsatisfactory, unfulfilled. At an early age he, of course, acquired a contempt for authority, a deep and ineradicable suspicion of his fellow beings, a desire to get even with society for all the vaguely defined but terribly hurtful things that seemed to go wrong with his inward life. And he combined all this, of course, with a brilliant, almost animal, shrewdness in discerning the main chance, and an intelligence limited in scope and compassion but supremely able in seizing upon and profiting from the weaknesses of others.

All of this had made him, of course, almost completely amoral, almost completely ruthless and almost completely cold and dead inside.

Thus he had surveyed, as he emerged from college, a country whose evils, inadequacies and inhumanities his teachers had drilled into him constantly, as they had tried, with considerable success, to do with a great many of his generation. Some had responded with a desperate, intolerant idealism which, in a peculiar, turned-around way, pushed them into wanting to destroy the system in order to save it. With Fred Van Ackerman this went one step further. He kept it to himself because he knew candor in this area to be self-defeating, but inside he harbored only contempt for what he referred to in his own mind as "the idealism stuff." He could see, however, that the idealism stuff was a perfect vehicle by which to rise to some powerful position, undefined at first but gradually clarified as he went on to law school and graduated with reasonably satisfactory grades. He decided quite early that if he played it right, he could use the idealism stuff as a springboard and then kick it away when he became strong enough. He had completed the first part of this program and now he could see its sequel approaching very fast.

The process had begun with his first election to the Senate six years ago. He had seized upon the opportunity offered by a dying incumbent to announce his candidacy without so much as an aye, yes or no from those who thought they ran the party machinery. He had appeared, apparently out of nowhere, to challenge the "old politics" of the too-complacent mossbacks, and he had succeeded. He was not, after all, deformed: at least on the outside. He was reasonably good-looking, relatively intelligent, supremely crafty, a powerful, demagogic speaker. Shrewdly and apparently with great sincerity spouting the clichés of the earnest left, he had stumped the state, an exciting liberal whirlwind in contrast to the bumbling conservatism of his much older opponent. Instantly this had won him not only state recognition but the sort of national attention that comes automatically, with great speed and warmth, to anyone who appears to challenge the basic worth of America's customs, history and tradition.

A DARING YOUNG FIGHTER TAKES ON WYOMING'S CON-SERVATIVES, *World* had trumpeted early in his campaign. WYOMING SENDS AN EXCITING NEW LIBERAL TO THE SENATE, *Time* had dutifully announced after it was all over. VAN ACKERMAN OF WYOMING: A NEW KENNEDY? wistfully inquired *Newsweek*, ever engaged on the ceaseless quest. The *Times*, the *Post* and the networks, kit, caboodle and all, had rallied 'round with glowing articles, flattering photographs, sycophantic interviews, fatherly, approving commentaries and editorials. He had fooled them all, and it was only after he had taken office and begun to reveal his contempt for the traditional customs, and the frayed but still valid decencies, of the national political game, that some began to become a little uneasy. He might, a few perceptive souls were moved to think, eventually turn on *them.*

But such queasy thoughts were successfully suppressed, even though his speeches and actions soon appeared to become somewhat erratic. The high psychotic whine of his voice under pressure disturbed all who heard it, but because he always backed the Right Causes and worked with the Right People, this was never commented upon in national publications or broadcasts. The media went with him, in fact, almost all the way through his fight in support of the first nomination of Robert A. Leffingwell to be Secretary of State. It was only after he had succeeded in blackmailing Bob's stubborn young opponent, Senator Brigham Anderson of Utah, literally to death, that a strong undercurrent of questioning and disapproval began to run through the media. And even then it surfaced rarely, because after all, he was still fighting on the Right Side for the Right Things.

In similar fashion, his association with COMFORT, the Committee on Making Further Offers for a Russian Truce, evoked only scattered, uneasy comment, no more than was accorded the sudden appearance of COMFORT itself. Destiny had brought the rising young Senator and COMFORT together the night Fred delivered a speech with the immortal line "I had rather crawl on my knees to Moscow than die under an atom bomb!" Prior to that, COMFORT had been a brand-new unknown, come, like himself in his early days, apparently out of nowhere to enter the American political scene.

He did not know for quite some time where its funds and its backing came from. By the time he began to get an inkling, their destinies were so intertwined that he probably could not have disengaged himself even had he wanted to. He did not want to, because a nationwide organization of COMFORT's wealth, skill and tenacity was indispensable to the ultimate plans that were beginning to form in his mind. And then Ted Jason had come along, with a rare and still baffling stupidity, to give him inadvertently the final weapon he needed. Almost absent-mindedly Ted had accepted the idea of NAWAC, and with it had sealed, as Senator Van Ackerman saw it, both his own fate and that of the American Republic as it had existed up to now.

Ted Jason, that weak, silly, egotistical, idealistic, arrogant nincompoop! Of all the people he considered his enemies on the political scene, and that was almost everyone of any consequence, the new President was the one for whom he had the most complete and withering contempt.

How anyone could reason as naively as Ted had concerning the formation of NAWAC, Fred could not understand. If you were smart you didn't permit your problems to be unified into one big bundle, you kept them fragmented. Instead of COMFORT, DEFY and KEEP, working at cross-purposes and generally hostile to one another, no real threat to the country or to him, Ted had naively, almost eagerly, embraced the casual suggestion that it might be easier to further his Presidential ambitions in cooperation with the various peace movements if they could all be brought into a single organization. The name, with its harsh and menacing acronym, had been entirely his inspiration: The National Anti-War Activities Congress—*NAWAC!* It could not have been more perfectly named if Fred and the man who actually originated the idea had christened it themselves.

And then Ted found that he had given his support to the birth of a monster, and the knowledge had begun the process of breaking him down that figured so vitally in the plans of so many today.

The beating of Crystal Danta Knox by NAWAC bullies outside the Cow Palace during the Knox-Jason nominating battle had been the first move in the dislocation and destruction of a personality. It had been done by an element that was largely Ted's creation, and Ted, for all his defiance about it to Orrin Knox and others, could not escape the burden of conscience.

Then had come President Harley Hudson's savage tongue-lashing of Ted before the convention, his support of Orrin for Vice President, Ted's defeat. This had been followed immediately by Fred Van Ackerman's own bullying of Ted as he had ordered him to be present at the formation of a third party to run against Orrin, a development canceled only by Harley's death on the way back to Washington.

Then, most importantly of all, had come the death of Ceil at the Monument Grounds, an event far less haphazard and unplanned than the world assumed. That had begun the real process of shattering, submerged but not halted when Ted was chosen to succeed the slain Orrin as the Presidential candidate.

Then had come the campaign, in which NAWAC had tried its muscle on a national scale and gotten away with it because the candidate apparently—either through fear, self-confidence, desire for office, or sheer inability to grasp its dangers—failed to repudiate it.

And then had come Ted's astounding inaugural address, idealistic in the eyes of his devout supporters but appallingly weak (though very welcome) in the eyes of Fred Van Ackerman and his friends—and in it the voluntary sacrifice of nearly all of America's few remaining advantages in dealing with the Russians. This had been followed instantaneously and inexorably by Tashikov's brilliantly ruthless and apparently successful gamble, culminating in the Moscow conference whose inner core Fred did not know but could shrewdly guess.

How could one feel anything *but* contempt for such a weakling? And what else could one logically do but proceed as fast as possible toward the dark, fantastic goal one had evolved out of one's bitter, harsh and twisted personality? Especially since it had now been made clear to him, through channels in NAWAC and elsewhere, that those whose help he would require looked with kindly encouragement upon his efforts?

It was true that there had been, in recent months, two events which had temporarily shaken him a bit. But he had survived the one and thought he knew how to triumph eventually over the other. His extremely narrow margin of victory, only a scant 106 votes, in his race for re-election to the Senate in November had been a shock, for defeat would have put an end to his dreams forever. But in its mysterious wisdom the electorate had just barely saved him. In the American system a miss was as good as a mile: you could be the victor by one vote, if it came to that, as long as you had the majority. He had won, and that was that.

The event had deepened his dislike for Ted Jason, if that were possible, because he had given Fred far less enthusiastic support than Fred hoped for and needed. The media had made a lot of the fact that Ted had spoken for him, but he had only spoken once, in a rather offhand way. It had been a mighty namby-pamby, delicate laying on of hands, in Fred's opinion, far more concerned with the necessity for sending Ted Jason to the White House than it was with the necessity for returning Fred Van Ackerman to the Senate. If Ted had really supported him, Fred would have won comfortably by a margin that could have gone as high as fifty thousand votes or more. As it was, he had left Fred to squeak ignominiously in. It was not something Fred would forgive him, even if he could.

The second disturbing event had been Ted's selection of Roger P. Croy as his running mate, but it had not taken Fred long to rationalize that to his own advantage. He could see why Ted could not choose him, the fuss from certain of the media and from Ted's idealistic supporters would have been too much. And Roger P. Croy, fatuous, pompous, arrogant and asinine stuffed shirt as Fred saw him, would be no great hindrance in the long run. Perhaps you needed a Kerensky for a while, until things were ripe for the Lenin to move.

For this, fantastic though it might sound, and unbelievable (happily and fortunately unbelievable, from his standpoint) though it might be for the great majority of his naive and well-meaning countrymen to grasp, was actually the way Fred Van Ackerman saw himself.

He knew what no one yet was quite prepared to believe, though some in the media were finally beginning to suspect—some he would take care of, he rather thought, before they had a chance to get to him —that there actually was a United States Senator who wanted to become dictator of his country, and who wanted to do so badly enough that he was accepting the covert and all-embracing help of the Soviet Union to achieve his desire.

And this in a wild, disjointed moment when the whole fabric of America, thanks to the President's genuine idealism and the Russians' ruthless response, was suddenly unraveled, and when no one could predict what might not come of it for the stern of purpose and the fleet of foot.

Nothing like this had ever happened in America—it just couldn't. But like so many other things that just couldn't happen in America, yet in these recent hectic decades had indeed happened, this, too, Fred believed, could come to pass.

He reflected, with a grimly sardonic humor, that it was rather like the old joke about Washington weather.

So it can't happen here because it never has happened here?

Wait a minute. . . .

Now the first overt moves were under way.

The uniforming and arming of NAWAC, tested tentatively during the convention and the campaign, had been sanctioned by the non-opposition of the President and now were established beyond his power to control.

"Help America" had been launched this afternoon on the Hill by the man who only four months ago had filibustered it to death in the Senate in its original form of "the anti-riot bill." Fred had reversed his field without a moment's hesitation when the Administration changed and it became certain that the bill could now be used against the general citizenry instead of against NAWAC. He had revised and amended it to give the government terrible teeth, counting on the political naiveté, ideological intolerance and lifelong educational conditioning of the new young members who came in on Ted's coattails to help him carry it through. He knew it would be a hell of a fight, but he felt he could either intimidate Ted into supporting it or intimidate him into remaining silent. Fred believed that Ted in his present condition was highly subject to being intimidated, and he intended to do so.

And around the world and in Moscow the other side of the pincers was closing.

The situation of fright and fluidity in which he saw his opportunities was hourly increasing.

At his back, on the two floors rented by NAWAC overlooking Connecticut Avenue, the computer memory banks were filling up with a steadily increasing stream of data on most of the prominent citizens of the country. Within a month virtually every American of any importance would be filed and catalogued according to his or her weaknesses. Much of this might not be necessary if the Help America Act passed, for then he intended to so arrange things that he and NAWAC would have access to all the vast records of the government. But this would give NAWAC a nice backup, just in case. The computers were the latest and most sophisticated, and there was very little they could not be used for in the hands of men unscrupulous enough to do it. It had always been only a matter of time before such men came along in America, as they had long since in the Soviet Union and other police states of the world.

Half-laughing, at beautiful "Vagaries" a couple of miles north in snow-hushed Rock Creek Park, Hal Knox had made a wry joke about spying.

Downtown overlooking busy snow-clogged Connecticut Avenue, NAWAC and its chairman weren't joking at all.

ABBOTT, MRS. KNOX, SENATOR HAMILTON ANNOUNCE FORMATION OF "IN DEFENSE OF FREEDOM" GROUP TO OPPOSE PRESIDENT'S POLICIES. IDF TO HAVE QUARTERS IN WASHINGTON, CAMPAIGN FOR STRONG RESPONSE TO RUSSIA, DEFEAT OF HELP AMERICA BILL. VAN ACKERMAN DISMISSES EFFORT AS "TYPICAL RIGHT-WING REACTIONARY ATTEMPT TO CRIPPLE OUR GREAT PRESIDENT." SENATOR PLEDGES ALL-OUT NAWAC FIGHT TO PASS HELP AMERICA, SUPPORT JASON IN ANTI-WAR POLICIES. HAWKS EXPECTED TO RALLY TO ANTI-JASON STANDARD.

PRESIDENT REMAINS SILENT WHILE MOSCOW CONTINUES TO CONSOLIDATE NEW POSITIONS AROUND GLOBE. NO WORD OF TALK TO NATION AS HEALTH RUMORS HIT CAPITAL. SUPPORTERS EXPRESS CONFIDENCE, CONCERN.

And not the least of these, on the morning of the day on which the two houses of Congress would start their bitter debates on S. 1776 and H.R. 1776, was the distinguished white-haired gentleman who now occupied the office of Vice President of the United States. Roger P. Croy looked every inch the confident statesman as he dismissed the worried questions of reporters when they cornered him just outside the Senators' Dining Room after an early lunch, but underneath a hearty facade a somber and increasingly desperate concern was gnawing away. This he managed to conceal, though he found it impossible to banish.

"Mr. Vice President," the Dallas *News* led off, "is it true that you have been unable to contact the President since his return from Moscow?"

"I have been in contact with the White House on several occasions—" Roger P. Croy began, but of course he was not allowed to get away with that.

"I said the President, sir," the Dallas *News* reminded politely but firmly.

"I am not privileged to disclose my conversations with the President," Roger Croy said, congratulating himself that this was true enough.

"Have you had any, sir?" the New York *Times* inquired blandly. With equal blandness the Vice President shook his head and smiled.

"Now, gentlemen, you know very well I can't answer that sort of question. Furthermore, I won't. So let's proceed to something else, shall we?"

"Mr. Vice President," the Washington *Star-News* said, quite severely, "you are aware that there is a substantial and growing concern in the country. The President's silence is disturbing people. Can you tell us anything about it?"

"The President," Roger Croy said thoughtfully, "has a great many things on his mind, right? He wants to be sure that when he speaks his words—and his actions—will contribute to a solution of the rather difficult situation in which we find ourselves, right? Therefore, I personally don't fault him at all for taking his time. And I think, on reflection, that you won't either."

"But when, Mr. Vice President?" the Washington *Post* inquired. "Don't you feel any sense of urgency about it at all?"

Roger P. Croy flushed and for a moment looked quite annoyed.

"Naturally I feel urgency about it," he admitted sharply. "This is a very grave situation we are in. At the same time, however, I am prepared to trust the judgment of the President of the United States, who will act at such a time and in such a manner as he deems best. After all, what are you gentlemen complaining about? You wanted him elected President, didn't you? Then have faith in him!"

"Mr. Vice President—" the *Post* began to reply with equal sharpness, but Roger Croy gave a toss of his silver head and turned on his heel with a last riposte.

"Have faith!" he repeated, and strode off, satisfied that their angry grumbles indicated that he had put them in their places.

He was not, however, at all satisfied with the way things were going, and as soon as he had taken a few steps down the hall a worried frown returned to his face. Earlier this morning he had tried twice to telephone the President, only to be fobbed off by the appointments secretary with some flimsy excuse. A little while ago he had tried again and this time the appointments secretary had snapped, "The President is only taking calls of major import, Mr. Vice President!"

"It is imperative that I speak to him," Roger P. Croy had said evenly, keeping his temper with great difficulty. "I want to know what he thinks I should—"

"He has other imperatives!" the appointments secretary interrupted brutally, and rang off.

The result of this, as with so many of the appointments secretary's arrogant rejoinders, was that it left his listener enraged and very much inclined to say, "To hell with you and the President too." Except, of course, that one did not say that, and certainly not in such an hour.

What Roger P. Croy really wanted to know—aside from a growing anxiety about the apparently unchanged international situation—was what attitude he should take toward the Help America bill. Should he stay on the job and preside over the Senate, thereby appearing to give some Administration sanction to the measure? Or should he turn the gavel over to someone else and make himself discreetly invisible, thereby indicating some Administration displeasure? If he did preside, should his rulings be relaxed and friendly to the bill, or should they be strictly by the book? Should he recognize mostly Senators who were in favor of it and suavely overlook those who weren't, or should he be strictly impartial and straight down the middle? If there were tie votes, how should he resolve them? The Chair did have *some* role to play, after all, and Roger P. Croy felt that he would very much like to know what the President thought it should be.

It was typical of him, and in a sense typical of the whole hectic situation at this moment, that the Vice President should be quite prepared to move either way according to the President's dictates. He felt no particular moral, historical or democratic indignation against the bill, and no great enthusiasm for it. He was there, he felt, to do the job the President wanted. He would just like to know what it was. If he didn't know, he would flounder, and that could open the door to results the President might not desire.

He felt frustrated, annoyed and rather helpless. A sudden hand on his arm, particularly when he spun about impatiently and saw who it was, did not make him feel any better.

"Yes?" he said, barely civil, for he instinctively disliked and mistrusted this particular individual. "What can I do for you?" And then, because he suddenly felt uneasy and on guard for no reason he could quite put his finger on, he added the name almost as an afterthought —"Fred?"

"Well, Roger boy," Senator Van Ackerman said, "let me come along to your office for a minute and I'll tell you."

"It's almost time for the Senate to convene—" the Vice President began, but a sudden angry, almost feral expression on his companion's face caused him to change his mind. "We have about fifteen minutes, I guess," he amended lamely. "You can come in, if you like."

"Good," Fred said, amiable again as suddenly as he had been hostile. "I like . . . Now," he said, when they had ascended to the second floor in one of the Senators' private elevators, nodded to the police and Secret Service at the door and entered the Vice President's ornate little office just off the floor, "sit down, Roger, and I'll tell you what's on my mind. What do you hear from the man downtown?"

For a moment the Vice President felt like bluffing. Then he abandoned it and spoke frankly.

"Not a damned thing. I haven't been able to get through."

"Neither have I," Senator Van Ackerman confessed with a scowl, and though what he said next sounded like a joke, something in his tone made the Vice President shiver a little. "That smart-ass little bastard who screens the calls has got to go. . . . Well, anyway, I guess that leaves it up to us. Since he's temporarily out of the picture for some reason I can't figure, we've got to decide on strategy for the bill."

"That's why I was trying to reach him," the Vice President said. "I don't know whether he wants it or not."

"Silence implies consent," Fred said shortly. "He's already missed the time to oppose it, if he wanted to." He frowned a little, then smiled an intimate, secret little smile and said, as if to himself, "He misses the time for almost everything, doesn't he? . . . *but,*" he went on, more brightly, "that's his problem, isn't it, Roger, and none of yours and mine."

"I don't know what you mean," the Vice President said stiffly, deciding that he must reject this apparent attempt to establish an unwanted intimacy, especially since he suddenly felt that at its heart lay a carefully calculated campaign to separate him from the President. "I just don't know what you mean."

"Sure you do," Senator Van Ackerman said comfortably. "It's obvious he's scared out of his gourd and the whole thing is drifting. So that leaves it up to you and me and our friends on the Hill to go ahead and do for him what we know he wants us to do, which is to pass the Help America bill and give him the tools to get the job done."

"What job?" Roger P. Croy inquired, hating himself for his uncertain, almost hesitant tone. This was no way to deal with Fred Van Ackerman, but in the absence of word from the President he was really on a spot.

"The job of keeping these lily-livered reactionary right-wing bastards under control," Fred Van Ackerman said in a suddenly vicious voice. "The job of keeping the damned dissenters from interfering with the policy of peace he was elected to carry out. *The job of showing them who's boss*—that job. You know we can't have these pantywaists tearing down the country and messing everything up for him, Roger. It's intolerable!"

"It's awkward," the Vice President conceded carefully, "but whether it warrants a measure as harsh as yours is in some respects, is another matter. After all, it's still a free country."

"It is?" Senator Van Ackerman asked, again with his secret, conspiratorial little smile. "Come now, Roger!"

"But it is!" Roger Croy protested, shocked out of his carefully held dignity. "Of course it is!"

"Well, it won't be for long," Fred said flatly, "if we let this damned protest and dissent get out of hand. They're out to destroy America, Roger, it's obvious that's their game. That's why we have to have this bill. That's why we've got to help America. The 'Help America bill!' That's what we've named it and that's what it is: to stop the damned dissenters and preserve law and order!"

"But you always used to be opposed to stopping dissent," the Vice President protested, rather foolishly. His answer was a scornful smile.

"I was opposed when the dissent was directed against something I didn't believe in," Fred Van Ackerman said, "but now it's against a man and policies I do believe in." His voice suddenly acquired a savage singsong. "Don't *you* believe in the President, Roger? Don't *you* believe in the great peace policies he's following? Aren't *you* for Edward M. Jason? Don't tell me the Vice President of the United States is betraying his President, Roger! Don't make me have to tell that to him and to the press!"

"*No!*" Roger Croy said so hurriedly and loudly he was sure the guards outside the door must have heard him. *"No!"* he repeated in a lower, insistent voice, ignoring the sudden ominous scowl his next words brought to the face across the desk. "Don't you pull any of your blackmail games on me, Fred Van Ackerman! I'm for Edward M. Jason and his policies 100 per cent! I believe in Edward M. Jason and everything he does! I believe—"

"Then stop gasping for breath like a silly old woman," Senator Van Ackerman interrupted with a harsh relish, "and help me plan strategy to get this bill through. I'm counting on you, Roger, and the President's counting on you. You'd damned well better keep the faith, hadn't you?"

"Well," Roger P. Croy said lamely, his voice still shaking with affront and anger, "of course I want to do what's right to help him. . . ."

But a few minutes later, after he had convened the Senate and then turned over the gavel temporarily to the president pro tempore, stately old Lacey Pollard of Texas, he again was unable to get through to the President. He thought it might be of help to let him know the mood and thinking behind the bill, but the appointments secretary, coldly efficient, blocked him again.

ADMINISTRATION FORCES RUSH HELP AMERICA BILL TO FLOOR OF BOTH HOUSES. SENATE JUDICIARY COMMITTEE VOTES APPROVAL 9–6 IN BITTER ALL-NIGHT SESSION. "YOUNG TURKS" ON HOUSE RULES COMMITTEE RAM THROUGH DECISION TO BYPASS JUDICIARY, SEND MEASURE DIRECTLY TO FLOOR. VAN ACKERMAN, BRONSON BERNARD TO OPEN DEBATE.

RUSSIAN FLEET RIDING ALL SEAS. GOVERNMENTS IN PANAMA, GOROTOLAND ANNOUNCE "COMPLETE PACIFICATION" AS FINAL AMERICAN PRISONERS ROUNDED UP. WHITE HOUSE ANNOUNCES PRESIDENT CONFERRING WITH TOP AIDES AS CRISIS MOUNTS. NEW ANTI-JASON GROUP REPORTS "MANY THOUSANDS" OF WIRES, MESSAGES SUPPORTING STAND.

The Picturephone rang, but when she turned on the receiver the screen was blank. Only a voice, husky and unidentified, said, "Mrs. Knox?"

"Yes?" she said coldly, though her heart gave a sudden hurtful leap. "Who are you and what do you want?"

"Just a friend, Mrs. Knox," the voice said. "Just a friend. One who wants you to be very, very safe and not very, very sorry."

"Who are you?" she repeated, indignation and courage making her voice stronger. "What is this all about?"

"I think you should return to your dignified widowhood, Mrs. Knox," the voice said, eerie and oily and obviously enjoying its own effects. "I don't think you should try to meddle in public affairs any more. After all, Mrs. Knox: one death in the family is enough, isn't it?"

"Are you threatening me?" she demanded sharply, reaching finally to snap off the picture transmitter so that her sinister caller could not see her expression. The voice chuckled.

"You—your son—your daughter-in-law—who knows who I might be threatening? But 'threat' is a nasty word, Mrs. Knox. Let's just say I'm offering a word of sensible caution to a very great lady whom I admire very, very much. Let's say that."

"You're wasting your time," she said shortly. "Kooks and psychopaths have been after the Knoxes all our public life. One more doesn't matter."

"There's already been one too many, hasn't there?" the voice snapped, a sudden cold rage snarling out of it. "Where's dear old Orrin now, Mrs. Knox? Where's that great, distinguished husb—"

But swiftly and instinctively, almost without conscious thought, she had snapped off the machine entirely and the room in the pleasant old house in Spring Valley was abruptly still.

For several minutes she sat trembling, her breath coming in shallow, almost sobbing gasps, her heart pounding painfully, her body covered with perspiration. Then she forced herself to breathe more slowly, forced herself to stop trembling, by sheer will power made herself calm again.

That finally accomplished, she switched on the machine and dialed the White House. The chief operator, efficient veteran of twenty-five years on the nation's most important switchboard, recognized her with a cordial smile.

"Why, Mrs. Knox!" she said. "How nice to see you. What can we do for you?"

"Nice to see you, too, Marjorie," she said, forcing herself to be sociable though her heart was filled with a sudden desperate impatience. "Is there any chance I might speak to the President?"

The chief operator's expression changed to one of brief but candid annoyance.

"It is so *difficult* to get through to him. I don't know *what's* going on over there. But—" and normal cheerful briskness took over again— "we'll give it a try. Hang on."

The screen went blank for a couple of minutes. Then she reappeared, expression regretful.

"I'm terribly sorry, Mrs. Knox," she said, and Beth could see that she genuinely was, "but the appointments secretary says—"

"Let me speak to him," she said sharply. The chief operator nodded with a wink and a fleeting but obvious expression of approval.

"Yes. I'll get him."

Again the screen went blank. Then a face she did not know, young, smug, self-contained and curiously closed-off, unwelcoming and unyielding, appeared.

"Yes?" he said sharply. "What is it, Mrs. Knox?"

"I must see the President," she said firmly. "Today."

"Mrs. Knox—" he began, the sharpness unchanged. "The President is extremely busy. He has given orders—"

"You tell him," she interrupted, her voice deliberately slow, authoritative and filled with what appeared to be an absolute certainty that he would comply, "that Beth Knox called and that I must see him personally *today* on a matter of great importance to us both. I expect you to transmit this message for me honorably, truthfully and at once. May I have that assurance?"

"Mrs. Knox—" he said angrily. But she could see he was not so sure of himself as he had been.

"May I have that assurance?" she repeated evenly, and for several seconds they stared at one another. Then his eyes dropped and with a sullenness suddenly almost little-boy, he snapped, "Very well! I will call you back."

Again the screen was blank, but before she could flick off her own, the chief operator reappeared for just a second.

"Good going," she said briskly. "I can't *stand* this new crew."

"Thanks," Beth said, feeling a return of amusement for the first time in half an hour. "I'll be right here, Marjorie."

"Stand by," Marjorie said. "We'll be back to you just as soon as possible."

And in ten minutes, amazingly, she got the answer she had hardly dared hope for.

"The President will see you at 3 P.M.," the appointments secretary said, expressionless. "We will send a car and a couple of Secret Servicemen to pick you up."

"That won't be necessary—" she began, and then stopped abruptly, her voice trailing away. His expression did not change.

"The President thinks it will be best," he said. "See you at three o'clock."

"Thank you," she said. And presently, after he had given a little half bow and vanished, and she had turned off her own machine, she added aloud to the silent room, "So apparently he does have some inkling of what's going on in the world, after all. . . ."

Heartened considerably by this, she spent the next ten minutes calling her son and the ex-President. Hal was on the floor of the House, his first response a hurried and impatient "What is it, Mom, we're about to start debate on the Help America—damn it, they've got me doing it too—dictatorship bill." But when she told him tersely why she was calling, he responded with great alarm, demanding to know where Crystal was—"Safely upstairs taking a nap," Beth said—and insisting that she call the police and ask that someone be assigned to guard the house. She promised she would, urged him to take care of himself and wished him well in the debate. He replied grimly that he thought they would lose but it would be a hell of a fight, and rang off, looking young, tense and worried but as stubbornly determined as his father would have been in similar circumstances.

William Abbott, whom she found in the Majority Cloakroom just off the House floor, sounded equally alarmed but with an extra edge of fury that indicated how perturbed he was by the drift of events. He too urged precautions, thanked her for calling, promised to watch out for himself—"although," with a grim little amusement, "I still have my Secret Service protection. They can't take that away from me— yet, anyway." She saved her most surprising information to the last. Bill Abbott was suitably astounded and immediately practical.

"Very well: so you're going to see him. I'm pretty sure you're the first outsider he's let in, you know. I hope you'll really impress upon him—well, everything."

"Don't worry, Bill. I will."

"Wake him up," the ex-President said bluntly. "Shake some sense into him. *Make him take hold.* My God, he can't let us drift any longer!"

"I'll do my best," she promised, "—if he'll hear me out."

"I think he just may," William Abbott said. "I have a sneaking hunch he's feeling desperately alone or he wouldn't have agreed to see you. He wants reassurance, he needs a friend. I think in some way, subconscious or conscious, he feels he needs the help of the Knoxes." His voice grew suddenly softer, and he used for Elizabeth Henry the nickname that only her husband had used. "You're going to be Orrin's stand-in, Hank. Do him proud."

"I will," she promised with a sudden shaky little laugh. "I will, dear Bill. And I'll report to you afterwards."

"Please do," he said gravely.

"You'll warn Cullee for me, too?" she asked. He nodded. "I'm going over to the Senate in a minute to talk to both him and Bob Munson. I'll warn them immediately."

"Good," she said, "God bless."

"You, too," he said. "Be very careful."

"Yes."

For a moment after the screen went blank she sat motionless, mind racing. Then she called the office of the chief of police of the District of Columbia; was put through to him at once; explained the situation; was promised the immediate assignment of two officers—"They're on their way," the chief said with a smile, "ten minutes ago."—and rang off, considerably reassured.

After that she got up, tiptoed silently upstairs; looked in on Crystal; found her sleeping with a childlike soundness; and tiptoed back down. Then she returned to the Picturephone and made the call she had been considering ever since the evil voice had violated her home an hour ago. The expression on the face that appeared on the screen was a study as its owner saw who was calling him. But she didn't give him time to think about it.

"Walter," she said firmly, "I think it's imperative that you know something. I don't know what you'll think you should do with the knowledge, but I think you should have it. Do you mind?"

For a second he looked quite nonplussed at the question. Then he shook his head with a cautious but not unamiable little smile.

"No, Beth," he said quietly. "I don't mind. What is it?"

While she described the voice he studied her face carefully and apparently without emotion. But when she finished he drew a deep breath and spoke with more genuine feeling and more genuine candor than he had ever revealed in all the years of his bitter opposition to her husband.

"*Christ*," he said. "What *are* we coming to?"

Something about the desperate unhappiness of his tone sparked an intuitive response and with a quick, shrewd glance she asked bluntly, "Have they been after you too?"

For a moment he hesitated. She was flattered that it was not for long.

"I never thought," he said wryly, "that I would find an ally in Beth Knox or she in me. But, yes, they have. They've been threatening many of us in the media for quite a while, now. Well back in the campaign, as a matter of fact."

"But why didn't you tell us?" she demanded. "Why didn't somebody—"

"Because *he* wouldn't speak out," he said with a dry bitterness. "And we wanted *him* to win. And we thought if we complained about *his* most violent supporters it would hurt *his* chances. And so we muttered a bit but generally kept quiet."

"And compromised your own integrity," she said levelly, and as levelly he answered with what she knew was the most honest word she had ever heard from Walter Dobius:

"Yes."

They were silent for a moment, studying one another. Presently he resumed in a calm and pragmatic voice.

"I am not defending this and I am not proud of it. By the same token, I am not going to waste your time or mine beating my breast about it. It happened and here we are. The question is, where do we go now?"

"You can't join the IDF, of course. But maybe you can work in parallel ways."

"Some of my friends and I have been discussing it," he said. "You didn't find the editorials about your venture so very severe this morning, did you?"

She smiled.

"Not at all what I expected. I even detected a certain—what might almost be called tolerance—in certain famous institutions. Not approval, of course, but tolerance."

"Nobody quite feels we can approve just yet," he said slowly. "But it may come, and very shortly, if things don't change." He paused and studied her for a moment. "Beth—can I use this information you've just given me, in my column?"

She hesitated for a second, a worried frown crossing her face.

"Not directly," she said slowly. "Not by name. If you want to say that influential organizers of the IDF are being threatened with violence by supporters of the President—"

"We don't know that for sure," he said quickly and with equal quickness she gave him an ironic glance.

"Now don't tell me you're going to hide, Walter. I thought we were in the same boat."

He blinked. Then he nodded with a conceding little smile.

"Will you allow me to say 'there is good reason to believe that these intimidations come from certain forces supporting the President?'" he inquired. "For the moment, that is? I can get stronger as I go along."

She smiled.

"I'm beginning to rather like you, Walter. I never thought I would."

It was his turn to be ironic.

"Spoken like a true Knox." Then his face became grim. "I am worried for our country, Beth. Desperately."

"So am I," she said, and decided to tell him her other news. "I am seeing him at three, you know."

He looked startled but immediately practical.

"Tell him—" he began, and then shrugged with a wry little smile. "I don't have to tell you what to tell him. Tell him everything there is to tell. Tell him to *move*."

"Will you tell him too?" she asked. "And will the *Times* and the *Post* and the networks and all the rest? He won't unless you all begin clamoring for it, too. There's got to be a great public outcry."

"Which, if it is to be effective with him," Walter Dobius pointed out, "cannot be too closely associated with IDF or mobs in Lafayette Square. It has to be respectable."

"You're telling me Bill Abbott and my son and Cullee Hamilton and I and the millions who look to us are not respectable?" she demanded with some asperity. "We're not mobs in Lafayette Square, Walter. But I can tell you this: unless we who *are* respectable can make our weight felt, and unless we can have the effective, even if not open, support of people like you in the media, then the mobs in Lafayette Square will take over and it *will* be mob against mob. And then the country really will be gone. This isn't a semantic game we're playing, this time. It may be the end of America."

"I know that, Beth!" he said sharply. "I know that! Why do you think I'm going out on a limb in my column day after day, even though they've been hanging around 'Salubria'—even though those vicious nonentities Van Ackerman, Shelby and Kleinfert came here four months ago and threatened to burn it down if I didn't go along with Ted Jason? *Threatened to burn it down!*" he repeated, his face contorted with a naked anguish of which she had never believed him capable. "'*Salubria!*' Burn it down! Burn it *down!*" He paused and struggled to regain his composure. "No," he said finally. "Events are forcing us all together, Beth. We're going the same road. We've got to."

"And we've got to *now*," she said. "I have this terrible feeling that he's sleepwalking. The Russians aren't pulling back a bit—Van Ackerman is pushing his bill on the Hill right this minute—everything's moving against us—and *nothing* is being done."

"You would think," he said slowly, "that if the Russians felt they had to make any concessions, they would do at least *one* thing, make at least *one* gesture. Let the prisoners go, perhaps, or abandon the attempts to blockade Alaska, or something—just *one* thing. They're acting completely arrogant, as though we're absolutely helpless and they don't have to do a thing."

"Maybe they're right," she said quietly. "Maybe they found him so weak that they feel they can do anything they want—or nothing. It's terrifying."

"And then, with that as an excuse, in comes the bill in Congress to impose the first steps of a virtual dictatorship upon us. Everything suddenly doesn't make sense any more." He shook his head grimly. "It *is* terrifying."

"You and your friends had better write fast, Walter. There may not be much more time."

"There may not," he agreed gravely, "though it seems utterly insane to sit here at the fulcrum of the American Republic and acknowledge the possibility. Are you under sufficient protection?"

"I think so. Are you?"

He shook his head.

"Not really. The local sheriff would try but it wouldn't be very effective, I'm afraid."

"You could always come in town and stay at the Metropolitan Club."

"And leave my home?" he asked sharply. "Never."

"No more can any of us leave," she said, her eyes widening in thought, "anywhere in America. We have to stay right where we are and fight it out."

"I doubt if many would want to do anything else," he said, "though I pray it may not come to fighting."

"Or other terrors," she said. "There are other terrors, besides fighting."

"Well," he said, "we mustn't be so gloomy. Everything isn't lost yet. I've got a column to write—you've got an organization to lead—you're seeing the President at three." He gave an ironic chuckle, sounding more himself. "Beth Knox at the bridge. Maybe you can save us all."

"It won't be for lack of trying," she promised with the return of a reasonable humor.

"I should think *not*," he said with a smile. "Tell me about it afterwards, if you think you can."

"Will you be home? I'll call you tonight."

"I'll be on the Hill. I'm going in as soon as I finish my column for tomorrow. I want to sit in on this debate."

"I may be there myself. If I don't see you, I'll call in the morning."

"Good. Thank you very much, Beth. Many old alignments are changing. I think it not too bad that we wind up together."

"Nor I, Walter," she said. "Be careful."

"You too," he said gravely. "You too."

How ironic it was, she reflected as his pompous, determined visage faded from the screen, that she and Walter Dobius should find themselves in tacit alliance: how typical of this chaotic moment in the country's history. The powerful columnist who had bitterly disliked and bitterly opposed her husband for so many years, the rigid and intolerant liberal who had so savagely denounced everything Orrin Knox stood for, the molder of public opinion who had always done his best to mold it in the leftward direction—suddenly an ally. And one, she admitted honestly, that she was very glad to have. With him would come many influential members of the media, perhaps not in open alliance but in many effective corollary ways that would help to bring a strangely paralyzed President to life again and return the country, if they were lucky, to self-respect and courage and a new start in the face of its enemies.

She listened for a moment at the foot of the stairs, heard Crystal gently snoring. She must wake her soon, for they both wanted to listen for a while to the televised debate on the Help America bill before Beth went to keep her appointment at the White House.

As she turned back to the kitchen to start water boiling to make tea for the two of them, she heard the sound of a car, tires in the driveway. She glanced out to see a police car pulling in. Three young officers got out and started up the walk. She ran the water quickly, put the teakettle on. Then she went to the door in answer to their ring, and let them in.

"You jes' give 'em hell, now," the Speaker had told him, scarcely fifteen minutes ago when he stopped by the ornate old office across the corridor from the floor. "You jes' let 'em have it, and I'll be right there backin' you up, because we sure as shootin' got to help the greatest President this country's ever had. Yes, sir!"

"Mr. Speaker," he had said, a little hesitantly, because there was one little nagging worry on his mind and he wanted reassurance before he went forth to make his grand debut upon the national scene.

"Yes, son?" Jawbone responded with the kindly, fatherly air he had begun to adopt toward many of his colleagues, particularly this young smart-as-a-whip crew that had sailed in on Ted Jason's coattails. "What is it, son?"

"Well, sir," said Representative Bronson Bernard of New York—"Bronnie" to his constituents, his family and his friends—"well, sir, it's this: are you sure the President really wants our bill? Is he really behind it? I'd hate to go out on a limb for him and then find out he wasn't with us. Has he told you he wants it?"

"Well, sir!" Jawbone exclaimed. "Well, now! What on earth makes you think that?"

"Have you talked to him, sir?" Bronnie Bernard persisted politely. "Has he told you so?"

"Well, now," Jawbone confessed with his ingratiating, puppy-dog smile, "I wouldn't say I've exactly *talked* to him, you know. Don't believe much of anybody *has,* as a matter of fact, since he got back from Moscow. He's been mighty busy since then, you know, mighty busy—"

"Doing what?" Bronnie Bernard inquired, fixing the Speaker with a gimlet gaze both innocent and implacable.

"Well!" Jawbone said, taken aback. "Well, doing what, yes, doing what!"

"Yes," Bronnie Bernard agreed pleasantly, "doing what?"

"Studyin'!" Jawbone said. "Workin'! Plannin' strategy to get us outa this! That's what! Can't be bothered with no little ole bitty Congressman, now—like either one of us, here!" he added hastily, as Representative Bernard's eyes narrowed, not so pleasantly. "Like you or me, both! That man's got high strategy on his mind, Congressman! Yes, sir, high strategy! He just hasn't had *time* to consult with you or me. But I know he wants this bill, now, I know he's just got to have it, to keep the country calm and u—nited behind him in this great crisis! *Why!*" he exclaimed with a sudden calculated indignation that did have its effect on Bronnie Bernard, who after all was only twenty-six even if he had won a seat in Congress against all predictions, "Are you telling me that you, a *brand-new* member here, are going to set yourself up to challenge the President of the U—nited States and maybe betray him, when he is countin' on you to be one of his best young lieutenants in the years to come? You goin' to be-*tray* your President, Congressman Bernard, the first time he turns to you for help? That what you tellin' your Speaker, now?"

"No, sir," Bronnie Bernard said hastily. "I'm not going to betray him, I just want to be sure he—"

"You be sure, boy!" Jawbone cried. "You jes' bet your bottom dollar you be sure! Now you get on out there and give 'em hell, like I tole you! You jes' give 'em hell and don't look back! The President's watchin' you, Bronnie! He knows what you're doin' is right, jes' like you know what you're doin' is right! Isn't that right, now?"

"I believe we do need legislation to curb disruptive outbreaks against the public interest," Representative Bernard said carefully. "I believe it is imperative that the President be free of radical public pressures while he formulates and administers his policies for peace. I believe—"

"Well, then!" Jawbone cried triumphantly. "You jes' believe and you keep right on believin', and before you know it we'll have passed this bill of yours and you'll be a great man, Congressman Bernard! A great man, and you'll get your reward for it, too! This Administration won't forget you, Congressman! You'll find we take care of our own in this Administration!"

"That," said Bronnie Bernard with an instantaneous icy disapproval, "is exactly the type of old politics most of us new members have come here determined to wipe out. You cannot bribe me, Mr. Speaker. I do what I do because it is *right,* and my reward is a conscience satisfied and at rest. You would not understand that in your generation but I suggest to you that it is the key to understanding mine. We do what is *right* because it is *right.* Try to grasp that fact, Mr. Speaker. It will make your duties here much simpler and more agreeable if you do."

And turning on his heel with a fine indignation, he strode out, narrowly missing collision with the newsmen who were beginning to straggle in for the Speaker's usual presession press briefing.

"Well," Jawbone called weakly after his sternly departing back, "you give 'em hell now, you hear? You give 'em hell!"

Which of course was exactly what he intended to do, Bronnie Bernard told himself with a still seething disgust as he took his seat toward the rear of the chamber. And he didn't need that dithering old Southern reactionary fool who unfortunately happened to be Speaker to tell him about it, either. He would like to have direct assurance of the President's support, but he was prepared to move forward anyway, because he knew as well as Swarthman did that the President really did want the bill. He wanted it, Bronnie knew, because he needed it; and concerning the fact that he needed it, Bronnie had no doubt. He had a conviction about this that was visceral because it was generational. Bronnie was a very bright product of a very determined educational process, and it was inevitable that he should therefore be the perfect instrument for what some called the Help America bill and others called the dictatorship bill.

In the mind of Bronson Bernard certain basic tenets had been implanted by his teachers at every stage from grammar school through college, and nothing was ever going to shake them. The United States of America was no damned good. Its ideals were a mockery. Its history was a fraud. Its purposes were corrupt. Its achievements were empty. Its hopes were a sham and its dreams were a lie. Whatever good might have come from it here and there over the years—and that was precious little—had been entirely inadvertent and accidental. It was sinister, hypocritical, imperialistic, racist, worthless and cruel. It was a mess, and if it happened to provide one with a substantial amount of material comfort and an amazing amount of personal freedom, that was entirely aside from its true nature and a dividend you shouldn't question but should just make the most of while you did your best to tear the country down.

So believed Bronnie Bernard and so believed many millions of his generation who had spent their adolescent years passing through American schools, reading American newspapers and magazines, watching American television and listening to American radio, absorbing with rapt and respectful attention the savage attacks and denigrations of American intellectual and cultural leaders. The end result had been to make of Bronnie and his like exactly what they were: human time bombs perfectly trained and programmed to go off, in due course, in every area where a nation must look to find its endurance and its strength.

Now in increasing numbers they were taking their places in the educational apparatus, moving into the law, being appointed to the courts, taking over medicine and public health, acquiring more and more control of the media and the arts, rising to ever more influential positions in the economy, being elected to city councils, school boards, state legislatures, Congress. The Jason landslide had been a turning point in more ways than one, for it had finally brought Bronnie and his generation close to full control of both houses of Congress. Given the number of wavering elders who still remained—those who had always been dreadfully self-conscious about doing anything that could possibly be labeled "illiberal" or "reactionary" by a relentless media and a vindictive intellectual community, those who could always be scared into line by a raucous hoot of "conservative!"—and Bronnie and his newly elected colleagues just about had it made.

And in all of this, of course, there was no "conspiracy," no "cabal," no "organized infiltration"—at least on their part. They were quite genuine, quite idealistic, quite honorable on their own terms and quite sincere. They were simply the raw material for the Fred Van Ackermans to use, the conditioned, willing, eager stooges of the manipulators who knew exactly where they were going and exactly how they were going to get there.

They were absolutely innocent, absolutely earnest, absolutely righteous and absolutely terrifying. They *knew,* because they had never been allowed to know anything else, that they were the children of a rotten country that had to be changed no matter what the change might do to liberty or to human beings. They were without objectivity, compassion, the power to analyze or any points of historical or moral reference because objectivity had been destroyed, compassion had been withheld, the power to analyze had been turned upside down, and history and the concept of moral reference had been deliberately and scornfully dismissed.

Bronson Bernard and his generation were the great innocents who could do horrible things to their fellow beings, simply because they had been taught no other way of dealing with them. And this they were now about to do.

He wondered impatiently why the House took so long to get down to business, and made a mental note to talk about it to his already rapidly widening circle of friends among the new members. House rules were antiquated, outmoded, inefficient, deliberately designed to permit the forces of reaction to retain their control of the democratic process. Bronnie and his friends would get to that in due time, he promised himself grimly. But first, of course, they had to get the Help America bill through. With a serene and absolutely sincere conviction that the bill was entirely necessary, and a serene and absolutely sincere inability to perceive any of its dangers to democracy, he arose when it presently came time for him to open debate and stated his case with a youthful and stirring fervor.

"Mr. Speaker!" he began, and the challenge of his tone disclosed that all those medals for debating at Harvard had not been ill-accorded. "We meet here in a grave moment for the American Republic—a moment which makes it imperative that we consult, not the old and outworn fears of the past, but the new and dynamic opportunities that have come to us with the Presidency of Edward M. Jason.

"Opportunities which, I submit to you, Mr. Speaker, come but seldom to a people. . . ."

"I'm sorry, Mr. Secretary," the guard at the East Gate said politely, "but the appointments office doesn't appear to have anything on the list for you—for any of you. Perhaps if you could come back later—"

"Listen," Ewan MacDonald MacDonald said with a rare show of anger, his clipped Scottish accent at its driest and most acerbic. "You get back on that phone and you tell the appointments office for me that the Secretary of Defense and the Joint Chiefs of Staff are on their way in, and if the appointments office wishes to shoot us down at the door of the Oval Office they are welcome to do so, because that's the only way we're going to be stopped. Come along, gentlemen."

And with an expressive whirl of his chunky body, he turned on his heel and started up the curving drive, dutifully followed by his colleagues of the armed services, bundled against the savage wind which tore through the city under a bleak and elusive winter sun.

Other guards, worried, upset, distraught, politely trying to follow orders but not quite daring to use physical force against the phalanx that bore down upon them, attempted to stop it at the east door, the entry to the corridor leading past the Rose Garden, the door to the corridor outside the Oval Office, the door of the Oval Office itself. Ewan MacDonald MacDonald, a stubborn man enraged and desperately worried by events, was an impressive sight backed by his admiral, his Army general, his Air Force general and his Marine general; and within five minutes after their arrival at the East Gate they were standing before the closed door of the Oval Office.

"Mr. *Secretary—*" the appointments secretary said in a tone of angry dismay.

"Announce us!" Ewan MacDonald ordered flatly, "And no more of your damned nonsense."

"The President—" the appointments secretary began, but with a sudden imperious, contemptuous gesture the Secretary of Defense stepped forward and threw open the door.

Hushed, orderly, impressive and serene, the empty office appeared before them, everything in place, not a single piece of paper, not even a pencil, on the gleaming expanse of the mammoth desk.

"Where is he?" Ewan MacDonald demanded. "What have you done with him?"

"*I* haven't '*done*' anything with him!" the appointments secretary spat out. "If you hadn't been so damned stubborn—he's over in the Mansion and he isn't receiving anyone this afternoon."

"He has *got* to receive us," the Secretary said, while behind him the Joint Chiefs of Staff gave worried, confirming nods. "The situation is deteriorating so fast we must do something. *We must.*"

"Mr. Secretary," the appointments secretary said, and for the first time in their brief acquaintance Ewan MacDonald perceived that he might be human too, "believe me, I am as scared as you are. I am as scared as hell. But all I can do is what the President tells me, and he's told me that he won't see anyone at all today or tonight, except Mrs. Knox. He has an appointment with her at three. In fact"—he glanced at his watch—"she's a little overdue already. I have orders to take her directly to the Lincoln Study, and she's the only person he's going to see today. Believe me, Mr. Secretary, I'm not being arbitrary or insulting to you personally, or to you gentlemen of the Joint Chiefs. It's just his orders. I haven't any choice."

"We can understand that," the chief of staff of the Army agreed, and again they all nodded, more friendly now.

"Well—" Ewan MacDonald said uncertainly.

"Why don't we do this?" the appointments secretary suggested. "Why don't you just sit down in here and wait, and I'll get word to him right away that you're here, and perhaps after he's seen Mrs. Knox he'll see you. All right?"

"All right," Ewan MacDonald said. "Fair enough." He offered his hand. "I'm sorry if I sounded—"

"No, that's all right," the appointments secretary said, accepting it thankfully. "It's a tough time for everybody. Have a seat, gentlemen, and I'll get back to you just as soon as I can."

But after they had sat for ten minutes in the fateful room, burdened now by history as it perhaps had never been before—after each had thought his long long thoughts about America and reviewed all his desperate fears and worries about it in this dreadful hour—the appointments secretary came back openly dejected, shaking his head.

"Maybe tomorrow," he said. "The request is in. I'll just have to let you know."

"Very well," the Secretary said. "Come along, gentlemen. I only hope," he said, trying not to sound bitter, "that Mrs. Knox can say something to him, since the rest of us don't have the chance."

"She's late," the appointments secretary repeated with a frown. "I'm going to have to check with our people who went after her."

On the second floor of the Mansion, in the little narrow room off the Lincoln Bedroom which over the years had come to be known, to those of his successors who had used it as a place to brood, ponder or exult, as "the Lincoln Study," the solitary figure by the window made no movement, uttered no sound as he watched them go out through the East Gate to be whisked away in their Pentagon limousine. Looking idly down on the street below as the minutes ticked past 3 P.M., he could see the traffic passing between the White House and the Treasury. It looked like the traffic of any other day. Nobody would know the world wasn't going along about as it always had. *What are you thinking, people?* he wondered. *Are you frightened too?*

But of course he knew they were, and he knew that inevitably he must sooner or later reassure them. They were looking to him for guidance, comfort, leadership, hope. They were looking to him to act and he knew he must act. He knew also that every hour that passed without action could only make action more difficult when it finally came. Yet he still had not found the key, and the one thing his exhausted mind still clung to was the certain knowledge that unless he had answers and a positive solution to offer, it would be better not to speak at all than to offer a feeble and ill-prepared response.

This, if ever, was the time for the American President to think. American Presidents were supposed to think. They were supposed to have the answers. They were supposed to know everything, be always confident, always strong. If and when they confronted Doomsday, they were supposed to know what to do.

All of them, that is, except the one who finally did confront Doomsday: who, through the lazy, overconfident hopes, the devious, too-clever-by-half maneuverings, or the careless, overly wishful trespasses of his predecessors, found himself and his nation suddenly naked in the gale of history with nowhere to turn and nowhere to hide and nothing to do but—what? Touch the button and blow up the world in an agony of lost hopes and failed purposes? Or surrender the nation and all its dreams, and close the book of time upon an experiment unable to triumph over the built-in potentials of its own destruction?

This was the choice he confronted, or so he believed; and down there in the street, on the Hill, in the great cluttered cities, the peaceful small towns, the farmlands, the deserts, the mountains, lakes and prairies, they did not know this. And therefore his silence only frightened them more.

He was aware of their fright, as he was aware of his own, and of the reasons for it which they did not know and which he perhaps might never be able to bring himself to tell them. Yet the responsibility was his. He had wanted it, he had received it, and he had tried to exercise it, in the way that seemed most enlightened and most worthy in the eyes of God, for his nation and for mankind.

"Why didn't it go right?" he demanded in a sudden anguished outcry, hastily choked off lest any unexpected servant wandering the Mansion hear him. But he knew the answer to his own question. And again he was silent and nothing broke the brooding hush of the Lincoln Study.

There must be a key: there must be a way out. In some almost superstitious fashion, as though he could draw from her some mysterious transfer of strength from her volatile, pragmatic husband, he clung desperately to the thought of Beth Knox, who would soon be here and might be able to give him advice and encouragement and work with him to discover and decide what he must do.

He waited and he hoped; and yet, when the appointments secretary presently entered, white-faced and shaking, to tell him that it was not to be, his tired mind seemed unable to feel surprise. One more horror on top of so many was not unexpected, somehow. It seemed to be the pattern of life that God had ordained for Edward M. Jason at this particular moment in time, and he was not really surprised to learn of another of its consistencies.

"Call the Attorney General for me," he said in a voice almost devoid of expression, "and tell him I said to do everything we possibly can to help."

"If you will forgive me, sir," the appointments secretary said, "I have already taken it upon myself to do that. He's got the FBI on it already."

"Good," he said in the same mechanical way. "Thank you."

"Yes, sir," the appointments secretary said, and hesitated, on the verge of some blurt of sympathy, some offer of assistance, some human gesture that might help the man whose burdens were so terribly great. But the President did not stir, the moment vanished. The appointments secretary, looking young and desolate, swiftly withdrew.

Patiently the silent figure in the rocker by the window resumed its perusal of the traffic in the street.

Sitting calmly at his desk, still in the front row on the majority side but now some seats away from the front seat on the aisle that he had occupied for so many years as Majority Leader, Robert Durham Munson of Michigan stared around what he kept thinking of as "the new Senate" with a thoughtfully somber air that was not lost upon the Press Gallery above. The afternoon was already half gone. He and Warren Strickland and a few others had managed to delay the start of debate on the Help America bill with a series of brief statements on other matters, routine insertions of material in the Congressional Record, elaborately prolonged discussions of minor issues and other time-consuming trivia. But now the time had come for the junior Senator from Wyoming to begin argument for his dreadful measure and the time of delay was over.

"Would you say Bobby and Warren have been filibustering?" AP leaned over to ask UPI in the front row of the gallery, as Fred Van Ackerman sought and received recognition from the president pro tempore, shrewd old Lacey Pollard of Texas.

"Not yet," UPI said with a grin. "Just practicing. The filibuster may come later. And," he said, smile fading, "not such a bad idea, if you ask me."

"Yes," AP agreed. "This is a damned peculiar piece of legislation."

"A damned frightening one," the New York *Times* said from the desk above. "Can't you see Freddy censoring the press?"

"I can," AP agreed. "That's what scares me."

"This new Senate," the Washington *Post* said with a certain relish, "is likely to do almost anything."

"Thank God we have a few old hands left," UPI said.

"A few," AP remarked glumly, "but not many. Have you talked to any of this new breed? They're getting ready to set up a guillotine."

"I don't think it's quite that bad," the *Post* said. "The Senate has a way of taming down firebrands."

"Mr. *Post*," the *Times* said dryly as below them Senator Van Ackerman cried, "Mr. President!" in a harsh and demanding tone, "meet Mr. Firebrand. He's got buddies, this time."

"Maybe," the *Post* agreed, though skeptically. "But I still think the Senate will tone them down."

"The Senate as we have known it is dead," AP said flatly as they concluded their sotto voce conversation and turned to the business of taking notes. "Believe me, this is a new breed."

Yet for a time it did not seem that the changes brought by the Jason landslide had done so very much to the United States Senate. It was true that there were some fifty new members, a relatively massive turnover brought about by the usual election of one third of the membership every two years plus an unusual number of vacancies due to death or retirement. But for those who had not had time to talk to many of them in depth—and in this last hectic week since inauguration, few had—they appeared on the surface to be much like any other group of newcomers to the Hill. The majority were under forty, several barely thirty, and most of those who were over forty were very conscious of, and self-congratulatory about, how well they "related" to their younger colleagues; but outwardly they had given little sign as yet of any unified desire to upset traditional patterns. They had defeated Bob Munson for Majority Leader, which had startled most experienced Washington observers, but that could have been brought about by many different causes. He had finally concluded, himself, that it was basically just a youthful desire for change, strengthened of course by the President's wishes. He had held the power for a dozen years and it was probably understandable, though hurtful, that a new President and a new group of his followers should want someone else. And it wasn't as though they had chosen anyone very radical: just waspish old Arly Richardson of Arkansas, who had a couple of years on Bob Munson and was certainly no flaming liberal.

He was pliable, though, Bob reflected, watching the sycophantic way in which he was following Fred Van Ackerman's every word: vain, egotistical, intellectually arrogant, intellectually flatterable: a

man who would go along, which was obviously what the President
wanted, as his letter to the Senate had made thoroughly clear.

But go along where, and with what? With this terribly dangerous
monstrosity of a bill that Van Ackerman had suddenly produced? With
this abject surrender to the Russians that appeared to be Ted Jason's
tacit response to their deliberate démarche against the United States?
With drift, paralysis, terrifying inaction at the head of the government
at a moment when America's whole world appeared to be collapsing?

What *was* the matter with the man? Senator Munson wondered for
the thousandth time. And what could be done about it?

There were plans afoot already to get up a deputation to call upon
him. Bill Abbott had dropped over from the House a while ago to
convey Beth's warning to him and to Cullee. They had agreed that
things could not be permitted to drift much longer—not later than
tomorrow, probably. They would have to rally a group that could not
be denied, and insist that the President see them. They would announce their visit to the press, and he would not be able to say no
unless he wished to destroy the last vestige of public confidence and
put the final cap on public fear.

But when they did see him, what could they accomplish? From
what he had experienced of Ted Jason so far, Senator Munson did not
have many hopes. He had seen him slide skillfully out from under too
many attempts to pin him down, to feel very sanguine about it. Except that this time he could not be allowed to slide out from under.
This time he could be allowed no escape, for, indeed, there was none.

Meanwhile, Fred Van Ackerman, ranging back and forth along the
center of the majority side, was stating the official defense for everything that was going on. Presently, Bob knew, he would rise to answer. For the time being, he could only marvel anew at the vast
rationalization that was comforting the President's supporters in this
hour when all their basic assumptions were being challenged.

You would never know the challenge existed, to hear Fred Van
Ackerman.

"Mr. President," he said, his voice still relatively calm though it
would no doubt soon rage up under pressure, "I rise to urge passage
of S. 1776, a bill to help America overcome the disruptive activities of
her enemies both foreign and domestic. I wish to give notice to all
Senators that I and the proponents of the bill intend to keep the Senate
in session until the bill is passed, even if that means an all-night session. The leadership tells me this is perfectly agreeable, considering
the desperate nature of the situation that exists in the nation. Am I
correct, I will ask the distinguished Senator from Arkansas?"

"The Senator is entirely correct," Arly Richardson agreed promptly, hardly bothering to rise from his seat. There was an approving murmur from many Senators, objections from a few, a little ripple of applause from the galleries, filled with the now customary scattering of NAWAC representatives. Lacey Pollard in the chair looked stern but did not rap the gavel. Fred went on, his voice beginning to fill with sarcasm.

"Now, Mr. President," he said, "there seem to be a few timorous people around who are worried about this bill. And they're even more worried about what's going on in the world right now—as they see it. I say to them, it's what's going on inside the country that's truly disturbing, not what's going on outside. Because, outside, things aren't so bad."

("How's that?" AP murmured to UPI. "Shh," UPI responded. "The indisputable logic will unfold.")

"Outside, what do we have?" Fred asked, and his colleagues and the gallery were quite still in the thought of what they did have. But Fred proved to them that it was different from what many of them thought.

"We have, it is true, an ill-advised and overreactive series of moves by the Soviet military. I think we all agree on the unfortunate extremism of that. But note this, members of the Senate: since those initial unfortunate Soviet moves, we have had no further overt attack upon the United States and its citizens. We have had no further—"

"Mr. President," Bob Munson said sharply, rising to his feet. "Is the Senator trying to tell us that the continuing incarceration of American troops from Gorotoland and Panama, the continuing harassment of American fishing vessels seeking to ply their trade from Alaskan harbors, the continuing pell-mell rush of Soviet sea power into the oceans of the world—"

"Mr. President!" Fred said with equal sharpness. "I did not yield to the Senator and I do not welcome his impolite interruptions!"

There was an approving smatter of applause from the galleries and he turned to address them directly.

"No, Mr. President, I do not welcome it, and I do not think the American people welcome it! We are aware of our difficulties, Mr. President, I will say to the Senator, and we agree that they exist. But not all of us are as quick to see deep, dark, sinister plots directed at the ending of the American Republic as he is! No, Mr. President," he said, as there was a little sarcastic, approving laughter from floor and galleries, "some of us are not that paranoid, I will say to the Senator! We can see, Mr. President, how a military organization can get out of hand and sometimes embarrass a civilian government, because God knows we've had that here, in Viet Nam, in Gorotoland, in Panama and in a lot of other places in recent decades. We know how easy it is for the military to get out of hand, and we know that's what happened the other day in the Soviet Union. But we know it's being brought under control, and we know as a result of our great President's journey to Moscow that we can expect a world of peace from here on."

"Mr. President," Cullee Hamilton demanded without even bothering to seek recognition from the chair, "how do we know that? What crystal ball is the Senator using? No one else knows what went on between the President and the Chairman. How come the Senator from Wyoming knows?"

"Now, Mr. President," Fred Van Ackerman cried with a fine indignation, "that is exactly the sort of thinking that hampers and cripples our great President in his search for peace! It is exactly that kind of conservative, reactionary, warmongering blindness that makes it so difficult for him to deal effectively with the problems he faces! It is exactly—"

"It is exactly," Bronnie Bernard declared to the packed and restless House and its packed and restless galleries, "what makes his task, and the task of all the millions who believe in him, so terribly difficult. It is exactly why all of us who support him must close ranks and turn a united front to his reactionary right-wing enemies. It is exactly why we must pass this Help America bill, so that we can not only help America, but help Edward M. Jason, the greatest President America has ever had!"

A roar of applause approved him, and in the chair Jawbone gaveled busily, but not too hard, for order.

"Mr. Speaker—" Bronnie's voice dropped to the low and solemn tone he had found effective so often in debates with the intransigent who could not be convinced and must therefore be overwhelmed, "I say to this House, we *must* pass this bill. We *must* preserve the domestic peace and tranquillity which furnish the only framework within which our great President can seek, and achieve, a viable and lasting peace. We *must* support him, Mr. Speaker, for *he . . . is . . . the . . . only . . . President . . . we . . . have!*"

And he sat down to another roar of applause that turned quickly to hisses, boos and grumbles of discontent as Hal Knox, William Abbott and half a dozen others jumped to their feet and sought recognition. After a moment's hesitation the Speaker said, "The distinguished gentleman from Illinois, great son of a great father!" with an elaborately kindly, heavy-handed graciousness. For just a second Hal gave him a look of mingled surprise and amusement that said as plainly as words, *Who are you kidding, old buddy?* "And a great mother, too," Jawbone added solemnly, and this time Hal grinned and gave him an obvious wink. It was the last moment of even moderate lightness in the debate of either house on the Help America bill.

"Mr. Speaker," Hal said, "I thank the Speaker for those kind words. And I appreciate his generosity in recognizing me so that I may attempt, albeit feebly, to answer the very able and very voluble gentleman from New York. Now, Mr. Speaker," he said, ignoring the little wave of hisses that greeted this disrespectful reference to Bronnie Bernard, who simply gave him a blank, exaggerated stare and shook his head in a pitying way, "the gentleman has been very colorful in his language this afternoon.

"He has told us of the many crimes of the United States of America, going back unto the first generation, and he has used them to justify perhaps the most repulsive and dangerous measure ever put before this free Congress.

"He has managed, in so doing, to absolve the Soviet Government and the Russian nation from any responsibility for anything that has happened in the world, as nearly as I can understand his argument, clear back to the Russian Revolution in 1917.

"He has painted a picture, and I find it a very familiar picture, because I went through the same schooling he did and I heard the same clichés—of an America cruel, rapacious, imperialistic and corrupt. He has balanced it with a picture of a Soviet Union pure, peace-loving, humanitarian and noble.

"And seeing the world that way, he has of course arrived logically at the conclusion that in this present crisis it is simply a rather absentminded piece of overreaching on the part of the Soviet military which confronts us. It is not a deliberate campaign by the Russian Government to embarrass and, indeed, destroy, the United States of America."

There were a few derisive hoots at this, but he ignored them and went on.

"And so, with equal logic, he arrives at the conclusion that all Americans who are in any way suspicious of Soviet Russia, are in any way concerned about the present crisis, are in any way upset and critical about the course of action—if it can be called action, Mr. Speaker, which is very much in doubt, it seems to me—of the President of the United States, are somehow traitors to the President, traitors to America and traitors to the cause of world peace.

"And so, with equal inevitability, he argues the conclusion that if free American citizens make any public demonstration of disapproval or dismay, they must be suppressed for the higher good of the future as conceived, formulated and directed by Edward M. Jason. They must be subjected to the restrictions of this bill, which are as sure a prescription for dictatorship in America as have ever been put before the Congress. The great American tradition of protest and dissent must be destroyed *because it offends the political ideas and programs of one man.* It has been implicit and inevitable in all the violent protests of recent years that sooner or later this would be proposed by somebody in this Congress on behalf of some President, but it strikes me as fantastic and even more dangerous that it should be proposed by 'liberals' in the interests of a 'liberal' President. Yet I suppose, Mr. Speaker, it has also been implicit and inevitable that when such a move came, it should come from the 'liberal' side, because only they can manage to find language pious and self-righteous enough to camouflage the true nature of the malodorous package they have put before us today."

But this was too much, not only for the galleries and many members, who hissed and booed and shouted, but for the bill's coauthor and introducer. Bronnie Bernard was on his feet, face twisted with anger, shouting, "Mr. Speaker!" in a tone that brooked no denial. Nor did Hal intend to deny it, for with an open contempt he snapped, "I will be glad to yield to the gentleman, Mr. Speaker!" and turned to Bronnie an expectant and grimly skeptical face.

"Mr. Speaker," Congressman Bernard said, and his voice shook with the disgust and contempt he felt for his antagonist across the chamber, "the Congressman from Illinois and I are new in this chamber, but I warrant you if we stay for a hundred years we will not hear such unfair and inflammatory language as the Congressman has just uttered here today!" Applause rewarded him and his voice raced on, furious, self-righteous and accusatory. "No one, Mr. Speaker, wants any dictatorship! No one is accusing the United States—except for clear crimes against humanity amply borne out by the historical record! No one is defending the Soviet Union—save for her many patient attempts to achieve world peace! Certainly no one is defending her military, who have temporarily exceeded the bounds of civilian control! And certainly no one is advocating a dictatorship in this free land! That is the farthest thing from the thoughts of any of us!

"No, Mr. Speaker, the gentleman will have to do better than that. He cannot scare us with these bugaboos—the work we have to do here is too important. We are engaged in no less than the saving of the world, Mr. Speaker. Let us address ourselves to it with the solemn dignity it deserves!"

Again he received applause, spontaneous and noisy, mingled this time with the boos, hoots and shouts of the bill's opponents. With a look of satisfaction he turned to face the tumultuous House.

"Mr. Speaker, I submit to you that this proposed bill does just three fundamental things: it guarantees to the President the climate of calm and national unity that he needs to meet the present crisis brought on by the temporary aberration of the Soviet military machine. It guarantees him the united public support which he must have in order to deal calmly and constructively with the peace-loving Soviet civilian government, which wishes so desperately to cooperate with us. And it guarantees that certain sinister reactionary elements, which will seize upon any crisis to mask their incessant attack upon this democracy and all its institutions, will not be able to advance their anti-democratic schemes behind a smoke screen of phony so-called 'patriotism!'

"That's what it does, Mr. Speaker, and I submit to my frightened friend from Illinois and all *his* frightened friends wherever they may be throughout this broad land—a land which is much more confident and much less afraid than they are—that this is *all* the bill does.

"They cannot frighten us into believing more, Mr. Speaker! They cannot stampede us with their divisive, reactionary, terroristic rhetoric into abandoning the greatest advocate of world peace who has ever come to the White House. They cannot stampede us—"

"Mr. Speaker," William Abbott interrupted, biting off his words in a way that brought immediate attention from the House, "will the gentleman from New York permit a brief rejoinder, or is the right of reply too reactionary to be included in his concept of democracy?"

"Mr. Speaker," Bronnie Bernard said angrily, "I yield to one of the major architects of our present troubles."

Even for the House in its present mood that proved a little strong. There was a gasp of surprise and a sudden silence. Into it the ex-President spoke with a savage and hammering deliberation.

"Mr. Speaker," he said, "I won't waste time on the personal attacks of the gentleman, which are about on a par with the rest of what he has been saying. He is very good at words. Unfortunately in my estimation most of them don't make sense.

"He and those who agree with him here have done a lot of clever arguing in an indefensible cause. The main point they've made, as near as I can figure it out, is that we have to have this bill because opposition to this President is undemocratic and can't be permitted.

"What kind of talk is that in a democracy, Mr. Speaker? And just what do they know about this President, anyway? Has *he* spoken to them? Have *they* spoken to him? What does he *really* think about this bill, I will ask the gentleman from New York, its principal mover? Does the gentleman know? Tell us what the President told you about it, Congressman. We all want to hear."

"Well—" Bronnie Bernard began, but William Abbott was onto his hesitant tone at once.

"Hasn't told you a thing, has he? You haven't seen him, you haven't talked to him, you haven't heard from him, isn't that right? He hasn't talked to anybody about anything at any time since getting back from Moscow, as near as I can find out. And yet you get up here in this House, and over there in the other body that great statesman from Wyoming is doing the same, and you claim to be presenting a bill in the President's name that you're trying to tell us he needs and approves of. How do you manage that, Congressman? Isn't that making pretty free with the name of the President of the United States?"

"He hasn't said he's against it," Bronnie snapped, "and God knows he's had plenty of opportunity!"

"True enough," Bill Abbott agreed. "And he hasn't said he's for it, either, and he's had the same opportunity. So I think somebody for some reason is trying to put over something pretty vicious on this Congress and on the American people. I can excuse you, because you're young and inexperienced here and haven't had time to learn that there are sharks in these waters. But I can't excuse those who are using you, Congressman. I can't excuse them at all, *because they know better.*"

At this Bronnie Bernard seemed to swell up and threaten to pop. But with great and obvious difficulty he forced himself to hold it and presently replied in a voice uneven with anger but under control.

"Perhaps my youth," he said shakily, "in contrast to the Congressman's age, is what this is all about. Maybe it takes us younger members to really appreciate what the President is trying to do. Maybe it takes *us* to understand how sincere he is, what a great leader he is, how dedicated he is to world peace and to all of humanity. Maybe it takes *us* to be unafraid to face up to what is required if he is to achieve this goal. Maybe it takes *us* to understand how he can't possibly achieve it if he is constantly going to be hampered and hamstrung by reckless and irresponsible protest and opposition at his back. Maybe we and the President *are* the future, I suggest to the Congressman from Colorado, and maybe he and his friends, even if some of them *are* young and reactionary, are the past."

Again he was rewarded by prolonged and hearty applause from floor and galleries. The ex-President let it die completely before he attempted to speak.

"If you are the future," he said slowly, "God help this Republic. And I'm not saying you're not, Congressman. I wouldn't be that certain about it. You may very well be. I hope not, I will say to you frankly, because I don't think you have the slightest concept of the Pandora's box you will open if you pass this bill into law. You think it will be administered fairly and idealistically, maybe, in some perfect fashion that will just restrain people a little, not really hurt anybody. But laws aren't administered fairly and idealistically, Congressman, no matter who proposes them: they're administered by men. And men can be terribly hard on other men when they come to administer a law—particularly if they are men, like yourself, who are absolutely—and I grant you, quite sincerely—convinced that they and they alone know what is right and best for everybody.

"I submit to this House, Mr. Speaker, that this is a monstrously dangerous proposal we have here before us, rushed to the floor by the Rules Committee without time for witnesses or adequate study. I submit that it will establish the machinery for the most arbitrary and absolute control of the individual citizen that has ever been seen in this Republic. I submit—"

"I submit," Bob Munson said, and the Senate and galleries were quiet as he spoke, listening intently to his summation, "that this measure, brought in here by the Senator from Wyoming and friends of his in the other body under God knows whose auspices, rammed through the Judiciary Committee in the wee hours of the morning by a narrow vote, will establish nothing less than a dictatorship in America." There was a titter of disbelieving laughter from somewhere in the room and with a sudden anger he snapped, "Yes, a dictatorship in America! We had better call it by its right name, right here and now before we go any further. You set up this Domestic Tranquillity Agency to peek and pry and tell us what to think—and write, Mr. President," he said, turning suddenly to stare up at the packed Press Gallery above, "*and write*, make no mistake about that—and you've got dictatorship. You accompany it with this so-called 'Special Branch' in the Department of Justice, with all its power to go into the private and confidential records of the citizenry—and you've got dictatorship. You will have gone a terrible way down the road from which free nations don't return. And it won't be lightly administered, Mr. President, don't let anybody fool himself on that. It won't be a joke. Those who support this measure *want* it, Mr. President, and they mean to use it if they get it. And we won't have the opportunity later to reverse it or repeal it. There won't be a second chance."

"Mr. President," Tom August said in his gentle, hesitant way, "would the distinguished Maj—ex-Majority—Leader yield to me for a comment, to be followed by a question?"

"Certainly I shall yield to my old and dear friend, the Senator from Minnesota," Senator Munson said, thinking, *God, now we're going to get things fumbled up,* "whom I find, to my sadness and disbelief, on the other side of an issue on which I had thought he of all people would stand foursquare for democracy and against dictatorship."

"Well, Mr. President," Senator August said, still gently, while a few partisans in the gallery laughed scornfully at Bob Munson's comment, "I am not going to argue those terms with the Senator from Michigan, who is *my* old and dear friend also, and who distresses me as I distress him, because he cannot see the reasons why we need some such measure.

"Let me postulate to him my view of the situation as I see it, and then let me ask my question. . . . I see, Mr. President, a President of the United States who campaigned for his great office on the constant pledge that he would go as far as might prove necessary in the search for world peace. I see him winning on that platform, and winning overwhelmingly, to the plaudits of the great majority of his countrymen and the plaudits of peace-loving men everywhere in this world.

"I see him appearing—scarcely a week ago, Mr. President, yet it seems a year, so tumultuous have been the events proceeding from that day!—in front of this building to make his inaugural address. I see him, perhaps more swiftly and more completely than many of us expected, perhaps more swiftly and completely than the more cautious might have advised, yet with a deep and I believe genuine sincerity, withdrawing from around the globe those naked expressions of American power which have for so long proved so offensive to so many peace-loving states and peoples.

"I see, then, a wholly unexpected, overly emphatic, overreactive response by the military forces of the Soviet Union, still apparently operating under a concept of the world which the President's inaugural made instantly and forever obsolete. And I see an intense inward philosophical and political struggle going on in the Soviet Union concerning this, culminating in an appeal to the President of the United States to come to Moscow in the hope that differences might be resolved and peace be everywhere restored.

"I see the President going, I see his return, and I see that all is not at once perfect, as my friend from Michigan and many other citizens had obviously hoped it would be. Apparently the battle has not yet been won in Moscow between those who believe in peace and those who believe in the outmoded expressions of power—as also, Mr. President, one must regretfully conclude that it has not been won here.

"So I see the President, carrying his enormous burdens, seeking a moment of quietude and reflection before he comes to conclusions inevitably profound and far-reaching—and I also see, unhappily, a vast wave of impatience, mistrust, intolerance and fear hampering and hindering him at every turn. I see protest and dissent carried beyond acceptable norms. I see riots and violence designed solely for the purpose of thwarting the peace efforts of Edward M. Jason, and I ask myself, as I now ask the distinguished senior Senator from Michigan:

"Can America afford this? Can we permit the peace efforts of this great President to be thwarted by protest and violence at home? Can we allow certain misguided Americans to destroy what may well be our last, best hope of peace—when we have before us now in this bill the means of assuring the President the domestic peace and tranquillity he needs in which to make the decisions so vital to us all?

"I wonder how the distinguished Senator would answer that?"

And he looked about in his shy, apologetic manner and sat down to a thunder of applause that began in the galleries and swiftly spread to the floor. The Vice President, who had returned to take over the gavel from Lacey Pollard, rapped dutifully for order but it was not restored until the outburst had died of its own steam. Bob Munson waited patiently for it to subside and then replied with an expression unmoved and unyielding.

"I will tell the Senator how I will answer that. I think it is so much pious, wishful, self-serving fiction to claim that there is any separation whatsoever between the actions of the Soviet Government and the actions of the Soviet military. There is not one iota of evidence, except the theory put forward by the President himself in private conversations with some of us prior to his departure for Moscow, which indicates in any way that there has been any internal Russian quarrel about this at all. What has happened has been a deliberate, cold-blooded gamble by the Soviet Government in all its branches, to seize upon the opening offered by the President in his inaugural and make the most of it.

"And," he added somberly, "there is not the slightest evidence of any kind now that the Russian Government and Russian military have the slightest intention of doing anything other than exactly what they are doing, no matter what decision the President may reach. He has sacrificed his advantages and no one, least of all the Russians, has any intention of giving them back.

"Mr. President," he said into a growing murmur of annoyance, disagreement and resentment, "I put this question in return to the Senator from Minnesota, and to all Senators who agree with him: *is* the President reaching any decision? *Is* he doing anything to meet this increasingly grave situation, which is rapidly becoming almost hopeless? Why do we need domestic tranquillity for a man to make up his mind, when he is sitting in the White House apparently paralyzed by shock and apparently incapable of making up his mind on anything?"

A great boo of anger and scorn gave him answer. But he only looked more determined, shook his head as though to knock off a swarm of hornets and continued in the same level, unimpressed voice.

"No, I will say to the Senator, it won't wash. There is a deliberate and carefully calculated plan here to relate this bill to the international situation. The President's silence encourages this plan. He has said nothing on the foreign situation since returning from Moscow. He has said nothing on this bill. Those who wish American democracy ill are profiting from his silence to link this most viciously repressive and dictatorial measure with the perfectly understandable and legitimate uneasiness and dismay of many loyal Americans who have become almost frantic at the spectacle of their President retreating into silence when history cries out for him to act.

"I tell this Senate, the two do not go together, no matter how hard the Senator from Wyoming, the Senator from Minnesota and their friends try to make us believe they do. Presumably in due course—and the sooner the better I devoutly pray—the President will emerge from his self-imposed silence and give us the leadership that is the job and duty of Presidents. Then we will know where we are going and be able to take hope again. Then the public outcry will die down. But if we pass this bill in the heat of this moment, *it* will not die down and go away. *It* will be law, and it will stay right there on the books to intimidate, dictate, threaten and control the life of every private citizen. We must separate the two. We cannot tie them together."

"Will the Senator yield?" Warren Strickland asked quietly from across the aisle. "Isn't the Senator overlooking one possibility—that the President, when he does act, may not satisfy those Americans who are dismayed and distraught, but may continue along exactly the lines of what I can only call retreat and submission—" there was an ominous rumble from the galleries and he repeated the phrase calmly—"retreat and submission? And is it not then likely that the protests of many millions of loyal Americans will not diminish, but will grow more desperate and frantic? And so are not the proponents correct when they feel, as they obviously do, that the time to clamp their yoke on the people's necks is now, rather than later when protest may be much better organized and much harder to control?"

"Mr. President!" a dozen Senators shouted angrily, popping up all over the floor like so many infuriated jacks-in-the-box.

For a second Bob Munson studied them carefully and then, with a shrug, said calmly, "Mr. President, I yield to the Senator from Wyoming, hoping against hope that he will be brief."

"Very amusing!" Fred Van Ackerman snapped. "But, Mr. President, not an adequate answer to the vicious slurs and innuendoes which the Senator from Michigan and his friends have been casting on the President and on this bill—this great bill to help America and her great leader in their hour of desperation and need.

"The Senator from Michigan and the Senator from Idaho are just making debating points, Mr. President. Whatever the President of the United States decides to do—and I am informed that top-level conferences are even now going on at the White House to determine our next moves—('That's a lie,' UPI murmured to AP, who nodded as his pencil scurried across his note paper)—whatever he decides to do, it will not remove the necessity for stopping disruptive and violent protests which seriously threaten our democracy and seriously cripple the President in reaching his decisions. I agree with the Senator from Idaho, the Minority Leader—protests are going to continue, all right, but it won't be because anybody disagrees with what the President decides to do. It will be because there is a group—yes, Mr. President," he exclaimed, his voice suddenly sailing into its high ranting whine, "yes, there is a group, which will always oppose peace, which will always oppose the efforts of decent men to get peace, yes, a group which will not be satisfied until it has used the bomb on the Russians and wiped them off the face of the earth! That is the group we are contending with here, Mr. President! That is the group that seeks to defeat this bill by inflammatory arguments and devious means! There is a group, Mr. President, yes, there is a group, and it is composed of all those who want to see democracy destroyed, who want to see riots and protests disrupt the country, who want to see our great President thwarted and betrayed in what he is trying to do for world peace, a group who want to see democracy, yes, democracy itself, destroyed! There is a group—"

"There is a group in this Congress," Bronnie Bernard told the House in his gravest, most effective tones, "and I could not believe my own eyes and ears until I became a member of this body and saw it for myself, who will sacrifice anything if they can destroy the freedoms of this country. Mr. Speaker, I used to hear about this group in college—about how reactionary they were, how rabid they were, how right-wing and uncaring of democracy, how selfish, how self-indulgent, how evil. But I didn't quite believe it, Mr. Speaker—no, not quite, although I could read in the newspapers every day, and see on television every night, the examples of this group's evil conspiracies against this free people. But now I see it in action, Mr. Speaker! In action right here on the floor of this House! An ex-President gets up here, a new Congressman gets up here, a handful of other leftovers from an old reactionary way of thinking—" there was a ripple of laughter and applause mingled with a few boos—"get up here and they berate and denounce the President of the United States, they try to deny him the domestic peace and tranquillity he needs to carry out his policies in the cause of world peace, they argue and they twist and they duck and they dodge, and what does it all add up to, Mr. President? Crap!" he said, probably the first time that term had ever been used officially in House debate, and there was enough tradition left so that it did produce a little gasp of surprise. So he repeated it firmly. "Yes, crap! Sheer, unadulterated, lying, hysterical, old-woman, poppycock crap!" The gasp turned to laughter, then to dutiful applause from the galleries and many on the floor.

"The opponents of this bill," Bronnie Bernard said with a fine self-righteous sternness, "are full of the awful things that it might do to democracy *if* some evil beings whom they don't identify, and whom *I* for one don't see anywhere on the horizon, should administer it. Well, Mr. Speaker, I am full of what a divided and disrupted country can do to our great President as he tries to make peace, and *I* am worried about the effect on our democracy if he gets pushed and bullied and harassed into doing the wrong thing. *There's* your problem, Mr. Speaker! *There's* your danger to democracy! Not in a bill to insure domestic peace and tranquillity, which we have *got* to have in these dangerous times, but in unrestrained and unbridled protest and dissent, running amuck every time some little group or alliance of groups disagrees with the policies of the President of the United States! We simply can't afford this any more. We're entering an era in which things are too tense, too difficult, too subject to being blown up by the errors of men. We need a united country as we have never needed it before. This bill guarantees it. Don't deny America and her President the certainty of domestic peace! We've got to have it or we'll go under. It is as simple as that."

And again he sat down, to heartfelt applause, though he knew that they would all be up again many times before this long day and night were over and the bill safely passed. As he expected—for in the past hour the debate had narrowed down pretty much to the two of them and the House was watching their contest with an intrigued and attentive interest—the new Congressman from Illinois was on his feet seeking recognition.

"My good young friend from Illinois," Jawbone said with a cheerful nod, "is recognized for more of his astute and enlightening remarks."

"Well," Hal said with a tartness that would have done justice to his father, "I appreciate the Speaker's jovial and avuncular welcome. I only wish it were matched by an equal perception and astuteness concerning the dangers of this vicious bill. Now, Mr. Speaker, I shall not try to match the inflammatory rhetoric of the gentleman from New York flame for flame. That would be impossible for my poor talents. But I should like to make a few points in response, if I may.

"The gentleman is very strong on the reasons why we should waive democratic procedures and, in my belief, clamp a dictatorship on this country in the name of a particular President and what his supporters see as his particular campaign for peace. Doesn't it occur to the gentleman or any of his friends what a terribly dangerous principle they enunciate? Democracy either exists or it doesn't exist. If you suppress it in the name of one President and his particular cause, then why shouldn't you suppress it for some other President and *his* particular cause? Indeed, if you pass this bill, you *will* have suppressed it, once and for all, because any President will be able to come along and claim that he has to have 'domestic peace and tranquillity,' for whatever cause. It may be a war cause one of these days, I will say to my friend from New York and his friends; it may not be a peace cause at all.

"This government wasn't established to fluctuate according to who happens to be in the White House and what he proposes. It was established to be flexible enough so that it could protect democracy under any President and any cause. It was established to be flexible enough so that no matter who the President or what the cause, the basic framework of freedom would be preserved.

"That is what I and those who agree with me think we are fighting for, I will say to the House. We say it doesn't matter how you invoke Ted Jason's name and wave the flag of peace—what you are really doing is trying to destroy the right of free dissent and peaceful protest —indeed, dissent and protest of *any* kind on *any* subject, for that is what the law will speedily become when it is once on the books. Sure, you think it will be gently administered in the name of Ted Jason for Ted Jason's cause—but what of other Presidents who will come, and what of their causes, and how will it be administered then? You can't tailor your democracy to the passions of the moment. It has to be a bridge and a continuation, otherwise it's no democracy.

"That is the basic issue on which I am arguing, and others are arguing. Sure, I'm afraid, I admit it—afraid of putting this kind of power in the hands of any government, because who knows what use can be made of it if evil men so desire?

"That's the basic argument, in my mind. And then there's another. It seems to me that all the proponents of this measure are very sure of two things: they're very sure of how the President feels about it, and they're very sure of how the Russians feel about it. Yet has *he* spoken, Mr. Speaker? Have *they* told us in the slightest way whatsoever that this is all an internal argument between the Soviet civilians and the Soviet military? Do we really know his mood, or theirs? Has *anybody* told us?"

He paused and there was an uneasy stirring in the room. But he went on quietly, talking now directly to the Speaker, who shifted uneasily but kept staring back, as if hypnotized, at the steady eyes that looked into his.

"There were others along, you know, Mr. Speaker," Hal remarked in an almost conversational tone. "The Secretary of State, the Secretary of Defense, the Majority Leader of the United States Senate—and you, Mr. Speaker," he concluded softly. "*You*. Why don't you come down here in the well of the House and tell us all about how nice and kindly the Russians are, and about what *you* observed and what *you* saw and what *you* listened to while you were in Moscow with these kind and loving people?

"I challenge you, Mr. Speaker. Come down here and tell us all about it, and then maybe we can believe."

He paused, and the room became very still as everyone turned to look at Jawbone, who, as he told Miss Bitty-Bug later in their apartment at the Watergate, felt like a squinch bug on a banana peel about to be gobbled by a goose. He looked about in some desperation as Hal persisted quietly, "How about that, Mr. Speaker?"

But at that point—and he told Miss Bitty-Bug he guessed it was just plain Providence, though of course he wouldn't for the world have wanted it to happen as it did had *he* had anything to say about it— two things came to his rescue.

One was Bronnie Bernard, leaping to his feet with an indignant shout of "Mr. Speaker!"

And the other, coming rapidly down the aisle to where Hal stood tall and unyielding, a little quizzical smile on his face, was a youthful page carrying a note. He handed it to Hal, who opened it and gave it a quick glance.

Simultaneously two more things happened. The Speaker said, "The gentleman from New York!" with a relief that would have appeared comic some other time, and Hal cried, "Oh, *no!*" in a tone of such agony that everything abruptly stopped and the room became deathly still.

"Does the gentleman—?" Jawbone began uncertainly. "Is the gentleman—?" And then abandoning protocol, in a tone of genuine concern, "Are you ill, Hal?"

"No, I—" Hal began, and then stopped, white-faced, struggling to get his breath, hands kneading and crumpling, smoothing and recrumpling, the note while the frightened page stared up at him. "I—I'm all right—I—I guess. But my—my mother—has been kidnapped"—there was a wave of quite genuinely horrified "No's!" from around the chamber—"and apparently—" he smoothed the note and read it through again, narrowing his eyes and squinting painfully, holding it far from him as though unable to believe its contents—"apparently the motive is not money. They say that unless I—unless I stop opposing this bill and actively support it—and unless the Congress passes this bill—she will be—be—'liquidated'—is the word they use. . . . I suppose," he said slowly, staring at Bronnie Bernard as though he were seeing him for the first time, "that this is—is your doing—or—or people like you."

"Well, now," Jawbone said hastily, as an ominous rumble began on floor and galleries "before we get into personalities, and I say we all sympathize most deeply, most dreadfully with my dear young friend from Illinois, before we say anything we'll all regret later, I suggest this House stand adjourned for two hours, and do I hear any dissent," he banged the gavel hastily, "it is so ordered!"

"I suppose," Cullee Hamilton said with a terrible bitterness five minutes later to Fred Van Ackerman when the news reached the Senate, "that this is your doing."

"I think we should follow the example of the House," Roger P. Croy cried hastily even as Fred's voice began to rise in an angry yell, "and take a brief recess to assess this development. Without objection, the Senate stands adjourned for two hours!"

SURVEY SHOWS POLITICAL KIDNAPPINGS COMMON FOR YEARS IN OTHER LANDS, the *Times* said in a special front-page article in its early edition, BUT BIZARRE KNOX EPISODE IS NEW FOR AMERICA. The article was written by one of the paper's youngest and brightest new members. Its tone was calm, chatty, informative, reasonable, matter-of-fact—even, it might almost be said, cheery. A fatherly air of this-happens-every-day-so-don't-you-silly-readers-get-yourselves-all-worked-up-now ran through it from beginning to end.

It was not a mood that could be found elsewhere in America that night, not even among those who really counted on the *Times.*

"My God!" Walter Dobius said in a tone so charged with rage and impatience that his colleagues on the Picturephone link-up were a little taken aback, agitated though they were themselves. "Is there no limit to the insanities of this insane age? And how much longer are we going to sit by and let them go along without our condemnation?"

"We're all condemning them," the editorial director of the *Times* said with a sharpness increased by worry. "You've seen an advance copy of our editorial—"

"Patty-cakes!" Walter snapped. "Patty-cakes! Polite deplorings, signifying nothing. I mean *give them hell.* Because we must, I tell you. *We must.*"

"I agree with Walter," the executive chairman of *The Greatest Publication* said gently. "I do agree with Walter. Today Beth Knox, tomorrow the world, so to speak. Or anyway," he said, his fine old face looking tired and wan, "tomorrow *us.*"

"Exactly," Walter said. "Exactly. And it's all so damned *pointless,* that's what gets me. The Congress is going to pass the bill anyway, God help us."

"But they need the Knoxes to make it respectable," the general director of the *Post* suggested.

"More than that," Walter Dobius said somberly. "They need something to shock and cow the public. They need *schrecklichkeit,* as Mr. Hitler used to say—*frightfulness.* I am worried to death for Beth, I will tell you frankly. I don't think she's coming out of this alive."

"Oh, now," the *Times* said. "There's no need to get melodramatic. What could they possibly gain from her death?"

"Just what Walter says," the executive chairman of *The Greatest Publication* told him. "Public shock. Much can be done, you know, with public shock."

"It defeats itself," the *Post* said shortly.

"As long as insanity is not in control of things," the executive chairman of the *G.P.* agreed. "When it is, then shock serves exactly the purpose Walter says—it cows people."

"Do you think her son will give in?" the *Times* inquired.

"She wouldn't want him to," Walter said, "but who knows what anybody will do, under such pressure? How come they didn't take his wife as well? That would have really done it."

"Apparently they didn't realize she was sleeping upstairs," the *Post* said, "and apparently they were so swift and silent with Beth that they didn't wake Crystal. It was a good half hour, you know, before the White House got really alarmed and began looking for Beth."

"And what is *he* doing, that great, brooding, silent figure?" Walter inquired bitterly. "Why is there nothing from him? Why doesn't he *speak?*"

"Our man at the White House just got through to the press secretary," the *Post* said, "wait a minute—" they could see him reach across his desk, take a piece of paper from a spindle—"'I am shocked, horrified and saddened by the kidnapping of Mrs. Knox. Such acts of political terrorism have no place in free America. No pursuit can be too ruthless, no punishment too severe for those who have perpetrated it. I have given orders to the FBI and all other law-enforcement arms of the government to join in the search for Mrs. Knox and the apprehension and punishment of her abductors. I trust the Congress' judgment on the measure now pending before it will in no way be affected by this cruel episode, which will be handled in the most effective way possible by your government.'"

"Well," Walter said with a savage dryness, "so he *is* alive."

"If he wrote it," the executive chairman of *The Greatest Publication* suggested, "it may have been the staff, trying to protect him."

"No," Walter said, "I think he wrote it, all right. I'll give him that. But it comes damned late in the day for one who has given silence and tacit assent to the rise of elements that could do a thing like this. And I repeat: we must all condemn them without any ifs, ands or buts. They are despicable—utterly despicable. And so is this bill. Is it not?" And with a sudden challenging air he searched their faces, filled with varying degrees of apprehension and concern.

"It is monstrous," the executive chairman of the *G.P.* agreed quietly.

"Absolutely inexcusable," the *Times* said.

"But not necessarily as bad as young Knox and Abbott and the rest seem to believe," the *Post* commented. "Now, is it really? Isn't it necessary to have *some* public quiet and stability if we are to come through this international situation all right?"

"Quiet and stability for what?" Walter Dobius demanded. "So insane fanatics can kidnap Beth Knox?"

"It isn't necessary to get hysterical about it," the *Post* replied mildly. "We can see plenty of dangers in this bill if it is poorly administered. But who says for sure it will be?"

"With George Wattersill in charge of the Special Branch?" Walter inquired.

"And God knows who at the head of the Domestic Tranquillity Agency," the executive chairman of *The Greatest Publication* agreed.

"Maybe Fred Van Ackerman?" the *Times* tossed in with an almost dreamy air. "Run that one up the Washington Monument and see how it grabs you."

"We still have some faith in the good sense of the President of the United States," the *Post* said sharply.

Walter Dobius snorted.

"Why?"

"Because," the *Post* said angrily, "we happen to believe that he is sincerely trying to work out a peaceful solution for this crisis and we happen to believe that he is going to do it. And we believe we have the obligation to continue to support him—actively—until events prove us wrong. That's why!"

"With the opportunities there are in that bill for control of the press," Walter said slowly, "and with the kidnapping of Beth Knox to disclose to you the state of mind of those who are behind it, you still think that? I admire your courage. Or deplore your stupidity."

"Walter," the *Post* said sharply, "you and I are old and good friends, but I will not take that kind of language from you or anybody. How do we know 'the people behind this bill' had anything to do with Beth Knox? How do we know this isn't just a diversionary tactic by the lunatic fringe to try to horn in on the situation, embarrass the President and make the search for peace even more difficult? How do we know his friends are behind this? What about his enemies?"

"Are you trying to tell me," Walter asked softly, "that this is a conservative, reactionary, right-wing plot? Oh, come now! Oh, for Christ's sake, come now!"

"Well," the *Post* said stoutly, "stranger things have happened."

"Not in our lifetime," the executive chairman of *The Greatest Publication* said quietly. "No, I'm afraid it won't wash, and I should hate to see the idea appear in any of our pages."

"Of course, it *is* true," the *Times* said thoughtfully, "that we may be prejudging this a little too fast. I could see where—yes, I could see the logic. What better way to kill the bill, hurt the President, sabotage peace? Just outradical the radicals, but keep your tracks well-hidden, and—yes, I can see where some mind sufficiently devious could think of it."

"Obviously," Walter remarked coldly, "such minds do exist. . . . Well, you do as your consciences tell you, but *I* tell you this: this crime against the Knoxes is all part of the same picture. It is carefully devised, not to hurt the bill, but to terrify the country, stampede the Congress, and give the government terrible powers over us—terrible powers. I have covered this town for almost twenty-six years, now, and I have never seen a piece of legislation or a mood in the Congress as dangerous to the freedoms of the country. You mark my words: if this bill passes, and if the President doesn't somehow retrieve the country from the perilous international situation we are in—though how in God's name he is going to do it, I can't see—then we will be next. Because they have to control the media, you know—that's the one element they have to have. And this bill and this crisis can be used to give it to them."

"Well, now," the *Times* said comfortably, "I'm concerned, Walter, I grant you that, but I'm not *that* concerned. This is a tough situation about Beth Knox, all right, and the bill does have dangers if it's wrongly administered, and things are tough all over, and all that. But there's *some* common sense left in the country, after all. And we still have a President who's sworn to preserve and protect the Constitution, and we've still got to rely on him, because there isn't anybody else. So I'm inclined to agree with the *Post*. It's rough, and you know from our editorial that we're already expressing alarm about it, but there are limits to alarm, you know. You've got to be reasonable. You can't be hysterical, or nobody will listen."

"Very well," Walter said, "*you* be reasonable. *I* shall be as concerned and as strong as I know how. You weren't so bland during the campaign when NAWAC was acting up. Things are a lot worse now. Why are you getting calm about it, all of a sudden?"

"We aren't getting calm about it, Walter," the *Post* said reasonably. "But, after all. We can't sound as though the end of the world is coming. We'd be laughed right out of town."

"Oh, I think not," the executive chairman of *The Greatest Publication* said gently. "I think not, in this case. I think *we* agree with Walter. Of course, it may just be—" his eyes narrowed thoughtfully—"it may just be that the degrees of our concern are not really going to matter. It may just be that we will all receive a quite impartial treatment, if Mrs. Knox is not recovered, and if this bill is passed."

"Well," the *Times* said shortly, "*we* will be strong, but *reasonably* strong. We're as concerned as the next man, after all."

"You've got to be concerned *in your gut*," Walter Dobius said, and for the first time in all his years as a national columnist they got the feeling that, wisely or foolishly, he really was. "Otherwise, it's all chaff. All chaff."

"Well, Walter," the *Times* said comfortably, while the *Post* nodded quiet, almost amused agreement, "you do it your way and we'll do it ours."

"And don't be surprised," Walter Dobius said harshly as he reached over to snap off his machine, "if we all wind up in the same jail together."

But this was too much, and their scornful though not unfriendly laughter followed him as their faces dissolved from the screen; only the executive chairman of *The Greatest Publication* giving him an understanding and encouraging look.

He had made his conference call from a booth in the House Press Gallery. He was about to go to a typewriter to begin work on tomorrow's column when the head of the gallery staff called, "Walter, incoming call in booth 6," and he obediently went to take it. The craggy, concerned visage of the ex-President appeared on the screen.

"We're over in Warren Strickland's office with Hal Knox," he said. "Why don't you come down?"

"Yes," he said, becoming more committed every second to the only course he thought consistent with America as he had always conceived it, "thank you, Mr. President. I shall be right down."

"Now, Mrs. Knox," the voice that appeared to be in command said pleasantly after it had finished reading her the contents of the note, "you see you really have nothing to fear from us."

"I don't believe you," she said, "but if it does something for your consciences to pretend with me, go right ahead. Why don't you untie my hands and take off this blindfold so that I can see you? What are you afraid of, one tired old woman against three strong young men? You ought to be ashamed of yourselves. What are you afraid of?"

"Mrs. Knox," the voice said, a little tighter but maintaining the pleasantness, "you may be a tired old woman but you are also a brave one. Whether you are a wise one remains to be seen. I have always thought so. Therefore I know you understand me when I say that you have nothing to fear from us. It is your son you have to fear now, Mrs. Knox. Your son and the Congress."

"The Congress is going to pass the bill anyway," she said. "And why do you need my son? Suppose he did give in to your blackmail. The world will know why. It will be under duress. It will be obvious that it isn't genuine."

"Exactly," the voice said. "That is exactly what the world will know—that he can be forced to do things under duress. That Knox principles are as weak as those of other men. That even the Knoxes have been forced to bow. And that will destroy the Knoxes as a political power in this country. And that's one of the things we have to do: destroy the Knoxes."

"But millions of people who believe in the name—who believed in my husband—who believe in me and my son—will continue to support us anyway," she said, making her voice reasonable and matter-of-fact despite her inward terror. "The very fact that this is all public, that Hal would be openly bowing to threats against my life—everybody knows this. They would simply understand it and dismiss it. So what do you gain?"

"We think the gain is sufficient to warrant the gamble," the voice said calmly.

"But what is the gain?" she repeated. "I don't understand it."

"Mrs. Knox," the voice said, "if you were not an intelligent woman, I certainly should not be wasting time arguing with you about it. The gain is, one, to demonstrate that the Knox name means nothing any more, that its inheritor can be cowed like other men; and secondly, to emphasize to all who believe in him—and—" the voice grew grim— "to everyone else—that no one is safe in his home any more and that we will not hesitate to do anything necessary to achieve what we want."

"Which is what?" she demanded, her voice suitably scornful and, she was pleased to find, strong and free from the tremors she was feeling inside. "Turn Ted Jason into a dictator? He may not want to be, you know. He may not be as evil a man as you apparently consider him."

"A clever thought," the voice said appreciatively, "but not pertinent. What we want will develop as we go along. No need to telegraph it in advance."

"What's happening to me isn't telegraphing anything?" she asked, still scornful. "Do you have any concept of the public horror and revulsion that are sweeping the country right now as a result of this? You don't seem to know Americans very well. Maybe you aren't one. That could explain it."

"Mrs. Knox," the voice said patiently, "does my English sound like a foreigner's? I think not. Anyway, that's so much quibble. I know horror and revulsion are sweeping the country. But something else is sweeping it too: fear. And it's growing even faster than the horror and revulsion, because the average citizen, I think, has been quite well-conditioned in these recent years of terrorism and bombings and kidnappings and assassination all over the globe to understand that horror and revulsion are quite powerless. Sure, people get horrified—even Presidents get horrified. But what good does that do? It hasn't stopped a million things and it won't stop a million more. And people know this. And so the fear grows stronger.

"Much can be done with fear, Mrs. Knox. Give people the certainty that nothing is really safe—that nothing save blind luck really holds their world together—that anybody who really wants to can invade and destroy it if he has sufficient ruthlessness and determination—and they become quite reasonable, Mrs. Knox. They forget many fine old democratic loyalties and traditions very fast. They lose their nerve and they become very weak. The foundation crumbles, the certainties go, the safe world collapses. And the strong, the ruthless and the determined take power and lead them.

"But it is for their own good, Mrs. Knox, you must believe that. It is in the cause of peace and world stability and an end to all these frightful wars. So much agony and so much pain! You are going to help us put an end to that, Mrs. Knox. It is not so bad a destiny."

"Then I take it," she said, still managing by sheer strength of character to sound quite fearless, "that I *am* going to die at your hands, and that you have no place in your plans for the President, either. Because you contemplate things that I honestly don't believe him to be capable of, and you also refer to the strong, the ruthless and the determined. And that is not the President as we know him in this moment."

"Mrs. Knox," the voice said with some sharpness, "there is no point in being so dramatic about your own future. I said you only have your own son and the Congress to fear, didn't I? And as for the President— well . . ." the voice became amused—"I grant you he is not noticeably dynamic at the moment. But he is, after all, the President. He has a place in the scheme of things."

"A 'destiny,'" she suggested dryly. "Subject to 'liquidation,' like mine."

"I repeat, you're a brave woman," the voice said admiringly. "But now we have some chores to attend to, so if you will excuse me I'll be leaving you for a while. You are still in the District, you may be interested to know, and quite safe. In fact, I am going to untie your hands and loosen the blindfold and after I leave this basement, you may remove it. There's a bathroom next door, and some food laid out for you on the table." Again the voice sounded amused. "You can eat it. It isn't poisoned."

"I don't believe you," she said, and a sudden tension gripped her heart, for she really did not.

"No, probably not," the voice said comfortably. "But you may find yourself growing hungry, even so."

"Are you going to communicate with my son again?" she asked as a chair scraped and she felt the bonds at her wrists fall loose and nimble fingers start to work on the blindfold.

"Maybe," the voice said. "Maybe not. The Congress is in recess at the moment but they'll be back soon. We'll await events. Now don't peek, Mrs. Knox. I may not be one of your original captors, you know. I may be someone quite different. Scouts' honor, now. No peeking."

"You are going to kill me, aren't you," she said with a sudden certainty.

The voice sounded impatient.

"Now, Mrs. Knox. *Please* don't dramatize."

"I hope my son says no!" she said loudly.

"Oh, I hope not," the voice said soberly as its owner stepped out and closed the door. "I hope not, Mrs. Knox."

"If you want us to," William Abbott said quietly, "we'll all recant and support the bill. I think everybody on our side is agreed on that. In both houses."

Around the table Warren Strickland, Bob Munson, Cullee Hamilton, Lafe Smith and Walter Dobius all nodded gravely, looking at him with a deeply troubled sympathy and an insistent, inescapable expectancy.

"What will I do?" he asked Crystal in a hopeless voice, his stricken face staring at her from the Picturephone. "What will I do? They're waiting for me to decide."

"I don't know," she said slowly, "but I think maybe what you have to decide first is what she would want you to do."

"Maybe she isn't capable of reasoning about it," he said. "Maybe she can't even—even think—at this point. Maybe they're—maybe they're—"

"Stop that!" she said with a sharpness increased by fear and worry. "Isn't the moment horrible enough without you going on like that? You ought to be ashamed of yourself!"

"I'm sorry," he said, eyes half-closed in pain. "But I just don't know what to think—or do—or anything."

"Which is exactly how they want you to feel," she said, more calmly. "I don't know what is—happening—to your mother right now. But for the sake of our own sanity, and for her sake, we have to assume that nothing is. What we can be sure of is that when she thinks about it, she wants you to stand firm. Wouldn't that be characteristic of her?"

"Yes," he said, "but it isn't for her to decide."

"Who has a better right?" Crystal demanded. "Think about her and not yourself, for a change."

"I *am* thinking about her!" he said with a sudden anger.

"No, you're not," she said. *"Think."*

"Jawbone," the ex-President said softly into the Picturephone, "aren't you, or your President, or any of your sleazy crew on the floor over there going to repudiate these damnable bastards? Isn't *anybody* in your camp going to speak out against this nightmare?"

"The President did, Bill!" Jawbone exclaimed, from the Speaker's office, looking aggrieved and harassed. "He did, now, Bill! He used strong words and he sicked the FBI on 'em! Now, that's a fact, Bill, it is, now!"

"Why doesn't he go on television?" William Abbott demanded. "Why doesn't he talk to the country? Why does he hide behind a White House press statement? Why doesn't he come out and name names? *Why isn't he brave?"*

"He's goin' to, Bill," Jawbone promised. "He really is goin' to, now."

"Who said so?" the ex-President inquired sharply. "He hasn't talked to you or anybody else, and you know it. The country is falling apart, Jawbone. Where is your President? More important, where are *you?* How come *you* don't condemn this bill now, Jawbone? You want to play with people who would do a thing like this to Beth Knox? You really think they're good for America, O mighty Speaker of the House? Tell me."

"Now, Bill," the Speaker said, and William Abbott could see his expression turn both frightened and stubborn, "you stop talkin' to me like that, now, always patronizin' and lookin' down and sneerin' like you always have at poor ole Jawbone. I *am* the Speaker now, and don't you forget it, hear?"

"And you feel as though you have some responsibility to America?" Bill Abbott inquired dryly. "Show it, then! Here's *your* cue to leave this damnable bill and join us. Take it, man! Show a little integrity for a change!"

"And kill Beth Knox?" the Speaker demanded, his eyes narrowing triumphantly. "That what you want, Bill? Help to murder that fine lady? Why should I do that, now, Bill? You can take her blood on your hands, Bill, that's for sure! I don't want it on mine."

"No more do I want it on mine," William Abbott said evenly, "and I don't think they would quite dare do such a thing. But they may, Jawbone: they may. But they'll think twice if the Speaker comes out against them. So you see, it does come back to you, Jawbone. You can stop the whole thing if you'll just prove to them that these tactics won't work in America. How about it? Got the guts, or are you going to go down like a jellyfish?"

"I'm not the only one, now, Bill," the Speaker said with a stubbornly desperate unhappiness. "You callin' from over there on the Senate side, right? Why don't you bully Roger Croy, Bill? Why don't you talk to *him* about integrity, get *him* to come out against the bill, make *him* lead the parade? How about that, now, Bill? How about the distinguished Vice President, over there?"

"We've talked to Roger Croy," William Abbott said with an annoyed contempt. "He's even scareder than you are, Jawbone, if that's possible. He says he can't do anything until the President takes a strong lead. He says he can't say any more than the President does, and all the President says is that he hopes Congress won't let this affect its judgment of the bill. He doesn't say what *he* thinks Congress ought to do, he doesn't say what *he* thinks about the bill. He doesn't support it and he doesn't condemn it. Doesn't do anything, really. Roger Croy says he can't do any more than that."

"Well, then," the Speaker cried triumphantly, "why should you expect me to do any more? Why do you keep after *me*, Bill? I can't defy my President any more than Roger P. Croy can. We're in exactly the same spot, Bill, exactly the same. So there!"

"And meanwhile," the ex-President said coldly, "Beth Knox may be dying or already dead, and those who took her may be about to get away with blackmail of the Congress—"

"Congress is ready to pass this bill," Jawbone said sharply. "You know that, Bill, you can feel it out there on the floor. This young crowd, Bill, they're different from you and me. They *believe* in Ted Jason, Bill, and they want peace. They're going to get it, no matter what. They're all set to pass this bill. You know that."

"But the country hasn't had time to find that out," William Abbott said. "It isn't really clear, yet. So if they pass it, whoever has Beth Knox —NAWAC, I suspect, is the obvious—can claim they did it. And that gives them immediately an enormous psychological leap in controlling this country."

"Be even more of a leap, won't it, Bill, if they *kill* Beth Knox?" the Speaker asked shrewdly. "Think how scared folks would be then, Bill."

"That's what they want," the ex-President agreed. "That's why you Administration fellows can't afford to give in. That's why you've got to take the lead."

"Can't do more than he does," Jawbone said, stubbornness returning.

"You know that, now, Bill. Can't defy my President if I want to keep on being Speaker here. This new crowd would kick me out in a minute, Bill. Simple as that. . . . *Anyway*," he added with a sudden sharp, shrewd look, "what about *your* side of it? What are *you* going to do when you get through lecturin' me, Bill? What about young Hal? What's *he* going to do?"

"He hasn't told us yet," William Abbott said gravely. "He's locked up in Warren's inner office right now, going through a hell we can only imagine. It's not an easy decision, you know."

"I know that, Bill," the Speaker said, not without a genuine sympathy. "But we're goin' back into session in less than an hour, Bill. Somebody's got to do *somethin'*, and soon, seems to me."

"I agree with that," the ex-President said unhappily. "But who, or what, doesn't seem to be clear, just yet."

"Is this Mr. Justice Davis?" the voice inquired from the carefully blacked-out Picturephone screen, and Tommy, who had not yet turned on the visual portion of his own machine, paused in mid-reach and slowly withdrew his hand.

"Yes," he said, trying not to sound as disturbed as this anonymous caller made him feel. "Who is this? Are you the ones who have Mrs. Knox?"

"Shrewd guessing, Mr. Justice," the voice said admiringly. "Very shrewd."

"And what are you going to do now?" the little Justice inquired, a growing anger and disgust strengthening his voice. "Threaten me too? Isn't one such monstrous and despicable act enough to win you the contempt and horror of the civilized world?"

The voice sounded amused.

"I think possibly you overestimate the scope, determination and moral vigor of 'the civilized world,' Mr. Justice. Its boundaries grow narrower, within the general mass of humanity, every day. . . . No. We don't want to threaten you. Why should we? You are not germane to our plans at the moment—except in this way: we have sent one message, as you know, to Mrs. Knox's son, and through him to the Congress. And now we wish to follow this up with a message to the President. We thought you might act as agent for us in getting it to him. Immediately. Before Congress reconvenes tonight."

"Why don't you send it to him directly?" Tommy asked. "You know where the White House is."

"We can't get through to him," the voice said. "You know no one can. Furthermore, we'd be traced instantly. And we don't want that. In addition to which, of course, it will help to have a messenger of your distinguished fame and stature. It will impress the civilized world."

"If it's a private message," Justice Davis objected, "how can it?"

"It won't be," the voice said. "It won't be. We expect you to hand-carry it and make its contents public."

"And suppose I refuse to do either?" Tommy Davis inquired coldly. "I have better things to do than be a stooge for terrorists."

"Ah, but Mr. Justice," the voice said in a gently chiding tone, "you are a friend of Mrs. Knox's, aren't you? And you do want her to live, don't you?"

"Yes," Tommy snapped, "I *am* a friend of Mrs. Knox's and I *do* want her to live. What guarantee is there that she will if I do what you demand?"

"None whatever," the voice agreed pleasantly. "None whatsoever. But the most complete guarantee that she will not live if you do not do what we—'ask,' I think, Mr. Justice, not 'demand.' 'Demand' sounds too crude."

"You are crude," Justice Davis said coldly. "Crude and awful and I hope *you* die for it."

"Not unless you and your colleagues on the Court reinstate the death penalty, Mr. Justice," the voice said cheerfully. "We couldn't possibly, no matter what we do, rape, pillage, devastation, desecration, or the death of Mrs. Knox. *No* way, Mr. Justice. Now: this is what we want you to do . . ."

"*What* the hell?" the head of the AP Senate staff demanded in the Press Gallery as they all clustered around the news tickers in response to the clattering of bells that indicates a bulletin. "Tommy Davis is going to have a press conference—at the *White House!*"

"I guess we'd better get on our horses and get down there," his counterpart of UPI said, grabbing his hat and coat and starting for the door, as many others did the same. "Keep an eye on things here, you guys. Maybe he's going to announce the release of Beth Knox."

"I'd like to think so," the New York *Times* said gloomily as they jostled hurriedly down the worn old marble steps of the Capitol and out into the freezing night to began frantically hailing taxis. "But I don't think there's too much hope."

"I think," he said, as he came back into the room and faced them at the oval table, his face drawn and sad and even more haggard than it had been when he left them an hour ago, "that I have a decision for you."

"Why don't you hold it up a little," Cullee Hamilton suggested gently. "Tommy Davis is about to make some sort of announcement at the White House. It could be they're going to let your mother go."

"I don't think," he said in a voice infinitely tired and sad, "that I am ever going to see my mother again. At least—alive. . . . So let's get our statement ready, and then as soon as—as Tommy's finished, we'll let it go."

"All right," Cullee said, turning to snap on the television set in its niche on the wall. "But don't give up hope yet."

"Why not?" he asked in a dulled, sleepwalking way. "Why not?"

JUSTICE DAVIS ANNOUNCES ADDED DEMANDS FROM KNOX KIDNAPPERS AT WHITE HOUSE. TERRORISTS [the first time the word had been used] SAY PRESIDENT MUST GIVE "CLEAR AND FORCEFUL ENDORSEMENT" TO HELP AMERICA BILL. DEMAND KNOX-BACKED "IN DEFENSE OF FREEDOM" GROUP BE DISBANDED IMMEDIATELY.

JUSTICE EMPHASIZES KIDNAPPERS APPROACHED HIM, SAYS HE ACTED AS "EMISSARY UNDER PROTEST." EXPRESSES PERSONAL HOPE GOVERNMENT WILL HAVE CULPRITS "BEFORE NIGHT IS OUT." URGES PRESIDENT TO REPUDIATE BILL "AND ALL THE SINISTER ELEMENTS WHO ARE APPARENTLY BEHIND IT." WHITE HOUSE PRESS SECRETARY SAYS PRESIDENT "CONTINUES TO DEPLORE INCIDENT BUT WILL HAVE NO COMMENT AT THIS TIME WHICH MIGHT JEOPARDIZE WORK OF FBI."

CONGRESSMAN KNOX, EX-PRESIDENT ABBOTT, OTHERS SILENT ON REACTION TO THREATS.

But not silent for long following Tommy's hectic and clamorous press conference in the White House Press Room. An obviously tired and worried Frankly Unctuous had the latest on the 6 P.M. news roundup.

"Here in this stricken capital of a tense and troubled nation which must work out its agonies squarely in the eye of the watching world," he began (in what some of his irreverent colleagues were wont to describe as his "invoking-the-whole-God-damned-panorama" style of opening), "the leaders of America await tonight the response that must be made somehow, by those who genuinely love America, to the vicious and heartless thugs who have kidnapped Mrs. Orrin Knox.

"Scarcely two minutes ago, just before this program came on the air, the response of Mrs. Knox's son was released to the media. While this correspondent was never particularly impressed by the policies of the Congressman's late father, no one ever truthfully denied that Orrin Knox was one of the most courageous men who ever served in American public life. Now his son has proven himself worthy of his father.

"IIis statement is brief and to the point:

"'Aware as I am of the threat to the life of my mother by those who are holding her as a means of blackmailing the Congress, the President and all who oppose the so-called 'Help America bill,' I am nonetheless unable to follow any course other than the one I think she would want me to follow. It is the course consistent with her principles and her courage, with my father's principles and courage, and, I hope, with mine.

"'Trusting in the ability and determination of the Jason Administration to speedily recover my mother and to ruthlessly pursue and prosecute those responsible for her kidnapping, I accordingly reject all of their demands and I urge all who believe with me in the traditional protections of this democracy to reject them too.

"'I shall continue to fight this bill with everything I have. I hope all who think as I do, both in the Congress and throughout the country, will do the same. There will be no relaxation or lessening of our efforts to defeat this vicious and potentially dictatorial legislation. And there will be no lessening or relaxation of our efforts to change a foreign policy we can only regard as completely disastrous for the United States of America.

"'I call on all citizens who believe in America—including the President of the United States—to join me. I do not think the consequence will be the death of my mother. But at the same time I do not think she would want me to do anything else.'

"So speaks," said Frankly in his most respectful tones, "the brave son of brave parents. To his statement are appended the signatures of the ex-President of the United States, Congressman William Abbott of Colorado; the Minority Leader of the United States Senate, Warren Strickland of Idaho; former Senate Majority Leader Robert D. Munson of Michigan; Senators Cullee Hamilton of California, Lafe Smith of Iowa; and—in a rather surprising addition, yet one perhaps not so surprising in view of his long devotion to the principles of this Republic—the name of America's most famous news columnist, Walter Dobius.

"I should have been happy and honored," Frankly said gravely, "had I been asked to append my own. And I am sure I speak for many of my more experienced and established colleagues in the media when I say this. . . .

"The name we do not see," he went on, and his voice became noticeably and surprisingly sterner, "is the one name that Americans would logically and rightfully expect to see, either in direct or indirect endorsement, on a document of this nature: the name of the President of the United States. Again we are faced with the greatest mystery of all that have surrounded his hectic first week in office: where is he? What is he thinking? What is he doing? What does he propose?

"The brief statements that have come out of the White House in the past four hours are correct and encouraging as far as they go. But not even the staunchest proponents of the President—and I should say that I have long been one of them—will claim, I think, that they have gone far enough.

"Still, at this late hour, we turn to the White House for guidance. Still, we await the leadership that should come from that fateful residence. And now, with the kidnapping of Mrs. Knox adding even further horrors to those piled upon us, we all but cry out, 'Speak, Mr. President! Lead us, Mr. President! At least—we beg of you—take us into your confidence so that we may find the hope we must have, Mr. President!'

"Harold Knox, brave son of brave parents, has shown the way. Now, as the Congress prepares to resume within the hour its debate on a most significant and possibly even ominous bill, and as the fate of Mrs. Knox herself remains a mystery in the hands of the evil beings who hold her, we beseech you, Mr. President: lead us! *Lead us!*"

And that, for Frankly Unctuous, was a break with the White House as startling as Walter Dobius' signature on Hal Knox's statement. It was duly noted in the places where the consequences of such actions were now being prepared.

But from the White House came nothing further to expand upon the terse word that the President continued to deplore, but would not jeopardize the efforts of the FBI by saying more. This satisfied some, increased the concern of others and solved nothing.

And so the debate resumed.

"Well, Mrs. Knox," the voice said, its owner speaking through the locked door, "it doesn't look too good, does it? We had hoped your son would be more sensible."

"I am proud of him," she said, though to her annoyance her voice trembled, too noticeably.

"You should be," the voice agreed. "He is, as our friend has just said on television, the brave son of brave parents."

"When will you kill me?" she asked, knowing that such bluntness had seemed to shock the voice before. It appeared to again.

"Mrs. Knox! How like a Knox, to be so direct! But also, as I have cautioned you before, so dramatic! Nothing is definite, nothing is clear—except for your son's attitude, that is. But he may yet come around. And there are other factors: the Congress—the President. We will simply have to wait and see what happens as the night draws on. Is everything all right in there? You've eaten dinner? The television is working satisfactorily? You can keep in touch?"

"I'm keeping in touch," she said dryly, her voice steadying.

"What do you think of our President?" the voice asked with a sudden humorous scorn. "Isn't he something else? Won't even help an old friend, apparently."

"He's helping according to his lights," she said, feeling an odd need to defend Ted Jason, of all people. "He has the FBI on it. He isn't sitting still."

"But he isn't *really* helping you, is he?" the voice persisted. "The FBI isn't going to find us, and if it did, I think I can assure you it would be much too late to be of assistance to you. He isn't helping you in the way we've suggested—he isn't taking up his option. Don't defend him, Mrs. Knox. He's a sorry soul, our President." The voice chuckled. "Which is quite all right with us."

"I think," she said quietly, "that you and your fellow fanatics are insane."

"In the world of the sane," the voice said amicably, "he who is insane is king. Particularly in this kind of situation. And you must admit, Mrs. Knox, this kind of situation is quite common around the globe, these days. And, of course, you know—you *do* know, because you're very intelligent—that 'fanatics' perhaps isn't quite the word. This isn't a pack of irrational crazies, Mrs. Knox. We're quite calm, quite cool, quite collected—and quite determined. Which I don't think your son, or our other friends in Congress or our strange, hermitic President quite realize, as yet. I think they too feel a certain contempt. It isn't wise. . . . Well"—with a sudden briskness—"I must be running along. Keep smiling, Mrs. Knox. No one can say when the dawn may break in the middle of the night. Let us pray it comes not too late."

"I pity you," she said, "because you are so lonely and so far from the rational world, and because what your tormented souls prompt you to do to one old woman isn't going to make that much difference to the world."

"Not so old," the voice said, "and quite a lot of difference. And don't," it said, suddenly sharper, "pity us, Mrs. Knox. Don't dare pity us. That is very dangerous."

"I know it is with people of your type," she said quietly. "But nonetheless, I do."

"*Don't!*" the voice said, almost in a shout. "*Don't*, Mrs. Knox! I warn you!"

"What does it matter?" she asked with a sudden indifference that she found to her surprise was quite genuine. "Pity or love—neither could reach you now."

"Mrs. Knox—" the voice began in an ugly tone, and then broke off as if overcome by some emotion too deep for expression. (How old was its owner? Hal's age, she imagined—if that.) And so once more she said quietly, for she knew instinctively, as she had for some time now, that these conversations were in all probability rapidly approaching their end, regardless of what her son, or the Congress, or the President or anyone might do:

"I pity you. You cannot begin to imagine how much."

But this time the voice said nothing. Instead two fists pounded the door in an expression of rage so recognizable and distinct that she could almost see it. And then footsteps hurried away.

She sat for what seemed quite a long time, thinking about what the voice had truly said: these were not fanatics in the old sense. These were conditioned, cold, intelligent and forever unreachable. These were the new breed.

Then she thought of Orrin, convinced now that he and Ceil had been their victims just as she felt certain she would presently be.

Then she prayed quietly, for a time; and presently, feeling at last somewhat comforted and serene, went to the television set and turned it on, so that she might keep in touch with the tumbling world and her sadly troubled country as they raced ever faster toward whatever destiny an inscrutable Providence might have in mind for them.

"Mr. Speaker," Hal said shortly after 2 A.M., face white and strained, voice controlled at times with difficulty but persistence unflagging, "I appreciate more than I can say the many expressions of sympathy which have been given me by members on both sides of the aisle since debate resumed. But I do not detect therein any change in sentiment as regards this bill, and therefore I wonder if—since the House is obviously going to pass it anyway—I might be recognized out of order to move to suspend debate on the bill temporarily and introduce, also out of order and for immediate consideration, a resolution stating this obvious fact to those who have my mother? The resolution calls upon them to release her at once, since their claimed reason for her kidnapping—namely, to influence the Congress—is entirely moot and unnecessary.

"The resolution also expresses the sense of the House that we call upon the President of the United States to state his position clearly and at once as being in favor of this bill, since that too is obvious, and since therefore the kidnappers' attempt to use the threat to her life as a weapon to force him to give the bill his endorsement is also moot and unnecessary.

"A companion resolution is even now, I believe, being introduced in the other body by its former Majority Leader, Senator Munson.

"I do so move to suspend the regular order, Mr. Speaker."

"Well, now," Jawbone said hastily into the uneasy murmuring that arose from the crowded floor and the galleries, "well, now, the gentleman knows that his request is entirely out of order, and in fact, I don't even know if it is possible at all under the rules of the House. If the gentleman will give me a few minutes to consult with the parliamentarian and other interested parties then maybe we can come up with some sort of suggestion that will be within the rules and still try to meet some of the gentleman's objectives. Would that be agreeable to the gentleman?"

"No, sir," Hal said evenly, "it would not. Naturally you must consult the parliamentarian, Mr. Speaker, but I don't want consultations with 'other interested parties,' and I don't want any 'suggestion' that would 'try' to meet 'some' of my objectives. I want a resolution that will meet all of them, just as I have stated it."

"Well, now!" Jawbone cried, looking around nervously as the uneasy murmur grew and in a few areas of the galleries turned to boos and hisses. "Well, now, I must say to the gentleman that he is really quite out of order in those comments, let alone in what he proposes. I must say to the gentleman—"

"Mr. *Speaker*," William Abbott said with an angry emphasis that quieted the House at once. "Mr. *Speaker*, if I may be recognized to comment, I should like to say that I—"

"Mr. Speaker!" Bronnie Bernard interrupted in an indignant shout. "Now, Mr. Speaker! I am going to have to insist on the regular order here if this sort of thing is going to be allowed to go on! The gentleman from Illinois and the gentleman from Colorado both know perfectly well, Mr. Speaker, that what is being proposed is an attempt to embarrass the President of the United—"

"What is being proposed," the ex-President exploded, an utter contempt in his voice, "is an attempt to save a human life! Have the gentleman from New York and his like become so bereft of all human feeling and decency that they wish to interpose themselves in the way of that? In the name of God, *what kind of people are you?*"

"The gentleman from Colorado," Bronnie Bernard said, turning white himself but standing his ground, "is a former Speaker and a former President of the United States, and he should be ashamed of himself for saying a thing like that to me and to my colleagues here. Of course we want to save a human life! Of course we sympathize with the gentleman from Illinois and with his mother! Of course we are not monsters! *But,* Mr. Speaker, neither are we so naive as to believe that there is not also an ulterior motive behind the suggestion of the gentleman from Illinois. Neither are we so innocent that we cannot understand this attempt to embarrass the President of the United States by making him do something he may not yet be ready to do. Neither are we so naive that—"

"And why?" Cullee Hamilton demanded bitterly as Arly Richardson peered at him like some spiteful old bird and on the Senate floor and in the galleries the tension grew, "*why* is it an embarrassment to the President of the United States, I ask the Majority Leader who makes the charge with such ringing rhetoric, to ask him to do what he can to help save Mrs. Knox? How can he possibly be embarrassed by committing himself to this bill which his silence commits him to already?" He paused and his expression and voice became somber. "I ask the Majority Leader this question direct: does this Administration intend to sacrifice Mrs. Knox? Are you ready to let her die?"

There was a great burst of boos and hisses and beside his front seat on the aisle Arly Richardson drew himself to his full height and spat out his response.

"The Senator from California talks arrant, insulting and, I am inclined to think, subversive nonsense. Certainly this Administration does not 'intend to sacrifice Mrs. Knox,' as the Senator so kindly puts it. Of course we are not 'ready to let her die,' to quote his extreme, nonsensical and despicable language. And we do not intend to accept this kind of two-bit, propagandistic interference with orderly debate on this bill, either, I will say to the Senator! There are rules in this Senate—"

"Will the Senator yield to me?" Bob Munson demanded, and proceeded before Arly could stop him. "Mr. President, what *is* this quibble? Has the Senate reached—has the country reached—a point so low that we are unable to bend our rules if necessary, yes, break them if necessary, in order to save a human life? Is that what the Majority

Leader is trying to tell us? Is he so protective of a do-nothing President—" there was a burst of startled and angry sound from the galleries and some places on the floor but he ignored it—"that he will attempt to block a simple humanitarian act? Is the President himself so afraid to take a stand that he will sacrifice the life of a helpless woman to avoid taking a stand on this bill to which his silence has already given assent? Why this strange protectiveness of him, Senator? Why this denial of a simple humanitarian act? Why hide behind the rules? We can suspend debate and take up this resolution, it's been done before. As anyone who has served here knows, I will say to the Senator, the Senate can do anything it really wants to. Why won't he let it?"

"Mr. President," Fred Van Ackerman said, rising slowly in his place, looking around floor and galleries with an appraising stare, "I don't know who has the floor at this point—"

"I do," Cullee snapped, "and I am not so sure I am going to yield."

"Well, the Senator had better," Fred said, his voice suddenly ugly.

"Why?" Cullee asked contemptuously. "Which will you have them do to me, Senator, kidnap me or kill me? Or both?"

"Mr. President," Fred cried with a sudden fury, "I will say to the Senator that some people had better not be so smart! Some people had better not be so smart, I will say to the Senator!"

"I repeat," Cullee said in the same contemptuous tone, "will you have them—" then he broke off with a disgusted shrug. "Go ahead, Senator. Tell us what you've got on your mind and get it over with. We've got business to transact."

"You bet we have," Fred Van Ackerman cried, "you bet we have, and I'll tell you what part of it is, Senators! We've got to find out what's behind this sudden tricky move at almost two o'clock in the morning as we near a vote on this most important and vital and necessary bill, why there is this diversion, yes, diversion, Mr. President, offered here and in the other body by those who oppose the greatest President this country has ever had! Our noble friends cry out about Mrs. Knox, and God knows nobody deplores this unhappy situation more than I do— *yes!*" he cried sharply as Cullee looked at him with a sarcastically ironic smile he took no pains to conceal, "and the Senator can stop smiling at me, I *do* deplore it—but where is the consistency in it, Mr. President? Why do they want the President to say what the Congress will do, when we haven't even voted yet? Why do they want to put Congress on the record, why do they demand the President put himself on the record, when *they* won't commit themselves to the bill?

"Oh, it's all very well for Mrs. Knox's son, the gentleman from Illinois over there in the other body, to act pious about the President, but

Congressman Knox is part of the deal, too, he's part of the demand. Why doesn't *he* commit himself to the bill as he ought to, instead of holding back and trying a tricky move to embarrass the President? Why doesn't he disband the IDF, instead of offering diversions? How about that, Senators? Why don't you talk to him, instead of trying to embarrass the President? You all signed his statement a while ago. Use your influence, Senators! Bring him to heel!"

"Now, that's enough of that," Cullee said angrily. "I have the floor, and that's enough of that. I shall not yield to the Senator further. This Senate and the Congress know very well that Congressman Knox and those of us who support him in his statement cannot in all conscience endorse this vicious bill—"

"Maybe the President can't, either!" Arly Richardson snapped, too quickly.

"Oh, then he's against it, is he?" Cullee demanded instantly. "Then he's really opposed to it, too, is he? Well, Mr. President, now that we have the word of the Majority Leader that the President of the United States opposes this bill—"

But the completion of his sentence, along with Arly's angry shouts of denial, were lost in the general booing that filled the chamber. Lacey Pollard of Texas, the president pro tempore, once more back in the chair while the Vice President was absent from the floor, rapped hard and furiously with the gavel, his handsome old face flushed with anger and excitement.

"The Senate will be in order!" he demanded. "The Senate will be in order, now! The Senate and the galleries will be in order! Be in order, now! Be in order!"

And after a few more moments during which no one appeared to pay any particular attention, and during which Lacey's face became even more heated and flushed—so much so that Verne Cramer of Oregon, a doctor, murmured to Magnus Hollingsworth of Wisconsin, "Lacey'd better watch it, he looks as though his blood pressure is about 300 over 250"—the floor and galleries finally quieted down and the Senate could proceed.

"Mr. President," Bob Munson said quietly, "will the Senator from California yield to me? . . . I thank the Senator. Now, Mr. President, it seems to me that we can make all kinds of debating points here for the rest of the night, but the basic fact of it is that a human life may be at stake—in fact, in my opinion *is* at stake, for I take these terrorists who hold Mrs. Knox at their word, I believe they mean business—and it is up to the Senate to act in all conscience to express its opinion and call for a speedy and safe solution to this dilemma. Mrs. Knox's son, who with his lovely wife, the daughter of the senior Senator from Connecticut, bears more tonight than a son and daughter should have to bear, has made it quite clear to all the world where he stands and why he stands there. The same cannot be said for the Congress and it certainly cannot be said for the President. The only way to get a decision from him, apparently, is to flush him out. That is what we propose in this resolution. If we cannot, Mr. President"—his voice became grave—"and if anything does happen to Mrs. Knox, then I can only say to him that he too will bear a most heavy burden and one he cannot escape when the reckoning comes."

"Mr. President," Arly Richardson said, his usual sarcastic tones quivering with anger, "the Senator from Michigan, as always, makes a very clever statement, full of nuances and innuendoes. He wants the Congress to express *its* opinion. Very well, then, stop getting in the way and let us vote on this bill! He wants the President to express *his* opinion! Very well, then, stop trying to harass him and let his Administration go forward on all fronts, as we are informed it is doing, to recover Mrs. Knox safely and apprehend her abductors! Let us get on with it, Mr. President! Let us stop procrastinating and stop this waste of time on a side issue! Let us—"

"Let us," Bronnie Bernard cried to a tensely listening House, "stop trying to evade and avoid the only real issue that confronts the Congress here this morning, namely whether we are going to support our great President in his search for peace, or whether we are going to let domestic disturbances and harassment tie his hands and thwart his actions at every turn! That is the only real issue, Mr. Speaker, and we must stick to it. We must stick to it! We cannot afford to wander away, the stakes are too important—"

"And my mother's life is not important?" Hal demanded in a sudden harsh outburst. "*That* is not important, the gentleman argues? *That* does not matter to anyone?"

"Well," Bronson Bernard said, and he paused and drew a deep breath. "Well—at the risk of sounding harsh, I think historical perspective compels the thought that while individual lives are of course important to those around them, they do not, in the long run, count so much as the historical imperatives that confront great states and societies. Therefore—"

"Mr. Speaker!" William Abbott cried, and Hal, who had turned pale and started an angry retort, deferred to him immediately. "Mr. Speaker," William Abbott said, his voice somber, "I had never thought to reach the day when I would hear so cold-blooded and inhuman a statement uttered in all seriousness on the floor of this House. I had never thought to hear the day when a member of the Congress of the United States would place human life at so low an evaluation—when he would have the utter callousness and gall to say to a son that the life of his mother is worthless and unimportant. The gentleman from New York cried shame upon me, Mr. Speaker. I say to him, for shame, and for shame, indeed, to say so cruel and heartless a thing! And God help us if that accurately reflects the heartlessness and cruelty of the new generation of leaders who are coming to power in this land where human life and individual rights once meant something."

"Mr. Speaker," Bronson Bernard said, and his expression, which had for a second looked upset and abashed, hardened into a mask of superior and self-righteous anger. "The Congressman from Colorado as usual uses inflammatory and derogatory language in his attempt to portray me, and those who think like me, as monsters. But that is not honest, Mr. Speaker, nor is it fair. I was simply saying what all intelligent students of history know, which is that the historical imperative in the life of nations in the long run overrides the lives of individuals, and that the lives of individuals must therefore in the long run find themselves subordinate to the needs of their nations. History shows this, Mr. Speaker. It is nothing new. It has happened in many lands, and it is sheer hypocrisy to say it has not happened in this. The gentleman from Colorado knows this."

"The gentleman from Colorado," William Abbott said coldly, "knows that an occasional historical happenstance is a long way from a formally enunciated and active principle of government and political behavior. It is one thing if it happens inadvertently in the course of things. It is quite another if it represents the cold-blooded policy of the government."

"How many American boys did the gentleman, as President, send to die in Panama and Gorotoland?" Bronnie Bernard inquired softly. "Was that an 'occasional historical happenstance?'" There was a little gasp of delighted laughter, and some applause, from the galleries. The Speaker banged his gavel sternly.

"Now, then!" he said. "Now, then, up there, you-all be quiet, now! You-all are guests of this House and you must be quiet. Does the gentleman from Colorado wish to reply to the question of the gentleman from New York?"

"Only if the gentleman believes I am a cold-blooded monster who enjoyed sending American boys to their deaths," Bill Abbott said with a savage dryness. "Does he?"

"The gentleman seems to believe equally derogatory things about me," Bronson Bernard replied with a deliberately offhand air. "I don't see that we're so different. . . . Anyway, Mr. Speaker! *Anyway!* Here we stand arguing a side issue while the President who does *not* believe in sending American boys abroad to die, the President who does *not* believe in 'an occasional historical happenstance' but who *does* believe in a positive program for peace, finds his policies hampered and disrupted by domestic protest. That is still the issue.

"Mr. Speaker, I sympathize with the gentleman from Illinois, but I really honestly do not think that one life, however valuable and important to those around it, must be allowed to stand in the way of action to help America in her hour of need. I must insist on the regular order, Mr. Speaker, in order to bar the resolution of the gentleman from Illinois and allow us to get on with the business of the House."

"Then if that is the case, Mr. Speaker," William Abbott said, "I must appeal to the chair for a ruling on the resolution, and I serve notice that if the ruling is adverse, I shall appeal to the House to override it."

"Mr. President," Fred Van Ackerman said, "I am sure we all sympathize very, very deeply with the Knox family, but, after all, there are things more important than one life or one family. The country is important, Mr. President! A leader who seeks peace is important, Mr. President! Working with our great friends in Russia is important, Mr. President! Mr. President, this resolution is a nice piece of sentiment but it is impeding the work of the Senate. I must insist on the regular order."

"Then, Mr. President," Bob Munson said, "I must appeal to the chair for a ruling on the resolution, and should it be adverse, I serve notice that I shall appeal to the Senate to override it."

CONGRESS PASSES HELP AMERICA BILL BY SURPRISINGLY NARROW MARGIN AFTER FOES FAIL IN LAST-MINUTE ATTEMPT TO BLOCK IT. ADMINISTRATION FORCES IN BOTH HOUSES BEAT DOWN SPECIAL RESOLUTION DEMANDING PRESIDENT'S ENDORSEMENT OF BILL, THEN PASS MEASURE 56–44 IN SENATE, 279–256 IN HOUSE. FATE OF MRS. KNOX STILL UNKNOWN.

But not for long.

It fell to Frankly Unctuous to announce the news in a special bulletin and commentary, as first light began to touch the gleaming white dome of the Capitol and the glistening white expanses of the snow-held morning city. He faced the cameras in one of the broadcasting booths of the House Radio-Television Gallery, deathly pale, drawn, almost, it seemed, crying. His voice trembled and he steadied it with difficulty, but there was no mistaking where he stood this day. He had made his decision—although, like that of so many, it came a little late.

"This long night is almost ended," he said, "and it ends with another terrible tragedy, this one wanton, unnecessary, savage and awful. It is my sad duty to report to you that the body of Mrs. Orrin Knox, widow of the late Secretary of State and late candidate for President, has just been found on the steps of the West Front of the Capitol. The discovery was made just moments ago by a Capitol policeman making a last check on the grounds as Congress adjourned after passing the so-called 'Help America bill.'

"Mrs. Knox had been shot once through the head. Her body, apparently with some care on the part of whoever did this dreadful thing, had been placed in the center of the massive ceremonial steps that overlook the city where she and her late husband served their country with such distinction for so many years. She was fully clothed and wearing a coat. FBI officials, already on the scene, believe that she was alive when brought to the Capitol and was executed—for there can be no gentler word—on the spot at some point during the final moments of the Congressional session.

"The purpose of all this," Frankly said, and he paused to draw a trembling hand across his forehead, "is, apparently, that there is no purpose—that it is simply frightfulness and horror for the sake of frightfulness and horror. It is true that Mrs. Knox's son, Congressman Harold Knox of Illinois, with whom all decent Americans must join in sorrow and mourning, had defied the kidnappers' demands that he support the so-called 'Help America bill.' It is true that President Jason, whose formal endorsement of the bill had also been demanded by the kidnappers, had ignored them. But if the basic objective of the kidnappers was to secure passage of the bill, as their statements seemed to say, then all of that was immaterial. The bill *was* passed—and all the kidnappers really succeeded in doing, during the time their captive lived, was to alienate some of the votes all observers agreed they had, so that the final margin was much narrower than they presumably desired.

"There is some presumptive evidence that Mrs. Knox's captors may have intended to release her alive at the Capitol, and that her murder was a sudden angry act of revenge because Congress, the President and her son had not behaved exactly as they were ordered. That motive is being speculated upon in this now hushed and saddened building, as shocked members of Congress and the media prepare to go slowly and unbelievingly away to their homes.

"But to those familiar with the methods of terrorists in other lands in these recent unhappy decades, it seems likely that a motive deeper and more sinister may well be present.

"This awful event may have been intended from the first. It may have been simply frightfulness for frightfulness' sake—terrorist horror for no other reason than to shake the American people—to put the country into a state of shock deeper than it is in already as the result of the assassinations last summer and the difficult and still-unresolved events that have followed the inauguration of President Jason.

"And it may also have been done to precipitate exactly the kind of domestic division and internal turmoil that would justify an immediate appeal to the extremely dangerous provisions of the so-called 'Help America bill'—a bill which this correspondent among others, may God forgive and help us all, at first believed necessary to assure the effective fruition of the policies of Edward M. Jason.

"Now those policies seem dreadfully precarious, the bill dreadfully dangerous to the liberties of this nation. Already anti-Administration demonstrations touched off by Mrs. Knox's death are being reported from many cities throughout the country, even though much of the nation, in time zones beyond the eastern seaboard, is still in the grip of night. The dreadful news is spreading fast, and with it come the first eruptions of what promises to be a most somber and fateful day for America. Because, of course, the demonstrations are not being allowed to pass unchallenged.

"They are being met already with force from the organization which many here, rightly or wrongly, are holding responsible for Mrs. Knox's death—the National Anti-War Activities Congress—NAWAC. Bloody clashes have already been reported from Chicago, Milwaukee, Des Moines, Boston, Richmond. And this is very likely just the beginning.

"Edward M. Jason must speak now. Even the most patient charity, the most charitable patience, can no longer excuse his silence in the face of all that is happening to this unhappy land.

"First he must issue the most forceful and powerful condemnation of the murder of Mrs. Knox, and increase to the utmost the government's search for her murderers.

"Then he must veto the so-called 'Help America bill' with a forcefulness that will guarantee that no such evil proposition will ever again be placed before the Congress.

"And then he must address the nation and take it into his confidence concerning his plans to meet what has now become the definite Soviet menace to the very future and existence of the American people and of the United States of America itself.

"Further silence from the President would be inexcusable.

"Already there is talk of impeachment in the air, up here in the Capitol. Grounds may not yet entirely or logically exist. But further silence and inaction from the President—in the opinion not only of his opponents but of many, including this reporter, who have long defended and supported him—may well provide those grounds: and harsh and saddening though it may be to acknowledge—justly so."

It was quite a profound and moving recantation, for one who had joined his colleagues so often in ringing denunciations of all those fellow citizens who had feared the basic trend of recent decades in the great Republic. But it did not impress at all those who had held Mrs. Knox.

They knew, as he had accurately surmised, that frightfulness—wanton, unnecessary, savage, awful—had its place in a nation's intimidation; and that a people, if you gave them a few sudden, sharp examples of it, could sometimes be shocked, stunned and nearly beaten before the battle was half begun.

There were still a good many, of course, who continued to fight on; and to them, for the first time in a week that seemed a year, the President of the United States gave encouragement with one hand, even as he drew it away with the other.

PRESIDENT LEADS NATION IN MOURNING FOR MRS. KNOX. STATEMENT DENOUNCES "MURDERERS AND SUBVERSIVE ELEMENTS FOREIGN TO THIS DEMOCRACY WHO ARE BEHIND THE KIDNAPPING." HE PLACES ATTORNEY GENERAL WATTERSILL AT HEAD OF DRIVE TO FIND AND PUNISH CAPTORS, PLEDGES "FULLEST RESOURCES OF GOVERNMENT." SIGNS HELP AMERICA BILL AS "STRONG NEW WEAPON TO AID IN BATTLE AGAINST ALL SUCH SUBVERTERS OF THE AMERICAN WAY OF LIFE." RIOTS AND DEMONSTRATIONS SPREAD ACROSS COUNTRY.

Events moved to a yet more somber beat and the foundations of certainty crumbled with an ever more rapid acceleration, in a land where everything seemed to have gone wrong in the place where it really mattered fundamentally—at the top.

In the hushed house in Spring Valley he looked at his wife in the ghastly dawn as though he had never seen her before.

"I'm sorry," she said.

"It doesn't matter," he said.

And for the time being, and as far into the future as he was able to see in that awful moment, it did not matter.

Nor did she.

Nor did he.

Nor did anything in all the ruined shambles of what was left of the once-bright dream of the fighting, independent, likable, loyal, cantankerous, freedom-loving Knoxes.

"Dolly is coming over," she said with a careful politeness.

"That's good," he said. Some tag-end of thought prompted an inquiry. "What about Mabel?"

"She just called. She isn't going to marry Lafe. She's going back to Utah with Pidge. She says politics is too evil. It killed Brig and now it's killed—it's killed—oh, *Hal.*"

And they were in each other's arms, finally, crying together as though they would never stop; although of course they would, eventually; and life would go on.

But his instinct was right.

The bright dream was over forever, for the Knoxes.

They arrived at the East Gate shortly after 6:30 A.M., riding four by four in two limousines, the Speaker's official Cadillac and Bob and Dolly Munson's Rolls-Royce: Warren Strickland, Justice Davis and Walter Dobius with Jawbone; the ex-President, Cullee Hamilton and Lafe Smith with Senator Munson.

They had gathered with a sort of uncoordinated inevitability in the Speaker's office just twenty minutes ago. William Abbott had said tersely, "Let's go!" The Speaker had started to protest, then fallen silent under the ex-President's sudden glare. Meekly he had turned to the phone, ordered his car. Bob Munson had done the same. Bill Abbott had placed two quick calls, to the State and Defense departments' switchboards; introduced himself, said the same brief words—"Tell the Secretary a group of Congressional leaders and myself are going to the White House immediately to see the President. Tell him to meet us there if he can." Then he had led the way out the door through the now deserted Speaker's Lobby to the elevator, down to the worn old stone steps of the East Front of the House where the cars were just drawing up.

Silently they got in and silently traversed the mile-long run down the Hill and west along just-stirring Pennsylvania Avenue to the Mansion. The skies were clearing, the dawn was growing steadily stronger; there was, at last, the promise of a sunny day. But a knifing wind blew off the frozen Potomac. It was still cold. Very cold.

As they drew up at the gate two other limousines moved in behind them. Under the portico the Secretaries of State and Defense stepped out, tired and haggard like the rest, clothes rumpled, eyes showing signs of all-night vigil. Not very many in official Washington had been to bed that night. Both Secretaries had been at their desks when the ex-President called. Both had welcomed the message. It was time, and past time, to end all mysteries, hesitations, duplicities, evasions.

If they could be ended, of which no one was sure.

Again, as with Ewan MacDonald and the Joint Chiefs, the startled guards made some pro forma attempt to stop them. But the habit of yielding to the ex-President's commands was still too strong; plus the fact that none of the formidable phalanx of ten somber men who stood in the lobby showed the slightest signs of taking no for an answer.

A call was obediently put through, word came back at once from a surprised valet that the President was taking a shower to freshen up before breakfast.

"Tell him President Abbott, two Cabinet officers and some members of Congress are coming up," Bill Abbott ordered tersely, hung up, turned to the captain on the desk.

"Alert the guards throughout the house that we're on our way," he directed—received a now-compliant, "Yes, *sir!*"—said again, "All right, gentlemen, let's go!"—and trudged off along the corridor past the Rose Garden to the family elevator, where they went up in a couple of loads, regrouping on the second floor. Down the long central hall a member of the Secret Service came to greet them, shook hands deferentially with William Abbott, gravely nodded hello to the rest.

"The President will be out in a few minutes," he said. "He has directed me to show you to the solarium. He wants to know if you want breakfast also?"

"Coffee, juice and Danish will do fine, I think," William Abbott said. "At least for me." The others nodded agreement, the Secret Service bowed and led the way to the solarium where they disposed themselves amid the casual chairs and sofas of the Mansion's most relaxed and comfortable family room. Across the Ellipse the Washington Monument confronted them, its tip touched by the first rays of sun, pure, white, shining, serene as ever. William Abbott gave it a long stare; for some reason he could probably not have defined, uttered a sudden snort in which impatience, annoyance and a sort of grim, sardonic humor were inextricably mixed; and turned away.

There was a bustle at the door. Instinctively they all stood up.

"Gentlemen," the Secret Service said solemnly, "the President."

He looked handsome as always but as tired and haggard as they, the fine eyes red-veined and haunted beneath the thoughtful forehead and the carefully combed swatch of silver hair. But at least he had the advantage of a shower, and the advantage of being President. They stared at him and he stared back, looking carefully from face to face, returning finally for a long, long moment, during which their eyes locked and did not waver, to the granitic and unyielding visage of his predecessor.

"Gentlemen," he said finally, "please be seated. They'll be bringing the food right in. After they have left—" he paused and a profound, almost inadvertent sigh escaped his lips, a small, desolate sound that disturbed them all greatly—"I shall tell you about my trip to Moscow."

BOOK FOUR

1. EVEN THEN, after what appeared to be the collapse of all his idealistic and well-meaning plans, it had begun in a suddenly revived mood that was close to euphoria.

Suddenly it was all playing games again—the landslide President, the mover and shaker, history's maker of miracles, the great rearranger of the globe, the man who in his first dramatic hours was to lead his people and the world out of the bondage of suspicion, hatred, vengeance and war, forever.

It was not until Air Force One and its accompanying press plane neared the Russian border that he finally realized irrevocably at last that the games were grown up beyond recall, that they would not change despite his desperate imaginings, and that the happy innocence and wild, popular hope of his election and inaugural were destined never to return.

"What is that?" Ewan MacDonald had exclaimed suddenly, somewhere over Poland, and they had all turned quickly to look where he pointed, ahead and to the right. At almost the same moment Jawbone, sitting at the window opposite, uttered a similar excited query, and he, too, pointed.

Ahead on both sides a swarm of Russian fighter jets materialized out of nowhere, rushed past the windows, circled and came back. Within two minutes the two American planes were neatly boxed in, front, rear, right, left, top, bottom. They were inside a hurtling cocoon. They were, as they knew with a cold and frightening instinct, imprisoned.

And so what was he to do, President of the United States, "most powerful man on earth," as his countrymen liked comfortably to tell themselves? It did not take the pilot's worried message over the intercom to tell him that communication with Washington was jammed: that was only logical, and even if it had not been, what could he have done about it? Ordered an attack on Moscow? Gone down in flames in one last, romantic gesture? Started a war and unleashed terror on the world? Sane men—if any of the world's leaders in this particular era could be considered really sane, in the everyday, normal sense of the workaday world—did not do such things. Particularly when there was always the chance that it could be—it simply had to be—not a genuinely hostile act, just an uncomfortable one—a flex of muscles, a show of power, one more method of saying, "See what we can do? Watch out, watch out! Look on our works, ye mighty, and despair!"

So he did nothing, for there was nothing to do; and after a few agonized seconds of looking at one another in inquiry and frustration, his companions settled back, grim and unspeaking, in their seats. The journey's tense remainder passed in silence, broken only by one brief message which the pilot transmitted over the intercom. It was in broken but reasonably good English: "You have just crossed the border of the Union of Socialist Soviet Republics. Welcome to the people's democratic country."

Soon after that, as they began the final stages of their approach to Moscow, they saw that the accompanying jets—there must have been fifty, although they had no way of making an accurate count—were dipping their wings in a salute which could only be considered ironic. Then they peeled away as swiftly as they had appeared. And the Americans landed to the cold, cold greeting, in the cold, cold city, of the minor functionaries sent by the Chairman of the Council of Ministers to do what he deemed suitable honor.

After such a convoy and such a welcome, so brutal in style and so implicit in contempt, it was all he could do to put a good face upon it. But Presidents were supposed to put a good face on things, always equable, always pleasant, always calm; and so he made the attempt, although its strains and difficulties were clearly apparent to the closely watching press corps (its members badly shaken by the circumstances of their arrival, although nearly all were agreed that its nature should be minimized or eliminated from the reports sent home, because there was no point in stirring up American uneasiness when world peace was so vital and so clearly the desire of their grim-faced hosts). The ceremonies were short and he was glad for their brevity, for it spared him the necessity of pretending more than the barest of civilities in return. It was in a deeply troubled mood that he and his countrymen found themselves whisked away in swiftly racing limousines to the Kremlin while the world, via direct live broadcast, watched them go and clearly grasped the nature of their welcome.

His still hopeful dream of dealing as an equal with a man he had naively believed to be as dedicated as he to solving the world's ills was gone in an hour. He knew he was meant to come as an inferior and a supplicant, and to his already great mental and emotional burdens was added the crushing weight of the knowledge that this, in fact, was very close to an exact description of what he was.

Yet he could not let himself really believe that, even now, or really let himself be controlled by it. In this his colleagues were of some help, for Arly and Jawbone, in particular, were indignant—still living (as Robert Leffingwell and Ewan MacDonald with a sadly troubled instinct obviously were not) in the old-fashioned world where such things were simply not done to the President of the United States.

But by the time they were ushered in to face the Chairman, the Foreign Minister and the Minister of Defense, all looking suitably, ostentatiously grim, Arly and Jawbone, too, were silent. There had been no concession to fatigue, no nonsensical courtesy of giving them a chance to rest a little before plunging into conference. They had been shown at once to their sparsely furnished rooms, offered no nourishment, given barely time enough to go to the bathroom. Stern knocks had come on the door, uniformed guards had beckoned them imperiously forward down the endless empty corridors. The Chairman's office was a startling contrast in luxury when they finally came to it. But it was obvious whose comfort it was designed for: not theirs.

Tashikov and his colleagues had not even offered to shake hands and after a tentative gesture which the Chairman ignored, the President made no further attempt to indulge in amenities. He and his party were grim-faced, too, but their somber cast was not theatrics. Their dismay was genuine, and with it a growing anger, as Tashikov gestured them tersely to seats along the big table at the far side of the room, and, with his ostentatious fellow basiliks, took up his station opposite.

"Now, Mr. President," he said abruptly, clipping off his words and letting them tumble forward in the angry rush so familiar to all who had seen him in action as Ambassador to the UN, "we shall get down to business at last. It is not enough that you come here with the blood of imperialist aggression on your hands, but you must also ignore my most generous and charitable invitation, you must ignore the demands of the civilized world as expressed in the UN, you must openly defy the wishes of peace-loving peoples everywhere, you must wait until there is no alternative but to demand your presence, you must—"

"Mr. Chairman," Ted Jason said, and there was a stirring among his colleagues, for they hoped his tone, polite but insistent, and, to their great relief, firm, might stop what appeared to be a building tirade. "Mr. Chairman, if you will permit me the common courtesy—"

But the tirade was going too well to stop, and its proprietor was too experienced in polemical debate to yield his opponent the advantage of common courtesy. So the Chairman raved on while the Americans sat silent, white-faced, furious, powerless, unable to defend themselves or their country against the fanatical rantings of their small, ferret-faced, dangerously powerful host.

For the better part of an hour this went on, a recapitulation of all the Communist attacks ever made against awful, corrupt, imperialist America. No charge ever parroted by the Communist press or radio throughout the world, no tortured lie ever dreamed up by history's masters of the vicious art of turning words and meanings upside down, was forgotten by Vasily Tashikov as he ranted on. He played his voice like the instrument he had learned to make it, now soft, now loud, now angry, now dismayed, now savage, now aggrieved, but always ugly. At times it sank to ominous ranges, at times it rose to a scream. Now he pounded the table with his hands, now he jumped up and down in his chair. There was nothing new in this: it is the way Communist imperialists have always been and no doubt always will be. But not since Nikita Khrushchev sent John Kennedy dazed and trembling away from his savage raking in Vienna years ago had the ordure been heaped with such savage ferocity upon an American President.

Now all the phony "spirit of Moscow" or "spirit of San Francisco" or spirit-of-whatever of the recent past was forgotten as though it had never existed—as indeed it never had, save in the minds of wishful Americans who really thought themselves so clever that they began to believe their own publicity. Now all the basic naked ugliness, the monumental irresponsibility toward mankind, of the rigid Communist ideology was displayed once again. And the President and his colleagues knew that the Communists would, as always, get away with it, because the world was not here to listen, and so the world—or at least much of that small portion of it which formed and controlled the world's opinions—would simply not believe the fact if anyone tried to describe it.

After what was literally almost an hour, fifty-seven minutes by the watch of the Secretary of State, who had glanced at it when Tashikov's carefully staged delirium began, the Chairman abruptly stopped and drew himself back in his chair with a smug and triumphant air.

"And now what lies will you answer me with, Mr. President?" he demanded. "What can you possibly say to excuse the insufferable, imperialist, peace-destroying actions of yourself and your government? Make them good lies, Mr. President! We wish to admire your cleverness."

For several moments the President said nothing, simply staring at him with a distant, thoughtful expression, which did, finally, make him uncomfortable. To cover it he snapped out, "Well, Mr. President?" in an angry tone. But still Ted Jason did not reply.

When he spoke at last it was in a perfectly calm, perfectly quiet, perfectly polite tone of voice. To the obvious surprise of his opponents, and to the surprise of his own people as well, he did not sound abashed, disturbed, afraid or otherwise thrown off balance. Bob Leffingwell was to tell William Abbott later that he seemed at that moment to have been "supported by some inner vision." Whether its origin lay in numbness, incomprehension or a genuine conviction of righteousness, no one would ever know except himself. But for the next few minutes, as long as he and Tashikov were talking to one another in the presence of their countrymen, it sufficed. And at first Tashikov appeared to listen as Ted point by point took up his allegations and denied them. It was only when the President reached his peroration that the Chairman stirred and let his fangs come out again.

"Mr. Chairman," Ted said slowly after almost forty-five minutes of uninterrupted rebuttal, "I doubt if it has ever ever been the sad task of an American President—or, indeed, of any sane individual—to listen to a pack of lies as monstrous as you have hurled at me. You are beyond belief, and you are also beyond the bounds of rational society. You sound insane. I hope, for your sake and mine, and for the sake of our peoples and of the world, that this is not the case. For if it is, awful things may happen."

"Not to us," Vasily Tashikov snapped. Again the President studied him thoughtfully before continuing.

"You have sounded here, in these past few minutes," he resumed, "as though you really believed that your government is entirely innocent of any wrongdoing against America and against the peace of the world. Well: let me tell you something. It is a lie and the world knows it is a lie."

"The world has voted," the Chairman noted coldly.

"The world has chosen to ignore the facts," the President said. "Mr. Chairman! Do you have any conception at all of the pressures I have been under this past week? Mr. Chairman, let me tell you something. You have no idea how much confidence I had in your word, and how much reliance I placed upon my belief that you were as genuinely dedicated to peace in the world as I am. No, let me finish," he said with a sudden show of anger, as the Chairman fidgeted in his chair and started to blurt out a retort. "Because of that faith and trust in you, I made what I sincerely believe to be the most genuine gesture for peace any President has ever made. I withdrew American power from many areas. I terminated American involvement in two unfortunate wars. I placed my hopes and trust in the ability of honest men to negotiate honestly. I defended you, Mr. Chairman. I said you were the captive of your military—" Tashikov gave him a sudden broadly ironic smile, but he ignored it and went stubbornly on—"I said you were a decent and peace-loving man who wanted as much as I to establish a viable and lasting peace. I accepted your statements in good faith—*I believed a Communist*. And I did so against the advice of many around me, and at the cost of great internal uneasiness and stress in the United States.

"How do you justify your betrayal of my trust, and of the hopes of my countrymen and, I think, of all the decent peoples of the world? I want to hear you tell me, for I have never quite believed that the mentality necessary to do this really existed in your government. And in fact—" and for the first time in his slow, patient recital, a heavy sigh escaped his lips, revealing a tension deeper than appeared on the surface—"I still cannot quite believe it, even now.

"Surely we can still negotiate this on a peaceful basis. Surely we can restore sanity to the relations between our two countries, and so bring peace to the world. Surely you are not as completely evil as you are now trying to tell us, Mr. Chairman. You are not that abandoned a soul. I cannot believe it."

For several moments after he concluded, Tashikov studied him carefully, eyes bright and intent, lips pursed, expression unyielding. Then he turned to his colleagues with a brisk, dismissing nod. Obediently the Foreign Minister and the Minister of Defense, who, like the President's companions, had said nothing, got up and walked out without so much as a glance across the table.

Following their departure the Chairman sat looking about him slowly with a sarcastic expression; and so, after a moment, the President looked at his colleagues and nodded too. Obediently they also rose and departed, to be marched back by their uniformed guards through endless empty corridors to their cold lifeless rooms.

Behind them they left two men staring at one another across a table. For several moments more the stare held, the silence remained unbroken. Neither let his gaze drop, and it was still with their eyes locked in a silent battle of wills that the Chairman of the Council of Ministers leaned forward and rested his hands upon the polished wood.

"Now, Mr. President," he said softly. "Let us, you and I, talk facts." He touched a button somewhere beneath the table's edge. An enormous map, covering the entire wall at the far end of the room, sprang to light. Ranged before it were two glass-topped tables, also now alight. On one of the tables was a thick-bound volume. His visitors had noticed none of this earlier, being absorbed in his carefully orchestrated hysterics.

"Now," he said with a satisfaction he made no attempt to conceal, "come with me, Mr. President, and we shall take a trip around the world."

He led the way to the map and the tables, and area by area, sea by sea, quadrant of sky by quadrant of sky, he described for his visitor the globe as it looked from Moscow. And although the President was aware that he had only the Chairman's unsupported word, and the thought occurred, for a minute or two, that it might all be a gigantic bluff, yet he soon realized with a terrifying certainty that Tashikov was telling the truth. He was too obviously like a little boy boasting of his frightful toys. He was too obviously delighted with what he had. There was no doubt his glee was completely genuine. He was so happy he was almost giggling.

A dreadful cold weight began to settle on the mind and heart of the President of the United States.

Little red lines of light, moving slowly yet inexorably even as the Chairman spoke, were the Soviet fleets moving out in all the seas. Other little winking lights, completely ringing the shores of continental United States and Hawaii, were Soviet submarines armed with atomic missiles. Tiny jet planes, each representing a squadron, were illuminated rapidly one by one at their stations at home, in Europe, in Asia, in Africa, the Indian Ocean, Cuba, the Bahamas, the Bering Straits and the far north of Canada.

"They don't know we are there, the silly Canadians," he said scornfully. "But who can track those endless wastes except us? We are the only ones who spend the money, take the time and *keep alert*. We are the only ones who *have the will*. Even before your inaugural, your surveillance had been cut back so drastically for lack of funds that you might as well have had none." He chuckled suddenly, a dry and chilling sound. "Someone of our people told me a lot of the money has been diverted for government housing, welfare, urban renewal and erosion control. We shall appreciate all of that, when the time comes."

"The time will never come," Ted Jason managed, but Tashikov rounded on him with a sudden contemptuous look.

"Never?" he demanded in a heavily sarcastic tone, sweeping his hand in an encompassing gesture across the lighted map and tables before them. "Tomorrow!"

"Not tomorrow," the President said with a dogged stubbornness, for it had to be true. "Never."

"Mr. President," the Chairman said with a pity as deliberate and heavy-handed as his sarcasm, "I have only shown you half of it. Look now."

And he touched another button, this one on the table with the book. A slowly rotating globe appeared, suspended in the concave center of the table. New winking lights went on, hundreds of them, in Russia, Asia, Africa, Cuba, South America, the Indian Ocean, the Arctic, the Antarctic.

"Those are missiles carrying multiple independently targeted hydrogen bomb warheads, Mr. President. And these—" another button, and a silvery, pulsating, never-still tracery of wires appeared around the globe's surface, tiny sparks crisscrossing it constantly in all directions —"are satellites for surveillance, satellites to kill other satellites, satellites armed with hydrogen and atomic bombs ready to descend upon your country if I so much as lift the telephone—" he did so, and listened intently—"and say—" he broke off with a chortle and then went on in a jovially joshing tone—"Ah, comrade! How are you? I was just checking your alertness. That is good. That is very good! Goodbye! . . .

"And in this volume here, Mr. President," he said, replacing the telephone, "are listings of germ and chemical warfare bombs and an exact description of where we have such equipment stored and awaiting signal. If you will just look at this first map—" and he opened the unwieldy book and laid it on the table before them—"you will see that we have quite a few items here and there in America, in old buildings, in storage warehouses, at power plants and dams, at many other similar locations. Some are on the persons of people who in the past week have begun just—traveling. Constantly—traveling. Many are in the very midst of cities, near or actually in city halls, police stations, other administrative centers. Yes, here we are: Detroit . . . Minneapolis . . . San Francisco . . . yes, Seattle, Denver . . . Des Moines, Atlanta, New Orleans . . . Kansas City, Miami . . . many others . . . and of course Washington and New York. Of course!"

He closed the book with a snap, turned to look again, with a happy and complacent satisfaction, at the winking lights, the model planes, the spider-web traceries, the symbols of a destruction so great as to be beyond the comprehension of all but the demonically insane.

"So there you have it, Mr. President," he said, touching a final button that returned it all again to darkness. "How do you like my exhibit? Let us go back to the table and talk some more. . . . Now!" he said when they were seated again. "You understand why you must swiftly cease this stupid and insane defiance of the will of the world's peace-loving peoples. You understand why the United States must *at once* withdraw from her many attempts to interfere in the world's affairs and assume the role which history has reserved for her hereafter, namely that of a peaceable and cooperative partner of the Soviet Union. Even, one might say—" and the shrewd little face broke into a merry chuckle—"a *junior* partner, for that is how we see it here in the Kremlin. And how we see it, Mr. President," he said with a sudden softness, "is how, we believe, it is going to be."

The President thought there must be some brilliant and effective retort to make to that, but all he could imagine was threat replying to threat, to be answered by threat, to be answered in turn by threat, to be answered in turn—his tired mind was overwhelmed and almost suffocated by the pointlessness of it all. So his answer was lame and he knew it. But there seemed no help for it.

"The Soviet Union," he said slowly, "has apparently violated every treaty, every arms control agreement, every understanding ever reached with the United States. How could you do such a thing, when we trusted you?"

For just a moment the Chairman looked at him with an expression of such profound disbelief as to be almost comical. Then he shook his head in an amazed and wondering way.

"Oh, Mr. President!" he exclaimed with a wry, almost amiable regret. "If the United States were not so evil it would almost be possible to feel sorry for it. So naive! So wishful! So childish! Treaties! Agreements! Understandings! Did anyone in America really think we would *honor* those things? Why on earth should we, when all we had to do was play upon the ego, the gullibility and the infinite capacities for self-delusion of your Presidents, your Congress, your intellectual community and your press? America has *begged* to be betrayed in these recent decades, Mr. President! Even if it had not been our intention, we should have been forced to oblige. How else could we have treated a great power whose controlling minds have had so little understanding of what it takes to *survive* as a great power, in this harsh world? The race goes to the strong, Mr. President. Were we supposed to be in the business of helping weaklings to save themselves? That is not the Communist concept, I assure you."

"What is the Communist concept?" Ted Jason inquired in a weary voice. "To threaten the world with all this—this—" he gestured to the darkened tables, the silent map—"galaxy of horrors?"

Tashikov shook his head.

"We do not threaten. It is simply there. We wanted you to know it, so that you might intelligently consider what to do next. After all, we don't have to convince the world, if they see we have convinced the United States." He smiled with a grim satisfaction. "They will fall in line soon enough. In fact—" his expression changed to one of open contempt—"they are scrambling already. You would not believe the number of diplomatic approaches we have received in this past week while you have been so silent, Mr. President. A great shift is already under way in the world. I am inclined to believe nothing you could do now could in any way reverse it. And anyway: what *could* you do now? Do you have any ideas?"

And leaning forward, elbows on table, resting his chin on the tips of his fingers, he gave Ted Jason a calmly insolent, blandly inquiring stare.

Again for several moments the President was silent, though his eyes did not leave those of his grand inquisitor. The basic assumptions of a nation, a policy and a human personality were swept away forever. Inwardly he was groping for something that could re-establish at least some faint semblance of sanity and reason to a world in collapse. Nothing came. The silence grew.

Finally he spoke, in a heavy, almost dulled tone.

"I could of course," he said slowly, "order an immediate attack upon the Soviet Union."

"How?" Tashikov interrupted. "From here? Of course all your communications are cut off. How would you get the message through? And furthermore, Mr. President—" and his eyes gleamed with a satisfaction long delayed but finally satiated, "what would you do it with? Acting under all these 'treaties'—and 'agreements'—and 'understandings'—the United States has dutifully cut itself back to the point where you really have very little to meet us with. Oh, you might get a missile or two through, although our interceptors by now are so sophisticated that even that would be sheer luck. And one or two of your submarines might be moderately effective. But supposing they were, Mr. President? We still have you outnumbered in every category by at least three to one—*and this by the United States' own doing.*

"I will say to you frankly, Mr. President—" he shook his head in a bemused, amused gesture—"that it has been almost awesome to us here in the Kremlin, it has been so unbelievable: every time there has been an 'agreement,' your government has dutifully cut itself back like good little boys. What on earth did your leaders expect us to do in return? What on earth—"

"Act in good faith, as people should who bear equal responsibility for the peace of the world!" Ted Jason shot out with a sudden choked anger that surprised Tashikov and seemed to surprise even himself. "Be honest! Be trustworthy! Show some sense of historical responsibility! Have some basic regard for humanity! Apparently you are ready to kill millions and millions of people in your insane drive for world domination. Millions and *millions* of people—"

"Oh, no, Mr. President," Tashikov said softly, "it is not *we* who would have the responsibility for killing millions and millions, it is *you*. *We* will not start anything. *We* are not going to attack anyone with all the power we have. It is *you* who will start the killing if anyone does. It is *you* who is talking about attacking the Soviet Union. . . . Of course, Mr. President, if you do, we will respond. But stop and think about it: do you really want to be responsible for starting an atomic war? Not only would the United States be instantly annihilated, but *you* would bear the responsibility in history forever as the one who launched the war that could very well wipe out civilization itself. Is that the honor history has reserved for Edward M. Jason and the United States of America? Think about it, Mr. President! *You* are the one who will make war, if war is to be made. Are you ready to take the responsibility?"

The President shook his head as if to clear it of some great cobweb. But he did not look as though he had succeeded.

"We thought—" he said in a voice almost dazed, "we thought you might have changed."

The Chairman uttered a short, sharp laugh, completely unamused.

"We will never change. We are educated, trained, dedicated Communists. Our methods may change, our goals never. We have never made a secret of this, either in our published statements or our actions, over six decades.

"Why are Americans always so self-deluding about this, Mr. President? We frown, and America becomes hysterical. We smile, and America falls down and rolls at our feet in gratitude. We have 'thaws,' we have 'détentes,' we have 'freezes,' we have whatever other easy, sleazy catchwords your media dreams up for us; but all the time we just go steadily right along, no matter who is in charge here, no matter what apparent outward twists and turns of policy we may find advisable: we still go steadily right along. We are programmed by history,

Mr. President: history says the triumph of communism is inevitable. So why should communism change, if victory is inevitable? Communism never changes. How ineffably childish, stupid and immature of so many influential Americans, so many fools in the West, to deny all the evidence, all the record of history, to self-delude themselves into thinking that we do!

"We are the servants and the instruments of this ideology, Mr. President. From birth, a majority of us, now, *have never known anything else*. What on earth makes Americans think we are going to change?"

"Then—" Ted Jason said, his voice beginning to sound ragged with emotion and exhaustion, "then war is indeed inevitable."

Tashikov made a harsh impatient, contemptuous gesture.

"No. Not war. *This*. You, the American President, sitting here in the face of our overwhelming power, unable to make a sensible or effective move in response. *This* is what has always been inevitable, implicit in what communism has always done, implicit in America's unbelievable and obliging acceptance of it. *This* is what has always been inevitable, the breaking of the American President, and with him the American nation. And now at last it has come."

"You are leaving me no alternative," Ted Jason said in a strangely naive, woebegone, almost wistful tone. "We have always been careful to leave the Communists alternatives. We have never pushed you to the point where it was either atomic war or surrender. We have never—"

"No, that is right," the Chairman said cheerfully. "You have never pressed your advantages when you had them, when you could really have contained us and made us follow a peaceful course. *You* were concerned with saving *our* face. So your leaders foolishly missed all those opportunities. I weep for them, Mr. President! I weep for *you!* But my tears do not blind me to the duty of the Soviet Union to lead the world to a new era of genuine and really lasting peace. We may sob a little for you, if we happen to think about it, but somehow we shall manage to struggle on with our task, Mr. President. It will be difficult, but we will manage."

"To think," Ted Jason said almost in a whisper, "to think that an American President should find himself in a position of such weakness as this."

"It was inevitable that sooner or later one would, Mr. President," Tashikov said, "considering the deliberate self-weakening of the United States in these recent decades. But how fitting," he said with an irony almost light, almost jolly, "that it should be Edward M. Jason the Peacemaker who has been chosen to join my country in *really* bringing peace to the world at last, by ordering home American power and giving up—permanently, at last—all the mad dreams of American meddling and involvement in the affairs of the world's peace-loving peoples. History has indeed reserved you a place of great honor, Mr. President, for you have been chosen to *really* make peace. I congratulate you!"

"How do you know," the President inquired, still very low, "that I will not leave here and go home and *then* order an attack upon you? How can you be so sure of what I will do?"

"Because I know the American conscience," the Chairman said in an almost indifferent, offhand way. "And I know your conscience, which is the official representative of it, and its operative arm. We have studied America for many, many years, you know. We have studied you. We know how you both operate. Even if such an action could succeed—even if we did not have you, as we do, completely and absolutely checkmated with our power, we know you still would not do it. You would talk and argue and fret and worry and struggle with your consciences. And your consciences—and we—would join hands and win together. . . . Mr. President!" he said, and his tone was heavy and emphatic. "You know no American President would do such a thing. You know particularly Edward M. Jason would not. Now, isn't that the truth?"

"You do not know what I would do if you push me too far," the President said, again very low. "Too far . . ."

"Mr. President," Tashikov said, his tone contemptuous, "we know you have given us all the indication and proof we need in your paralysis of these recent days. We did not really expect a response in Gorotoland or Panama, but when you failed to defend *Alaska! Your own territory.* We knew then, Mr. President," he said simply, "that we had you."

"I was only trying to avoid a confrontation that could mean war," the President said, and he knew it sounded lame and whining, and he hated himself for it: but it was the truth.

The Chairman snorted.

"We understood your motivations, Mr. President. In the dream world in which America has lived, we knew they would be considered admirable by many of your countrymen. But that did not make them admirable—or intimidating—to us. To us they simply seemed appallingly weak, abominably misguided and, indeed, somewhat pathetic. But if that was the way you wished to present your head to us on a silver platter, Mr. President, we were not, of course, averse to accepting it. Why, Mr. President!" he said, and oddly there was almost an indignation on Ted's behalf in his voice. "Do you have any concept—do you have any understanding—do you know that we issued orders throughout the world to withdraw *at once* if you had shown us the slightest sign of resistance?

"Of course we did! But you turned the other cheek. And enough of your people applauded you to persuade you that you had somehow saved the world by being so utterly misguided and weak. We would have appreciated and respected a strong response, Mr. President. But *that!*" An expression of pitying contempt crossed his face. "It was too much, Mr. President, *too* much. . . .

"Now!" he said, and he became abruptly cold and businesslike. "These are the things we want you to do:

"First. You will continue the withdrawal of American power which you so kindly and voluntarily began at your inaugural. There will be no reversal of *those* orders.

"Second. You will recognize the democratically formed peoples' governments of Gorotoland and Panama, and indeed all other such democratically formed peoples' governments, wherever they may be, which the United States has not already recognized.

"Third. You will begin immediately to curb the disruptive elements among your population which are opposed to the establishment of a genuine and lasting peace brought about by close and obedient cooperation of the United States with the Soviet Union." His lips twisted with an angry contempt. "And by this I mean: *get rid of them!*

"Fourth. You will similarly curb the disruptive and hostile elements in the American intellectual community and in the American media which are opposed to this cooperation with the Soviet Union. And by this I mean: *force them into line or get rid of them!*

"Fifth. You will invite me to come to the United States within a month's time to sign a formal agreement of friendship and cooperation between our two countries, pledging your loyal support for our peace-seeking efforts and an end forever to attempts by the United States to meddle and interfere in the affairs of the world's peace-loving peoples.

"Sixth. You will conduct yourself at all times with the greatest circumspection, restraint and respect toward the Soviet Union, both when you leave this city and hereafter. You will not tell your people of the power we have here—for indeed, how can you admit to such weakness?

"If you do not do these things, I promise you there will be retaliation, swift, sudden and complete. There are no divided counsels and no wishy-washy consciences in *this* building, Mr. President. We have proved that in Hungary, in Czechoslovakia and in many other places.

We already hold several thousand of your soldiers captive, you know, and more are coming. If need be, we shall execute them one by one in Red Square—*and you know there will be nothing you can do about it except sit and take the horror and the humiliation for your people.* And if that does not suffice to keep you in line, Mr. President, well—" he flicked a button and the wall map and the tables sprang again into light—"there are, as you know, other means and methods. . . .

"So," he said, rising abruptly, "that is where we stand. Thank you for coming to see me. I must now retire. Stay where you are. The Foreign Minister and the Minister of Defense will join you shortly to give you a detailed briefing on all our little toys."

"I wish to leave," the President said, eyes haggard but voice becoming stronger again.

"When the briefing is over," the Chairman said coldly. "We cannot let you leave this room until it is finished. Remain, please. I shall see you in Washington in one month. Goodbye."

"Mr. *Chairman!*" the President cried, his voice a mixture of anger, hatred and exhaustion.

But Tashikov was at the door, and gone; and after a few unbelieving moments Edward M. Jason the Peacemaker sat slowly down again, his eyes staring with a vacant despair at the brightly lighted map, the winking lights, the spider traceries darting above the model of the tortured globe . . . until another voice said with a cold, peremptory air, "Mr. President, if you please! Come over here and let us explain to you—" . . .

. . . "And so presently," he said into the utter silence of the Oval Office, "when they had decided that they had sufficiently convinced me, they let me go . . . to come home to a country racked by a fear that I should only have increased had I taken you into my confidence, and clamoring for a leadership I could not at the moment provide because I literally did not know what to do."

"Do you now?" William Abbott asked with an equal quietness; and with a candor and honesty the ex-President had never seen in him— a candor and honesty so completely without defense that they made William Abbott inwardly flinch—the President responded with one word:

"No."

The desolate negative brought an uneasy stirring, a shifting in the room, a protest silent yet emphatic: *You cannot do this to us. The President must know what to do, that is the job of Presidents. You must know.* And after a moment, as if in response, he too shifted in his chair, sat up straighter. His expression changed. Some shadow of the old, dominant Ted Jason came back.

"However," he said—and there was a sudden release of tension, an abrupt relief prompted by what for the moment appeared to be a returning decisiveness—"I wanted you to understand why I have acted as I have in these recent days, and why I have a little hope—a little—that if I continue to act very carefully and patiently, we may yet come through."

"I should like to hear that," William Abbott answered for them all, though he sensed instinctively, with a sinking despair, that he already had the answer. But he put a good face on it, looked sympathetic, encouraging, attentive; sat back and listened, as he had known he would, to another variation on the theme of his successor's inability to understand his times, his position, or the needs of his country—now that it was too late, of course, for understanding, even if it existed, to be of much help to any of them.

"I have felt," the President said, "that if I continue to—lie low, so to speak—for a little while, I could perhaps avoid provoking them into any further harsh actions. It has taken me a while, of course—" he looked about the somber circle of faces, appealing for their sympathy which of course they could not deny him, so dreadful was his predicament and with it their own—"to recover, you might put it, from that interview." The faintest trace of an ironic smile crossed his face. "I am not used to being browbeaten in that fashion. Jasons are not used to it. Presidents of the United States are not used to it." (*Note the sequence,* the Secretary of State thought in unbelieving wonder. *Note the sequence.*) "It was not, as you can perceive, a pleasant experience. It has taken me a while. In fact—" and he uttered a sudden deep sigh that did not seem to relieve his tensions much—"in some ways, I may never recover. But life has to go on. . . .

"So, then," he said, more strongly, "I have, essentially, been playing for time in these past several days. I have tried to do so without yielding too abruptly to his demands—"

"Mr. President," Ewan MacDonald asked in an odd, uncertain tone, "what do you mean by 'yielding too abruptly?' Do you mean you intend to yield to them *at all?*"

The President shook his head with a certain impatience that also seemed odd, under the circumstances.

"Not really, no. Not openly. I'm counting on events. And so far, events have helped me to some degree. One of his points I can probably comply with, because it is already a fait accompli. The wars are over in Gorotoland and Panama, I think that's obvious. Even my predecessor—" he smiled a dry smile at silent William Abbott—"would not, I suspect, reopen them under present conditions. It is simply a practical, pragmatic matter to recognize the new governments in Panama and Gorotoland. What would we gain by being stubborn? Possible Soviet retaliation and not much else, I should think. On the other hand, we would, I think, gain much international respect by recognizing the simple facts as they exist. Isn't that true?"

And he looked around the circle again with a tired but defiant challenge. No one replied. Presently he gave a satisfied little nod and continued.

"So I will ask you, Mr. Secretary of State, to prepare a statement to that effect and present it to me by noon, for release at 3 P.M. All right?"

"But—" Robert Leffingwell began.

"Please," the President said quietly, in a tone permitting no objection; and after a moment the Secretary said, "Yes, sir," his face devoid of expression.

"And the Congress," the President said, and now a strange, almost lighthearted note came into his voice, "has, of course, already aided me in another matter, and very well aided me. No one, of course, intends to make very much of the Help America Act, but at least it is a gesture in the direction of what they want. It is a bone—a very small bone—that we've tossed them. It doesn't have to be implemented, but there it is. I think in that instance, although not understanding all the implications of the situation in which I find myself, the Congress has served me well."

"That is how you see it?" Bob Munson asked harshly. "I wish Beth Knox could have seen it like that."

For a moment the President did not reply, flushing with anger, then obviously controlling it.

"Please. Please, Senator. I have expressed my regrets over that, I have assigned all the agencies of government I could to it, *I am doing my best.* So, please: if you don't mind. . . . Now," he went on presently, his voice again firm and strong, some plan in mind, again managing to stir them to a little hope. "In much the same fashion, I want the Congress to cooperate with me on something much more fundamental." He paused as though savoring his little surprise, then let them have it. "I want it to pass, at once, a massive rearmament bill. And when I say 'at once,' I mean at once. By—let's say—next Tuesday. Can you do that, gentlemen?"

With a somewhat dazed expression Jawbone Swarthman looked at Bob Munson. After a moment Bob responded.

"Well, as you know, Mr. President," he said with some dryness, "you have taken pains to see that I am no longer responsible for the course of events in the Senate. But as nearly as I can assess this new Senate, what you want it will do. If you don't want to express yourself outright, then of course the word can get around discreetly behind the scenes. Of course, I'm pretty sure that in that event the media, and the Russians, will pick it up. But the public facade would be preserved. You personally would not be calling for massive rearmament."

"No," the President agreed with an air of satisfaction, "particularly when I shall then veto the bill."

"But, Mr. President, sir—" Jawbone began in a dismayed tone.

"And you will then, of course, pass it over my veto," the President said, satisfaction now open. "And we will then proceed posthaste to build up our strength so that I shall never again—" the handsome face darkened, the intelligent eyes showed a genuine anger, the voice grated—"I shall never again be in the position of having to take that kind of bullying from any man."

"I assume the United States would not be, either," William Abbott could not resist, but his successor's only reply was a rather startled, blank stare. The Speaker decided to fill the ensuing pause with a nervously cheerful burble.

"Now, Mr. President," he said hastily, "I think that's a mighty clever strategy, now, I really do. I think that's mighty clever *and* mighty farseeing. I think that's really statesmanship, Mr. President, I really do!"

"Well, I don't," Cullee Hamilton said with a sudden explosive release of frustration. "I think it's pathetic. Absolutely pathetic."

"So do I," Warren Strickland said quietly. "As pathetic as the American President sitting numbed and speechless in the office of the Chairman. As pathetic as this great nation crippled and foundering. As pathetic as are all feeble, clever tricks in the face of history's implacable challenges to men. Mr. President," he said to the suddenly pale-faced figure behind the desk, "why will you not handle this as the President should? Why will you not come before us, take the Congress and the country into your confidence, lay all the cards on the table, appeal for help and support—demand immediate rearming, and get it?"

"And risk a war?" the President cried with a genuine anger that broke through his carefully controlled composure.

"He won't go to war," the ex-President said bluntly. "He told you so and he meant it. They don't want war. They want you to give in without a fight. Just as you are doing," he added, an expression in which disgust, dismay and a sort of helpless bafflement, combined, crossed his face. "Just as you are doing. . . ."

"I tried to tell you what I saw there," the President said carefully. "I tried to describe it. Didn't you believe me?"

"We believed you," Bob Munson said. "But I agree with Warren. The only way out, the *only* way, is to *act as though* you are not afraid, and proceed with your duty as the head of this nation in the outward —and, I hope to God, the actual—conviction that what you are doing is right, and that it will succeed. Because you can't bluff it. You're going to have to mean it. Congress won't go along with you on these back-door tricks—even your new Congress. They're all set to be suspicious of everybody except you. They still expect you to deal with them straight because you, in a sense, are their creation, as they are yours. If you betray that faith, they will turn on you like the pack of young savages I believe they are. . . . Again, and for what may be the last time, God help us, I beg of you: *lay it on the line.* Don't be clever. Don't be devious. Don't be tricky. Don't be starry-eyed in the face of evil. *Don't be scared.* You can't afford to. You *must* be decisive and daring. There is no other way."

Again the Oval Office was completely silent while its occupant struggled to master what appeared to be surging and terrible emotions. But when he spoke it seemed to them that he had hardly passed through an ordeal by fire at all. From some deep recess, perhaps of reviving, if unfounded, confidence, perhaps of some certainty known only to Jasons and to this one in particular, perhaps even of some "inner vision," as the Secretary of State had put it, came finally what appeared to be a composed and quite reasonable answer. At least the tone was reasonable, although to his Congressional critics, and indeed to his two Cabinet members, it seemed with a sudden wave of hopelessness that they must be confronting one of the great fanatics of the age, transported by the shattering of his hopes and the savaging of the Communists into some world where nothing could reach him any more.

For the ex-President and his friends, it was a devastating thought: The President might no longer be rational.

But he had to be.

He had to be.

And so he appeared outwardly, as he said at last, with a calm conviction that brushed aside their arguments as though they had never been,

"So, then. I may count on your cooperation, gentlemen?"

Again a silence, deepening, widening, more and more dismayed.

Into it Walter Dobius spoke with an abrupt harshness that seemed to startle even the President.

"I should hope not!" he said in a choked voice. "I should hope not!"

"Well, now—" Jawbone began, but America's most distinguished political commentator turned on him like some avenging tornado.

"And I don't need *you*," he said with an acid anger, "to confuse everything with your asinine chatter."

"Well!" the Speaker said. "*Well*, I—"

"Be quiet!" Walter snapped, and turned back to the President, who surveyed him with a speculative and growing anger in his eyes.

"Mr. President," Walter said, "no man, I think you will agree, has supported you more actively or done more to assist your political career than I have. I feel this gives me some right to speak. Over and above," he added harshly, "my right as a concerned American citizen— a *very* concerned American citizen.

"I think the ex-President is entirely right. I think we are in a situation demanding desperate measures but *practical* desperate measures. I don't think playing tricky games with Congress, the country and the Russians comes under that heading. I think it is a time for absolute honesty, all around.

"I cannot, of course, speak for my colleagues of the media except in a general way, but I think I can safely say that if you do level with us, if you tell the whole country the situation as it exists and call us to our own time of blood, sweat and tears, then you will have such an upsurge of popular backing as you cannot conceive. Certainly you will have the backing of most of the media, I think that's safe to say. And you will have the Congress. And the country."

"But not the Russians," Arly Richardson said with a sort of sour triumph in his voice. Walter rounded on him as he had on the Speaker.

"No, not the Russians!" he agreed with a savage impatience. "But who, now, gives a damn about them—*really* gives a damn about them? I grant you everything they showed the President was probably genuine, they probably do have all those horrors, they probably could destroy us in an instant if they were so minded. But I agree with President Abbott—"

"Why?" Senator Richardson demanded, still sour, still unimpressed.

"Because I believe as he does that they still don't want a war with us. Why should they?" Walter asked, and his mouth took a sudden bitter twist. "When they've gained so much over so many years because of fools like me? Yes!" he repeated angrily, "fools like me! Like all of us who excused them and rationalized them and justified them, all those years when they were moving into position to cut us down. Who were always so clever and so biting and so arch and so superior when some of our countrymen tried to warn of the trend of events. Who were always so smug and perfect." Again his mouth twisted in a bitter, ironic way. "Smug and perfect! That was us, all right. And now we're caught in the gale of history, just like you are, Mr. President. Just like you. . . .

"But," he said, firm and forceful again, "I believe the situation can still be saved if you will go to Congress—go this afternoon, indeed, why not, the sooner the better—and be absolutely candid and ask for help. . . . Of course," he said, and a certain irony came into his eyes, "that would mean admitting you have made a great mistake, Mr. President. And maybe you can't do that. But maybe the situation is serious enough so that you wouldn't mind. Anyway, I agree, as I say, with William Abbott: you must do this. There is no other way out."

For a moment after he had concluded the President said nothing, merely studying him with a careful look as though he were seeing him for the first time, as it was true they were all seeing this particular aspect of Walter Dobius for the first time.

"That is all very well for you to say who don't have the responsibility for war," he said finally, and Tommy Davis protested with a dismay that seemed to surprise even himself,

"But, Mr. President—!"

"Yes," the President said more strongly, "for you who don't have the responsibility for war. Where is your certainty that this will work?"

"No certainty, Mr. President," Walter Dobius said. "Absolutely none."

"But an absolute certainty," Lafe Smith said into the quiet that again fell on the stately room and its frantically worried occupants, "that if you do nothing, the speedy end of this Republic is inevitable."

Again the President was silent. When he answered it was obvious that they had accomplished nothing.

"I am sorry," he said, "but I must do it my way. They understand that I will not oppose them openly—"

"Did you enter any agreement?" William Abbott demanded sharply. Edward M. Jason shook his head.

"I think they understood."

"Then *why*—" the ex-President began. But his successor raised a cautionary hand, and he fell silent.

"So I come back to my original plan," Ted Jason said quietly. "I shall expect the Congress to act just as quickly as possible, because time, as we are all aware, is very important."

"All right," the ex-President said, and his tone was suddenly cold and unyielding. "You've said what you 'expect.' Now I'll tell you what we expect. We expect an open declaration, an address to Congress, a call to the country to unite—*an honest approach.* And if we don't get it, my friend, there is a reasonably large group of us still left on the Hill to make things really uncomfortable for you. God knows I sympathize with the President's right to be supported in times of crisis, but I can't go along with this back-door tricky business which is still, to my mind, too much Ted Jason and not enough President. Yes!" he repeated as his successor gave him a sudden angry glare. "Too much Ted Jason and not enough President. Now, you listen to me, Mr. President, because it's the last time I'm probably going to talk to you, about this or anything.

"If you try to do this behind the scenes, I'm going to get up on that House floor, and I expect Bob and Warren are going to get up in the Senate—" his glance brought nods of confirmation—"and tell the whole wide world exactly what you're up to. And that, I suggest," and his tone was as savage as though he were physically slapping Edward M. Jason across the face—"is going to make you look even more pathetic than you do already. And I don't know what it will make the Russians do. . . .

"So I'd suggest you act like a President, Mr. President, because this may be your very last chance. . . . We want your promise," he concluded somberly. "And we want it now."

"And," Walter Dobius spoke up, as Jawbone and Arly Richardson stirred uneasily but this time did not quite dare interrupt, "speaking on behalf of my profession, we want your promise that you will immediately denounce the Help America Act, state that you will never activate it, and seek its immediate repeal."

For the last time in their desperate and doom-hung conversation, silence filled the Oval Office. The President appeared pale but composed. The handsome silver head did not yield, the tired dark eyes did not waver from the contemplation they seemed to have taken up, of Abe Lincoln on the wall. With a fearful intensity his countrymen studied him for some sign of defiance, capitulation, anger, remorse, fright, determination—anything. It did not come.

At last he sighed and lowered his eyes to stare into those of his predecessor who sat, stolid, powerful and adamant, across the enormous desk.

"I go to Moscow and get browbeaten," Edward M. Jason said softly, "I sit in my own office and get browbeaten. I recognize the motivations are different, but the effect upon me is very close to being the same. . . . Very well. I cannot promise you anything. I can only promise to give the most serious consideration to what you have proposed. I shall have to think about it. But I will. You have my word on that."

"Then," William Abbott said, and his voice was filled with a growing relief, for in situations so perilous well-meaning men will grasp at any cause for hope in their leaders, no matter how much they may think cause for hope does not exist, "if you will really do that, Mr. President, I think we can go away in good spirits. Because I don't think, after you have really thought it through, that you can do other than we ask."

"I shall hope I can," the President said. "Thank you for coming." He stood up and held out his hand gravely to each of them in turn, and each shook it with a suddenly fervent, sentimental, deeply emotional vigor. There were even tears in many eyes, of relief, of love of country, of reviving faith in Ted Jason, of reviving hope that everything would yet, somehow, be well. . . .

But under the awning of the South Portico while they waited for the limousines to drive up, as a savage wind blew off the Potomac and the swiftly rising sun struck enchanted sparkles from the ice-hung trees and shrubbery, Walter Dobius said to William Abbott:

"Do you believe we accomplished anything?"

And the ex-President, with a sigh that seemed to come from the very depths of his being, a sigh for his country, for her President, for all the teeming millions here and everywhere whose lives hung dependent upon decisions still to be made in this fateful, haunted house, gave him a sadly troubled look and replied:

"I'm damned if I know."

U.S. RECOGNIZES NEW REGIMES IN PANAMA, GOROTO-LAND.

WHITE HOUSE PRESS SECRETARY DENIES RUMORS JASON WILL ASK CONGRESS TO REARM AGAINST RUSSIANS. PRESIDENT NAMES WATTERSILL HEAD OF "SPECIAL BRANCH" IN CHARGE OF HELP AMERICA ACT, PICKS VAN ACKERMAN TO HEAD "DOMESTIC TRANQUILLITY BOARD."

HINT ABBOTT MAY INTRODUCE IMPEACHMENT RESOLUTION IN HOUSE TOMORROW. HE AND MUNSON ANNOUNCE IMMEDIATE APPEAL TO SUPREME COURT TO OVERTURN HELP AMERICA.

NAWAC, IDF FORCES BEGIN TO CONVERGE ON CAPITAL AS ANTI-JASON MOVES GAIN STEAM.

BOOK FIVE

1. "WE DO NOT know," the Washington *Star-News* said somberly in its lead editorial, which hit the streets shortly before 11 A.M., "what pressures have prompted the President to move forward with so quick and drastic an implementation of the highly suspect 'Help America Act.' But we do know we deplore it.

"We also deplore the fact that he is still keeping the country in the dark on what plans, if any, he may have in mind to reverse the alarming trend in world affairs touched off by the startling concessions to Soviet power which he made in his inaugural address. We give him full credit for his sincerity, but in this instance the personal sincerity of the President may not be enough. The safety of the whole American experiment may well be at stake.

"It seems to us that serious.

"As for the 'Help America Act,' we of this publication long ago concluded that George Henry Wattersill and Fred Van Ackerman are of no real help to anybody but the misfit and the mistaken. We believe this has been amply demonstrated by the careers of both. We have been uneasy ever since the President named Mr. Wattersill to the post of Attorney General, the office most directly concerned with the liberties of the citizen. Our uneasiness is compounded by his recruitment of Senator Van Ackerman, who comes trailing clouds, not of glory, but of NAWAC. We do not think the appointments mean anything good for the country, nor do we think they mean anything good for our profession. On the contrary, we think the free press and media of the United States of America are suddenly in jeopardy as they have never been before in the more than two centuries of this Republic.

"The liberties of the citizen, we have always believed, in basic measure stand or fall with the liberties of the media. Sometimes, we will admit, some in the media have sadly abused their liberties and with them, in many indirect but inescapable ways, the liberties of the citizen. We do not condone those lapses, some of which we have ourselves no doubt been guilty of. But that does not change the basic fact of it: a free press is vital to the continuance of a free democracy.

"Suddenly it is a question how much longer the press will be free.

"We do not think the President can be lightly excused for this, even though he is obviously under terrible pressures. His duty to American freedom still remains, even in the midst of what seems to be the collapse of all his hopes, and ours. We still hope he will respond strongly and without equivocation to the challenge from Russia, particularly now that he has been to Moscow and savored for himself the plans and purposes of that enigmatic state. But we are deeply and earnestly alarmed if he thinks putting two of the nation's most ruthless and arbitrary men in a position to threaten the free media of the land is one of the ways to meet the challenge."

In similar vein, though not quite so harshly as regards their long-time pet Wattersill—they were more critical of their more suspect friend Van Ackerman—spoke the *Times*, the *Post*, the Boston *Globe*, the L. A. *Times*, the St. Louis *Post-Dispatch* and the rest of that particular sector of the media. In similar vein spoke NBC, CBS and ABC as the morning wore on. So wrote Walter Dobius at "Salubria" for to-morrow's column. So buzzed the world, or at least that portion of it that had control of newsprint, picture tube and airwave.

The members of the media were suddenly scared to death. Like so many other things made vulnerable by the Presidency of the man they had helped elect to office, their own position was suddenly thrown into glaring light. Suddenly their high and mighty, unaccountable-to-anyone position seemed not so inviolate after all. For years they had screamed, "Wolf!" at the slightest challenge to their self-assumed right to describe the world as they pleased: now, abruptly, it appeared the wolf was here. After protesting hysterically for decades against the frequently justified criticisms of the fair-minded, it suddenly appeared that they were about to be done in by their friends. They found it quite unbelievable but also quite terrifying. In the privacy of the handsome offices from which they had hurled such thunderbolts against the clodlike public they secretly deplored, they were petrified. Significantly, almost none of them protested the rumors that the ex-President might be preparing a resolution of impeachment against his successor. The clear implication was that, while they did not yet (maybe never would) dare say so openly, they were beginning to conclude that this might be the only way out of a situation they themselves had done so much to create and now stood to suffer from as much as, if not more than, anyone in the country.

Whether or not he was planning impeachment resolutions, William Abbott refused to say to the reporters who besieged him in the lobby of the House shortly before noon. In fact, he refused to say anything, except, tersely, "Come with me."

"How's that?" the head of the AP house staff asked blankly.

"I said," said William Abbott, getting his hat and coat, " 'Come with me.' "

"That's funny, we thought you said, 'Come with me,' " AP remarked. "Where?"

"You have no spirit of adventure," the ex-President told him.

"It's weakening," AP said as his clustering colleagues joined him in rather wan laughter. "Do we have time to get our hats and coats or do you want us to freeze to death?"

"I'll meet you downstairs in ten minutes," William Abbott said.

"How about cars?" UPI inquired.

"Don't bother," Bill Abbott said. "We'll walk."

"What the hell—?" AP said as they tumbled over one another getting to the elevators, up the stairs, into the Press Gallery, down again. "In weather like this? Is the old man reviving the LBJ Memorial Walkie-Talkies?"

But when they joined him just inside the entrance, some thirty or forty of them suited up for the steel-cold sunshine that awaited them outside, they could see it was no lighthearted expedition but grimly serious business. Senator Munson, Senator Strickland and Senator Danta had joined the ex-President. They nodded gravely to their friends in the press corps but indulged in no banter. "Come," William Abbott said. Obediently they followed, out the door, through the archway, toward what they had guessed would be their destination: the Supreme Court, standing stately and sedate, white against the white of the winter world, across Capitol Plaza.

"And so, Mr. Chief Justice, if it please your honorable Court," the ex-President concluded gravely, "petitioners, who include those you see before you, plus Representative Harold Knox of Illinois, absent because of a monstrous bereavement we all know about, plus several other members of both houses of Congress whose names are appended, request this honorable Court to pass judgment at once upon the constitutionality of the so-called Help America Act, Public Law 1 of this Congress signed yesterday by the President. We shall be glad to answer any question you or other members of your honorable Court may wish to propound to us. And," he added, looking somberly around the small, dark, red-velvet-marble-and-leather room at George Henry Wattersill, Senator Van Ackerman and Congressman Bernard (all of whom had appeared, breathless and taken by surprise, a few moments before), "we will also be glad to answer any who may wish to oppose our petition.

"In summation, it is our position that this law is unconstitutional per se and on its face; that it gives to the government of the United States, in the person of the President and those he may designate to exercise his authority for him, very vast and dangerous powers over American citizens and American institutions; that censorship, suppression of free thought, suppression of dissent and actual physical control of the thoughts and the actions of the individual citizen and many very important American institutions are both implicit and unavoidable in the language, the intent and, I am afraid, the purpose of the law; and that it is basically repugnant and horrendous to the liberties of a free people and particularly to the free people of the Republic of the United States of America. We respectfully urge your honorable Court to expunge it from American history before so much as another day goes by. Its provisions are too dangerous in the wrong hands, or indeed in any hands, for it to remain on the books even an hour longer.

"We so respectfully petition, your honor."

During the interval while he sat down and George Henry Wattersill prepared to rise, there was time for the tensely watching group of newsmen to glance quickly around the room and appraise the leading participants in this latest episode in the on-racing career of Edward M. Jason the Peacemaker and his distraught country. There was also time to hear a rising murmur, at first far-off then rapidly nearer and louder: the sound of NAWAC, the IDF and their respective friends, supporters and hangers-on, hurrying up from the city below to swarm in ever-increasing numbers into Capitol Plaza. It was an animal sound, ominous, ugly and uneasy: the sound of a human volcano, building up.

It was obvious that the implications of this were not lost upon the occupants of the small, sequestered room. The first to take official notice was the Chief Justice, that actually aging but outwardly still-youthful figure appointed soon after the end of the second Nixon term. Hurriedly he beckoned to the bailiff, hurriedly the bailiff hurried away. Within moments extra guards appeared at the doors and presumably, although no one inside could know for sure, along the corridors and outside at the great marble portals that looked out upon the roiling park. What good they could actually do against a determined assault, being most of them aging pensioners of the Court or elderly constituents who had been given their jobs as the Court's obeisance to the powerful chairmen of the House and Senate Judiciary committees, remained to be seen. But it was obvious they were prepared to do their best if they had to.

In the room, from which the public had been cleared twenty minutes earlier so that it was now occupied only by the petitioners from Congress, their opponents from the Administration, the media and the Justices, it was obvious that these preparations, and their cause, were making everyone nervous. But there was a job to be done, and a most serious and fundamental one; and so for a time they managed to proceed as though everything were the same in America as it had always been, and that by so proceeding, they could keep it that way by sheer force of institution.

Beside the ex-President in the front row sat his colleagues from the Senate. Further along sat the Attorney General, Bronnie Bernard and the junior Senator from Wyoming, clothed now in all the dignity of his new position as head of the Domestic Tranquillity Board. The dignity did not seem to extend too far, for Fred Van Ackerman was too obviously enjoying himself as he sat glancing with a sardonic air of superiority at William Abbott and his group. Fred, in fact, appeared to be the only man really enjoying himself at the moment. Even George Henry Wattersill and Bronnie Bernard looked tense and serious.

Equally tense and serious were the members of the Court, called now to pass upon one of the most fundamental, if not the most fundamental, questions ever to come before them. This time there was no protective shield furnished by what they always called "the courts below." Nobody beneath their august level had cushioned the shock of the case by ruling upon it first. This came to them *ab initio* and they stood exposed in the eye of the hurricane. It is not a position the Court relishes, and it was obvious it did not relish it now. Its members appeared distinctly worried, uneasy and apprehensive.

This was true of the Chief Justice himself and of Justices Grant, Osborne, Stevenson and Mulvaney to his right; and it was true of Justices Davis, Montgomery, Cappola and Madam Justice Watson on his left. In the quick whispered tallyings and analyzings of the media, it was generally assumed that the Chief and Justices Davis, Osborne, Stevenson and Mulvaney would, on the basis of past track records, vote to deny petitioners and uphold the government; while Justice Cappola, Justice Montgomery, Justice Grant and Madam Justice Watson would vote to uphold petitioners and defy the government. It therefore came as something of a shock when, just as the Attorney General was tossing his famous leonine mane and getting ready to deliver another of his famed oratorical salvos, Justice Davis spoke up from his position, as senior justice, on the C.J.'s left.

"I trust the Attorney General," he said quietly, "will refrain from extraneous oratorical flourishes and address himself directly to the very serious issues raised by petitioners. I think the Court would appreciate that, Mr. Chief Justice. At least I would."

("Well, what do you know," the *Post* whispered to the *Times*. "Is Tommy going to be the swing man?" "I wouldn't have believed it before," the *Times* whispered back, "but suddenly everything has become unpredictable.")

"Well, Mr. Chief Justice," George Wattersill said, obviously flustered by this gentle but firm interruption, "of course I—of course I—"

"*Let him have it,*" Fred Van Ackerman whispered fiercely at his side, and this seemed to give the Attorney General a boost.

"I shall of course defer as much as possible to the wishes of the Court for expedition," he said with a somewhat defiant firmness, "but I cannot, of course, slight what we believe to be the merits of the government's case."

"Mr. Chief Justice," the ex-President said, rising, in an ominous tone of voice, "in this instance I think we can dispense with the term 'the government' in the arguments of counsel opposite. My colleagues and I, I will remind the Attorney General and his friend, are members of 'the government' also, fully coordinate and coequal with anything he may represent. I would suggest we just talk about 'the Administration,' if my distinguished opponent will be so kind."

The Chief Justice nodded, without other comment, and after a moment of annoyed silence George Wattersill proceeded.

"Very well, your honor, the Administration, then. We in *the Administration* believe we have merit on our side. We in the Administration believe petition should be denied. I will tell the Court why, if it pleases your honors. If there be flourishes," he added dryly, giving Tommy Davis a look and gaining confidence as he went along, "then that, I am afraid, must just be put down to my characteristic style of argumentation. This Court, other courts and numerous clients, I will say to Mr. Justice Davis, have not found it insufferable."

"Nor I, Mr. Attorney General," Tommy Davis said, "as long as it doesn't get *too* windblown. We are under some pressures here to expedite. As witness," he added as there came a sudden swelling, cause unknown, in the distant roar and everyone turned to glance with varying degrees of concern and apprehension at the guarded doors, "what is going on outside."

"It is exactly for that reason, Mr. Chief Justice," said George Henry Wattersill, "that I do not want to do less than justice to the govern—to the Administration's case. This is too important a matter. Too many great imponderables of American stability are involved. Too many citizens are directly concerned in the outcome."

"All citizens, I should think," said Justice Cappola in the drawl of his native Dallas. The Attorney General accepted the amendment with a grave nod.

"*All* citizens. . . . Petitioners come here, your honors, on the spur of the moment, without warning, springing surprises on us, seeking apparently to catch us off balance. I shall not dwell on these aspects of it, except to say that we in the Administration are a little surprised that the Court should have accepted this move with such alacrity and set aside its regular business so expeditiously to accommodate this kind of trickery. But," he added hastily as several justices stirred uneasily and he thought he perhaps had gone too far, "we accept it and proceed as directed, even though it places some handicaps on our preparation.

"However, if it please your honors, I think we can refute the arguments of petitioners almost as expeditiously as they have been made. To wit:

"It is a fine thing, Mr. Chief Justice and your honors—" his expression and voice both became indignant—"for the very man who originally proposed this legislation to come here and argue that it is 'unconstitutional per se and on its face'; that it confers 'very vast and dangerous powers' upon the President; that 'its provisions are too dangerous in the wrong hands, or indeed in any hands.' It was all very well for him to propose it when he thought it could be used upon those who were opposing *his* policies. Now that it is offered as a means of protecting his successor from frivolous and sinister dissent against *his* policies, it is another matter. Where was the Constitution six months ago when this bill was first introduced under the kindly aegis of the ex-President? In hiding, I presume!"

"Mr. Attorney General," Justice Davis inquired gently, "was the measure vigorously pushed by President Abbott six months ago? Did he make any real attempt to secure its passage? Did he not permit your colleague, Senator Van Ackerman, to filibuster against it, for instance? Was it not, perhaps, simply a political gesture at the time, rather than a serious proposal?"

"I'll answer that, your honors," Fred Van Ackerman said, coming forward quickly to the lectern, brusquely brushing George Wattersill aside. "The individual who originally proposed this bill meant it, don't anybody be foolish enough to think he didn't. He wanted to stop all dissent and protest when it was directed against him. He didn't give a —he wasn't so worried about the Constitution then, believe me. And furthermore," he added, and a real annoyance entered his voice, "he didn't 'permit' me to filibuster the bill to death, I'll remind this Court. He tried to stop me but he couldn't. Oh, how he tried! But I killed it. *I* killed it!"

"Then why," the Chief Justice asked, "were you so eager to revive it? Why were you the one to reintroduce it?"

"And why," Tommy Davis inquired, leaning forward intently, "did you add new provisions to it which petitioners argue are unconstitutional and dangerous to the liberties of American citizens and American institutions? Provisions which were not in the original bill, provisions which petitioners are therefore perfectly justified in arguing against?"

"Well," Senator Van Ackerman said—and his voice was such that AP muttered to Reuters, "Oh, oh, here goes Freddy"—"*well,* your *honor,* I will tell you why I did. Because a great President is struggling desperately to save the peace of the world! Because a great President is giving us the benefit of his leadership, his vision, his idealism and his courage! Because that President needs the support of every citizen in this land in this desperate moment *and because* petitioner and his colleagues are leading a dangerous and yes, Mr. Chief Justice, I will even say a subversive campaign to thwart, defy and destroy the efforts of our great President for peace!"

There was a stunned silence for a moment. Against it the distant roar of the now completely filled plaza rose and fell and rose again. Presently Madam Justice Watson ran a hand through her close-cropped gray hair, adjusted her pince-nez and leaned forward in her customary professorial manner.

"Does counsel actually argue," she inquired slowly, "that petitioners are being *subversive* in seeking relief from this Court against what they sincerely believe to be a measure dangerous to the nation? Does the Senator actually think we have reached a situation in America in which disagreement with the sitting President and his Administration is somehow . . . against the law?"

"It is against this law as it now stands," Fred Van Ackerman snapped, "and this is the law passed by Congress and signed by the President. What other law controls?"

"The Constitution, I presume," Justice Watson said quickly and as quickly Fred Van Ackerman replied,

"If a majority of this Court says so!"

"Do you think it won't?" Justice Davis asked and Fred Van Ackerman turned on him with a contempt he made little attempt to conceal.

"What do you think it will do, your honor? Listen!" he said abruptly, and he flung out his arm in a gesture toward the ominous rumble, now much louder outside. "*Listen!* There speak the American people who have elected this great President, who love this great President, who trust and believe and follow this great President! There is your final arbiter, Mr. Justice! *They* know where justice lies. And *they* won't forget," he added, a relish in his voice that made the blood of quite a few in the room run cold, "who is for justice this day, and who isn't!"

"Are you threatening this Court?" the Chief Justice demanded with a note of real anger. But it was apparent the Senator from Wyoming was past being impressed by a judicial annoyance that would in other times have intimidated any counsel before the Court. He obviously believed himself to be allied with a greater intimidation now.

"*I* am not threatening this Court, Mr. Chief Justice," he said with an offhand air as he turned away to sit down again. "The American people are, and today they will not be denied."

"The Attorney General," the Chief Justice said after a moment with a reasonable show of dignity, though it was apparent that he and several of his colleagues were more shaken than they would have liked to admit, "will proceed with his arguments if he has more to offer."

"Yes, your honor," George Wattersill said, speaking more harshly now that Fred Van Ackerman had shown the way, "I do.

"Petitioners—and some members of this Court who obviously have already decided to associate themselves with petitioners in spite of the obvious public sentiment noted by my colleague—seem much concerned about provisions of the Help America Act which were added after the then President failed in his attempt to impose his will upon those who disagreed with him. The ex-President—and those members of this Court who seem to wish to associate themselves with him— make much of alleged unconstitutionality, supposed censorship, presumed dictatorial control over American citizens and institutions.

"Nothing, Mr. Chief Justice and your honors," he said with a sudden profound gravity, "could be further from the minds of this Administration. *Other* administrations may have had such sinister purposes in mind when they proposed *their* version of this bill, but not this one, your honors. Not this one. These are exaggerated fears, unfounded and ungrounded. The purpose is solely and exclusively to secure for this Administration the climate of calm and cooperation that we must have if the President is to succeed in his search for peace—that search for whose success not only his own nation, but all mankind, joins in prayer."

"Mr. Attorney General," Tommy Davis asked with a certain quiet but persistent tenacity, "when you speak of 'calm and cooperation,' is that out there—" and he too gestured to the thunder beyond the doors— "the sort of thing you have in mind?"

"It is not," George Wattersill said quickly, "but it is the sort of thing that will speedily replace calm and cooperation if this Administration is not given the means of securing calm and cooperation. I suggest your honor consider that!"

"Oh, I am considering it," Justice Davis said, sounding not at all abashed, though several of his colleagues appeared to be, by the harshness of the Attorney General's tone. "I am considering that very carefully, I will say to counsel. And I must confess," he added, peering slowly about the silent chamber like an earnest little owl, "that it does not impress me. Not one little bit."

"Well, your honors," George Henry Wattersill said bluntly, "I would suggest it had better impress you all, because I think it not too extreme to say that this nation stands on the brink of revolution at this very hour. Yes!" he repeated as there was a gasp from somewhere in the room and a noticeable, uneasy shifting along the bench. "On the brink of revolution! That fact, I would suggest, imposes something of a burden on this Court to save us from so dreadful an eventuality. I would suggest your honors take it into account as the fact—perhaps the paramount fact—to be weighed in reaching your decision."

"You seem to be threatening us again," Mr. Justice Cappola remarked. "Are you suggesting that the law is not the paramount fact for us to consider in this matter?"

"The law is not much good without a country around to obey it," the Attorney General said in an offhand, almost scornful way; and a little silence, shocked, dismayed, uncertain, grew in the room.

"Well," the Chief Justice said finally, "is that your principal argument, Mr. Attorney General?"

George Henry Wattersill shook his head impatiently.

"No, of course not, your honor. But it is one, I respectfully submit, which must be given major and important place in your deliberations. For, hark!"—and he, too, gestured grandly toward the angry susurrus beyond the doors—"There speaks the American people. And it is a voice that cannot, I respectfully submit, be denied."

"But," Madam Justice Watson suggested, "not all the American people. And not the united American people. I have not been out there, but I rather suspect there is some division of opinion present.

Unless," she added with a sudden sharpness in her voice, "you already have them so terrified that honest dissent is afraid to show itself."

"Madam Justice!" the Attorney General said sadly. "Madam Justice! How prejudiced and unfair can your honor become in the heat of the moment! No one is suppressing dissent. No one is intimidating or terrifying anyone. I am simply trying to place in perspective the potentials of what could happen if the Administration is denied the means with which to secure the law and order it must have if it is to carry forward the great objectives of peace enunciated by our President. That is all. Nothing else."

"That is not all," Tommy Davis said with a sharpness that brought an instant hush, against which the murmurous roar outside swelled and grew louder. "That is not all, I submit to the court of my brethren and to the court of world opinion which is still represented here by the press—still," he repeated ominously, "but, if the Administration has its way, not much longer.

"No, Mr. Attorney General!" he said, as George Henry Wattersill made a movement of angry protest and started to open his mouth. "No! It is inexcusable what the Administration is attempting to do here, and you know it. The bill was monstrous when the Senator from Wyoming and his young colleague in the House introduced it, it was monstrous when it passed the Congress as a result of Administration pressure, and it became even more monstrous when the President signed it into law. I do not know what possessed him, I say to my brethren. I do not know what has become of the Edward M. Jason who once stood so tenaciously for the free expression of honest dissent. He is no longer with us, my brethren. He has left us and gone somewhere else. Now he wants no dissent, he wants only agreement. He has become terrified of liberty. And I for one, I will say to this court of my peers, am finally, but I am afraid irrevocably, becoming terrified of him."

"Your honor!" Fred Van Ackerman cried, leaping to his feet as the dignified chamber became filled with a sudden burst of sound, startled exclamations, unbelieving comments, angry disagreement, angry support, even, here and there among the media, a little applause, furtive, quickly hushed. "Your honor, Mr. Chief Justice, I demand—the Administration demands—the disqualification of this man, who has proved himself in that single comment to be completely unworthy, completely unfit to sit in judgment on this issue. He is completely partisan, your honors! He is completely unfair! He has removed himself deliberately from the tolerance, the integrity, the judicious, careful, unemotional judgment which alone can qualify a man to sit on this Court! We demand his removal from this case, and in due course, your honors—in due course, after your honors have decided this issue in the only fair and honest way it can be decided, namely to reject petitioners and uphold our great President and the Help America Act—then, in due course, I promise you the matter of Mr. Justice Thomas Buckmaster Davis—that *great jurist!*—will be brought before the Congress for action. We will see then what can be done to rid this Court and this nation forever of one who has become a simple scold and nuisance, your honors, yes, a simple scold and nuisance without any qualifications whatsoever to mix and mingle in the affairs of this Republic! A man completely dangerous to, and defiant of, the democratic process, your honors! A legal dictator who would superimpose his judgment upon that of the American people and override the needs of this great peace-loving free society in its time of gravest peril! Get rid of him, your honors! Disqualify! Disqualify!"

And in a few seconds, roused by some means of communication not visible within the chamber but evidently efficient nonetheless, the roar outside for the first time took on coherent form. There began a sullen, heavy chant, loud enough so that they knew the building now must be surrounded on all sides:

"Disqualify! Disqualify!"

For several minutes within the room no one spoke, no one even moved. Then movement began, hardly perceptible, hardly conscious, perhaps instinctive, but pointed nonetheless: from Justice Davis there was a slight but definite withdrawing on the part of several of his colleagues, among them the Chief Justice on his right. It was not lost upon the media or upon anyone else.

Presently Justice Montgomery, one of those considered certain to be against the Administration, leaned forward and peered around Tommy Davis at the Chief Justice.

"Why are you shrinking away from Justice Davis, Mr. Chief Justice?" he inquired with a dry contempt consistent with his reputation for savage repartee. "Are you intimidated by the rabble beyond our gates? Are they really going to dictate to this honorable Court and frighten us into doing their bidding? For shame, I suggest to you, Mr. Chief Justice, for shame!"

Again there was silence in the room while outside the angry chant continued. Justice Davis stared impassively straight ahead, the Chief Justice flushed with anger, Justice Montgomery continued to fix him with an unyielding eye, their colleagues looked at them with varying degrees of interest, uncertainty or alarm. The media, whose members realized suddenly that they had a great deal riding on Tommy Davis, studied them all with an intensity in which a considerable apprehension was beginning to appear. The usual wisecracking exuberance of the profession was not present now. Abruptly it was all deadly serious as it became obvious that perhaps not even the Supreme Court was immune to the cancer of the times. If the Court went—and the Congress went—and the White House went—then what would be left to protect them from the savage rush of dissolution?

To protect them or anyone?

A great uneasiness grew.

Into it the Chief Justice finally spoke, obviously controlling his annoyance with some difficulty but managing a reasonable outward calm.

"I will not dignify the comment of Justice Montgomery with reply other than this: this Court will not, as he puts it, be 'frightened' by anybody. It will perform its duty as it always has. It will take into account the facts put before it and it will decide thereupon and forthwith." Then his firm tone changed, subtly but unmistakably, and the worry quotient in the room shot up again. "It is true, of course, that there may be some valid question raised concerning the propriety of Justice Davis' remarks, in that they do appear to show a certain amount of bias in his consideration of the issue now before us. This could possibly be misconstrued. It could possibly be seized upon for the advantage of one side or the other. It could possibly be an embarrassment to this Court. Perhaps he would care to explain his rather peculiar and, in my opinion at least, unwarranted attack upon the President of the United States, which, coming from this bench, falls oddly upon the ear."

Now it was Tommy's turn to remain silent for a time, during which the ex-President and his friends silently but fiercely exhorted him in their minds to stand firm and remain true to his convictions, which were now, obviously, the same as their own. They need not have worried. The reply of the little Justice, when it came, was slow, thoughtful and unimpressed by the Chief's disapproval.

"Mr. Chief Justice," he said mildly, "and my brethren of the Court: I am so sorry if my candor has dismayed you. I hope it will not be used, as the Chief Justice suggests, by one side or the other. I hope it will not embarrass the Court. Above all, I hope that it will not be misconstrued. For I meant," he assured them quietly, "exactly what I said.

"I am afraid of the violent elements in the country, as exemplified by the mob we hear outside at this very moment. I am afraid of the 'Help America Act,' which is a measure desperately dangerous to democracy. I am, above all, afraid of a President who could convince himself that he should condone and sign so vicious a piece of legislation. I think it must spring from a great desperation and a great fear. And that, I regret to say, makes me very much afraid of *him*.

"Some of us in this room—" and his eyes flickered briefly over the ex-President, Bob Munson, Warren Strickland, Walter Dobius sitting crowded in between the *Times* and the *Post* in the press section—"were at the White House much earlier today. We were in the presence of a very complex man, but one, I think, at wit's end. It is terrifying to me— and terrifyingly sad, as well—that in his desperation he should be turning away from democracy—that he should have lost faith in the processes of free government—that he should be seeking the easy way, which is the way of force and suppression—the force and the suppression that will flow inevitably from this measure if it is allowed to remain on the statute books.

"I do not know what the ultimate outcome is going to be, of the President's experiment in turning the other cheek to the Russians. But I do know it must not be a domestic tranquillity secured at the price of the liberty of his own people. That would make of both his dreams and his actions history's most awful mockery. I care not what others here may do, but I will not be a party to it. I simply will not. And I am ready to so vote. And the quicker the better."

("That makes five against the Administration, as I see it," the *Times* whispered to Walter, who nodded grimly. *"Disqualify! Disqualify!"* insisted the angry roar, just outside.)

Again there was a silence. Into it the Attorney General finally spoke with a fierce and quivering indignation, which the Chief Justice at first made some pretense of checking, then shrugged and let it flow.

"Your honors!" George Henry Wattersill cried in a tone so aggrieved it would have been laughable under any other circumstance. "What an extraordinary performance! What an extraordinary scene! A Justice of the Supreme Court of the United States attacking so viciously a President of the United States! So personally, so openly, so unbelievably, so inexcusably! For shame, indeed, Justice Montgomery, for shame indeed! But not shame upon the great Chief Justice, who is doing his best to provide a fair judgment here for the Administration of a great President, but shame upon a member of this Court, and upon all colleagues who side with him, for his unwarranted, unjustified, unconscionable, *unjudicial* assault upon our great President! Disqualify him indeed, your honors, for he has forfeited all right to be considered a fair and objective member of this Court! . . .

"Mr. Chief Justice, and your honors," he concluded, more quietly, suddenly all grave, all statesmanlike, "we submit that Justice Davis is no longer fit to sit upon this Court in this case, or possibly in any other. Certainly he is not fit to sit in this one. He has disqualified himself by his own intemperate and unjudicial words, he has removed himself from the high company of this distinguished and noble bench. We ask you to make certain that he will not vote by formally disqualifying him, your honors. Simple fairness and justice require no less. The nation expects no less. We earnestly and respectfully request that you consider the matter of his disqualification before all else."

"*Disqualify!*" urged the chant outside. "*Disqualify, disqualify!*"

For a moment the Chief Justice hesitated; long enough for William Abbott to rise to his feet and say, with a firmness that assumed he would receive no denial, "Mr. Chief Justice, I wish to address myself to this question, if you please."

"Your honors," George Wattersill began indignantly, "your honors, this is most irregular—"

"Oh, stop it!" the ex-President roared with a vehemence that startled them all. "Stop this damnable hypocritical nonsense of yours! You have just had your say about Justice Davis, and now, damn you, I am going to have mine!"

"Your honors," the Attorney General repeated, but with an obvious uncertainty, "your honors, this is most irreg—"

"Petitioner may speak," the Chief Justice interrupted. "And then," he added, to a sudden heightening of the already almost unbearable tension in the room, "the Court will, if it please my brethren, decide the matter of Justice Davis' worthiness to pass upon the pending issue."

"Mr. Chief Justice," William Abbott said, more calmly, "I, too, was among those present at the White House very early this morning. I agree with the analysis of Justice Davis. This President is drifting. He thinks he has a plan, but it is a plan of desperation. He is clutching at straws. Meanwhile this monstrous bill has been passed by the Congress, in an equal mood of desperation, in his name. He has signed it. He really thinks, I believe—although no one really knows what he thinks—that it will assist him in some way to meet the situation in which he finds himself. It will not. It will only destroy the liberties of all Americans, using the pretext that he must have 'domestic tranquillity.' For what, your honors? So that he may pursue the course of surrendering to the Russians all hope of saving the independence of this country and the liberties of her citizens? He will give us domestic tranquillity, all right—the tranquillity of the grave.

"Yes!" he repeated angrily, as George Wattersill, Fred Van Ackerman and Bronson Bernard stirred restlessly in their seats. "The tranquillity of the grave! . . . Mr. Chief Justice, spokesmen for the Administration, like all who argue from weak law, offer strong dramatics. They wish you to disqualify Justice Davis for expressing his opinions. Exactly so, your honor. Exactly so. *That* is becoming the new crime in America—expressing opinions. Particularly if they are opposed to the Administration. That is what will be written into law here if you uphold this dictatorship act. That is what will be established if you disqualify Justice Davis. Make no mistake about it: this nation stands on the edge of the abyss. Don't let this honorable Court push it over."

"Is not your argument really based," the Chief Justice suggested in an unimpressed tone, "upon the fear that if Justice Davis is disqualified this act will be upheld?"

"And is not the argument of the Administration based," the ex-President snapped, "upon the fear that if he is *not* disqualified this act will be thrown out by this Court?"

"I am not asking you about their argument," the Chief Justice said bluntly. "You are not responsible for their argument. I am asking you about your own. . . . Of course"—his tone became thoughtful, almost dreamy—"perhaps it need not come to a showdown at all. There are many precedents. Justices have disqualified themselves heretofore, when they felt themselves to be, and have acknowledged themselves before the world to be, personally prejudiced on one side or the other of an issue. Perhaps an honorable man might even disqualify himself from voting on his own disqualification. That might show a real integrity."

"Oh, no, Mr. Chief Justice," Tommy said quickly, in a voice so sharp that Bill Abbott, with a grim little smile, sat slowly down and left him to his own defenses, which appeared to be good. "Oh, no, you don't! Precedents there may be for justices to disqualify themselves, and precedents there are for justices *not* to disqualify themselves. There is no precedent at all, I might point out, for the Court itself to arbitrarily disqualify a justice.

"I will not disqualify myself from voting on the question of my own disqualification," he said flatly, "for the simple reason that I believe we are finally right up against it, in this country. I think it is finally coming to us, the terror, the disaster, the betrayal, the end—unless some of us somewhere hold the line.

"It is not being held in the White House.

"It is not being held in Congress.

"This is the last place. . . .

"Now, just suppose," he said—and he looked from one side of the bench to the other, at briskly efficient Madam Justice Watson; at easygoing but tenacious Justice Cappola; at Justice Montgomery, lean and sharp-tongued; at the Chief Justice, outward stateliness not always successfully concealing the rigid partisan inside; Justice Grant, tall and dignified, unyieldingly conservative in all his approaches; Justices Osborne and Stevenson, equally unyielding on the other side; Justice Mulvaney, usually a swing man, not a man of great personal courage or principle, one whom mobs could conceivably impress and intimidate—"just suppose, my brethren, that I did disqualify myself on the question of my own disqualification. And then suppose—not that I am predicting, for I have no knowledge how you would vote on the matter—("Not much," *Newsweek* remarked dryly to *Time*)—that your vote should be 4 to 4. A tie vote preserves the status quo, does it not? I should not be disqualified. I should remain right here. And if there were indeed four who think as I do, I should then join them, and 5 to 4 we would uphold petitioners, dismiss the Administration's argument, and declare the 'Help America Act' unconstitutional and void, as I believe it is."

"And by the same token," the Chief Justice pointed out calmly, "if by one means or another you *were* disqualified, the same principle would apply. We would vote 4 to 4 on petitioners' appeal—a tie vote would uphold the status quo—and the Help America Act would be declared constitutional and in full force and effect, which happens to be *my* way of looking at it."

"But I am not going to disqualify myself, and I am not going to allow myself to be disqualified," Mr. Justice Davis replied cheerfully. "So we seem to have reached an impasse, have we not? Therefore, Mr. Chief Justice, I think we should entertain a motion on whether or not I am to be disqualified, don't you?"

"I move that Justice Davis be qualified to vote on the pending matter," Mr. Justice Montgomery said promptly.

"I offer an amendment to that motion that Justice Davis be disqualified," said Justice Osborne with a stern and equal promptitude.

"Oh, for God's sake," Justice Cappola snapped, his usual equanimity suddenly worn thin. "Does it matter whether the issue is stated negatively or positively? Will Mr. Justice Osborne stop playing games and let us get on with it?"

("Hot damn!" the *Post* murmured gleefully to Walter Dobius. "Now we've got a real dog fight!" "Stop talking like a child," Walter told him harshly. "This is too serious for that.")

And presently Justice Osborne seemed to agree; for after glaring at Justice Cappola, who glared back, he finally shrugged and said, "Very well, Mr. Chief Justice. I withdraw my amendment. Let it stand on Justice Montgomery's motion."

"Mr. Chief Justice," Justice Mulvaney said in his characteristic worried and uncertain manner, "I don't think there are any precedents for the kind of spectacle this Court is making of itself this afternoon. I really don't."

"Basically," Tommy Davis said, before the C.J. could reply, "this isn't a time for precedents anyway. There are no precedents for what is happening to America right now. This is a time for getting to the guts of things. So, Mr. Chief Justice, may we have a vote?"

"Mr. Chief Justice," Justice Stevenson said angrily, "at least let us not make a spectacle of ourselves in public! At least we can go into chambers on this! *This* is most irregular, this sort of public sideshow the Court is putting on today! I object, Mr. Chief Justice! I most emphatically object!"

"I think we'd better do it in the open," Justice Cappola said calmly. "It's gone much too far now to hide ourselves behind a fig leaf. How about Justice Montgomery's motion, Mr. Chief Justice?" he inquired with a sudden sharpness. "Let's have it."

The Chief Justice gave him an openly hostile look; but after a moment, having really no choice, conceded.

"Very well," he said shortly. "With a proper seconding."

"I will second," Justice Cappola said promptly.

The Chief Justice paused for a moment, took a deep breath, mouth pursed, eyes grim; looked to the colleagues at his right hand, looked to the colleagues at his left hand, shrugged and began his poll, starting with the most junior.

"The question is, shall Justice Davis be qualified to vote on the pending issue. Mr. Justice Mulvaney."

"No," said Justice Mulvaney with a stern satisfaction.

"Madam Justice Watson."

"Aye," she said crisply, looking more than ever like a spare and determined schoolmarm.

"Mr. Justice Stevenson."

"*No!*" said Justice Stevenson with an angry emphasis.

"Mr. Justice Cappola."

"Aye," said Justice Cappola.

"Mr. Justice Osborne."

"*No!*" said Justice Osborne as sternly as Justice Stevenson.

"Mr. Justice Montgomery."

"Aye, of course," said Justice Montgomery.

"Mr. Justice Grant."

"Aye," said Justice Grant with a stern satisfaction.

"Mr. Justice Davis," the Chief Justice said, glancing with a dislike he could not conceal at the small determined figure on his left.

"Aye," said Tommy with a blandly cheerful smile.

"And I vote No," the Chief Justice said in an exasperated tone, "and the vote is five Aye, four No, and the challenge to Mr. Justice Davis' qualification is dismissed."

("Tommy called it," the *Star-News* murmured. "He knew he had the votes, all the time," the Boston *Globe* agreed.)

"And now, Mr. Chief Justice," Tommy said with a sudden severity, while the packed chamber buzzed and murmured, and outside the multitudes, unknowing, still shouted *"Disqualify! Disqualify!"* from time to time, "I would suggest we speedily get on with it, take a recess, retire to chambers, vote on the pending matter and report back not later than—let's see, it's now almost two o'clock—not later than 4 P.M. In fact, I so move."

"Mr. Chief *Justice!*" Fred Van Ackerman shouted, shooting out of his chair as though propelled by the strength of his own carefully orchestrated indignation. "The Administration must protest this absolutely inexcusable attempt to railroad this matter through the Court!"

"I thought you wanted to railroad it," Justice Cappola snapped. "You're the one who's been in such an all-fired hurry to put pressure on us and get a vote here today. What's the matter now?"

"Mr. Justice," Senator Van Ackerman said, a little more calmly but still giving the impression of a boiler about to explode any second, "it seems to the Administration that this is a most unwarranted and, yes, unjudicial attempt on the part of Justice Davis to foreclose all reasonable argument on this matter. Why, Mr. Chief Justice! We have only been discussing this, as he says, for about two hours. Certainly we want speed, I'll admit to Justice Cappola, certainly we want a quick decision so that this great President can proceed, unhampered and unhindered by phony, inexcusable protest, in pursuit of his great goals of peace. But not at the cost of virtually *no* discussion, Mr. Chief Justice and your honors! Not at the cost of a half-made argument which would allow petitioners to win their points virtually *nolo contendere!* Why, your honors!" he cried, and it was with a fine, noble fury, "how unfair can you be? How ruthless, undemocratic, unjust, inhumane can you be? There must be a limit, your honors! There must be a limit!"

"You don't think the Help America Act goes beyond those limits?" Madam Justice Watson inquired sharply, and for a moment Senator Van Ackerman looked quite taken aback. But not for long.

"There, Mr. Chief Justice and your honors!" he cried. *"There!* That's an example of the sort of hostile, prejudiced, closed-minded approach of some members of this Court! *That's* why we need more time, your honors! *That's* why you shouldn't rush this! *That's* why there must be solemn and patient deliberation on this issue, not the steam-roller approach of Justice Davis and some of his colleagues here! That kind of attitude, if it takes root in this Court, which is literally the court of last appeal, would indeed be fatal to democracy, your honors! There must be at least a few hours of deliberation away from the stresses and strains and pressures of this proceeding here! There must be!"

He ceased as abruptly as he had begun, and from outside came again the insistent roar: *"DISQUALIFY! DISQUALIFY!"*

"Why don't you go out there and tell your—your *minions,*" Justice Grant suggested with an indignant distaste, "to go away and leave us alone? That would be *your* contribution to a few hours of deliberation away from stresses, strains and pressures!"

"That's a good idea," Justice Cappola agreed. "Anyway, tell them to get a different chant. Tell them Justice Davis isn't disqualified and isn't going to be. At least bring your bullyboys up to date, Senator. They aren't helping the Administration now."

"I must demand," the Chief Justice said with a sudden vigorous anger, "that justices maintain at least a minimal dignity and decency in this courtroom! I don't think we need unprincipled, inflammatory statements to help us with our deliberations here!"

"How can you be so unfair?" Justice Montgomery demanded harshly. "You let *him—*" and he gestured with an open contempt at Fred Van Ackerman, still in insistent and demanding stance at the bar, "say any inflammatory thing he pleases, yet when one of us that you don't agree with tries to say something perfectly honest, you—"

"The Justice will be in order!" the Chief Justice cried, rapping the gavel angrily. "The Court will be in order altogether! . . . Now," he said, breathing heavily, when the room had become deathly still following his outburst, "I think we must consider calmly and sensibly what to do."

"It's about time," Madam Justice Watson said, and for a moment it seemed he would lose control and turn on her with some harsh and personal retort. But there were high stakes involved, and after a moment, obviously working at it, he spoke in a tone as flat and reasonable as he could make it.

"It probably would seem in order," he said carefully, "as Justice Davis suggests"—at his side Tommy made him an elaborately ironic little bow, but though he flushed angrily, he ignored it—"that we now go into recess and have further private discussions of this issue. I think this Court, like all in this room, and indeed all in the country, is perfectly well aware of the major arguments on both sides. I doubt if further presentation is necessary. If that is agreeable to both sides?"

"Perfectly agreeable to us, your honor," William Abbott said.

"The Administration has no objection," George Wattersill agreed, and was rewarded with a sour scowl from Fred.

"Then perhaps," the Chief Justice said, "we can take a recess to a time certain. It seems to me that Justice Davis is a trifle optimistic about the hour of 4 P.M. as a goal for reaching a decision, but perhaps some other member would wish to suggest an hour?"

"How about 8 P.M.?" Justice Cappola proposed, his tone reasonable and calm once again now that the flurry appeared to be over. But of course it wasn't.

"Mr. Chief Justice!" Justice Osborne said sharply. "I don't want any arbitrary limits put on a full and free discussion of this matter, it's too important."

"I couldn't agree more," Justice Stevenson backed him up firmly.

"Nor I," said Justice Mulvaney.

"Nor, I suppose, I," agreed Madam Justice Watson. "But surely by midnight—"

"Your honors," George Wattersill said, "at the risk of intruding—"

"You are," Mr. Justice Cappola said—"it does seem to the Administration that if you go that late, you might just as well go to noon tomorrow in the regular order. We would be prepared, of course, to remain here all night if necessary, in case you wished further clarifications, but—"

"Why don't we, Mr. Chief Justice?" Mr. Justice Grant inquired.

"Which?" the Chief Justice asked.

"Run all night. As long as necessary. Not establish an arbitrary hour. I'm not in any hurry."

"Nor I," said Justice Davis with a bland little smile. "None at all."

"*Vote! Vote!*" demanded the roar outside, and Justice Grant started and then turned upon Senator Van Ackerman a dry and withering smile.

"Ah," he said with a savagely gentle sarcasm. "I see you have informed them."

"Mr. Chief Justice—" Fred began in an ominous tone, but Justice Grant gave him a brusque, dismissing wave. He subsided, face suffused with a vengeful anger that might have disturbed Justice Grant if he had not already looked away. Many in the media observed it, however, and it did not make them feel easy.

"Justice Davis wanted the deadline," the Chief Justice pointed out with an indifferent air. "Will he allow us to continue beyond it?"

Tommy gave him a sunny smile.

"Why, certainly, it was just a suggestion, your honor, just a suggestion. I'm quite content to go on until *all* hours, if that suits the Administration. I don't really think, on the basis of the vote just held, that it will matter much to the outcome."

"Don't be too sure," Justice Osborne said dryly, a remark made in all innocence which would come back to haunt him later.

"Well," the Chief Justice said abruptly, forestalling what apparently was about to be a rather sharp retort from Tommy, "we needn't go into that sort of thing again, it seems to me. If it is agreeable to my brethren, we will terminate the public hearing at this point and continue our discussions in private later, beginning possibly around 8 P.M. and running as late as we wish from there on. Would that be agreeable to the Court?"

He looked along the bench at his colleagues on each hand, they all nodded, he turned back. Right on cue from outside came, "VOTE! VOTE!" Justice Cappola leaned forward and spoke in a dry, emphatic voice.

"I would suggest, Mr. Chief Justice, since the Court is for all practical purposes under siege, that you ask the Justice Department for additional marshals and the District police for additional officers to be sent up here to protect us; and I would also suggest that justices be extremely circumspect and not venture out of the building for any purpose whatsoever until our deliberations are concluded."

"Oh, that is absurd!" Justice Stevenson said angrily.

"It is?" Justice Cappola asked in the same dry tone. "Step outside, John: be my guest. I'm sure the President would welcome the opportunity to fill a vacancy on the Court so early in his term."

"I have nothing to fear," Justice Stevenson said with the slightest emphasis on the pronoun. Madam Justice Watson was on it like a ferret.

"Exactly!" she said. "Exactly so! *You* have nothing to fear because *you* will do their bidding, while we who oppose them may be subject to bodily harm. Is that what you're trying to tell us, Mr. Justice?"

"Not at all," Justice Stevenson said indignantly. "Not at all!"

But Justice Watson had obviously scored a point, and his denial fell uncomfortably into a widening pool of silence, unbroken until the Chief Justice said finally,

"I have already sent the marshal of the Court a note requesting that he do as Justice Cappola suggests. Some minutes ago, in fact."

"Oh," Justice Davis said brightly. "Then we *are* under siege."

"I do not wish to assign labels to anything," the Chief Justice said in a tired tone. "I am telling you I have already taken steps. I join Justice Cappola in suggesting we remain in the Court. There is ample food on hand in the restaurant, we are in no danger inside the building—or out, either, I suspect. However, precautions are available and we will take them. If our deliberations carry over until tomorrow, justices, of course, can sleep in their chambers, which are fully equipped for overnight use. . . . So, then, gentlemen," he said, addressing the ex-President and the Attorney General, who rose to come forward and stand side by side at the lectern, "if it is agreeable to you, we will conclude this public session, to resume in private at 8 P.M. If you wish to remain, quarters will be found for you and you may do so. I rather doubt that we will need to call you again for questioning, as the basic arguments are very clear. But we may."

"Then we on our side are prepared to remain," William Abbott said.

"And we," George Henry Wattersill agreed.

"And the media?" the Chief Justice inquired. There was a silence. The *Times* at length stood up.

"Your honor," he said, "speaking for myself and perhaps for my friends, I should like to remain and watch out this historic decision."

There was a general murmur of agreement. The Chief Justice nodded.

"The press officer will make suitable arrangements," he said. He looked along the bench once more, first to his right, then to his left.

"Very well, gentlemen," he said. "This public hearing is terminated and the Court stands in recess until 8 P.M., at which time we will take up the pending issue *in camera*."

He rose, his colleagues rose, everyone rose. The Clerk cried, "This honorable Court is now in recess until 8 P.M.!" The red velvet curtains parted, the justices turned and disappeared, the curtains fell into place again behind the empty bench. A milling about began. Into it Bronson Bernard cried out in a strong, commanding voice,

"I will hold a press conference outside the door in five minutes!"

"What the hell?" said many a reporter. But obediently they jostled out and took up their stations in the echoing marble corridor. A disgruntled murmuring came from beyond the walls, a last, rather half-hearted cry of "Vote! Vote!" The news had already spread and many in the mob were apparently preparing to disperse until 8 P.M., when they would resume their vigil. Miraculously there had been no really bloody clashes between NAWAC and the IDF during the past couple of hours, possibly because NAWAC had immediately appropriated the areas closest to the building and invested them in depth. An inner core remained in place as the fringes began to wander off. Enough remained, however, to fully warrant the *Star-News'* final edition headline:

SUPREME COURT UNDER SIEGE AS JUSTICES PONDER FATE OF "HELP AMERICA."

"The reason I'm having this press conference," Bronnie Bernard said in a noticeably defensive tone, looking about the circle of attentive, worried faces, sensing that for the first time in decades a liberal figure was facing an openly hostile and suspicious press, "is because I intend to return to the House at once and introduce a resolution of impeachment against Justice Davis. I think he deserves it. I think the country deserves it. I think the time is now."

"Why does he deserve it, Congressman?" the *Times* inquired sharply, revealing that a feeling of this-is-*my*-neck can be a marvelous educator for man or institution. "Just why does he?"

"Because he is obstructing the policies of a great President," Bronnie began. "Because he—"

"Congressman," the *Post* broke in harshly, also revealing a surprise-ing deathbed conversion, "aren't you simply parroting all the clichés we've been listening to from the Administration side for the past two days? Isn't this just a naked power play to drive Justice Davis off the Court so that the Administration can have its way with this dictatorial bill?"

"Listen to that!" Bronnie Bernard cried with an abrupt, blazing indignation. "Listen to that, will you! Talk about clichés! Talk about a prejudiced one-sided press! I never thought I'd live to see the day— *Yes,* so the Administration can have its way! *Yes,* so a great President can work out the terrible problems that face him without a lot of crap from you guys! *Yes,* so we can have peace! What's wrong with peace, I'll ask *you!* Let the media tell us, right here in front of television—" and he waved, somewhat wildly, at the cameras dutifully transmitting the brightly lighted scene in the historic white hallway—"let the press and the media tell us what's wrong with peace! Go ahead! Go ahead!"

"It isn't a question of peace, Congressman," the Boston *Globe* said coldly, "as you know damned well. It's a question of a law which comes closer to dictatorship than we've ever seen yet in this country. Or ever will see, if it passes, because there won't need to be anything more. This is it, right here. And you know that just as well as we do."

"I do *not* know that," Bronnie Bernard cried bitterly. "I do not know that! My God, *I'm a liberal!* I've been a liberal all my life! How can you imagine that I would support anything dictatorial, anything that wasn't for the good of all the people, the good of all this country?"

"What makes you so sure this is for the good of the country, Congressman?" the Los Angeles *Times* demanded.

"I *know* it is!" Bronnie Bernard cried. "I *know* it is! Any fool can see that!"

"And so all fools have to accept it," Walter Dobius said bitterly, "because *you know* it is best for them and so you and your precious Administration *will do it*, no matter who it hurts or what it destroys."

"'Hurts!' 'Destroys!'" cried Bronnie Bernard with an almost hysterical scorn. "Listen to clichés, will you listen to clichés! My God, I'm a liberal! *I'm a liberal*, can't you crazy fools get that through your heads?"

There was a silence as they glared at one another, there in the great hall of the Supreme Court of the United States, while many an old god toppled and many an old faith crashed. Finally the Congressman spoke in a voice that he managed, with a terrific effort, just barely to control.

"I am returning to the House, as I said, to introduce a resolution of impeachment against Justice Davis—"

"Do you really think you can get it through in time to stop the proceedings here?" the *Post* interrupted with an open sarcasm.

"It has to go to the Senate for trial, you know," the *Times* agreed. "It could take weeks. They're planning to vote here in hours."

"I am assured by Senator Van Ackerman," Bronson Bernard said carefully, "and he tells me he has been assured by the Majority Leader, Senator Richardson, that the Senate will be prepared to take it up immediately."

"It still will take days," the AP said shortly. "Who are you kidding?"

"I'm kidding no one!" Bronnie Bernard cried, flaring up again. "No one! The Court has its responsibility, we have ours! Ours is to remove an illiberal, conservative, willful, reactionary old man who is standing in the way of this Administration and everything it wants to accomplish, in foreign affairs and domestic affairs, too. Everything!"

"In other words," Frankly Unctuous said quietly, extending a microphone to Bronnie's lips to be sure and capture the answer, "you have to break the Court, don't you?"

For a long angry moment Congressman Bernard glared at him without reply. Then he snarled an answer quite clear and specific.

"I have better things to do than waste my time talking to you fucking bastards! I'm going over and impeach Justice Davis!"

And striding straight ahead without looking right or left, he shoved them roughly out of his way and stalked off down the hall.

"I'm afraid Tommy's right," the *Star-News* said quietly as they stood in a dazed semi-circle watching him go. "This *is* the last place."

"And it's going," Walter Dobius said bitterly.

"Tommy, baby," the head of the AP House staff said fervently, "you'd better take care of yourself."

"So had we all," Walter said, bitterness, if possible, even deeper. "So had we all."

At the doorway, far down the great corridor, Bronnie Bernard turned back for one last moment.

"We're going to impeach that reactionary old fool!" he shouted, his voice bouncing eerily off the marble. "We're going to impeach him! Don't you make any mistake about that!"

But there were, of course, simpler and more efficient ways available to those who wished to use them; which, it should be said to his credit, he in all his innocent and liberal youth knew nothing about.

He felt solemn, but also satisfied and confident of his course, as he sat in his silent chambers and waited for them to come up from the kitchen with the frugal meal he had ordered.

This was the second time Mr. Justice Davis had defied the massive weight of Ted Jason's political appeal compounded by the violent pressures of Ted Jason's more radical supporters. He had won the first time, when he had ruled against Ted in the bitterly contested National Committee battle for the nomination after Harley Hudson's death. He was certain he would win this time, and for the same reason: because he was right.

Tommy was still old-fashioned enough to think, at this late date, that the righteous cause could win in America.

Partly he was confident of this simply out of the old-fashioned goodness of his heart and the basic morality in which he had been reared, back in a simpler age when moral principle and devotion to democracy really meant something in government. Not everything, of course, because Lord knew, and he knew, that there had always been the trimmers, the cheaters, the subverters and the corruptibles in America, always, from the beginning. But he had grown up while there was still some sort of balance, some sort of equaling out—when decency and the cause of liberty still had a fighting chance.

He had seen this condition change very drastically in recent decades, when those who really wanted to destroy democracy—and those who were too clever by half as they tried to appeal to all the pressure blocs with one hand and yet save democracy with the other—had, between them, come close to bringing democracy down.

The world now was not the world he had grown up in, the world in which he had made his mark as a young anti-trust lawyer, become a leading figure in liberal causes, risen swiftly to national attention and finally, in his mid-forties, received the ultimate accolade of appointment to the Court.

Tommy had seen many things besides water pass under the bridge, particularly the original meaning of the word "liberal." When he began "liberal" had meant real liberalism, with all its passionate, impatient, but still basically tolerant devotion to the common weal. Now that he was in the final years of his life and service, "liberal" had come to mean the rigid, ruthless, intolerant and unyielding orthodoxy that had finally and inevitably produced the mood, the spirit and the fact of a "Help America" Act.

Yet he remained confident that right and liberalism, as he conceived them, would prevail: and not just because he, Tommy Davis, was cast in the role of Horatio at the bridge, Dutch boy with finger in the dike, or whatever other clichés of heroism he might be representing at the moment. He wasn't the only one standing at the bridge: he had become sharply, if ironically, aware in the last few hours that he had much strong company. From Walter Dobius to Tommy's old crony, the general director of the *Post,* the leaders of the media were suddenly, as the *Post* had put it to him a short while ago in a hurried chat on the Picturephone, "scared as hell."

"You've got to stop this law, Tommy," the *Post* had said, his usual sniffy-superior expression changed to one of desperate earnestness. "It all depends on you."

"It does?" Tommy could not resist inquiring with a little twinkle. "Doesn't it depend on you too?"

"I think," the *Post* said, his expression turning somber and genuinely honest at last, "that we've muffed it. I think it's past time when it could depend on us."

"And whose fault is that?" the little Justice had inquired with some asperity. But the *Post* gave as good as he got.

"Yours and ours, both, Tommy," he said. "Yours and ours, both. How many phone calls have you made in this town, how many visits, how many little notes and letters, urging, urging, urging the liberal cause? Going by my own experience, it must run into the millions."

"That was in the cause of real liberalism," Justice Davis said tartly, "Not in the cause of the Van Ackerman kind."

"Where did we go wrong, Tommy?" the *Post* inquired in a tone of genuine puzzlement. "Where did the one kind slide over into the other kind? How did we stray so far from home base?"

"I think it began," Tommy Davis said thoughtfully, "on the day we all decided that those who disagreed with us should not only be disagreed with in return, but should be punished. When we began to lose tolerance for the opposing point of view. When we began to use our decisions, our editorials, our news stories, our broadcasts and commentaries and evening news reports, to deliberately stamp out and suppress all other points of view but our own. When we became so arrogant that we thought we and we alone knew what was best—and that anyone who disagreed must be denied his fair hearing, be suppressed, destroyed, sunk without trace. Now," he said, somber himself, "it has been turned back upon us and *we* are the ones to be destroyed. And all in the name, God save the mark, of a 'liberal' President."

"Unless you can stop it in the Court," the *Post* said. "And you will, won't you?" he pursued, his expression openly worried. "There won't be any slip-up, will there?"

"I don't *think* so," Tommy said thoughtfully, "but of course you never know. I think the vote will hold just as it went today in the session. But we are still surrounded here, you know, and the mood is very ugly, and one or two might waver—although I don't really think so. I think we have the votes. Although even then—" his expression became, if anything, more moody, more somber—"it may not be that easy. 'The Court has made its decision,' Andrew Jackson said, 'now let the Court enforce it.' It's been a long, long time since a President said that, but when you come right down to it, upon what does our power depend? On that same old thing—'the consent of the governed.' And when that consent is withheld, as it could be by an extremely popular and determined President backed by a violent and lawless constituency which recognizes no law but the law it can force upon others—then what, my friend? *Then* what?"

"We look to you to save us, Tommy," the *Post* said quietly. "Which sounds dramatic, but expresses the fact."

"I shall," Justice Davis said firmly. "If the Lord is still with America, and I feel He is, I shall. I must be on this Court for some reason—much" he interjected with a sudden smile, "as many of my critics over the years may have doubted that there was one—and perhaps this is it."

"I'm sure of it," the *Post* said. "It has to be. . . . Do you think you'll vote sometime tonight?"

The little Justice nodded.

"I expect so." He smiled again. "My impeachment may take a little longer."

"The vote will change that," the *Post* predicted. "It will be forgotten. The vote will change the whole emphasis and trend of everything. This is the watershed."

"I think so," Tommy Davis said. "I am approaching it in that spirit."

And so he was, as his friend's troubled visage faded from the screen and the silence of the book-filled, leather-bound room reclaimed him. He was coming as close to praying as he had in a long time; telling himself, with a trace of his old impish humor, still lively even in this heavy hour, that this was directly violating the separation between church and state. Hadn't he handed down several ringing decisions on this subject? Of course he had! *Well, Lord,* he thought with a wry little smile, *that's our little secret, right? I know You will forgive me, and be amused, as I am.*

Which was really, he thought as a sudden renewed burst of sound outside drew him to the heavily curtained windows, about the only thing left to inspire amusement at the moment. The thought was strengthened as he lifted his hand to draw the curtains very slightly apart so that he might peek down at the mob below. As he did so a great shout went up and simultaneously some heavy object hurtled through the window and crashed, muffled by the draperies, to the floor.

Instinctively he jumped back, then approached it cautiously as another shout, this one quite distinguishable—"KILL PIG DAVIS! KILL PIG DAVIS!"—arose outside. He paused. It might be a bomb, it might be a grenade, it might be any one of a dozen lethal things. They who were shouting meant it, he could tell that from their tone. He decided to leave whatever it was where it was and retreated to his desk, where he sat down, trembling a little inside but even more determined, if possible, than he had been before.

"You will not change me, rabble," he said aloud to them in this room which had really been his home, above all others, for more than twenty years. "You will not change me, at all."

And presently, when nothing exploded and nothing further came in, he quieted the trembling altogether and composed himself for a little prayer, which he began a trifle self-consciously but soon found he was quite open and unabashed about.

"God," he said quietly, "give me strength to help my country, which is so mixed up right now. I know her heart is still good, her purposes still valid. I accord to the man who leads her the same sincerity, though I think he is dreadfully mistaken—dreadfully mistaken. But I do not accord that sincerity to those who have gathered vulturelike behind his banner, for them I believe to be killers of the hope and murderers of the dream.

"He wanders, God, bemused by their importunings and their pressures, and shattered, I think, by what he found in Russia. Since he wanders, his foot must be held to the path. He must not be allowed to stray toward dictatorship and suppression of the thing that has made America unique: the right to voice opinions freely and openly as long as they are peaceable and non-violent, and as long as those who voice them do not attempt to deny the right of expression to those who disagree with them.

"That is the issue here, God: that is the issue. Bemused, uncertain, possibly terrified, the President lends his name to dictatorship in the wan hope that it will somehow strengthen his hand and make the bad things go away. But the bad things do not come from the honest worries of his own people: they come from abroad. He cannot strengthen himself by punishing his own people for what others do. If he does that, he plays their game and helps give them what they want. He runs the risk of destroying America altogether, under the pretext that denying her freedoms will somehow save her. . . .

"So it has come to me, Lord," he said with a heavy sigh. "So it has really come to me. The deciding vote is mine, and great are the pressures against me. I am not afraid of them, and with Your help I shall defy them and do what is right for my country. If—" he paused and his eyes widened in somber thought—"if this brings upon me retribution, even death, then I hope I shall meet it unafraid. . . .

"I love this country: she has been good to me, and good to so many. Her record is not perfect, her justice not infallible. Her treatment of some of her children has sometimes been cruel and downright shameful. But always her nobler elements have tried to correct those things, constantly they have striven to make those things better; and more often than they are given credit for, they have succeeded.

"The heart is here and the heart is good. Help me to defend it, Lord, as I believe You have chosen me to do. Guide me, strengthen me, encourage me, sustain me—and I shall do justly in Your eyes, and in the eyes of my country when, after storms have died and tempests passed, it renders final judgment on what I am about to do."

He sat for a moment staring far ahead, far away. Then he rose and went firmly to the window, stooped down and retrieved the object that had come through: a rock wrapped in a paper whose message, no doubt scabrous, he did not bother to read as he tossed it into a wastebasket. A sharp blast of air came up from behind the draperies, outside a sudden savage roar greeted the sight of their agitation as he moved them and let them fall back. He returned to his desk with an impassive face, sat down, took a yellow legal notepad from a drawer, began to draft his decision: remembering as he did so some of the phrases he had just articulated in his prayer, and thinking, with a wry little bow to heaven, *Lord, I think You may have helped me get a good start on writing my opinion.*

He was deep in the task when there came a discreet knocking on the door. He looked up with a smile, thinking this must be his dinner, finally, from the restaurant—said, "Come!"—and looked up to see, not Henry, the waiter who usually served him, but one of the young law graduates who came to the Court regularly as clerks to the justices— the newest, he believed, whom he had only seen around the Court in the past few days, and whose sponsor's name he had not yet had a chance to find out.

"Yes?" he asked pleasantly, as two more young men entered after the first and quickly and firmly closed the door upon the ancient, amicable Court policeman outside. "What can I do for you?"

JUSTICE DAVIS FOUND DEAD OF HEART ATTACK IN CHAMBERS. WORRY, STRAIN OF HELP AMERICA BATTLE BELIEVED CAUSE AS BETHESDA HOSPITAL PANEL FINDS "ABSOLUTELY NOTHING BUT NATURAL CAUSES" INVOLVED IN SEIZURE.

COURT PAYS TRIBUTE, THEN UPHOLDS HELP AMERICA ACT ON 4 TO 4 TIE VOTE.

BLOOD BATHS BREAK OUT IN PANAMA, GOROTOLAND AS MOSCOW ANNOUNCES "ALL SOVIET FORCES NOW AT FINAL STATIONS AROUND THE WORLD." PANAMA CANAL CLOSED TO ALL BUT COMMUNIST-BLOC COUNTRIES.

EX-PRESIDENT ABBOTT INTRODUCES RESOLUTION TO IMPEACH PRESIDENT JASON. HOUSE LEADERSHIP CLEARS WAY FOR IMMEDIATE DEBATE. CONFIDENT ADMINISTRATION LEADERS IN SENATE, CERTAIN HOUSE WILL DEFEAT PROPOSAL, PLEDGE SPEEDY TRIAL—"IF, WHEN AND AS."

"Mr. President—" Walter Dobius said in a guarded voice, somewhere around 1 A.M., "Bill—I have just received information I think you should have for the debate."

"Yes?" William Abbott said, coming full awake from a troubled, uneasy sleep in his comfortable bachelor apartment at the Sheraton-Park. "What does it concern?"

"Several—departures," Walter said carefully.

"Where are you?" the ex-President demanded. "At home?"

"Downstairs."

"Come up at once. I'll notify the Secret Service to let you through."

"Are they safe?" Walter asked with a harshness he could not keep out of his voice.

"*Mine* are," Bill Abbott said grimly. "I offer no guarantees of any others."

2. "MR. SPEAKER," Bronson Bernard began, first on his feet as Jawbone gaveled the House to order after the prayer and the routine morning business, "Mr. Speaker, I want to warn the House—"

"Mr. Speaker!" William Abbott cried angrily. "Regular order, Mr. Speaker! Nobody warns anybody until we get this debate properly under way. Suppose you let the proponents of this resolution have their say as they should have and then we'll have warnings from this—this other crew."

"*Mr. Speaker!*" Bronnie cried with an equal anger and a greater grievance. "Mr. Speaker, how can you permit—how can you countenance—oh, the language, Mr. Speaker! We're not a *crew*, Mr. Speaker. We're the *people* who represent the *people*. We're—"

"Well, now!" Jawbone said sharply, giving his gavel a smart rap that brought them both up short. "The gentleman from Colorado and the gentleman from New York don't realize it, but there's a messenger from the White House waitin' there at the door, he's just come in, now, and we've got to hear him, so you-all be quiet!" And he rapped the gavel sharply again as a sudden silence fell on the packed chamber and everyone turned to look, with a piercing and devouring gaze, upon the nondescript and obviously quite nervous individual who stood just inside the door, carrying a briefcase under his arm.

"Mr. Speaker," the messenger intoned solemnly, "a message from the President!"

"A message from the President!" Jawbone echoed solemnly.

In the customary way the messenger then came forward down the attentive aisle, opened the briefcase, took out a sheaf of papers, handed them to the Clerk of the House, closed the briefcase, turned on his heel and departed as he came.

The doors closed behind him. The tensely expectant silence closed in again.

"The message has been duly received and will be appropriately referred," Jawbone said hurriedly in the customary way. "The Chair will now recognize the gentleman from Colorado to continue the debate on his resolution."

"Mr. Speaker," William Abbott said in a tone of annoyed disgust, "for *heaven's* sake. This is the first word we have received from the President of the United States in days, while all sorts of hell has been breaking loose. At least shouldn't we know what it is? Is it just a routine appointment of a postmaster or is it something more vital to this House which we should know about?"

Jawbone flushed and spoke sharply to the Clerk.

"Very well! Hand it up here!"

The Clerk obeyed. Jawbone glanced at it quickly, looked up with a sudden gravity.

"I apologize to the gentleman and to the House, I really do, now. It appears to be a message on the national defense."

"I suggest the Clerk read," Bill Abbott said, looking both surprised and skeptical.

"I'm gettin' to that," Jawbone said with a certain testy dignity. "Read, Mr. Clerk."

"Yes, sir," the Clerk said in his flat, somewhat singsongy voice. "A message on the national defense. To the Congress of the United States—"

"Who writes these things?" Bob Munson murmured to Lafe Smith ten minutes later in the Senate, where the message was also being read, and where it was obviously in its final moments. "How do you say so little in so many words?"

Lafe nodded.

"Why send it at all? It doesn't mean a damned thing."

And indeed, as the reporters in the Press Gallery above dashed out to try to make something of it for the wires, and while the broadcast reporters retired to their booths in the Radio-Television Gallery to do likewise, it was obvious that it did not. But it was also obvious that they had to write and broadcast as though it did, for the President, as often happens with the occupant of that office, had them on the hip. It might not have meant anything in a realistic sense but in a political sense it meant all it needed to mean, right at that moment. It meant that the President was in the White House, on the job, and concerned about the welfare of the country. It meant that anyone who wanted to impeach him was just silly, because he was right where he was supposed to be, doing what he was supposed to do. How could anyone argue otherwise?

Yet there were those, of course, who tried.

"Mr. Speaker," William Abbott said when the Clerk of the House had concluded and Jawbone had stated the usual formula: "The message will be referred to the Foreign Affairs and Armed Services committees for appropriate action"—"Mr. Speaker, I cannot imagine why the President sent such a message. It says nothing, Mr. Speaker. I tried to jot down its salient points on this piece of paper—" he held it up for the House to see—"I have no notes. Nothing but clichés. Nothing but empty words. He urges us to be concerned for the national defense— he suggests we study its needs with great care—he commends us for our diligence—he expresses faith in our wisdom—he fades away. No notes, no sense, no nothing. What are we supposed to do about it? How is it supposed to enlighten or encourage us? Does anyone know?"

"Yes," Jawbone said with a sudden nervous decisiveness, "I think I do, and if the gentleman from Tennessee—" he beckoned to one of his cronies, who obediently came forward—"will assist me here by takin' the chair for a bit, I'll try to tell the House what I see it to mean. . . . Now," he said, when he had come down to the well of the House and taken his stand at the lectern, "first of all, one thing it means is that we have a President, I'll say to my old friend from Colorado, we *have* a President. We don't have some silent little ole do-nothin' figure who jest sits there and *sits* there, Mr. Chairman. He's *there,* Mr. Chairman! He's not a figurehead or a do-nothin', Mr. Chairman! He's a real live President and he's *on the job!*

"Furthermore, Mr. Chairman, he sees our nation's need *and he wants us to do somethin' about it.*

"He's tellin' us to get busy, Mr. Chairman, he's tellin' us to *get on the ball.* He's sayin': get with it, Congress! Face up to this touchy li'l ole situation we're in! Give me a strong rearmament bill, you-all! Let me have it! Give me the money to buy the missiles, the bombers, the submarines, the air-eo-planes—"

But here, of course, Jawbone lost his youthful constituency, and with it, insofar as the national defense was concerned, the House; as in exactly the same fashion across the Capitol, Arly Richardson lost the Senate. Both had seen the light—they thought. Both had found a tricky way out—they thought. Both were swamped immediately by the noisy objections of their restive and unruly colleagues.

"Mr. Speaker!" Bronnie Bronson cried, all sincerity, indignation and genuinely honest dismay.

"Mr. President!" cried Fred Van Ackerman, all insincerity, phony indignation and shrewdly exaggerated outrage.

"Mr. Speaker," Bronnie said, obviouly struggling to master his horror at this abrupt resurrection of the ghosts of militarism, imperialism, industrialism and all the other awful isms his education had trained him against, "how can the Speaker say such a thing? How can he offer so inexcusable and dreadful a suggestion? *Where* in this message of the President does he find any call to arms, Mr. Chairman? *Where* does he find a warrant for his reactionary attempt to return to the long disgraced and discredited ways of old-style big-stick diplomacy? *Where* does he find a warrant for trying to blast any possibility of negotiating with the Russians by offending them with a sudden move towards rearmament?

"I say this is not the meaning of the President's language. I say this is not the answer needed by the times. If that is what members are going to try to read into this brief statement from the President, Mr. Chairman, then I say let it indeed be buried in the House Foreign Affairs and Armed Services committees *and may it never see the light again!*"

"The Majority Leader astounds me!" Fred Van Ackerman cried with equal fervor in the Senate. "Absolutely astounds me, I will say to this Senate! Of all the topsy-turvy, upside-down, bass-ackward interpretations of the simple honest language of a great President! *Where* does it say he is calling on Congress to rearm? *Who* says he wants us to increase the military strength of America as a substitute for honest negotiations? And *who* is so naive as to think we could possibly build up our forces in anything less than a couple of years anyway?

"What would be the purpose of such an idle threat, Mr. President? It is sinister—oh, *it is sinister!* I am astounded and dismayed by the distinguished Majority Leader. I thought he was on our side, Mr. President. I didn't think he was with the reactionaries, the war lovers and the peace destroyers! If he is, he stands alone, Mr. President! He stands alone!"

"Well, I—" Arly Richardson began in a dismayed tone. "Well, I—nobody wants, Mr. President—nobody wants—"

"Well, now," Jawbone cried with an aggrieved haste. "Well, now I will say to my young friend—"

"I move the message be referred immediately to the Foreign Affairs and Armed Services committees with instructions that they do *not* report back to the House on its contents," shouted Bronnie Bernard.

"Second!" and "Question!" shouted everyone at once.

"I move the message be referred to the Foreign Relations and Armed Services committees with instructions that they do *not* report back to the Senate on its contents," shouted Fred Van Ackerman.

"Second!" and "Question!" shouted everyone at once.

"This is most irregular, now!" Jawbone cried, his eyes meeting and then scooting away from William Abbott's bitter glance.

"This is most—irreg—Mr. President—Mr. President—" Arly Richardson shouted, as all around him Senators were on their feet, shouting too.

"VOTE!" demanded the House. In a moment a great roar of "Aye!" welled up.

"VOTE!" demanded the Senate. In a moment a great roar of "Aye!" welled up.

"And now," Bronson Bernard said, breathing hard but triumphant, all innocent, righteous youth and liberalism, "let us get on with the vicious, partisan attempt to impeach our great President. I want to say a few things on that myself, after the *gentleman* from Colorado has given us his unfair, one-sided comments."

"And now," said Fred Van Ackerman with a savage relish, all craft, calculation and ruthless determination to pursue his own dark purposes, "I'd suggest we have a little discussion of this impeachment question, so that we can dispose once and for all of this vicious, inexcusable attempt to embarrass our great President in his search for peace."

"The Senator is out of order," said Lacey Pollard, overflushed and overexcited, in the chair in his capacity as president pro tempore. "The Senator knows the Senate cannot act on impeachments until the House has voted to have an impeachment trial. The matter then comes to us and we conduct the trial. The Senator knows—"

"What the Senator knows," Fred Van Ackerman said with the same harsh relish, "and what the Senate will do, I will say to the distinguished president pro tem, may be two different things. Is the president pro tem going to deny me the right as a United States Senator to comment on anything I want to comment upon? Is he going to deny my right of free speech in this Senate?"

"The chair," Lacey Pollard said, visibly struggling for breath in a way that made Verne Cramer, the doctor, lay a warning hand on the arm of his seat mate, Johnny DeWilton of Vermont, "is going to enforce the regular order and the regular constitutional procedures, he will say *that* to the Senator—"

"Mr. President," Fred Van Ackerman demanded, his eyes glistening bright with battle, "I move that the Senate debate the impeachment move against our great President."

"The Senator is out of order!" Lacey Pollard cried angrily.

"I appeal the ruling of the chair, Mr. President!" Fred said.

"VOTE!" cried what the Congressional Record would refer to next day as MANY SENATORS.

"Question!" said Arly Richardson, suddenly capitulating and scuttling back to join the group.

"Mr. *President!*" shouted Bob Munson with a furious indignation.

"Question!" shouted Arly and others.

"Regular order!" shouted Lafe, Cullee, Warren Strickland and others.

"QUESTION!" roared Arly and friends.

"The Clerk," Lacey Pollard said, struggling ever more noticeably to control his breathing, "will call the roll."

"And now, Mr. President," Senator Van Ackerman said triumphantly a few minutes later into the hush of the suddenly silent, temporarily exhausted Senate, "let us turn to this most inexcusably vicious attack upon the President which is presently under way in the other body. Let us send the word so clearly and loudly that even a grotesquely vindictive ex-President can hear it, that it will do him and his friends no good to try to impeach Edward M. Jason because *we won't have it.* Send them word to *stop their nonsense and leave our leader alone!*"

"Mr. Speaker," William Abbott said solemnly into the suddenly silent, temporarily exhausted House, "the President's men have done his bidding: they have let him make a tiny gesture toward the security of the nation, and they have combined their forces to bury it without trace, thereby relieving him of the embarrassment of following through on something he never really said, anyway. If anything ever demonstrated why this man should be impeached, this episode is it. And," he said with a sudden significant change in tone which caught the attention of even those who despised him most, "there are other things."

But as the afternoon drew on, baffling Walter Dobius who sat above in the Press Gallery and stared down intently like some somber little buddha, he did not go into them, nor did he, really, even remotely hint. Walter did not understand why, but the reason, in Bill Abbott's mind, was quite simple and quite overriding: there still remained, in himself and a good many others of the older generation in politics, some basic decency which made them recoil from using upon their opponents the ultimate weapons they might possess.

A Fred Van Ackerman in such a situation would not have hesitated. Even a Bronson Bernard, whose youthful righteousness infuriated the ex-President even though he could not help but respect its essential innocence, might have been strongly tempted. But most of the older hands were still playing the game the way they had always played it: roughly, sometimes, but still with some essential decency which, as they were beginning to suspect—though it was too late to remedy— disqualified them in the new world of the new breed that was closing down, with terrifying rapidity, upon America.

So as Walter passed back and forth across the Capitol during the afternoon from House to Senate, listening to a bit of the debate on one side, following it for a while on the other, the conviction began to grow that it was going to be up to him. It was not clear to him, just yet, exactly how he would use his knowledge. But he knew he must.

At one point, around 5 P.M. when the House debate had lapsed into one of the exhausted lows that came quite regularly between the emotional peaks as Edward Jason's critics battled with his friends, he felt he had to confirm this impression. He went to the press lobby and sent in word to William Abbott. The ex-President came out at once and they retired to a couple of chairs among the newspaper racks, in the members' reading room just off the floor.

"Why don't you use it?" Walter demanded without preliminary, his voice lowered, face carefully impassive against the curious glances coming their way from other members, some of them strongly pro-Jason.

"Walter," Bill Abbott said simply, "I can't do it. Not on the floor of the House in public debate. I'm sorry, but I just can't do it. My resolution's lost anyway, we all know that, and it would just be attacking a man terribly to no real purpose—at least for no purpose of the debate. I can't do it, because basically, I guess, I'm sorry for the poor bastard." He smiled and shook his head with a wry disbelief. "I am actually sorry for Edward Jason, though I think he is the man who has—probably already, beyond recall—destroyed America. How's that for one of life's little ironies?" He lost the smile, made no pretense to hide his somber expression, which matched Walter's own, from the observant eyes all around. "I tell you what I'll do, though. I'll go to the White House with you and we'll confront him with it. I think Bob and Warren may want to go too."

"Another of these endless little delegations calling on the President that don't do any good?" Walter inquired bitterly.

"Walter," Bill Abbott said, "*something* has got to reach that man. It has just got to."

"What time?"

"Tonight. As soon as the debate ends in both houses. Whenever it ends: midnight, one, two—no matter. We'll go. There's no time left to space things out gracefully, it's all moving too fast. As soon as we're free, we'll go."

Walter studied him for a long moment. Then he shook his head with a sudden decisiveness.

"No, I guess not. I'll go by myself."

"Why?" the ex-President asked blankly.

"I just feel I have an obligation. On behalf of myself—and the media —and a lot of people. I think I'd rather see him alone."

It was William Abbott's turn to study him. Finally he nodded.

"Very well. But call me and let me know right away what the results are, please. And, Walter—don't get yourself too far out on a limb. These really are dangerous times. You have the proof that some people are not stopping at anything."

"Is cowardice the answer?" Walter inquired. "It isn't for you. Or caution, either."

"No," the ex-President said slowly. "But I have certain protections, still."

"I think I do, too," Walter said. "And if I don't—" he shrugged, his eyes suddenly bleak—"well, maybe I deserve it."

"Be careful," William Abbott said. "Be very careful."

He stood up quickly, shook hands, departed.

Walter, staring blankly at the other occupants of the room as though he did not see them, as perhaps he didn't, departed too.

"Mr. Speaker," Bronson Bernard said shortly before 8 P.M., "we are nearing the end of this historic debate, and I submit that the proponents of this impeachment resolution have not produced one single piece of evidence to warrant any such drastic, preposterous and fantastic action as they propose. All they have succeeded in doing is to demonstrate the paucity of their own arguments. Against that standard, Edward M. Jason towers like a giant: peace lover, peacemaker, statesman, leader. The gall of this proposal, Mr. Speaker! The monstrous, sheer, unadulterated, unmitigated presumption of it! How dare the ex-President and his friends? How dare they?"

"How dare they?" Fred Van Ackerman cried, taking the floor once more after the three new Senators from Minnesota, Wisconsin and South Dakota had joined him in ringing denunciations of the impeachment group, ringing defenses of Edward M. Jason. "How dare this cabal—this corrupt, evil, sinister cabal that has found its inspiration and guide in a jealous old man in the other body—how dare this cabal attempt to besmirch and demean—attempt to actually *throw out of office*—one of the greatest patriots who ever sat at 1600 Pennsylvania Avenue? It is impossible to believe unless they have gone insane, Mr. President. I think they have. I am convinced of it."

"Mr. President," Cullee Hamilton said patiently, "will the Senator yield?"

"No, I won't!" Fred cried, his sudden upward-soaring hysteria beginning to break through. "No, I won't yield to the Senator from California who is such a lackey for the cabal! A lackey, Mr. President, a lackey! . . . Mr. President," he said, abruptly calm again, "I have a resolution here I want to offer and I ask for its immediate consideration."

"Now, Mr. President—" Bob Munson began.

"I offer it, Mr. President," Senator Van Ackerman said, "and I am going to read it. And then I am going to insist on a vote. It reads as follows:

"Whereas, a sinister attack has been launched upon the President of the United States by certain unprincipled members of the other body; and Whereas, this attack has taken the form of a completely partisan and unjustified resolution of impeachment; and Whereas, the President of the United States is striving with all his heart and soul, with all his integrity and honor, to bring peace to the world and should not be hampered by partisan attacks of this nature from enemies who hope to thwart his plans for peace; and, Whereas, the aforesaid resolution of impeachment is indeed such a hampering and partisan attempt; Now, therefore, be it resolved by the Senate that the Senate approves of the policies of peace being followed by the President of the United States, condemns without reservation the resolution of impeachment offered in the other body, and declares the sense of the Senate that if such resolution should pass the House and come to the Senate, it will be rejected by the Senate, and declared null and void by the Senate, and no trial of impeachment of the President of the United States will be held thereunder."

("How's that for being unconstitutional, out of order and generally no damned good?" the Chicago *Tribune* inquired wryly of the Honolulu *Star-Bulletin.* "*And* lovable, into the bargain," the *Star-Bulletin* said. "We should have cut him down years ago," the *Post* said. "You were too busy working on Orrin Knox and people like that," the *Star-Bulletin* remarked; "meanwhile, your little friend crept up. It's too late to catch him now." "I hope to hell not," the *Post* said. "A truly pious hope," said the *Star-Bulletin,* "but not one I'm putting any money on.")

"Mr. President," the new junior Senator from Massachusetts asked cautiously into the silence that had fallen upon the chamber, "is a resolution like that possible? I mean, I'm new here, and I don't know all the ropes, but I have the impression that if the House passes an impeachment resolution, we don't have any choice. We have to try it, don't we?"

"Certainly," Lacey Pollard said tartly. "The Senator is absolutely correct. There is no way out of it. The resolution of the Senator from Wyoming is absurd."

"Oh, it is, is it?" Fred Van Ackerman cried, his voice sailing again into its ranting register. "Absurd, is that what the president pro tempore calls it? Is that what our great, distinguished presiding officer has to comment, just an empty word like 'absurd?' Well, I'll tell you who's absurd, Mr. President: you are! Utterly and completely and beyond any peradventure of a doubt. An old," he said with deliberate cruelty, "out-of-date, used-up, absurd leftover from an earlier time—and not such a worthy time, either. You won't be here after the election two years from now, you know that, don't you, Senator? The voters of Texas are going to retire you because you're so absurd. That's what's going to happen!"

("What the hell is Fred taking after Lacey for?" Johnny DeWilton murmured to Verne Cramer. "I don't know," Verne Cramer said in a worried voice, "but Lace had better watch it or he's going to have a heart attack, and I'm not kidding.")

For a moment, indeed, it seemed that he might right then and there; but somehow, aided by years of discipline in Senate debates, many of which he had successfully dominated in his younger days, he managed to display a reasonable calm as he said quietly,

"I shall not dignify the Senator's remarks by any answer. His resolution is absurd and falls of its own weight. Surely the Senate has better things to do than waste its time on such an absurdity."

"There you *go* again," Fred said with a furious impatience. "I *told* you not to use that word on me, being so absurd yourself."

"Mr. *President*," Bob Munson said, "I must insist that the Senator take his seat if he is going to use such insulting language to the chair, or to anyone else on this floor. We can't have any kind of debate if Senators descend to billingsgate. It destroys the whole democratic process."

"Destroys the democratic process?" Fred cried, and here and there over the floor came a snicker of supporting laughter from some of his new young colleagues. "Who is destroying the democratic process, I will ask the chair? The democratic process has recently elected a great President who is trying to bring the world to peace. But great noble Senators here and little noble Representatives over *there*—" and he flung out a contemptuous arm in the direction of the House—"are doing their best to cancel the democratic process with a resolution that says to the American people, 'No, you made a mistake, you can't have your great President, we're going to take him away from you with a sinister, evil, partisan impeachment.' How does that square with your great democratic process, Mr. President? Is that democracy?"

"The chair is not going to engage in debate with the junior Senator from Wyoming," Lacey Pollard said in his most dignified voice. "He has done that before, many times, and has always come away defiled by the pitch which he has touched."

"Senators!" Fred cried, turning to face the attentive circle of faces, back to the chair, arms upraised in anger and indignation. "Senators! You heard the language just used upon me by the president pro tempore of this Senate! Is that what we want as president pro tempore? Is that what we want to preside over this Senate? Is that—that—*individual*—what we want to represent us to the world? *That* is the presiding officer of the United States Senate? My *God,* how low can we get!"

("What's he up to?" Stanley Danta murmured to Bob Munson, and Bob Munson gave him a worried frown. "I don't know. He's trying to do something to Lacey, I don't know quite why." "*I* do." Stanley said with a sudden conviction. "By God, *I* do." After a second Bob Munson nodded and rose to his feet.)

"Mr. President," he said, "will the Senator from Wyoming yield to me?"

"For what purpose?" Senator Van Ackerman demanded suspiciously.

"To put an end to this bullyragging of a man old enough to be the Senator's father," Senator Munson said coldly, "and get on with the business of the Senate."

"He *is* the business of the Senate!" Fred Van Ackerman cried. "We don't *have* any other business at this moment more important than the character and ability—and, yes, the alertness, since the Senator mentions age, I didn't—the alertness of our president pro tempore. What else is more important to this Senate?"

"I thought the Senator's resolution about impeachment was," Senator Munson said scornfully. Fred Van Ackerman rounded on him with an angry stare.

"The Senator, and some other Senators too, and some members of the House, can be just too clever for their own good one of these days! Just too clever! All right, then, if my resolution bothers the Senator, I'll withdraw it for a little while until we get this matter settled. I do so withdraw it, Mr. President. Temporarily, I withdraw it."

"The Senator has withdrawn his resolution," Lacey Pollard said with a scorn as withering as Bob Munson's, "knowing full well that it was an impossible resolution, an unconstitutional resolution which could not possibly have been passed. He was only threatening the House, I think, only making mischief. That is all the Senator was doing, trying to muddy the waters, stir up the country and make mischief. Not a very worthy pastime for a United States Senator, I think. Not a very worthy pastime."

"Mr. President," Senator Van Ackerman said, not quite concealing the triumph in his voice, "I move that the office of president pro tempore of the Senate be declared vacant immediately and that the Senate proceed forthwith to the election of a new president pro tempore."

("So *that's* his game," the L. A. *Times* said in a tone of utter disbelief to the AP. "He'll never do it," the AP predicted grimly. "You hope to God," said the L. A. *Times*.)

It was obvious the same thought had leaped instantly into the minds of many of the older members. They were astounded by the sheer audacity of it. No one would ever know whether Fred had been carrying the plan in his head right along or had simply seized on a target of opportunity, but its ultimate implications were clear enough: the president pro tempore of the Senate was third in line for the Presidency, following the Vice President and the Speaker of the House.

It was no wonder at least a dozen Senators were on their feet at the same moment, all shouting, "Mr. President! Mr. President!" in a frantic attempt to gain recognition.

"The distinguished Minority Leader, the Senator from Idaho," Lacey Pollard said, his face suffused with its overrosy glow, his voice husky as his breath grew shorter with strain and excitement.

Warren Strickland turned to face the Senate.

"Senators," he said, "I shall not waste the time of the Senate with any lengthy attack on the motion of the junior Senator from Wyoming. The least important thing to say against it is that it is out of all order and tradition of the Senate. But since—" he raised a hand instantly with a grimly ironic little smile to meet the murmur that greeted the words— "since we appear to be entering upon an era in which the order and tradition of the Senate do not mean very much to many of its members, that is a minor thing. Much more serious is the fact that the motion, if it succeeds, will simply throw the Senate into a bitter and divisive battle at a moment when we, like all agencies of government and all Americans everywhere, should be concentrating on just one thing, namely: how do we get the country out of the terrible pickle it is in?

"What is the point in changing the president pro tempore at the present time? Simply to satisfy the pique of the junior Senator from Wyoming? Many of you are new here, but we who are veterans can assure you that there is no point in trying to do this, for he has a pique that springs up at any hour, for any cause, on any occasion. It is impossible to satisfy him. And, Mr. President," he said with a sudden gravity as Fred Van Ackerman stared at him with a blankly angry scowl, "it could very well prove very dangerous to do so. Because it is obvious, at least to many of the older hands here, that he is out for much bigger game than the scalp of Senator Pollard. Taken together with the far-reaching authority over civilian thought just granted him by the President of the United States, it becomes a downright ominous thing."

"Mr. President," said the new young Senator from South Dakota, rising from his seat with an earnest if somewhat elaborate manner, "will the Senator yield? Could the Senator explain something that has struck me as very curious, since I've arrived here? There seems to be a very strong and very personal undercurrent of dislike, among the older members, for the Senator from Wyoming. Yet as far as I know, and as far as I have been able to see—and I think this applies to a good many of us newcomers, Mr. President, because we've had some discussions about it in the past few days—he doesn't appear all that bad. Sometimes he's a little outspoken and a little overvigorous, maybe. But outspokenness could be considered honest candor, and vigor could be considered a virtue, in the strenuous world of legislative battle. Why is it, I wonder if the Minority Leader could tell me, that so many of his seniors despise him? It tends to make many of us newcomers rather sympathetic towards him, I think. I wonder why it is?"

For a moment Warren Strickland did not answer, as through his and other veteran minds passed the sad story of the death of Brigham Anderson and all the bitter, unhappy memories surrounding Robert A. Leffingwell's first nomination to be Secretary of State. For a second he was tempted to try to explain. But how could you, if your listeners were not really interested, and if you knew you could not convince them? Brigham Anderson was only a name in old newspapers to them— Bob Leffingwell actually was Secretary of State, now—what had all the fuss been about?

He sighed, so impossible was it to convey to these bright young men why the Senate had acted as it did then, and why it had all been so important and had so many implications reaching to the very heart of U.S.-Soviet relations in those days so recently past.

The era was already as dead as Brig himself.

"I could say many things on that subject," he remarked finally, "but you would not understand them and you would not believe them. Suffice it to say that resentment, in the opinion of many here, is well-founded. And suspicion of motives and future intentions, is, we believe, well-justified on the basis of past behavior. That is not the issue here today, however—"

"Oh, yes, it is, Mr. President!" Fred cried, interrupting without even the minimal courtesy of seeking recognition. "Oh, yes, it is! There is a little clique in this Senate which is out to get me for one reason pure and simple: because I am the President's man, and any way they can strike at the President is fine, in their minds. Why, Senators!—" and he turned again to face the Senate, appealing to it directly, "do you suppose there would be this animosity against me if I didn't support Edward M. Jason, the greatest statesman we have ever had in the White House? Do you suppose if I hadn't been actively leading his campaign for the Presidency ever since—yes, even before—yes, *well* before—he announced his intention to run, that they would be attempting to stop me now? Do you think if he hadn't entrusted me with great responsibilities to assure domestic peace and tranquillity so that he can have the climate of cooperation in which to put forward his great plans for peace, that they would be hostile to me now?

"Oh, no, Senators! Oh, no! That wouldn't be their game. What is their game? *It's to discredit and eliminate Edward M. Jason,* that's what it is! Fred Van Ackerman is just an incidental, just a convenient little whipping boy. *It's to eliminate Ted Jason,* and don't you let them tell you differently! Watch it, I say to you new, earnest, sincere, liberal young Senators who have just taken your seats! Watch out for this old mossback, reactionary, vicious clique which is trying to run this Senate! You went a long way toward cleaning house when you voted out that *great* statesman, the *distinguished* Senator from Michigan as Majority Leader. That cleared the way enormously for the President's programs, just as he said it would. *That's why you did it.* Now let's clean house the rest of the way! Let's get rid of the last holdover! Let's eliminate the last mossback! Let's don't let them kid you into eliminating Edward M. Jason in the guise of an attack on Fred Van Ackerman! You know better than that!"

And he sat down with a shrewdly triumphant look as many on the floor and in the crowded galleries burst spontaneously into applause.

For a couple of minutes there was no response from the scattered remnants of what worried members of the media were rapidly coming to think of as "the old Senate"—the Senate that had mustered sufficient moral indignation and integrity to censure Fred for blackmailing Brigham Anderson to death; the Senate that had nurtured doggedly a certain concept of what America ought to be in the world; the Senate that had acted, in its slow, rather stodgy, but ultimately just way, like the Senate. That Senate had vanished, decimated and revolutionized by the landslide victory and coattails of Edward M. Jason.

This was "the new Senate." In it, Fred would have to capture the votes of most of the freshman members on both sides of the aisle, plus a good number of the holdovers as well.

Troubled hunch and frightened instinct told experienced observers that he might well do it. While there remained perhaps forty who despised him, there were many in both parties who leaned in his general political direction, many who believed in "You've got to support the President," many who were skeptical, for reasons of philosophic disagreement or youthful resentment or long-held grudge, of the old guard that had for so long run the Senate. It was obvious that in the last couple of minutes he had made enormous headway with his cleverly aggressive statement.

In this unhappy realization, those members of the Senate who feared and disliked the Senator from Wyoming looked instinctively to the man who had led them for more than a decade. Convinced with a cold sickness in his heart that it was already a lost cause, Bob Munson stood up slowly and with meticulous care addressed the chair.

"Mr. President," he said, "do I have the floor?"

"The chair recognizes the distinguished Senator from Michigan," Lacey Pollard said, in a tone so unconsciously but openly woebegone that for a moment there was a little flicker of amusement, not kind, across floor and galleries. Bob Munson waited gravely for it to pass and then spoke with a solemn and somber mien.

"Mr. President, the junior Senator from Wyoming says some are attempting to attack the President through him. That is not the issue. We are trying to stop the increasing acquisition of power by a Senator who is ruthless, unprincipled and, many of us believe, inimical to the basic principles and human decencies of the democratic system as it has been practiced for more than two hundred years in America.

"No, Senator!" he said sharply as Fred leaped to his feet and opened his mouth to start an indignant clamor. "Don't try to yell about my language or get high and mighty about my saying personal things about you. No one has done more in the past six years to lower the tone of debate in this body than you have, and we're not going to waste time on your phony complaints after the language you have consistently used on other Senators, both today and in the past. So sit down. I'm going to speak your own language now. Is that clear?"

"Mr. President—" Fred began furiously.

"*Is that clear?*" Bob Munson shouted suddenly, an open hatred his friends had never heard before in his voice. That, too, was deeply disturbing, for it indicated as well as anything how things were disintegrating on the Hill under the pressures of the times.

"Well—" Fred said; and dropped it as abruptly as he had begun, shrugging with an elaborate indifference as he sat down.

"Now, Mr. President," Senator Munson said, mastering himself with an obvious great difficulty, "whether new members here see it or not, there is a pattern in these recent days. A very sinister pattern, in the judgment of many Americans, including some here who have known the Senator from Wyoming a lot longer than you have. His organization known as NAWAC has become openly hostile, openly threatening. A dictatorial measure has been imposed. Mrs. Knox has been murdered. Extraordinary powers over the citizenry and over the media have been granted the Senator from Wyoming. Justice Davis has died at a very opportune moment—"

Again Fred started to surge angrily to his feet, but the new young Senator from Oregon beat him to it; and after a second, realizing he had allies eager to do his work for him, he sat slowly down again.

"Mr. President!" cried the young Senator from Oregon. "Oh, Mr. President! Surely, *surely* the Senator from Michigan is not implying that there was something sinister in Justice Davis' unfortunate death! Surely he is not attempting to link the Senator from Wyoming to all these events which he sees as sinister. Surely he is not charging that the Senator had a hand in all these things. Now, that is too much, Mr. President! That is *too* much. I don't know how other Senators are affected, but as for me, I've had it. The Senator from Wyoming might be the worst man who ever sat in this body, but when the Senator from Michigan says things like that, I just rebel and refuse to go along with him. I just can't take it, Mr. President. It's too much."

Again there was an explosion of applause from the galleries; and at Bob Munson's side Lafe Smith whispered worriedly, "He's probably right, Bob." But the Senator from Michigan was no longer as rational and well-balanced a debater, no longer as shrewd a manager of the Senate, as he used to be. His own defeat and the anguish of these terrible days had finally got to him. He plunged ahead.

"Senators say they just can't take it, Mr. President. What have the Senate and the country had to take from this individual already? What more will they have to take in the days ahead? His influence is evil now, it has always been evil. But there is one difference: before, he was powerless, even in this Senate—except to do mischief, which maybe was power enough. Now he is getting power outside, real power, and the mischief he can do is growing in geometric proportion to the power he is acquiring.

"We cannot stop the President giving him power. That is one more of the many baffling destructive decisions this President has taken in the last few days. But we can stop the Senate from giving him power—"

"Oh, no, you can't!" said the new young Senator from Arkansas in a half whisper that cut sharply across Bob Munson's voice and brought a murmur of ironic laughter in its wake.

"We can try!" Bob Munson said angrily. "By God, we can try! Because mark you, my smug new friends, mark you: this Senate knows the Senator from Wyoming, and it knows what he is like and—"

"Mr. President," the earnest young Senator from South Dakota said smoothly, "will the Senator yield? I repeat what I said a while ago— *we* don't know the Senator, and *we* don't know what he is like, and why should *we* believe all these hostile and unfriendly statements about him? I repeat, I'm baffled. It doesn't add up, somehow."

"It wouldn't be, would it," the young Senator from Oregon inquired with an exaggerated naivete, "that older Senators simply disagree with a liberal? Because if that's the case—" he grinned amicably, and a number of his freshman colleagues joined him in pleasant laughter, "good heavens, there are a lot of us here who are in for a hard time!"

"The Senator is deliberately reaching for something to confuse the issue!" Bob Munson snapped. "No one here has discussed the Senator from Wyoming's liberalism, or lack of it. There are some of us, I say for the information of the Senator from Oregon, who were 'liberals' while the Senator from Wyoming was in nursery school. Real liberals. Genuine ones. People who favored social progress and worked for it, fought for programs, put laws on the books—really made liberalism mean something. And at the same time remembered that personal liberty makes for social progress and not the other way around; and that when there has to be a choice, personal liberty has to come first, or the whole thing goes under. That's the kind of liberals we are, I will say to the Senator from Oregon. His friend is far from that."

"Mr. President," the Senator from Oregon said smoothly, "now I think the Senator is just being disingenuous. He knows and we know that the motivations behind this unwarranted and unfair attack upon the Senator from Wyoming are exactly what the Senator from Wyoming says: he backs the President and he's a liberal. All else is so much chaff. I think the Senator from Wyoming has a very good point about cleaning house. Why don't we get on with it without a lot more talk?"

"Because I have a right to talk!" Bob Munson said angrily. "Because that's what the Senate is all about—talk, the right to be heard, the right to express a viewpoint, the right to agree or dissent. And that, I suspect, is what the move of the Senator from Wyoming is all about, too. He—and presumably his President—wants to bring this Senate under control and stop it from talking. It's too uncomfortable, too bothersome, all this opposition, so out with it! Plus another factor: that the Senator from Wyoming sees another opportunity on the horizon. President pro tem of the Senate isn't all that important an office, except in one contingency. We all know what it is."

"Oh, Mr. President!" the Senator from Oregon said with a mocking laugh. "Is the Senator from Wyoming really engaged in a deep dark plot to make himself President? Then why doesn't he support the resolution of impeachment instead of doing his best to block it? Why doesn't he join this slimy campaign to scuttle Ted Jason? If that's his game, Mr. President, he's missing a big bet, it seems to me, a really big bet. . . . No, Mr. President, with all respect to the Senator from Michigan, I think he's outstayed his time and his welcome and his purpose for being around here. I think many of us," he added blandly, "feel the same way about you, Mr. President. Can't we have a vote? Please?"

"Mr. President," Senator Munson said with a harsh contempt, "Senators who connive in what is going on here at this moment have no conception of what they are engaged in. They have no background, no perspective, no understanding. They are being led like lambs to the slaughter."

"And, Mr. President," the Senator from Oregon said with a bored humor, "no doubt they will live to rue the day, right? Can't we have a vote, Mr. President? Please?"

And from floor and galleries he received support as many Senators and many visitors joined in an impatient cry of "VOTE! VOTE!"

"Mr. President," Bob Munson said angrily, "I yield the floor, but before I do I will just say this: the Senate is at a turning point this afternoon. Very likely the country is too. New Senators here take it all very lightly, full of fun and frippery. Many of them are obviously not subject to persuasion, I can see that. To those who are less closed-minded, and to all who are veterans here, I say only: much more rides on this than whether the Senator from Texas stays or goes as president pro tempore. Think, I beg of you, *think*. We *must* think. The hour," he concluded somberly into the momentary hush that greeted his impassioned peroration, "grows very late."

"VOTE!" came again the cry that was becoming characteristic of these turbulent days in which the methods of democracy were being used shrewdly and skillfully to drive democracy down. "VOTE! VOTE!"

"I'm afraid I overdid it," he confessed gloomily to Lafe Smith as he settled back in his chair. "But—" his face became contorted for a second with a look of naked hatred he made no attempt to conceal from the now sympathetic and avidly watching press, "I despise him so."

"He is an evil, evil man," Lafe said in a comforting tone, though he agreed with Bob's own analysis of his performance. "You did the best you could in the face of this crew. Listen to them!"

"VOTE!" demanded the galleries, and "VOTE!" demanded many on the floor.

For several moments Lacey Pollard looked about him with an angry and affronted glare.

"In a minute," he said finally in his dignified old voice, and there was something about it, heavy and shaking with emotion, about his overflushed face and about his manner, almost painfully dragging and slow, that silenced the clamor and made Verne Cramer again stir uneasily in his seat. "In a minute, we shall vote. But first I think I have a right to say a word or two in my own defense, and in defense of the Senate. You will grant me that, I hope. If you don't, I shall say it anyway. . . .

"Now," he said, and the voice that had so often thundered to the Senate suddenly lost its strength and sounded weak and strained, "I am being personally attacked, and through me, this Senate is being attacked as an institution. As for me, I can take it, although it comes as a bitter thing at my age, which is seventy-seven, after thirty-two years of honorable and I hope effective service in this body.

"It comes as a bitter thing because I am not being attacked for my personal merits or demerits, or even because, as he so kindly phrases it, the Senator from Wyoming considers me an 'out-of-date, used-up, absurd leftover from an earlier time.' Oh, no, that isn't it. The reason I, together with old friends here who believe as I do, am under attack, is *because we are in his way*. More or less incidentally—because I don't think the two are parallel at all in spite of his shouting about it—we are in the President's way.

"I say 'more or less incidentally' because I don't think the Senator from Wyoming really cares whether the President lives or dies, or whether he succeeds—" there was a start of harsh and ominous booing but he overrode it with a trace of the old fire for a moment—"whether the President succeeds or fails. His success, I think, would be worse than his failure, in the mind of the Senator from Wyoming.

"The success of the Senator from Wyoming would be dreadful for this Senate and dreadful for the country.

"That is why it is mightily important that this vote be carried against the motion of the Senator from Wyoming. Not because I am an issue. Not because my age or my political philosophy is an issue. But because it would open the way for domination of the Senate by the Executive, and even more important—more desperately important—it would open the way, potentially, to put the Senator from Wyoming in direct line of succession to an office which I hope and pray to God he may never even remotely come near to occupying."

"Mr. President!" Fred Van Ackerman shouted triumphantly as again the dutiful chorus of boos began. "Mr. President, I challenge you on that point! Look who is talking, Senators, about the line of succession! *Look* who is talking! A man seventy-seven years old, who disagrees entirely with the President in every respect, who stands three heart-beats away from the Presidency, who may die at any minute—yes, Senators, *any minute*—that man has the infinite gall and presumption to say *he* should be kept on in this most important office. Look at him, Senators, look at him! *Seventy-seven years old! Seventy-seven years old! Seventy-seven years old!*"

And he sat down with a quick, belligerent, satisfied nod as a buzzing started and applause rewarded him.

For what seemed like quite a long time but actually was probably no more than half a minute, Lacey Pollard paused, hesitated, looked about with what appeared a sudden vagueness. Verne Cramer and the Senate's other three doctor members braced themselves. Then he seemed to regain control for a moment.

"I think," he said very slowly, "that when members come to examine closely this proposal . . . I think when Senators . . . it seems to me that when—that when Senators . . . when Senators—"

"Mr. President," Bob Munson said in alarm, jumping up and going forward as did Senator Cramer and his medical colleagues. "Mr. President, let me take the chair—"

And presently Lacey Pollard, breathing heavily, still conscious but appearing dreadfully unwell, was taken out on a stretcher hastily summoned from the office of the Capitol physician; and presently Senator Munson in the chair gaveled for order and found himself confronted by just one Senator seeking recognition.

"The Senator," he said, and his old friends had never heard such a burden of anger, hurt, contempt and dislike in his voice, "from Wyoming."

"Mr. President," Fred Van Ackerman said into the tense silence that held the room, "*now* may we have a vote on my motion?"

And after it had been approved 43–20, with many abstentions, the new young Senator from South Dakota arose and said quietly, "Mr. President, I move that the junior Senator from Wyoming be named president pro tempore of the Senate."

And after the roll call had been taken in the somber hush, Senator Munson announced the result in a voice which he now kept, at great cost, totally devoid of any feeling of any kind.

"The vote is 51 Ayes, 49 Nays, and the junior Senator from Wyoming is hereby declared president pro tempore of the United States Senate."

"And now, Mr. President," Fred said softly, not bothering just yet to come forward and claim the chair, "I reintroduce and call up for an immediate vote my resolution condemning the move to impeach the President of the United States."

And after that too in due course had been approved 53–47, Bob Munson brought down the gavel and declared the session at an end.

Hurrying up the Press Gallery stairs to dash to the teletypes and file this latest bulletin of the day from the Senate side, UPI looked at AP with a deeply troubled glance.

"The Senate has gone insane," he said in a voice both somber and unbelieving.

"The Senate has gone," AP replied, equally somber. "—Period."

And so also, it seemed to those who did not support Edward M. Jason, had the House, which shortly before 9 P.M. voted down 387–136 William Abbott's resolution of impeachment. Its defeat was followed by another hour of speeches, most of them filled with a bitter dislike of the ex-President and his friends, a quiveringly angry and ominously vindictive note of triumph, as opposing members gloated over his repudiation and the endorsement of his successor.

At 10:07, not really knowing quite how he felt about things now that it was all over, Jawbone brought down the gavel with a masterful rap to end the session. At 10:10 Walter Dobius was in a cab on his way to the White House.

3. "SCARCELY TWO YEARS AGO," Frankly Unctuous began his concluding commentary from the House Radio-Television Gallery, "he was censured with unprecedented severity by the Senate and warned in the strongest terms that he would remain a member only on the suffrage of his elders.

"Three months ago he won re-election to the Senate by the very narrowest of margins, leading his opponent by only 106 votes.

"The militant organization for which he serves as principal spokesman is increasingly arrogant, increasingly paramilitary, increasingly dangerous to all the principles that used to be lumped generally under the loose tent of what we have known as 'American democracy.'

"Yet today he stands at the head of the Senate organization as president pro tempore, and in the broader arena of public affairs he has been entrusted by the President with vast and potentially very dangerous powers over the citizenry and the media.

"How has Fred Van Ackerman, junior Senator from Wyoming, done it?

"At first glance it does not seem to make sense—until one takes into account the very strained and peculiar atmosphere in which all Americans are living at this crisis point in their history. Then it fits a pattern of sorts—a pattern which disturbs many Americans greatly, but a pattern which in these hectic days seems to be gaining an increasing hold upon the nation.

"The Senator's censuring by the Senate and near rejection by the voters of his state occurred in one era of American life—prior to the inauguration of President Jason. His election as president pro tempore of the Senate, and his appointment to head the Domestic Tranquillity Board come in another—after the inauguration of President Jason.

"Rarely have two eras been so different, and rarely, perhaps never, has one led so rapidly into, and been so rapidly absorbed by, another.

"Tonight's Senate vote—like the House vote a little later to kill by overwhelming majority ex-President Abbott's resolution of impeachment against President Jason—serves to symbolize the vast confusions that rage through the country at this moment. Many in the Senate still do not like Fred Van Ackerman, many in the House are deeply uneasy about the policies of President Jason. Yet the old appeals to 'support the President—don't rock the boat—uphold national unity' —have combined in a most peculiar way to produce tonight's events.

"Partly the Senator's victory came simply because he saw an opening and was audacious enough to go after it. Senator Lacey Pollard of Texas, whose retirement from the Senate itself will now probably be forced by reasons of health, has served very long in the upper house. His age disturbed some of his colleagues, his conservative record disturbed many of the incoming new liberals in the Senate. When his obvious poor health was added as a factor, Senator Van Ackerman had only to seize the moment and use it to further his own ambitions. The brazen swiftness of it successfully bowled over opposition that might otherwise have formed against him had it had time. Those who know him well enough to dislike him but wanted to support the President, whose man he cleverly pictured himself to be—and, apparently, is— voted for him. Those who do not know him well enough to dislike him voted for him. Those who were uneasy about Senator Pollard voted for him. Those who wanted a change but were given no alternative voted for him. He moved fast, too fast for his opponents: and he won. It is typical of the gambler's streak in him, which has been apparent to all who have reported his activities in the six years he has been in the Senate.

"Now the broader implications enter in. They were touched upon in the debate by the Senator's opponents but in the heat and haste of the moment they were not effective. Sober reflection calls them to mind. Firstly, he is not the most stable of legislators or the most devoted to American liberties. Secondly, he now holds, as president pro tempore of the Senate, the position of being third in line to the Presidency after the Vice President and the Speaker of the House. Presumably the possibility is a very long shot and will never concern the country. But it may—it may. And certainly his general free-wheeling attitude toward traditional democratic procedures must be an immediate worry as he embarks upon the chairmanship of the Domestic Tranquillity Board, with its very broad and very ill-defined authority to encourage a public atmosphere 'conducive' to support of the President's policies.

"Almost lost in today's shuffle was the President's message on national defense—if message it could be called. It was, as some of its opponents accurately said, basically an exercise in window dressing, a collection of clichés which did not add up to the strong call for massive rearmament which such defenders as Speaker of the House J. B. Swarthman attempted valiantly to read into it. Because of its very vagueness, it was easy for the peace faction—or perhaps more accurately the do-nothing faction—to shunt it summarily aside in both houses. So much for the strong call to massive rearmament—another example of the 'strong, decisive leadership' his supporters profess to see in President Edward M. Jason.

"It left the Congress unmoved and the Russians, presumably, not at all deterred from whatever further plans they may have for our discomfort.

"The country is left with a puzzle and a threat. The puzzle is, what further, if anything, does the President contemplate to meet the Communist advance?

"The threat, which now takes its place alongside all the others beleaguered America faces at the moment, is the junior Senator from Wyoming.

"It is not easy to decide at the moment whether the puzzle or the threat poses more problems for this tense and unhappy nation."

And that, Lafe thought as he switched off the set in his new home on Foxhall Road and considered idly for a moment whether or not to mix himself a nightcap, is something you can say again, Frankly, boy.

The threat or the puzzle: which was worse. He decided with a heavy heart that there wasn't really all that much difference between them. Both meant trouble for an already deeply troubled land.

He had been one of those who had wanted to debate the President's message, which could have provided the springboard for a full-scale Congressional review of the last few days' events. But the angry momentum generated against it by Fred had foreclosed this in the Senate, as had Bronnie Bronson's in the House. The message had died the innocuous death which he suspected the President had intended. And Fred's momentum had carried him on to a triumph Lafe would never have believed possible in a million years.

But: there it was. And from it, he knew with an instinctive certainty, many ominous things could flow. Lafe had long ago passed any point of charity with Fred. He did not put anything past him. He was one expert on Fred Van Ackerman who did not consider it at all unlikely that Fred, if he had the chance, would do what he could to shorten the line of succession, now that he had joined it.

Even without anything as melodramatic as that, there was still all the damage he could do as head of the Domestic Tranquillity Board. If Ted Jason exercised no more control over his appointee than he seemed to be exercising over the flow of world events, then God help the democracy, in Lafe's opinion. The job was so ill-defined, as Frankly said, and its potentials for real thought control were so great, that an ambitious and vindictive man could make of it virtually anything he pleased. Fred was both of those and then some. If he worked in close cooperation with George Wattersill and the new Special Branch in the Justice Department, there was almost no limit to what might occur.

And so, what to do? Lafe found himself, like any decent and well-meaning citizen, up against a stone wall when it came to dealing with genuine evil. He had cast his vote in opposition, but once that was done, what else could he do? Fred would be able to do certain things to his opponents, and Lafe had no difficulty at all in imagining what they might be. But Lafe himself could no more imagine himself doing those things to anyone than he could imagine himself flying. Lafe belonged to that great mass of well-meaning people (he suspected, the overwhelming majority of mankind) upon whose hesitant impulses and general inability to recognize and comprehend evil, let alone cope with it, dictators and tyrants build their worlds. He was more sophisticated than many: he could see and believe in the evil. But he was as helpless as they because he could not bring himself to adopt evil's methods to defeat it.

Basically, he was just a human being, like most around the globe, who wanted to go on living his life as peaceably and constructively as he could. He was not equipped to be constantly on guard against the predators of the world, or as ruthless as they in his defenses against them. So the predators grew great, as had ever been the case.

It was a gloomy world, as he saw it tonight from Foxhall Road, and he did not perceive many bright spots in it. He looked about the pleasant, comfortable room and thought of the three people he hoped soon to have here: Mabel Anderson, anxiously and fearfully seeking some safe haven after Brig's dark tragedy, bright little Pidge sparkling about the world like a mischievous sunbeam, Jimmy Fry, locked away in his silent citadel that as yet gave no one entry.

Those three hearts, Lafe thought fiercely, belonged to him; and he wanted them close about him as the icy winds of winter and the even icier winds of history beat in on Washington. It was a time for the good to gather together, it was a time to be close: there appeared to be, even to the most optimistic and well-balanced of people, as he generally was, little else.

He thought of Mabel and Pidge, staying temporarily at the haunted household of the Knoxes in Spring Valley; of Jimmy, temporarily quartered in Bethesda Naval Hospital, undergoing a final checkup before being released to come here to his new home. He thought of himself, one United States Senator, now very much in the minority, struggling desperately against the terrifying downhill slide of his country which every day grew more rapid and more terrifying. And he did not know whether the goodness in four such hearts, combined with the goodness he knew to exist in many millions of other hearts, would be enough to save what must be saved. For the first time in his life he really did not think so. He really saw the possibility that America, always heretofore strong through all her weaknesses, decent through all her indecencies, great through all her faults, might really be coming to an end.

He got up with a sudden angry, impatient movement and started toward the phone. Then he paused, irresolute. He had already called the hospital about Jimmy, found out that he had stood the day well and was sleeping placidly; had already talked once, an uneasy, inconclusive conversation earlier in the evening, with Mabel. Now it was getting on for midnight. There was no point in checking on Jimmy again; the house in Spring Valley would be silent as its occupants tried to sleep and gather strength for Beth's funeral tomorrow afternoon. Who should he call? Why should he call? What good would it do?

Slowly he went to the bar, slowly mixed himself a light bourbon and soda, slowly returned to his chair by the now dying fire. Outside he heard the wind, inside he heard the wind. There was no crevice and no stout heart it did not penetrate, this night.

"Val," Patsy said with a rising exasperation as the family sat in the solarium and looked out through the swirling snow toward the luminous, barely visible sliver of the Washington Monument across the Ellipse, "sometimes I think you are perfectly AWFUL. As if he doesn't have ENOUGH problems, without you coming along and lecturing him like some old *biddy*. He's too kind to tell you so, but you're really just AWFUL."

"You *are* laying it on a little thick, old girl," Herbert agreed, peering at Valuela severely over his glass.

"Yes, Val," Selena said. "It isn't as though it were the end of the *world*, you know."

"The end of a lot of things," Valuela said grimly. "Maybe the world. Anyway, a lot of things. Maybe even America, if her President doesn't do something more than he has done to save her."

"What would you suggest, Val?" he asked quietly, looking as tired as these dreadful days of strain and worry had made him, yet still haggardly handsome, commanding, impressive, statesmanly.

"You have done so many things that seem wrong to me," she said bleakly, "and have let so many things that seem wrong to me either slip by you, or you have actually encouraged them, that I don't know, now, what I would do." She paused, her eyes widened in thought. "If I were sitting in that chair down there"—she gestured toward the Oval Office, below and to their right in the West Wing—"right now, as of this moment, with all that has happened . . . I should make some single symbolic answer to the Russians, I think—maybe bombing their trawlers in Alaska. Then I would weed out all the trash around me, such as Senator Van Ackerman, I would ask Congress to repeal the 'Help America' Act, I would call in all the old, wise heads such as President Abbott, and I would form a national coalition government, insofar as that's possible under our system. And I guess," she added with some bitterness, "that anything *is* possible under our system, these days."

"And then?" he asked, still quietly. "Suppose the Russians retaliated for my bombing their trawlers? Suppose Congress refused to repeal the act? Suppose Abbott and the others refused to serve?"

"They'll serve," she said. "They're desperate to serve . . . It's too late to take counsel of your fears, Ted. You must be resolute—*resolute*. Nothing is left to us but your courage, I'm afraid. And I guess," she said, giving him a sudden penetrating glance, a combination of concern, affection and pity, "there isn't too much of that, right?"

"Val," Patsy said sharply, "you haven't any right—"

He raised a quieting hand. "Yes, she does, Pat." For a moment a little of the old Ted came back. He smiled. "She may be the last guardian of the indomitable Jason legend. We're family; she does. . . . I would just say one thing, though, Val: you don't know all that I know, and you don't have the responsibility that I have." His eyes grew somber and faraway as she replied impatiently.

"No, of course not, of course not, who does? But that doesn't mean that the basic situation changes. That doesn't mean that it doesn't come down to a matter of character in the final analysis. It's your character against the Russians. You're in a worldwide game of bluff, it seems to me. How tough are they? How tough are you? That's the essential."

"But," he began with a sudden anger, "it's past time—past time for—"

"It's never past time for character," she said. "Jasons used to have some."

"Really, old girl," Herbert protested. "Really, you are getting to be too much. He knows what he's doing, now leave him alone. Actually, I can't see it's all that bad. You could look at it as being simply the redressing of a balance in world affairs which for years has been grossly and inexcusably weighted on the side of this country." He gave the sudden, sunny, open smile the photographers had captured in so many peace marches and demonstrations down the years. "Why shouldn't the Russians have their day in the sun? Haven't they got as much right as we?"

"That's exactly what I say," Patsy agreed. "They've been a little crude about it, perhaps, but I can understand their point of view. I expect it will all settle down comfortably before long. If you and all the others, Val," she added sharply, "don't succeed in throwing him completely off balance with this constant caterwauling."

"We've got a law to stop that now, haven't we?" Selena inquired lazily, passing her glass to her brother for a refill. "Watch out, Val!" She chuckled. "You may be in a concentration camp before you know it!"

"Very funny," Valuela said sharply. "Very amusing, I'm sure. You think that's a joke, Sel? You think it isn't going to start happening to people very soon now, with this new law on the books? Ask Senator Van Ackerman. Ted may be an innocent but I'm sure Van Ackerman has plans."

"Oh, bugaboos!" Herbert said grandly, "Bugaboos, bugaboos! Things like that just couldn't happen in America, Val, you know that as well as we do. They just couldn't happen."

"The hell they couldn't," she said. "The hell they couldn't. What's to prevent it? The law is there now. All it needs is the right mentality to operate it. The Senator has that, I'm sure. Why did you appoint him, Ted? Whatever possessed you? In fact, whatever possessed you to sign the bill at all? And then to put a worthless thing like that in a position of such power—it baffles me." She sighed. "It baffles me. You've done such very strange things in the last few days."

"I don't think he's such a thug," Patsy said stoutly. "He was one of the very first to support Ted for the Presidency, and he's always been a fighter for the Right Things. Fred Van Ackerman has been a REAL liberal, Val, and don't you forget it. He may be a little crude, sometimes, and he *does* get a little excited now and then, but basically, he's a good man. A GOOD," she repeated with a burst of enthusiasm that seemed, somehow, a trifle forced, "man."

"You can always count on him to be on the Right Side," Herbert agreed thoughtfully. "He backs the Genuine Causes, Val, you have to admit that."

"He's a thug," Valuela said flatly. "A thug and a disgrace to this Administration. He has been a very dangerous man with his NAWAC association, and now that he's fortified by a law he's going to be even more dangerous. It was a dreadful appointment, just as it's a dreadful law. Neither should have received your support for a minute, Ted. Not a single minute."

He shrugged, a curiously detached and uninvolved gesture that made her give him a sudden sharp look, as though she wondered if he were really with them.

"He has been a faithful supporter," he said, "and George Wattersill, who has direct responsibility for administering the law, wanted him. So I appointed him. I trust George to keep him under control." He smiled with a certain irony. "It would be to his interest to do so, I should think."

"And as for the law, Val," Herbert said, "you must admit there have been most dismaying demonstrations against Ted. Most dismaying. How can he possibly function in such an atmosphere? He has to have some protection, goodness knows. There wouldn't be any kind of government in a tense period like this if everybody was permitted to attack it and try to tear it down. Now, that's just common sense."

"Why wasn't it common sense for them to have a law years ago to stop people like you and Selena from demonstrating against things?" Valuela demanded. "Why shouldn't that have been done long ago?"

"But we always demonstrated against bad things," Herbert said comfortably. "We were on the *Right Side,* Val. It would have been absolutely undemocratic and absolutely *illiberal* to have tried to stop us."

"It would," Selena said firmly, "have been unconstitutional and a terrible threat to our democratic liberties."

"Well, then, why—" Valuela began. Then she stopped abruptly and shook her head in a gesture close to despair. "You are beyond belief. What a rationale. What a rationale! And there are millions of you. Millions!"

"It is a rationale," Selena pointed out with an almost prim smugness, "which has supported the faith and belief of millions of people in this country and abroad for years, Val, simply *years.* You are quite correct on that. We couldn't have kept *going* if we hadn't been able to demonstrate *against* things and *for* things. Nor could this democracy, either."

"That's exactly—" Valuela began. "That's exactly—" Then she stopped and shook her head with a shrug that was genuinely helpless.

"Now, let's stop badgering Ted and let him work it out in his own way," Patsy suggested firmly. "His OWN way, Val. He IS the President and HE knows BEST. So stop badgering. Just stop it!"

Valuela stood up, looked once more through narrowed eyes at the Washington Monument ghostly in the storm. As she did the lights went out, denoting midnight. Nothing was out there now but the cruel wind and the heavy flakes splatting wetly against the big glass windows of the solarium. She turned back to face them, a stout, elderly, rather garish lady, overly made up, overly bejeweled, overly dressed, but possessed of a certain solid dignity nonetheless.

"I think I am going back to the villa in Positano. I'll be leaving early in the morning. I'll probably have breakfast sent to the room, so I expect I won't be seeing you all again for a while. I'll say goodbye now."

"Are you afraid, Val?" Patsy asked tauntingly as they all stood up. "Are you trying to HIDE?"

"No, I'm not afraid," she said. "I'm the Jason who isn't afraid, don't you remember?"

"None of US is afraid either," Patsy said brightly. "What makes you think WE are? I still think you're trying to hide."

"Where is there to hide?" Valuela asked simply. "If they get away with this with the United States, all of Europe will fall to them in six months because there won't be anybody left to protect it. I expect to see Italy go in a week, if that long. . . . No, I'm not going there to hide, I'm just going there to wait it out in my own home, among the things I like best. I'm going there," she said, and for the first time her voice quivered a little, "because I don't want to stay here and see it happen to my own country. . . . Teddy—" she stepped forward, took his head between her hands, kissed him tenderly on the cheek—"my dear—try to be brave, try not to worry too much, try to do what is best. It may yet work out all right for you, and for all of us. God! It has to. . . . Selena—" she gave her sister a quick, impersonal brush of the check—"Herbert—" she did the same—"Patsy—" the same—"everybody, goodbye. I may be back in the spring if everything is all right. If it isn't—" she shrugged, her eyes darkened, she seemed close to tears. But she straightened her back and lifted her head with something of Doña Valuela's own indomitable air. "If it isn't, then I hope you may meet it as I intend to do, with dignity and with courage. Good night, all."

And she turned quickly and left the room.

"WELL!" Patsy said after the door closed. "If THAT wasn't a dramatic farewell!"

"She's always been that way," Selena said indifferently. "She'll get over it when everything calms down again."

"So will we all, I expect," Herbert said cheerfully. "Good night, all, also. I think I shall toddle along. Have to be up and demonstrating tomorrow, you know! Assuming, that is," he said with a complacent irony, "you will permit me to do so, Ted?"

He nodded and managed a smile, more moved by his aunt's valedictory than he wanted them to see.

"It's permissible," he said. "I'll talk to Fred Van Ackerman."

"You do that," Herbert said with a jolly laugh. "You do that very thing! Good night!"

"We're coming along too," Patsy said; and suddenly she too stepped forward and kissed her brother. "You're all right, Teddy. We're your family and WE have faith in you. You can always count on *us*, you know that."

"Right," he said with a quick nod, for it seemed to be all he could manage as they turned away. "Right."

Alone after they left—utterly alone, as he felt in some dark, dimly grasped way he had been ever since Ceil's death—he too stood staring out at the swirling storm. It was very heavy, and for the last few days had been very persistent, blizzards seeming to pile upon blizzards, coming out of the west to savage the continent with record winds, record snowfalls, record temperatures from California to the eastern seaboard. He wondered for a moment if this came from the third table —the weather table, which Tashikov had carefully kept darkened during their talk, but which Tashikov's aides had later illuminated for him with many smirks and satisfied, significant looks. As long ago as the mid-sixties, scientists had been working on controlling the weather for military purposes. By the early seventies they were within sight of their goal. Now, the Russians told him, they had achieved it. He had not believed that, though he believed the rest. It seemed too much a horror, too much the science-fiction nightmare. But the scientists had been working, working, working in their incessant damnable busy, busy way. That was historic fact. It was not at all beyond possibility that they had succeeded. He knew America's own scientists were well within reach of it. Perhaps the Russians had been telling the truth.

Yet in some curious dream sense, as though he were faraway looking down upon himself—that lonely figure in the solarium who bore the hopes of his nation and of all those helpless and defenseless peoples around the world who still, for all their constant bitter criticizing, looked to the American shield for their protection—he did not care. It did not matter. Nothing more could possibly add to the heavy weight he was carrying, nothing more could possibly increase the staggering load of terrors that bore him down. If it were true, it was just one more thing—just one more thing. Just something more to meet, when he already had so much.

Valuela, like most women, oversimplified; but how he wished he could act as simply and directly as she would have him do. The Russians had, he acknowledged that; but they had acted first, using the elements of long-range secret preparation—carefully gathered, overwhelming force—cruel and ruthless surprise. That was not the American way. Americans had been conditioned over many years by their educators and their opinion formers to doubt themselves, question their motives, hesitate, agonize, temporize—retreat. Americans had been conditioned, in fact, to lose. And now, with the greatest idealism and the best will in the world, he had offered the Russians voluntary concessions that could not be taken back, once the Russians had moved, without blowing up the world. And so, under his Presidency, it at last was beginning to seem almost inevitable that America would lose.

Almost—but perhaps not quite. Perhaps there was still something to be found in delay, in equivocation, in playing for time.

He had done what he could to secure its advantages while, it seemed to him, moving in ways still open to him to strengthen his position. And if his position was strengthened, surely that strengthened the position of his country. How could the two be separated?

So he had permitted the Help America bill to go through Congress and had signed it into law: because now, with the situation as desperate as it was, he really could not allow or afford to his domestic opponents the luxury of seeking to interfere with every move he felt compelled to take for the sake of his country. They did not know what he knew, as he had told Valuela. They could not be allowed to interfere, through ignorance, however patriotic and well-meaning. Later on, no doubt, after the crisis had eased somewhat, he could consider requesting a repeal of the law. Right now he felt he really must have domestic peace and tranquillity in the face of the Communist threat, if he was to find the way out.

The action of the Court in upholding the law had confirmed him in his belief. It was true the Court's decision had been essentially negative, 4 to 4, and it was true that Tommy Davis' sudden death from heart strain and overwork had been amazingly fortuitous. And yet might not that, also, be regarded as some indication that he was doing the right thing? Certainly the fact that the Court in any event was so narrowly divided indicated that there was a substantial body of opinion which upheld his point of view and endorsed his actions.

The appointment of George Henry Wattersill to head the new Special Branch in the Justice Department, and the nomination of Fred Van Ackerman to work with him as head of the Domestic Tranquillity Board had to some degree been forced upon him because they were the most vocal and available leaders of the forces that supported him. But he was not as worried as his predecessor and others seemed to be about the two men. George Wattersill was a fatuous fool, basically, and could be controlled. Fred Van Ackerman, though he sensed in him something potentially more dangerous, could be played off against George, and vice versa, to keep him in line. And the President knew, as his uncle knew, that fundamentally there was no real need to fear that the act would be administered unjustly or undemocratically, because this was America, and in America things like that simply just didn't happen. The mere existence and threat of the law, he was sure, would be enough.

And finally, there were the actions of the Congress tonight. He had been dismayed that his supporters had apparently not received the signal in his message on the national defense, that they had, innocent and earnest, insisted on rejecting it as a gesture offensive to their peace-loving souls and offensive to the Russians. But in the long run, maybe their instinct had been right. Maybe, having committed the nation to peace, he should be prepared to stay with it and not flirt, even indirectly, with a return to older, less popular methods. It would take months to rearm anyway—more likely years. All the attempt would have accomplished would have been to annoy the Russians. And that would only complicate his problems more.

He regretted, now, that he had let the ex-President and his friends browbeat him into even that half-militant gesture. It had made him look, to the perceptive who went behind the facade of things, faintly ridiculous; and Ted Jason did not like to look ridiculous. Nor could he afford to, when all he had left to bring to the situation was his own popularity, and the respect a united people might be able to give him, to strengthen his hand.

His popularity, in fact, was the one thing that seemed to be surviving in reasonably good shape. If the Congress represented the people, and that one had to believe, his popularity was doing all right. The votes in the two houses on the impeachment question had demonstrated that. The House had voted directly on the issue and endorsed him overwhelmingly. The Senate had not had any legal right to vote on the matter at that stage at all, yet it had ignored legalities, defied the Constitution and given him equally overwhelming support.

The Congress was united. The people, if not entirely united, were generally for him, and when the Help America Act began to have a real impact, would be even more so. He was still the leader of his country. No one would, or could, take that away from him.

He stood up at last, feeling somewhat better, and was about to turn out the lights and go along to the Lincoln Bedroom when the intercom buzzed beside his chair.

Walter Dobius, they said, was at the East Gate and wanted to see him; and after a moment, startled and once more disturbed and uneasy for reasons he could not quite define, he told them to let him in and bring him along to the solarium. He called the pantry and ordered coffee for two. Then he sat slowly back down in his chair while the storm, taking a yet more savage turn, snarled and tore at the beleaguered old building.

"This is Walter," he said abruptly, and in the Sheraton-Park William Abbott, once again roused abruptly from sleep, said sharply,

"Yes? You've seen him?"

"I've seen him," Walter said slowly.

"And—?"

"Nothing," Walter said, in a tone heavy with unhappiness and disbelief. "Nothing . . . except that he has it, but he can't release it because it would offend the Russians and he doesn't dare do that. . . . His own wife," he said unbelievingly. "*His own wife.*"

"So what are you going to do?"

"I already have a column written. I'm at the *Post* and I'm going to send it out on the syndicate wire right now. He asked me not to, for his sake 'and the sake of the country.' The sake of the country, my God! I don't feel I have any choice."

"Walter," William Abbott said, "be very careful. You know what they can do, now."

"I know what they can do," Walter said bleakly, "but somebody's got to be brave, Bill. *Somebody's* got to be brave. It's so late. So awfully late."

"Can't we all do it together tomorrow?" Bill Abbott suggested.

"No, we can't. We can't because I got hold of it and I feel it's up to me to decide what to do with it, and to take the consequences, whatever they may be. I feel I owe it to myself. I feel I owe it—" he paused and then went on—"I owe it to a lot of people who were probably right . . . when I was wrong. This is the least I can do for them, now, I think . . . the least I can do."

"Be careful," the ex-President urged again.

Walter uttered a wry little sound, somewhere between laughter and desolation.

"The admonition we used to utter in casual joking farewell, back in some other world before Ted Jason—'be careful.' But it's real now, isn't it, Bill? It's real now."

"Let me know if there's anything I can do," the ex-President said earnestly.

"I will," Walter Dobius said, "but don't wait up, because I don't really think there is."

He snapped off the Picturephone, turned back to his typewriter, picked up his column and read it through one last time. He knew it was the most fateful piece of writing he had ever done, both for the country and for himself. He had wasted no time on what his colleagues called "typical Dobius touches," but had reported it straight as it had come to him—in one quick, anonymous, frightened moment in a crowd, and in one quick, anonymous, frightened telephone call of the type that historically had provided the inspiration and basis for much of Washington's investigative reporting.

"This correspondent has learned from sources he believes to be reliable that the President has received an official report linking the deaths of President Harley M. Hudson, Secretary of State Orrin Knox, Mrs. Knox and Mrs. Edward M. Jason to—" (Yes, he had thought wryly, he would have to use the funny words he and his colleagues had scorned and derided so many times over the years, for they were true)

"—a Communist conspiracy whose implications and tentacles stretch directly to domestic and international enemies of the American Republic.

"This correspondent has also learned that there is extremely strong presumptive evidence that the death last night of Justice Davis of the Supreme Court was also caused by this group. It was not, as the Bethesda medical panel pronounced, precipitated by 'absolutely nothing but natural causes.'

"This information, in official form, is on the President's desk.

"If these allegations are true, and this correspondent is convinced that they are, the country has entered upon a time in which political assassination as a method of influencing United States policy to suit Russian purposes is no longer a fantasy. It has arrived, with the grimmest possible implications for all Americans.

"The information concerning the Hudson, Knox and Jason deaths is contained in the report of the official commission appointed by President William Abbott following the assassination of President Hudson. The commission's authority was subsequently extended to cover the deaths of Secretary Knox, Mrs. Jason and Mrs. Knox.

"This reporter received a copy of the top-secret report from an anonymous donor who placed it in his hand last night as he was leaving the Supreme Court after Justice Davis' death and the Court's vote on the 'Help America' Act.

"The donor fled. His action was so hasty that this reporter was unable to see his face or otherwise identify him. But this reporter is convinced, on the face of the report, its language, manner of presentation, certain words and turns of phrases—plus the signatures of commissioners and the experience of a quarter of a century of Washington correspondence—that it is completely authentic.

"Similarly, this reporter is convinced that the anonymous telephone call which he received concerning Justice Davis was also completely authentic. Certain internal evidence in the conversation verified this.

"What the commission report says, in essence, is this:

"The death of President Hudson in the crash of Air Force One at Andrews Air Force base eight months ago was not an accident. The craft's altimeter had been tampered with and there was at least one crew member, more likely three, under instructions to divert the pilot's attention and, if necessary, use force upon him to cause a crash. A companion assassin was waiting at the gate in case this plan failed. The latter individual died in the flaming wreckage along with the President, the crew, several members of Congress, and members of the media.

"The assassinations of Secretary Knox and Mrs. Jason at the Washington Monument Grounds in August were planned and executed by the same group responsible for the death of President Hudson. This group is composed of native America fanatics of the left, some of them in very high positions in the National Anti-War Activities Congress—NAWAC. These native fanatics of the left are working in close conjunction with members of the Russian secret police, the KGB, posing as staff members of the Soviet Embassy in Washington.

"The names of these Americans are known to the FBI.

"So far, the Justice Department has not acted on this information. There is reason to believe it is being restrained from doing so, on the ground that punitive action would be regarded as 'hostile to the Russians' and 'upsetting to the cause of world peace.'

"The commission report further states that the assassination of Mrs. Jason, far from being an accident as most assumed, was in fact a deliberate move to affect severely the morale of President Jason, to make him less able to withstand Russian pressures and more vulnerable to psychological and other moves to weaken his leadership of the United States in the face of a determined Russian challenge.

"It is this correspondent's belief, based upon direct personal observation, that this goal was achieved.

"The murder of Mrs. Knox was part of the same pattern of deliberate terror, in this instance designed to shatter the morale of those who oppose the President's appeasement policies toward the Soviets as expressed in his inaugural address and as implemented by him in the days since.

"The essence of the information received on Justice Davis is this:

"There was found on the inside of the Justice's left ankle a tiny oval lesion which experienced medical examination recognized as the insertion of a syringe into a vein. Blood analysis revealed no trace of poison or other foreign element in the body. Therefore there is a strong conviction among members of the medical panel, even though they suppressed their misgivings because they believed silence to be in the best interests of national stability—" (and also, he could have said but did not, because they were terrified of reprisals)—"that there very likely was injected into the Justice's blood stream the simplest yet most effective of killers—air.

"Well-documented reports over many years from Czechoslovakia, Poland, Hungary, Rumania, Latvia, Lithuania, Estonia, the Soviet Union itself and many other places confirm this as a favored Communist method of inducing so-called 'heart attacks' and 'fatal seizures.'

"This correspondent has seen the President and has urged him personally to release this information to the country. The President, while not questioning or denying the essential facts set forth herein, has refused to do so.

"Therefore this correspondent is releasing them on his own responsibility."

Which, given all the circumstances, was really an extraordinarily brave thing for Walter Dobius to do. But no one, however critical, had ever said that Walter was not a good reporter, or that he lacked personal courage. He had, as many saw it, his faults of interpretation and bias. Inaccuracy and cowardice had never been included among them.

It was a time to be brave, and Walter was. Indeed he felt he had no choice, for he believed he really was witnessing, and participating in, the last days of the American Republic.

As he had foreseen, the consequences were immediate, vast and far-reaching.

COLUMNIST RELEASES SECRET PRESIDENTIAL REPORT ON RECENT POLITICAL DEATHS. DOBIUS CLAIMS PRESIDENT SUPPRESSING DOCUMENT CHARGING COMMUNISTS PLOTTED HUDSON, KNOX, JASON DEATHS. ALLEGES MEDICAL PANEL KNEW JUSTICE DAVIS' DEATH NOT DUE TO NATURAL CAUSES. WORLD SENSATION. WASHINGTON IN UPROAR AS NEW CRISIS HITS JASON ADMINISTRATION.

But though the headlines were cautious—"claims" and "alleges," those two down-putting, skeptical, subtly mocking favorites—that was simply a matter of legal protection. There was no doubt that Walter's colleagues accepted his story completely, and there was no doubt that they were as alarmed by it—and as brave about it—as he.

"The sensational disclosures by world-famous columnist Walter Dobius this morning," the *Times* wrote soberly in an unprecedented front-page editorial accompanying Walter's column, "can only shed a most appalling light on the present domestic state of the country.

"We believe every word of what he says, for we have known and admired Walter Dobius as a stouthearted liberal seeker after truth for more than a quarter of a century. And we believe that he acted nobly and courageously in releasing this shocking material on the tragic deaths of President Harley M. Hudson, Secretary of State Orrin Knox, Mrs. Knox, Mrs. Edward M. Jason and Supreme Court Justice Davis.

"We also believe, though it saddens and disturbs us dreadfully to have to say it, that Mr. Dobius is telling the truth when he says that he has discussed this information with President Jason, and that President Jason has refused to release it officially. We suspect, on the evidence of recent days, as Mr. Dobius does, that this Presidential decision is due to some desperate last-minute fear of 'offending' or 'upsetting' the Soviet Union, thereby jeopardizing what he may still regard as a valid chance for peace.

"Sadly but finally, we must say that we do not agree with this. We have supported Edward M. Jason consistently in his drive to reach the Presidency. We have supported, though with deep concern and misgivings, his idealistic attempt to deal with the Russians on a generous-minded, generous-hearted, truly Christian basis of concession and withdrawal.

"But we can go with him no longer.

"His partisans in the Congress yesterday successfully and overwhelmingly beat back an attempt to remove him from office. We doubt that the outcome would have been any different even had the material released by Mr. Dobius been generally available to the legislators before they voted. It is also highly unlikely that another attempt could be made to impeach him, or that it would be any more successful than that of yesterday. Nor is there anything in the material released by Mr. Dobius which would warrant impeachment. It is only the way the President is handling it which has a bearing; and we doubt if that would be compelling, except with the most astute and perceptive students of men.

"Not too many of those, we are afraid, can be found in the ranks of the generally youthful and inexperienced new members who now, apparently, dominate the Congress.

"But we can, insofar as it lies in our humble power and influence, attempt to stand forth as bravely as Mr. Dobius has done against the President's methods and against his policies.

"We are desperately saddened to have to say it, but we believe Edward M. Jason has failed already as President of the United States; and we believe that all patriotic Americans must now oppose him, as the last means of saving the Republic his policies have already come close to destroying."

Equally emphatic and, at last, equally courageous, was the *Post:*

"The revelations of political assassination and conspiracy by Columnist Walter Dobius would be suspect, if not utterly laughable, coming from any other source. From America's most distinguished political commentator they must command belief, respect and action.

"We have known Mr. Dobius as a great reporter, concerned human being and truly liberal journalist for more than a quarter of a century. We have implicit faith in his accuracy, his integrity and his courage. Although it goes against all of our past convictions and experience, we believe him when he says that a Communist conspiracy was behind the five violent deaths which have disfigured and tortured American politics over the past year.

"We also believe him when he says the President has refused to release this material to the public, for reasons that can only be surmised —in order, we suspect, not to 'antagonize' or 'upset' the Soviet Union. This reason seems to us fundamentally and terribly mistaken. It also seems something more.

"It seems pathetic.

"No political leader, no public institution, no member of the media has been more outspoken, more consistent or more devoted in support of Edward M. Jason than we. No one, we think, has therefore a better right to deplore and criticize when we see him, as it seems to us, abandoning the courage, the decisiveness and the force which may be the only way we can survive in the face of the Russian threat.

"We did not wish to see him impeached yesterday. We do not wish to see him removed from office now. We only wish to see him the strong, fearless, farseeing leader we have always believed him capable of being. But we are finally convinced that he cannot do it alone. We are convinced that his friends do him no favor when they refrain from the criticism and opposition he so obviously needs if his balance, and the nation's, is to be restored.

"For ourselves, we cannot travel further with Edward M. Jason along the path he has chosen for himself and for the country. We accepted his inaugural concessions to the Soviet Union with great misgivings, because they seemed to us too swift, too one-sided, too unprotected by any kind of quid pro quo. We admired the liberal spirit but we were deeply worried about the too-liberal execution. And basically, we were worried about Edward M. Jason himself.

"It makes us grimly unhappy to have to say it, but we have come to the reluctant conclusion that Edward M. Jason is simply not measuring up to the demands of his office. We think he has already made errors which could be fatal to the very survival of the United States. We think he desperately needs the help of his friends. We think that such help can best be given, at this unhappy juncture of his career, not by support but by opposition.

"We call upon all his friends to openly and strongly oppose, as we do, his policies and his methods of handling the crisis—indeed, the whole complicated web of crises, both foreign and domestic—that has grown out of past national errors and his own wishful and well-meaning actions.

"Being wishful and well-meaning is not enough. He has failed us and we must help him. *Now*. By mobilizing public opinion, by bringing pressures to bear upon Congress, by a constant drumbeat of concerned and emphatic opposition.

"He must not lead us one step further down the road of drift. The country simply cannot stand it."

In similar fashion and similar mood wrote many another distinguished journal as the day wore on. In similar mood spoke Frankly Unctuous and his major colleagues of tube and airwave.

It was all very indignant and very brave; and it was all, of course, years too late.

During that day NAWAC and the IDF found themselves swamped with new applications for membership as the national mood turned even more disturbed and ugly.

During that day Edward M. Jason, locked away in his unapproachable house, did not act.

Others did.

It might have been entitled, had there been a wry historian to record it, "The Day They Took the *Times* and the *Post*"; and it posed for many Americans—who did not then have, and would never again have, the opportunity to answer them—many questions:

How would you react, for instance, if you were walking down a street in New York or a street in Washington, and suddenly you saw some sort of disturbance going on at the doors of two distinguished newspapers? Not a big disturbance, you understand, just a minor sort of scuffling, a quick coming and going, a few frightened people, a flurry, a fuss?

Just the sudden arrival at the doors at the same moment in each city, of a couple of police vans . . . the sudden entry into both buildings of small groups of armed and uniformed men . . . a pause of perhaps ten minutes . . . and then the emergence of the uniformed men, hustling along between them a handful of other men, handcuffed or with guns at their backs, obviously angry, terrified, protesting, some dressed in business suits, some with coats off and sleeves rolled up, some, perhaps, crying with a bitter irony, "But this is the Times! *(or the* Post!) *You can't do this to us!" . . . and then a swift clanging and locking of doors, a sudden roaring of engines, a sudden disappearance down the crowded street . . . and then, just visible from the sidewalks, a momentary cluster and swirl of frantic people inside . . . and then their abrupt, hurried, almost furtive dispersal, so that all is quiet again . . . and the streets returning immediately to their normal hustle and bustle, the uncaring rush and hurry of life, after an elapsed time of perhaps a quarter of an hour. . . .*

Just exactly what would you do, in such a circumstance? Would you shout out frantically to your fellow passers-by, "Help! Help! They're taking the Times! *(or the* Post!) *Help, citizens! Help, freedom lovers! Help, fellow believers in American democracy! They're taking— they're taking—they're taking—the press?"*

Would you immediately leap forward, in company with all your fellow citizens, alerted and made knowledgeable by your cry, a great, angry, overwhelming mass, noble and not to be denied, to rescue in savage scuffle, yourselves unarmed against armed and ruthless men, the once arrogant but now wan and horrified souls being dragged off to—who knows what?

Would you, if rescue failed, throw yourselves heroically in front of the vans, the sheer weight of your massed bodies stopping their escaping surge with a sickening and bloody crunch?

Would you cry havoc and let slip the dogs of civil rebellion to save your free press?

Why, no, of course you wouldn't.

In the first place, two thirds of you wouldn't even glance up from your busy scurrying down the streets on your own private affairs.

And of the third of you who did notice, perhaps only a handful would be informed enough and sophisticated enough to have an inkling of what was going on.

And of that handful, half would think, very quickly, Well, it's none of my affair, I'd better get on by just as fast as I can and forget about it, I can't afford to get involved.

And half again would think, Oh, dear, they can't do that, but how can I stop them, oh, dear, I might get hurt, I guess I'd better not try to do anything, oh, dear.

And of the three or four left, perhaps one or two of you might half start forward—and then as abruptly stop, appalled by the unbelievable occasion, paralyzed by the knowledge of your own unarmed vulnerability, aware that you were almost entirely alone, aware that you might very well be instantly shot down. . . .

And so they would take the Times *and the* Post, *and any others across the country they might want to take, in exactly the same way . . . and in the offices so swiftly and smoothly made vacant, other men would suddenly appear, from outside, perhaps, but more likely from other editorial desks, or from obscure offices on other floors, rising from their places in the composing room, or converging swiftly from the library stacks, or entering from the business department—just as they actually have in so many other newsrooms in so many other doomed lands . . . and presently, without the world being aware of even a pause or a hitch, the presses would roll again . . . and next day, just as always in the world where the* Times *and the* Post *and their sister publications are such permanent, immutable and reassuring fixtures, the regular editions would appear, containing editorials, headlines and news stories fervently praising the President of the United States, hailing his Administration and all its works, endorsing his policies in every phase—praising, praising, praising the Russians for their forbearance and cooperation—urging, urging, urging the people of the United States to accept with a docile and unprotesting compliance the yoke so shrewdly, cleverly and unanswerably prepared. . . .*

He had sent out his column, received the first startled phone calls from his colleagues, emphasized his belief in what he had written; received assurances of their belief and support; left his office at the *Post* and walked through the bitter cold to the Metropolitan Club (since it was too late for Roosevelt to come with the car and drive him back to "Salubria"); taken a room and slept fitfully until about eight, when he had arisen, dressed and come down to breakfast.

A few of his fellow members had been in the dining room and one or two of them, carrying the *Post* or the *Times* with their stark headlines, favorable editorials and his column, had come over to shake hands and talk with him for a moment in quiet tones. But the tones were not only quiet, they were muffled, even furtive; and while others in the room had looked at him with startled recognition, they had abruptly looked away and buried themselves in their papers; and with a prickling of his scalp he had realized that there was something new in the Metropolitan Club: fear, as palpable as though he could see its ugly paralyzing presence seeping through the halls and public rooms.

He finished his light meal quickly, signed his check, got his coat, went down to the lobby. There he had the same experience several times with old friends from the Hill or the departments who had never hesitated before to greet and fawn upon him. He knew instinctively that they had believed him—but he knew also that they were afraid to be seen talking to him. This made him sad at first. Then it made him angry. He was tempted to shout, "My God, don't you see we've all got to stand together, otherwise they're going to pick us off one by one?" But you didn't shout in the Metropolitan Club or anywhere else where skeptical, civilized men foregathered in their skeptical, civilized way; and he knew, with a crushing certainty, that it was almost at the point where it no longer mattered: they *were* going to be picked off one by one, anyway.

In five minutes or so Roosevelt arrived, and Walter sensed before he spoke that something was upsetting him.

"What is it?" he demanded sharply.

"Arbella," Roosevelt said tersely as he opened the door and helped him in. "She scared. She scared good and plenty."

"Why?" he demanded again as the doors closed and Roosevelt moved the limousine carefully out into traffic to begin what would be, with snow-clogged streets and snow-clogged country roads, at least an hour and a half drive to "Salubria."

"She dream about you, Mistuh Waltuh," he said. He paused and then added soberly, "An' de house."

"What about the house?" he asked sharply, the familiar knifelike apprehension starting inside.

"You know, Mistuh Waltuh," Roosevelt said quietly. "You know."

"Where is she?" he asked at last.

"Down de road a piece."

"Safe," he said.

Roosevelt nodded.

"Safe."

"Good," he said. *"Hurry."*

"Fas' as I can, Mistuh Waltuh," Roosevelt agreed softly. "Fas' as I can."

But it was not, of course, fast enough.

They passed through Leesburg, turned off on the familiar lane, began the rolling, twisting run along the worn old ruts through the snow piled high on either side. As they neared the final bend in the woods he saw the great pillar of smoke rising above the trees and heard a raucous clanging behind them. The local fire engine slipped and slithered past on the bend, its occupants giving him friendly shouts and encouraging waves. But he knew there was nothing to be encouraged about.

The car turned the bend. Dimly as through a great screen of darkness he heard Roosevelt draw a sudden sharp breath.

Before them they saw all that remained of "Salubria," dancing bright against the sullen sky.

Around 10 P.M. that night, after a day in which the nation hung suspended in fear, foreboding, inaction and uncertainty, there occurred at the gates of St. Elizabeth's insane asylum in southwest Washington an odd and interesting sight. No television cameras were there to record it, no reporters from the *Post*, the *Times*, the *Star-News* or any other publication were on hand avid with their pencils. But the media were well represented, and in a way it was a pity that the distinguished members who were present could not have reported it. For it was a historic jest and jape, filled with the ironic horror that had filled similar occasions in half a hundred other lands.

Five armored vans drew up to the door. Fifty-six men under heavy guard were brought out.

It could have been observed, had anyone other than the wardens been there to watch it, that four of them had very familiar faces: one was Frankly Unctuous, the other two were his ranking news-commentary colleagues from the other networks, the fourth was Walter Dobius, whose picture had appeared at the head of his column for twenty-five years. The others had rarely appeared before the general public, so they might not have been recognized: general directors, editors, publishers, leading reporters and editorialists of the *Times*, the *Post*, the Associated Press, United Press International, *The Greatest Publication*, the New York *Post*, the Boston *Globe*, the St. Louis *Post-Dispatch*, the Los Angeles *Times*, the San Francisco *Chronicle*. All were disheveled, distraught, looking as though they might indeed be on the verge of taking leave of their senses, shivering in the wind.

Just as they were about to be hurried through the gates a small Mercedes-Benz drew up. A guard went forward deferentially and opened its door. The president pro tempore of the United States Senate got out, on his face a smile happy, triumphant, almost innocent, like that of some horrible child about to pull the wings off butterflies.

"I just wanted to say, gentlemen," he said with a savage joviality, "welcome to your new home. Don't be lonely. We're rounding up other company for you and we'll have more tomorrow. And after that—more. And after that—more. So you won't be alone. After all," he added with a sudden, humorless chuckle, "we don't *want* you to be alone. That might drive you insane!"

And with an elaborately sarcastic bow and wave he hopped back in his car and zoomed away.

Had anyone been there to observe he would have seen that for a few moments after Fred Van Ackerman left there was a certain undecided milling about, a hesitation, almost a holding back as though the wardens could not quite bring themselves to do what they had been ordered to do. But the observer, if such there had been, might have known that there was no cause for concern. The wardens did indeed have their orders, and as with anything, next time it would be easier, and after that, routine.

"Get along," the one who was apparently in charge said at last. "Get along in. All of you."

And presently, dazed, stumbling a bit, prodded by the guns of their captors, the miserable little group obeyed. As it passed out of sight and the heavy gate began to close, one last anguished cry, so desperate and filled with pain that it would have moved the observer, had observer there been, came from the lips of Walter Dobius.

"We did it!" he cried. "*We* did it! *We* did it! *We* d—"

But who he meant by "we," and what it was that he thought "we" had done, was never to be divulged, for at that point he was summarily, and no doubt roughly, choked off. The gates clanged shut and no further sound escaped the walls of St. Elizabeth's.

FAMED COLUMNIST, TOP PRESS COLLEAGUES JUDGED UNBALANCED BY PUBLIC HEALTH SERVICE DOCTORS. WALTER DOBIUS, OTHERS TAKEN TO ST. E'S ON COMPLAINT OF DOMESTIC TRANQUILLITY BOARD AND JUSTICE DEPARTMENT SPECIAL BRANCH. PSYCHIATRIC TREATMENT EXPECTED TO LAST SEVERAL MONTHS. OFFICIALS PREDICT REHABILITATION WILL BE SUCCESSFUL SO MEDIA BIGWIGS CAN RETURN TO "HELPFUL AND CONSTRUCTIVE ROLES IN PUBLIC LIFE."

"It is more in sadness than in anger," the *Times* said in its lead editorial, "that we print the news that columnist Walter Dobius and other formerly prominent figures in American journalism, including several from this newspaper, have been confined to a mental institution for treatment because of their inflammatory and clearly unbalanced attacks on the President of the United States and his policies for world peace.

"In some other era, when the press was less earnestly and patriotically dedicated to the success of those policies, this newspaper and others might have professed alarm and concern at such an action by the government. Today, knowing how desperate is the situation in which we find ourselves, and how imperative is complete and unquestioning support for the President, we can only applaud, however regretfully, a step which is clearly in the best interests both of the government and of the journalistic figures concerned.

"There has been little doubt for some time that these men have been approaching a state of genuine mental disturbance in their writings and commentaries upon the President. It is for their own good, therefore, as well as for the country's, that they should receive the kind of superbly skilled and highly effective psychiatric rehabilitation which the government plans to provide for them. They will emerge, in due course, restored to sanity, restored to balance, restored to their rightful places as loyal and fervent supporters of a great President and his great policies.

"Their incarceration will be temporary, their treatment profoundly good for them, their re-entry into public life in a new and more constructive mood a boon to all Americans. We applaud the government's action, which was, saddening though it is to admit, well-deserved and long overdue. . . ."

Similarly spoke the *Post*:

"The commitment of Walter Dobius and other former major figures of American journalism, including some from this paper, to temporary incarceration and intensive psychiatric rehabilitation in St. Elizabeth's is, in our opinion, an unfortunate but necessary step by the government in the best interests of all Americans.

"For too long certain reactionary forces that had worked themselves into the upper echelons of the media have been writing with hysteria and deliberate malice toward President Jason and his peace policies. If those policies were to succeed, which all patriotic and law-abiding Americans devoutly hope they will, it was imperative that such attacks must cease. And cease they have, and in an effective yet genuinely humane manner which can only bring good to the men involved, and can only reflect credit upon the government responsible.

"If there was ever any valid doubt as to the wisdom of the Help America law, this action by the Jason Administration removes it. It proves that the law, despite the fears of the fainthearted, can be, and is being, enforced in the best interests of all the people.

"Under this law, men whose published writings have proved them clearly and demonstrably unbalanced are now going to be afforded, at government expense, the most compassionate and thorough mental rehabilitation. They are going to be returned, once their aberrations have been successfully removed, to an honored, respected and loyal place in American society where they will be able to devote their great abilities, as they should, to the constructive and complete support of the President and his policies. They will be, we predict, genuinely and publicly grateful for the considerate treatment they have received—a treatment which, in its compassion and forbearance, should prove an example to the world.

"It is proof, once again, that American democracy, for all its imperfections, *does* work. . . ."

And that evening, on the "Opinion" segment of the news roundup, the successor of Frankly Unctuous, a suave and earnest young man with an appealing manner and a skillful turn of word, conferred his accolade too:

"Washington is thoughtful yet proud tonight: thoughtful because some of the nation's leading media figures must undergo a temporary and well-deserved psychiatric rehabilitation to bring them into line with the best interests and unanimous thinking of the American people —proud that there is an Administration in office possessing sufficient compassion and sufficient tolerance to provide them, freely and generously, with much-needed help for aberrations that were becoming increasingly dangerous to the country.

"Walter Dobius, our own Frankly Unctuous, the editors of the *Times* and the *Post* and their colleagues across the country—plus those others from the media, from the academic and theatrical worlds, from the world of business and industry, even from the Congress itself who are, we understand, slated soon to undergo the same generous assistance at the hands of a kindly government—are not, all observers here agree, bad men. They have simply been misguided. They have simply been led astray by evil, reactionary, anti-democratic influences. They have simply been suborned and seduced into a way of thinking and a way of writing which could have resulted, if left untreated, in a most desperate weakening of American democracy.

"Now American democracy has the opportunity to emerge strengthened and made more hopeful by the rehabilitation of these valuable, if misguided, citizens. The event is proof anew, if proof were needed, that the forces of American liberalism, acting through a liberal American President, can always find the solution for the nation's problems, when given half a chance. . . ."

But of course there were, as always with any forward-looking innovation in American life, the gripers and the carpers and the holders back, unwilling to accept the wisdom of the government and the manifest destiny of the people.

Some of them, perhaps because of their youth and lack of maturity, became quite violent about it.

"But you can't *do* this to the *Times!*" Bronnie Bronson cried, his voice rising to a near shout in the Capitol office of the president pro tempore, down the hall from the Senate floor. "I grew up on the *Times*. I have read the *Times all my life*. You can't do this to them! Or to *anybody!* It's undemocratic! It's dictatorial! It's—it's just plain *horrible!*"

"Sure, Bronnie-boy," the president pro tempore said with a lazily amused agreement, "but it isn't illegal, is it? *You* guided that bill through the House, didn't you, buster? *You* told off poor old Bill Abbott and his reactionary colleagues. *You* beat the drums for Ted Jason. *You* helped to pass the law. So what's your gripe? Can't you take it?"

"We never meant it to be like this!" Bronnie protested, so desperately earnest and upset that Fred Van Ackerman could not refrain from grinning openly in his face. Not that Fred wanted to refrain, because if there was any type he couldn't stand it was this wide-eyed, lily-livered, namby-pamby, games-playing Babes-in-Toyland liberal type, Fred wasn't playing games any longer, and it annoyed him intensely to run into these innocents who managed to convince themselves anybody still ought to be.

His rejoinder was not kind.

"Listen to me, you sniveling little fool," he said and there was a savagery in his tone so profound and beyond the bounds of civilized dealing that Congressman Bronson could only gasp and blink in rather laughable dismay. "Listen and get it straight, because I'm not going to waste my time repeating it to you every ten minutes:

"This Administration has a job to do and it is going to do it regardless of reactionary fools like Bill Abbott or so-called liberal fools like you. What in the Christ kind of game did you think you were getting into, anyway? Drop the handkerchief? We've got a country to run, and thanks to you and your silly pals in both houses we've got the law to do it with. And we're going to enforce it to the limit and don't you forget it, Bronnie-baby: *to—the—limit.* And that means you, if you don't watch out. There's plenty of room in St. E's for bright young men who don't want to help their great President and support their country. Want me to put you on the list?"

And he gave Bronson Bernard a contemptuous and frighteningly inquisitive look that made the Congressman turn pale and actually move back a little in his chair. But Bronnie was brave as well as idealistic and the one reinforced the other. He leaned forward again and returned Fred look for look.

"Don't you threaten me," he said angrily. "Don't you threaten *me,* you monster. I'm not afraid of you and your phony psychiatric gimmicks. I want you to stop trying to set up a dictatorship over this country, or—or—"

"Or what, Bronnie-boy?" Fred Van Ackerman inquired softly, with a dreamy and chilling detachment. "Just—what? What are you and your little pals going to do about it? What *can* you do about it? *We've* got the guns, you know. *We've* got St. E's and all the places like St. E's all over the country. *We're* the government. What are you going to do, little crying liberal who suddenly finds the kid games are all over and it's grown-up time, now? Shoot us dead, bang, bang? More likely we're going to shoot *you* dead, Bronnie-boy, so don't wet your pants. Keep calm and just follow along behind our great President Ted Jason and you'll be quite all right. O.K.?"

"I can't believe he's condoning this," Bronnie Bernard said in a desolate, far-off voice. "I just can't believe it."

The president pro tempore gave a sarcastic snort.

"He doesn't know what he's doing or what anybody else is doing," he said with a dry contempt. "Don't you understand that, Bronnie-boy? He's all gone, that man. He just isn't there any more."

"I'll get to him," Bronnie shouted with a sudden desperate rage. "I'll get to him! I'll tell him what you're doing! I'll take it to the floor this afternoon and I'll—I'll—"

"You'll what?" Fred interrupted savagely. "Look around you when you get there, friend. You'll see everybody's scared to death. It's *too late*, don't you see that? It's just too late. It's been done and there's no way out. You and your friends should have thought of that while there was time. There isn't time now."

"But," Bronson Bernard said, and his voice was despairing and his eyes were haunted, and now he looked fully as young, idealistic and desolate as he was, confronted by the awful consequences of a misguided but terribly well-meaning idealism, "we just wanted to help him save the country . . . we just wanted to help strengthen him so he could fight for liberal causes we all believed in . . . we just wanted—peace."

"Yes," Fred Van Ackerman said, and there was almost a kindness in his voice. "Well. You just run along now, Bronson. Don't worry your head about the way things are going any more, because there's no point in it. It would just weaken you, and you're needed. He needs you right here on the Hill, he has a place for you, you're going to be one of his bright young leaders, just as you always wanted to be . . . because if you aren't—" his voice became dreamy again. "Well, if you aren't, there's always St. E's, where you'd have a lot of company from the Hill, because we have some names on our lists who are going to be surprised in their beds some night soon. And up there in Manhattan, you know, there are two nice little old people, Mommy and Daddy, quite defenseless, you know, quite defenseless. And Sonny-boy is way down here . . . so you'd better get along back to the House, Bronnie. We need you there."

"Monster!" Congressman Bernard said, white with rage, fear and horror. "*Monster.*"

Fred Van Ackerman grinned.

"Somebody," he said cheerfully, "should have thought of that, a long time ago. . . ."

And so much, he thought with a savage satisfaction as he returned to his desk after showing his shaking visitor out with an elaborately ironic courtesy, for pipsqueak little baby-faced dreamers who thought they could pretend their way through today's real world. It wasn't their hoped-for earthly paradise any more, never had been, never would be: it was a jungle. In the jungle Fred Van Ackerman, predator, stalked with the best.

The clock on the wall gave a sudden loud click, the buzzer sounded twelve noon. The Senate was in session. He thought with a sudden amusement that he would go over and frighten the Vice President out of the Chair. If he made his tone sufficiently menacing, Roger P. Croy would hand him the gavel in a flustered, pompous, frightened hurry.

So he went on over, a pleasant little smile on his face, sidled up to Roger earnestly after the chaplain finished his worried prayer, and whispered, "I'll preside for a while."

"But," Roger P. Croy protested. "But—"

"I said," Fred Van Ackerman repeated, making his tone suddenly ominous, "I'll preside for a while. Or do you want me to make a great big public scene, right here?"

"Why—why, no," Roger P. Croy said hastily. "Why—why, no."

"Then git," Senator Van Ackerman said happily. "Just—*git*."

"Why, er—yes," Roger P. Croy agreed, in a flustered, pompous, frightened hurry. "Why—yes."

4. THE WIND whipped across the haunted hillside, haven of Kennedys and many others gone, in one way or another, in the service of their country; and to the small but valiant band of mourners who moved slowly between two new graves it seemed to bite with an extra savagery on this desolate morning.

Elizabeth Henry Knox and Thomas Buckmaster Davis were being laid to rest, not far from one another; and at the request of the Knox family and the little Justice's sole surviving brother, the services at National Cathedral and the interment at Arlington National Cemetery were being held together.

Now finally, to Hal and Crystal, to the Justice's brother, and to the handful of intimate friends who had braved the weather to attend the twin ceremonies, the fact of irrevocable termination was at last coming home, though two such vigorous spirits did not leave easily, and in a sense, of course, never would. Whatever might have to be faced by those who were left, something of Beth Knox and Tommy Davis would remain, indomitable and unchanging, to strengthen them for it; if, indeed, such strengthening were any longer possible, or could help.

The services at the Cathedral had been muted, short, almost furtive, in contrast to so many other high farewells of state that had been conducted there. The dean of the Cathedral, whose assumptions of a lifetime were in ruins like those of so many others, had gotten through the ritual low-voiced, subdued, bereft of his usual glamour and glittering words: he felt this as he had felt few other such occasions, and he knew as well as anyone what its implications were. Indeed, he only needed to glance at his morning newspapers to have his most somber misgivings confirmed: neither *Times* nor *Post* had carried so much as a word. To have done so, he suspected with a desperately worried bitterness, would have been to run counter to that domestic peace and tranquillity so necessary to the success of the policies of the President.

He himself, in fact, was probably counter to that success; and like so many others in the past forty-eight hours, he too was now expecting the knock on the door, the terror in the night. How long would he be permitted to remain before a more sympathetic presence in that fashionably influential post became necessary to the new order of things being imposed upon America? Not much longer, he imagined. The foreboding showed in the intonation of every word and the sad, more than usually elegiac, farewells he uttered for two old friends.

Noticeable also was the size of the funeral party that gathered, silent and barely nodding to one another, to pay their respects and then follow the two hearses across the Potomac to Arlington. Very few represented the hundreds who would have been there in steadier days. Perhaps a hundred only, the bedrock of those who used to honor the names of Knox and Davis: the ex-President, Hal and Crystal, Bob and Dolly Munson, Stanley Danta, Warren Strickland, Justice Cappola and Madam Justice Watson, Lafe Smith and Mabel Anderson, Cullee Hamilton and Sarah Johnson, a few other members of Senate and House, the Knoxes' maid and gardener, some clerks, some secretaries, a scattering of anonymous citizens, some sincere, some curious. Surprisingly, and also, perhaps, at serious risk to themselves in these new times, five were present from the diplomatic corps: the British Ambassador and his lady, the French Ambassador and his, and the Indian Ambassador. There was no formal representation from the White House. Only the Secretary of State, in a gesture that would have been expected a week ago but now seemed suddenly very brave, was present from the President's official family.

After the words had been said, the hymns played, the tears shed, the gathering dwindled even further. Six cars only formed the cortege that moved swiftly, almost apologetically, along the broad avenues and over the frozen water to the beautiful hill. There the interment services, also delivered by the dean, were extremely brief, again almost apologetic, almost furtive. The flags draping both caskets were removed, dirt fell, the earth began to close over Beth beside Orrin, Tommy a few yards away. Slowly, by twos and threes and fours, the mourners straggled back down the hill toward their cars. Some would disperse into the tense city, some fly home across the uneasy land. A handful would move on to "Vagaries" in Rock Creek Park, where Dolly Munson had suggested they stop by for a bite to eat and a visit together. She had done her best to make it sound as though it were not the last one but the thought lay behind all their careful words. Only Celestine Barre was typically direct and pragmatic.

"Events have been moving so swiftly on center stage," Dolly had said yesterday when she called her, "that we haven't been able to get together off on the side and discuss them as we used to do."

"And may not be able to again," Celestine had said in what was, for her, a rare volubility.

"Oh, I shouldn't like to think that!" Dolly had exclaimed, obviously thinking it.

"Nor I," Celestine had replied. "But it is there, dear Dolly. It is there."

And so it was, as the cars drew up under the portico of "Vagaries" and their passengers got out. How many times had cars drawn up before those lovely columns, how many times had these same people, and many more besides, stepped forward to enter the all-embracing warmth of the Munson's beautiful home! And when would "Vagaries" see the likes of those happy days again? It was a thought they did not care to contemplate but were unable to ignore.

Nonetheless, for a little while their host and hostess tried to put the best face on it; and aided by the fact that the first few minutes of such conversations are always grave and filled with emotion and thoughts of the dead, they were able to keep away from it. But presently the necessary things had been said, the necessary release had been achieved; even Hal and Crystal, though wan and somber, appeared to be a little more relaxed. And as was inevitable in a gathering of political people in that political house in that political city, someone said the first word, and they were off.

"I notice," Krishna Khaleel said in his brightly chirpy way, "that our distinguished journals did not mention the services today. I wonder why."

"You know why, K.K.," William Abbott said calmly. "These were the non-services of non-persons. As such they were non-reported in non-newspapers, which is what we now have in America."

"Oh, Bill!" K.K. said cheerily. "Always so gloomy, always so pessimistic! It is only temporary. Nothing has changed. Nothing *could* change. This is America, Bill! *America!*"

"We are leaving on Monday," Raoul Barre said with a certain bleak, matter-of-fact calm. "We have been recalled."

The Indian Ambassador looked at him in surprised dismay.

"Yes?" he said. "Yes?"

"Yes," Lord Maudulayne said with an equally fatalistic bluntness. "We too."

"But why?" Krishna Khaleel demanded in an aggrieved tone. "Why, dear Claude, dear Raoul? Surely, you are not afraid that—"

"*I* am afraid," Lord Maudulayne said with a kind of savage calm. "I am afraid. Also, I believe, my government now considers that Britain must have in Washington an ambassador who is a little more—tolerant, shall we say—of what is going on here. It is felt in Whitehall, in other words, that it is time for us to begin to adapt to the new United States which is suddenly—appallingly—unbelievably—but actually—beginning to emerge. It is believed," he added bleakly, "that we must make our peace with the new situation, or, in due course, die. Therefore a new man is needed here. I am considered to have been much too close to the *ancien régime*. I am considered to be too sincere a believer in democracy and too open in my sympathies toward it. The New Day requires new men. Ergo—we bid you farewell, Tuesday week."

"But surely—" the Indian Ambassador said with a genuine unhappiness, "surely, it is not so. Surely, there is some—surely, your government cannot think that—"

"Oh, but our governments do," Raoul Barre interrupted. "They do, K.K. They do not take quite the long view that is taken in Delhi. They must deal with the situation here and now, right across the Atlantic. A great change is now under way in the world, beginning with the inaugural of the distinguished new President and accelerating every day, as things do in international affairs when certain barriers are suddenly knocked down. We, too, like our colleagues across the Channel, must adapt or die. Not so you Indians, of course. You have always been so—flexible. You, no doubt, will stay right on here, K.K., smiling with your usual sunny good will upon all that passes, serene in the knowledge that India has always been so sympathetic and understanding that her preservation can be taken for granted. India will give no trouble—*you*, K.K., will give no trouble. But Claude and I—we are too old to change. We have believed the wrong things for too many years. We have to go.

"And soon, of course, in Paris and in London, many others will have to go, too. Whole governments will have to be restructured to meet the new situation in Washington. The United States cannot change without the world changing. And so it will be done: all will come, in due course, neatly into line. We are but the first indications. There will soon be many, many more. . . . So you see, dear Dolly, this is indeed the last gathering of our happy group at dear, delightful 'Vagaries'—which I believe comes from the Latin 'to wander,' and can be held to mean 'a wild fancy; an extravagant notion.' . . . What a wild fancy," he concluded with a sudden heavy bitterness, "that men are, or of right should be, or are capable of being for any great length of time, free! What an extravagant notion!"

And rising suddenly he went to one of the room's great windows and stood staring out unseeing at the cold white day, hands, locked behind his back, twisting and turning as though possessed of some unhappy life of their own.

There was silence in the room for a time, broken at last by Dolly who had long ago adopted the social rule: when in doubt, ring for the maid. Two presently came, with coffee, tea and an ample cold buffet which they spread upon the two marble-topped Louis Quinze tables that stood along the wall. When they withdrew Dolly said firmly,

"Now, there is food, everyone, and I think we should all have something. And I don't think we should have further gloomy talk."

"Why not?" Hal Knox inquired slowly. "It's true, isn't it? Not many of us will ever be here again. This kind of life isn't going to last, Dolly. It's going to be the first to go. 'Vagaries' has had it. And so has all that 'Vagaries' represents."

"I won't have you say that in my house!" Dolly said with a sudden harsh, startling anger. Then quite abruptly she began to cry, as Senator Munson stepped forward and placed his hand, which she grasped, alongside her cheek.

"Maybe better not," he said quietly. "It doesn't do any good and only upsets everybody."

"It's upsetting *me!*" Mabel Anderson said with a sudden explosive force, the abrupt release of a shy and indrawn soul assailed beyond endurance. "I can't take this city any more. I never could. Not even when Brig was here. And then when he—left—I left, and I didn't intend ever to come back. But I did, because I thought—" she stared at

Lafe, who looked completely shattered and taken aback—"because I thought there might be some peace and stability here, after all. And maybe there could be if it were just—us. But it isn't just us. It's Ted Jason and Fred Van Ackerman and all the rest of them, and what they're doing to things. It's fear, everywhere. It's what the future holds for all of us who don't agree. It's horrible things about to happen to our country. And I can't take it," she said, beginning to cry in a forlorn, woebegone, little-girl fashion. "I just can't take it any more. I'm taking Pidge back to Utah and I'm never coming back. Never, ever, ever!"

"But you can't hide there," Lafe said in a gentle, pleading tone. "You and Pidge won't be any safer there than you will be right here with me. Really, you won't."

"Safe with *you!*" she said, a terrible bitterness breaking through the tears. "Who says *you're* safe? There isn't a member of Congress who's disagreed with him—there isn't *anybody* who's disagreed with him— who's safe. You're all on the list. Nobody is going to escape these people, nobody!"

"As members of Congress," Lafe said, trying to keep his voice steady and reasonable, trying to hang onto traditional patterns of thought because they were rapidly becoming the only things left to hang onto, "we have immunity from arrest for what we say on the floor. They can't arrest us. They wouldn't dare."

"'Wouldn't dare!'" Mabel said with a hopeless, forsaken, bitterly scornful little laugh. "'Wouldn't dare!' You'll see what they dare, pretty darned quick!"

"Oh, really, now," Krishna Khaleel said with a nervous jocularity, as though speaking from some other, almost-forgotten world, as indeed he was. "Oh, really, now—"

But they all turned and stared at him blankly and after a moment his voice trailed away and he murmured, *"Oh, really, now!"* once more to himself in a worried, rather absent-minded little whisper, and subsided.

"Is that your final answer?" Lafe asked, very low. Mabel stared at him for a long time, her eyes wide, making no attempt to stop the tears that rolled steadily down her cheeks.

"That's it," she said at last. "That's it."

"But it's a time to stay together!" Lafe cried with a sudden harsh bitterness. "It's not a time to stay apart! We're all lost, if that's what we do!"

"I'm sorry," she whispered. "I'm not very brave, and I guess—I guess they've won, as far as I'm concerned. . . ."

They were all silent, staying as they were, making no attempt to get up and move toward the food, making no attempt to be "social," though it might have eased the moment. The gesture seemed suddenly very pointless. At last William Abbott spoke, in a musing, faraway tone.

"*Somebody* must do *something*. . . ." His eyes met those of the Secretary of State, somber and deeply unhappy, across the room. "I don't know what it is, but *somebody* must do it. . . ."

"Are you suggesting," Bob Leffingwell inquired with something of the old, wry dryness, "that I shoot him?"

"Are you suggesting," the ex-President said with a deliberately matching dryness, "that *you* will not be shot, if it suits the purposes of some people in your Administration to do so?"

"Well—" the Secretary of State began almost angrily, almost impatiently. Then he stopped. His voice trailed away. Finally he smiled a little, though without humor.

"You do reduce it to essentials."

"That's where it's at," Bill Abbott said crisply. "That is definitely where it's at." He gave the Secretary of State a long, appraising look. "Why don't you and Ewan MacDonald," he suggested softly, "discuss it together?"

For a moment Robert A. Leffingwell looked absolutely flabbergasted while the others suddenly became very, very quiet.

"But Ewan MacDonald," the Secretary of State said at last in a disbelieving near whisper, "is Secretary of Defense."

The ex-President nodded calmly.

"Exactly so. Is anyone here going to report me for the suggestion?"

He looked slowly and carefully around the room, face by face, until he was satisfied at last that not even the Indian Ambassador would dare. Then his gaze returned to the Secretary of State.

"Well?"

Robert A. Leffingwell shook his head, hard, as if to clear it, and spoke in the same bemused near-whisper.

"If I understand you correctly, you are advocating treason."

"What is treason, now?" the ex-President demanded, quietly and without rancor. "Who can say where treason lies, any more? Who can say where duty lies? Each must judge for himself. And only those who still can act must try to find the answer. Talk to Ewan MacDonald. He's a practical Scot and, I think, still unafraid of the right as he sees it."

"Do you think I am afraid of it?" Robert Leffingwell asked with a sudden sharpness.

"No," William Abbott said calmly. "That is why I suggest you talk to Ewan MacDonald."

"Oh, dear!" Krishna Khaleel exclaimed. "Oh, *dear!*"

On which note, leaving untouched Dolly's carefully prepared luncheon, the members of the last party at "Vagaries" of the *ancien régime* bade one another hurried farewells and went somberly and swiftly away, not knowing when, if ever, they would see each other again.

Now he too, at last, felt fear; and the principal cause of it sat across the enormous desk in the Oval Office, staring at him with an impudent and unyielding insolence. The President had demanded his appearance in a furious telephone call at 9 A.M. And now, at approximately 3 P.M., he had condescended to drop by.

It was immediately apparent that he had not been in the least impressed by the furious phone call, nor by the cold and angry expression on the President's face that had greeted his deliberately tardy arrival. Edward M. Jason simply did not have that kind of credibility any more; and now, after only a few seconds of conversation with the junior Senator from Wyoming, he was finally beginning to realize it. The knowledge, coming after so many other things, was a shattering moment he did his best to conceal.

Fred Van Ackerman, with the instinct of a ferret, was not fooled.

"Sorry I couldn't get down here sooner," he said with airy contrition, adding almost as an afterthought, "—Mr. President. . . . We've been pretty busy on the Hill today, you know, and—"

"Doing what?" the President inquired sharply. The president pro tempore shrugged with an amiably scornful smile.

"Oh, listening to a lot of crap from the likes of Munson, Danta, Hamilton and Smith. That sounds like a second-rate Washington law firm, doesn't it? Or a run-down vaudeville team." His expression became suddenly vicious. "Well, that's what they are, all right. They and their buddies."

"What were they concerned about?" Ted Jason asked, trying to sound as though he did not know. Fred ignored the pretense.

"You know. You've been getting reports. A lot of who-struck-John about your crackdown on the press."

"Not my crackdown," the President said with a sudden almost desperate anger. The response was predictable.

"No?" Fred said with an elaborate surprise. "Well, I'm damned. I thought you were the President of the United States. Or—" his expression became innocent and wide-eyed—"has someone else slipped in when you weren't looking?"

"It was never my intention—" Ted Jason began. But he was interrupted.

"What were your intentions," Fred Van Ackerman demanded coldly, "when you backed this—" and his voice became mimicking, mocking and singsong—" 'dictatorial, un-American, frightful and abhorrent' law? When you put in charge of its enforcement 'one who is completely amoral, ruthless, undemocratic and hostile to all the principles of freedom?' When you gave him the power, and said and did nothing to stop him, to 'launch a terrifying assault upon the free media of the United States' in order to transform its members into 'whipped lap dogs tethered on chains behind the chariot of Edward M. Jason?' Where were you when all these things were going on, Mr. President? I thought—" and Fred's voice became soft and gentle, "that you were right there backing me every inch of the way. That's what they think on the Hill, Mr. President. How are you ever going to convince them differently? It's too late now. 'Way, 'way too late. Everything has been done."

"I order you," the President said, keeping his voice level with an enormous effort, "to release those men at once and restore them to their rightful positions."

"They're in their rightful positions," Fred said blandly, "being re-educated to support properly, as they should, the peace-loving policies of the greatest President who ever sat in this office. Yes, sir," he added, looking around with a speculative air that literally raised the hairs on the back of Ted Jason's neck, "and some office it is, too. Wow, man!" he exclaimed with a subtly sardonic mockery. "Like I mean, it's great!"

"And it is not to be demeaned," the President said, still levelly, "by the likes of you. I repeat, I order you to release those men at once and cease all plans to imprison anyone else. *Anyone else,* I don't care what sector of the population he comes from, media, academic, business, labor, whatever. I don't want *anyone else* subjected to this. It must stop, or I shall have you arrested, if that's what I have to do to stop this madness."

"On what grounds?" Fred inquired reasonably. "For heaven's sake, on what grounds? Carrying out the law of the land? Administering the authority vested in me by the President of the United States? Doing the job my great President appointed me to do, assisting him in his great peace-loving plans? I swear, you baffle me. I don't understand what you're getting at, at all. I just don't understand what you're trying to do in this office."

"I am trying—" the President said, and suddenly he felt a weariness and weight so great upon his head and shoulders that he lost his thought for a moment and quite obviously struggled to find it again as the Senator from Wyoming studied him with a bright and attentive eye. "I am trying—trying to save this nation from collapse and this world from war, and I am under great—great pressures—from—from everywhere. You don't know," he said, with an appeal in his voice he hated because he knew it was wasted here, but he did not seem to be able to keep it out, "you just don't know the pressures I am under."

"It's tough," Fred agreed judiciously, "all over. . . . Anyway, that doesn't change our problem, does it? It seems to me it just makes it all the more imperative that you have a united country behind you."

"But not united by fear!" the President said angrily. "Not united by fear!"

"How, then?" Senator Van Ackerman inquired, still judiciously, still reasonably. "How, Mr. President? Tell me. All I want to do is help."

Ted Jason started to speak; stopped; studied him with an angry yet somehow supplicating bafflement; and finally spoke with a bitter distaste.

"You really are a monster."

Fred Van Ackerman uttered a cheerful laugh.

"Everybody seems to be calling me that lately." He shrugged. "But —here I am, doing the job you appointed me to do. And you haven't answered my question: how can we unite the country, at this late date, in any other way than we're doing?"

"You can stop saying 'we,' for one thing," Ted Jason told him sharply. "This is my responsibility, and I am the one to do it."

"Exactly what I say," Fred agreed promptly. "And you are, too. Working through me and a few other strong men who don't flinch from what has to be done."

"I order you—" the President tried again; but again was interrupted.

"Order me to do what?" Fred demanded with a sharpness and anger of his own. "Order me to let every half-assed columnist and commentator in the country continue to attack you at will? Order me to sit idly by while those bastards on the *Times* and the *Post* and all their little buddies around the country try to sabotage and subvert everything you're trying to do? Order me to step aside and let them come back and block every step you make toward achieving peace in the world? That's what I'm supposed to do? Maybe you'd better get yourself another boy!"

"Very well," the President said. "I accept your resignation."

"Oh, no, you don't," Fred cried with an exasperated harshness. "Oh, no, you don't! If you want me out of here you'll have to come right out like a big, brave man and fire me, Mr. President. You won't trick me into it. You'll have to *do* it. So, go ahead. Go ahead, and see what that gets you from your true supporters! Why, listen!" he said scornfully, abandoning the ranting tone in one of his typical lightning changes, "do you want NAWAC in the streets in five minutes rioting against *you?* Do you want this country *really* turned into an armed camp? It can be done now, Mr. President, and you know it. *You know it.* So you just tell me how you want it, and I'll be happy to oblige."

And staring with a fierce intensity at Edward M. Jason, he leaned forward and waited for an answer.

From the President, who realized now with a sickening foreclosure of all hope that he had indeed created a Frankenstein's monster who could no longer be contained, there was, for a few moments, no answer forthcoming. He knew with a chilling sense of vacuum that there was here, for himself and his office, only a basic contempt; and also, even more chilling, the will—and the capability—to shift ground in sheer ruthless self-interest and cause great trouble. He was about to try, as the last resort of desperation, to reason with his antagonist, when his antagonist, in another of his baffling changes of mood and technique, leaned back in a suddenly relaxed and earnest fashion and began to reason with him.

"Really, Mr. President," he said in a perfectly rational voice, "there is nothing to be gained by our fighting each other—nothing at all. It's the enemies of America that you and I have to fight—and fight together. Not apart. Not separately. *Together.* I've already taken major and effective steps to stop the most obvious elements opposing you. Now, surely, you don't want to undo all that and start a great fight inside the Administration, open everything wide up so all the subversives in America can attack us and destroy what we're trying to do. Surely that isn't what you want, Mr. President. *Surely* not. Why, it would be—it would be a *hell* of a thing. It would tear the Administration to pieces! And furthermore," he said, leaning forward again in a confidential, man-to-man manner, "think of what it would do to the millions and millions who believe in you, who understand and support your great mission for peace, who want you to succeed because they know that only through your success can America succeed! Why, it would shatter them completely. It would ruin their morale forever. It would *destroy* them. There wouldn't be anything or *anybody* they could believe in. You couldn't betray them like that, Mr. President!

Please don't, I beg of you! You just couldn't do it. You just *mustn't.* Please, Mr. President. *Please.*"

And earnestly, beseechingly, moved by what could almost seem a fervent conviction, he again stared, with an intensity now humble and deeply concerned, into the troubled eyes across the desk. The moment lengthened.

"Unbelievable," the President said at last. "Unbelievable."

"But right, don't you think?" Fred inquired pleasantly. "You simply cannot betray the people who believe in you, Mr. President. What is the point to your life, if you do?" Again came the blandly insolent look. "Why have you bothered to live?"

"I have bothered to live," Ted Jason said with a sort of dogged determination, "so that I might do what I could to help my country and the world. Some things haven't worked out quite—quite as I would want them to do—but that has been my motivation. I am still trying. I cannot accomplish what I must do if—" he shook his head as if to clear it—"if—"

"If all these disruptive elements are attacking and upsetting you," Fred agreed in a tone soothing, almost fatherly. "Exactly what I'm saying, Mr. President. They *must* be stopped so they are *being* stopped. Now you will be free to proceed unhampered and untroubled in the great work you have to do. Now your life *will* be meaningful and worth living, as few lives, even of Presidents, have been. Isn't that right? Think about it, Mr. President," he said softly. "Think about it!"

There was a silence in the Oval Office while Edward M. Jason did think about it, his face somber, seemingly strong yet subtly helpless, his eyes far away. Finally he spoke, so quietly that Fred had to lean forward to catch it.

"I think you had better go."

Fred stood up promptly.

"Sure, Mr. President." He held out his hand expansively. "We'll stop 'em," he promised with a satisfied conviction. "They won't bother you any more."

The President did not respond, either to the hand or the comment, but remained seated, still staring far away, as the Senator from Wyoming, ignoring the snub, gave him a cheery farewell wave, and left the room.

For perhaps two more minutes the President remained immobile. Then he swung around abruptly and reached for the Picturephone. He had barely touched it when the appointments secretary knocked discreetly to inform him that the people he wanted to see were already waiting to see him. Slowly he replaced the phone; nodded; and stood up with a sudden surge of returning confidence and decision that indicated that he saw, at last, some way out of the endless and inexorable tunnel he seemed to be in.

But of course it was not to be.

The road chosen by Edward M. Jason must be traveled to the end.

"Mr. President—" Bob Leffingwell began, and stopped. An uneasy sensation stirred somewhere in the back of the President's mind and moved rapidly to the front.

"I am glad you have come," he said quickly, pushing the warning signal aside, concentrating upon their earnest and troubled faces: the Secretary of State, the Secretary of Defense, the four members of the Joint Chiefs of Staff, who today, oddly, were wearing full uniform, glittering with medals. "I was about to call you to come here. I have something of the utmost gravity to discuss with you."

There was a silence.

"And we with you, Mr. President," Ewan MacDonald MacDonald said finally.

"Oh?" the President asked. "Perhaps you should proceed first."

"No, Mr. President," the Secretary of Defense said in a hesitant yet dogged tone. "We think you should."

The President looked from face to face. His visitors were obviously terribly troubled and uneasy, yet it seemed to him that an obdurate and ominous rigidity possessed them all. The warning signal grew sharper. He fought it down and spoke with the calm conviction he knew he must.

"I must ask your help in regaining control of the government. I have just had a talk with Senator Van Ackerman and it is obvious that he is in a state of almost open rebellion against me. He and his gangs are going to have to be brought under control by sheer physical force, I think. I may have to ask the armed forces to help. I expect you to do so if requested."

"Mr. President—" Ewan MacDonald began; and stopped.

"Mr. President—" Robert A. Leffingwell began; and stopped; and started again.

"Mr. President," he said, his voice trembling with emotion but determined. "I think we have something more fundamental to discuss with you."

"What could be more fundamental than that?" he demanded sharply.

The Secretary of State drew a long breath but stood his ground.

"The question of your remaining in this office," he said quietly.

"Suppose I were to declare a state of national emergency," the President said rapidly, deliberately not giving himself time to think of the fearful implications of what his Secretary of State had just said, "and ordered you, as your Commander in Chief, to help me enforce it. Then what?" And again he glanced sharply from face to face; and again sensed a bafflement, a desperate unease, something close to helplessness—but an underlying obduracy and a frightening determination, too.

"What is it?" he demanded sharply. "Surely you are not supporting Van Ackerman against your President?"

"Mr. President," Bob Leffingwell said carefully, "perhaps you did not understand what I said. We have come to discuss the question—" he paused and added firmly—"we have come to discuss the wisdom—of your remaining in this office. Nothing else is as important as that. That is what we are here to discuss, Mr. President."

And now a silence absolutely somber and absolutely deathlike settled upon the Oval Office. A fearful chasm had opened at their feet, a thing without precedent in American history, a moment for which there were no guidelines or patterns of the past to help any of them work his way out; least of all the man who faced them from behind the enormous desk, head trembling but erect, face pale, eyes filled with many unfathomable things.

For what seemed a very long time, but perhaps was only a minute or two, he did not speak, nor did they: only staring at one another as in the grip of some horrid paralysis whose implacable hand they did not know how to dislodge. When he finally spoke they felt nothing but a vague surprise that he had finally done so; and it was in such a low voice that they all instinctively leaned forward a little to hear.

"You are talking treason."

"God knows, Mr. President," Bob Leffingwell responded, also very low, "we would give anything in this world if we did not have to do so. But you have permitted events to deteriorate to such a point that it is beginning to seem to many people that you are—" again he paused and took a deep breath—"that you are no longer worthy or capable of discharging the responsibilities and obligations of President of the United States."

And now abruptly Ted Jason was on his feet, a man desperately frightened but desperately angry, too; the anger, springing from some deep well of personal affront compounded by resentment at the affront to his office, for the moment overriding all.

"I command you to support me!" he said harshly. "I am your President and your Commander in Chief and *I command you* to stop committing treason and support me as you are legally, constitutionally and morally sworn to do. I *will not accept,*" he added, and he grated it out although the trembling that seemed to have seized his body did not abate and his face remained ghastly pale, "any other course of conduct from any of you. *Is that clear?*"

"Mr. President," the Secretary of Defense said with an unyielding quietness that obviously cost him much, "you may no longer be in a position to command such things. For, if you have broken your contract with the country, as we have come reluctantly to believe you have—and if the people beneath you, on whom you must depend to carry out your orders, will not obey you—then who is to enforce your will? And what point is there in your remaining in office if you no longer have the power to enforce your will?"

Still with the same blazing anger, and still with the same shattered but unyielding aspect, the President turned to the Joint Chiefs of Staff.

"Arrest these men," he snapped, "for grave and heinous treason against the President of the United States and the liberties of this Republic."

Again there was silence, broken at last by the Chairman of the Joint Chiefs, the Chief of Staff of the Air Force.

"Mr. President," he said, looking fully as tired and strained and emotionally upset as any of them, "I am afraid we cannot obey that order."

"Then this is rebellion," Ted Jason said, almost in a whisper. "Then this *is* rebellion." And in a tone that almost broke them emotionally, so like a lost child did it sound, he asked of no one in particular, staring out the window at the cold winter lawn, "What am I to do? What am I ever to do?"

For a time, again, there was silence, while their minds were filled with all the swirling, awful, inexorable things that had conspired to bring them to this dreadful moment. Bob Leffingwell spoke at last.

"Mr. President," he said gravely, "no one here wants to commit treason, or to drive you from office, *if you will only act in the interests of this country.* If you will only," he said, and his voice was both respectful and pleading, "stop taking counsel of your fears, and just—be brave."

"You know why I can't 'be brave!'" the President cried with what seemed to be a sudden harsh recovery of purpose. "You know why I can't respond to that silly, empty, worthless cliché! I have told you my situation vis-à-vis the Russians and I have told you completely and frankly right here in this very room. How dare you give me that silly cliché! *How dare you,* when it would mean the absolute certain destruction of this free nation!"

"And will your present course mean anything else, Mr. President?" Ewan MacDonald inquired softly. "Will it, then, mean anything else?" And with a sudden bursting anger of his own, as though he could hold it back no longer, he reverted instinctively to the brogue of his childhood and cried out harshly, "For God's sake, man, will ye no act like our leader and not like a poor wee mouse!"

For a while the President made no response, staring directly yet apparently without anger at his Secretary of Defense. When he spoke it was in a voice level, drained of emotion, without resentment, fear or anything other than a calmness born of both desperation and conviction.

"The only body in this land constitutionally empowered to judge me," he said quietly, "is the Congress of the United States. It has done so. It has been given the opportunity to impeach me and it has overwhelmingly rejected that opportunity. Who, then, are you, to come here and threaten me? Who, really—" and he looked at them as though for the first time, as though he had never really seen them before and was appraising them, new and baffling individuals, "are you? . . . I have done my level best since I entered upon this office to do what I thought was right for my country and for world peace. That my efforts have been misunderstood and taken advantage of by our enemies is not my fault. I have been honest, I have been straightforward, I have been sincere. I shall die in the conviction that what I tried to do in my inaugural was right: you can never shake me from that. . . . Now, as for you—" and his voice grew harsher and more personal —"you should be shot, all of you, literally stood up against a wall and shot, for coming to me with denunciations and threats as you have. How dare you attempt such a thing with the President of the United States? *How dare you?* I could have you imprisoned and executed in a matter of hours for such a thing . . . but I will not. You will return to your respective duties and you will perform them as your Commander in Chief requires. And we will hear no more about it, because we have a much greater problem to solve together. And we *must* solve it, for the sake of this land."

"Mr. President," Bob Leffingwell said, and his voice too was level, drained of emotion, unyielding, "it cannot be solved with you in this office unless you reverse your policies both foreign and domestic. Are you going to do so?"

"I have told you—" Edward M. Jason said, his face beginning to flush with anger. But the Secretary of State interrupted in a tone that indicated that he and his colleagues were also having no more of it.

"You must change them, Mr. President," he said quietly. "Otherwise you will be required to resign from this office."

"I shall go to the country tonight," the President said. "The people will support me. I shall go over your heads to the armed forces, and they will support me. If you wish to persist in treason and create civil war, we shall see who wins."

"The country's too confused and divided to support you," Ewan MacDonald said, his voice almost pitying in tone. "And how could they do it, anyway? The only organized support you would have would be NAWAC and Van Ackerman—and you've already shown us that you know how reliable he would be. And as for the armed forces—" he looked at the Joint Chiefs of Staff, who nodded agreement—"my colleagues will support me when I say that you could not command them, either, if you go over our heads. The military works through channels, Mr. President: there are ways of doing things, orders come down in an orderly fashion, authority must follow a clear, agreed-upon line and be authenticated every step of the way. Orders may come *from* you but they must come *through* us. If you tried to go over our heads you'd find the military confused, uncertain and unwilling to act, for fear they'd be doing the wrong thing and would be punished for it later. So there's nothing there for you. . . . No, I think you had better consider our proposition, which we put to you, I say for all of us, only with the greatest reluctance and agony of heart. You *are* our President. We *don't* enjoy forcing your hand. It goes against all tradition, all law and all our hearts want to do. But you leave us no choice, Mr. President. . . . This we have concluded, after great pain and soul-searching."

The President stared again out the window; spoke at last in a flat, almost sardonic tone.

"And what deadline do you propose to give me? Any?"

"We were thinking in terms of noon tomorrow," the Secretary of State said, his tone both relieved and impersonal. "That would give you time to prepare a speech, which could, quite appropriately, be delivered to Congress."

"You choose the place," Ted Jason said dryly, "and, no doubt, you write the speech."

"We should expect to assist," Bob Leffingwell said evenly.

Again Ted Jason stared out the window while they waited, hardly daring to look at him, hardly daring to breathe.

So abruptly that it almost literally made them jump, he swung back with an air of sudden and complete resolution.

"Very well," he said quietly. "Very well. . . . No," he said, raising a hand as some indeterminate sound, relieved, delighted, encouraging, grateful, humble, inchoate, came from them all. "I don't want any congratulations, any anything. Just go, now. Bob and Ewan, come back at eight tonight and we will work on the speech. For now—just go." His voice sank lower, seemed almost to break. "Just—go . . . if you please."

Murmuring confused expressions of relief, gratitude, support, encouragement, while he sat immobile and almost pathetically unresponsive behind the great desk, they did so, hastily, almost guiltily, now that their fearsome objective had been achieved.

Outside under the South Portico, waiting for their limousines in the icy afternoon, the Secretary of Defense turned suddenly to the Secretary of State.

"My God," he said in a voice both awed and frightened, "we're nice people, we're good men, we believe in the laws of this land. *My God, what have we done?*"

"What nice people and good men sometimes find themselves forced to do, by events," the Secretary of State said bleakly. "What they must."

Inside, in the historic office still warm with their presence, a man driven to the wall, who also considered himself a nice man, a good man, and one who had always believed in the laws of his land, did what he, too, felt he must.

PRESIDENT ISSUES INVITATION TO RUSSIAN LEADER TO COME FOR IMMEDIATE CONFERENCE. TASHIKOV ACCEPTS JASON BID, ALREADY ON WAY TO FATEFUL WHITE HOUSE MEETING. WORLD SEES LAST HOPE FOR PEACE.

SPECIAL BRANCH MOVES AGAINST ANTI-JASON CONSPIRACY "AT HIGHEST LEVEL." RUMOR SECRET ARRESTS OF "POWERFUL MEN AROUND PRESIDENT." JUSTICE DEPARTMENT TO RELEASE NAMES TOMORROW.

And so now, hardly thinking, hardly daring to think, he was embarked on the final curve of the trajectory begun at noon on Inauguration Day. Inexorably, step by step, his own good intentions—the ruthless opportunism with which the Kremlin had taken advantage of them—the blindly stubborn and uncooperative attitudes of his more conservative countrymen—had conspired to bring him to a point he had never dreamed: a point so far from where he had begun that he simply could not afford, now, to let himself contemplate all its results and all their implications.

It was shortly before 9 A.M. After very little sleep and a half-hearted attempt at breakfast he was again sitting alone in the Oval Office. Around him the White House was beginning to come alive. Soon secretaries would be opening mail, taking telephone calls, replying to telegrams, typing reports, working on the endless assembly line of paper work that comprised the executive routine. Appointments would be made, plans would be argued, staff meetings and conferences would be held, the structure of the day would go forward like other days—or would it?

He suspected the heavy oppression of events would hang over these corridors as it hung over him.

The staff would go through the motions but like people everywhere they would be half-hearted, automatic, near-somnambulistic.

Like people everywhere, they would be waiting.

Like himself, they would be waiting.

He knew that none of them would have to wait very long, for he had already been notified that the Chairman of the Council of Ministers had landed at Dulles International Airport at 7 A.M. and was even now on his way from the Russian Embassy with the Foreign Minister and the Minister of Defense. For a single bleak moment he realized that he himself would have no such support in their meeting. Then his mind closed angrily against the thought and a harsh and bitter mood overcame it momentarily: *they deserved it for what they tried to do to me and I can't afford to grieve for them now.*

Or for the loss of things that their absence represented.

In a strange way, which perhaps revealed more about his inner condition than he knew, he was almost glad of this—almost glad that he had to face alone the men who had almost destroyed the dream he had given the world when he took the oath of office. Almost destroyed it—but not entirely destroyed it—for was he not still its keeper? And was there not still, in him, the strength of conviction and the idealism of heart to face them down, in the end?

He did not know why he felt confident of this, for certainly his last meeting with Tashikov had produced no such result. If the Chairman had been brutal and gloating then, what would he not be now? Yet in some last, stubborn, desperate way, the President of the United States *knew*—because he had to know—that he would yet win out.

If he could not believe this, what was left?

In a curiously dreamlike state he became conscious of a sudden bustle and stirring in the hallways, a quickly cut-off vibration of motors in the distance, the abrupt termination of sirens which a second before had been screaming through the streets.

His visitors were here.

In the same unreal, almost hypnotic state, in which his mind seemed to float somewhere slightly above the surface of events, amazingly serene and untouched, he arose and stood quietly behind his desk. He would not go forward: they could come to him.

The door opened, the appointments secretary, tense and nervous, made his announcement and withdrew. Edward M. Jason's visitors entered and approached. And the dream collapsed.

"Mr. President," Vasily Tashikov said, making no attempt to shake hands or show any but the most cursory deference. "I knew you would call on us for assistance but I had not expected it quite so soon. May we sit down?"

"Please do," he said, sitting down himself, and they did so, the Foreign Minister on one side, the Defense Minister on the other, Tashikov squarely in the center like some shrewd little terrier, facing him across the gleaming desk. "What makes you think I called on you for assistance?"

"Is it not obvious to you?" the Chairman inquired. "It is to all the world. Your country is in chaos, your Administration is in collapse, your democracy is in ruins, you are surrounded by traitorous men you cannot trust—you call for us. Or so it seems to the world. More importantly, Mr. President, so it seems to us." He leaned forward and inquired gently, "Is it possible we are mistaken?"

"I felt it was time to resume our discussions of the situation you have created in the world," the President said stiffly.

"You felt it was time you needed help," Vasily Tashikov said bluntly, "and we are here to give it to you. We commend you, first of all, upon the firm hand you have shown against the enemies of world peace who have attempted to destroy your plans for cooperation with the peace-loving programs of the Soviet Union. Nothing could have advanced our mutual interests more surely than their removal. We could not have asked for more. It was a superb, courageous and worthy decision on your part. We thank you for it. First you rid your country of the troublemakers of the media, and by your actions last night you eliminated the only remaining ringleaders who might have successfully defied you."

And he took folded copies of the *Times* and the *Post* from beneath his arm and shook them out to display the names of Leffingwell, Mac-

Donald, the Joint Chiefs, in banner headlines; the two-column front-page editorials in both now-subservient papers that praised the President in the most fulsome terms for his noble and fearless elimination of these traitorous enemies of America's freedoms.

"And now," Tashikov said, neatly refolding the dutifully groveling journals and placing them precisely on the desk in front of him, "you have no one else to turn to. And so you turn to us. It is as we expected. It is as we planned."

"'Planned?'" he inquired in a voice dull, almost stupid. "How could you have 'planned' it?"

"Because for three years now," the Chairman said with a quiet but obvious satisfaction, "we have been studying the personality of Edward M. Jason. There is very little about you we do not know—the overriding ambition, the arrogance of family and of mind, the strange, erratic, impulsive quirks of what you choose to regard as idealism and sincerity, the willingness to compromise with the violent when political advantage seemed the reward, the inability to suffer opposition without being persuaded to strike back blindly, the fatal tendency to let yourself be backed into corners from which the only escape has been by sacrificing yet more of the few remaining principles of this flimsy and dying democracy—above all the weakness under pressure, the weakness in power, the weakness, the weakness, the weakness!

"Oh, yes, Mr. President," he said, and the satisfaction was open and self-congratulatory now, "we have studied Edward M. Jason very well. And everything we have done has been based upon that study. From the moment you failed to respond to our calculated challenge after your inaugural, we knew you would do as you have done. Everything has followed, just as we had foreseen, from that first challenge which produced so weak a response. From that moment to this moment we have predicted you accurately every step of the way. And you have not failed us once, we will say that for you, Mr. President. You have shown an unwavering, if from America's standpoint fatal, consistency, every hour of every day. It has been beautiful to watch . . . and to take advantage of. . . .

"And so," he concluded, his tone abruptly harsh and emphatic, "here we are, to tell you what will happen next."

"Who are you," the President demanded in one last show of anger and fear, too alone and too far adrift now for it to sound anything but petulant, desperate and hysterical, "to tell me what to do?"

"We are your new allies and your intimate—very intimate—collaborators in the great adventure of bringing lasting peace to the world,"

Vasily Tashikov said smoothly. "And this is how we are going to go about it, together. . . ."

JASON, TASHIKOV CONCLUDE DAY-LONG WHITE HOUSE MEETING, ANNOUNCE ACCORD ON NEW U.S.-RUSSIAN "AGREEMENT OF FRIENDSHIP AND COOPERATION." HINT AMERICA TO WITHDRAW PERMANENTLY FROM MAJOR PO-SITIONS AROUND GLOBE, ACCEPT SOVIET LEADERSHIP IN FOREIGN POLICY, WORLD PEACE-KEEPING.

TWO LEADERS TO MEET IN FORMAL SIGNING CEREMONY AT CAPITOL AT NOON TOMORROW.

WORLD HAILS NEW ERA OF STABILITY AND GOOD WILL.

"It is with the utmost rejoicing," the *Post* exclaimed in its lead edi-torial, "that we hail the conclusion of the historic 'Agreement of Friendship and Cooperation' reached between the President of the United States and the Chairman of the Council of Ministers of the So-viet Union. Its signing will truly mark a new era of stability, serenity and hope, not only for the great American people and their great Rus-sian allies, but for all of humanity which has been so long harassed and endangered by the foolish, pointless, inexcusable rivalry between the two superpowers.

"If there be those Americans who grumble—and inevitably, as al-ways, there will be some—at what may appear to be a voluntary ac-ceptance by this nation of a somewhat secondary role to the Soviet Union in world affairs, then we can only say to them, 'Oh, ye of little faith, await events and see!' To do any differently, of course, would invite the immediate and righteous anger of the state.

"For we know, as our two great and farseeing leaders know, that from this willing, voluntary and realistic readjustment of the world situation by a great American and a great Russian, there will come only good for mankind—an end to tension, an end to suspicion, an end to fear and aggravation, an end to the eternal nagging threat of ideological explosion and world war.

"Is there more sane men could ask?

"We suggest to the Nobel Committee that this year's Peace Prize should logically have, not one, but two recipients, their names and achievements to be engraved equally forever upon the hearts of a grateful humanity—Edward M. Jason and Vasily Tashikov.

"If there be those elsewhere—in China, let us say—who do not like this, we say to them: 'Do not interfere with the inevitable tide of history as it runs toward peace. Those who stand in the way of peace in today's world can only destroy peace. The consequences, now, could only mean annihilation.'"

And from the *Times*, its customary self-conscious judicial air enlivened by its new proprietors' obvious joy at the turn of events, a commendation equally emphatic and grateful:

"'Agreement of Friendship and Cooperation!' At last the world hears the words it has longed for decades to hear from the two superpowers who rule the globe!

"Now the doubts and fears of almost three generations have at last been swept away by the farsighted and fearless statesmanship of two great men, one an American, the other a Russian—Edward M. Jason and Vasily Tashikov, whose names will go down forever in the annals of a grateful humanity. We suggest that this year's Nobel Peace Prize go equally to them both—a very small beginning to the tribute which will grow and swell and surround their names with honor as long as men anywhere believe in peace.

"For peace, we think, is now at last within the world's grasp. To those Americans—and inevitably, there will be some carpers, bewailers, men and women of little faith—who deplore the apparent decision of the United States to accept a somewhat lesser role in world affairs and rely upon the wise leadership of the Soviet Union and the great Russian people, we urge patience, understanding, trust and hope. All are inherent in this new and more practical readjustment of world realities which will lead in turn to world peace. There is also a practical reason for acceptance: while the great venture goes forward, protest would not only be futile. It would be treasonable, and as such, bring harsh reward.

"And to those elsewhere—Peking is one obvious place—who would seek in some way to thwart and subvert this great new move toward world peace, we would point out only that those who stand in the way of history in the end find history rolling over them. It is a lesson we commend to the one nation in the world which perhaps does not applaud, because it does not understand, the new reality of power that now exists in the world. It would do well to adapt, for the consequences of non-cooperation there, too, would be both futile and disastrous.

"So the world enters a new day, and the signing at the Capitol this noon will symbolize it as nothing else could. It is a great day for America, for Russia, for the world; but greatest of all, perhaps, for Edward M. Jason, President of the United States. Idealism, patience and the truest type of statesmanship could do no more, nor could they bring any greater personal satisfaction."

So caroled the new press of the nation (lesser journals across the land, even when not yet overtly controlled, following the lead very rapidly, self-preservation being the wonderful convincer that it is); so said the successors of Frankly Unctuous and friends who now spoke the new tongue from TV screen and radio; so echoed many from pulpit and hall of academe, from haunt of Thespis and nest of legal eagle. So sounded the New Day—new day in truth, and with a vengeance.

From the private words of many troubled citizens who viewed the newest development with the utmost of appalled concern, one conversation might have been selected as typical. It was monitored and recorded, of course, and very shortly was to bring upon its perpetrators the same consequences already meted out to those who had shown themselves to be too blind and reactionary to march with the enlightened times. It was earnest, honest and sincere in its expression of anguish, and so could have remained something of a historical symbol —had it not, of course, been erased and obliterated as soon as it had been used to produce the desired result from the new justice of the New Day.

"Bob," the ex-President said and his voice sounded old and very weary as he spoke from his office in the House of Representatives shortly before 10 A.M. on the day of the signing, "I think—"

"I know what you think," Senator Munson said, and he too sounded very old, very weary. "I agree with you. It's all over."

"But it *can't* be all over," William Abbott protested. "It *cannot.* America *cannot* go down as easily and swiftly as this."

"Who's to prevent it?" Bob Munson inquired bitterly. "Not you and I, certainly. Not Walter Dobius or Frankly Unctuous or their friends from the *Times* and the *Post,* undergoing God knows what in St. E's. Not Bob Leffingwell or Ewan MacDonald or the Joint Chiefs, awaiting drumhead trial at Fort McNair. Not any of our steadily dwindling band of friends up here, all of us subject to arrest at any moment. We won't any of us *be* here in another week, Bill, you know that as well as I do."

"I cannot believe," Bill Abbott said, "that this great Congress, in which you and I have served together so long, with all its profound traditions and habits of democracy, with all its proud record of two centuries of free men solving their own problems in their own way, with all the great history of parliamentary government behind it, can be wiped into nothingness almost overnight on the whim of a—of a—"

"Dictator," Bob Munson supplied, "for that is what he has become. And the worst sort, if there is any better or worse in that category—a weak dictator, a scared dictator, a dictator being driven under by a bigger and tougher and stronger dictator, a desperate dictator, a terrified dictator, a frantic dictator, striking out blindly at everybody and everything in search of scapegoats and justification. I don't think he's sane any more. How could he be, with every pressure in the world on him in these past few days and months?"

"And he is taking us all down with him," the ex-President said bleakly, "because he would not listen and he would not let us help. He knew it all, he couldn't be convinced, he couldn't be warned, he couldn't be persuaded: he knew it all. He could play with all the violence in the country, he could hand our enemies the world on a silver platter, he could let people he should never have trusted become more and more ruthless with those who dared oppose him, he could go all the way down the bitter road until now we face the end of the Republic, never to be reborn again as Americans have known it for more than two centuries. . . . It makes the heart cry, Bob. It makes the heart cry."

"And all so unnecessary," Senator Munson said. "Each step so clearly dangerous in its implications, so clearly fateful in the eyes of thoughtful and prudent men. But he was not a prudent man. He was a man in love with his own good intentions, eager to accept the assistance of anyone, no matter how evil, who could pretend to be in agreement with his purposes and sufficiently flattering of his ego and his public image. And weak . . . weak . . . weak."

"And always, be it remembered, adored by a majority of his people," William Abbott said, "who love a handsome face, the statement of high ideals and the glamor of high position. . . . Well: I suppose bitterness is childish and doesn't help. But what does, Bob? What does?"

"Nothing," Senator Munson said, "except to remain true to the Republic as we have known it, to continue to act as we have always acted in the democratic tradition . . . and to be brave enough to take the consequences when they come, as inevitably, now, they will."

"Yes," the ex-President said with a sigh. "We will be brave, you and I and our friends, because we have the character to be brave, and also because in a sense it doesn't really matter to us: our lives are fairly well along, even in the case of such as Lafe and Cullee or young Hal: the pattern is set, we have done what we could, we will all do it to the end, whatever the end may be. But what of the new generations coming along, Bob? What kind of America will they have?"

"The kind of America they know," Bob Munson said. "And since it is the only America they will ever have known, they will probably be reasonably content, if they have enough to eat and sufficient shelter. I am sure history will be rewritten to leave no wistful memories of the dream of free men that died. Give the thought manipulators twenty years, and there will be no memories of anything but things as they are then. This has been the pattern in other countries, and every day new inventions make it easier to achieve in America."

"I hear the agreement calls for 'the closest possible coordination of programs between the two governments to guarantee a mutually friendly climate within each nation,'" William Abbott said. "This in addition to the abandonment of bases and the subordination of foreign policy. It may not take twenty years."

"It will take an hour," Bob Munson said. "Books, records, documents, national memories—they can be destroyed or changed by computer in an instant nowadays. It will be very simple and very swift once the process starts in earnest. . . . Are you going to the signing?"

"I have been invited to sit on the platform," William Abbott said. "One of life's grimmer ironies. I am not going."

"Nor I. Nor perhaps a third of the Senate."

"And about as many in the House. Not that our protest will be of any importance. But it may give a little heart to some."

"I hope so," Senator Munson said. "I intend to watch it on television, however. I want to see him sign us away."

"I still cannot believe it," the ex-President said. "I still cannot."

Outside the Mansion he heard again the preparations for departure to the Capitol, the myriad busy bustlings of pomp and circumstance that just a short while ago had heralded his triumphal progress to inauguration. In an hour or less they would come to tell him that all was ready, and that the time had come to keep his appointment with destiny.

Then they would bear him away, along Pennsylvania Avenue between the solid human walls of his frantically cheering countrymen—for only those who would cheer would be allowed to be present this day. Those who would not cheer would not be allowed to be present, nor would they be allowed to mar his progress, ever again.

As usual in these recent days he had slept very poorly, risen very early, eaten very little; talked briefly to Patsy, Selena and Herbert, who had called from Dumbarton Oaks at nine to wish him well; responded to their anxious questions with the assurance that he was "all right," whatever is meant by that all-inclusive, all-purposive phrase; given orders to his staff that he was not to be disturbed because he was going to draft a few appropriate remarks to make at the signing; and then had retired to the Lincoln Study to do so, equipped with pens, pencils and yellow legal writing pad. Now, an hour later, he had two lines. He knew at last, with a great and final certainty, that no more would come.

Confronted by this knowledge, inescapable, unchangeable, unbearable, he sat for some time unmoving, the jumble of his mind at first turbulent and chaotic, then moving into some suspended state where at first nothing stirred to break its abandoned desolation. But in time —he did not know how long, five minutes, ten, twenty, thirty—two things did. On a sudden impulse he called the Vice President, conducted a conversation—very brief on his part, quiet, unshakable, strangely serene; ending in tears and sobs and anguished protestations on the part of Roger P. Croy. Then he rang for his secretary, directed that the portraits of Ceil and Doña Valuela be brought up from the main hall; and now was thinking a little more clearly, aided by the two faces which for him had always meant stability and certainty and a world that made sense.

In some last, desperate, curiously comforting way, it still did—for a minute or two—as he looked at his wife, so lovely, so straightforward and so honest, and at his grandmother, so determined, so indomitable, so wise and also so honest.

"I tried," he said aloud to them at last, like a child seeking their approval. "I really tried. I wanted it all to be so right for the world and so good for America. It all went wrong, but you know I tried."

His eyes filled suddenly with tears, he sounded like a lost little boy, which indeed, in history's unending parade of well-meaning hearts and ill-managed hopes, he probably was.

"I wanted to be good," he told them earnestly. "I really tried."

But the two faces, frozen forever in time and place, were unable to answer and now, at last, unable to help; and presently, turning his eyes away from them, trying carefully to look at nothing at all, he did what the honor of a President of the United States, accepting at last without reservation or self-protection the full responsibility for his actions, seemed to him to require.

At almost the same moment, standing outside the Vice President's office in the Executive Office Building just across West Executive Avenue from the White House, the worried little group of nervously gossiping secretaries and Secret Service men heard a single, sharp sound.

The girls screamed, the Secret Service rushed in. Pompous, ambitious, overly clever but at heart well-meaning, Roger P. Croy had kept his appointment with honor too.

Now the sun, having struggled since dawn, broke at last through the sullen icy haze and cast its pale but determined light upon all the glittering and glamorous scene in front of the Capitol.

It shone upon the stolid ranks of soldiers, sailors, marines and airmen as they stood, facing outward, rifles ready in an enormous U that framed the central steps of the building. It shone upon the inaugural stand which, more than half-dismantled, had been hastily resurrected during the night and now stood surrounded by a mounted honor guard. It shone upon four members of the Supreme Court, perhaps two thirds of the members of Congress, upon George Henry Wattersill and the remaining members of the Cabinet, upon many foreign ambassadors, officials, dignitaries and friends who, deeming it best to be there, filled the viewing stands on either side. It shone upon the eager members of the new media who crowded the press section below, avid to report this day so full of hope and glory for long-beleaguered mankind.

It shone upon the numerous Russians who mingled with the Americans in the stands, jovial, laughing, excited, indulging in many heavy jests to which their new allies responded gamefully, though, it must be admitted, with a certain forced friendliness, uneasy and uncertain. It shone upon the many thousands who filled Capitol Plaza beyond the heavy ranks of military—at least two hundred thousand, the new media reported, though the old media might have seen no more than fifty thousand and many of them unhappy, although afraid to show it.

It shone upon the two flags, side by side everywhere, flying together from the top of the Capitol, snapping together around the inaugural stand, arranged on trees and lampposts, draping government buildings and private establishments, red-star-and-sickle, red-white-and-blue, red-star-and-sickle, red-white-and-blue, all down the Avenue and all along the main arteries of the city.

It shone upon the Russian jets, passing in perfect formation, back and forth and back and forth again, at regular three-minute intervals, over the cold, cold city.

The sun shone upon the Speaker of the House, increasingly nervous as the clock moved toward, and then beyond, 11:45 A.M. He didn't know why, Jawbone confessed to his wife, but he jes' had a little ole hunch things weren't goin' right, he jes' didn't know exactly what it was but he jes' had a hunch. "Hooush!" Miss Bitty-Bug ordered, soft-voiced but vehement. "All these people goin' hear you maunderin' on like an old fool, Jawbone. You jes' keep calm, now, and *remember who you are*. Ev'-thang's goin' be *all raight*."

The sun shone, too, upon the Chairman of the Council of Ministers, seated in his armchair to the right of the lectern, opposite the one awaiting the President, smiling and beaming and waving cheerfully to the crowd, which responded with applause and cheers each time he greeted them: applause and cheers that seemed a little forced, somehow, but this did not disturb him. He was used to that kind of applause in Russia, and he knew that his countrymen who had arrived with him to assist in the new arrangements with America were used to it, too. It would not bother them any more than it bothered him. The applause came on signal, did it not? Its nature did not matter. The fact of it was all that was necessary to satisfy the eyes of the watching world.

And the sun shone on the president pro tempore of the Senate, seated in the row behind, looking about him with an interested, satisfied, triumphant air he took no pains to conceal. Fred Van Ackerman was a happy man this day and he did not care who knew it. All was going according to schedule, and he saw no reason to complain about or fear the future, for he believed it to be his.

So the clock moved on toward noon—reached noon—passed noon; and presently, through all the crowd at the Capitol and all down the Avenue and all over the world where satellites carried the scene there began to run little questionings and murmurings. For there came up, from the snowbound city and the Avenue below no surge of welcoming shouts, no sound of advancing motors, no sirens of triumphal progress.

Instead a great hush seemed to be falling, and after a few minutes, as the hour moved on to 12:05, 12:10, 12:20, it seemed to have come down upon all the world. Here and there someone coughed nervously, a restless child cried out, a horse whinnied. Other than that, a vast and troubled stillness lay on the world as they waited, with growing uncertainty, for the President of the United States.

"Shall I step forward?" Jawbone finally whispered frantically to his wife. "Is he comin' or i'n't he? Oh, Lord, Bug, *what shall I do?*" And this time Bug could not advise.

In the clever mind of the Chairman of the Council of Ministers the obvious possibility of a trap occurred and was immediately dismissed. The Russian jets still continued their rhythmic fly-over every three minutes, Russian aircraft carriers and long-range missile submarines stood along the eastern seaboard from Boston to Baltimore, eight more subs were at anchor in the Potomac channel from Anacostia to Kennedy Center. At many other places around the periphery of the North American continent many trained fingers were poised to push many decisive buttons to send off many deadly greetings, should the need arise. There was no trap, Vasily Tashikov knew, though it could be that a certain annoying and embarrassing stubbornness had suddenly developed. Yet where could he turn, this naive and thoroughly checkmated President who had delivered up his country? What good would stubbornness do now?

In the clever mind of the president pro tempore of the Senate, something nearer the truth suddenly occurred; and with it, a slow and contemptuous smile, as he contemplated what would be left, should his flash of intuition prove correct. Roger P. Croy, that simple-minded, old-fashioned liberal fool, would be child's play to scare into resignation or a heart attack within a month. That would bring into the White House that other fool, Jawbone Swarthman, and he, too, would be child's play to remove. And that left—

He swung about restlessly in his seat with a savagely satisfied smile that contrasted startlingly with the sober expressions that had developed all around him as the silence lengthened. As he did so he caught the eye of the Chairman of the Council of Ministers, whose glance, inspired by some sudden intuitive hunch of his own, seemed to have sought him out. Impulsively Senator Van Ackerman clasped his hands, raised them to chest level where Tashikov could see them, gave the prize fighter's self-congratulatory shake of triumph.

With a sudden look of comprehension the Chairman nodded, bowed and turned away as Fred smiled happily. The Senator from Wyoming had plans and now, more swiftly than he had thought possible, they were about to unfold for him. Like all the simple egomaniacs of history who have not been Communists but have thought they could use communism for their own ends, Fred was, temporarily, content.

So they waited for the President of the United States, whoever he might be; and presently, in a soft, secretive way that went unnoticed by anyone around him, the Chairman of the Council of Ministers also began to smile.

Fred Van Ackerman, savage child of a savage age, was not the only one who had plans. Nor was he the only one whom history would fool.

For the Chairman, whose smile turned savage too before he removed it with a sudden furtive haste, did not know, of course—as men never really do know, however much they may believe they know it philosophically—that in due course his plans as well, and those of his strange, misruled, misguided country, would in their turn crumble into dust and be forgotten in the merciless, inexorable, implacable unwinding of time.

All, all had gone wrong for the President of the United States.
And not from evil intentions.
But from good intentions, foolishly applied.
And so America in her turn learned the lesson:
Great states are *brought down, great nations* are *humbled, great dreams* are *destroyed.*
It can happen here.
No one had ever really believed it.
Until now.

October 1971–February 1973